Mancheste[illegible]

Laurie Pimblett

Manchester Hill

Matador
9 De Montfort Mews
Leicester LE1 7FW, UK
Tel: (+44) 116 255 9311 / 9312
Email: books@troubador.co.uk
Web: www.troubador.co.uk/matador

ISBN 978 1906221 348

Typeset in 11pt Stempel Garamond by Troubador Publishing Ltd, Leicester, UK
Printed in the UK by The Cromwell Press Ltd, Trowbridge, Wilts, UK

Matador is an imprint of Troubador Publishing Ltd

This book is respectfully dedicated to the officers and men of the Manchester Service Battalions of the Great War – The Manchester Pals – whose many acts of heroism and self-sacrifice at the Somme, at Passchendaele, at St. Quentin and in countless other engagements now long forgotten deserve the remembrance and esteem of posterity.

And it is dedicated most particularly to the fond memory of Albert Buckley, Tom Burton, Frank Eaton and Charles Pimblett who gave unstintingly of what little time they had left to share with the author their recollections of Hell.

ACKNOWLEDGEMENTS

My thanks are particularly due to my wife Yvonne, who weathered three years of angst from me during the preparation and writing of this book; also to Michael Keane, Archivist of The Manchester Regiment Museum , for his diligence in unearthing several priceless documents; to M. and Mme Mesenge and the people of Francilly-Selency who befriended us on our visits to Manchester Hill; and lastly to my colleague Leanne Horrobin whose inexhaustible patience and expertise enabled me to make some sense of ICT.

This book is not intended to be an historical analysis of the Great War.

Whilst it is based broadly on actual events, and whilst some of the characters who figure in the book are historical figures it remains essentially a work of fiction. Any inaccuracies of fact are due to the author alone, and are regretted.

'It was an epic ; there was never a greater stand...
than that of the 16th. Manchesters
on the immortal little hill in front of St. Quentin...'

Maj. General T.H. Shoubridge

'...None more devoted, and none more valiant
have passed in this war
through the Valley of the Shadow of Death.'

Lieut. General Sir James Willcocks

I

Chapter 1

A PATCHWORK of hedges, byways and coverts gave shape to the hazy greenness. Stands of beech and elm punctuated copses of lesser trees, while here and there the symmetry of a hoary oak or a line of poplars traced out some obscure lane. A mile or two distant a river gleamed intermittently in the beams of the late afternoon sun. It twisted and turned by degrees to the west, still pursuing its age-old course between banks scoured through the soft sandstone of the Cheshire Plain.

Shielding his eyes from the sun's glare with his cap, a small boy stood motionlessly observing the passage of a distant bird. He wondered fleetingly what sort it was, and where it was bound. As the speck dwindled rapidly into the haze he lowered his hand; and consigning guesswork to the winds, resumed where he had briefly left off. With his right boot he aimed a swingeing kick at a pebble, roughly shaped like a small rugby-ball, and drove it erratically along the still unmetalled surface of the road. As it bounced tiny explosions of dust puffed up until it spun to a halt; then the whole procedure was repeated.

'*Warrington to the line* !' shouted the boy to an invisible, cheering crowd. Picking up the pebble he clutched it tightly to his chest and ran as if his life depended upon it, ducking and diving as much as his tightly-laced boots would allow, as if avoiding unseen opponents. Darting across the way he reached an imaginary touch-line.

'*Try*!' he shouted, ramming the pebble down; '*Warrington gets another*!'

Tiring of this the boy abandoned the pebble where it lay; and becoming suddenly conscious of the temperature, wiped his brow with the sleeve of his heavy serge jacket.

The day was hot, and getting hotter. The dusty air seemed to roll down the road toward him in scalding waves; and the exertions of his rugby game had brought him to boiling point. Still clad in jacket and cap and lugging a heavy leather schoolbag over his shoulder, he trudged on for another hundred yards, then dropped down from the raised level to a lush depression adjoining a small paddock. Through it flowed a clear spring which passed at an angle beneath the road.

He knew of a shoal of tiny fish which lived in the pool where the stream widened, and the current slowed. Entranced he had watched their every movement, their sinuous dartings and curves, and the lightning speed with which they scattered if alarmed. He had tried his hand at fishing for them, despite owning nothing in the way of proper gear; and had been surprised at the ease with which they had fallen victim to no more than a small red worm tied to a length of cotton. He had found that if he threw the bait ahead of them and allowed the current to bring it down in a natural fashion the little fish would seize it greedily; and by swallowing the worm in one to prevent the others from getting it, would be caught. He thought he might give it a try now, and cool his feet as well.

Millwain Place was approached by a long winding drive, thoughtfully planted with shrubs to shield the house and outbuildings from the new public road a hundred yards distant, and from the gaze of the new public soon to pass along it.

Ida and Clarence Rusholme had found the plot five years before; and whilst her husband had remained indifferent Ida had seen its potential immediately. Spurred on by her, Clarence had negotiated with the developer to acquire the adjoining site; and though the expense had been considerable, Ida never once had cause to regret her decision. Some ten years younger than her solicitor husband, she still possessed the sparkle and youth which had always been hers, and seemingly never his. She had thrown herself into the design of Millwain Place as she had no other project, and had carried it off judiciously. The result was neither extravagant nor showy, but stated in its restrained but substantial style the confidence of an affluent people who looked towards the New Century with quiet conviction and without reservation.

The hallway was of contemporary design -spacious and very much in keeping with the loftiness of the house itself. Its oak front doors were flanked by glass panels depicting romantic scenes from Scandinavian legend, the doors' massiveness contrasting with the delicacy of the glasswork To the left a naked blonde maiden with prominent breasts swept valkyrie-like across a cloudless sky, while her companion on the right stood resplendent in fanciful Nordic armour, flaxen hair blowing, wielding a sword. Created by a young Manchester artist of rising reputation their eyes had been so positioned as to gaze fixedly upon the visitor wherever he stood. Despite her eclectic tastes Ida had nevertheless been rather taken aback when confronted by the results of her commission; but with the easing of the initial shock she insisted that they were 'growing on her'. Clarence Rusholme had adjusted his spectacles, looked, adjusted them again, and said nothing. A viewing of the panels was a highlight sneaked by every youthful male visitor to Millwain Place, and many were the compliments received by Oliver Rusholme and his older brother on their hallway.

It was to this comfortable home that Oliver returned on that hot afternoon in June 1908. Running up the broad flight of stone steps to the main door he pressed the bell-push – an electrical model, and very much the latest thing. Nothing happened. After a brief pause Oliver yanked hard on the mechanical bellpull which his father, with his deepseated mistrust of modern gadgetry, had insisted be left in place. A distant ringing echoed from a side corridor which led to the kitchen and the scullery. Shortly after a stout figure – even more distorted by the window-glass – could be seen making its way heavily down the hallway. The figure muttered ill-humouredly to itself as it plodded.

'Good afternoon, Alice'.

The old woman looked disapprovingly at her employers' son, and wiped flour from her broad arms.

'Oh. Master Oliver. I wasn't expectin' you to be so early home. Now *why* can't you use the side doors as your Ma told you to? You *know* the trouble it puts me to if I'm bakin', *an'* Phoebe's had to go an' see her Dad in Stockport Infirmary.'

'Didn't think, Alice. I'm awfully sorry.'

'That's as may be, *Master* Oliver; I'm in two minds whether to tell your Ma.' And to emphasise her sense of grievance, she added significantly '*an'* Albert's gone to Manchester to fetch your Pa'

'Don't tell, Alice. Please don't.' They had made their way together down to the kitchen, and now Oliver, perching himself on the corner of a massive pine table, helped himself to one of a cluster of little cakes left to cool on a stand.

'Well, I don't know… I *ought* to. You an' your brother! You'll put me in t' work'ouse, you will. Look at your boots! An'leave them cakes alone! What '*ave* you been doin'in 'em?'

Oliver knew from long experience that this signalled the end of hostilities,and he capitalised on it.'Can I have another cake? Just one? *Please*?' The old woman selected one with a small piece broken away, of the kind she called her 'stales', though they never were. Then shaking her pinafore –front at the boy, she drove him out of her kitchen.

A life spent poring over legal niceties has its price, and time had been ungenerous to Clarence Rusholme. An angular man with thinning hair, he had not aged well; and he wore that dessicated look which suggested the onset of premature old age. The senior partner in a highly respected and successful firm of Manchester solicitors he was at the peak of his career, and perhaps should have appreciated the hand Fate had dealt him; but he did not. He had no pastimes, and no interests in literature or the Arts other than the regular visits made with his wife to the Halle's orchestral concerts; but these he would carry out in a perfunctory way, from a mingled sense of form and duty – and in the unswerving belief that his wife must be accompanied – rather than from any desire to hear music. He was unmoved by drama and could see little point in sculpture or painting, though Ida had been allowed from time to time to squander money on works by contemporary artists. Yet though aesthetically arid, Clarence was astute enough to recognise that virtues might well lie hidden in those creative genres to which he himself was blind. So he did not condemn or censure, but attempted to understand the appreciation that others – and especially his wife- showed; and he even indulged them, in a mock censorious way.

With her imposing stature Ida Rusholme was rather more handsome than beautiful. Tall and poised and energetic, she seemed the very reverse of her ageing and stuffy husband. Though she was his junior by twenty years, the gulf between them was not simply that of two decades, but of an Age. For she possessed a *joie de vivre* which celebrated modernity, imbued with an ambitious and optimistic view which looked steadily forward to a rosy future, a feature which distinguished her as being one whose childhood and adolescence had been shaped in the late Victorian mold.

Her mother had been constricted by the crinoline. She too had been a child of her time; a decorative doll resplendent and glittering and intellectually sterile. But Ida was the product of an age of social enterprise, when a girl might follow higher academic or cultural interests without necessarily encountering the blank walls of male derision and contempt. So with a mixture of realism and genuine commitment Ida had pursued her studies in literature and the Arts, sharing her student years equally between the Victoria University of Manchester – red brick and progressive – the dangerously heady atmosphere of Paris and the Montmartre, and Bremen. This last was not by chance, and not entirely by choice; for though born a Mancunian, Ida's parents were members of the city's considerable German community – an industrious people who had played a central role in its economic and cultural growth, and who had prospered hand-in-hand with their adopted city.

Ida had received an exceptionally liberal upbringing – though she had been indulged rather more by her father than by her mother who considered her daughter headstrong and unlikely to settle to anything appropriate, and feared for her. But Ernst Roemer had winked at his daughter's caprices, and indulged them all the more.

Bremen had been his attempt at compromise. When first the subject of spending a year in her mother's old home surrounded by a crowd of half-known relatives was broached, Ida had responded with undisguised aversion; but when the chance of a place at an Academy of Fine Arts beckoned – a heaven-sent opportunity to pursue her love of sculpture – she gave in instantly.

A year later she had returned, loaded with bronzes and a more refined German accent to resume her Englishness in her parents' Victoria Park villa.

The success of her marriage to Clarence Rusholme had confounded the sceptics. Though never passionate their relationship was caring enough, founded upon mutual loyalty upon which the pair continued to build. Three children had been born to them; Helene was first, in 1890; then Godfrey in 1891. Oliver had followed as something of a surprise in 1896 – a year which had been one of warmth and sunlight for the family. They and countless others of their generation looked forward with mounting anticipation to the genesis of the Twentieth Century – and to the New Age that seemed poised to accompany it.

1896; a year whose children would prove to be amongst the most ill-starred in history.

Chapter 2

'AREYOU intending to go to the City tomorrow,Dear?' Ida enquired. Her husband pursed his lips over his after-dinner coffee and considered. 'The Oldham matter needs to be worked at, certainly; and I've a few items which require my attention, so yes I think I might.' He adjusted his spectacles and glanced over them to the window and at the evening sunbeams flooding into the dining-room. ' The weather certainly promises to continue fair and hot'

'Then if you're going, you'll have told Albert to have the trap ready?' queried Ida.

'Well... no... No, my Dear.I don't recall *mentioning* it to him.'

'If you're to go early, we had better send Phoebe down with a note, don't you think? He'll need to get *Damson* harnessed '.

Clarence nodded, and smiled. In that smile which was uniquely hers lay the affection of an unlikely husband for an equally unlikely wife. And she smiled back.

'Actually, Ma, I was thinking of taking a walk down towards the village myself a little later on' interrupted a youthful male voice;'so to save Phoebe the trouble, I'll stick my head round Albert's door and let him know.' The speaker was a young man who because of his imposing build and almost Latin good looks could have passed for twenty or so, but was in fact barely eighteen.

A natural affability caused him to be both respected and liked at Hugh William's School. With his immediate peers he was universally popular, and as a Senior Prefect and Head of House he was held in awe by the younger boys. Now in his final year in the Sixth, he intended to follow in his father's footsteps and go up to Oxford to read Law – a step which had seemed gratifyingly logical to Clarence, but about which Ida had mixed feelings. Yet he and his father had ultimately prevailed over her ambivalence towards what she regarded as a somewhat threadbare profession. He had already paid his first visit to Goldring College and behind the lattice windows and the ivied walls of the Dons' rooms, the deal was done; he would take his place at the start of the Autumn Term.

'I'll pop in on Albert when I'm down.' Ida smiled her agreement. 'Might I be excused?' His father nodded,slowly stirring his coffee. Godfrey rose, inclined his head respectfully to his parents, and left by the scullery door with Oliver close at his heels.

'Pa, if you're proposing to make a trip into Manchester tomorrow, could I come with you, please? Only, there are a few particulars that I need – canvas, for a start… .'The young woman who had spoken was very much the female physical counterpart of Godfrey; for that same olive handsomeness had in her been transformed into a striking beauty, of the kind which causes men to draw breath, and look again. Hers was the same openness of mien which gave rise to the common belief which prevailed beyond their childhood that she and her brother were twins, which they were not. When arguing a point she would stress each word with quiet emphasis, and. her eyes would become charged with passion, and flash with a dark fire When amused her laughter was almost bell-like; it rang around the room, and made an entertainer regret he had no more jokes to tell. It was the former quality which her mother appreciated most; but the latter which her father loved.

'… and some more of those Reeves' pigments that worked so well – 'specially the sienna and the aquamarine. And I want to have a *really* good look at the new sables that they're doing. Mine are rather bald. A bit like Pa!' she laughed.

'*Helene!* That's unkind.'

'Pa knows I don't mean it.Don't you, Pa?'

'She's quite right, Dear. I'm decidedly thin upstairs. Rather *wispy*, one might say 'said Clarence. Since her infancy Helene had possessed the innate power to summon from her father all that was lightest in his nature, distilling from his muddiness a crystal spirit which he found quite heady and intoxicating. He did not care about being the butt of her gentle humour; indeed he secretly revelled in it, because of that laughter.

'I'm leaving early, you know. No time for slacking!' he said with mock severity. 'I think I might keep Albert with me – he could have some of the morning to himself – and rest up *Damson* at the Bridgewater Livery.' He placed obstacles artfully in the way of his daughter's request, knowing that she would become more animated, and the more engaging.

'Pa, you *know* I'll be ready ! And anyway, May Atherton and Dulcie Grady are going to wait for me at Forsyth's; Dulcie's Pa is going to treat her to a new piano for her birthday. He says we'd better help her choose, as she's so silly she might come out with an *accordion* !'

'Well, Dulcie does have her moments, I hear.' said Ida.

As the details of the morning were being finalised, Godfrey was sitting on a rough bench by the washhouse door after collecting his walking-boots from the nearby boiler-room – a snug little den where Albert relaxed for a smoke after mucking-out the stables and watering the family's two Welsh cobs *Damson* and *Cherry*. There he would sometimes be joined by Oliver, who petted the horses and helped whenever he could with the brushing-down and feeding – simple pleasures which his father frowned on as being 'low'.

For the present Godfrey was struggling with his boots. High-ankled and made of unforgivingly stout leather they seemed to be engineered for discomfort, getting your foot in being equally as difficult as getting your foot out. Lolling on the arm of the bench as he swung his legs to and fro was Oliver. He watched each movement of his brother's hands, minutely following the lacing process though he'd seen it countless times before.

'Godfrey?'

'Yes, old chap.'

'Would you mind it if I walked down to the village with you?'

'Not in the least… tell Ma you're coming' Godfrey replied abstractedly 'Right! *That's* on.'

He stamped his booted foot hard for emphasis. 'Tell Ma. And remember your boots. I'll wait by the stile.'

By the time Godfrey had sauntered down through the grounds his younger brother reappeared breathlessly, clad in well-worn tweed trousers and randomly laced boots.

'Before we go a step further we'd better sort those out.' Godfrey said 'you couldn't march half a mile in them. '

As they swung easily over the stile and dropped into the adjoining meadow, Oliver looked across to his brother. Godfrey caught the movement and smiled back. This would be a cardinal point in Oliver's recollections, and it was how in after years he would always choose to remember Godfrey best. Nothing would ever again give him greater pleasure than their rambles through the fields and lanes of North Cheshire; and no other memories, greater sorrow. As they walked the aloofness of an older brother towards a younger – unwritten but maintained as a part of the code when at school- evaporated like dew in sunlight. They chatted and laughed about this or that idiosyncrasy of the Masters, the merits of the batting and bowling of the First Eleven in the present season, and who was likely to make the First Fifteen in the next.

At times they would fall silent, listening awhile to Nature oozing or trickling or warbling about them; and sometimes they would pause and drink it all in. It was in these moments that the boy unconsciously committed himself to his lifelong affair with the one great miracle as he gained a glimpse of the intensity of existence,and learned to love it for the beauty of its infinite forms and phases. They might halt briefly by the neighbouring badger sett; and hardly daring to breathe, would await the appearance of one of its wary occupants. Or perhaps they might catch sight of a fox, scudding along furtively. And just once they came upon a roe deer, grazing quietly by herself. On scenting them she started away in panic, crashing through the adjoining undergrowth and passing so close that Oliver caught the fear in her wild eyes.

Skirting the crops they would track in single file, Oliver following in Godfrey's footsteps, trying to make out the imprints left by his brother, and place his own feet in them. So it was on that evening as they headed by obscure ways to the village, switching with hazel wands at the frowsy heads of cowslips, and toppling their crowns with imaginary sabre-cuts.

'Will you be going to Camp, this summer?' Oliver asked.

'Oh, yes; it's all been planned for some time.'

'I wish I could go.'

'I'm sure you'll get your chance. Let's see… the rules are, you have to be fourteen to enter the Corps. You're getting on for thirteen, so that means you've only a year to wait.'

'But by *that* time you'll have left and gone up to Oxford. So by the time *I* get to join, you'll have handed your kit and everything in, and I won't get into your platoon.'

'Well, I shall certainly be back from time to time. The University terms aren't particularly long, so it's likely I'll be nipping down to put you through a spot of drill.'

'But it won't be the *same*.'. Then after a pause Oliver added 'Have you got your uniform ready for the Review?'

'I should say so! You know how RSM Oldham and The Pod take to a shabby turnout.'

'I shall miss you when you've gone' Oliver said, almost inaudibly.

'And I'm sure I'll miss you, too, old chap.'

From the lower meadows the path wound through a spinney of young willow saplings, planted and cropped from time to time by a family of basket-weavers. Their premises stood hard by in a tiny red brick cottage lit by equally tiny windows. It was roofed with large slabs of sandstone – far heavier and thicker than Welsh slate- whose bulk had caused the structure to sag, and give the whole a curious bent-in-the-middle cast. Down the overgrown passage adjoining the cottage wall the two made their way. Encroaching elder stems forced them to stoop; and spreading their arms wide to balance themselves they slithered down the bank of the Gorebrook, negotiating the derelict wooden footbridge which had kept dry the feet of farmworkers long gone, and which nobody could now be troubled to replace. The lane to Desbury village now stretched away to either side before them, glowing in the evening half-light which dappled its surface with russet and gold as the leaves shifted with the breeze. Ancient elms lined the route as far as the eye could see, and beyond; till their overarching boughs melted into a twilit indistinctness, and then dipped entirely from sight. The brothers struck out to their left, keeping to the lush grass of the verge whose exceptional width told of its purpose as a drove-road, down which generations of fat Cheshire cattle had made their way to the markets of Shudehill and the Shambles, to feed the City. But now the softness underfoot was preferable to the vagaries of its surface, rutted by the steady flow of builders' wagons in damper seasons, then baked hard by the July sun to the consistency of terra cotta.

Desbury was less a hamlet and more a large courtyard fringed by small terraced cottages through which the road passed. Constructed in curves and to the clear pattern of some long-gone architect, each dwelling wore a neat and comfortable air. Some were of rendered brick, limewashed white; while one or two were of the same soft brown sandstone which walled the older fields and byways, and which was still used in stylish gateposts for the affluent. At the heart of this community stood *The Red Hen*, an imposing structure built in the latter part of the eighteenth century to take advantage of the burgeoning coach-trade. It still retained its rather grand arch, raised high enough to allow the most top-heavy vehicles and their teams to pass beneath and into the cobbled yard and stables beyond. But none but the most ancient residents of Desbury could remember the mailcoaches, though several local families had in their time made their livings from them.

The poor of Manchester whose ninepenny fare (third class) took them to Desbury station as a welcome respite from factory or mill, and who came in increasing numbers on Sundays to ramble the lanes and gaze at the houses, would -after considering the *Hen*- decide it was too imposing, and beyond their limited means. Instead they crossed the divide from the more affluent to the more homely, entering the saloon of *The Sceptre* opposite where they found ample refreshment at a reasonable price – though in fact the tariffs of the two rival public houses varied by hardly a penny. And it was on the neatly-painted door of a cottage adjoining *The Sceptre* that the brothers now knocked.

It was answered almost immediately by a small child with startling flaxen hair. Perhaps nine years of age, she was clad in standard uniform of snowy white pinafore, black stockings and lace-up boots.

'Who is it, Dolly?' came a man's voice from the kitchen.

'I don't know' trilled the girl over her shoulder 'it's two gentlemen.'

There was a pause; then ' *ask their names*' said the same voice.

Dolly turned back to the callers. 'Dad says *Who are you? What's your names? If* you please.'

'Will you tell your Dad that it's Godfrey and Oliver – *Master* Godfrey and *Master* Oliver. From the House. We wish to speak to him.'

Dolly had no need to relay the message. Immediately the figure of Albert Chadderton emerged from the rear of the cottage as he brushed crumbs from his waistcoat and struggled with his top button.

'Here, Dad. I'll do that for yer.'

Albert stooped dutifully before his daughter, who deftly secured the button.

'Ta, pet. Now you shoo in to yer Ma. She needs some help.'

Albert turned apologetically to the visitors. 'I'm awful sorry, gentlemen. I didn't know it was you. We weren't expectin' company.' Deferentially he indicated a door to the right.

'Would you step in, please? Into t' parlour, if you don't mind?'

He ushered them into a tiny room floored with a drabbet rug –a room hardly large enough for the mock-Jacobean cupboard and heavy table and chairs which dominated it. There was a mustiness about the room, an unlived-in odour accentuated by the fireless hearth.

It was as a rule reserved for 'best' use, only. Guests in that house were generally family or close friends who when visiting gravitated automatically to the warmer and more welcoming quarters centred on the kitchen and its glittering iron range. Nervously Albert took out his handkerchief; and after dusting the seats of two chairs invited the boys to sit.

'We have a message from our Pa, Albert. He asks that you drive him to Manchester tomorrow, early. Would you arrange to have *Damson* harnessed and ready, for seven'o'clock prompt? Miss Helene will accompany him.'

'I'd be right pleased to !' came the immediate reply.. A major consideration was that he would be paid to go on a jaunt to Manchester, and with a bit of luck have a fair bit of the day to himself. And Mr. Rusholme was generous as to treating him to his dinner – on condition that he took it at *The Temperance* – and there was sometimes a five shilling tip to crown the day. But a Saturday run to Manchester at the reins of the Rusholme's smart little turnout – flying up the Wilmslow Road at a crisp pace with *Damson* in the shafts – was not what Albert deemed hard work.

It was a source of perpetual delight to him. His fancy sped him along at the same tempo, for it savoured of what life must be like for the class who raised the big houses, and lived in them. As he dropped his passengers off at *The Exchange*, the entire rig – the leather, the brass, the polish – would be his, for a while. Dressed for the occasion in best suit and stiffly starched collar, he would assist the ostler at the Livery to unharness and stall *Damson* with a proprietorial air, making the occasional kind but firm suggestion as to the horse's wellbeing.. Then he would saunter across to Piccadilly via *The Atheneaeum,* perhaps taking a turn round the gardens of the imposing Infirmary. So the day would pass in a leisurely way, until the time came for the homeward journey and his collection of the Master and Miss Helene. Though he would hardly have recognised it, he was deeply fond of the family and loyal to them; and he delighted in listening at intervals to the light-hearted conversation about the day's doings which passed between them, and sharing vicariously in their pleasure.That he would be required to attend to his boiler-duties later in the evening did not weigh much in his reckoning.

'Yes, certainly Master Godfrey ' he said, grinning 'I'll be more than pleased to.'

Chapter 3

THE OLD HALL seemed to have been designed primarily as a framework into which doors could be installed. There were dozens of them, ponderous affairs hefty enough for a gaol, and hung on iron hinges which despite their massive appearance were slowly succumbing to the years. The countless openings and closings of school doors when coupled with a chronic lack of oil invested each with its own arthritic voice, ranging in pitch from a shrill squeal to a malevolent grumble. As the pupil progressed from class to class he learned almost as a catechism the sequence of dissonant sounds telling which room had been entered or left, and where the unseen walker had been heading. As solo voices they were merely discordant; but when they opened in unison at the ringing of the school bell they combined to produce a racket which was amplified tenfold by the high vaulting of the roof.

The Old Hall was a place of acoustic episodes. The chorus of doors would be followed hard by the impact of boots on heavily planked floors, cut about and worn by five generations of hurrying feet. The percussive roar caused by a movement from one Master's room or study to another would then die back as abruptly as it had arisen, as lessons were resumed. Then the third phase would begin with the narcotic drone of male voices – one declaiming in Latin or Greek, another holding forth about Euclid while yet another expounded upon the History of Empire.

Though the sun was hot and beat down relentlessly on the adjoining Quadrangle, its rays did not penetrate far into the dusty recesses of the room in which Oliver Rusholme sat. He wriggled uncomfortably but not so energetically as to cause his desk to move and creak, thereby attracting the attention of the Master. He was perched in one of some two dozen similar desks ranged in three precise lines. These quaint contraptions resembled small Santa Claus sleighs but lacking in festive purpose. A boy had to climb on board rather than sit behind, negotiating his way in via a narrow gap between the uprights of the desk bit at the front, and the frame in which the seat was attached at the rear. This was operated in turn by a counterbalancing weight which seemed to invest the whole assembly with a fiendish will of its own; for the luckless pupil had to time the arrival of his backside perfectly in order to avoid trapping his fingers as the seat came down. Time it too late, and he would miss the seat entirely and collapse in a heap beneath. Those experienced in the idiosyncrasies of such furniture had developed the grotesque manoeuvre of groping between their legs to secure the seat before descending, then waddling forwards with the offending panel gripped firmly. It was unseemly but unavoidable.

Other strategies had been tried including the extension of the leg to tilt the seat of the boy in front, but they had met with limited success, as those hampered by shorter limbs swiftly discovered. And the reckless technique of hurling the seat down then leaping aboard before it began its ascent was shortlived. As, almost, was its inventor.

But the desks remained – partly owing to the frugality of the Board of Governors, and partly out of a curious sentimentality; for on the lids were carved the names of generations of boys who had fleetingly occupied that spot during their school careers. To any other school plagued by graffiti this might have been a sound reason for their removal and certainly no grounds for their preservation; but many of these names differed from the usual scrawlings in that a good few of their owners had served with distinction in the armies of the Empire. The military history of the School –and indeed of Britain herself- was scratched there; Alma, Inkermann, Magdala, Lucknow, Delhi, Omdurman, and more latterly Ladysmith and Spion Kop. There was something far more human about the boy who had affirmed his identity with a pen-knife fifty years before; and it made his subsequent death in some remote corner of the Empire the more poignant and personal. True, the names could be found inscribed with gilded dignity on the lofty tablets raised in the Great Hall. But the retention of their desks was accepted almost with one accord as a simpler and more affecting memorial.

Some of the survivors had found their way back to William's after their retirement, to teach, having discovered that Her Majesty's Armies could be harsh even to Her Commissioned Officers. The School provided a home of sorts, for those in straitened circumstances and for those who had simply nowhere else to go.

Such a one now considered Oliver Rusholme as the boy leaned on his elbow and gazed balefully out through the dust-blued panes.

'Rusholme.'

Oliver did not stir.

'Rusholme!' A few of his classmates tittered, and there was some anticipatory shuffling. Schoolboy loyalties did not extend so far as to pass over the fun of someone else 'catching it' for a change. Oliver was directly in the line of fire, and the glee became tangible.

'*Rusholme*! What *ails* you, boy? Stand up at once.' Startled from his reverie and the sunlit outside world Oliver sprang to his feet and drew himself upright as his seat crashed shut.

'Well? Would you care to repeat what I have just said?'

Oliver paused. 'I… .I can't, Sir.'

'*Why* pray?'

'I'm afraid I didn't hear it, Sir.'

'Is my voice particularly *quiet* today, that you did not hear? Or have you developed an impediment? *Deafness*, perhaps?'

The irony drew an appreciative guffaw from the audience. 'Wiskus' Bonnard's wit was recognised and relished throughout the school. Though not on top form today, he did not disappoint. And nomatter how popular the target of 'Wiskus's' repartee, the fun was redoubled by the simple fact that you yourself were not the recipient.

With a melodramatic flourish Capt. Bonnard stroked the feature which had gained him his nickname amongst the younger boys. His moustache was his pride, and he cultivated it with a topiarist's care.

Oliver made a bid to draw the matter to its conclusion, regardless of the risk.

'I 'm afraid I wasn't listening to you, Sir.'

'Then, *Master* Rusholme, if you feel you are unable to listen in my lesson time, you will have to learn to listen in your own. Attend in my study at luncheon, if you please; there it will be made *painfully* clear to you.Sit down.' Oliver sat, to a whispered refrain of '*whackwhackwhack*' from the grinning faces around him.

The hours leading to his appointment with Wiskus weighed like lead on Oliver. Even his closer associates added to the misery by speculating on the outcome. 'Well, you're in for it this time' said the spotty Cedric Gosling dolefully. But the condemned gave little reaction, lost as he was in apprehension of what he had to face.

Lunchtime eventually arrived, though Oliver had lost his appetite. Struggling against the flow of other boys of his year who were heading for the refectory, he made his way irresolutely across the Old Hall and through one of its many doors. This gave onto a narrow corridor lit only by a fanlight,and closed off at its further end by yet another door. Approaching it Oliver knocked timidly. There was no reply. He knocked again, this time more firmly.

'*Enter*!'

Oliver stooped to negotiate the narrow flight of wooden steps which descended steeply into Captain Bonnard's study. The master sat entertaining a couple of his colleagues who reclined in old leather chairs from which the horsehair protruded in places. Together with clouds of tobacco-smoke and the leisurely attitudes of the visitors, the atmosphere was less that of an educational establishment and more of a rather shabby clubroom. Its walls were hung with the clutter of a military and sporting lifetime; mildewed harness and a guidon, a sepia photograph of moustached officers posed stiffly by a line of tiger- carcases, mounted shooting-trophies, a decorated native musket, zebra-skin shields, a rack containing fishing rods, a huge salmon in a glass case, and a hundred other things. In short, all the trappings of a Victorian soldier-wanderer for whom each item held a memory and a virtue. They represented almost the sum of Bonnard's worldly possessions and were there simply because he had no space in his lodgings to put them. Surrounded by them he felt their constancy, like old friends.They did not change, as his life had changed, and each was the dilapidated symbol of a place or an event long-gone, and by which the passage of his life could be charted. And though that life had been one of ceaseless movement those mementos and the school in which they had ultimately been housed,had a shared immutability. In a curious way they belonged there, more than anywhere else; for these visual manifestation of what the boy of fifty years before had done with his life, invited no judgments, neither for nor against. They were merely a statement of what had been. And anyhow, their accommodation had been stoutly refused by the landlady of the small private hotel hard by Alexandra Park where Bonnard lodged – together with a number of other masters as elderly and as homeless as he.

Oliver approached slowly, then stopped outside the circle. 'You wished to see me, Sir.'

Recognising the official nature of the visit the other two masters rose heavily from their chairs; and looking down distastefully at the boy, made their slow exit.

'Not Rusholme *again,*surely?'

'Nothing like his older brother… '

'Big disappointment to the parents, I should imagine… '

'Got a long way to go to match-up… '

Captain Bonnard remained seated.

'You know why you are here, Rusholme?'

'Yes sir.'

'Kindly explain to me why.'

'Inattention in your lessons sir.'

'That was not my meaning. *Why* do you not attend?'

'I don't know sir.'

'No more than I, Rusholme. No more than I. You have proved intelligent, and have shown some ability when you have taken the trouble to apply yourself. Consider your older brother. Look what he has accomplished in his time at the School. First Eleven, First Fifteen and now to cap it all, a senior NCO. And he will be going up to Goldring shortly. Your father must be very proud of him.'

'He is, sir. We're all very proud of Godfrey.'

'*There* you are! My *very* point!' Captain Bonnard brought his hand down emphatically. 'When one is fortunate to have a brother who sets one such a fine example, ought one not to take a leaf from his book, so to speak? This drifting- off of yours. He was never prone to it. Yet this is the fourth time at least, this term. This inattention… it is as though you were entirely indifferent to your studies. Why do you allow yourself to succumb?'

Oliver looked down at his boots, and then out through the window, to the distant trees at the school's boundary and back to his boots again.

'I can't say, sir.'

Bonnard noted the glance, and how the boy's eyes had wandered. He considered for a moment, then raised his eyebrows resignedly ' Well, Rusholme. You know the consequences. What will it be? Short and sharp, or Saturday afternoons, for two weeks? *Look at me.*'

Oliver looked up not in compliance with the master's order but in surprise that the latter option had been granted him at all. Under normal circumstances there would be no choice whatever- particularly given that the offence had been a repeated one. So what *was* Whiskus about? Oliver weighed –up the Saturdays. Less painful, certainly, and a soft way out. But his Pa would certainly find out, with the ensuing explosion and post mortem. And to lose *two* Saturdays! The week was a jungle through which he struggled to reach Saturday, which stood prominent like an island of leisure amidst the shoals of school life. To lose them was too awful a prospect. The other way, though fearful, was preferable for its brevity.

'I'll take it short and sharp, sir.'

Captain Bonnard looked at the boy through narrowed eyes. He was unsure himself as to why he'd allowed the alternative. But it was of no matter for it had been resolved for him.

'You know the procedure by now I think.'

Oliver dutifully bent over the desk and braced himself for the onslaught. Wiskus took down a willow wand from a nail, and flexed it as duty required. He brought it down smartly on the boy's trousered backside. And again. Oliver grit his teeth, and readied himself for the third blow.

It never fell. 'Get up, Rusholme. That's enough.'

Two! It was unheard of. And in a school where Senior Prefects were allowed to administer beatings to younger boys, five was usual. But *two!* As one who had experienced more than his share of the punitive system and its vagaries, Oliver felt a mixture of relief mingled with an odd sense of having been cheated out of the glories of withstanding a major whacking.

Whiskus replaced the wand on its hook. 'Now return to your lunch, Rusholme. And think seriously about what I have said.'

'*What would Pa say if he found out*?' Oliver stood remorsefully before his older brother in the Senior Prefect's study. 'You *know* how the only thing that gets him in a state is your attitude; yet you damn' well go on.' There was genuine anger in Godfrey's voice, and he stared obliquely at Oliver, coldly, bitterly. That expression – which the boy saw but rarely, and hated – seemed to illuminate with a chill light the one dimension of his brother which he had cause to fear. A fissure would open, albeit briefly, onto something dark and ruthless, and remote. Physical punishment he could bear willingly; but estrangement from Godfrey–when a gulf suddenly yawned between them which for a time seemed unbridgeable – made him feel very alone; yet somehow the situations cropped up with monotonous regularity.

'How many times have you been in trouble since Easter? *Three,* is it? Or *four*?'

'Five.'

'Five?'

'*Including* my last one with Wis… .. Captain Bonnard, I mean'. 'What were they? *Remind* me, if you please.' Oliver winced inwardly at this use of sarcasm by Godfrey, as the only times he resorted to its use seemed to be in such circumstances as these, and he felt the pain of it and of his failings acutely. With a heavy heart Oliver related each of the offences he had committed. 'I'm sorry, Godfrey; *very*.'

'But you don't make any effort to improve, do you? You simply can't be bothered, like you can't be bothered about *anything* that's of importance. It's not enough that you seem to be getting a reputation as a thoroughly bad lot in the School;but now *I've* had to answer for your behaviour to people, who want to know what's going on.'

'*Which* people? Was it Captain Bonnard?'

'No it was *not* Captain Bonnard, though I'm surprised he hasn't sent for me. If you *must* know, it was Warrington.'

This was a crushing blow. If there was one member of the school whose opinion Oliver valued even more than Godfrey's it was Warrington's.

Gerald Richards Warrington. Head of School, Captain in his turn of the

First Fifteen *and* of the First Eleven, revered as a demi-god by younger boys, and who in some perverse way seemed to exercise greater authority – and influence – than many of the masters. He seemed in every sense to epitomise all that the system was about.

Of imposing build and severe good looks, he exuded a spirit of power from every inch of his athletic frame. A grandson of General Sir Charles Richards Warrington, his future at a school with such distinctly military leanings as William's was assured. He found himself inexorably spiralled upwards to Company Sergeant-Major – the most senior rank attainable in the Corps.In an environment where academic achievement frequently came a poor second to sporting or Corps prowess – the two were inseparable in the mindset of many –the holders of the cricket or rugby captaincies were naturally expected to hold senior rank in officer training. The example set on the games field gained them the respect and admiration of other, lesser boys; by according them rank and dressing them in splendid uniforms the system thus ensured a steady flow of enthusiastic followers, and recruits. Warrington was assisted in part by the waxed and bullish Drill Sergeant Veitch, a veteran of the Cheshire Regiment who though employed nominally as the school painter, still spent rather more time in uniform than out of it.

With all the trappings of rank Warrington could have assumed the role of drill martinet, had he wished. Certainly he enacted the part, with Veitch at his shoulder as mentor, prompting him to adopt the requisite swagger and invective.

'Push'em'*ard*... kep'em *at* it... watch yer line... *watch yer line!* With respect. Mr.Warrington, *Sah!*'

Yet for all that there was another element in him which impinged on his leadership. Whether it was one factor more or one less, Godfrey could not say; but there was a something – a deficiency- which caused him a vague disquiet, albeit that he was on friendly terms with Warrington,and that he - even he – was to an extent in awe of his immediate senior. But he could not get any closer to identifying this hazy enigma in his friend's character. There was nothing – not a shred of evidence on which to base his reservations, and in consequence he tried to dismiss them entirely from his thoughts.

So Oliver's string of misdemeanours had been brought to Warrington's attention. While this was heavy news, at least his father didn't know; and that was a relief, certainly. But Oliver's assumptions were premature; and his sense of relief, misplaced. At the conclusion of a meeting at his offices, the senior partner of Gosling Peaphy and Co. observed to Clarence that his youngest child was becoming '*quite a wag*'.

When Clarence expressed his ignorance, all that Cedric Gosling's son had reported to his father about *'that bad and lazy Rusholme boy'* was again smugly related.Humiliated, Clarence travelled home that night 'in a high old mood' as Godfrey put it as he met Oliver on the stairs; 'you'd better keep a good lookout, that's all.' Another hazard to be encountered; but worse still was the sinking sense that perhaps it was his own brother who had been the source of this poisonous information.

'Godfrey!' he said appalled ' you didn't *sneak* on me, did you?'

The look that flashed from the elder's eyes precluded any further comment.

As Oliver faced his father in the library Clarence tersely delivered the indictment. He asked neither for explanation, nor defence. Though calmer now than he was, his son's conduct still appalled him; it had brought the family's good name into disrepute, and had been a source of considerable personal embarrassment. And whilst Oliver had sought to defend himself when confronted by Godfrey, against his father's accusations he chose to offer nothing in extenuation. He was guilty as charged, and that was that.

Clarence looked perplexedly across at his son.This dryad standing sheepishly before him, still fresh-faced from a romp in the adjacent corn field, seemed to him bound by codes far different from those which he himself had been constrained to follow. He had tried to like the boy, had tried to find some common ground which might serve as a congruent point for them both; but Oliver's interests were simply not his. There was no convergence, no consensus. The boy remained a mystery; one who seemed to Clarence to breathe an alien air, and who communed with spirits to which the ageing man was deaf and blind. Somehow this child had come to them, differing in every material way from his predictable and reliable brother and his engaging sister; and his very being somehow stifled Clarence's sense of paternal pride. It perturbed him that he felt thus; but it seemed to him then that there was a chasm between them. One was too young; and the other, simply too old. Of the child's desperate daily struggle to conform, and to find that elusive formula for pleasing his father – *to be in Pa's good books* – Clarence Rusholme was entirely ignorant.

A month of weekends restricted to his room. Oliver felt the punishment was intolerably severe. For a boy of his nature it was about as bad a fate as could be imagined, and one which threatened to asphyxiate him.

To some of his classmates confinement indoors might have been no more than an irksome and boring interlude. But to one who grasped every opportunity to spend time outside regardless of the weather it was too awful to contemplate. Nomatter how comfortable his room it was still imprisonment It seemed that his supply of oxygen was in the process of being turned off.

'Father?' There was a stony silence. '*Father*?'

'Yes, Oliver.'

He resorted to desperate measures in a last ditch attempt to have the sentence commuted. '*If* I try really hard to improve, and *if* I don't break the rules, do you think I could possibly get my weekends back? I mean, instead of that, you could whack me, or take my allowance off me, for instance. I wouldn't mind either of them as much.'

'You will not be physically chastised. You know that well enough.' Clarence was curiously ambivalent about corporal punishment. He wincingly recalled the floggings which had been a part of his own schooldays, and which few had escaped; yet paradoxically he harboured no resentment against a system which, despite his compliance, had made his time at school one of wretchedness and terror- a system which continued to advocate the practice of beating as a sure remedy for building character. But in his house it was nevertheless proscribed- a testimony to the more enlightened and enlightening influence of Ida.

Clarence remained impassive, and unmoved by his son's appeal.

'That is *precisely* why you will receive the punishment I have decided upon. I have spoken to your Mamma about it, and she agrees with me absolutely.' This was not entirely true. Knowing her son well she had foreseen the distress these sanctions would cause, and had only agreed to them because no other means of censure seemed weighty enough to emphasise her own disappointment in him; and she remained unswervingly loyal to her husband.

'But I will *hate* it up there… all shut up with nowhere to go, and… and it's summer.'

Oliver had throughout his ordeal refrained from crying; he had accepted all that an unfair world had chosen to hurl at him without demur But now,slowly at first then more quickly, his whole frame was shaken by heavy sobs, rising upwards from far within.He closed his eyes tight to stop the flow of tears, but they came nevertheless, hot and scalding and unmanly. Clarence was nonplussed by this lack of reserve, this display of passion. His fingers clasped and unclasped repeatedly, not in anger but rather from a mingled sense of embarrassment and impotence – the former because what Oliver had succumbed to was just *not done*, and the latter because while he felt his duty was to offer comfort, he was powerless to do so. All he could do was fumblingly give Oliver his handkerchief – the boy never had one – and conclude by telling him to 'get a grip on himself' and dismiss him shortly to his room.

As the boy left, Clarence rose and briskly strode to the windows where he stood with hands behind him, contemplating the gardens below. He heard the door quietly open, and someone enter. He did not turn.

'After you told him your decision, was he *very* upset?' The voice was Ida's.

'He was. He… *ahem*… .wept, rather.'

'At your speaking to him, or at the punishment?'

'Oh, at the punishment, of course. Confound the boy!' he added emphatically.

'Yes. He *is* a confounded boy. Well, let's not allow it to cause too much unhappiness amongst us.' She pressed the button to summon the maid.

'I shall ask Phoebe to bring some tea. Will you take it here?' Clarence nodded noncommitally. 'Actually, I think I'll go down myself; I have to speak to her about something.'

Ida left the room; but instead of heading for the kitchen, made her way instead to the upper rooms where she knocked gently on Oliver's door. There was no reply. She knocked once more, and heard a voice in muffled tones order whoever it was, to go away and leave him alone.

'It's Mamma, Oliver. I would like very much to speak to you.'

'Well *I* don't want to speak to you or anyone else at the moment, *thank* you.'

'Will you let me in?'

'No!'

'Then I think we must have our little talk through the door; and that will be *most* inconvenient.'

'Well I don't have to talk to *anyone*. And you can't say I'm bad just because I don't want to.'

'I don't think you're bad; and I certainly wouldn't want to make you. It's just that I thought *you* might.'

'*They'd* think it was bad *enough*, at school. If I talk, I catch it. When I don't, I catch it again. I'm always in hot water. I don't want to be.'

'I know you don't. And we're not at school now, are we?'

'Pa seems to act as though we are. He's just like the masters.'

'He had to do *something,* Oliver. He couldn't let it pass.'

'But why my *weekends*? It's just about the worst thing that could happen.'

The door was unbolted from within, and opened slowly. Oliver turned away from his mother and shuffled abjectly to his bed,wiping his eyes roughly with the back of his hand.

'There's nothing wrong with crying' said Ida, gently. 'It's very human to weep, you know. Lots of people do it.'

Oliver's puffed and reddened eyes made a masculine denial of his state impossible.

'Not at school, they don't.'

Not at school, they don't.

She approached,her skirts softly rustling. And sitting by him on his bed, enfolded him in her arms.

Chapter Four

THEN CAME the long-awaited cricket season. Ida dredged out Oliver's kit, which was found to be ludicrously small. It had been usual for him to receive Godfrey's old whites and boots, and this he had done uncomplainingly; but this year there were no hand-me-downs available. Despite her husband's objection that it would be seen as a reward the next weekend Ida took Oliver to the Manchester firm of Tyldesley and Holbrooks, to be fitted for a new outfit – his first. Oliver awaited it with growing impatience. A fortnight later the kit arrived. Tissue-paper was peeled back, revealing an immaculate set of 'whites' complete even to the school crest embroidered on the pullover, and a blazer in the most fashionable style. Each evening Oliver would stand before the wardrobe mirror admiring his new sporting image, perhaps slouching nonchalantly with his new bat and eyebrow alike raised as if posing for a photograph, or perhaps making a powerful cut. As he peered at his reflection out of the corner of his eye he still innocently equated this caricature of himself with success, believing implicitly that it would prove to be the turning of the tide in his estimation of himself, and more particularly, in others' estimation of him. Yet the new finery and the patch it applied to his deflated self could not for long dispel the growing irksomeness of his lost weekends, and the novelty faded as he grew accustomed to this new persona. As the second weekend of restriction loomed he chafed to be out and away, having long exhausted his indoor resources by the close of the previous Saturday. But what was to be done? Slumped on his bed with a few unread books scattered about him he would leap to his feet in frustration and pace from bedroom to bathroom, pay an unnecessary visit to the lavatory then prowl the landing for a while. His mother listened below to his caged ramblings, and was concerned. His father listened too, and was not.

Uneasily Ida made her way softly up to his room. She tried the door but it was locked from the inside. Pressing her face close against the panels, she enquired whether he was comfortable, and if she could bring him anything? Oliver's light-hearted- almost animated- reply quieted her concern; and reassured that all was well she went down once more to the drawing-room and picked up her copy of *Jude* where she had left off.

At that moment Oliver was scouring the bottom of his wardrobe. All that was visible of him were his legs and backside, wrapped in a dressing-gown. There was a muffled exclamation of triumph and he emerged clutching a pair of faded canvas deck-shoes. He kicked off his slippers, pulled them on and tied them swiftly; then stripping off his dressing-gown he seemed transformed; for beneath he was dressed in the grubby old trousers and jacket which he wore when out rambling. He turned off the light; then furtively opening the casement window he leaned out, looking about him. The dusk was now falling rapidly as the sun percolated through a distant beech coppice. Far beneath the drawing-room lights stretched out across the upper garden, distorted and elongated by the slope of the lawn. He had not allowed for it being quite so well-lit; and the contrast with the twilight made them seem still brighter. With the agility of a cat he slipped one leg noiselessly over the sill; then the other, swinging himself over to an adjacent downpipe. Massively cast, it was easily capable of bearing the weight of a twelve year-old boy. Nevertheless it was not a manoeuvre which he relished, despite his talent for shinning up all the climbable trees in the locality.

With reckless confidence he grasped the pipe tightly between both arms, and for a moment hung diagonally half-in, half-out of the casement. Then his hands slipped a little and his whole body came round like a pendulum, bringing him abruptly against the unyielding iron. While he hung there momentarily winded he considered the absurdity of his position for the first time. He could call for help, and risk all the problems that would create. He could let go, and risk the long fall to the flowerbed. He might get some sympathy, if anyone believed it *had* been an accident; but his common sense told him that nobody would. The only realistic alternative was to continue downwards, since he had got this far. The descent proved easier than he'd thought, however. Footholds there were in plenty, created by the ridges in the decorative stonework. By hunching himself up he found that his feet could be planted flat against the wall; then slowly at first, but with gathering speed as his confidence grew, he simply went down monkey-fashion. His elation at reaching the ground in one piece would have been no greater had he managed to break out of the condemned cell at Strangeways Prison.

Euphoric with success he repeated the process not merely as an encore, but because he knew that his triumph would be shortlived if a return *up* the drainpipe proved impossible. And he suddenly recalled with a sinking feeling that he had left his door bolted firmly from within. His anxiety on that count evaporated when he found that the ascent was, if anything, even easier. Just to prove the point he scrambled up and down several times, once even climbing back into his bedroom.

But now he was skirting the upper garden, keeping to the very fringes of the trees, taking advantage of every pool of darkness they afforded, and scudding from one to the other like a wraith. Within a minute he had attained his objective. Vaulting the stile he dropped into the meadow, and freedom. Then he ran in the shadows, simply for the joy of running, careless of the cuts and scratches to his hands as he stumbled and fell and picked himself up and ran on. For they were honourable wounds, ones you couldn't get from being safely closeted in your bedroom. They were almost something to savour, because they had been gained in *his* world, the one *they* didn't even begin to understand, and they were a memento of the regaining of freedom, and the illicit time he had won for himself.

Weekend detention suddenly seemed more tolerable. He began to anticipate his nightly escapes with relish, and his mood brightened appreciably. His wanderings became a source of excitement and of pride, for he found that he could negotiate a course unerringly and with growing skill. How much or how little of the landscape was moonlit became progressively less important, for he learned early to orientate himself by taking a bearing on any still visible feature. He was a quick and perceptive learner in such situations, and the mistakes he made became fewer with each expedition. He found he had a talent for reading a map nomatter how complex, and for committing the finest detail to memory. He took to studying the Ordnance Survey maps of the district, making mental notes of interesting tracks and byways which might be worth further investigation.

His mother smiled at the change in his interests and mood; as it seemed to coincide with a new sense of purpose – one which continued long after his weekend confinements had lapsed – she felt it was all to the good, and provided practical encouragement by ordering those maps he had difficulty in obtaining himself.

She would make a point of spending time each evening with him, when they would huddle over this or that sheet, and Oliver would point out to her the features of the region, proud that he had something to share with his mother – something which genuinely interested her, and which she valued. Ida voiced her pleasure to Clarence one evening as they were preparing for bed. '... and he shows such a facility for reading and remembering *every* detail, and describing every part, almost as if he'd been there himself. He really does!'

Her husband sniffed sceptically from his dressing-room. 'Then I suppose he'll have to earn his bread drawing maps or mountain-guiding, or whatever.'

Rarely did a cross word pass between them; but this gratuitous sarcasm at Oliver's expense both hurt and appalled her. Ida rose furiously to defend him.

'How *can* you speak so? I think that's utterly despicable! After all, you have yourself commented frequently on how aimless he seems. Yet *now* when he takes an active interest in something practical, you criticise! You *persist* in having a low estimation of him… Oliver can do nothing other than displease you. I feel quite put out by the opinion you have of him.'

The heat of her argument took Clarence completely unawares. Recognising that there was truth in what she had said he attempted to mollify her.

'I am *of course* as pleased as you are, my Dear, that Oliver is showing interest in something. I *only* meant to imply that if this new-found enthusiasm were to manifest itself in school, how much more gratifying it would be… '

'I doubt that is what you meant, at all.' Ida retorted ' I feel that you have no interest in the boy, nor any good expectations for him. And I believe that *he* feels it, too.'

Meanwhile Oliver, compass around his neck, was in the process of slipping out by his accustomed route; then doubling quickly away through the grounds he sped off into the meadow beyond. It was a night of scudding cloud which from time to time cloaked the moon in a bluish veil; shadows came and went, patching his path and giving a strange unearthly quality to the whole. Moonlight had divested the world of its colour, and now the landscape seemed lighter than the sky, as if the two had been inverted by some cosmic freak of nature. As he passed them, the boles of trees stood black as sable against the grey; and he noticed that their leaves, agitated by a stiffening breeze, were edged with silver as they caught the moon's rays.

He made his way resolutely towards a gap which yawned blackly between adjoining stands of elms. As he reached it the ground fell steeply away before him as he knew it would; and he braced himself as he descended, crossing and recrossing the incline with the confidence and surefootedness of an accomplished skier. In this miniature gorge summer always seemed a remote and tardy visitor, and last autumn's leaves still crackled underfoot. It was walled on either side with crumbling sandstone bluffs whose trickling waters fed its perpetual dankness, even though elsewhere the hottest of summer days might be crisping the wheat in nearby fields.

He reached the bottom without difficulty and skirted a little brook for a few yards; then cut across it diagonally, placing his feet on age-washed stones whose location he had memorised. Attaining the opposite bank he rapidly made his way upwards over the soft earth, ducking beneath a fern-hung outcrop and feeling the bite of the icy droplets which showered him. Tossing them from his hair like a dog he continued his ascent until he regained the higher ground once more. He sensed then that what he was engaged in somehow transcended time; and by revealing to him the inconsequence of his troubles when contrasted with the vastness of the universe, he felt comforted.

Rising once again from the gully he cut across country until he reached the night's objective – a small hill which rose gently from the east and descended more precipitately on its western side.

A clump of gnarled oaktrees – ancient survivors of a long – forgotten forest – clung precariously to life around its summit. Oliver paused for a moment, listening to the sough of the wind in the branches, and feeling it run like unseen fingers through his hair. To the North lay the shimmering gaslights of Manchester. Turning from them he climbed up among the limbs of the outermost tree and shuffled himself round until with the aid of the luminous compass needle he had aligned himself to the west. With eyes screwed up he scanned the horizon for the merest hint of light. At first he could make out nothing whatever on the mantle of the Plain spread before him. But by degrees he saw – or thought he saw – a faint glow, distinguishable only in that it seemed to him less dark; and within that glow he caught the occasional twinkle, which his imagination told him were street lamps. *That would be Liverpool… and Birkenhead… and Wallasey,* he thought. He then shifted his gaze further to the south, where he knew for certain there rose the mountain ranges of North Wales.

North Wales. A favourite with his parents, they had spent their honeymoon in a warm Llandudno hotel from which they had made daily sightseeing excursions in a hired trap. It was a favourite with Oliver, too; for rarely did a year pass but the whole household would decamp, bag and baggage, and travel in style on the Holyhead boat-train bound for Llandudno or Conwy or Bangor. And once there he could be as free as the wind; for from their rented house or cottage he would wander with the comforting knowledge that the only restriction was his attendance at mealtimes.

Deprived of companionship of his own age, he had of necessity to fall back upon his own resources. Thus, strangely, the visits never disappointed; for a sensitive nature and a creative imagination enabled him to make of them what *he* wanted, to people their landscapes and shape them into the image of what his holiday should be. The loneliness was there, sometimes, for he was a boy who liked to share; but he resigned himself to it as the price of the freedom he valued so highly.

This year, Ida had told him, their destination would be Ridland, a village lying rather to the North of their usual holiday spots. But she had read about it in the guides, and it seemed ideal for the family's purpose. A large rectory had been rented, and they would leave at the end of the School Term, though Godfrey and Clarence would make their own way there later – the former because his attendance was required at Corps Camp, and the latter because there were always loose ends to tie up in the firm.

Oliver took one last lingering glimpse westward; then swung himself under the branch, and dropped to the ground. With his spirits buoyant at the prospect before him and his heart big with affection and nostalgia for past holidays he swiftly retraced his route. Within the hour he had reached the meadow bordering the house, and was about to make for the stile when he heard voices. He instinctively froze and listened. Two people – one male, the other female – were locked in heated argument. Though hardly rising above a whisper, it was clear from their tone that the issue between them was contentious and passionate. His schoolboy code despised eavesdropping as the practice of a sneak; but his coming on them unawares like that had not been his fault. His arrival there had not been noticed; but his withdrawal might well be.

'Can't you stay? *Only* for a little longer?' begged the masculine voice

'I can't... don't press me. Oh, I can't, not now... 'The girl's reply was charged with emotion. 'Don't you see?' she continued 'that we can't continue like this? Can't we simply remain the best of friends, as we started?'

'You *know* that would be quite impossible 'said the other 'how could I regard you in any other way?'

'It's simply not right... the time, everything. It's far too soon to be... to be... committing ourselves to something we would both regret.'

'You can't mean that.'

'I do.'

'How do you *know*? No-one can see into the future.'

'I know we'd have regrets, because I regret everything already. The deception, the telling lies, and all that. And that feeling... being tied up. I don't want to *belong* to anybody, not in the way our parents have to. We've got so much to *do* yet, in our lives, you and I. I don't want to tie myself to anything, don't you see?'

'Or anyone, including me?'

The girl did not answer at first.

'*And including me?'* he pressed her again ' tell me once more, and look at me. *Tell me that you don't care for me. Tell me that you want me to go.'*

The girl falteringly maintained her dignity

' I don't care for you. And I *do* want you to go. *Please.'*

The effort with which she controlled her words – pronouncing them slowly for fear of yielding to her feelings – showed those feelings to be plainly at odds with the sentiments she had uttered.

The young man turned abruptly on his heel without another word, and left. His athletic figure and his physical bearing, bowed as it was with the misery of a lover, were unmistakeable. Aghast, Oliver watched the departure of his erstwhile hero Warrington.

Other eyes followed him into the gloom; and though they had remained dry until then, as they caught the reflection of a distant lamp they could be seen to be brimming with tears.

Slowly the weeping girl made her way back to the house, whereupon she straightened, bringing herself upright by sheer strength of will, and pulled out her handkerchief. Having regained her composure to a degree which made it possible to re-enter safely, she shook out her hair behind her, refastening it neatly; then quickly smoothed down her dress.

Oliver was an unwilling party to his sister's secret.

Chapter Five

THE LOWER Vale of Clwyr stood in rich contrast to its more austere upper reaches; for here the river wound through lush dairylands whose fertility had long been recognised and valued – not least by the invasive English aristocracy who coveted it and seized it for themselves. The great manors of the Clwyr were picturesque now, and attracted many on walking or bicycling holidays; but their mossed and ivied fortifications told of a more troubled past, when rights of tenure were guaranteed by force of arms rather than by any document. Centuries of peace had witnessed their gradual decline, however; for the builders of barn and shippon raided the ancient walls for convenient supplies of building material, ready-dressed. And here the Old Testament proverb of *swords into ploughshares* was realised again – not this time in metal but in stone.

In its passage through these meadows the Clwyr was at its finest and richest; for from the trout–ringed pools, pebbly shoals and undulating willow-groves it meandered into tidal marsh and mudflat, home to flocks of waterfowl whose voices then as now invested winter evenings with a particular melancholy. Here the tidal river possessed a distinct grandeur – a darker and more dramatic beauty of its own- rendered more forbidding by the skeletal magnificence of Ridland Castle which for six centuries had frowned upon it. Edward's grey bastions and keep had been built strong, resisting the most diligent efforts of Cromwell and his gunpowder to obliterate them; and even in their drunken leaning state, still had the power to impress and intimidate.

Lying within the shadow of the castle's derelict gatehouse, and built largely from its venerable stones sat a square Rectory, ringed about with gardens.Its mottled limestone walls were sun-traps, absorbing and reflecting the heat of the day throughout the early hours, and adding to the prodigious growth of every herb and shrub planted there.

When the Rectory became available as a holiday retreat, Ida decided to take it for the summer. Alice and Phoebe went ahead some days prior to the Rusholme's departure for Wales, loaded with bedsheets, cooking utensils and cleaning paraphernalia – and despite the agent's assurance that all would be ready in time.

The only one who remained buoyant throughout their journey was Oliver. Whilst his mother and sister lost themselves in popular novelettes he stood with face up against the compartment window, watching the passage of each landmark and feature, scoring them off his mental map and envisioning them as he had so often done during his midnight rambles. And he knew instantly and with certainty when the train had crossed the border into Wales. There was a quality which though indefinable led to a subtle sensory change, and which told him the moment that England was behind. Perhaps it was the light striking the rising ground of Flintshire, where the winds shaped the clouds and where brilliance and shadow seemed thrown into greater definition than on the softer English Plain. Or was it the sounds? A million tiny nuances of water and wind which differed from those of home, or the fluting breezes playing against the crags, or the call of creatures strange to him. Or could it be the smells – of sunbaked drystone walls, of creeper, of pine-resin, of sheepfold, of tarred timber, estuaries, and the sea? He reckoned he would know it blindfold, and told his mother and sister so. But the comment aroused no interest, and they kept to their books.

But whatever its origin, the point of entry into his beloved Wales never failed to ratify his childish faith in dreams. And as he assumed another self – an elemental being of waters and winds and colours – he became more attuned to the subtleties of his surroundings, listening and observing and breathing with greater awareness. The physical shortcomings of the trip were nothing to Oliver; for he let anticipation shut them out.

The house and its grounds were the first on the list for exploration. Left entirely to his own devices he investigated every room and cellar with the zeal of an estate agent, probing the remoter corners and savouring the places that he knew the others would not go. His own bedroom, on the upper floor, was snug enough – a heavily carved bed, washstand and chest of drawers the only furniture. Everything smelled sweetly of beeswax, and had a well-used sheen to it. And like every other part of the Rectory the colour-scheme was monochromatic – whatever was not washed a blinding white had been painted jet-black. He thought the whole building resembled a huge humbug as he looked at its snowy walls and glistening black doors and windowframes.

The secrets of the garden were soon secrets no more; and guided by the bowed old gardener Jonas he uncovered the hiding-places of slow-worms and grass-snakes, and found where the barn-owl nested; so the first few days were spent within the garden's buzzing warmth, collecting snails for Jonas or picking vegetables for Alice. These attractions were soon exhausted, and as Ida and Helene had resumed their interest in watercolour landscapes, Oliver was as usual alone again.

Early next morning, after dashing his face with cold water and gulping down a hurried breakfast Oliver left the house armed with a packed lunch and bottle of ginger-beer, prepared to follow wherever the path might lead him. With his fascination for water it was natural that his course would tend downhill to the river. The Clwyr was at this point tidal, as the worn piers of the medieval bridge clearly showed. Little of the lower masonry was visible, so dense were the clumps of bladderwrack which hung dripping from it. The stonework at water-level had been scoured by centuries of neaps and springs, each of which ground away at the diminishing surface with its load of sand. Piers which had been fashioned by medieval masons to resemble bows of ships no longer parted the flows effectively but bulged against them,causing the currents to whirl and eddy in a sinister fashion, which made Oliver shiver appreciatively from his vantage point above.

Turning back across the bridge he vaulted lightly over the crumbling stone parapet at the landward side, and dropped down to a sheep-path worn into the bank. Following this closely Oliver set off on his first expedition to trace the river's course from the bridge to the sea, armed with an Ordnance Survey map.

Now that the sun had burned off the last of the early mists the temperature began steadily to rise, so that within half an hour of leaving Ridland Oliver was sweating despite having removed his jacket. Soaking his handkerchief in a trickle of fresh water he placed it squarely on his head and immediately felt refreshed. Shading his eyes he scanned the path in both directions. From there to the bluely-obscure bridge it was entirely empty, and his own. No other living creature was visible- neither man nor beast – for it was used only infrequently by a shepherd and his flock or by those in search of edible mussels. It was often inundated by the spring tides which ran particularly high in those parts; and would then prove impassable for a week or more because of the mud.

Today Oliver was entirely alone with river and tide, but was not at all not put out. Indeed quite the opposite; for though a sociable boy who enjoyed the crowd, he had long been compelled to depend on his own resources in the absence of companions. He might have become increasingly independent in spirit, but for the Achilles Heel of his relationship with his father. Despite this – or perhaps, partly because of it – he retained a taste for adventure, for exploration, for escaping the strictures which elsewhere hemmed him in. It was a salve to his soul, and by enabling him to place his perceived inadequacies in truer perspective made them more remote, like the hoary old bridge whose defects were now invisible to the naked eye.

There was no-one there to censure – no-one to direct his feet on any course other than that chosen by himself, and Oliver was content with that. For a few minutes he stopped to watch the motionless intensity of a fishing heron and admire the lightning speed with which it struck at its quarry. Then seeing movement beneath the surface of a deeper tidal pool ahead of him, he crept with the sureness of a cat to the very edge. There hidden behind a tussock he thrilled to see several long grey shapes detach themselves from the darker greys of the bottom and rise leisurely to inspect objects floating past. What species of fish they were, Oliver could not guess; but to him, accustomed as he was to the minnows and loaches of Cheshire streams, they were huge. And their closeness – for he felt that he could reach out and touch them – magnified them still further in his mind. He whiled away the minutes, observing the ease with which the great fish turned in the current, sometimes holding against the steady flow with barely a twist of their tails, at others gliding together to disappear entirely beneath the undercut bank on which he perched. As quietly as he had approached, he withdrew again, making a mental note of the pool's location for a return visit.

From here the river now widened appreciably, spreading out into an estuarial pool of some hundred or so yards in width. Its furthest landward margins were marked at either side by the skeletal remains of two old wooden ships, beached long before as protection against erosion. Their planking had given up the struggle against time and tide but their massive timbers remained even yet, pointing defiantly skyward from the ooze into which they had settled. They had been substantial seagoing vessels in their day; and it was still possible to make out the lines of the nearest, and visualise from the graceful rake of her bow and the sharpness of her stern how splendid she must once have been.

As he contemplated the ruins Oliver's imagination restored her vanished deck and absent masts; and in the breeze he heard the flap of canvas against the yards and in the cry of the gulls the voices of her long dead crew. He pictured in his mind's eye the romantic places she might have visited, and saw her running before a stiff Atlantic gale, America-bound. As a keen reader of Stevenson it was not difficult for him to place her in some far-distant port of long ago and feel her riding gently at anchor, her masthead -lamps glowing warm in the twilight. And now she had fetched up here, abandoned at the mouth of an obscure river to serve as a cheap form of coastal defence.

Having scrambled down the banking he found himself standing ankle deep in mud right within the heart of the ship, in a place which once must have been dark and pungent and creaking but which now lay broken open to all weathers. He would have loved to have known her name, and what she had been. Within the embrace of her curving timbers he was reminded of the colossal ribcage of a whale which he had seen in a museum; and at first glance they appeared just as archaic and pointless as the display, and just as dead. On drawing closer however, he saw that what he had assumed to be lifeless wood in fact teemed with a multitude of living things both plant and animal – weeds, barnacles, mussels, limpets – and hordes of little crabs which scuttled away to new hiding places when he disturbed them. Excitedly he picked a few up, and then for want of somewhere to put them pulled out his pocket handkerchief and wrapped them tightly in that. Then for fear of killing them he immediately unwrapped them and released them again.

Following a gentle bend in the river he came upon the first sign of habitation. Despite the distractions along the way he had walked further than he had expected; and now he saw a wisp of blue smoke trailing up from the lower horizon, soon followed by the whitewashed stone cottage from whose chimney it came. This was the first and only building a walker encountered on the river path from Ridland to Fforyd, and was the most remote of its dwellings. For all its isolation it nevertheless seemed a cheery little place with its freshly whitened walls, stubby chimneypot and tarred front door. Its builder seemed to have erected it as near to the river as was possible without actually siting it in the water, for on the seaward side it possessed its own miniature jetty which was basically no more than an elongation of its front yard. Against its hoary stones knocked a stout rowing-boat moored so close to the door that with little effort one could step straight from the house and be afloat in seconds.

While attempting to pick his way around the piles of nets, crab-pots and other equipment which obstructed the pathway, the path led him close to the front of the cottage. Threading his way through he noticed several cane fishing rods propped against an adjoining wall. Their worn silk whippings and dulled varnish testified to the long service they had given their owner; but they nonetheless looked to be of the finest quality. He was stooping to inspect them more closely when he heard movement within the cottage. Someone coughed, and there was the clatter of a pan-lid. Then the latch rattled, and the door began to creak open. Instinctively feeling guilty Oliver took to his heels, and fled back along the path down which he had come.

Chapter Six

FOR A WEEK the weather continued exceptionally fine. Awakened by the first stirrings of the household, Oliver would rise with the morning mist, and having snatched a swift breakfast in the kitchen and begged a lunch from Alice he would speed away down the drive to the crunch of gravel beneath his boots. Then off down the now–familiar path to the bridge, and over the wall. He would pause at the pool where he had seen the grey shapes, expecting them at any moment to materialise as they had when he had seen them first, like ghosts from the darkness; but unversed in the movements of the tides and their influence upon wild creatures, felt a pang of disappointment when they did not. He would listen to the lap and gurgle of the current and the hiss of the grass, and he revelled in the solitude. This landscape was fast becoming his friend; he conceived of it as being a living and breathing entity and he was conscious of a growing intimacy with it, a sense of belonging to it as surely as it belonged to him. His contentment deepened as he breathed in the virgin airs of the morning and exhaled the troubles of school and home and father.

There was nothing in the outward appearance of the cottage to suggest it was anything other than a simple fisherman's dwelling. But there had been the fishing-rods; certainly they were not the commonplace tools of an ordinary man, whose monthly wage would scarcely have been enough to buy them. Their presence against the wall had been incongruous – as odd as finding that the local farmer ploughed with a thoroughbred racehorse, or that the village shop was a branch of Fortnum's. Oliver trod warily round the cottage, giving it a wide berth;but at the same time it retained an attraction for him. Though there was somehing familiar about it- some factor or quality it possessed which struck a chord in his senses – he was at a loss to know what it might be. But it was less a sense of fear and more one of caution that caused him to bypass it, keeping it constantly in view and glancing warily across at it as he made his way through the meadow behind. Half of him took pains to avoid it, whereas his other half was drawn to it as inexorably as a needle to a magnet.

Then the weather turned. Hazily benevolent only hours before, the expression of the mountains changed to a frown which shrouded the peaks with truculent black cloud. It poured from the heights like a chill lava flow, overwhelming pasture and paddock and obscuring all but the most immediate surroundings. Despite the constant threat of it the rain held off, though the effects were much the same. Every object outdoors seemed to have been drained of its previous colours, substituting instead a drab mockery of the brighter original in which greys and browns predominated. The Castle's walls now assumed a uniform charcoal shade, causing the ancient mass to glower with redoubled malevolence upon the town.

Outdoors everything dripped. Wherever you stood – beneath trees, beyond them, under the eaves or beneath the sky – every object was heavy with runnels of water which coalesced into leaden drops far larger than the usual rainy sort, and which produced a miniature downpour at the slightest movement of branch and leaf. Ida Rusholme looked doubtfully at the sky from the study window.

'I don't think it would be a good idea for you to go far tomorrow, Oliver ' she said 'The weather is set to change quite for the worse, and the barometer is dropping off alarmingly.Mr Owens at the Post Office says that there is likely to be a heavy rainstorm because of the heat. He knows a lot about the weather hereabouts.'

'But Mother, I could wear my oilskins… and I've got my sou'wester,' Oliver protested,'and I've nothing to do in the house.'

'I'm sure there are *plenty* of exciting places to explore within the grounds' Ida replied shortly '- and perhaps you might catch up on some of your reading.You haven't been doing as much as you usually do, and you know how you enjoy it.'

'I haven't brought any books.'

'Then we'll borrow some. Perhaps from the Schoolmaster in the village. I'm sure he would be glad to lend you one or two. Besides, I have received a telegram from Papa to say that he hopes to conclude business at the office by today at the latest, and expects to join us by tomorrow afternoon's Holyhead train.' This was heavy news indeed, and Oliver's face fell visibly.'I'm sure you'll want to be here to meet him. He would be *very* glad if you were' she added brightly.

She saw that her attempt to encourage him was inept. She was constantly troubled by the strained relationship between her husband and her youngest son, and understood – or flattered herself that she understood – the reasons behind it. But she put it down to a childish phase which, like a sore throat, would run its natural course and fade with time. She perceived this dimension of father and son but indistinctly, and her mistake lay equally in choosing to view it as superficial, and in refusing to recognise that the poisonous seed of future estrangement was being planted ever deeper. Though a modern and a liberated woman for her time, further intervention on Oliver's part – beyond what she had done already – was unthinkable.

For his ranging spirit the prospect of forced enclosure within the bounds of the Rectory was bad enough.But his father's *humphing*, and those censorious looks over the rim of his spectacles... Oliver banished himself to the gardens and sought what amusement there was amongst the wooden seedtrays and sieves in the greenhouse.But it was thin fare; and the solitude of river and estuary which had invigorated him because it had purpose, now became simple loneliness when under constraint. Then the rain settled into a steady drizzle and Alice was sent to hunt him out amidst the debris. There she found him, damp and dishevelled,and ordered him firmly inside. 'An' when you come in, you can wipe them boots an' all' she said, eyeing him up and down with distaste. Oliver wondered about Alice's preoccupation with the condition of *his* boots, for it seemed that any conversation with her was always predicated by a comment the state of his footware. But while Alice was outwardly severe and abrupt, there nevertheless existed an unspoken bond between them. From the time that Oliver had taken his first tottering steps she'd had a special affection for him, though she would have been the first to deny it; and Oliver, grateful for the many little kindnesses she did him, was equally devoted to her.

Like a creature trapped in a diminishing rockpool by the receding tide, confinement indoors represented a further and alarming contraction of Oliver's territory. In frustration he banged about the Rectory, clumping up and down stairs and slamming doors until warned off by both his mother and Helene.

He'd had little to do with his sister during the holiday so far.Their paths had crossed at evening dinner, when their talk was polite but inconsequential. At other times they had met only infrequently and then quite by chance as Helene was packing easel and paints ready for the days' excursion in the trap. But that evening her conversation had become brighter and more animated, and more inclusive of him. Oliver put it down to the imminent arrival of their father, whose favourite she was. He did not begrudge her that status and regarded it as being hers almost as of right.

Oliver could not recall his sister having ever engaged him so much in conversation before. She quizzed him lightly about what he'd been doing, and what he proposed to do. He in turn told them of the Clwyr's hidden beauties and of the creatures he had seen.

Altogether the evening passed extremely pleasantly and Oliver was able to defer gloomier thoughts about his father's arrival. But the morning came, nevertheless.

'Well, Oliver. Your Mama tells me that you have been behaving yourself and have taken care not to get into scrapes. I am pleased to hear that you have kept yourself busy. Nothing comes of idleness. You look very healthy.'

'I am, thank you, Father.'

It was much as Oliver had expected – the coldness of Clarence's paternal routine toward him never surprised; but because of the boy's misplaced but irrepressible optimism, always disappointed nevertheless. His father extended a hand formally to him as if he were greeting a legal adversary. Oliver took the outstretched hand deferentially.

'You have been spending a great deal of time by the river, haven't you my dear?' Ida interposed.

Oliver nodded.

'Is there much to do, down there?' asked Clarence coolly.

'Oh, lots, if you look hard enough' said Oliver.

A faint shadow of annoyance clouded his father's face.

'I wonder if there is.' There was a hint of suspicion,and Oliver felt the barb. The comment was unkind and unnecessary, and he sensed the oblique reproach. Nomatter how well intentioned his conduct it always failed to please; he was condemned without even being charged.

His fatherly duties completed, Clarence Rusholme removed the heavy travelling-cape which he wore irrespective of the season or the weather. Now for once it had been appropriate. He shook the raindrops from it and handed it to Alice. Then he turned to the others, and his manner brightened.

'Well! From what I hear, we *might* be receiving a surprise visitor in the course of the next day or two' he said mysteriously. Clarence liked springing surprises like this, and it was the closest to lightheartedness that his nature allowed. 'Alice. Would you see to the airing of one of the guest rooms?'

'Straight away, Sir. I'll get Phoebe to light a fire. It'll cheer it up grand.'

Oliver was intrigued. He had his own ideas as to the identity of the anonymous guest; but as his opinion was not sought, he kept it to himself.

Next morning dawned bleary and grey. Oliver had risen with the lark in the vain hope of being greeted by the early sun; but one glimpse at the muddy sky as he folded back his bedroom shutters told him that he was in for much of the same.

With the arrival of his father breakfast now reverted abruptly from the casual affair which Oliver had made it to the laconic, newspaper-rustling ordeal of Millwain Place.Clarence Rusholme was punctilious about attendance at meals, to the point that it had become almost an obsession with him. Watch and clock would be scrutinised, newspapers would rustle even more, there would be emphatic sighs; then the meal would commence promptly on the hour, or on the half. The only one capable of disarming him for her lateness was Helene. Generally a smile of apology was enough to deflect Pa's – though not Ida's –irritation. In Helene lateness was the unavoidable corollary to a busy and creative life, and it assumed the role of an engaging character trait. But woe betide Oliver if he was late. In him it was a vice. So he went down early to obviate any problems, though his punctuality was only remarked upon by his mother. Clarence grunted to him from behind his *Times*.

The day passed slowly and uncomfortably. Pleasantly cool in the heat of the North Welsh summers, the limestone of the Rectory now become dank and chill overnight.Fires had to be lit not only in the guestrooms but throughout the house to dispel the cellar-like atmosphere which pervaded everywhere. Oliver sought the outermost limits of the garden where he could remain as inconspicuous as possible, and the day dragged on to a still damper evening. As to who the enigmatic visitor might be, he had a pretty shrewd idea that it would prove to be Godfrey. Camp would be finishing that weekend and the distance from Shrewsbury to Ridland was substantially less than from it to Manchester. It was logical enough that Godfrey would take the shortest route – and anyhow, his father's manner hinted strongly in that direction. But for all that, whilst the element of surprise was absent, the sense of anticipation which Oliver felt at the prospect of his brother's arrival was undiminished. He thought of all the things they could do together; how he would take Godfrey down to the Clwyr and show him his bridge and his seapool and his wrecks and how they would listen to the seabirds and the wind.

He was roused from his reverie by the clop of a horse coming slowly up from the village, and the rattle of a cab's ironshod wheels on the road. He looked up eagerly as it swung heavily in through the Rectory gates. The driver drew rein, and a tall masculine figure descended. Cases and a trunk were handed down – Oliver could not make out by whom, for from his vantage point some sixty yards distant his view was obscured by the body of the cab itself. The driver was paid, and saluting smartly, clicked his tongue to the horse and turned for home. In the misty twilight Oliver could not see clearly enough to make out the figure; but he heard voices engaged in light banter, and laughter. Surely there must be two?

The main doors of the Rectory were thrown open and orange light poured out onto the drive, illuminating the figures standing there. As they turned Oliver caught sight of his brother's profile. The other face was that of Gerald Warrington.

Oliver had expected to have Godfrey to himself; this he regarded as his of right. He had not considered the possibility of another guest accompanying his brother, and his plans were thrown into confusion by it. As a devotee of the sporting idol Oliver was flattered that Warrington had seen fit to visit them, and was prouder than ever of his brother who was enhanced still further in his eyes by bringing such a guest to their house. On the other hand Warrington introduced an atmosphere of School-invisible but nonetheless present. He epitomised that system, moreso even than Godfrey, and with him came an aura of implicit censure. Oliver knew the alternative 'non-school'aspects of his brother's character intimately; and whilst he deeply admired and respected him as an icon of the school system, it was the other side – the more human side – which he loved. Oliver was ignorant of any equivalent quality in Warrington; he was exclusively School, albeit its most acceptable face. And then, of course, there was the matter of Helene; and whilst Oliver would have preferred to forget all that he knew, it was not that easy.

The meeting with Godfrey had been warm enough; but Oliver detected a new reserve which he did not doubt owed its origins to the presence of Warrington, and which made him smart with resentment. Somehow by just being there Warrington had unwittingly modified his brother's boyish sense of fun and had instead caused it to be supplanted by an urbanity which seemed unnatural and rather forced.

From the hosts' point of view dinner went splendidly. There was much laughter at the doings of various people at Camp and as a popular and honoured guest Warrington was the main focus of attention, though Oliver noticed that whilst Helene had greeted him in a friendly manner and smiled politely at his anecdotes she alone seemed to maintain a cool distance from him, limiting her exchanges to a clipped sentence or two, and those seemingly out of courtesy alone. Oliver recalled how animated his sister had been on the previous day, and had wondered at her high spirits. On reflection it seemed that they had arisen almost from a sense of expectancy,as if she had been privy to news which had been kept from the rest of the family. But his mother *knew* of the intended arrival of his father, so that was certainly no secret. He came to the conclusion that Godfrey must have written to his sister and asked that his visit be kept from them, though why only from his mother and himself he could not fathom out.

He was not alone in his reservations. Ida was not blind to her daughter's fey mood,and now saw how their guest's initial attempts to engage her in conversation brought a momentary flush of colour to her cheeks. She also noted how Helene averted her eyes from Warrington's, looking indifferently elsewhere after he had spoken to her and how she fell into deep discussion with Clarence about some trivial matter.

'Have you noticed anything about Helene?' she asked as they prepared for bed 'about her attitude, in general?' Clarence stopped undoing his collar and considered.

'I doubt it's anything of importance,' he said. 'Perhaps a little too bubbly, tonight? She certainly talked a great deal- at least to me. Why do you ask?'

'Oh, nothing really. No reason, in particular. It's just that she seemed rather... well, *strange.* Just at certain moments. Please don't concern yourself about it; I'm sure it's nothing'

'Probably misses her friends, you know. They're such a chatty lot when they're together; quite the *life and soul*, so to speak. Couldn't she ask them down?'

'She has written to them, certainly. She tells me that May Atherton has replied with apologies – she's off to Italy with her parents. But Dulcie Grady says she'd love to come, though she's unsure when. That's rather Dulcie, I'm afraid. Always something of a butterfly.'

Dulcie Grady fluttered through life irrepressibly and buoyantly, and rarely downhearted, always putting a positive gloss on the gloomiest situations. What she lacked in poise was compensated for by her ability to cheer others. Corpulent since childhood she possessed a round figure and a moonlike face with a mouth which dimpled into an irreverent grin and eyes which creased readily into a smile. This, topped off with a shock of curly blonde hair and a taste for white dresses caused her to resemble an enormous giggling meringue. Though some thought her shallow she cared little for opinion, either way. At heart a realist she had a talent for stripping off pretentiousness and seeing people for what they were.

She had considered herself in the mirror and after a long cool look had decided pragmatically that she would never resemble the *Gibson Girl* nor stood a chance of ever getting close. She sniffed at her reflection then smiling wistfully, shrugged her shoulders and walked away from it, resolving to be her own person from that day on.She was of a rare breed; irrespective of what you thought of her, you could not help liking her.

She and Helene Rusholme had been fast friends and confidantes since their schooldays, and each was foil for the other – in looks and in character. Clarence had a soft spot for his daughter's light-headed friend and was tolerant of her apparent superficiality.

'Dulcie?' he said equably. 'Of course. Why not?'

At that moment Helene was shrouding herself in a warm travelling cape against the clinging night dampness. Her heart throbbing in her ears she tiptoed silently down from her room. With the fleetness of a cat she made her way through the pantry and along the stone-flagged corridor which gave on to the vegetable garden. In the darkness she fumbled for the handle of the outer door. It turned but would not open. She stifled a little cry. Again she tried the handle, and rattled it up and down as loudly as she dared. It seemed to her that every sound was amplified tenfold, that the slightest movement echoed and roared throughout the house. Someone must *surely* have been alerted by the racket she was making? She paused a moment. Apart from the beating of her heart all remained still and silent.

Again she pulled at the door, her emotions adding fire to her efforts. Still it would not yield. She stepped back and reconsidered as coolly as she could, absently brushing back an invisible lock of hair.

Matches! She sped back to a kitchen still bathed dull red by the coals glowing in the range – the only fire still burning in the house. Swiftly she searched the high mantel – shelf where she knew Alice kept her pot of lucifers and spills. Soon – though not soon enough for her – she was scanning the area of the door by a faint flame. Immediately to the left of the lock hung the key. Chiding herself for not having the sense to check it out beforehand she seized it and with a trembling hand rattled it into the keyhole. It turned unwillingly, but she was out at last.

Clutching the collar of her cape about her against the chill of the sea-mist she picked her way along the cobbled path. There hardly ten paces before her she could make out a darker shadow. It seemed to turn toward her as she approached.

'Gerald?' her voice was tremulous. 'Gerald? *Is that you*?'

'I wondered if you'd come.'

'I have... oh Gerald, I... have… ' A sob rose up from deep within, choking her further words. In a second Warrington had covered the few yards separating them and they were enfolded in each others arms, clinging tightly, fiercely, possessively. They hugged and caressed and kissed each other as if in defiance of the world, indifferent to all else. He smoothed her hair with his hand; she ran her fingers through his; and as he wiped away her tears with his handkerchief she caressed his cheeks. Then arms closely about each other they made their way stumblingly to a little gazebo by the lawn. Warrington lit a tiny oil lamp. There by its faltering rays they sat closely together in silence, for a long while.

'Since we parted I've just lived my life an hour at a time.' Warrington's voice contrasted starkly with his forced levity at dinner. 'I've just waited and waited, counting the days off to our meeting which all along I thought might never happen. It's been a torment. *Why* did you never reply to any of my letters? That was cruel of you' he added reproachfully. 'You *did* get them, didn't you?'

'I did. And I'm sorry.'

'Then why… '

'Because of what I said the last time. I hated myself for saying it, but it was true then.I have to stand by it'. She paused, trying to regain her composure. 'Time hasn't changed anything.It's just as true now.' She pronounced the words slowly and emphatically, in a vain attempt to mask the tumult of feelings within her..

'You can't believe that. Not really.And anyway 'he said with passion 'Time *does* change things It has with me.I'm more certain than ever about my love for you.'

She made no attempt to answer.

'Do you love me?' he continued 'You said you did, once.' Again there was a pause. 'Helene! *Do* you?'

'You know I do.'

'Then I think it's outrageous that we should have to creep about like this – like thieves in the night. What have we to feel guilty about?'

'I don't want anyone to know… about us. Nobody must! And I don't want our relationship to go beyond… what it has already. We've gone too far, as it is '

'You *can't* mean it. Not after what… after the way we met. Doesn't your heart tell you anything? You can't deceive it,or me. I think you're being dishonest with yourself. And with me, for that matter.'

'I'm trying not to be. I don't want to pretend to you, of all people There's a *part* of me which says this is all wrong. That we're too young for each other… for all this. We can't get tied up in knots, so soon. We've years to go before we could ever marry. I *do* believe it.'

'But Helene! you admit that is only one part of you. What does the *other* half tell you? What does the *real* you want?' He squeezed both her hands vehemently. She made no reply at first, and looked out unseeingly into the dark. '*Well*?'he urged.

'You.' Her voice was almost inaudible. Warrington laughed aloud for joy at this.

'Sssh!' Instantly the depressive atmosphere was banished from the hut, and the very mist seemed to lift a little around them 'Be quiet, you silly!' she giggled girlishly shaking his arm 'Do you want to wake the whole house?'

'I don't mind! And I don't care! I really don't! We love each other and that's everything!'

Again they kissed passionately and long, she covering his face with caresses, he seeking her lips over and over.

'Gerald' she said, tearing herself free 'we *have* to be realistic. We *can't* get engaged, or anything. Mama and Papa would be furious. They wouldn't give their consent or their blessing to it. And I don't want to hurt their feelings.' Now it was Warrington's turn to be silent

'You do see the logic of my point,don't you? Gerald?

'Yes. Yes, of course.But then, my Pa is twenty years or so older than my Ma.'

'But that's not it exactly. My Pa's a lot older than my mother too. It's not about age differences, don't you see? Our parents married when they could – when our fathers had established themselves in their professions. You've got at least three if not four years ahead of you at the University. And there's so much that I want to do, here and in Bremen; I *must* go back to the Academy. That would bring us to 1914 at the earliest. Then you'd need a couple of years as pupil before you could become a barrister in your own right. And *then* you'd have to find Chambers and begin to make a name for yourself. That could be as late as 1917 before we could hope to marry.'

'You're being a bit of a Job's Comforter' he said, but noted hopefully that she had spoken of marriage without his mentioning it.

'Gerald,my darling, I'm trying desperately to face the realities for *both* of us. We have to face up to them, sooner or later.'

'We can go on seeing each other, can't we?' he pleaded. 'I mean, there'll be vacations. Oxford's's terms aren't particularly long,and there'll be weekends too. And we can write.'

'We can write'.

'But will you..?'

There was a pause. 'Yes,of course I will. I was wrong-headed. I thought I could fight this thing off by ignoring it, trying to deny its existence… and you. I'm so sorry I hurt you so.'

'So are we lovers, at last?'

'No, not exactly' she prevaricated. 'Let's just say we are friends who love each other.'

Her tautology was lost on Warrington, whose uncomplicated nature was unable to distinguish between the subtler calibrations of a more sophisticated mind. But he accepted the distinction uncomplainingly; as far as he could see there was little in it.

They sat together twined in each others arms until the first ragged light of dawn filtered through the gaps in the planking of their shelter. A casual observer might have passed them by seeing only motionless shadows against the dark.

Distant clattering in the kitchen awoke them immediately from their reverie. '*It's Alice*!'Helene said in panic.' She's always first to rise, even before Phoebe. We've spent far too long here! What shall we *do*?'

'We can't go back in together.'

'Of course we can't ! Gerald, how did you find your way out here?'

'Well, I came through the conservatory, and out by the garden door.'

'Then you'd better go back the way you came. Remember to lock the doors behind you. Go now. I'll wait a little longer.'

Another lingering kiss, and they parted, Warrington slipping away into the pre-dawn greyness which instantly swallowed him. Helene suddenly felt the cold as she was deprived of his physical warmth, and she wrapped the cloak more closely about her and sat still and silent, listening to the homely noises from the kitchen. Her pulse raced – not only because of the fear of detection – but because the feelings rekindled by Warrington glowed on undiminished.

After what she considered a sufficient interval she rose, dusted her clothes down and arranged her hair as best she could. Then she cautiously made her way back along the path to the kitchen door. She turned the handle and entered the passage, now lit brightly by the made-up kitchen fire. The atmosphere was heavy with breakfast smells, as Alice bustled about frying her own and Phoebe's meals. Helene closed the outer door silently behind her – for once it did not creak – and turned the key in the lock. Then she crept past the opening where she could see Alice's round figure stooping over something on the range. But any hope Helene might have entertained to slip past unnoticed was vain. Alice gave a start and spun round with a speed belied by her size.

'By gum, Miss! Miss Helene! You *did* give me a fright! I nearly jumped out of my skin.' Once over the initial shock the old woman looked her up and down critically. ' What are you doin' about at *this* time o'the mornin'? she asked suspiciously 'Been out on t' tiles by the look of it.'

Alice considered the figure which stood before her, her eyes dwelling on the girl's face. With a knowing look she turned back to the range to prevent the contents of a pan from boiling over.' For some time, an' all' she continued, half to herself. 'Pardon me for sayin' so, but you look a *right* mess!' she added sternly. 'You'd best take care not to let your Ma and Pa see you like that; they wouldn't be overpleased.' A denial would have been futile, and somehow insulting to the old woman. It would have been hard to dissemble. Despite the warmth in the kitchen Helene suddenly felt icy cold and weak. She sank silently down onto a bench and buried her face in her hands. Alice was beside her in an instant, arm around her shoulder. The voice which spoke now was filled with compassion

'Now then,lass! It's Mr.Warrington, isn't it?' Helene just nodded her head. 'Ah,well! Just you get nice an' warm here before you go back upstairs.Let's get a hot cup o' tea down you. Works wonders, does that.' While the tea brewed she cradled the girl's slim frame in both her arms, Helene's head nestled into the curve of her ample bosom as she had so often done in years long past, when the child had run tearfully in to her for a plaster and for comfort.

Then they had tea together; and though they refrained from speaking, the silence between them was eloquent.

Helene rose to go. 'Now make yourself presentable' Alice said.

'In the scullery you'll find a mirror, and I'll lend you me hairbrush. Also, there's some of your clean nighties in t' laundry-room. Slip into one o' 'em, tak'off them wet shoes and cape, and stump up t' main stairs bold as brass. No-one'll even guess where you've been.' Helene changed her clothes as she was bidden. Now dressed in her nightgown and with her hair braided, she looked as if she had just risen. Apart from her eyes.

She put her head around the kitchen door. 'Thank you Alice' she smiled. Then she stepped across to the old woman and kissed her tenderly on the cheek.

'Thank you.'

'Silly stuff!' came the retort. 'I'd do t'same for me own, if I'd had any,' and the habitual archness reasserted itself.

Then she took the girl's hand and squeezed it to emphasise her point. 'There's nowt to fear from this quarter, Love. Your secret's safe wi'me.'

As Helene left the room, she called after her 'but for God's Sake, Lass! be careful.'

Chapter Seven

NEXT DAY the prevailing wind shifted from an easterly to a drier southerly, and with the change the drizzle promptly ceased. A fresh but pleasantly warm breeze displaced the dankness and the massed columns of cloud, scattering them far out over the Irish Sea. Oliver watched the shifting patchwork of blues and creamy whites, and his spirits rose. And as the weather lifted so did the injunction confining Oliver to the Rectory.

At breakfast he seated himself beside his brother and Warrington who included him in their general conversation, asking his opinion of this player or that, and of the Rugby teams' prospects for the autumn. His sister's arrival a few minutes later than everyone else went unnoticed and unremarked on except by the two who had a particular interest in her at that moment. Despite Helene's indifference to Warrington at dinner on the previous evening, Ida Rusholme noticed that her greeting was this time in contrast friendly and attentive. Her daughter had tried to slip as unobtrusively as possible into her place; but the young men had already risen to receive her and as she seated herself there was a fleeting glance across the table in Warrington's direction.. For a second their eyes met.

Ida saw it but remained unsure as to what it might imply. Was she reading too much into what might well be no more than innocent good manners? she asked herself. And if Warrington did find Helene attractive, it was hardly surprising. What concerned her was that it should not lead to emotional dalliance or an entanglement of any sort. That would be most unacceptable. Unconventional though she might be in many ways, she was unflinchingly conventional in this. Affairs of the heart were to be conducted with the express consent and under the approving eyes of the parents. There was a time and place for everything, she thought, and such a time – if it came about at all – should be far in the future. If indeed there was any attachment such things were usually transient, she told herself, and attributable to young men's tendency to infatuation. For now Ida dismissed her thoughts as being mere speculation, and nothing more.

'And what have you decided to do today, Mr. Warrington?' she enquired brightly; 'the weather is set fair to be a quite dry and warm; much more appropriate to the season, don't you think?'

'Absolutely! In fact, Godfrey and I were wondering if young Oliver here might wish to accompany us – to act as guide, as it were. We hear he's become quite knowledgeable about the landscape hereabouts. That's only if he's got nothing better to do, of course.'

'Would you like to, Oliver?'

A sudden unwillingness to take Godfrey *and* Warrington on his river-walk – the walk he had reserved to share exclusively with his brother – caused him to hesitate.

'Well, I suppose there are one or two places we could go… ' he said reluctantly.

'Oh, but what about the *fascinating* walk down by the river that you told us about?' interjected his mother 'some of the things you described sound most interesting – the great fish, the herons, and that old wrecked ship. He described them so well for us didn't he, Helene?'

Helene nodded emphatically. At that moment Oliver could blithely have done away with his mother and sister. Apart from compromising his intended walk with Godfrey they were clearly patronising him; they were talking 'adult talk' – the way some grown ups have of altering the manner in which they speak to children when there are other adults present – and he resented it.

'It'll be too muddy. It's been raining like anything. And besides there's been a high tide.'

'He's got a point there,' said Godfrey. 'I for one don't want to get absolutely plastered in mud – not if there's somewhere else to go. We'll have a good look at the map after breakfast.'

The two young men with Oliver unwillingly in tow made for the study, where the map was spread out on the desk. There was little Oliver could suggest as an alternative destination, for his time had been spent on the Clwyr and he was virtually ignorant of everywhere else. Consequently he felt rather redundant. They decided on a route without really consulting him much, and it was presented to him as a *fait accompli*.

Their ramble took them down byways and overhung lanes to tiny stone hamlets where they were stared at by inquisitive cottagers and where the young men's clear English attracted the attention of those to whom it was still probably a foreign tongue. In different circumstances Oliver would have revelled in it; but as it was he draggled behind – and was encouraged to *try to keep up, there's a good chap* as if he was some truculent child. This only worsened matters and from having made little effort to communicate at the start of the walk he now became downright taciturn. Having tried and failed to engage Oliver in conversation his older companions fell back upon their mutual interests, discussing people and joking in a language which was almost as foreign to him as it was to the Welsh villager. Oliver recognised the laughter but not the idiom; it was exclusive and he felt marginalised.

As the excursion drew to its weary close Godfrey dropped the final bombshell; they would be leaving the next day for Manchester. Whilst they had always intended it to be a flying visit, circumstances had arisen which required their prompt return. Abandoning silence Oliver now put as forceful a case as he could as to why Godfrey should stay a little longer with them. He could see that Warrington might *have* to go back – after all, his Ma and Pa must be expecting him – but surely there was no need for Godfrey to race off quite so soon? Yet nomatter how winning his arguments, they were politely but firmly countered by Godfrey. It seemed to Oliver that Warrington was less convinced of the necessity to leave than his brother,and this was doubly hurtful. But it had been agreed between them that there was nothing for it. They *had* to go. This pitched him headlong back into his uncommunicative mood once more.

There was a quiet knock on Oliver's door. He had taken himself off to bed early on the pretext of feeling tired but had lain there in the dark very much awake. Try to shut them out as he would, the events of the day kept turning over in his mind like a bad case of mental indigestion,and he still smarted with a sense that it was all acutely unjust.

'Come in'. Nothing happened, and the knock was repeated. 'I said *come in.*'

The door opened and Godfrey's head appeared around it. 'You're not going to bawl at me are you, old chap?'

'No. Why?'

'You seemed rather loud, that's all.'

'I didn't mean to be.' Oliver slowly sat himself upright, and turned up the flame of the oil lamp.

His brother's manner seemed almost apologetic as he stood at the foot of the bed. Though puzzled by this unexpected visit Oliver maintained a stony silence. Godfrey shifted uneasily, 'I think we need to have a little talk.'

'What about?'

'Well, about today, for a start. I was a little surprised by your… attitude.'

Oliver made no reply.

'You were very offhand, I think.'

'What do you mean *offhand*?'

'You seemed very sulky. To Warrington, and to me especially.'

'Was I? I didn't mean it.'

'I think you did. I was under the impression that you liked and respected Warrington.'

'Well, I *do*. But it isn't *that*' Oliver said resentfully 'it doesn't matter if I like him or not. I thought just you'd be here, so we could go and do things together, like we used to.'

'I really hadn't considered it like that' Godfrey said ' about bringing Warrington along. He really was most keen to come and see Ma and Pa again – you know how popular he is with them – and with *Helene* too, I think.'

Oliver could find no further words to say. Godfrey looked at the small figure in the bed, looked at the sorrowful white face and the accusing eyes, and felt a sudden pang of conscience. He saw how much his brother must have anticipated his visit and how insensitive he had been in taking Oliver's agreement for granted.

'I'm sorry I hurt your feelings, Oliver' he said quietly. 'It's the last thing I'd want to do. Can't we part friends?' He stretched out his hand. Oliver slowly extricated his own from beneath the counterpane where he had stuffed it. At once the iciness between them thawed and the old friendship and closeness reasserted themselves.

'I really am looking forward to taking that ramble down by the river, you know. Ma and Helene were most impressed by what you'd told them; they weren't ribbing you, truly.'

'It jolly well seemed like it, at the time.'

'I think you were being a *little* too prickly. You should have seen your pout!'

Godfrey grimaced horribly in imitation of Oliver, complete with rolling eyes.

'I didn't! Not like *that*, did I?'

'Oh, yes you did!' retorted Godfrey in a sing-song pantomime voice 'a beastly ghastly ghostly scowl, with great big slobbery lips dangling almost to the floor. But no-one happened to notice… .'

His performance was cut short a pillow hurled by Oliver, which Godfrey swiftly returned.

'But seriously, Godfrey; have you *really* to go – tomorrow, I mean? Can't you put it off just for a day or two?'

'Fraid not. It just can't be done. I've got an appointment at the outfitters tomorrow afternoon. If I miss it, it'll mean that my stuff simply won't be ready when I go up to the University. It would be unthinkable.'

Oliver reconciled himself to it; but it was still impossible for him to conceal his disappointment.

'Oh well, p'raps we can go on my walk next time then.'

'Yes, of *course.* We'll make it a binding contract, as Pa would say.'

'Promise?'

'I promise.'

It would prove to be a contract that one of them would not live to fulfil.

A watery sun emerged uncertainly from the east as Godfrey Rusholme and his friend Gerald Warrington piled aboard the trap. Each had said his farewells to the family that morning prior to the departure for Rhyl Station, and now with a selfconscious flourish they climbed up and perched themselves alongside the driver.

It was the second time that Warrington had taken leave of the girl who had been the sole object of his visit, for they had said their protracted goodbyes hours before in the privacy of the garden. Now with true emotions carefully masked there was no more than a knowing look or a lingering glance to hint at the depth of feeling between them.

The trap jolted abruptly into motion speeding the visitors down the drive and away through the gates; then they were gone: and as the rattling of wheels and the tuneful ring of harness faded to nothing, the family turned back once more to their holiday.

With his father showing no inclination to share in any of his pursuits Oliver was again left to his own devices. He took up where he had left off, and headed directly for the river; but Godfrey's flying visit had brought home to him the extent of his loneliness, and it was with diminished enthusiasm that he took up his foraging of river and rockpool.

The rains had caused a rise in the river level, and in consequence access to some of the more interesting parts of the Clwyr was limited. Gentle glides of only a week before were now transformed into turbulent whirlpools, brown with silts scoured from the upper reaches. Branches, leaves and other debris were spiralled around and off downstream to the sea, and gravelly runs of barely a few inches now lay hidden beneath many feet of sullen river.

Though his usual haunts were largely submerged, Oliver religiously continued his daily wanderings finding a curious attraction in the morose power of the flood.It was that sense of being so close to something elemental and untameable, something in which Mankind has no part, or say; the flood pursued its course unheeding and unstoppable, distainfully sweeping aside every obstacle or carrying it off rapaciously. Even the Ridland bridge which seemed to Oliver to have stood forever would, he could see, one day inevitably succumb to that irresistible force.

The unexpected recall of his father to Manchester and the office some days after Godfrey's departure was to remove the final impediment to his taking up where he had left off.

Oliver had been present to bid his dutiful farewell, though his sense of relief must have been evident. As Clarence Rusholme climbed stiffly into the carriage he had given his son a large amount of advice but nothing material in the shape of money – not from meanness but rather from a fear of what uses the boy might put it to. Oliver had not minded, much; it was nothing out of the ordinary. He was perpetually hard-up and because he had learned from experience to survive on few extra luxuries he had long since ceased to be demanding; he recognised that there was simply no point. By far the best thing his father could do for him at that moment was to go back to the city.

He maintained his daily watch on the river, which because of his growing love for it and because he had yet to encounter another living soul on its banks, he had begun to regard ever more as exclusively *his.* He noted with satisfaction the steady drop in its levels as it quietened down from its irascible mood and settled to a more sedate pace, and it intrigued him that after the torrent it returned to a course different from that which it had left – a bank had subsided here, a new shoal had appeared there. It was still recognisable as the river he had known, but in the aftermath of the storm it had changed, had adapted and reshaped its route to the sea. And still it flowed on, undiminished; if anything it had enlarged itself, becoming more expansive and more powerful. His wanderings took him past the whitewashed cottage again – its curious magnetism still attracted, he could still not think why – and on one particular morning he was intrigued to see activity there. Apart from the usual wisp of smoke rising from its one chimney he saw that the cane fishing rods which habitually leaned against the rear wall were now waggling to and fro like the antenna of some colossal insect. Their invisible owner was clearly preparing for a fishing expedition, as tips dipped away behind the wall to reemerge with brown silk lines threaded through the rod-rings. Oliver was fascinated, and immediately abandoned his plan to visit the wreck. Shortly after came the sound of oars being pushed into rowlocks, and of a chain clinking against stonework as it was being loosened. Then came the rhythmic *clunk-swish* of steady rowing, as the angler and his craft quit the little jetty for the open river. Oliver sped off through the field to a point which would bring him out downstream of the cottage, and which he knew would give him an unimpeded view of the lower reaches. Neither boat nor boatman could be seen. With a sense of urgency he reversed his direction and headed back to the stile, vaulting over it in one jump. Dropping onto the soft ground beyond he ran as fast as the muddy path allowed. He shielded his eyes against the sunlight dappling the water and was relieved to catch his first glimpse of the unknown fisherman. Though too far away to make out the man's face, Oliver could see from the outline of his heavy frame that he possessed considerable physical strength. Broad shoulders bent to the oars with the skill of an accomplished boatman, and each thrust powered the craft against the stream at a good walking pace. Oliver kept his position well abreast of the rower, skirting along the bankside and feigning indifference should he look by chance in Oliver's direction.

From time to time the movement of the oars would cease as the man studied the river; then the rowing would begin again, though now the oarblades were lifted from the water leaving hardly a ripple in their wake – the emphasis now apparently being on stealth rather than speed. These halts were repeated some three or four times until the chosen spot was reached. A round stone weight was silently lowered to the riverbed; then rope was paid out as the boat drifted back and was held motionless in the current. At first the man was preoccupied with some small detail as he bent over the fishing rod; then standing upright he began working it back and forth, simultaneously drawing line from the reel.

With supreme skill the line and artificial fly which was attached to it were extended yard by yard across an area of deeper water lying behind a tumbling shoal. The series of actions were blended by the sunlight into one combined movement,as the curve of rod and line were caught in a symmetry of flickering and flashing; then the pattern shifted, from an oval to a figure-eight to a zig-zag. Mesmerised, Oliver watched as the lure was dropped at the head of the pool. Then stooping slightly the fisherman froze into a cat-like immobility, save for the stealthy drawing-back of the line with his left hand. Having worked that run through with no result the figure drew itself upright once more, and relaxed; then the whole process was repeated, this time with the fly dropping a foot or so to the left. Again the angler poised to strike, but again there was nothing.

A dozen or more casts were made across the pool, to no effect.

The man paused awhile, and Oliver could see him remove a battered old hat, and scratch his head. There was something about the way he carried out that simple act which made it almost a mannerism, and which seemed vaguely familiar; but Oliver could not associate it with anyone he knew.

Clearly a change of strategy was called for. Rummaging through a tackle-box the figure produced something and quickly substituted it for the fly he had been using. Once again the line was extended and cast, and once more the pool was searched, inch by inch. At first it drew a blank. Nothing. The second slow retrieval. Still nothing. But at the third attempt the rod tip was galvanised into sudden action. It twitched like a thing possessed, and the angler struck. Oliver's heart seemed to rise into his mouth. Now the line stretched taut as the fish shot to and fro, and was rapidly brought to the landing-net.

Oliver's could see the silver form struggling in the man's hands as the hook was removed. Then it seemed to Oliver that the man looked admiringly at the creature for a moment before slipping it gently back into the river. With barely a splash it was gone again.

Oliver was as entrapped as the fish. The man checked the state of the lure, and recast. For some time nothing happened. Then at the third drift down the rod again bent into action.

It was clear that this time it was no small fish. For a second or two there was no movement other than that caused by immovable resistance on the other end of the line. Instead of the scuttering of the tip only, the whole rod now curved itself into a shapely arc. As the realisation dawned that it had been hooked the quarry turned and powered off upstream at remarkable speed, stripping line from the shrieking reel. There was nothing the fisherman could do but hold on, controlling the drum with the palm of his hand as the rod bucked and kicked in his grasp. Oliver could see the bow-wave of the fish as it quit the depths of the pool and headed for the shallows beyond, and towards the remains of a tree brought down by the flood. The fisherman saw it too, and with a Herculean effort succeeded in turning the fish away from the snag. Now the battle continued in open water with the creature making doggedly for the next pool above. But by applying constant sidestrain the fisherman skilfully steered it round until it was following a diagonal course downstream, and back into the pool where it had been hooked. Still it fought on, powering to right and to left, but each rush served only to reduce the distance between it and the boat by a foot or two. And as the great fish was drawn alongside it summoned all its ebbing strength in one final bid for life and freedom, thrashing the water into a foam. As its struggles became feebler and more infrequent the man reached for a lasso-shaped contraption and deftly slipped it over the fishes' tail. The noose tightened and with one heave it was drawn bodily upwards and over the gunwale.

For a second Oliver caught the iridescent gleam of great silver-scaled flanks; then it disappeared into the well of the boat. Oliver had abandoned any pretence of being a mere passer-by; in his excitement he had stood upright from his crouching position and now, watching the closing moments of the fight he found himself clapping instinctively, as he would have for any other sporting *coup*. The distant figure turned and acknowledged the applause by doffing his battered hat to Oliver. Then the man stooped down again to the captive. An implement was raised, and a single blow fell.

The next day and the day following Oliver returned to the river in the hope of witnessing the fisherman repeat his triumph. But the rods leant in their usual position by the wall, and the boat knocked quietly against the stone jetty. Of their owner there was no sign.

On the following Sunday morning, as chapel-bells called the faithful to prayer, Oliver's path took him as usual down to the river.He was in a troubled state of mind, for his mother – hitherto quite content to allow him as much latitude as he wanted, had now begun to express those reservations planted by her husband about how Oliver spent his many hours of freedom. The evening before she had suggested worryingly that they ought to spend more time together, and explore further afield – perhaps he might wish to look at some castles?

Mulling over the implications of his mother's announcement he followed the well-trodden path which brought him to the first of the deeper pools. The night's tide was now dropping rapidly and the current swept into this natural basin, causing the surface to boil rather more powerfully than normal. Oliver pricked up his ears, alerted by a faint but regular drumming of wood against wood. Though distant, there could be no doubting it; the fisherman was making his way steadily upstream.

Within a minute or two the same old figure, clad as before in weatherstained tweeds and deerstalker, hove into view, emitting occasional puffs of tobacco-smoke as he bent to the oars.

The boat glided into position against the far bank and anchored in a deep eddy. Watched intently by Oliver the fisherman explored every overhang and ledge, every shallow and deep, paying out line here, drawing in line there. Small fish were hooked, landed and returned, and others were hooked and lost; but the success of that first day was not repeated. He wound in his line and secured the cast to his rod. As he stooped to haul in the anchor-stone he glanced up and noticing Oliver on the distant bank, raised a hand in greeting. Oliver saw the gesture, and waved back. The fisherman sat down on the bench and turned the boat, allowing the flow to carry him downstream through a shoal of fast water and into the pool below. Oliver followed as best he could, arriving in time to see the first cast coil out over the water. As before, little enough seemed to be happening. The fisherman struck hard at a take but missed it entirely, the sharpness of the strike causing line and cast to flick back over his head and become entangled in an overhanging tree. For once Oliver saw him discomfited as he retrieved his line minus the cast and fly.

Once more the pool was searched systematically as the replacement fly was worked back and forth. At the conclusion of the third cast the rod twitched and the fisherman's frame visibly stiffened. Again it twitched, and the hook was struck home. This fish was if anything greater and wiser than its predecessor, for without delay it set out on a scorching run of some fifty yards or more across the river, making straight towards a tangle of roots and brambles immediately below Oliver's perch. Despite every effort to slow its first surge there was little the fisherman could do to head it off; the creature was wily and old, and it had not lived so long nor grown so huge by being stupid. It knew well the location of every established snag and bolt-hole upwards of five miles from the sea and it had every intention of using its knowledge and its considerable strength to evade capture now.

With a mingled sense of excitement and shock Oliver watched as the invisible giant headed across the river, the only clue to its whereabouts being the tiny v- shaped wake as the line cut through the water. He looked from the snag to the line and back again, seeing in an instant what the fishes' objective was. What impressed him most perhaps was not the speed so much as the irresistible force which headed so unwaveringly toward him, and the creature's intelligence. As it approached the nearer bank it slowed for a moment, presumably to get its bearings. Then with one final sweep of its tailfin which caused the water to boil it drove beneath the overhang, neatly hitching the cast round a fallen branch. There it went doggedly to ground, believing itself impregnable.

The fisherman' s exasperation could be heard right across the river. Nomatter how hard he pulled and irrespective of the direction the cast remained attached immovably to the branch. There was no alternative to snapping off, and parting company with cast and fish.

Then the fisherman's eyes narrowed in disbelief. It seemed hard to credit, but the boy had climbed down the crumbling bank and was now balanced precariously only inches above the flow. He had evidently got himself a stick from somewhere and was trying to untangle the cast from the snag. At first he was unsuccessful, and in his wilder sweepings seemed only likely to entangle himself. '*Get back, boy! Get back*!' bellowed the fisherman as he saw the danger ' *There's no need*!' Oliver heard the man's voice, and the alarm in it; he recognised it in an instant, and smiled to himself. Breaking off the loose ends of his stick he fashioned it quickly into a rough 'Y' shape.

With one hand clinging to a protruding root he leaned out from the banking and by using his stick as a fork was able to untangle the cast from the branch. He waved his hand to the fisherman, shouting 'It's free again, sir!' but as he did so, he momentarily lost his footing and slid rather than fell into the water below. The chill percolated through his thick woollen trousers and made them instantly as heavy as lead. For a moment he hung there, up to his waist in the river. Then with a snapping like a rifle shot the root to which he still clung broke, and Oliver was pitched headlong into the glide below.

When he had first looked down the river at that point seemed to run black and glassy. It occurred to him that it was deep, and he had shivered at it. But the speed of his descent carried him down under waters far deeper than he had supposed. An olive darkness swept about him, and swallowed him; the sounds of the world above suddenly became remote and deadened and for a fleeting moment he was conscious of the mouth of a cave yawning beneath the overhang; then to Oliver's horror something huge and grey emerged from it, and gathering speed forced its way violently past him.

This added a further impetus to his instinct to save himself as he struggled gasping to the surface and attempted to regain the bank; but the buoyancy provided by his jacket could only be temporary, and was counteracted by his hefty boots. Despite all his efforts he was swept backward by the current and began to sink for a second time. Oliver would have met his end there and then had his jacket collar not been seized in a vice-like grip which hauled him rapidly upwards back into the daylight. With one heave he was dragged over the gunwale and was dumped unceremoniously into the well of the boat. There he lay, his head spinning, feebly coughing up river-water.

' Breathe in, boy. Get it all up! Onto your side, now. That's the ticket!' Oliver turned his head to the speaker. Sad old eyes returned his gaze from beneath a battered hat. 'Really, Rusholme! You *are* the limit!' but there was no reprimand in the words; only relief.

'But the *fish*, sir! *The fish!*' Oliver burst out as he recalled the reason for his near-drowning.

'Hang the fish, boy. I'd lost him, anyway.'

And Captain Bonnard smiled.

Chapter Eight

THEY SAT in the black and white study of the Rectory. To one side stood Oliver, scrubbed and pink from a hot bath and in dry clothes. Before him sat Ida, and beside her, Bonnard.

'I really think this has gone *quite* far enough, Oliver' his mother said 'your Papa foresaw that this – or something rather like it – would happen. I blame myself for it *entirely*, Captain. What your opinion must be, I dread to think!'

The old man carefully put down his teacup, but said nothing.

'I simply can't imagine where it will end, if he continues in this reckless fashion.' Ida looked severely at Oliver.

'If I could say a few words in mitigation, Mrs Rusholme... ?'

'Please *do,* Captain.'

'Firstly, I do not think that things are nearly so bad as you fear'.

'How so?'

'Well, you see, while Godfrey has of course received the highest accolades that School has to offer, he is not alone in showing promise. I have held the view for some time that young *Oliver* here has resources which have yet to be tapped.' Oliver stood and listened as if transfixed.

'In what direction do you think his... *resources*... might lead?' Ida asked doubtfully.

' I can only hazard a guess. His potential has not assumed any particular form, as yet. But I believe it will, given time. I think he has *vision,* if you take my meaning. He sees far – and though we all might wish he paid at least *some* attention to,well – forgive me – to the present –I nevertheless have high expectations of him.'

'Well I have to say that he nearly put an end to any future whatever by his foolishness this morning. And I hear that he has been by the river every day, with the intention of spying on you and has intruded upon your privacy and your sport. I can only apologise and assure you that it will *not* be repeated.'

Oliver felt the blood drain from his face. It seemed that his whole footloose world was in imminent danger of being restricted to the Rectory, or to visiting ruins. But his mother intended a far worse fate for him.

'I am considering sending him back to Desbury as soon as is practical. Alice will take him. I shall write to my husband to see if he agrees with my proposal.'

This was now assuming the proportions of a nightmare. Returned home in disgrace! Torn from his beloved river, to face the cold wrath of his father. The prospect was appalling. Then Captain Bonnard spoke.

'I do not think his conduct was particularly foolhardy. I did not think it then, and I have not changed my opinion.'

Oliver's mother bridled at this, but Bonnard pressed on. 'You see, I do not believe he would not have acted so had he not been trying to help. Oliver saw that I was about to lose perhaps my best fish of the season, and tried to help. That was all.'

'It was still reckless'

'Of course; but judged by the risks boys will take, it was a small offence indeed. I cannot deny that I did as much and more when a boy, and as a young subaltern in India. I think I might have done the same, in his shoes.'

This defence of her son from such an unexpected quarter coupled with the Captain's frank admission, rather nonplussed her. Ida Rusholme made no reply.

'And as to spying on me, Madam,' Bonnard continued, 'Oliver was merely watching me fish; many boys like to do that. There is no offence in it, and I take none.'

'I appreciate your generosity, Captain.'

Bonnard inclined his head in acknowledgement.

'Could I suggest that Oliver needs to direct his energies towards something practical? After all, there is little to occupy a boy on his own in these parts.'

Ida considered her son in silence. When she spoke again her tone was changed 'Perhaps it is my negligence rather than his... What would you advise?'

'I think that any boy permitted to roam without instruction will at some time or another fall into scrapes.' Though unintentionally critical, Bonnard's comment struck home. ' And life is full of risks' he continued 'which we must all encounter daily. We should equip ourselves to deal with them as best we can'

'And your meaning, Captain?' Ida's tone was altered.

'You tell me that you propose to spend several more weeks here at the Rectory?'

She nodded.

'Then allow Oliver to accompany me as I fish. I would be glad to instruct him in watercraft – which he is sadly in need of – and I undertake to return him daily safe, sound and *reasonably* dry!'. The Captain looked inquiringly across to Oliver who simply smiled his thanks broadly across the room.

'I'm really not sure, Captain… ' Ida wavered.

'He might learn to fish too, with your agreement. And I think his company would be most welcome.'

Oliver found voice at last. 'Oh *please*, Ma! *Please* may I? I promise I'll do everything Captain Bonnard says.'

His mother relented. 'Well, if I have your word on it,Oliver. At the slightest sign of trouble, Captain, you must return him here.'

'Absolutely. *Straight* back! And… as to that letter… ?'

'Ah. The letter. Well, I haven't written it yet… '

'Nor, perhaps, is there any further need for you to. It was a minor incident, when the lad got a bit too wet- a holiday incident. If he were to bathe in the sea he would get just as drenched, and with your blessing! It has all ended well, and we are none of us the worse for it.'

Ida could certainly see the advantage in not having to inform her husband,for there was no point in exacerbating the already poor relationship between Clarence and her son. Uncomfortably she also recognised that it exonerated her from blame.
The letter was destined never to be written.

The following two weeks were to prove a Seventh Heaven for Oliver. Not only had he been reprieved from the sentence contemplated by his mother, but he had been transported from the very prison-gates to play a part in a world in which till then he had only been a bystander. Early the following morning, clutching his dinner and a bottle of cold tea, he arrived in front of the tarred door of the cottage. For the first time he felt he had a legitimate reason for being there; and holding his breath he knocked. As the door swung ajar and he was welcomed with a gruff 'Step in, lad, don't stand on ceremony!', another door opened within Oliver – opened onto a dimension which in the dark years to come would provide some respite to a soul in torment, and a reprieve of an entirely different kind.

He stepped from a pool of morning sunlight into the cottage. Two small windows made of tiny panes of glass were set deep and low into the stonework, and on the windowledges stood several leafy plants in earthenware pots. The sunlight penetrating their foliage cast a greenish shadow onto the flagstones of the floor, and exaggerated the boy's feeling that he was entering a place which owed its origins more to Nature than to the hand of Man. The furnishings were simple and few – a table, chairs and a tall cupboard- and against the windowless rear wall stood a little pine dresser bearing rows of willow-pattern crockery.

The cottage – fixtures and fittings included – had been bought by Bonnard on his retirement from the Army in 1898. By adding his savings to his gratuity he had found the combined funds were just sufficient for his purpose. The asking price had been low on account of the very remoteness that he sought; and as its location had offered seclusion together with a mile and a half of excellent salmon and sea-trout fishing, he had purchased without hesitation. So whilst he roomed at the lodging-house during term time, he would slip away at the beginning of each vacation and return to Manchester on the day prior to the start of School.

'Take a seat, boy – either one will do.' The Captain gestured to the chairs with the stem of his pipe. Though still gruff, the tone was not yet that of the Master-Pupil sort, to which Oliver was accustomed; the biting edge was missing.

'Tea?' The old man opened a cupboard and produced two stoneware mugs. 'Leave the fancy stuff to the ladies, eh?' he joked, removing the kettle from the hob.

As the Captain occupied himself with brewing up Oliver's attention shifted to two gilt-framed photographs carefully placed on the dresser so that they faced each other. The first was of a young woman whose clothing suggested that the picture had been taken many years before. Oliver could not think quite when, but guessed it might have been in the eighteen-seventies. She sat stiffly upright on a highbacked chair, hand on a half-closed book; and the tiny smile which played about her lips made her doubly pretty as she turned her dark eyes upon him.

The second photograph was of a young officer clad in a Boer War uniform, with dress-jacket and shining buttons and peaked helmet held jauntily along his forearm. The officer's face, like the young woman's, was turned in the observer's direction, but the eyes seemed focused on some remote spot far beyond. Oliver detected a resemblance between the image and the Captain, though the young man's features were finer and darker.

As Bonnard brought over the teapot he followed the boy's gaze to the shelf. Oliver instantly coloured up like a guilty child. The old man set the pot down hurriedly and as if handling the most fragile of treasures gathered the frames closely to him. Then with a tenderness which touched Oliver despite his embarrassment, the old man placed them in a drawer which he pushed shut decisively. He stood beside the cupboard a moment or two longer, as if contemplating something. Then letting out an audible sigh he turned back to the table and Oliver and took up where he had left off, as if nothing had happened.

Their tea passed off with casual chat, Bonnard speaking disarmingly to Oliver as if he was eager to redeem any offence his actions might have given. Then as abruptly as he had concealed the photographs he piled the crockery onto a tray and stomped through a tiny door into the scullery. Having cleared the table he opened another drawer and began to pass a number of black-lacquered containers of various sizes over to Oliver, motioning him to lay them out across the table

'*These* are the key to it all, boy' he said 'these, and knowing your river. Open'em up!'

As Oliver prised open the lids his gaze was met by row upon dazzling row of exquisitely tied flies, replicas of every sort of insect imaginable and some of such fabulous design that they could never have existed in Nature. No milliner could ever have conceived such beauty, nor created objects so tiny nor so precisely made. He gingerly ran his finger over the iridescent reds and blues and greens, feeling the faint brush of the feather against his skin. 'Take'em out,' urged Bonnard 'don't concern yourself about damaging'em. They're tougher than they look.'

Oliver lifted out a particularly striking specimen composed of wings of peacock herl swept delicately backward and picked out with a single stripe of crimson. Its slim body was finished with silver tinsel and a bushy black hackle shaped to resemble insect legs.

'They're *wonderful*!' breathed Oliver 'I've seen ones like them in that shop in Manchester. Did you buy them there?'

'No, not a bit of it,' said Bonnard with some pride 'Tied 'em myself. You can improve the design to suit conditions on the Clwyr. Now *that* one you are holding is called an *Alexandra*. Used to work pretty well on the sea-trout in the lower pools, but during the last season or two I've done rather better with *this* pattern.'

He indicated a row of flies with black and white wings and turquoise hackles. 'Of course it's sometimes necessary to vary the hook size on a *Teal and Silver*, if they're a bit finicky or taking short' he added. 'If you'd like, I'll teach you how to tie them yourself. When the tide's in, that is.'

On Oliver's arrival each morning the procedure would be much the same. Captain Bonnard would outline the programme for the day, adding details necessary to convert the boy into a competent boatman and angler as need arose.

Watercraft had to come first. Stepping down from the stone jetty and into the boat for the first time required something of a balancing-act from Oliver, and as it started to move sideways away from him he clung desperately to an iron ring set in the wall. In an instant Captain Bonnard grasped Oliver's wrist in a steely grip while with his foot he steadied the gyrations of the boat.

But despite this and other small mishaps the boy proved to be an enthusiastic and able learner, and he rarely made the same mistake twice. The Clwyr was not an easy river, and was as temperamental then as it is now.The aptitude Oliver showed as apprentice waterman surprised his teacher, and skills which would have taken someone of reasonable ability weeks to learn, he had mastered within a few days.Nor was his progress limited to boating only; for when not on the water the Captain would give instruction in the art of tying a fly.

One morning Oliver entered to find only the Captain's legs visible, his body having disappeared through a little hatch in the ceiling. Then with a heave the legs were drawn up, followed by the sounds of rummaging.

'Here, boy. Take this from me, would you?' A slender brass-bound wooden tube appeared through the hole, and was waved about until Oliver grabbed it. 'And this. Take care not to drop it.'

The Captain's hand now emerged, clutching a dusty leather box resembling a small travelling-case. As they were caked in dirt Oliver carefully laid the two objects by the rear door. The Captain's legs reappeared, then the rest of him, every part of his visible body being coated with soot. Oliver took one look and despite his regard for the old man, burst into a fit of laughter.

Bonnard peered down at the boy, and scowled. 'I fail to see what amuses you, Rusholme, in my appearance!' But the pomposity of the comment coming as it did from such a ridiculous source made it all the more absurd, and Oliver could not contain himself.

For a fraction of a second it could have gone either way – the old magisterial distance might have reasserted itself, and the barrier once raised would have then proved irremovable; but something in the clear peals of Oliver's laughter rang remotely in Bonnard's memory. As he lowered himself through the trapdoor he was reminded of another boy, and the recollection moved and pained him. As he reached the floor he happened to glance at his image in a shaving-mirror hung on the wall, and saw the white teeth and eyeballs staring back at him. He looked again a second time, in disbelief at his own bizarre reflection. Suddenly he too was convulsed,his whole frame shaking hilariously. Oliver joined in, and the two stood roaring with glee until the tears ran down their faces, and made runnels in the grime on Bonnard's cheeks. He had not laughed so deeply for more years than he could count, and as he laughed he felt a lightening in his soul and the release of an iron constraint about his heart which had long held him in its grip

'I… I think I'd better visit the pump' he said indistinctly 'you just… just bide here, old chap.'

Yet as the Captain quit the cottage a change came over him. The tears which still flowed were no longer those of joy but of profound grief, long suppressed. He made his way blindly to the pump but made no attempt to draw water. Instead he leant against the wall like a drunken man as he gave in to his wretchedness – all the more poignant in one hitherto so reserved.

'Edward… .Oh, *Edward* !' For the first time in his life he was powerless to resist as the tide of his distress overwhelmed him; and as the long unspoken name rose once more to his lips the steely fabric of denial which he had woven about himself collapsed to its foundations. And even as he gave voice to it the name evaporated like a sweet sad fragrance cast to the winds; and as they spirited it away the pain he had borne so long gradually eased. By degrees the storm in his soul abated until it had assumed the proportions of a simple sorrow.

How long he leaned there, he could not guess; but suddenly mindful of his young visitor he turned his face abruptly from the wall. Then drawing himself upright he busied himself with pumping water into the trough. Stripping off his waistcoat and shirt he plunged himself head first into the chilly water and scrubbed vigorously, as if bent upon washing away not merely soot, but the accretions of many years. Though neither knew it then, Oliver Rusholme's indebtedness to the gruff old master was in the process of being repaid.

Chapter Nine

BONNARD placed the tube and the leather case on the stone scullery- slab and proceeded to clean away the grime. Unscrewing the brass top he shook the tube, and pulled out a slender canvas bag containing a small built- cane fishing-rod.Bonnard turned his attention to the case.'Open it up,boy' said the old man shortly, turning round and handing it across to Oliver 'and don't drop what's inside.'

Oliver took it carefully in both hands and carried it to the table where having unfastened the strap-buckle he cautiously levered up the lid. Encased in ruby velvet was a fishing-reel, which he took out and laid beside the rod. Each was a smaller and more delicate version of the mightier rods and reels which he had seen the Captain use, and each was clearly of the same superb craftsmanship and quality. The reel, made of bronze and silver, bore on its rotating face a feathery coat- of –arms, and a single ivory handle. The rod was whipped in matching silks, and it too bore the same mark. Though clearly quite old, their condition nevertheless suggested that they had not been used much or heavily. Bonnard picked up the rod-sections and fingered them awhile, as if associating them with some distant memory. Then returning to the task in hand he squinted along them piece by piece with a practised eye. 'True as ever' he grunted. 'Thought they would be.'

Line was wound on to the reel; then making their way out to the cow pasture behind the cottage Bonnard took the rod and after threading the line through the rod-rings, attached a cast.

'Now watch closely, boy!' With easy sweeps of his left hand Bonnard drew off loops of line from the reel whilst simultaneously working the rod back and forth. Each forward stroke caused the line to extend a yard or two further until fully fifteen yards of green silk were whistling overhead. With a deft flick of the wrist Bonnard dropped the cast at precisely the spot he had indicated.

'Now, Oliver, you have a try. Remember,*work the rod as if you were driving in a nail.*'

He set to with a will to master this most graceful and challenging of all angling skills, and the morning passed swiftly in a blur of green silk and the flickering of the rod in the sunlight.

By noon of that same day enthusiasm and talent had combined in him to ensure that the rough novice of only four hours' previously was now an accomplished flycaster.

In the early evening light he and the Captain tiptoed cautiously along a shallow gravel bank positioned below a glassy pool. The sun was way past its zenith and was now gilding the uppermost boughs of a poplar, throwing useful shade onto the water. From time to time its smooth face dimpled mysteriously as insects were waylaid by unseen fish.

Aim above him, and let the fly drop like gossamer. Oliver did as bidden, but the fly descended like lead. *You've put him down. Try him later. There's another!... there where the flow eddies round...*

This time the fly dropped perfectly, a yard or more above where the fish was holding in the current. Oliver's heartbeat drummed in his ears. The fly passed over the spot, and there was a small swirl as the creature rose warily to inspect the lure, and turned away doubtfully. *Leave him a minute, and go back to him.* Oliver paused, and recast. Again the fly landed beautifully, and drifted over the fish. Again there was a swirl,but this time... *this time he could see no fly* as the rise died away – only his cast slowly disappearing beneath the water as if through a tiny hole. *He's taken you!* Oliver raised the rod tip with a twist of his hand, and in a moment had hooked his first trout.

Oliver and the old man knelt beside the landing-net as the fish was unhooked. The boy paused to enjoy a moment in which his life seemed totally fulfilled. At that juncture of elation and achievement he could neither have demanded nor desired anything more than this. Entranced by its speckled silver flanks as it wriggled and turned, Oliver thought that he had never seen anything so close to perfection.

The old man reached into his pocket and produced a small metal bar. Oliver was too lost in contemplating the fish to notice what he intended. When he did, it was too late.

The bar rose, then fell with a sharp crack; and the fish lay still. Oliver let out a stifled cry. Bonnard seemed not to notice. 'I say, what a beauty!' he beamed, holding the fish up. 'It's close to a pound, I think. Well done indeed! You should be *very* proud of yourself!' Oliver forced a smile and assured the Captain that he was; but his sense of pride was tinged with shame and regret. Fishing was wonderful – inexpressibly so; but he had not sought to bring about the creature's death – and the destruction of something which seemed the epitome of beauty. Yet now he felt as though he had actively conspired in it.

So when he took the fish home that evening and presented it in the kitchen the rare praise showered upon him by Alice only seemed to redouble his sense of shame. It did help a little that his Mother declared fresh trout to be her favourite dish, and he felt that the act of killing was to a certain degree vindicated. Nonetheless he still firmly refused to try even a mouthful of it.

More particularly he wondered why, as he left the cottage with his fish, Captain Bonnard had bidden a cheery goodnight to someone called Edward.

His accomplishments grew with each day spent by the Clwyr. Inwardly delighting in the progress made by his pupil, Captain Bonnard gradually withdrew from the role of instructor,and instead took along his own well-worn fishing-gear. Confident in the boy's skill and resourcefulness he would sometimes leave Oliver to try one promising pool while he moved upstream to try elsewhere; whereas at another time they might fish alongside each other and work the same wide run. As fish were hooked and landed they would exchange grins or words of congratulation; but while the old man took a fish or two *for the pot* Oliver would always find some excuse for releasing them. Bonnard noticed this and wisely refrained from comment, seeing in it the boy's tacit acknowledgement of the sanctity of life. He saw it all, and respected it.

Alice did not. 'It's a waste o' time an' effort, all that fishin', if you're goin' to bring nowt 'ome, Master Oliver.' Oliver laughed, but still returned fishless.

Dulcie Grady's arrival at the Rectory was conspicuous, dispelling in a clatter of luggage the serenity of both the building and the warm afternoon which bathed it. The little cab crunched its way up the drive, and even before it ground to a halt its door was kicked open to reveal a female backside clad in a white cotton dress The garment had become caught up on an obstruction within, and the two stout legs of the wearer were unflatteringly revealed. The young lady struggled to free her clothing with one hand while at the same time collect her hat and travelling-bag with the other. The cabbie was sauntering round to assist his fare when he was met by a substantial pair of bloomers complete with legs protruding from his vehicle, the rest of the passenger being lost to sight. The man stopped dead in his tracks then retreated rapidly in the direction he had come, muttering something in Welsh about English women. From its tone it was unlikely to have been a compliment

'Oof! *Well!*'Dulcie puffed while some of the more inaccessible areas of her dress were put in order by Alice. 'I say, oh, that tickles a bit! Are you sure it's all smoothed down? I was *so* embarrassed! Do you think he *saw* anything – I mean the cabbie, and my underthings? I'm certain he couldn't have! Do you remember that perfume you said you liked?well I've got you a bottle only don't tell Mrs. Rusholme about it, probably not a good idea actually...'

Alice had put on her inscrutable face – the expression which she habitually wore when dealing with the trail of minor mishaps which inevitably followed in the wake of Miss Helene's friend.

'It *is* smoothed, Miss. I'm *sure* he didn't. I *do* remember, and thank you *very* much for the kind thought. And it's probably *not* a good idea. There! You look a treat, Miss! Fresh as a daisy! No-one would ever know you'd travelled all the way from Manchester. Did you have a pleasant journey?'

Alice's question, though asked only out of courtesy, was equally not a good idea.

'Well, Alice it's strange you should ask that, because the answer is yes *and* no. You wouldn't *believe…* .' But the account of Miss Grady's travelling woes was cut short by the arrival of Helene at the top of the stairway. *I'll tell you later, Alice!* Dulcie whispered conspiratorially.

Arms outstretched she ascended the stairs as Helene came down to meet her. Their embrace was affectionate and genuine – their friendship had lasted too long for it to be otherwise – and Helene drew Dulcie off to meet Ida, who was finishing off a canvas she'd been working on.

Alice stood listening to the retreating hubbub, shaking her head. 'A really nice an' kindly lass, Miss Dulcie' she said to herself 'but my, she's daft as a brush!'

Dinner that evening was lively, in contrast to the quiet meals and quieter conversation of the preceding weeks. Dulcie's generous nature was such that she did not mind in the least that the joke was frequently on her; she told of her silly doings, seeing herself as a rather ridiculous figure. Yet because those qualities of self deprecation and self–effacement were recognised as genuine by her hosts they laughed with her rather than at her. Thus the arrival of Dulcie Grady instilled some sparkle into the Rusholme's temporary household. Oliver – though not one for the company of young women – invariably enjoyed her presence. She never excluded him from conversation and spoke to him as an equal, listening attentively to what he had to say. And furthermore, with Dulcie you never quite knew what *she* might say. Her forthrightness and her mastery of the unexpected always supplied extra zest to the conversation. Some anecdote or other of hers would be received amidst the laughter with scandalised exclamations of ' Oh, Dulcie, how *could* you!... Oh they *didn't* find out, did they?... What *will* you do next… ?'

Dulcie affected not to mind, nor to care a great deal.

But there was another side to Dulcie; less flippant, less devil-may care than the outward image. For deep within her lay a vein of humanity and compassion which ran unseen by all but her closest friends. It was this quality which caused her to be sought out as confidante by not a few who had troubles. Though she could be garrulous in the extreme about her own affairs, they knew that in the matter of others' secrets she was as tight-lipped as a clam. And her advice was something to be valued. It was this Dulcie who late in the evening sat by Helene in the twilight of their room. For months she had secretly agonised for her, reading much from her letters and suspecting more. The tone had changed from one of levity to one of melancholy and foreboding; and Helene's former frankness had become tainted with a reserve which troubled her friend. Some weeks before she had received a note which contrasted oddly with its predecessors. Its mood was effervescent to the point of feverishness, though Helene had still given no clues as to the cause. Dulcie had found this letter to be all the more disturbing in that those which followed had again reverted to dark introspection. Such mercurial change she knew to be foreign to Helene, and it gave her increased cause for concern.

It was with this uppermost in her thoughts that she had decided to make a visit to Ridland; but despite her growing unease she resolved to allow events to unfold by themselves and leave the initiative to Helene.

Their conversation ran lightly and superficially at first, concerned only with the doings of mutual acquaintances and how they had passed their vacations. Dulcie was outwardly admiring a folio of watercolours and sketches which Helene had opened before her, though she was focused more on the tenseness of her friend. They were considering the pictures' merits when Helene quietly closed the case without a word and set it aside. Still she said nothing but sat there with an expression of utter despair on her face, her eyes focused unseeingly on some shadowy corner. It struck Dulcie that this was as it had been in her letters – a veneer of normality which Helene had employed to mask some terrible dilemma. But now the veneer had cracked and the mask was falling away even as she watched her.

'Dulcie?' Her voice was almost inaudible.

'Yes, Helene.'

'How long have we been friends, do you think?'

'Well we started together at Miss Tierney's, and we were friends *then*, certainly. So let me see… it *must* be twelve years, at least. That long!'

'We've always been friends, haven't we?'

'Always.'

'You've always been very special to me. If..if I'd ever had a sister, I would have liked her to have been you.'

'That's one of the nicest things you've ever said to me.'

'At the moment… I just don't feel I have anyone I can turn to, but you. I feel so hopelessly alone.'

'I'm sure things aren't as bad as you fear they are.'

'I don't know where to start.It's such a tangle, and I can't see any way out.Will you listen to me, and tell me what you think I should do.?'

'Of course, Helene' Dulcie said, squeezing her hand reassuringly 'if it's something where I *can* help you.' If it was an affair of the heart, as she suspected it to be, then how was she qualified to offer advice to anybody?

Helene told all, falteringly at first then with growing passion. Of her first chance meeting with Gerald Warrington when he was visiting Godfrey; of the immediate attraction they had felt for each other, and how they found it difficult to pretend before the others. How she would not give in to some mawkish relationship which would shackle her hand and foot, and which would put paid to all her ambitions in the arts. So she told Dulcie.

She continued to tell how they had met but a few times, but had corresponded more; and how she had tried to distance herself *from* herself, and him. How she was torn apart by her consuming love for one who was barely into manhood, and her junior by several years; and how she was possessed entirely by one whom she could not exorcize from either her mind or her heart.

The beautiful eyes now flashed fiery through the tears. Helene caught up a handkerchief and wept into it, in a hopeless attempt to choke back the pain.

'And now you know it all. Oh… when he came here last… I thought… we could end it, and remain as friends… but I didn't know *myself,* Dulcie, and how utterly impractical the idea was or how the misery *gnaws* at you. I feel betrayed by my own emotions, and I can't survive this storm in my soul. If I cut *him* out, it'd be like cutting away a part of my own existence.'

'Does he return your feelings – in the same way that you love him? I have to ask.'

'If anything he's more committed and intense about it. I'm sure he's just as wretched as I.'

'Is there anyone else who knows – or suspects – about… you and him?' Dulcie asked gently.

'Alice knows… .that I have an *involvement*. She knows it's Gerald And she's true as steel.'

'Does anyone else?'

'I sometimes think Mama *suspects* something- she's looked at me in a strange way, once or twice.'

Dulcie considered her sympathetically. 'I'm envious of such a love as yours, Helene. I've seen Warrington about, and even met him once, socially; he's a handsome chap, and very accomplished. But I'm also really sorry that you are hurting so deeply. Other people will notice the change in you. I did… It's not really the *limitations* that you fear most though, is it?' she added, after a pause. 'It's your age -difference. Isn't it?

'You're so sensitive, and my dearest friend. You know me better than anyone else.'

'Even so Helene; I wouldn't presume to judge you. What you have is different, that's all. From what you've said it's lovely; there's nothing wrong in it.' Even though Helene was used to Dulcie's unconventionality this came as a considerable surprise. 'But if you wish to guard your secret from the world you must be more careful.Do you write much to each other?'

'Not much, until recently. When he came we agreed to write more often.'

'Then you've got to make sure that your letters are passed through another source – you can use me, if you like – and I can forward them on to you. Then you've got a Desbury postmark on them and not an Oxford one, and your Mama knows my handwriting. No-one will be the wiser.'

'*Would* you, Dulcie?' she said more brightly 'You're a friend in a thousand!' Then abruptly her brow clouded again.' And it's kind of you. But what do I do about all this?'

'Do as you have always done 'Dulcie said simply. 'The only thing different in you is that you're in love with someone, but that doesn't have to destroy your life. Try to see the positive side. Why should you have to give up anything that you value because of it? Has your Mama had to give up her painting or sculpture?'

'No.'

'Has she had to forego anything since marrying your Pa?

'Not that I know of.'

'Well *there* you are, then!' Dulcie boomed triumphantly 'Marriages these days are becoming far more… well, *modern*.And look at the age-difference between our parents! Why shouldn't the rules apply equally to women? The fusty old traditions of the past don't have to concern us, or necessarily bind us, either. Girls are doing *all sorts* of things these days!'

Helene laughed in spite of herself.

'And if you *can't* marry him just now, well you'll just have to wait. *Is he worth waiting for?'*

'Yes.'

'And he'll wait for you?'

Helene nodded.

'Then you'll have so much to look forward to, and I'm happy for you both!'

Helene flung her arms about Dulcie's neck, and kissed her.

Chapter Ten

OLIVER LOOKED anxiously the calendar and was shocked to see how little of August remained. There were disturbing signs that the household was planning its return to Desbury, and to the world of Manchester and work; less necessary items of clothing were packed into cases which now stood about the landing like ominous milestones, marking for Oliver the end of a period.which for him had been one of unqualified contentment. He could not recall any time in his short life when he had been happier, and its impending conclusion hung over him dismally. He did not know when, if ever, he would return; and it was that which caused him to wander the river again in search of impressions which he could lock away in his memory, to be unearthed at will on dark winter nights like old photographs or postcards. And the uncertainty of it added immeasurably to the nostalgia.

As the Summer drew gently to its end Oliver saw that every plant and shrub now hung glittering with the morning's dewfall, and the droplets on spiders webs caused them to bounce like miniature trampolines in the faintest breath of air.Sunsets grew more glorious and protracted, somehow emphasising the endless rolling of the Earth and how precious and how brief Time really was for him. He became suddenly aware of a crispness which he had not noticed before, and the clarity of the air gave greater definition to the distant mountains as Oliver and Captain Bonnard fished the Clwyr together for the last time.

It was not a successful day for Oliver, and he ended it fishless, distracted by his mother's announcement that morning. His father had written to suggest their departure be brought forward to the Friday since Helene and her friend had already returned, and so that after the office he might meet his wife and son at Central Station. Oliver thought his father's timing bad in the extreme, and resented it even more because in one fell swoop Clarence had accelerated the end of the one period he had been truly happy. And all for *his* own convenience.

As Oliver prepared to leave the cottage he handed the old man a note which had remained forgotten in his jacket-pocket until then. Bonnard opened it, and smiled. Then he took out a sheet of paper and an envelope, and wrote a reply which he addressed and gave to the boy.

'Captain Bonnard, sir? I've got a few things which I borrowed from your fishing-tackle'.Oliver extracted a small tin of tied flies from a canvas bag, and placed them carefully on the table.' And I've put your rod and reel over there by the dresser. I've cleaned and oiled them for you.'

'Good.'

Oliver drew himself up straight and extended his hand to the old man. 'Thank you sir for teaching me so much and letting me fish your beautiful river and everything. I've had a *wonderful* time; I'll never forget it.' His face glowed with gratitude as he spoke.

The old man took the outstretched hand.'On the contrary, Oliver, it has given me the greatest pleasure to have such an able student. I have appreciated your company more… .well, more than you might imagine. And I feel we've learned a lot together, don't you?'

Oliver looked back over his shoulder, and waved to the grizzled old figure framed by the cottage doorway. A hand was raised, and waved back. Oliver wondered if he would ever tread the path to the cottage again.

That same evening found Oliver in his room, where he had been ordered to get his things together for Phoebe to pack. But few though his possessions were, in his reluctant mood he nevertheless managed to drag the task out interminably. He was looking balefully down at the mess that represented the sum of an hour's efforts when he heard the door-knocker rap loudly. He listened indifferently as a visitor was admitted. Dismissing it from his thoughts he flopped down on his bed to await the dinner – gong. He lay there, staring idly at the beams above, and speculating on how miserable the next term at school was likely to be. Having considered the options he came to the depressing conclusion that there was nothing whatever to look forward to. He was content that he had established a good relationship with Captain Bonnard. He was truly grateful to the master, for he acknowledged that much of the old man's vacation had been devoted to *him*. But he had no right to expect anything more from that quarter; and besides, what was he *really*, to the Captain? In the manner of one constantly reminded of his failures by others and who in his own opinion had achieved little, he set about disparaging himself.

Then the dinner gong echoed up from the hallway. Oliver swung his legs off the bed and reluctantly made his way downstairs and into the dining-room., where he was surprised to find Captain Bonnard seated in an armchair enjoying a glass of something.

The old man stood up politely and, though they had parted only a few hours previously, again offered his hand. Oliver took it firmly and noticed that despite the old-fashioned tweed suit and waistcoat he cut a most distinguished figure, from the mirror-polished boots to the starched wing-collars. The beard and famous moustache had received a trimming and gave an impression, though faded, of the dapper young cavalryman he must once have been. Ida Rusholme smiled warmly to Oliver and motioned him to sit beside her.

'Captain Bonnard has kindly agreed to join us for dinner, Oliver' she said. 'and at short notice too! I've been hearing his very flattering opinion of you. I'm gratified – and *proud* – that you tried so hard to be good, and learn all you could from him.' Oliver appreciated the compliment, and saw that it came equally from both of them. When on more recent occasions Ida had smiled at him it seemed that the warmth had been tempered by reservations. Now her affection seemed unqualified, and he glowed in it.

The evening passed quickly and pleasantly, not least because it was unknown for a pupil to dine at the same table as a master. The times spent by the river had been wonderful, but somewhere in the background there had still been the master-pupil element, nomatter how kindly the instruction. Now they were face to face across the table, and dimensions in the man were revealed which Oliver had never once suspected.

The Captain proved to be a most genial guest, regaling them with stories of his own boyhood in Devon and his years spent in Kashmir. He spoke of his servants, and the great hunts, and the durbahs, and the hill-country, and the bungalows with their evening verandahs; and his affection for India filled the room like incense.

The meal drew to a close; and after a brandy and a cigar Captain Bonnard rose to thank his hostess, and wish them good night. With the decorum of a past age he drew himself to attention and bowed to Ida, and kissed her hand. Oliver suddenly felt deeply saddened by the old man's departure. Now he was leaving he discovered that the Captain mattered far more to him; it was as if he was bidding farewell to a dear old friend. Oliver knew then that he would never have a closer.

As Bonnard moved towards the hallway he turned to Ida. 'Forgive me Madam. Am I correct in assuming that you and your family might take future vacations elsewhere in the country, or perhaps even abroad?'

'Quite possibly, Captain. Helene and I – and my husband – have been considering that very thing. We wondered about Paris, perhaps; and we hear that Rome is quite enchanting.'

'Indeed it is Madam. And worthy of a visit by an accomplished artist such as yourself.'

She smiled modestly as he continued. 'Yet it seems to me a pity that

Oliver might never in the normal course of things have an opportunity to return to the Clwyr. I feel quite a selfish old stick with my river and all, and I've no-one now to share it with. I'd like to extend an invitation to your family -and most particularly to Oliver – to visit as often as you or he likes. For myself, I spend my vacations nowhere else.'

Oliver felt light-headed with gratitude. Ida thanked the Captain, and promised to put the generous offer before her husband on their return.

As he was pulling on his overcoat Bonnard stooped down and picked up two objects which he had brought with him, and placed unseen by the hatstand. The shapes were too familiar for Oliver to mistake them, as the Captain handed them to him. The rod and reel which had been lent, and which the old man had handled with such care. Oliver held them uncomprehendingly.

'They have been with me many years, Oliver. They once belonged to someone... someone who was close to me. I'd like *you* to have them.'

'Oh, but Captain Bonnard!' Ida said 'we cannot *possibly* accept things which mean so much.'

'It is for that very reason I wish to make a gift of them to your son. They were made for someone rather like him... very like him, in fact. I fancy that Oliver will use them as they were intended, and value them as much as I. And he will certainly put them to better use! I truly wish him to accept them.'

Bidding them goodnight he turned on his heel and was halfway across the gravel before Oliver caught up with him. Bonnard paused and turned. For a moment Oliver stood before him, unsure as to quite why he had acted in that way. Nothing was said; but on an impulse he suddenly flung his arms around the old man and hugged him. Then breaking away as abruptly he raced back to the house and upstairs into his own room.

Chapter Eleven

THE AUTUMN TERM did not prove as dreary as Oliver had feared He had chosen to follow a more enterprising course of study in the sciences – then very much the New Thing and regarded with distaste by many of the Senior Masters. *All muck and smoke* was one epithet doing the Senior Common Room rounds. Bonnard smiled at it, but refrained from making judgements. 'Not quite the sort of stuff The School's reputation was built on, eh?' grunted one of his colleagues 'and furthermore, have you seen the *paraphernalia* that young Crossley's cramming into his so-called laboratories? Who's going to *pay*, that's what I'd like to know!'

That Young Crossley was a sour reference to the newest member of the teaching staff. Having gained a Double First at the Victoria University Percy Crossley had resolved to enter education out of pure altruism. Chronically myopic, he was a young man who because of his private income could indulge himself and still maintain a moderate lifestyle, albeit eccentrically. Part of that eccentricity was his offer – eagerly seized upon by the Head Master and the Trustees – to equip several laboratories at his own expense, installing the latest electrical and chemical equipment.

Crossley's particular expertise lay in the field of biology. Elderly colleagues glared balefully in the direction of the new 'Science Labs' as cages and glass vivaria of every size were delivered. But the reaction was as nothing compared to the horror with which they greeted the arrival of their occupants. Language became more colourful with each exotic mammal or fish.

'Feller's turnin' The School into a damn' zoo'… 'bloody menagerie, more like'… ..'the cove'll have a circus in The Quad, next… '

But the jaundiced views affected Crossley not at all. 'And after all, it's for the boys, not for them,' he said to another master as young and as ostracised as himself.

One of the first recruits to this Babylon was Oliver. Clarence Rusholme had raised no objections, on the sound principle that as he hadn't had his money's worth from a classical education his son might as well waste his time on the Sciences, instead.

Oliver's decision inevitably came under the scrutiny of the Senior

Common Room. After a particularly caustic comment about the odds in favour of Oliver blowing himself or the whole school up, Bonnard sprang ferociously to the boy's defence. 'That's uncalled for, Paterson, and you damn'well know it!' he barked. 'One of these days I think you'll be forced to eat your own blasted words!'

'*Blasted*'s certainly apposite' came the sneering rejoinder; 'some relative of yours, no doubt?'

'No he's not. And even if he were, I'd certainly not be ashamed of it. I for one believe Rusholme has considerable promise!'

The opposition retreated muttering.

Oliver remained blissfully unaware of this Common Room warfare. He found in Crossley an inspiring teacher who delighted in speculation and in sharing the wonder of discovery. In his turn Crossley fostered the boy's own gifts – his receptiveness to ideas and his desire to conjecture and investigate until he *knew* and understood. The change in him was as singular as the change in Captain Bonnard. People noticed it, but did not associate the two. Both smiled and joked more, and seemed generally more optimistic. Oliver became less gauche, less conscious of failure and more attuned to success. No longer the shambling figure with head cast downwards, he looked forward rather than back. And his fear slipped from him.
Except, that is, where it concerned his father.

It proved to be a year of rare triumph for Oliver. At its conclusion his glowing Report was read and reread by a disbelieving Clarence who could not or would not accept the sea-change which had transformed his failure son. The praise heaped on Oliver's accomplishments by a beaming Mr. Crossley did not lessen Clarence's scepticism. Rather it increased his suspicions that all was not right, and there was something distinctly odd about it all. *Leopards don't change their spots to that extent* he reminded himself. Though unable to account for the remarkable shift in her son's motivation Ida's reaction was quite the opposite and she drank in Crossley's eulogy, it being to her a novel experience. She increasingly resented her husband's disparaging attitude toward Oliver, and found his interrogation of Crossley increasingly offensive.

'Are you *sure* we have the same boy in mind?' Clarence persisted ironically. 'After all one can make mistakes- with one's register of marks, for instance?'

'No mistake' Crossley answered archly. 'No mistake, I assure you. You see clearly from the percentages that your son is far beyond the other boys in his form. He is proving to be quite an outstanding pupil. And, you will be pleased to hear, his successes are not limited to sciences alone; he has made considerable advances in his trigonometry and mathematics.'

Peering at Clarence through his thick spectacles, Crossley wondered how the boy had progressed as far as he had with this man for a parent.

'So I gather that, with what you have set before us *here*.' Clarence waved dismissively toward the register '… that a career in Law will be out of the question?'

Crossley let his inexperience and lack of years betray him.

'In my opinion it would be quite wasted, sir. His path lies in other directions, I believe.'

'A career in Law is hardly *wasted*, young man!' Clarence bridled. 'Though I say it myself, I have made a considerable success of it. As, I may add,has my eldest son Godfrey, who has gone up to Oxford and is in the process of carrying all before him!'

Ida Rusholme placed her hand on her husbands arm in a bid to restrain his outburst and felt him trembling. 'Clarence dear, please!' she interjected 'Mr. Crossley was only expressing… '

'I heard quite clearly what *Mr.*Crossley was expressing.'

Clarence Rusholme rose stiffly ' Good evening to you, sir. My wife and I will find our own way out.'. Crossley remained at his desk, entirely lost for words.

It was with difficulty that Ida persuaded her husband not to have Oliver withdrawn immediately and placed in another school where a *more appropriate education* would be provided. Clarence's reaction had been disproportionate; and though she had always regretted the difficulties between her son and husband she had until now remained hopeful that in time they would be resolved. Now she saw that despite all Oliver had done to redeem himself, the rift had deepened to a chasm. She was fated to spend many sleepless hours vainly attempting to rationalise her husband's irrationality. Oliver's detractors- amidst whom Clarence was foremost – had in the course of three short terms been proved utterly wrong. Her husband's unbending prognosis was that the boy would fail; in an odd way it was *expected* of him. Perversely, Clarence felt that Oliver had let him down.

A week later Ida announced quietly that she would be paying an extended visit to her family in Germany.

Oliver missed his mother, but not perhaps to the extent that he would have done only a year before. His attainments had surprised him as much as they had others; but the boost they gave to his confidence and feeling of self-worth reduced his emotional dependency and enabled him to enjoy the fruits of it. He and his father encountered each other only at dinner, and the atmosphere was generally cool except when Helene was present; then conversation assumed a relative normality. After a cursory greeting Clarence would bury himself behind *The Times*, and Oliver would extricate himself from the table as quickly as manners allowed. He could generally time to the second the optimum point to ask permission to leave, which was usually granted with a grunt. Then he would speed up the stairs to his room and immerse himself in one of his increasingly large collection of scientific texts. Some were on extended loan from Percy Crossley who had an ample library and who never pressed for their return; but by far the majority of them had been bought by Oliver himself from the many secondhand bookshops in the streets and alleyways around Deansgate.

Crossley added fuel to the flames which he had already ignited in the boy's mind by inviting him to attend the laboratories after school. There, fortified with sandwiches and tea, Crossley would continue his research into the cellular biology which had won him his Double First. Oliver was an apt disciple, and the easygoing teacher sowed the seed which would in less than two years secure his pupil a coveted Scholarship at the University Medical School.

After some months Ida returned from Bremen. She was outwardly calmer, insisting that the change had done her good; but she was more thoughtful and reflective. 'It's curious' she said one day to her husband ' but I didn't feel quite as at home with Tante Ursel and Onkel Karl as I used to. There are many changes taking place, things happening which make one feel, well, *an outsider*.'

'What changes had you in mind?' Clarence asked indifferently, as if expecting them to relate to streetlighting or wallpaper.

'Well there's the German Army, for a start. One sees more soldiers about than ever before, I'm certain of it. And they're not there for mere pomp, either – though I know how fond the Kaiser is of his glittering Reviews. No, they're busy with all sorts of things – drilling, marching to and fro, digging holes and filling them in again, and not in dress uniforms but in *Feldgrau*. The whole place is buzzing with something which you couldn't say was *militarism*, exactly; but it is the nearest thing to it. And there are people making speeches, too; the papers are full of them.'

Clarence set aside his *Times*. 'What sort of speeches, precisely?'

'Some are just a list of complaints about territory and borders and such like, but others are quite inflammatory. Do you remember when we visited Opa Bauer, just after we got married? You were introduced to a little boy who hid behind the hangings? Well, that was my cousin Hilde's son Otto. He came to visit Tante Ursel while I was there. He's a soldier now- an officer in an infantry regiment, I think he said. He looked very smart in his uniform, but he talked with an intensity which... well, I found somewhat alarming. It was almost arrogance, and he said there might be a war, and if there was, then Germany would certainly win it.'

Clarence frowned, and his voice became more animated. 'Will she, indeed? *Will* she? Our Empire's Armies and Navies might hold a different opinion, I think. If they try anything on with *us* they'll get a bloody nose, and more besides. We're not *French*, they'll discover.'

'Otto did say that there could never be a war between Germany and Great Britain.' Ida continued placatingly. 'It would be unthinkable. After all, The Kaiser is quite closely related to our own Royal Family. I'm sure they would patch up any differences between them in a civilised fashion. And besides, their dispute is about territories in Europe, in which we certainly have no say'

'We have given guarantees – undertakings, if you like – which are *binding*.' Clarence said emphatically 'and I would expect us to honour them, particularly if Germany were to attempt to intimidate a smaller nation like Belgium. It would be the only decent course of action.One might even say we have a moral duty to act. I personally hold to that view. And I think that the Germans would be *most* ill-advised to attempt to tangle with *us.*'

Clarence returned to his *Times*, and Ida to her watercolours. But the doubts lingered, and their relationship changed as a consequence.

As the year 1912 passed into 1913, and as the passage of the months gathered momentum toward the events in Sarajevo, Ida had never felt so foreign, and her husband never so British.

Once his father's initial opposition had been overcome by the intercession of his mother Oliver spent at least some of every vacation at his beloved Ridland. Albert would pack cases containing Oliver's fishing-tackle, books and a few clothes into the trap and deliver him to Central Station where the Holyhead train stood waiting. He would visit the Captain for a few days or a week at a time,crushing himself and his gear into the cottage's tiny lean-to where a camp-bed and oil-lamp had been installed, and where the welcome was as warm and as genuine as it had always been.

The Oliver of later years would be recalled by the voices of those pre-crisis times to the precious, luminous days where the fishing seemed more splendid, the river more beguiling and the landscape greener and more vivid than anything he would know after the Apocalypse.

II

Chapter One

THE LIGHT hovered briefly far above, like some species of malevolent comet. Then almost leisurely it weaved its way downward, a bluish flame which hissed venomously to itself as it fell. A column of ashen smoke trailed in its wake, marking the path of its descent. The vapours wrapped themselves languidly around the wire entanglements out in front before dispersing entirely, and the murk swallowed everything once more.

Nothing happened for a good few minutes; then the process was repeated. As the next flare sputtered into garish life it illuminated a figure pressed hard against the earthen walls of a trench. It was shrouded in a gas-cape which glistened faintly in the rain, and from its motionless attitude it might have been mistaken for a corpse had it not started involuntarily as the flare ignited.

Its colour was indescribable, because it had none. Everything there – man and trench alike -seemed painted in the ghastly non-hue with which burning phosphorus invested them. Another figure could then be made out, discernible only because of the shadows which moved at its approach, and because what light there was twinkled faintly from the raindrops on its nodding helmet. Caution was in every movement as it skirted the outer wall of the trench; and where the parapet had subsided the figure ducked lower still, scrambling over the mound of earth which had been brought down in the collapse.

It slipped alongside the gas-caped sentry with experienced ease, and turned to peer through the same loophole towards the indistinct masses of wire lying some fifteen yards beyond. The silence seemed as impenetrable as the dark

'Anythin' doin'lad?' The voice was hushed and its tone of enquiry was kind – reassuring to a young soldier on his first night duty.

'Nowt, sir' the boy whispered in reply. 'Except when there's flares I can't see nothin'. They just keep puttin' 'em up every couple o'minutes. I can't think what for.'

'There's snipers about tonight. Like most nights in this sector. We must be right popular. Look sharp, *keep yer'ead down, an' you'll keep yer head* as the sayin' goes. The Boches never sleep. You must learn *that* as one of yer first lessons. And yer *second* lesson is, I'm a sergeant, and that's what I'm called..

Keep yer *Sirs and Salutes* for th' officers. Didn't they teach you *owt* at Training Camp?'

'Well they did, sergeant, but I couldn't see who yer was.'

'What's yer name, lad?'

'Broadhurst, sergeant.'

The older man fell silent for a moment as he squinted into the dark.

'*No. It's nowt…* ' he muttered absently. ' When did yer get sent up?

'The night before last. With the replacements.'

'Where are yer from, lad?'

'Levenshulme, sergeant. That's just outside… '

'Aye, I know where it is, right enough. Now, Private Broadhurst, if you want to get *back* to Levenshulme in one piece, take heed of any advice yer given, particularly by t'sergeants. The recipe for a long life out'ere is *savvy*. Startin' with, *where's yer rifle*?'

'Down 'ere' As the boy turned to retrieve his weapon yet another flare ignited above them and in that fraction of a second something whistled through the tiny loophole at immense speed, smashing into the timber revetment with astonishing violence.

The distant report of the sniper's rifle was followed by a crackling of return fire from hitherto unseen positions along the British forward trench. It swelled to a rattling intensity for a minute or two, flickering and stabbing blindly at the enemy, then died down as abruptly as it had risen to no more than a few sporadic shots; and the silence reasserted itself over No Man's Land again.

'Are you all right, Broadhurst? *Broadhurst! Answer me! 'Ave yer been hit?*' He groped about in the dark, trying to get hold of the boy to check his condition.

'I'm sorry, Sergeant' said a small voice 'I didn't want to get me rifle dirty, an' all, so I kept it out o't' mud.'

'You *silly* little bugger! What d'yer think it's for? Wrap the breech in sackin' if you haven't a bag. But keep it loaded an' cocked an' in the firin' position!' In the hushed darkness he could hear the boy's teeth chattering uncontrollably. 'Never mind, lad' said the Sergeant more amenably 'he missed, an' that's all as counts. Even if yer *did* get one of us nearly killed. Keep awake an' keep a sharp lookout. I'll be along again shortly.'

The Sergeant completed his rounds of the sentries and made his heavy way back along the trench. Cursing to himself as he caught his hand on a sharp piece of wire he stealthily picked his way past the gaping holes which were the entrances to various dugouts, and a latrine whose location proclaimed itself by the foul reek rising from it. Getting his bearings from this he felt his way a further ten yards, then ducked down an invisible sap which gave onto the right. His path was now made easier by a dull crimson glow which percolated faintly through canvas hung over a sandbagged opening. He reached behind the cloth and groped for a spoon dangling from a piece of string. This he tapped gently against a tin plate similarly suspended.

'Enter!' called a voice which seemed to rise from the very depths of the earth. The Sergeant slipped behind the canvas and made his way down through a fog of tobacco fumes and along a tunnel which channelled the light upwards. Though it came only from a half-dozen oil-lamps he stood wincing in the relative brilliance.

'Permission to enter, Sir?'

'Come on in, Sergeant Chadderton'. The man propped his rifle against the wall and removed his helmet,revealing a broad face set off by a squarely determined jaw. A scar the colour of raw liver ran between the corner of his right eye and his ear and disfigured an otherwise not unhandsome appearance. He was evidently a man of exceptional physical strength for though short he possessed a width of chest and athletic bearing which would not have been out of place in a middleweight boxing ring. His greatcoat and indeed every other part of him from the waist down was plastered with mud, and his puttees and boots were clogged with it. He looked about him at the four or five officers who sat there on a motley collection of chairs and stools, and turned to address one who had risen at his entry.

'Good evening, sir.' Albert Chadderton – groom and stoker and handyman at Millwain Place in an earlier life – brought himself to attention as best he could in the cramped dugout; and in spite of the filth in which he was caked, saluted smartly.

The officer who returned the salute was recognisable immediately as the eldest son of his former employer.

'Good evening, Mr Rusholme.' Chadderton said.

The face of Lieutenant Godfrey Rusholme of the 16th. Service Battalion The Manchester Regiment – *The 'Manchester Pals'* – nodded in acknowledgement of the Sergeant's greeting. It was a face which had changed markedly from that of barely two years' previously. Though its lines were still full and youthful and outwardly those of a young man – he had not yet reached his twenty-fourth birthday – the eyes which turned to Chadderton suggested a different story. They were almost unrecognisable. There was a disquieting depth to them which told of a chasm in the soul, and which suggested that a lifetime's trials had been compressed into the period between his enlistment and now. The light within came not from a young man's knowledge of the world but arose from the bitterness of adversity, and from witnessing that which no man should ever have to witness, scenes of the unspeakable which lacerated the mind. For Godfrey and countless others the war which was to be won by Christmas seemed to grind on relentlessly and mechanically and mercilessly until the inevitable happened, the body blow which knocked you out temporarily, or forever. You hoped and prayed for the former; for a nice safe wound which didn't disfigure or mutilate or emasculate, but which got you admission to a nice clean hospital where you could shuffle around helped by V.A.D.nurses. Their looks didn't matter; it was the tranquillity which mattered, and freedom from all this shit, and the constant bloody small-arms and the H.E.shells which dropped into your trench or dugout and obliterated you and the rest of the poor buggers round about.

But the nice clean wound *had* happened for Albert Chadderton.

The first round had caught him in the thigh, and as he'd fallen the second got him in the face. He'd been lucky, nonetheless, because the momentum of the *first* had spun him round, and because of that the bullet glanced off. That was what that Orderly had told him in the Forward Dressing Station where he was patched up before being sent down the line on a stretcher which was more red than khaki.

It *was* off his skull, though, and in consequence of that and the other wound which was a Blighty one Albert had been shipped back to Military Hospital – or rather an empty Girls' School commandeered to provide more beds because of certain setbacks at the Front.

He'd received visits from his wife (though not the children, who'd sent him little cards done up with pressed flowers from Desbury's fields, and a note from his grandfather *congratulating* him, which made Albert smile, wrily.). Then a Vicar came and said how noble their sacrifice was, and how Victory Always Went to the Just. And just as soon as he could hobble Albert returned to F Company 16th. Battalion without complaint and with an odd sense of relief. And his wounds had healed, almost.

'Mug of tea, Sergeant?' He accepted it gratefully, and stood clasping the warmth of the tin between his chilled fingers, though not at ease.

'Have you anything to report? We heard an outbreak of firing some time ago.'

'Nothing o' note, Sir. I didn't think it necessary to Stand 'em To. One of the new draft, sir- very temptin' for them Boche snipers. Had a crack at 'im which missed an' then the whole o' C Company opened up down by Maricourt. It weren't necessary. But they shut up pretty quick. Nothin' else to report sir except that the forward trench has been knocked about a bit, just by Pendleton Sap.'

'How bad?'

'Well, it's down, sir, an' the parapet's gone. Wizzbang earlier this evenin'. No casualties, though.'

'Detail some of the men to repair it, would you? I'll come along myself, presently.'

The work was completed under the cover of the darkness, while a macabre game of hide-and-seek was played out between the working –party from F Company and a lone German machine gun which swept the area with monotonous regularity each time a flare was fired. The high explosive shell which had brought down the parapet had also thrown up a low ridge of earth beyond them which to a degree provided some shelter for the diggers; but in spite of this makeshift cover Lt. Rusholme as Platoon Commander had to direct his men to crawl on all fours to keep below the line of fire. They sweated profusely despite the rain which now fell more heavily, and the chill wind which accompanied it. At each flare they would drop down or freeze motionlessly, gritting their teeth and cursing while bullets whistled barely inches above them. As the flare and the firing died off they would turn back to their evil task, hacking at the foul-smelling soil to refill new sandbags, then grunting and wheezing they heaved them upward to renew the battered parapet. The earth itself was dangerous and noisome, a mixture of every imaginable fragment of the detritus of war. Razor-sharp shrapnel hid treacherously amid mounds of foetid material – old rations, rusting tins, spent ammunition, strands of barbed wire, human waste, and human decomposition. A cut would almost immediately become diseased – often dangerously so. Many who had received only light wounds would later succumb to what was euphemistically termed 'blood poisoning', or gangrene. In the absence of any other disinfectant a wound would have to be cleaned with carbolic solution, or cauterised with boiling water;but such measures were frequently *too little, too late*; and amputation of the infected limb was often the first rather than the last resort.

Still their fevered labour dragged on, lit only by the minimal glow shed by a dark lantern. Several of the working-party had been detailed to excavate the sloppy mess which had all but filled the trench, and somehow dispose of the spoil back into No Man's Land. Of the remaining ten men four 'drew the short straw', having of necessity to work above the parapet itself as they drove down new baulks of timber to secure the smashed revetment.

Though the pelting rain and wind provided some cover for their efforts they still took the precaution of padding the timber with sackcloth in an attempt to muffle the impact of the sledgehammers. Whilst it protracted the job it made it substantially quieter; and every reasonable step must be taken to avoid alerting Fritz to what you were up to. Most worked silently and desperately, muttering only to themselves; and communication between them was clipped to a minimum, though frequently punctuated with the foulest curses.

It was this language which had caused Godfrey to wince when first he'd heard it; but now it was as much a part of trench existence as the ubiquitous lice and the rain; you got habituated to it and after a while it became almost as nothing. Most of the private soldiery were upright chaps – as upright as you could hope to find anywhere; but Godfrey noticed that the effect upon those condemned to life in the trenches – albeit a life too often cut tragically short – was degrading in almost every respect. Generally when returning home on leave the men were able to suspend their trench invective for the interim and revert to what they remembered of civvy speech; but it wasn't the same, and nor were they. They had changed as much as he – a change as irreversible as it was irredeemable.

Do Not Use Language Of Which Your Mother Would Be Ashamed exhorted the posters and 'pulpit professionals' alike. But any credit for his moderation was due less to them than to the inherent decency of the average Tommy who tried as best he could to slough off the permeating foulness during his brief respite in Blighty. But a week of the forward trenches sufficed; and Godfrey wondered as he looked then at the exhausted and rain-spattered faces of his platoon if even a few days of this were not enough. Obscenity flowed naturally from life in the trench – from the vermin and corpse-infested surroundings, from the non-world constricted within earth wall and dugout and latrine and fatigues. Godfrey Rusholme could not judge them.

He hated detailing men for *this* of all duties-this and wiring, and going on patrols and raids. But he went *with* them, then. Now he looked up at the perspiring muttering figures above him, and he felt a fraud,and cowardly.

'Beasant, get down.' Little Beasant, who looked barely sixteen, and was; who should still have been at school. At first the boy did not hear the hissed command but continued to strain hopelessly with the last of the heavy beams. He was unequal to it, any fool could see that. He could barely lift the bloody thing. As he struggled again and again to support it he attracted the withering scorn of the other three – kindly men all, and in other circumstances considerate; but they were exposed, and above the parapet; and the next sodding flare was due any time, the Krauts would see to that. The sooner they were done, the sooner out of this f——-g hole.

'Beasant, *get down! Beasant!*' Rusholme scrambled up the loose earth and grasped the boy's boot. Beasant looked below to his platoon commander, his haggard face framing eyes rounded with fear. '*Get down! Now!'* The boy slithered down and arrived in a heap at Godfrey's feet.

'Stay here and help the others with the shoring.' Beasant picked up a trenching-tool and joined his comrades in the relative safety of the trench. He turned gratefully to Godfrey as one would a deliverer; but his Commander had already made his way up the unbroken firestep on the left, and had crawled to the other three still contending with the last beam. At the arrival of the Officer quick looks were exchanged between them. Then the four set to as one, manhandling the timber with a united strength borne of desperation. Again a flare went up, and again the German machine gun burst into rattling life. As usual each man dropped like a stone and lay as if dead on the sodden ground. But this time – whether it was because a carelessly dropped baulk had dislodged a part of their flimsy cover, or whether the enemy gunners had elevated their weapon to fire more directly downwards – *this* time, the bullets did not pass overhead. There was a sickening crack, as of metal splitting through thick bone; a body was seen to jerk itself backwards and forwards convulsively like some demented marionette; then came a ghastly bubbling noise.

Then stillness. Indifferent to the fire Godfrey was instantly on his feet, attempting to drag the weight of a man's body into the trench. He hardly felt the stroke of something pass by his shoulder. In a moment all four were back below the parapet; three living, and one dead.

'Who is it, sir?' The question was almost non-committal, coming from a seasoned campaigner who had learned from bitter experience how to mask his anguish at the death of comrades.

Godfrey Rusholme took his torch and flashed it on the form lying crumpled in the mud. Gently – almost tenderly – he turned the man's body by its limp arm.

' *Christ! Oh Bloody Christ!'* The face was recognisable as that of Formby – just Private Formby, for no-one seemed to know anything about him, not even his first name. But the back of his head was entirely missing. As was much of his brain.

Godfrey fought to regain his composure 'Sergeant... Sergeant Chadderton?'

'Yes, Mr. Rusholme. Here, sir.'

'Find a stretcher... detail two men to take him down. To the rear Dressing Station. They'll want him there. Make sure that all equipment is returned. Dismiss the men.'

The voice was outwardly calm and detached. Godfrey walked slowly along the trench as if possessed by a dark dream. Then as if suddenly aware once more of his duties he turned back. Stooping over the body he unbuttoned the pocket of the battledress and pulled out Formby's wallet, and a few crumpled envelopes. These he pushed into his trenchcoat pocket.

Another flare rose and lit the dripping heavens. And then another. No machine gun pattered this time. Only a dull silence as the phosphorescent eyes hung there and glowered down on them.

The significance of it was immediate and terrifyingly obvious to both Officer and Sergeant

'*Down the trench, quick. Into the sap! All of you ! Drop everything! Run!*'

Just as the last man cleared the trench and dived left into a cleft cut deep into the rear they heard -or rather felt- a thud which caused the ground to vibrate beneath them. It came from the enemy lines. There came a slow drone like the passing of some huge insect. Then silence again.

'*Cover your ears! Cover them!*'

It seemed that a volcano had been unleashed beside them. For a second the Front Line was lit as bright as day. Then came the blast which caused the earth above and below them to heave with an infernal and deadly power, sucking air from lungs and striking flesh with fire.

And the roar which followed in its wake was terrible beyond all things as it mounted steadily in intensity to a demonic howl. Ears and noses bled freely, and the working party huddled together as they sheltered from the onslaught of the trench mortar rounds – monstrous projectiles which had dropped in the same Forward Trench where they had laboured so long, and where Formby's body still lay. Then like a malignant finale to the performance a wave of soil and metal broke upon them, half-burying them in the ruins of the sap where they had sought refuge.

An acrid vapour swirled over the devastation. Whistles blew in the distance, and all along the remaining Forward Line return fire broke out. Someone somewhere called for artillery support, and the British batteries replied, with a bombardment which scoured and searched in a welter of flame and shrapnel, ranging forward and back, forward and back.

Godfrey Rusholme pulled his battered body and his battered mind out of the wreckage of the sap, and collected those that were left of his working party, and bleeding and deafened they hobbled back together as best they could to the support trenches, where their Platoon Commander saw to the wounded. And then those who could still walk returned to their dugouts and to duty. After the skirmish and the barrage no signs were spotted of any impending enemy movements, so the Battalion was stood down, and sentries posted.

Hours later – or was it days? for his sense of the passage of time had become unreliable and imprecise – Lieutenant Rusholme slowly peeled back the sacking door of the Officers' Dugout – euphemistically nicknamed the *Hippodrome* – and made his way falteringly down the red-lit tunnel. The scene before him was outwardly the same, though some of his fellow-officers were still clad in trenchcoats, and all were plastered with mud. As he entered they sprang to their feet in evident relief at his reappearance.

'My God, Rusholme! We'd all but given you up for dead!'

'Rumours of my death are somewhat exaggerated' he replied, loosely paraphrasing Twain. But he spoke quietly, and though a young subaltern cackled Godfrey's voice had no humour in it, and the older and more senior officers stayed silent. The subaltern ceased his laughter, red faced.

'Sit down, old boy. Rest the pins a bit.' A thin-faced man who bore the insignia of a Captain on his sleeve rummaged around in a wooden crate and produced a bottle of brandy. He poured a tumblerful, and placed it before Godfrey. 'Drink up!. You'll feel better.'

None asked the details of the night's debacle. They did not need to know. They might have guessed that of the working party of sixteen, five had perished that night, with two 'light wounds.' It was always thus, more or less. And it didn't help to dwell on such things. There was nothing you could do about it. You could joke or drink or go mad with it all. But they were relieved that a popular fellow officer had been spared, together with his excellent sergeant.

Godfrey Rusholme had been spared, and Albert Chadderton his friend, with him. But the anonymous Formby had not; and neither had Beasant.

Godfrey eased himself down into a chair and took a pull from the glass. He felt no sense of relief. He wondered vaguely if it was the alcohol which made him so light-headed or the clammy heat of the dugout. He stood suddenly, trying to loosen his Sam Browne belt and holster. His efforts grew feebler and the room spun around him as his legs gave way. Two officers hurried to support him and half-carried half-dragged him to a bunk.

'Water, quick!'

'Take off his coat… ..My God. Look at his back!'

In the top left shoulder of his mackintosh were two blackened holes some four inches apart. The reason for their presence became all too apparent. The waterproof rubber lining had concealed the blood which was still flowed profusely from an as yet invisible wound. His entire shirt was drenched, as was the back of his trousers. Scissors were found, and the saturated crimson shirt was cut away and cast aside.

Godfrey had been hit at the top of his arm and the bullet had passed clean through the flesh of his shoulder, tearing a jagged hole in the muscle from which a flap of tissue dangled limply. A field dressing was hurriedly applied and bound tightly around his chest. Despite the pressure the flow hardly abated, and even as they tightened them the strips became bloodied and wet.

'We *must* move him; he'll bleed to death, here. There's nothing further we can do. He's got to get to the Field Hospital.'

After seemingly endless delays they got a stretcher from somewhere; then carried by two men of his own platoon who had volunteered for the duty, Godfrey was jolted away on his pain-wracked journey down the line. At best their speed was slow, but at worst it was punctuated by dead stops as the stretcher-bearers faltered time and again, lost down the multitude of blind trenches and saps. Manhandling the stretcher over the shambles caused by the last bombardment they reversed and retraced their staggering way a dozen times through mud which made every step a herculean task.

An hour into the journey Godfrey cried out weakly for a drink of water. The bearers halted; and stooping to the stretcher one applied a flask to his lips. Godfrey's appeal seemed to inspire the jaded men to one final effort; and a mixture of dogged resolve and luck brought them at last to the Advanced Dressing Station – no more than a ramshackle assortment of sheets slung hammock-fashion between the walls of a ruined farmhouse.

The canvas bellied in the ceaseless drizzle, maintaining a constant trickle of rainwater which pattered down onto the rows of wounded men lying in the mud beneath. A few RAMC orderlies slithered to and fro amongst the misery, bending over dressings, administering medicines, trying vainly to take notes with the aid of a flashlamp.

To the rear was sited what had once been a pig-sty, but was now transformed into a makeshift mortuary. Here in lines four deep lay the grim harvest of that day's guns, each sewn up in a sack and neatly tagged and ready for transfer to one of the many temporary cemeteries which proliferated thereabouts.

The stretcher bearers wished Godfrey good luck as they handed him over; and he turned to them with gratitude on his white face, and tried to raise his arm in farewell as they disappeared back into the murk.

Chapter Two

HE FELT exposed in the crimson light – a light the colour of flesh. It probed and it scalded, and he struggled to conceal himself from it, and from the Enemy. Voices speaking in undertones intruded into the welter of disconnected thoughts and images which flickered before and about him. There was a strangeness about these voices; disembodied, remote voices, they were not those of his platoon at all. And the smells. They were strange too. Nothing was what he was accustomed to, and he was seized by sudden irrational fear.

Sergeant Chadderton would know! If anyone could make sense of all this, *he* could. He'd be there, all right! Godfrey Rusholme tried to raise himself, but the pain was sickening. His hands scrabbled at the sheets which covered him – scrabbled frantically and feebly, and to no avail.

'Sergeant Chadderton!' There was no answer directly, but the voices ceased. '*Chadderton? Are you there?* Where are we?'

A shadow leaned over him. 'Sergeant? Is that you? Has the working party reported back yet? Are they back... ? Pendleton Sap... Draw sufficient timber. Order the Lewis gun forward... order it *forward...* '

A soft hand was placed on his forehead. It was cooling and comforting and it soothed his burning thoughts. He was at home. That was it. He was ill with something, and was at home.

'Alice! *Alice*?'

'Ce n'est pas Alice, Monsieur. Vous etes blesse. Vous etes a l'Hopital du Saint Maurice.'

Slowly the dream cleared with his vision. He blinkingly refocused on the face which looked down into his and it assumed a female shape – oval, pale with patient eyes and expressionless mouth. The voice was as soft as the hand on his brow.

'Vous etes blesse. Je m'appelle la Soeur Martine.'

The figure rose from him and left. Godfrey turned slowly and watched as the dark shape of Sister Martine glided noiselessly down the ward.

Loss of blood from such a wound when combined with severe concussion would have killed a weaker man; but Godfrey Rusholme fought against their debilitating effects and began to make slow but significant progress. The stitches in his shoulder pained him greatly; but after two weeks of care at the hands of the nuns of St.Maurice Convent he began to rally, and was to be found sitting upright in a chair in the garden-room where he smoked and thought and where he kept himself to himself, for the ward troubled him.

A hush of subdued voices emphasised the nature of the place, for many there had been wounded physically and mentally far worse than he. Cleanliness and a respite from the filth would have been welcome in almost any other place or context; but *this* cleanliness and the all- pervading odour of disinfectant and dressings spoke eloquently of the gravity of so many of the patients' conditions.

The whispering of the nuns and the episodes of calm urgency when doctors clustered round a screened-off case horrified him in a way far different from observing death at the Front. And the ward at night was in its way as much a place of death as was the Forward Trench. Men died there just as regularly. The calls of tormented minds and bodies plagued him incessantly in the dark hours, so that to have any rest at all he was obliged to decamp to the garden room, with a blanket or two. He politely disregarded the protests of the nuns at this, and after a while they ceased bothering him about it. But sleep did not come easily even there.

One evening a Sister came to him with a parcel done up with string.

'Your possessions, Monsieur. Your comrades, they have sent them for you.'

Godfrey loosened the ties, and unravelled the paper. Inside together with a brief note of greeting were things he recognised instantly and with a surge of affection as old friends – his pipe and tobacco, his field lighter, his wallet with some French francs and a few British sovereigns. And there were his photographs, too. He looked at the sepia images and smiled. The first portrayed his parents standing rather stiffly opposite each other, with Helene seated in between on a carved chair whose bulk accentuated the slenderness and elegance of its occupant. Her hair was tied back in the fashion then current, and her neck and face stood out creamy white against the russet backcloth. *To Godfrey* read the inscription in ink *from Your Mother Father and Sister.* It was written in Clarence's precise hand.

He turned over another photograph. It contrasted somewhat with the family group. It was the portrait of a tall young man with a faintly mischievous face, dressed in a stiff suit, with waistcoat and watchchain to match. He looked every inch the young doctor that he aspired to be. But despite the plainness of the looks, animation was given to the whole by the eyes which twinkled with life and the smile which played around the mouth. It was a most engaging likeness.

To My Dearest Brother ran the dedication *from Oliver.*

Godfrey squeezed the cardboard as if it had been Oliver's hand, and set it carefully on one side.

Though he had considered the pictures many times before, he looked at them again as if for the first time. Perhaps it was the light in which he had contemplated them whilst at the Front,and the light in which he looked at them now. Now he was struck by the change that Time had wrought in all but his mother. She, as calm and as serene and as in control, as always. She was exactly as he remembered her, wearing the dress which she had worn at their parting, though they seemed to have taken leave of each other in a different age, when things could be seen more distinctly than in the clouded and distorted images of the present. But Clarence seemed smaller, and diminished, and dried up. What hair he still possessed hung in lank wisps about his temples. How much older he appeared, and how wintry the light in his eyes. There were marks about his mother's face that suggested she had contrived the cool stare – had forcibly suppressed the affection which he knew she had wanted to show. But Clarence's coolness of mien seemed more naturally his own, and genuine.

Godfrey's gaze shifted to his sister's image. The girl he had known had gone; and in her place was a woman of great beauty whose dark eyes reflected an enigmatic spirit and a depth which he had not noticed before. She sat at ease, contemplating the camera serenely but without affectation, her white slender fingers clasped together on her knee. An outsider might have judged the set of her neck and shoulders to be contrived, but Godfrey knew better. This *was* Helene, certainly; but there was another dimension present –perhaps it lay in the eyes, in the mouth or in the turn of the head, or a combination of all three -which marked her transformation from the girl he knew to a woman he could only guess at.

And Oliver? The boy too, had departed and the confident young man who stood there in his place exhaled an air of serene independence. He had arranged to have his photograph taken separately from the rest of the family, and everything about the picture proclaimed the reason why. He was his own man, with a fierce individuality which declared itself in every nuance and shadow of the image. How he would love to see Oliver again! He packed the pictures away in his wallet.

His attention was drawn to something which seemed out of place. It was another wallet, one which he did not immediately recognise. Thoughts of his family had for a while dispelled other darker broodings, and he could not immediately associate the odd presence of this wallet with anything. It was certainly not his. He assumed it had been sent to him in error, and picked it up with the purpose of finding out its owner.

The leather was water – stained, and had a musty smell. He opened it and some papers fell into his lap, and yet more photographs. He glanced at them, puzzled. One was of a roundfaced little woman with her hair tightly knotted in a bun. She smiled shyly at the camera, lowering her eyes demurely. She was very plain, but had a kind face. On her knee sat a little boy dressed in a diminutive Khaki soldier-suit. He stared out of the picture proudly, his hat rakishly set at an angle – a gesture probably more to be credited to the photographer than the child. Yet neither face shed any light as to the identity of the owner of the wallet.

Godfrey turned to the papers. There were two letters. From its crumpled and well-thumbed appearance the first had been read and re-read many times. The other had been written quite recently; though damp its paper had not been handled much other than to fold it once with the undoubted intention of putting it into an envelope.

Godfrey opened the letter and read its contents.

F Coy 16th. Battn.
The Manchester Regt
'Somewhere in France'
My Dearest Lilly

I write these few Lines to you Hoping they will find you in as Good a State of Health as they Leave me and I thank you for your Dear Letter of the 6th.which arrived safely with the Nice Things you sent. You must be careful not to be too Extravagant, but they will go down a Treat. I will certainly share them out with the Boys. What a feast we will have.

Well here I am a soldier at Last. I said I would get through and I have though the Training was quite hard at times and the billets very cold. Now I am finally Somewhere in France as they say and with a proper Regiment too. The chaps in the dugout are as fine a bunch as you could hope to meet and we get along swimmingly together. We are having a rare old Time I can tell you for they have all made me very welcome in the Company and I feel very much at Home.

Our Sergeant is very tough but fair and his bark is worse than his Bite. He has been in some scraps in his time by the look of it. Our Officer is a real Gentleman. He is very kind and asked me how I was the other day. He is an absolute toff, brave as a lion and all the Men think the World of him and they would do anything for him.

Now my Dearest do not be worried by the rumours you will hear, about it being dangerous at the Front. Ignore them for it is not as bad as they say. I would not be anywhere else in the World, except with You, my Dearest Wife.

Tell Alfie I will get him a real Hun Helmet when I can,one of those with the points on that he wants so much. Tell him I will bring it for him on my next Leave. Give him a big Hug from his Daddy, and a kiss. And I send this with as many for You as I will Give you when I come home again. I have to close now because the Sergeant is calling us up.

So No More at present from Your Loving Husband

Tom. xxxxxxx

PS the picture you sent of yourself and our Alfie together is a topper! He looks very smart in his uniform. I should not think any other boy has one. I have got him the Manchesters cap badge which he asked for and which I will send, because I have a spare one.

PPS I carry the picture in my pocket, nearest my heart.

Godfrey Rusholme closed the letter and gently folded it. He pulled out the Soldier's Small Book from the wallet's inner leaf, and read there what he feared;

Name of soldier:-Thomas Joseph Formby
Enlisted:-Ardwick Bks, Manchester 19/3/1915
Age :- 28 years 2 months
Trade or calling:- mill-hand
Rank:- private
The Soldier's Next of Kin now living:-Mrs. Lillian Formby
Address:- 12 Elbow Street Longsight Manchester.

Godfrey did not read further. The Small Book fell from his fingers as his hands involuntarily shifted to the arms of the chair, and his grip closed about them until the knuckles showed white through the skin. The letters and the photographs slipped unnoticed from his lap onto the floor.

So it was Formby's letter – the simple bid of a man to conceal the loneliness and isolation and homesickness from those he loved and whom in his misguided innocence he had enlisted to defend. The memory of that hideous pelting night which Godfrey had till then consigned to the darkest corners of his mind rose again like a corpse in a pool. He recalled how he had taken the wallet from the body and put it in his pocket. They must have sent it along with the other things, assuming it to be his.

It was Formby, the man whose forename had remained unknown, and which nobody – including himself – had taken the trouble to discover; the lifeless Tom Formby who could never now be found, and who would even be denied the dignity of a grave.

Though he had imagined himself desensitised by the writing of too many letters of condolence to next of kin, or responses to polite, heartbroken enquiries as to how someone's lad had died, the composition of this letter had for some reason become harder than most. Indeed, it had become as harsh a message as he had ever written. His professional detachment was no more than affectation, a confidence-trick perpetrated on himself in a desperate bid to retain his sanity. As a protective shell it was only paper thin, and the charring of his emotions continued relentlessly behind it.

He rose and took a sheet of paper from a nearby desk and steeled himself to tell the half-truth about her husband's life and death to the little round-faced woman in the photograph – to Mrs. Lilly Formby of Elbow Street, who had by ill-chance become more alive to him at that moment in Time than any other being. He drew out his pen and embarked on the letter which he knew would confirm that which she had long dreaded, and which would shatter the life of the little family. He imagined how it would drop through the door, and how she might hear its fall; how she would pick it up but not recognise the hand and be perplexed, at first. In his mind he heard her open the envelope and draw out the letter, and he followed her eyes as she read it again and again in disbelief. And he fancied he could hear her cry out in anguish as the unspeakable truth of *his* message – the message created by *his* pen and *his* hand, and this war– finally struck home.

He hoped there'd be someone in the house with her; but not her son Alfred, not yet. There *must* be time – a decent pause, surely? -between what she herself *had* to face, and what she had to tell him.

He drew out a Woodbine and lit it with an uncertain hand. He could play the coward, and leave it all to the indifference of the Official Telegram, or the bloody Casualty Lists; but to do so would be shameful -a betrayal of Tom Formby and his widow Lilly. If he had failed them thus far, he would not fail them in this.

My Dear Mrs. Formby he began

It is with great regret that I have to tell you that your husband Thomas... He thought better of the formality, and substituted Tom... *that your husband Tom has lost his life while on active service. His comrades share with me the sense of grief at the death of a fine soldier and a fine man. He was courageous to the end and did his duty to the last. He was as plucky as anyone in the company and his friends regarded him highly as a loyal pal.*

I was beside him at the time he was killed and he did not suffer. Of this I am certain. He died instantaneously, helping his comrades in a moment of great need while repairing a section of trench.

I have taken the liberty of returning his wallet and some other things of his which I feel sure you would want to have.

Please accept my deepest and heartfelt condolences, and my assurance

that he will be greatly missed by his comrades and by the Officers alike.
Yours most sincerely
Lieut. Godfrey Rusholme. 7 Platoon F Coy.
16th.Battn.The Manchester Regiment

He sealed the letter in an envelope and placed it on the table. On looking down he was surprised to see Formby's few possessions lying scattered around his feet. He retrieved them and parcelled them up carefully, ready to send. Then as an afterthought he reopened the package and took out the private's last message to his wife. With his pen he purposefully scored out the section relating to himself, completely obliterating the eulogy it contained. At the side of the deletions he wrote *censored*. He wrapped the items up a second time together with the badge which he had taken from his own cap, and addressed it.

He sat motionless as the short dusk closed about the hospital. He watched the shadows in the garden lengthen and spread until having engulfed the outer world entirely, they invaded the room and him. His evening meal lay untouched where the Sisters had left it; despite their quiet encouragement he had eaten nothing. His eyes glinted in the dark, reflecting the guttering flame of an oil lamp in the nearby corridor. With an almost physical effort of will he extricated his mind from the convent, from the Front-line chaos and the canvas sacks and the coughing, and found his way back to a time before there was a war. He remembered with a pang of sentiment the heady days of Oxford colleges and the ancient warm stones of Goldring, clad in its mellow coat of ivy. He recalled the bicycling picnics with the wicker baskets and the straw hats, and the snowy jackets, and the snowier girls. It had been so straightforward, so certain, so settled, back then.He admired, and was admired; and the gaining of his Blue for cricket had brought his final year to a summit of perfection. He pictured the light playing on the willows, and the river whose easy and unhurried flow seemed to mirror his former life in its glassy waters. How could there be any return to all that without an act of massive self- delusion on his part, of reliance on a specious contention that neither he nor the world had been changed forever despite the appalling evidence to the contrary? Some sort of return was possible, but with few if any of the old certainties intact. And what would that make it? A submergence of his other self – his truer self, as he feverishly imagined it to be –under the mantle of a threadbare order which had led to *this.* Amidst his attenuated emotions there was a part which yearned for peace, and a return to that nebulous world on whatever terms might be dictated. But the side of him which he fancied was the realist scorned any such hopes, and derided them as futile.

His wound pained him more than usual. Rising heavily he made his way out to the garden, and crossed to the old convent well which now lay surrounded by lawns. He let down the bucket and heard its splash echo up to him from the darkness below. The act of winding the handle as he drew it back up was absurdly comforting with its simple predictability, and as he swung the full bucket onto the wall he glanced into it. The black surface of the water reflected nothing but the stars which shimmered and shifted faintly as the breeze ruffled it. Captured so fleetingly their images seemed immeasurably distant, and cold, and ancient beyond imagining; and their eternal remoteness seemed to diminish Mankind, and place his conflicts and his troubles into icy perspective.

The darkness which cloaked Godfrey became suffused with red at its very edge; and raising his eyes to the far horizon he saw that it was now animated with lights which flickered and leaped in wave upon wave of tiny scarlet tongues. He recognised them for what they were, and waited with racing pulse for the drumming which would announce the onset of another artillery bombardment. He stood a while, detached and distant from it all at first. He watched as the barrage grew steadily in ferocity and raged across the Front lines – whether British or German, he could not tell – and was struck by its precision and control and how oddly impersonal the whole process of destruction seemed to have become. In that dark and lonely moment he looked upon the war as a remote phenomenon, in much the same way as he perceived the starlight; neither seemed to correspond to anything vital in him. Abstracted from its grisly immediacy he could distinguish the logic of its mechanisms, its industrial mass methods and its massed resources; and note how the deaths of thousands was being engineered and refined as the byproduct of victory.

Then one by one the spectral faces of the men of his platoon rose before him as he saw them cowering in some stinking hole, amidst it all. They were human faces, lost faces. He wondered where they were, and who amongst them still lived. And as he thought of them sanity and compassion reasserted themselves once again, and he asked himself how he could possibly have entertained the ideas of only minutes before.

He turned and walked back, and slowly reentered the garden-room. Closing the double doors behind him he suddenly noticed how cold it had become; and wrapping himself in blankets he curled up as tightly as his aching shoulder would allow, and sought escape in sleep.

Chapter Three

BUILT PIECEMEAL in the early years of the nineteenth century, Nelson Street still retained a genteel and well- proportioned charm with its neat small bricks and fluted columns and porticoes. Russets predominated in its walls, and whites in its restrained stone- and plaster-work; and up to each fanlit entrance there ran a wide flight of steps, donkeystoned to whatever shade of yellow or ochre the housemaid had to hand.

A knot of workmen had gathered that evening around an ornate cast-iron railing fronting one of the houses. It was the final section remaining in the whole of Nelson Street,all the other corresponding ones having been stripped down as far as the low stone walls on which they had perched for a century or more. While the men contemplated this last panel others piled the remainder on to the back of a flat wagon. Wielding hacksaws it took them no more than a few minutes to sever the uprights, and with a deafening crash the entire section toppled forward onto the cobbles. What had seemed to be solid iron was less so, however; on the impact a cloud of reddish rust billowed from the casting, as a choking mixture of powder and flakes detached itself from the corrosion beneath. One of the workmen lifted a sledgehammer, and with a resounding blow drove it into the middle of the railing. With a dull thud the whole panel sagged and broke into a hundred pieces. 'Last of 'em' grunted the workman as he wiped his brow. 'An' more for t' bloody guns.'

A tall well-proportioned young man in a tweed suit was making his way along the gaslit pavement, attempting to read a book which he held in one hand while in his other he carried a case bulging with yet more books. Only when he was right up against the obstacle did he raise his eyes to discover the impossibility of any further progress down that side of the street. Sidestepping the sweating workmen he managed to continue for some yards on his way; then turning abruptly left into Number Seven he sprang up its flight of steps, taking two at a time. Without pausing he passed through the door and into the spacious hallway where he deposited a battered umbrella in the stand. 'Evening, Mrs Monaghan! Back!' he bellowed,pausing to sniff appreciatively at the aromas floating from the rear kitchen. A door opened at the further end of the corridor and a lady clad in a black crepe gown and white pinafore bustled out. She greeted him with the kindly but firm smile which she reserved for her *Young Medical Gentlemen* as she liked to call them – the emphasis which she placed upon *Gentlemen* carrying with it as much a note of censure as of respect.

'Good evening to you. There's dinner at seven, as usual. Have you seen me railin's?' she humphed. As it was far more a statement than a question the young man did not bother to reply. Mrs.'M' as she was known by all, was formidable in the extreme. She was the *doyen* of the lodging-house ladies who accommodated students from the world-renowned Victoria University Medical School, and her house was famed for its cuisine.It was difficult to stay thin while in Mrs.M.'s care, for she took the enlightened view that the effective feeding of the mind was impossible without feeding the body. Despite the privations caused by the War she ensured that her five *gentlemen* – medical students all – lived and dined far better than most. Her rule of iron forbade every form of *shenanigans, daftness and what-not* on the premises – a rule which was certainly necessary given the tendencies of medical students, then as now; but despite it the prevailing climate was benign, albeit that it arose from something approaching benign despotism. And there were ways to sidestep rules, if required.

Like the proprietor, the house was large and well-built and comfortable. Constructed at the time of Trafalgar by a wealthy cotton spinner it had been the first house in the street and was called Nelson Place in honour of the hero. But the century had moved on; and despite its illustrious name its previous owners had forsaken the grime of the industrial suburbs for the leafier world of Chorlton, leaving their once grand mansion to settle into a period of temporary decline. Yet the foundation and expansion of the University had breathed new life into Nelson Street and other neighbouring streets and squares. Enterprising ladies of whom Mrs Kathleen Monaghan was but one were quick to spot the opportunity, and seize it. Over the years the streets had experienced something of a renaissance as the houses were snapped up and refurbished; and the quarter was reinvigorated by the comings and goings of a new and younger academic world.

Oliver Rusholme had done well to obtain rooms at Mrs. Monaghan's; they were justifiably sought after, and a place under her roof was coveted. From the outset he had resolved to leave his parents' home at Millwain Place as soon as circumstances allowed; it was inconvenient for a number of reasons for him to remain there any longer than was absolutely necessary.

His relationship with his father had not improved with the years, and despite his success which was regarded by all but Clarence as being little short of meteoric, Oliver's departure was a mutual relief. It would have been difficult to travel to the Medical School on a daily basis from Desbury, anyway. The University's award of the Bridgewater Scholarship to him had come as a bolt from the blue, as had his secret nomination by his friends Captain Bonnard and Percy Crossley. The award caused Oliver to view himself in an entirely different light, and gave him a renewed sense of confidence and self-worth which he sorely needed.

When added to the allowance made him by his parents, the monetary value of the Scholarship was found to be sufficient to secure him a considerable degree of independence – an opportunity which he had grasped with undisguised enthusiasm. Thus he had moved out *bag and baggage* from Millwain Place the same summer that he had finished at Hugh Williams's; and though his mother had tried to persuade him to change his mind he had stuck to his purpose and had left the house as soon as he was able.

Seeing that her son's resolve was unshakeable Ida had bowed to the inevitability of it, and did all she could to assist him in what he had decided to do. Together they visited houses recommended by various members of the Medical School, and it was in the course of this that they had lit upon Mrs. Monaghan's. Each side had been impressed with the other, and the agreement was entered into without unnecessary delay. It turned out that one of her *Gentlemen* had secured his first placement at Liverpool and was at that moment in the process of moving out; consequently his rooms would become available within days.

That had been three years ago. Oliver had stayed put ever since, finding his rooms equally ideal for study and for their closeness to the City. His trips southward to Desbury became rarer with the passage of the months, for any residual need to visit Millwain Place gradually dwindled to nothing and it was only the leaden sense of duty which compelled him to go at all. On his increasingly rare visits home there was the inevitable atmosphere, with the indifferent politeness of his father and the transparent truce between his parents which failed to mask the deepening gulf between them. And then talk would inevitably shift to the War and Godfrey and his letters home, and his doings first at the Training Camp and then at the Front, with Clarence's jingoistic pride in his son's commission inflaming the conversation and turning his usual pallor to a bellicose crimson. Ida had been appalled by Godfrey's abrupt announcement of his intention to suspend work in Chambers and join up with his friend Warrington, and her husband's sentiments troubled her still more. Clarence applauded his son's decision, asserting that it was the duty of every subject loyal to Crown and Empire. It would be the making of him, he said, as though Godfrey had signed up for some outdoor Finishing-School. Ida thought otherwise and said so, fearing what effect such an experience might have on her son's career and indeed on his personality. She deeply mistrusted the military ideal and what she had seen of the mentality which seemed to empower it. She was wary of militarism and suspected the motives of those who pushed army service as a somehow ennobling experience, like some desirable Rite of Passage necessary for the attainment of Manhood. Despite her genuine efforts to understand she could find no merits in it, and she arrived at the unavoidable conclusion that it had none.

With Godfrey as the sole topic of conversation Oliver's interest soon waned; not because he resented Godfrey's pre-eminence in any way – he still worshipped his older brother and was fiercely loyal to him– but because the letters sent to him from the Front had begun to tell a different story from those which his parents continued to receive. Theirs were upbeat and optimistic, filled with trite anecdotes from the Officers' Mess and life in behind-the-lines France. Those to Oliver had begun in similar vein, but had gradually assumed a more candid and sombre tone. There was a blackness in them now. Sometimes they were the briefest of notes, scribbled in frantic moments snatched between the crises of Front-Line duty; while at other times they were protracted outpourings which rambled on page after depressing page; and in all of them hope seemed a fragile commodity. Oliver wondered at the difference between his and his parents' letters, concluding that Godfrey had constructed an elaborate smoke-screen behind which he was concealed growing reservations about the War. He had no doubt whatever that the real Godfrey was represented in the lines penned to *him* and not in the ones composed for his father and mother.

In his most recent letter Godfrey had repeatedly warned him against making

.... *the gullible fool's mistake of joining up. You must resist at all costs the blandishments and pressure which others will inevitably apply... . for frankly it's a mug's game. I could not bear to think of you out here in all this. I don't see how you could last, Old Chap. And surely one fool's enough for any family...*

The voice was hardly recognisable as that of his brother, and Oliver was deeply troubled by the state of mind it revealed. But he kept his fears to himself, and looked forward all the more to Godfrey's intended return home on convalescent leave.

Oliver might as well have proposed travelling to the moon as to Desbury, so mentally and emotionally distant did his former home seem compared to the worlds of Nelson Place, The Medical School and Ridland where he spent his time now.

The lodestone of Manchester and its University increasingly drew him like steel to a magnet, and it was northward to the great beating heart of the metropolis that his path increasingly tended.

Not that he was a particularly social or outgoing person by nature. He was liked and respected by his circle of student friends without exception. But years spent learning to exist in a world in which parental affection and friendship were scarce had left him able to survive well enough with his own company if necessary. Sometimes when not occupied in library or laboratory he would walk the streets of Manchester and observe the diversity of the milling crowds surrounding him – the millwright, the lawyer, the foundryman – and absorb it almost through his skin. He liked people, but enjoyed and valued his anonymity more.

There were of course the odd times – after exams, or at the end of the University Term – when he was persuaded by his friends to join them for an evening's *refreshment*, when a public bar of the sleazier sort would be chosen as the main port of call. This would inevitably be followed by a raucous trip to the *Palace* Music Hall, and a final stagger to another pub for a 'nightcap'. Then there would be the tiptoeing return to Number Seven and a slurred conversation at the door as to how best to avoid the wrath of Mrs.M. On the previous Hallowe'en some comic in the party had acquired a large pumpkin from Shudehill Market. Oliver had adopted the monstrosity and after carving a grotesque leer with matching eyes in it, had shinned up a column of Number Seven's portico. In his drunken devil-may –care state he perched this vegetable – now sporting an admiral's hat fashioned from cardboard – directly on top. Then he set about altering the premises' name slightly from *Nelson Place* to *Nelson's Face* with a stick of chalk.

Next day Mrs.M had wondered at the laughter directed toward her premises by passers – by; and her outrage was redoubled when she was made aware of the cause.

The joke misfired badly, however, for whilst Oliver as the main culprit owned up promptly to the offence, it might have cost him his rooms at Number Seven. Only with difficulty was the crimson Mrs.M pacified, and only then after Oliver had fetched a ladder and dismantled and erased the decorations of the night before, despite a ghastly headache. But such behaviour was very much the exception, and beneath the fury Mrs M. still liked him, and would never really have carried out her threat.

It was to Nelson Place that he returned that evening, just as his brother Godfrey was opening the fateful parcel from the Front.

Oliver stretched himself out in his armchair before the roaring fire and picked up a pipe and tobacco-pouch. He loosened his boots wearily and kicked them off, perching his feet on the fender and wriggling his toes in the welcome heat. Having filled his pipe he picket up a battered textbook and turned to a page marked with a slip of paper. No sooner had he become engaged with the subject than there was a knock on the door which promptly opened followed by a tousled head which poked round it.

'Evening, Rusholme ! Still at it? You'll wear the jolly old eyes out the way you're going!'

The visitor assumed that wheedling tone which always indicated he was going to ask for something. 'I came to see if you still have any of those essays you wrote last year about the function of the spleen. They were jolly good, I know. Got you yet another distinction in the Royal Coll.'s third year finals, as I recall… Wouldn't let me have a quick glimpse of them would you… ? Just a *quick* one, no more… need to get my bearings… direction… whatever. You know how it is' he concluded lamely.

Oliver smiled tiredly back. George Gillbank – a Second Year pre-med student and junior to Oliver by a year – seemed in a perpetual state of confusion. He struggled with most things of an academic nature, and particularly with meeting deadlines set by the martinets who taught them.

Oliver did not resent helping someone out, though he wondered how Gilbank had managed to pass his First Year General papers – none of them by any means a walkover. Oliver rose from his armchair and stepped across to a brass-bound filing cabinet in a corner of his room. Drawing out the top compartment he considered briefly, then pulled out a brown manilla file. Having checked the contents he handed them across to his visitor.

'Most decent of you, Rusholme! Really kind!. I'd *really* like to read'em in the comfort of the ol' study, if you don't object. Only, that is *if* you don't object.'

'Help yourself.I doubt I'll need them in the near future, if at all. Let me have them back when you've done with them.'

Still thanking him profusely Gilbank exited the room, and left its owner to resume his pre-dinner reading.

Oliver Rusholme was oblivious to the near – reverence in which he was held by almost all his Third Year fellow students, and by all the Seconds and Firsts. From the dismal failure of only six years' previously he had developed into an academically gifted young man for whom the study of medicine held no fears. He was naturally attuned to the complex of interrelated subjects which formed even then the core of this most demanding of disciplines. Though he did not suspected it, he was felt by many to epitomise the qualities of the finest of medical students; and his tutors privately predicted great things for him.

Prominent in his circle of admirers was Captain William Bonnard. The old man – though now advanced in age and prone to absent-mindedness – could still to be found holding forth to another generation of boys perched in the same desks which had caused their predecessor such pain. Bonnard delighted in reading out his protégé's frequent letters to a captive audience in The Senior Common Room, and scourging Oliver's former detractors with details of the boy's most recent achievements.

'*Told* you didn't I? *Told* you Rusholme'd make good! Only sneered, didn't you! Eating your bally words *now* though, aren't you! Hah!'

It would have been fitting for Percy Crossley to have been there. He could have heard about his pupil's continued success and how his faith in the boy had been vindicated; but the philanthropic teacher had resigned his post immediately at the outbreak of war in 1914; and volunteering for service with the Manchester Pals, had enlisted as a private soldier. But Oliver continued to write to him also, just the same.

The relative shortness of the academic Terms provided Oliver with opportunities to stride down to Manchester Central, rucksack on back,to catch the Holyhead Boat Train. Then with the wind and the steam about him like familiar spirits he would speed his way to Wales. From the compartment window he would still count off the well-known fields and forests as he had done ever since his childhood, until at last he approached Ridland and the Clwyr.

There he would renew his old acquaintance with the cottage and the Captain and his salmon-pools. He could have passed more time there than the old man himself, had he chosen to do so; for Bonnard had given him the counterpart key – a huge rusty iron contraption; but despite the Captain's invitation to treat the cottage as his own and call in whenever he liked, Oliver refrained from doing so. Though he loved the old man and the place equally, to enter in the absence of the Captain was somehow an intrusion into the home of another, nomatter how welcoming and open it was. There was a private side to the old man which he did not know, and Oliver sensed that part of the secret rested within. On his own there he found that it surrounded him – the very walls and flagstones and the fireless grate proclaimed it; yet he did not seek to know it.

Despite the conversion of the lean-to into a more permanent and comfortable lodging, Oliver felt it incomplete without the Captain.

The Captain; seated in his familiar place, puffing away at his battered meerschaum pipe as he struggled to read the local paper. On his first and only visit alone Oliver had looked at the sagging armchair and recognised the depth of affection he felt for the old man – an affection which he knew was reciprocated. Theirs was a mutual regard; the fatherless son, and the sonless father. He had returned to Manchester by the next train.

But there were times when they would meet up, either at Central Station or at the Cottage; or knowing how much frailer the Captain had become, Oliver would go down a day or two beforehand. Then he would get the fire going to dispel the river's dampness, re-tar the planks of the boat which was now as advanced in years as its owner, and generally put the place in order.

Oliver was thinking fondly about Ridland when the gong sounded down in the hallway to notify them of dinner. Normally it was necessary to strike it only once or twice at most as the appetites of the young men added sharpness to their hearing; but this evening some invisible person was giving the gong an absolute hammering. Having completely forgotten to change, Oliver hurriedly splashed his face and hands with water from his washstand jug, then tearing off his collar and tie he rapidly replaced them with fresh ones which he took from a chest of drawers. Slicking down his hair with the palm of his hand he glanced at the less dishevelled image in the mirror. It would have to do, he decided; and he set off on the three-flight descent to the rear dining-room.

'Evening, Rusholme'. Oliver duly returned the greetings which came from his four fellow-residents seated around a large mahogany table. 'Inhale, Pottinger!' Oliver edged his way past a stout red-faced young man and squeezed into his seat. He surveyed the table with satisfaction. Mrs.M.'s people dined as well as she could manage, with genuine E.P.N.S. cutlery and cruet-sets, all neatly laid on a blindingly-white tablecloth of Irish linen which had as always been starched stiff as a board. The general impression was most pleasant as the greenish flames of the gas-lamps glittered off the silverplate and the crystal – electric light not having as yet arrived at Number Seven.

Oliver poured himself a glass of water from the decanter and turned to the others. 'Decent day?'

'So-so'

'Phys. is proving quite a headache, if you'll pardon the pun'.

'Why so?'

'Well, it's that new chap MacIntyre… '

'*MacLeish,* you mean' interrupted Gilbank 'I'm sure it's MacLeish.

'Well, MacWhoever' retorted Wilfred Hallett testily. Exceptionally tall and thin –faced, he was notable equally for his acid wit and shortness of temper. It did not pay to cross Hallett. '*As* I was saying, this new chap's lecturing is about as clear as mud. Not a patch on old Bill Aplin.' Professor Sir William Aplin, one of the cornerstones of the School and foremost in the field of diseases of the bone, had recently taken a sabbatical to visit his native New Zealand. His return – though awaited with anticipation by his students who knew a good thing when they saw one – would not be for some considerable time. Hence the appointment of his deputy Prof. James MacIntyre.

'He seemed easy enough to follow, as I recall' said Oliver 'though he *was* only dealing with compound fractures at the time.' he added disarmingly. 'He was my tutor last year, y' know.'

'Tutor or not, *I personally* find the cove damn' hard to make sense of!' retorted Hallett.

The discussion might have become more heated had not the double doors swung open as Mrs Monaghan and a maid came in, laden with a tureen and a tray of bread rolls. Their attention were immediately diverted from The School to the more pressing issue of food.

Serving dinner was a moment of drama for Mrs. M. She would enter with a flourish, and assess the degree to which her cookery were received in terms of appreciative noises from the diners. An astute newcomer soon learned which way the wind blew in this regard; and also saw that to remain in her good books it was wise to join in the chorus with the rest. It had become *quite a sauce of humour* as Hallett drily put it, and the fun lay in feigning ecstasy without giving the game away or offending the generous-hearted lady whose devotion to wholesome food was beyond question.

Tonight she planted the tureen squarely in the middle of the table and removed the lid. The contents certainly were appetising, and the usual chorus of appreciation was genuine enough. Ample portions were ladled into soup-bowls, and as they were being passed along Mrs. Monaghan motioned to the maid to offer rolls to the diners.

'Gentlemen' she announced 'as you know, the last maid has been unable to continue in our employ' she raised an eyebrow significantly. 'In consequence o'that this girl has replaced her. She is called Dolly. I hope she'll be a quick learner.'

'Ah! The gong! *Thought* we'd a new player!' said Hallett. Oliver glanced at the girl who was about eighteen, and saw that she had reddened with embarassment. There was also something vaguely familiar about her, too.

The gentle eyes, the resolute chin, the flaxen hair tied neatly back; Oliver thought her quite pretty. 'I'm sure Dolly'll do just splendidly!' he said cheerfully, in a bid to ease her discomfiture. The girl returned his glance gratefully. 'Now where's that roll, to complement this excellent chicken soup!'

As dinner was drawing to its close and Dolly was clearing away the things, Mrs Monaghan brought two envelopes across to Oliver. 'I'm quite forgettin' meself Mr.Rusholme' she said apologetically. 'These two letters came by this afternoon's post, an' I clear forgot 'em with the rush to get dinner ready, an' that racket outside, an' all.' Oliver picked them up and considered the handwriting. One was in his father's inimitable spidery script, while the other was in an elaborate hand which he did not immediately recognise, and which seemed foreign. It bore neither stamp nor any mark other than the telltale franking FIELD POST OFFICE. He opened his father's letter first.

It was couched in the usual formalities of the time;

Millwain Place
November10th. 1915

Dear Oliver it read *Your Mama and I send our cordial greetings to you in the hope that you are progressing well with your studies…*

Despite their enduring estrangement, the icy goodwill which this opening line conveyed still caused him to wince involuntarily; his father was a good marksman. There was no news from home; no insignificant titbits which might have made the letter a little less impersonal, and more affectionate. Sentiment was wanting, utterly

The niceties dispensed with, Clarence got down to business without further delay.

You were no doubt as concerned as we on hearing of your brother Godfrey's gallant wounding in action, and have rejoiced with us that the injury he sustained is only slight. However we have now heard from the War Office that he will be returning home to England, hopefully by the weekend of the 24th. We propose to hold a celebration on the day following his arrival here, and have invited some of his immediate friends. Your Mama and I express the hope that you will be able to attend.

Kindly let us know of your intentions in early course, so that the appropriate arrangements may be made.

Yours.
Father.

Tight-lipped, Oliver replaced the letter in the envelope. He picked up the second and slit it open. The script was wandering and indistinct, and it was only after a second attempt at reading it that he began to decipher the message.

Base Hospital No. 6
Amiens
Nov. 7th.

Dear Ollie,

I hope you'll forgive the illegibility of this. For some reason I've had an attack of the 'shakes' of late, and my hands seem to be the main victims – or culprits – I don't quite know which. But I think my shoulder's on the mend, however; and that's what matters.

Thanks for all those letters which you sent me. You don't know just how much a letter means to someone in my predicament, and yours have always been the most welcome of all; they're so kind and cheery. I'm sorry that I haven't replied very often, or indeed at all, to some of them. It's not indifference, believe me; they have all mattered hugely. It's just that I have not always felt up to it, if you see what I mean. But here goes, as they say.

Well old chap, they tell me I'm destined for a trip Home to 'Blighty'. Not quite the sort of circumstances under which I'd have liked to come, but they'll have to do.

I can't tell you how I look forward to seeing you again, and picking up the loose ends with our friends and most especially you. Do you recall those rambles we took together, when we went off into the blue yonder? I think of them often, when I try to get my mind away from things. Perhaps we'll be able to do one or two, when I'm feeling a little better. I'd really like that.

I've heard pretty regularly from Ma and Pa, and Helene, too. Ma tells me you've been doing exceptionally at your studies to be an M.O. You're a dark horse, Ollie! Never a word to me about your triumphs. You shouldn't be so reticent to 'blow your own trumpet', you know.

Helene writes that she has heard from Warrington; he's landed some cushy job as an aide, apparently. We've rather lost touch, he and I, since he was elevated to the High and Mighty at Sandhurst and I got my posting to the 16th. I'm not surprised, given his connections. Still, I wish him well; and he was always a jolly good friend.

You haven't given in and enlisted, have you? Remember what I said, and ***don't*** *yield to mindless sentiment. You will do far more good where you are.*

I'm looking forward to seeing you very soon.

Your most affectionate brother

Godfrey.

P.S.*I've asked one of the nuns to address the envelope so there is at least an even chance of it reaching you.*

Oliver squeezed the letter in his hand while in an Amiens hospital Godfrey sat looking at the photograph.

Chapter Four

THE LITTLE TRAIN wheezed its way through a cutting which guided the single track to Desbury Station. It drew to an asthmatic halt at the platform to allow a handful of passengers off. Even fewer climbed aboard, for the deeper the line penetrated into rural Cheshire the less desire for travel there seemed to be amongst those who lived in its remoter villages. The Stationmaster's whistle shrilled and the engine huffed and groaned the three carriages away into the dusk at a steady twenty miles per hour.

Oliver Rusholme stood watching it away as its red tail – light was swallowed by the growing gloom. He had climbed out of the rearmost carriage; and now, having picked up his case, began to make his way past a porter engaged in lighting the platform's oil-lamps. Directly ahead of him a short line of passengers had collected at the barrier, waiting to have tickets clipped. Amongst them was a knot of khaki-clad Tommies, noisily home on leave, who with cigarettes in mouths laughed and flirted with a pair of plump office-girls. His attention shifted to a taller figure, also dressed in khaki, but whose cap and tailored coat marked him out as an officer. Despite the man's considerable height the attitude of his body seemed bowed and careworn. In the shadows thrown by the lamps Oliver could not make out his features; and as the man searched feebly for something inside his jacket he seemed utterly at a loss. Heart pounding Oliver stepped up to him; and clearing his throat and with eyes brimming with tears, asked as calmly as he could 'Can I help you, Godfrey?'

The figure turned and peered uncomprehendingly through the gloom at Oliver. 'That's very kind of you, I'm sure' his brother said 'but I have mislaid my rail warrant somewhere.I had it about me but it's… .' He continued to search for a moment, then paused and looked up. 'You called me Godfrey… it *can't* be, surely… ?'

'Don't you recognise me, old lad? Don't you *know* me?'

'Ollie… ? Is it *really* you?' Oliver enfolded his brother gently in his arms and hugged him.

'Yes, it's me all right.' he said indistinctly.

''Ave yer no 'omes to go to?' the ticket collecter enquired brusquely as they reached the barrier 'Everyone else 'as, as you can clearly see.'

Oliver handed over his ticket 'I'm afraid that this gentleman has mislaid his travel warrant. But he is a serving officer, as *you* can clearly see. That means he must have one.'

'That's what they all say' retorted the collector dubiously 'No ticket? Double the fare' adding as if it were a concession '*single*, o'course.' He motioned them across to the diminutive ticket – office, and peered out officiously at them from behind his window. ' Now, we'll *assume* yer journey were from Exchange; so that's tenpence doubled… .makin' one – an' – eight, all told.'

Oliver was unwilling to argue and dampen the moment still further, and was even less inclined to go through Godfrey's pockets as if he were a child. He paid over the money without demur. 'Lucky for you there weren't a First Class on tonight. Otherwise it'd 've cost yer more.' the collector added sourly. *Lucky for you, you weren't at Loos or Arras* Oliver thought; but resisted the temptation to retaliate.

Shouldering both bags he led Godfrey out onto the leafy broadway. His brother drew himself upright and breathed in the sharp night air.

'You can't know how good it is to be back.' he said.

'I doubt any of us here can' Oliver replied 'but I do know how good it is to have you back, safe.'

Godfrey smiled quietly at his brother. 'Yes. Safe.'

Though still in a weakened state, he insisted that they walk to Millwain Place rather than struggle down to the village in the faint hope of hiring a cab. 'Anyhow,' he added, 'it'll be a pleasant stroll.'

'Ma and Pa will be expecting you; they' ll know what train you caught.'

'Well, an hour either way isn't going to topple the world now is it? And I want so desperately to *walk* home. I hope you understand.'

So, deep in conversation they headed slowly but steadily back to their boyhood home. The dusk had plunged swiftly into a moonless night; and though sure of every byroad and lane for miles thereabouts the two young men found disconcerting changes in the new houses which had appeared along the main thoroughfare, and whose electric lights now illuminated the once – dark meadows as they passed by.

At an easy pace they reached the drive to the house within the hour. Godfrey's mood had brightened appreciably as they plodded along, and with it their conversation had become more animated and more like former times as his strange vagueness gradually evaporated. It occurred to Oliver that consciously or otherwise his brother was struggling to dismantle some obstacle within himself; and he saw the necessity of their walk in the dark together. Now, despite his tiredness, Godfrey appeared quite cheerful as they talked about this and that; but as his brother evidently did not wish to speak of France, Oliver studiously avoided making any reference to it.

As they approached the familiar doorway and the stained glass panels through which light streamed Godfrey halted. 'You go in first, Oliver, if you wouldn't mind.' The uncertainty of the railway platform seemed to have returned suddenly. 'You… you go in and prepare the ground, there's a good chap. I need to get my breath back… get my bearings a little, that's all.'

Oliver was filled with renewed concern, but he did as he was asked. Quickly ascending the flight of steps he tried the door and found to his relief that it was unlocked. Pushing it open he stepped inside.

At the sound a flurry of sudden activity came from within. First to emerge was Ida, her eyes wide with expectation; then from a side-room Clarence beamed, fully resplendent in evening-suit and tails. As their gaze lighted on Oliver Clarence's disappointment was tangible. 'Oliver… ah, yes… good evening.It's good to see you.' He did not offer his hand; but Ida swept up to Oliver and embraced him. 'We got your letter by yesterday's post. We're *overjoyed* you managed to come.'

'Hello Ma. Hello, Pa.' Oliver said quietly. 'What else *would* I do?' He held his hand out to his father who shook it briefly, and let it fall.

'We're still waiting for Godfrey.'

'I know.' Oliver could have said immediately where his brother was, but sensed that in Godfrey's fragile state he would need as much time as possible *to get his bearings* before having to confront such a welcome as this.

'You speak as if you have already met him' said Clarence tersely.

'I have, Father.'

'Then why in thunder did you not say so, at first? *Where is he*?'

'He's taking the air outside. He said he wished to, before coming in.'

'You mean that you left your *own* brother – your *wounded* brother – outside in the cold while you yourself came in? I find your behaviour preposterous and unthinking – and selfish.'

'He *specifically* asked to be left alone for a while… .to collect his thoughts' Oliver returned hotly. He had expected the usual frosty reception from his father, but had not anticipated that his hostility towards him would have surfaced quite so soon, or so venomously.

'I'm sure he has his reasons, Clarence' Ida interposed, attempting to head off the imminent clash.'Shall we go out to greet him?' But her husband was already out of the door and down the steps.

'Godfrey! Godfrey my son? Where are you?'

A figure approached slowly, becoming more distinct as it materialised from the darkness which had shrouded it. 'I'm here, Pa.'

The evening had not been a particularly pleasant one in spite of Godfrey's return. Oliver excused himself from the family circle clinging round his brother, and beat a retreat to the kitchen. There he found Alice up to her elbows in flour, as always. She spun round as he entered and her old face lit up 'Eh, lad, it's *grand* to see you ! What a fine figure of a gentleman you cut now ! Stand back, Master Oliver, let me' ave a good look at you.' He stood back as instructed; and as she considered him with pride he reflected sadly on the contrast between the depth of affection in her greeting, and the shallowness of his father's.

'An' your brother, Master Godfrey. He's back, too! *An'* a brave wounded soldier! It'll be just like the old times'.

'Not *quite* the old times, Alice. I think things have changed quite a lot, don't you?'

'Well, it was only in a manner o' speaking.' The smile faded from her face. ' I'm right concerned about the War, Master Oliver, an' what it's costing people. But I know its our patriotic duty, despite all... ' Then she brightened 'An' did you know that Miss Helene is comin' down tomorrow, an' Miss Dulcie… and Mr. Warrington is expected too?' The disarming way in which Alice introduced Warrington in the same breath as his sister sounded a warning in Oliver's memory.

He had not seen much of Helene over the last three or four years, and had heard relatively little about or from her. They had gone their own ways – she to her artistic milieu of London, and he to his medical studies. He felt a momentary pang of guilt that he had given such little thought to his sister; but the years had passed so quickly, and he had been so preoccupied. Yet now the memory of that impassioned farewell which he had reluctantly witnessed long before came flooding back. And together with it came the realisation that Alice knew about them, too. Just how she had become Helene's confidante, he could not guess. But her artifice had been enough for Oliver.

'They sorted me out enough to travel here, providing I reported regularly to the local hospital to have it checked.' Godfrey sat white faced and tired on the edge of his bed, while with his right hand he abstractedly caressed the counterpane. The left hung stiffly at his side. Oliver sat before him on a chair, leaning forward attentively. Silence descended on them for a while, as Godfrey's gaze seemed to wander to places and events far away; his mind absent from the room and from his brother. And as he sat there his hand ceased stroking and instead clenched itself into a fist, the knuckles shining even whiter through the whiteness of the skin.

Oliver broke the uneasy quiet. 'Do you want to talk, at all... about it?'

Godfrey shook himself out of his reverie. 'What... ? I'm sorry... what did you say?'

Oliver repeated his question gently. 'Do you want to talk, old chap?'

'No... no, not now. It's the bloody shoulder... pains me, sometimes. In fact, would you mind...'

He pointed to his bag. 'The rest of my kit's being sent along later by carrier. But I've all the necessaries in there, for now. I need to put a fresh dressing on. I wouldn't ask anyone else... but would you mind awfully... ?' His tone was apologetic.

'Of course, Godfrey! What are medical–student –brothers for?'

Slowly Godfrey's jacket was peeled off. Then tenderly Oliver removed his tie and undid the shirt buttons. Godfrey started in pain at an unexpected movement.

'I'm sorry' he said 'I'm a poor patient.'

'I'll go easily.'

'The strapping runs up from my back and over onto my chest. There's quite a lot of it.'

'I can see.'

Oliver turned to the muslin bag of dressings and bandages which he had taken from Godfrey's valise.

'You'll have to use one of those larger ones. Or possibly two.'

Oliver's studies had required him to examine the human body, both living and dead. He had witnessed surgery on hands mangled in mill-accidents, on legs shattered by cart-wheels, on faces pummelled in fights. But nothing in his experience had prepared him for what he saw as he peeled the last bloody dressing from his brother's wound. He winced involuntarily, shocked; and turned away for a second to regain his composure. Godfrey noticed the movement.

'It's not very pretty, is it? I haven't seen it myself, though. They don't permit mirrors in the hospitals.'

Oliver breathed deeply. He reached for the antiseptic lotion which he applied to a wad of cotton wool, working inward from the wound's ragged edges as gently as if his brother was the most delicate of children. Once cleaned he dried and redressed it in the same manner. Then he collected the used dressings and bandages and disposed of them in an earthenware bowl.

Godfrey leaned back a little, exhaling slowly as he let his muscles relax. 'I know you're my brother, Ollie, but it feels better already – better than it's done in ages.'

'You're only saying that! I'm a real tyro at this sort of thing.'

'I wouldn't say it if I didn't mean it. Truly.'

Oliver busied himself with tidying up.

'Godfrey?'

'Yes?'

'Do you recall that Albert Chadderton had a daughter… a very fair-haired child? Blue eyes?

There was no reply at first. And when it came it was uncharacteristically abrupt.

'Yes I do. Dorothy… or Dolly, as he calls her. Dolly Chadderton.'

'He *calls* her? Have you met him recently?'

'A few weeks ago.' Godfrey's voice had changed. 'Chadderton's my sergeant. And he's the finest and the best.'

Oliver bit his lip. 'I'm so sorry, Godfrey. I didn't mean to raise… '

'No matter. Now… help me get ready for bed, there's a good chap!'

Oliver assisted him to undress and put on his pyjamas. Slowly he eased his brother's legs round and into bed, making him as comfortable as he could. 'Don't forget, call out if you need anything at all. I'm in my old room, just down the corridor.'

'Thank you, Ollie. I promise I will. Goodnight.'

'Goodnight, old chap. Sleep well.'

Oliver went straight to his room. He did not wish to spend any more time in the company of his father than was necessary, though he knew that his parents still sat on in the lounge below. He undressed and got into bed but in his unsettled state found sleep impossible. He heard his parents retire to their distant rooms on the other side of the house, and listened as Alice puffed her way up to her attic. He rose heavily and dressed once more. Despite the cold he threw open the window and leant out, and listened. Nothing. Not the bark of a fox, nor even the wind in the adjacent elms; apart from his own breathing the silence was absolute.

The sight of that shoulder still haunted him. He felt Godfrey's pain almost as if he had received the wound himself, and pity for his brother rose in his throat. Yet it was not that alone which troubled him, but one bitter recurrent question; that if a single bullet could cause such appalling injury, what was the true scale of suffering? Just how terrible was it?

He had heard about the new hospitals being established in almost every Manchester suburb to accommodate the growing tide of war casualties.

Schools, colleges, institutes – indeed almost any large building with plentiful rooms and the potential for hygienic management were being annexed and equipped under the ambiguous title of *2nd. Western General* – neutral sounding enough, and one which until now had excited only mild interest amongst Oliver and his fellow students. But now he began to wonder about the true extent of the casualties, for the Lists in the newspapers seemed unending. And rarely was reference made to the wounded.

He had heard rumours from other students that the Authorities now shipped in many during the night – they had seen the wagons and their wretched occupants with their own eyes. What could the reason for this possibly be? He felt sure there was a valid excuse; but could there not be some ulterior, darker purpose? Uncertainties grew in his mind as simultaneously another certainty took hold; for with his brother's return Oliver had begun to view his calling in a different light. He closed the window silently, and lay down fully clothed on his bed.

How long he had lain there he did not know, but in his semi-conscious state he imagined that a wind had sprung up while he dozed. He rubbed his eyes and sat slowly upright, glancing blearily at his wristwatch. It was five to one. He listened again to the sound. He realised that what he had at first mistaken for the wind was in fact a low moan which rose and fell intermittently, and echoed throughout that part of the house. Oliver opened his bedroom door silently. The sound was louder, now. It came from Godfrey's room. Amidst its terrible ebb and flow he could make out disjointed words, though they seemed devoid of meaning. He sped back to his room and fetched his lamp.

Silently he slipped through his brother's door and stepped towards the bed. Holding the lamp aloft he could see that Godfrey was curled up in a blanket. His eyes were starkly open, glowering far away into profound darkness. And as he stared he moaned and talked as though addressing an army of phantoms. Oliver placed the lamp on a table and fetched a bowl of water. With a flannel he washed the perspiration from Godfrey's forehead and face, all the while speaking soothing words to him. Then he silently drew up a chair, and sat down.

'Oliver? What are you doing here?' A gentle hand touched his shoulder. Once more he shook himself awake.

'What time is it?'

'Six or thereabouts.'

Oliver turned painfully to his mother who stood just behind him, still wearing her dressing – gown. She looked down at him and at Godfrey, who lay in a deep sleep.

'How long have you been here?' she asked.

'Oh… not that long, really.'

'Really? You need a shave. Go down to the kitchen and ask Alice to make you a substantial breakfast. And some black coffee, too. I'll sit with Godfrey for a while.

Oliver rose stiffly and began to make his way to the door.

'Oliver.' Ida's tone was grave but kind. He stopped and half-turned toward her.

'I know what you did for Godfrey, and what you will continue to do. Try to forgive your Papa. One day he will know it too.' Oliver cast his eyes down at his slippers, and shuffled off downstairs.

Chapter Five

THE SEASON which ought to have been Spring was still ice – bound.Every feature of the landscape – brake, field and fence –had been liberally sprinkled with its touch. Except for the tussocky grasses in the immediate foreground the lower meadow was obscured by a low belt of freezing mist; and through this the upper boughs of oaks protruded like limbs of quicksilver. Oliver and Godfrey stood close together, overcoated and muffled against the biting air, and contemplated the horizon as though peering across a vague white sea.

Oliver knocked out his pipe on the top of a fence – post and refilled it. His brother lit yet another cigarette from the stub of the previous one, and pulled his collar up.

'I think I slept well last night'

'I think you did.'

'I had some dreams, at first.They come, from time to time. But I can't easily recall them, when I wake… Was I any trouble?'

'No. None at all. How's the shoulder?'

'Passable. Easier than it's felt in a while.'

'You must let me dress it for you before the others come.'

'Oh.The others. I *have* looked forward to seeing them all you know, and its splendid of Ma and Pa to lay on such a 'do'. He seemed almost apologetic

'They've been anticipating it for quite a while. It's their way of expressing their affection – Pa especially. I suppose we have to try to see things from their perspective. But I imagine it's a lot to face, isn't it?'

'It is. I knew that if anyone *could* understand, it would be you.'

'I doubt that I will ever understand, fully.'

'Maybe not; but you can see, can't you, that there's a huge contrast between *this,* and what's happening over there. I simply wanted to come home… to have as quiet a time as possible. A little bit of peace, away from it. But you take it with you, like the mud.'

'Perhaps a party is just what you need?' Despite his apparent optimism Oliver sensed that the party and the attention Godfrey would unwillingly attract was what his brother feared most, because he could cope with it least. 'Give it a shot, old man' he added encouragingly' 'I'll be there, too, to help you get through it.'

'It's cowardly and mean to say it, but it's an ordeal I'd rather not face.'

'I know you'd rather not. And it's neither cowardly nor mean.'

They fell silent for a few minutes, each wrapped up in his own thoughts. Then Oliver said more brightly 'Shall we plan that walk? Tomorrow? I've still got my old Ordinance Surveys on my bookshelf, and I've decided to stay on for a day or two. What d'you think, Godfrey? We could go as far as we want – as far as you feel you can manage.'

Godfrey rose to the bait, and he became infected with Oliver's enthusiasm:

'Well, it looks as though the weather is going to stay pretty constant, and the barometer's up. I think it's a capital idea.' Then a thought crossed his mind 'But what about Medical School? I can imagine how hard they push you, and what's expected. How can you spare the time?'

'Aha! It's all allowed for in my impeccable plan. *Firstly,* I got ahead of myself with my various essays and papers; they're already submitted for the remainder of the term. *Secondly* I paid a little visit to my tutors who were most accommodating – surprisingly so; and *finally,* they've granted me a week's leave of absence!' In his triumphant conclusion he omitted to say that he had obtained it on compassionate grounds.

The group of friends and acquaintances had continued to swell as the afternoon drew on. Some had come by cab – booked especially by Clarence – while others more affluent had parked their motor-cars along the driveway; and when that was full, had occupied the front lawns. A thin covering of snow made the scene doubly festive as the lights from the house seemed to take on its pristine whiteness, reflecting bluely upwards into the surrounding trees and the evening sky.

In the kitchen the chauffeurs of Clarence's partners sat over steaming mugs of tea, getting in Alice's way as she clucked and fussed over the final preparations. As the doorbell rang guests were ushered in; and while they admired the patriotic display of flags in the hallway their coats and cloaks were whipped away by the flustered maid who brushed the snowflakes from them as she ran. But the host himself was ill at ease. Though she had confirmed by telegram there was still no sign of Helene. Clarence knew that she had intended to travel up from London the night before, but she had also added that she might stay over with friends before pressing on to Desbury that day. Dulcie Grady had already arrived, as could be heard from the tumult in the main lounge; but as a trainee VAD nurse living-in at the Royal Infirmary, she was unable to shed any light on her best friend's whereabouts. Dusk was already well advanced when the doorbell rang and an apologetic Helene finally entered the Hall. 'It's been *such* a journey, Pa!' she burst out, forestalling Clarence's protest. 'My train was late, and had it not been for a friend of Godfrey's I think I should have had to walk the *whole* way. Still, you're not *terribly* annoyed with me, are you?'

'I did arrange for three cabs to be permanently at the station, to convey guests to the house. Did you not see them?'

'I'm awfully sorry. I didn't. I probably need spectacles!' The bell-like laughter chimed in Clarence's ears and he instantly succumbed, as she knew he would.

'Well… well… ' he said genially 'you're here, and that's what counts, my dear.'

Ida was not so forgiving, however. Drawing her daughter aside she whispered her displeasure

'… and how *could* you leave your arrival so late – indeed, after almost all the other guests, whom I'd hoped you'd be here to welcome; it's *most* inconsiderate of you.'

Hardly five minutes later yet another guest was heard to ring. Phoebe opened the door and admitted a striking figure dressed in full military attire. Heads turned as he walked down the hallway; some he nodded to, and they nodded back, beamingly appreciative of having been acknowledged.

The mirror-like riding boots complete with spurs, the polished Sam Browne, the glittering insignia on epaulettes and the crimson band on the immaculate hat spoke every inch of the Staff Officer. As he was relieved of his coat his handsome face searched the gathering crowd for closer acquaintances. They all seemed to be that, or wished they were. Soon he was engulfed by a group of admirers of both sexes, and all ages. Smiling broadly,Clarence swept forward and seized his hand.

'Welcome! Welcome *indeed*! I'm so very glad – on my own behalf, and on my son Godfrey's-that you were able to do us the honour of attending. We know how preoccupied you must be, with matters of war.'

'Well, not so preoccupied that I couldn't pop across to see an old chum, fresh from the Front, what?'

The accent had changed, with the figure; the vowels were longer, and more languid.Certainly the same sportsman was there, but he had been recast in a military mold.

'Welcome again to our house, Lieutenant Warrington.'

'Actually, It's Lieutenant no longer. It's Captain, with effect from this week.'

'I see congratulations are *indeed* in order' Clarence gushed 'clearly grounds for a double celebration! Helene?'

'Yes. Pa?' she said, stepped forward with a demure smile.

'*Do* see to the needs of *Captain* Warrington, would you my dear?' He turned again to the officer. 'You have met our daughter – Godfrey's sister – before, have you not?'

'Actually… ah… 'Warrington was momentarily lost

'Well, Pa,' Helene interjected. 'It was this *very* gentleman who so kindly gave me a lift from the station in his own cab, would you believe – so we are already acquainted, in a manner of speaking.'

'Splendid! Splendid!' Clarence could not believe how well the party seemed to be going. 'Now, if you young people will excuse me, I have things to attend to!'

The young people exchanged knowing glances.'Captain Warrington' said Helene, smiling up at him with the aplomb of the accomplished hostess 'let me introduce you to some of our dearest friends' and taking his arm she steered him off into the party scrum.

Upstairs Godfrey sat in the light of a sole oil lamp. Opposite sat Oliver, perching forward on his chair. They both listened to the swelling hubbub from the party below.

'You can't stay up here. We have to go down, you know; after all it is for you, Godfrey.'

'Then get me a whisky.'

'*Whisky?'*

'Yes, *whisky.* And make it a large one!' The tone was almost savage.

Oliver went down by the back stairs and in through the kitchen. Amidst the crowd of drivers and piles of cakes and other dainties, Alice turned to him 'Master Oliver, haven't you got Master Godfrey down yet? It's high time. All the guests are waitin'. '

Oliver replied over his shoulder without stopping 'He's still getting ready, Alice. He's coming, don't worry.'

He sidled through to the smoking room, and by keeping a low profile succeeded in avoiding notice. There he knew there was a cabinet in which spirits were kept. He slipped in, cautiously.

He quickly found a bottle, and was heading back towards the stairs when he encountered his father.

'Where's Godfrey? And what have you got there?'

'A bottle of whisky' Oliver replied simply. He was in no mood to dissemble.

'What on earth are you doing with that?' Clarence snapped.

‘I need it… for medicinal purposes.’

‘Medicinal! Indeed! ’ Clarence knew what medical students were like, but he wasn’t going to make an issue of it, not now at any rate. ‘Make yourself useful, and try to find Godfrey. He must be down, soon.’

Oliver retraced his steps to Godfrey’s room. His brother was sitting in the same position as when he had left him, and was still dressed in the clothes he had worn that morning

Oliver became exasperated. ‘For Heaven’s Sake! You have to make some effort. What do you wish to wear? Shall I set out your uniform for you?

‘Did you fetch the whisky?’

‘It’s here.’ Oliver produced the bottle from within his jacket.

‘Have you a glass?’

‘Damn! I clear forgot it in the encounter with Pa.’

‘Met him on the way up, did you.?’

‘Yes. And he wasn’t pleasant, not when he saw what I’d got.’

‘No matter.’ Uncorking it Godfrey took a long swig. Oliver stood watching him, appalled. His brother lowered the bottle and looked sideways at him. ‘Shocked? Yes, I suppose you are. And why not? You’ve every right to be. War does funny things to people, Oliver. It twists and turns them – warps them, if you like – from what they were to what it needs them to be. You become what *it* requires.’

‘Don’t say things like that! It’ll do you no good to speak in that way’

‘Why not? Why shouldn’t I? Bit like my shoulder, really; it’s a gruesome caricature of what it was. And it’s no different in here’ he tapped his finger on his forehead ‘it scrambles you in here, too.’

He held the bottle against the light, examining the lowered level. ‘Ah, well. Another snort of Dutch Courage, and we’ll make a move.’ He took a last pull then patted back the cork. ‘Some of us run on this stuff, y’know.’ he said, swinging the bottle to and fro. ‘Can get you through to the next day. Or even the day after. Helps with what you’ve got to face.’

‘I doubt that it does, Godfrey.’

‘We’ll not argue the point… .anyway, I’m not wearing my uniform.’ His voice became almost petulant.

‘Ma and Pa will be very disappointed.’

‘Let them be! What am I – some sort of bloody entertainment? I’ll wear a suit, fair enough. But not my uniform. Not tonight. Who the hell’s the party for? Them or me?’

Oliver did not attempt an answer ‘Godfrey’ he said deliberately looked straight at him. ‘For the sake of our family and our friends, *please* wear it. Or if for no other reason, do it as a favour to me.’

Godfrey hesitated.' Alright, then,if it means that much to you.'

Oliver fetched the uniform which had been cleaned and pressed by Alice. Pulling his reluctant brother to his feet he assisted him into his trousers and jacket – and finally squeezed him into his boots. A little pomade on Godfrey's hair and he looked outwardly most presentable. Oliver resolved that he would stick with him throughout the evening, as he knew that the apparent robustness was only skin deep.

He led the way down by the rear stairs once more. To go down by the main ones would drop Godfrey right in where the throng was at its thickest and most vocal, as a few shouts from below clearly indicated 'Where's the Man of the Moment?' someone bellowed. '*Godfrey*! We're *waiting*!' trilled another more feminine voice. It was obvious that things were getting lively.

The back stairs would be far less conspicuous and would give Godfrey time to acclimatise, Oliver decided. They had just arrived in the rear lobby when his brother halted, perspiring freely as he listened to the dull hubbub on the other side of the wall. 'I can't go in' he said falteringly.

'You must. You've faced far worse. And I'll stay with you.'

'What do I tell them when they ask?'

'Tell them nothing. Simply that. You're a lawyer; sidestep their questions.' Oliver opened the door to the kitchen.

Alice turned to them as they entered. 'Pardon me for sayin' so,' she commented archly, 'but it's about time! You'll meet yerselves comin' back if you leave it any later. Still' she added more warmly ' you look *right* smart, Mr. Godfrey. An' *you're* not too dusty, neither' she said, nodding to Oliver. 'You make a sight for sore eyes, the pair of you. *Will you excuse me*?' she said, trying to wedge her round frame between two drivers ' Any road, it's time you went in to your Ma and Pa. Go on, now!'

She sho'ed them out of her kitchen in the same way she had sho'ed out two small boys long years before. The brothers looked at Alice, and exchanged glances with each other; Oliver exploded into fits of uncontrollable laughter, and Godfrey followed suit. It was like the bursting of a safety valve, and in one instant it appeared to have transformed the complexion of the evening. 'Now for it'

As the door opened they were struck by a wave of mingled heat and noise emanating from the hall and lounges. Confronted by a near-impenetrable wall of backs they remained unnoticed as the guests continued with their conversations, and the brothers were able to sidle their way through without at first exciting notice. Then Godfrey was spotted by an old Chambers chum.'Here's the Man himself! Good – oh! Godfrey's here at last!' All discussion was suspended mid – sentence as the eyes of the fifty or more present shifted to the guest of honour. He scanned the expectant faces.

'Ah' he said lamely 'good evening, everyone.' As if at a predetermined signal he was pounced upon by those nearest to him and hauled away to divert them with his adventures in France.

Few seemed to notice Oliver as he trailed along in their wake, and apart from the routine pleasantries nobody wished to engage him in conversation. The degree of anonymity it afforded suited him well enough; but true to his word he kept as close as possible to his brother without giving the impression of overprotecting him.

'No, it's not like they say in the Papers... Yes we have done some fighting... No, I don't know if I've personally killed any Huns... Yes it can get very muddy... No I haven't met Kitchener'

Oliver listened as Godfrey fielded their incessant questions, parrying their unthinking shafts with considerable skill. Only Oliver suspected what it cost him when a bright young thing draped in a diaphanous gown asked him *whether it was fun going over the top, as she assumed it must be.*

'Rather like playing rugby with explosives' came his terse reply.

The Party wore on, and as the guests found Godfrey's lack of stirring anecdotes rather tame fare – *hardly think the chap's done much at all, frankly* – they dispersed into their natural coteries again, and took up the chatter where they had left off.

'I think you're through the worst of it.' Oliver whispered.

He was wrong, however. As they extricated themselves from the ruck of young people and escaped to the rear library they were confronted by an older group headed by their parents and consisting largely of Clarence's colleagues and their wives.

One particularly clear voice could be heard holding forth about the War. It drawled somewhat, and had a slightly southern nasalty about it; but despite the affectation there could be no mistaking the speaker. All attention – and especially that of the ladies – was focused upon him as he stood before the fireplace, glass in hand and legs braced, expounding on the High Command's theories as to how the War would undoubtedly be won.

'Of course, this is pretty hush – hush stuff, y'know' he confided to his appreciative audience 'so not a word to the Bosches!' Amidst the ensuing laughter he turned to the door. 'And if I'm not mistaken, here's one of our war-winners now!'. As they entered Captain Gerald Warrington extended his hand sincerely to Godfrey and shook it heartily. There was a subtle change in his manner as he looked across at his old school friend and spoke to him, for

Oliver thought that the voice had lost some of the self-assurance it had possessed only seconds before.

'Well, old man it's good to see you back, and in one piece.' Warrington said 'I'm certain everyone here feels the same.'

Their handshake lingered until a genial Clarence waved Godfrey over. ' This, my friends, is my son ' he beamed ' in honour of whose return from the Front this gathering is being held.'

As Oliver was neither mentioned nor even acknowledged he remained a shadowy presence on the outer fringe of the group. Godfrey was ushered to a chair which had been placed centrally and everyone leaned forward in anticipation. A heady mixture of alcohol and Warrington's monologue had put the gentlemen in a particularly jingoistic frame of mind, and before them they had an opportunity to hear a bit of *daring- do* from a Front-Line man in the flesh.

The Front- Line man perched uneasily on his chair and looked around at the encircling faces. 'I'm not sure quite what you'd like me to say. I'd... I should thank my parents..for throwing this splendid party. It's... it's good to meet some of my friends again.' He looked across to Warrington 'and thank you all for coming'. There was an uncomfortable silence.

'I'm sure we would all love to hear what life is like in the Trenches' Clarence said encouragingly.

'It's not like what they tell you in the papers. And I don't know how many Huns I've killed. And going Over The Top's like playing rugby with explosives.'

Godfrey spoke in a mechanical monotone, hollowly repeating stock answers to questions which had not yet been asked.

As Oliver listened with growing alarm his gaze shifted to another in the audience who was almost as troubled as he. Their eyes met, and the expression in them was one of mutual concern for their brother. Helene sat a little to the rear of the main group, behind Ida. This had been her first encounter with Godfrey since his return from the Front; clearly her parents had been unable to enlighten her as to his true condition, and Oliver in their infrequent correspondence had said nothing. The changes wrought in him shocked her and in a fraction of a second she took in how Oliver had somehow dedicated himself to supporting him- shielding him, even.

Brandy had made Cedric Gosling Snr. particularly expansive that evening. He removed the cigar from his mouth and wagged it in his stubby fingers to emphasise the significance of the point he was about to make.

'Well, from everything *I* have read in the papers we are certainly giving the Bosche a dose of his own medicine, what? It's one thing to come up against a crowd of Frenchy peasants armed with nothin' more than the odd pitchfork… ' he paused and smirkingly acknowledged the laughter '… and *quite another* to come up against our gallant Tommies. Heroes all, what? Resourceful in a tight corner, and an absolute scrapper. You just can't knock 'em down. Wouldn't y'agree, Godfrey?' he concluded generously.

With mounting concern Oliver watched his brother's pallid cheeks twitching convulsively.

'Agree? *Do I agree*?' Godfrey's voice was unnaturally blithe. To those who knew him least it appeared he was sharing in some party joke. Innocently they grinned with him..

'Oh, I agree, all right! He's a scrapper, every one.' As Godfrey seemed at last to be warming to the subject the audience eagerly leaned forward in their seats.

'E*very* one… ! It might interest you to *know,* that since I took over my platoon with the 16th. I've had nearly fifty men under my command, together with replacements. My sergeant and eight others are what's left of the original lot. They were all good *scrappers*, to a man That's *ten* of us, if you include me.'

'Not *killed*, though, surely?' came an enquiry from a small man with a glistening bald head.

Godfrey looked across to the questioner, his father's accountant, contemptuously.

'*Killed?* No! You can rest easy, there. There's... let me *see*… only nineteen of *them*; and three are still 'Missing In Action' as your papers term it. So we can't *really* count them, can we? Nobody knows where the Hell they are, and we don't want to give the wrong impression. The stiffs in No-Mans Land stop being recognisable after a bit, y'see? and the last two or three will never be found, anyway.'

His audience began to shuffle uneasily, but Godfrey pressed on regardless.'As for the rest,one's blind, and a good few are crippled for life. Or their wounds were so severe that they've been discharged as Medically Unfit and have died since, maybe at home; I wouldn't know. And one corporal went quite barmy. Lack of Moral Fibre, or something of that sort, they said. So they've locked *him* up in a madhouse. Ironic, rather, isn't it?' he grinned. '… So you're quite correct, of course. Not *all* killed. And I've got away almost scot – free, as you might say.'

Godfrey's tone was becoming distinctly unpleasant.

'Tell us, Godfrey,' said a pink – faced vicar brightly 'have you managed to bring back any mementos from France?' His bid to steer the conversation away from the morbid was well-intentioned but misguided.

'Funny you should ask that because I *have*, as it happens.' Godfrey rose suddenly. Oliver feared what might be coming next and moved swiftly into the midst of the gathering. 'Yes, I have! I haven't *seen* it myself, exactly, because of where it is; but all the M.O.s including Oliver here reckon it's really quite impressive. Would *you* like to see it?'

The direction Godfrey's thoughts were tending was now becoming increasingly evident to all but the most befuddled. Parents and guests alike exchanged uncomfortable looks, and shifted in the opposite direction as quickly as they had moved forward. Oliver gently took his brother's arm. 'I think it's time to go, old chap, don't you?' he whispered.

'*But they haven't seen it!*'

'I'm sure everyone can imagine what it must be like. Shall we go back upstairs?' Without another word Godfrey bowed stiffly and strode from the room. Before following him Oliver turned to the discomfited guests.

'I'm sure you realise that my brother has a little way to go before he is fully recovered from his wound. He is still very fatigued by it. He begs you to excuse him, and overlook anything untoward. I'm certain that he regrets any offence which he might unintentionally have given.'

As he made his way out he caught a glimpse of his father's expression. Clarence had listened to Godfrey's talk with growing consternation; as host, should he intercede to stay his son's ramblings? But how? And at what point? And what would Godfrey's reaction be? This favoured son who seemed to have returned from the Front a stranger to the household, and to him. Intervention might well make things worse and precipitate... God only knew what.

Clarence had been at a complete loss, up to the point at which Oliver stepped forward. Now he modified his view of his youngest son, a little. He had seen what he had done, and how tactfully he had managed his brother. Now he acknowledged – albeit grudgingly – that the situation had been redeemed somewhat, and a social crisis averted. As Oliver passed him his expression was a confusion of reluctant gratitude and relief.

'Now,ladies and gentlemen,' he said recovering himself 'I'm so sorry that my son was unable to spend as long with us as we would have liked... but I'm sure you all understand. Now, where's Phoebe got to? I have a toast to propose, to our gallant officers and men at the Front... '

Oliver meanwhile sped up to Godfrey's room. He knocked on the door, but there was silence. Gently he turned the handle and let himself in.

'Godfrey?' No answer. 'Are you there, Godfrey?' The room was in darkness.He turned the light-switch on the wall.The room was as they had left it barely an hour before. Concern for his brother now deepened to anxiety as he fruitlessly scoured the house. Party-rooms, bathrooms, bedrooms – even the cellar; nowhere could a trace of him be found. Oliver paused and considered. *Where would he head off to? Think!* Not the front parts of the house, certainly – he'd avoid them like the plague. He'd want to be on his own, naturally enough; but not outside, in this weather surely? As the thought struck him he knew. 'Alice' he gasped as he again entered the kitchen 'have you seen my brother? *Alice! Have you seen Godfrey?'*

She turned from a pile of pastries which she was loading onto Phoebe's tray. 'He went out a while back, sayin' he wanted to get some air. Hasn't 'e come back *yet*? An' it's still snowin'.'

Oliver paused only long enough to catch up his overcoat. Descending the rear steps he both blessed and cursed the snow in equal measure, for before him one single set of footprints trailed away from the house in an unbroken bluish line. The snowfall had been light, and had barely covered the tracks. Gingerly Oliver followed them down through the gardens, and away to where they had stood only that morning. Godfrey seemed to have hesitated at that point; then he had turned right, walking parallel to the field-fence bordering the meadow. Ahead of Oliver was a rustic shelter made of wicker panels.

The footprints led to the front of the ramshackle structure, which was effectively open to the elements on two sides.

'Godfrey?' There was no reply, but Oliver sensed that his brother was within feet of him. 'Godfrey? It's Oliver. Can I come round?'

There was silence at first. Then he heard his brother breathe out heavily 'Oh, Ollie. Can't they leave me in peace? It's not much to ask.'

'This is the place to find peace, alright, if you want to freeze to death.'

He quietly stepped into the shelter. By the unearthly half-light he could make out Godfrey's form curled on the bench within. He had been there sufficiently long and remained sufficiently motionless for a sprinkling of snow to settle on him; and now his hair, shoulders and knees alike were given a strangely statuesque definition by the white layer covering them.

'You'll catch your death, old man.'

Oliver slowly dusted the snow away from his brother's clothes and head. His hand touched by chance against Godfrey's cheek; it was icy cold.

'Come on' Oliver said encouragingly. 'Let me wrap this around you.' He took off the overcoat which still carried the warmth of the house within it, and placed it about Godfrey's shoulders.

'Thank you, Ollie.' Then without another word the same shoulders began to shake violently, and Godfrey buried his face in his hands as the tears fell onto the snow at their feet.

Oliver said nothing, sensing that the pain his brother felt was too deep for any consolation he could offer, and that in its way Godfrey's anguish was a necessary salve for his invisible wounds- those which none could see to bandage.

How long they sat there he did not know; but the storm in his brother's soul gradually abated, and Godfrey slumped despondently with head bowed. Oliver pulled out his handkerchief, and without a word handed it to him. Godfrey took it slowly and wiped his face. 'God, you must think me a weak specimen! I'm very sorry,' he said thickly.

'No, I don't. And there's nothing to apologise for.'

'I can't think what possessed me. It's never happened before.'

'It's not important. It's only important that you feel better… Do you?'

'I... think I do… a little. I don't expect you to understand.'

Oliver made no attempt to answer. He turned and looked out across the meadow, watching the snow which was beginning to fall more steadily.

'Don't you think we ought to go in, now? It's getting colder by the minute.'

'I can't; not just yet. I made such a bloody fool of myself in front of everyone. I can't imagine what their opinion of me must be.'

'We don't have to go back to the house. We could try the boiler-room. It's never locked these days and I promise it'll be as snug as anything in there.'

Godfrey rose and shook himself, rotating his shoulder and neck.

'Still painful?'

'Still.'

They walked back up the slope together and regained the light which seemed to swirl about them as it caught the snowflakes.

The boiler-room door had not been secured and as they slipped inside Oliver took down the paraffin–lantern kept there for emergencies, and soon they were bathed in its orange glow. Albert's replacement had stoked-up the coals almost to bursting point, and the atmosphere in the little building was close and fiercely hot; but neither of them was unduly troubled by it. Oliver pulled out a packet of cigarettes and offered one to Godfrey. They sat and smoked silently as the snow thawed from their boots, and watched as the flames in the furnace danced and flickered, projecting their animated shadows onto the wall behind.

'It's sometimes very like this' Godfrey said. 'In the Front Line dugouts, I mean. If it's quiet, and the Bosche haven't anything planned. Whenever I can, I go up and see the men. We'd managed to get some braziers and a few sacks of coke across to them, just before I got hit. You'd be amazed how much a little warmth cheers everyone up.' He stopped, gazing intently into the fire as though he had been diverted by something he had seen amidst the flames; and Oliver feared for a moment that the reticence might be reasserting itself.

'They don't ask for much, you know' he continued suddenly '... and how in Hell's name they stay as cheerful as they do, beats me. I mean, while it's pretty unpleasant for *us* much of the time, it's damnably worse for them. I think it's their gratitude that cuts deepest, somehow; they're invariably grateful for whatever you do for them. And what's more, they'd do anything in return for you... D'you know, two of my chaps carried me over a mile, out of the Line and all the way back through the Reserve Trenches? We were at it for hours. And they never grumbled... They're only kids, most of them. I've one or two who don't even shave yet. But then it's not the sort of place that you can grow old in.'

And as they sat on in the semi-darkness Godfrey told Oliver all that he could bear to tell.

As the last guests noisily departed the brothers slipped back into the house and up to their rooms, where having seen to the shoulder Oliver settled Godfrey down as comfortably as possible. Returning silently to his own bedroom he sat up in expectation of a repeat of the previous night; but physical and emotional exhaustion had taken its toll; first he nodded, then unwillingly fell into a deep sleep.

A sharp rapping on his door awoke him with a start.

He fumbled for his watch. It was barely a quarter past six, yet curiously light. He felt disoriented at first, unsure even as to where he was. But by degrees he recalled the events of the party and anxiety for Godfrey rose suddenly within him. Perhaps the caller had come to tell him of something which had occurred during the night, whilst he had slept on regardless?

The rapping was repeated. He jumped from the bed and was reaching for his clothes when the door opened slowly.

'Godfrey?' He was not sure which aspect of his brother startled him most – was it his presence there at all, or that he was dressed in the well – used rambling jacket from pre-war days? Or was it the expression on his face? Godfrey stepped halfway into the room, and he smiled. It was a broad, easy smile, though still a little wan. There was no artifice in it, just affection and gratitude. His apparent serenity so contrasted with the darkness of the preceding days that Oliver contained his spontaneous surge of relief at the change.

'You feeling better, old chap? You certainly look it.'

'Much. I feel quite a new man – more rested than I've felt in months, to be frank. It's as if I've got a dead – weight off my mind. I think it was probably last night when it all finally came to a head.' He looked steadily into Oliver's face 'And you were there. As you've been from the moment I came back.' he added emphatically; 'I can't say how much I appreciate what you've done to help me, Ollie.'

'Nonsense! You've got yourself to thank for that.'

Godfrey put his arm round his younger brother's shoulder.

'No, Ollie. I know the truth of it.'

'Well, one step at a time. You're getting better. Don't rush your fences.'

'And talking of steps and fences, have you had a quick look outside yet? Or have you been lying there wasting the morning away?'

'Have you seen the time, you idiot?' Oliver joked back 'It's barely daybreak!'

On drawing his curtains back a burst of silver light filled the room, reflecting from the ceiling and throwing into contrast recesses which had hitherto always been gloomy and obscure. The fall had held; and now they looked out onto a vision of inexpressible beauty. Their everyday landscape had disappeared; and the angularities of roof and beam, tree and post, had been rounded into softer contours by the snow.

'Let's go for that walk!' Godfrey pressed him, 'I'm sure it'll finish the job off, and I'm sure it's *just what the doctor orders*!'

Alice beamingly approved of the change; for though Oliver had always been her particular favourite, she doted on them both.

Godfrey's arrival had filled her with anxiety; but the young man who sat eating bacon and eggs amidst the laughter seemed more substantial and less abstracted and wraith-like than the one of only a few days before. And shrewdly she saw the hand of Oliver in it.

They were poring over one of Oliver's maps and finalising their route when the door opened quietly and Gerald Warrington came in. At first he did not notice them, and seemed preoccupied. Both Godfrey and he were equally taken aback – the former by finding Warrington still at Millwain Place,and in full military rig; and the latter by the presence of his old friend there at all, in such apparently good spirits after the previous evening's eccentricities.

Warrington's face dropped, and he flushed crimson. He had just descended from a guestroom where he had passed some of the night, and was now in search of breakfast himself.

'Good morning... ' he said lamely. 'What an unseasonable night it was! I'm afraid the weather prevented my leaving – damn' unfortunate, it closing in like that. Hadn't got much kit with me, but your housekeeper sorted me out alright.' The disarming affability of their greeting did not lessen Warrington's perplexity at the sea-change which just a few hours had wrought in Godfrey.He shook his hand firmly, and the handshake was as firmly returned.

Godfrey offered him a chair, and while Alice was clucking over them they talked in neutral terms of this and that – the weather, their intended walk, how he would get back and so forth. Had it not been for Warrington's uniform it could have been any leisurely meeting in peacetime, as they spoke of the soft days at Oxford and after. Reference to the war was studiously avoided at first, as if there existed some tacit agreement between them that it was in some way improper to broach the subject under the circumstances.Yet there was clearly some burning issue which Warrington was eager to raise; he was ill – at – ease, and excitable, and several times he seemed on the verge of speaking out. Godfrey decided to seize the initiative.

'Is there anything on your mind, old boy?'

'I'm sorry, Rusholme? How d'you mean?'

'Oh, it's just that I had a feeling there was, that's all.'

'Well, actually there is, if you don't mind me mentioning it'

'About the war?'

'To be quite blunt, yes.'

Godfrey smiled wrily.'I'm not yet so addled that I can't face speaking of it. Fire ahead'

Warrington explained that while he had been quite fortunate to have secured firstly a posting to Officer Training at Sandhurst and a subsequent promotion as aide to a Major-General, he felt that there was something lacking in the chauffeured and champagned *milieu* in which he now found himself. He freely acknowledged that many might think his good fortune arose from family connections, and had resolved to do something to counter this misconception.

'In fact,' he said, leaning forward over the table in his enthusiasm 'I've already made up my mind. I'm putting in a request for a Transfer to Active Service as soon as possible.'

Godfrey remained silent for a moment. Raising his eyes to Warrington's he looked steadily into his face. 'It's not a game, you know, what's going on out there. It's deadly, and once you've committed yourself you're stuck like a bug on flypaper.'

Warrington bridled. ' I'm surprised that you think my decision was made lightly. It wasn't, I promise you.'

'I apologise if I gave that impression. But irrespective of your motive, it doesn't change anything. Your request is misguided, my friend; and I urge you to withdraw it at once.'

'I can't.'

'Then I'm sorry for you, Warrington. Truly.'

Godfrey and Oliver were not the first to learn of Warrington's decision. In the early hours of that same morning and after bidding Helene a passionate farewell in the privacy of her bedroom he had told her of his intentions. She too had begged him to reconsider – wasn't he serving patriotically enough in his present position? Why should he feel it necessary to prove himself like this – in some boy-scoutish gesture which might end with him being wounded, or worse?

What he would not or could not tell her was that he acutely felt himself to be a fraud. He was inordinately proud of his uniform and enjoyed the privileges and status that went with it; but on examining himself he had found himself wanting in a factor crucial to his self-esteem.

He wondered increasingly whether he was entitled to the high regard in which others held him. When at William's or at Goldring he had *earned* the accolades by fair means, and in competition. He had won the captaincy of the School First by merit alone; he *knew* he had been the best –both as player and as leader – and the rewards had followed logically from it. None begrudged him, and he had accepted the prizes as of right. But his dissatisfaction with himself had grown; for the reading of dispatches – bloody though they often were – stirred him in a way he could not easily ignore. They inflamed him with a desire for action – he felt he understood the risks well enough – but it had been his meeting with Rusholme which had hardened his resolve, and precipitated the fateful request. The encounter with his old friend had unmanned him – a friend who though an inferior in rank had gained glory for himself as a battlefield commander; and in comparison with whom Gerald Warrington felt almost emasculated.

Despite the desperate entreaties of his lover, and despite the terse advice of his friend – advice given from bitter experience and from a sincere wish to forestall a rash decision taken in ignorance – despite all that others might do or say to dissuade him, Warrington's purpose was unshakeable.

Chapter Six

TWO FIGURES stood on the brow of a hill known thereabouts as Shrigley Beacon. It was the same remote place to which Oliver had frequently made his way as a boy, to climb in the branches of the oaks which still clustered tonsure-like about its summit, and look far away into the west. Though almost a decade had passed and the boy had gone, Time had changed little else.

The brothers' gazed over the snowscape ranging far beneath them, and they screwed up their eyes against the glare of the reflected sun. They stood as motionless as statues and as silently, lost in their own thoughts as they contemplated an immaculate and tranquil world where not a human form seemed to exist except for them.

If only it could always be like this Oliver said inwardly; *dear old Godfrey, and me. And there would be no war to claim him back, and drain away the life from him, as I know it will.*

At no point in the recent past had he felt closer or more in harmony with his brother, nor yet more apprehensive about the future. He had a chill foreboding that circumstance would intrude and put paid to it all. The snow's transient beauty had transformed an imperfect world for a while yet would be gone within hours; their remaining time together would be measured out in days only, and the rest was dark. The moment was a bright interlude in a sombre existence, and in consequence Oliver resolved to embrace it all the more. He did not know what would become of Godfrey when he returned, for return he would; and he feared the worst.

As if divining each others thoughts they turned as one, and looked back across the miles they had come together, back across snow-capped hedgerow and spinney and farmstead towards the distant house which had once been their shared childhood home, and which was now obscured by the icy mists of evening. Godfrey passed his hand across his eyes.

'What's troubling you?' Oliver asked

Godfrey did not answer at first; then he said quietly 'This. And going away; and coming back at all.'

'Why coming back?'

'Because it makes leaving a more *bitter* pill to swallow... and the contrast's too stark to reconcile yourself readily to it. There's no easy way. '

They passed through a deep cutting where the sun had not penetrated at all and where the snow still lay knee – deep.As they scrambled downward the almost vertical banks seemed to enclose them on all sides, dropping them from the lingering daylight above into a gulf of shadows and snowdrifts within the space of a few yards.

'Will you stay long?' Oliver asked.

'Probably not. No longer than I have to, to get *this* reasonably serviceable again.' He motioned to his shoulder with a twist of his head. 'There's a part of me – the alive bit, if you like – which recoils at the very thought of going back. It sickens me to the pit of my stomach. But there's another side which urges me to return; it's a siren – voice, all right.And it's insistent. *Wanting* to go sounds so ungrateful; and it's the wrong word. I'm not trying to get away – not from the family, and especially not from *you*. I simply don't have any choice. '

'I disagree; that shoulder's made it for you'

'It's not so, Ollie; if only it were that simple. I've left others to face things which I've shirked by being in hospital and by coming back here. Inadvertently,perhaps; but I *have* to return. '

'You've hardly been home more than a couple of days; you couldn't help being wounded.'

'Maybe not. But I've been away for longer than I care to consider – weeks, in fact; and I often think about the chaps still at the Front.To tell the truth they've been on my mind constantly, and still are.'

'You can't *contemplate* returning until that shoulder is healed ' Oliver protested 'No–one could ask it of you.'

'But I *demand* it of myself.That's a difficult one, isn't it?

How long do you estimate it might take to be tolerable, at least? '

'I've not had wide experience of such things… but in my view it certainly couldn't be less than a month from now- maybe longer.'

They returned to Millwain Place under a night sky laced with starlight. They paused briefly before climbing the stile, and turned one last time to survey the meadows through which they had passed.

'It was a splendid day.' Godfrey quietly said. 'One worth remembering. Thank you, Ollie.'

'My pleasure, old chap.There's plenty more walks we might do, as you get stronger. And I can always come down from Manchester for the weekends.'

'Yes… I suppose you could.' It seemed that he had said it for form's sake only and it sounded hollow. 'Of course, I'd look forward to that!' he added, with more conviction.

They shook hands, and made their way up to the boiler-house where they left their boots to dry, and returned to the house.

A week had passed since Oliver's return to Nelson Place and to his studies. Together with a rapid thaw which clogged every track with mud and slush, events had so fallen out that it was impossible to find time to go for another ramble. So Oliver had said goodbye to those at the house – some more warmly than others – and had tramped through the trickling lanes to the station with Godfrey. Before boarding the train he had secured a promise from him that he would try to join them at Mrs. M.'s for a day or two in the course of the next fortnight. The Halle Orchestral Season was in full swing despite the number of players who had enlisted.- perhaps he might like to take in a concert or two? Or if he had a taste for something earthier and more robust, there was always the music-hall.

Godfrey was genuinely keen on the idea – seeing it as an opportunity to free himself from the asphyxiating climate of Millwain Place – and it was with his visit in mind that Oliver now stood before the door leading to the kitchen. He rapped on it smartly.

At first there was no answer so he rapped again. He heard a light footstep approach, and the door was opened by the new serving – maid.

'Good evening, Dolly' he said politely. 'Is Mrs. Monaghan available? I'd like a word with her, if it's convenient.' Dolly looked up at him with her startling blue eyes.

'Good evenin', Mr. Rusholme. I'm afraid the Missis is out at the moment. She'll be back about ten o' clock. Can *I* help you?'

'No… ' said Oliver vaguely, considering. ' No thank you.'

'Then goodnight, sir.'

Oliver was about to about to walk back along the corridor when he was struck by an afterthought.

'Dolly?'

The door opened again.

'Tell me – did you once live in Desbury?'

'Yes, sir. My Ma still lives close by *The Sceptre*, on the Square. An' my brothers an'sisters.'

'Do you remember – many years ago now – that two boys used to visit from time to time, with messages for your father from Millwain Place?'

'I remember it well sir.'

'I was – still am – Master Godfrey's brother.'

'I know, sir. You're Master Oliver.' Dolly smiled innocently up to him, revealing a perfect set of white teeth.

He cleared his throat 'How is your Grandpa getting along, these days? I hope he is still well?'

'Oh, well enough, sir, though he's had to move in with my Aunt Mabel for the winter. His rheumatism.'

'Ah, yes. And your Pa? I hear he's in the Army, in France.'

Her smile faded. 'That's right, sir. We worry about him awfully – especially since he was wounded, the last time. Me an' my brothers an' sisters couldn't go to see him, but Ma did, an' she was very upset by it.'

'Did you know that he's Master Godfrey's platoon sergeant? My brother speaks very highly of your Pa.'

The girl's eyes shone. ' An' Pa thinks the world o' Mr. Godfrey. He says there's no better officer in the Battalion.' She hesitated, thinking that she had been too familiar. 'Excuse me, sir, I didn't mean to… '

Oliver raised his hand to silence her.

'There's nothing to *excuse*, Dolly. I'm proud that he should be so highly respected, and by men of the calibre of your Pa.'

The girl looked enquiringly up to him.

'Sir? Could you please tell me… how is your brother coming along? I'm sorry if it's out of place, sir, but Pa asks in every letter home, *can you find out how Master Godfrey is?* He says he was badly wounded. All the men in his platoon would very much like to know, as well.'

'He's coming along excellently, Dolly!' Oliver beamed 'You can write to your Pa to tell him that! In fact, you might be able to ask him yourself. It's about his intended stay here that I've come to see Mrs Monaghan. But never mind ' he concluded as he turned to go 'I'll see her tomorrow.' He halted briefly. 'Incidentally' he added 'you don't need to call me *sir* all the time. Not when it's just the two of us talking. I'd rather you just called me by the old name.'

'Master Oliver?'

Or just Oliver he would have liked to have said, but knew that the invisible barriers which stretched like a fine steel mesh between them would not allow such familiarity.

'If you wish' he said. 'Goodnight, Dolly.'

'Goodnight… Master Oliver.'

The girl smiled once more up to him, and the door closed.

Oliver slowly climbed to his rooms in a pensive mood. 'My goodness!' he said to himself, and was at a loss as to why he had said it.

Early the following day Oliver enquired as to the availability of a guestroom. Whilst no places were formally kept for the purpose, there had been occasions in the past when a closer relative – in the main a brother – had needed to visit; and somewhere had been always been found. As usual Mrs.M. cavilled a little, pursing her lips to emphasise the difficulty Oliver's request had put her in; but when told briefly of Godfrey's circumstances her reservations whether real or fictitious vanished as she thought of the kudos a genuine *Front Line* officer would bring to her establishment. Though small there was a snug little room at the rear of the second floor. It was presently being used as a store for linen; but in it was a bed and some furniture and a fireplace, too. She would instruct Dolly to make a start immediately, and light a fire in the grate to air it.

As Oliver greeted him off the Desbury train Godfrey paused to inhale the smoke- and steam-laden air of Central Station.

'You'll make yourself bronchitic!' Oliver warned him 'A lungful of this miasma is what you most certainly don't need!'

'Nonsense!. For the first time since I've been back it smells to me of… of *normality*; just the City, going about its business, as it's always done. I've not felt as settled as this for a long time. And I feel as though it's good to be back, at last.'

The evening dinner was an unqualified success. Kathleen Monaghan and Dolly surpassed themselves, having begun the preparations hours before; and once Godfrey had been installed in his room the brothers went down together when summoned by Dolly on the gong. Godfrey was accorded the head of the table by Oliver's fellow – students, who had awaited his arrival almost as keenly as Mrs.M.. The only disappointment for her – and it was a fleeting one – was that the soldier had not seen fit to wear his officer's uniform. In her mind's eye she had pictured the tall handsome figure from Oliver's photograph striding up the elegant steps of Number Seven sporting khaki,cane and immaculate riding – boots. It was the same handsome figure, right enough, who only an hour or two before had smilingly shaken her hand;but he was clad in a sober grey civilian suit and waistcoat from which a watchchain dangled – all well-tailored and very fashionable, but no more resembling the hoped-for military man than any other city gent She consoled herself with the thought that he would certainly *have* to wear his uniform sometime. Oliver had warned his fellow residents off the one subject which, though it might be foremost in their minds, should remain taboo unless raised by Godfrey himself.

But despite the injunction – or perhaps because of it – conversation flowed smoothly and good-humouredly. Even Wilfred Hallett's caustic tongue was silenced, and he shared in the laughter with the rest. Mrs.

Monaghan fussed over Godfrey like a long-lost son, asking him a dozen times whether the courses were to his liking? Godfrey assured her that they were; then standing suddenly upright he brought himself to attention and saluted her. It was an odd gesture in that context, and those present who had been enjoined not to raise the subject of the war were unsure how to take it. Oliver had been relieved that normality was apparently beginning to reassert itself over the darkly depressive mood which had plagued Godfrey; but the gesture of the salute – fleeting though it was –troubled him disproportionately. He shrugged off his unease for the present and willingly yielded to the pervasive party spirit, returning to the immediate problem of what they should do with the rest of the evening.

A small group of young men stood damply beneath the arches of the Free Trade Hall, having spent some ninety minutes listening to a thin programme of orchestral music. They pulled up the collars of their overcoats against the drizzle, though their dissatisfaction did not relate to the weather.

'Well! 'grunted Wilfred Hallett 'I feel in need of a 'pick-me-up' after that. Where *do* they get that stuff from?'

'The Saint-Saens was first-rate ' Oliver observed mildly 'but I agree about some of the 'Olde English' pieces. A bit too *earthy*, for me.'

'Exceedingly patriotic, though' interjected Gilbank 'I'm partial to a tune which makes you proud to be British.'

Hallett shot him a scornful look, but refrained from comment.

'Problem is, where to now?'

'I fancy a bit of ragtime, and a laugh.'

'If nothing else, we've got to get out of this blasted rain. 'Cos if we don't we'll all be candidates for the eminent Sir Bill… '

'*Diseases of the bones, my boy… diseases of the bones…* ' someone said, affecting the heavy accents of Sir William Aplin.

'*There's a world in' em, young man…* '

'Examine this arthritic vertebra, if you will,' mimicked Pottinger, assuming a grotesque Quasimodo – like stoop, '*it's a classical example of its type'* and still bent double he lurched off down Peter Street at an alarming pace, pursued by the others, including Godfrey.

'*Don't touch him!'* Hallett called out to other concert-goers ' he'll be alright shortly, *providing you leave him alone.'*

'It's just a little phase he has, from time to time' Oliver explained to a portly lady and gentleman. 'He's escaped from us, you see. We promised the

Asylum we'd keep him in check, but he's given us the slip again. He's not *really* dangerous... '

'How frightful!' the gentleman exclaimed. 'Poor boy.'

Turning the corner into Lower Mosley Street they all caught up with the 'escapee', now incoherent with laughter.

'Now where to?'

'I think a visit to the *Palace* is most definitely called for. Are you up for it, Godfrey?'

'I should say so!' and Godfrey began laughing again. Like the very antithesis of his misery of only weeks before, the peals came from him like a pure shout of joy. It was the sound of the careless undergraduate once more; and the evening's pranks and lightheartedness continued the process of healing.

The Six Brown Brothers were, according to the posters, scheduled to top the bill at The Palace Music Hall that evening.

The young men had absolutely no idea what sort of act they were, and didn't care providing they had a good time. With Pottinger restored from his temporary fit, the latecomers piled into some vacant seats some five or six rows back. It might have been any one of a dozen similar crimson –and-gilt music halls dotted around the city; and the khaki-clad soldiery seemed there with the sole object of squeezing as much fun as possible into the brief time remaining to them. They was already raucously jolly on account of the previous act, a comedian calling himself *Handsome Harry Burton, the Ship Canal Dog*. His *risqué* ' 'ello,'ello,'ello' jokes had had the required effect; and the crowd was in a mood for more of the same. As the friends squeezed their way to their seats Oliver toppled backward, narrowly avoiding an undignified landing in the lap of a heavily rouged young lady. Her ample frame and large feathered hat irritated a spidery little man perched directly behind her, who dodged back and forth in an attempt to catch a glimpse of the stage. She looked up at Oliver as he extricated himself and winked a wicked eye.

'Yer can sit there later if yer've a mind,chuck,' she sniggered. Oliver declined with a courteous smile, and continued to wedge himself past her and her equally well-endowed friend.

'Phew!' he exclaimed to Godfrey 'that was a close call!'

'Never mind, old chap. Strike while the iron's hot, say I.'

Oliver was unsure as to what Godfrey was implying, and perhaps wisely decided not to ask him to elaborate. A fug of tobacco – fumes hung over the auditorium like a blue mist; and the contrast between the clarity of the chill dank streets and the tropical heat of the interior was almost asphyxiating. Collars together with decorum were stuffed into their coat-pockets, and they settled down to enjoy the show.

Next act on was a skinny young woman introduced as *'The Delightful Miss Mimi Cabott, Direct From New York'* Her transatlantic origins were questionable, however, as from time to time she slipped from her broad American into a distinctly Lancashire vernacular. Accompanied by the sentimental tones of a lone violin she recounted the heart-rending tale of an orphan who, trusting to Fate and her dastardly Protector, had fallen as only a girl could.

The conclusion of her performance was so execrable as she raised her round cowlike eyes heavenward that the audience laughed and stamped and booed in equal measure. When a turnip landed squarely on stage before The Little Lost Lamb she returned it with a kick which belied her small frame, and startled the hecklers.

'Yer can 'ave *that* back, you old bugger' she retorted to the sport who had thrown it, and stomped off stage. Riotous applause ensued, with cat-calls from the audience for 'We want Mimi Cabbage!' 'Bring back The Little Lost Turnip!' and other comments of a similarly tasteless sort. Oliver looked across at Godfrey, who was helpless with laughter. 'It's the b..best ruddy night out I... I've ever had!'he choked 'I can't remember when I enjoyed myself so much!'

Then came another comedian dressed up in a Tommy's uniform who cavorted about the stage while telling ribald jokes about Germans and the Kaiser. Godfrey laughed again and as heartily, and even joined in the mawkish patriotic song which finished the act.

Finally came the bill-topping *Six Brown Brothers*, announced by the barker as 'Masters Of The Saxophone'. Five men dressed up as pierrots complete with absurd pointed hats treated the audience to a singular demonstration of that instrument, from the tiny sopranino whose buzzing resembled a bee trapped in a jar to the digestive rumblings of the grotesque bass. The whole show was directed from the piano by the Sixth Brother who, no doubt in a bid to add even more zest to the act, had seen fit to black his face and don a curly wig. Whilst it was definitely a performance more appreciated by the *connoisseur* than by the generality, there was no doubting the *Brothers'* competence and some of the tunes were almost catchy. After their earsplitting finale the performers bowed themselves off to polite rather than exuberant applause; but despite this somewhat insipid anticlimax to the evening's fun the spirits of the Nelson Place residents were in no way dampened. Oliver had enjoyed himself hugely, as had they all; and he was heartened to see how his brother had contrived to slough-off his despondency – at least for that evening. He had talked and joked animatedly and with an easy grace, just as he once had done, and it was as if the peacetime Godfrey was engaged in the process of rediscovering himself in the company of his brother and his new friends. Oliver wondered if this improvement could be sustained; but was content for Godfrey to live life one day at a time, and regain himself in his own way.

Then there was also the excellent news about the shoulder. With the nearest hospital some hours distant Oliver had effectively taken over the direction of his brother's treatment. In consequence the healing –process had accelerated. He had left clear instructions in addition to the rather cursory ones issued by the military medical authorities about the care and hygiene needed, and how the wound should be dressed. This advice Ida Rusholme had punctiliously followed; and it was she who when acting as Oliver's *locum* saw to the washing and dressing of the shoulder. And it gratified her, for she again had in her hands the care of one of her beloved sons, and was carrying out directions for his wellbeing at the behest of the other.

The next day being Sunday and a day of rest for all but medical students, Godfrey decided to return to Desbury after a lunch provided by the persuasive Mrs. Monaghan. Leaving the *Palace* after the previous evening's show they had noticed from a flyer for forthcoming events that the famous George Robey – the self-styled *'Prime Minister of Mirth'*- would be appearing there the very next week. This was an opportunity not to be missed, and they had decided to reserve a box – the only way seats could definitely be secured in advance.

Godfrey and the five *gentlemen* sat in the lounge after an excellent lunch prepared by Mrs. Monaghan and served attentively by Dolly, who had hovered about the guest like a moth round a candle-flame. They chatted lightly about the doings of the previous evening, dissecting every moment and laughing over them anew. Godfrey had risen to take his leave when Oliver caught sight of Dolly's eyes fixed on him from the doorway. At first he could not account for the intensity with which she was looking at him – a mixture of expectation and anxiety. He walked casually over and asked politely if there was anything he might do for her.

'Mr. Oliver! ' she whispered urgently ' don't you remember? You said you might… I might be able to speak to Mr. Godfrey… about my Pa?'

'My goodness, Dolly!' he exclaimed, cursing himself for his own forgetfulness. 'It had gone clean out of my head, with this weekend. It was thoughtless of me.'

'I apologise for askin' you, sir, but it's the last chance, isn't it, before your brother goes?'

'Don't apologise, Dolly; I should apologise to *you*. How *could* I have been so inconsiderate?'

The girl averted her eyes from him, and reddened.

'Do you think he might spare me a minute, Mr. Oliver?' she asked softly. Looking down at her he was once again moved by feelings beyond the simple desire to make good his forgetfulness.

'If it's the last thing I do, Dolly, you'll get a word with my brother. And I'm truly sorry' he added again, in a tone which was distinctly tender.

The screens were drawn shut across the dining-room, and some twenty minutes later Dolly Chadderton emerged from her meeting with Lieut. Godfrey Rusholme, her beloved Pa's officer.Dolly's face was flushed with pride and gratitude as she came out, and she smiled her thanks across to Oliver as she returned to the kitchens.

'Grown into a pretty little thing, Dolly Chadderton' said Godfrey musingly as he and Oliver sat on the platform awaiting the arrival of the Desbury train. '... in fact, she's quite an eyeful' he added, oblivious to the effect that his comments were having on his brother who had been thinking along the same lines.

For the first time since Godfrey's return Oliver felt irritated by him. 'Yes. Very pretty' he replied shortly. 'I've noticed *that* for *quite* some time'. Godfrey glanced sidelong at him and raised a quizzical eyebrow. He in his turn made a mental note to avoid a certain topic in the future.

As Oliver made his way back to Nelson Place after seeing Godfrey off he began to wonder what his sentiments really were towards the girl. Having expended a considerable part of his emotional capital in trying to make sense of the feelings of others, it came as a new and disconcerting experience to attempt to make sense of his own.

Chapter Seven

'*THE PALACE*' was packed to bursting, with every seat taken in the stalls and in the pricier boxes; and even the Standing Only area at the back was crammed.

The crowd stood shoulder to shoulder, impatiently awaiting the arrival of the top billing. Previous turns were received with impatience and ill-humour, and there had been some barracking from a crowd of Lancashire Fusiliers parked high up 'in the Gods' which required the intervention of the 'barker'.

But George Robey did not disappoint. Half the battle for any stand-up comic is to win the audience, and for Robey the work had already been done. His name and his reputation had gone before him, and a roar of laughter arose from the audience even as he entered dressed in a long frock-coat and with whitened face.

The friends had filed their way out of their box at the conclusion of the show and were still chuckling over one Robey gag or another when their attention was drawn to a young infantry officer waving frantically at them from the other end of the foyer.

'Hello,there! I say! Rusholme!' he bellowed 'Godfrey Rusholme!' The officer took a while to reach them as he fought his way through the tide of bodies flowing against him. Godfrey had looked towards the young man as he called out,and as recognition dawned the twinkle of fun died in his eyes. While the crowd moved inexorably forward the officer laboriously worked his way back; and as the distance between the two narrowed Godfrey's face assumed a progressively more sombre and unsmiling cast.

'My *goodness*, old man ! Fancy bumping into *you* of all people. And here, as well.!'

'Hello, Salini.' Godfrey politely took the outstretched hand and shook it, returning the smile of greeting with as much sincerity as he could muster.

'This is 'Bobs' Salini' Godfrey said by way of introduction 'and this is my brother Oliver... and our friends.' Salini nodded affably to each and shook hands with them all. 'Salini was – or rather is- a fellow platoon commander with the 7th.Company' Godfrey continued flatly; 'we've shared in one or two scraps, have we not?'

'One or two.'

'How are things going, in the Battalion? Still the same sector?'

'Til we were pulled out,' said Salini in a clipped manner. 'Second time in two months, actually. Can't understand it, myself. Word has it that there's something big in the offing,' he said confidentially, lowering his voice. 'On for the Summer, so they say. Couple of weeks ago we caught it hot, few nights in succession. Then just as they'd started it, the Bosche stopped again. No apparent reason. Then, withdrawn to support lines, and a bit of rest. '

Salini scanned Godfrey up and down, as if looking at him for the first time. 'Glad to see you looking so chipper, old man' he said 'Take it the Old Wound's coming along well. Certainly look in the pink, anyhow.'

'Thank you' said Godfrey shortly. 'Many casualties? Amongst the Battalion, I mean.'

'Some, but no more than you'd expect. Thirty or so, all told. Great pity about Walt Houghton. S'pose you heard?'

'No.' Godfrey had gone paler still. 'No, I've heard nothing. What about him?'

'Killed by a whizz-bang while inspecting a forward sap. Couple of O.R.s copped it too. Just as if Fritz had planned it that way, and was waiting his chance.' Unwittingly he let the casual facade slip briefly, and Salini bit his lip hard as he remembered.

'It was terrible, actually. Quite terrible. Not outright, you see. Lasted a few minutes, though Christ only knows how. He shouldn't have. Cut to bits… he was all over the place. I was there – had to clean up, actually. My bods and I.'

'I'm sorry old chap.'

'Ah, well!' Salini said, affecting his breezy indifference once more 'War's war, old boy. Things do happen, don't they?'

The death of Major Walter Houghton was a dreadful blow.

Their senior both in age and rank he had shared the same billets and table as his junior officers, and they had learned much from his experience as a knowledgeable field commander. But more than that, all had known him as a considerate and generous man who had understood well the daily ordeal suffered by those men and officers condemned to the Trenches. He had led by example, and courageously. And now he was dead. At that moment it seemed to Godfrey that a chasm had opened beneath his feet, and he felt immensely grateful that his wound had prevented him from being there, and witnessing it.

'And my platoon?' he asked 'Any news of my platoon?'

'Actually, largely intact, as far as I recall. Couple of losses… from the new draft, though; so you wouldn't have known them, anyway.'

'Thank you.'

Salini looked at his wristwatch. 'Got to fly, Rusholme! Dinner with the

Fair Sex! Keep on with that convalescent leave – it's doing you the world of good.' And bidding them goodnight he turned and disappeared into the press of leavers.

For the remainder of that evening and into the following day Godfrey was uncharacteristically quiet, as he ruminated on his chance encounter with Salini.

On the Monday Oliver attended a lecture on *hyperacidity and the digestive system* delivered by an expert invited from The Manchester Royal Infirmary. The subject-matter was interesting enough,but the eminent person's delivery was so monotonic that the students were reduced to a state of torpor within the first thirty minutes of the three-hour lecture.

As it droned to its conclusion Oliver slipped out from the rear bench where he had purposely stationed himself. Normally a conscientious student who regarded the cutting of lectures as a cardinal sin, today he had decided to make an exception. It was a decision which would alter the course of his life.

He stood hesitantly before a panelled mahogany door on which a brass plate was mounted. Oliver read the words engraved there, and raised his fist to knock.But he hesitated once more, and his hand again dropped to his side. Though by no means faint-hearted, on this occasion his resolve wavered and he was about to beat a swift retreat when he heard footsteps approaching.

'Well, young man. Will you knock, or will you think better of it and give it a miss?'

Oliver spun round to find himself facing a heavily-set man dressed in a well-tailored dark suit. The aura of distinction which cloaked him was enhanced by his exceptional height and a shock of white hair crowning his head like a snow-peak. He was of uncertain age; for one could consider the face and swear that he was no more than forty; yet look into the eyes and conclude that he was at least twenty years older. It was these eyes which now contemplated Oliver; calm and grey, they seemed to be evaluating him even as he stood there

'Which way? In or out?' he smiled, indicating the options by raising his arms sideways.

'In, sir.'

'*Then in it is*... Rusholme's the name, isn't it?' Oliver was surprised that he knew.

The door was opened for him; and as Oliver passed through it he glanced once more at the engraved plate.

Professor Sir William Aplin

F.R.C.S.

He was ushered through a small anteroom where a secretary rose to receive them, and into a study whose panelled oak walls were hung with cartoons and caricatures of famous medical men. The door was closed behind them and Oliver was politely shown to a chair.

Aplin opened a drawer in his desk and drew out a sheet of paper, skimming it briefly to reacquaint himself with the contents. Leaning back in his seat he remained silent for a few moments, pursing his lips and tapping the paper against his chin as he gazed abstractedly through a window and deliberated. He turned to Oliver.

'I have read your letter with interest, Rusholme, and have given every consideration to your request. I have to say that I sympathise with your sentiments and understand well the motives for your desire to contribute in the most constructive way you can. I think that as a young man I would have acted very much as you have. However, your lack of experience in what is proving to be by far the most challenging field in medicine – by virtue of its very diversity – must preclude you.'

Oliver's face fell, his disappointment evident.

'You have to understand, Rusholme, that we cannot simply adapt a whole syllabus to accommodate one person's aspirations, nomatter how praiseworthy... When do you commence your final year?'

'In September, sir.'

'Not long off, admittedly. But you see the School's position in this.'

'Well, sir. If I cannot do such work as part of my studies, might it not be possible for me to do it *in addition* to them?'

'Physically impossible. The academic demands placed upon you over the next twelve months will be insupportable if you devote your spare time to this, as you must.'

'Even so, sir. I would like to do what I can.'

Sir William considered Oliver across the leathertopped desk.He had taken an instant liking to this young man whose openness and quiet resolve had impressed themselves upon him. He had heard much about him, and had followed his career with interest. And everything he had heard pointed to a student of quite exceptional ability; indeed, *gifted* was a term used more than once in Oliver's context.

Aplin rose and walked to a cabinet from which he drew a cardboard file. He thumbed through its pages and grunted approvingly as he read.

'Well, Rusholme. Your results have for the last three years been more than satisfactory'

'Thank you, sir.'

'You realise that *if* I were to put your name forward you must bid farewell to what leisure time you have? That you will almost certainly be required to reside there whilst on duty?'

'I do realise that, sir. I've thought about it carefully.'

'I've no doubt that you have, Rusholme. No doubt at all. You realise that you will witness much that is distressing.'

'I'm a medical student, sir; how am I to learn, otherwise? And it can't be any less distressing for the casualty.'

'No. Of course not. Forgive me, Rusholme. I can promise you nothing however. The request you have made is somewhat out of the ordinary. I will make what representations I can, on your behalf. I will let you know the result in early course.'

Oliver rose to go. 'Thank you, sir. Very much.'

Sir William took Oliver's hand and shook it warmly.

'We'll see. But well done, lad. Well done.'

As he returned to his desk Sir William Aplin picked up the telephone. 'I'd like to make a call to a colleague of mine… 'he told the operator.

By Wednesday Oliver had received a note requiring him to present himself before the medical officer in charge of 2nd. Western General Hospital.

It had been agreed that Godfrey would return to Nelson Place the following weekend. These visits were fast developing into a regular thing, and he had earlier expressed the hope to Mrs. Monaghan that the room might be kept for him for the duration of his convalescence. The hospitable Mrs M. had warmly agreed to this proposal, and looked forward to the prospect of having an officer and a gentleman in residence, if only for the weekends. So it was that Oliver, returning from a visit to Sherratt and Hughes' bookshop the following Saturday afternoon was greeted by a radiant landlady who informed him that *Lieutenant* Rusholme had arrived already, and was in his room. Oliver was mildly surprised at his brother's early appearance, for Godfrey had himself insisted that to avoid compromising his brother's studies he would come by the early evening train.

But Oliver was always more than happy to see him, and was eagerly climbing the stairs when Kathleen Monaghan's voice rose up to him from below. 'He looks so smart, Mr. Rusholme. I *knew* he'd wear it.' At first Oliver could make little sense of this ambiguous message; but then a sudden thought occurred to him, and with it came the icy chill of misgiving. He sprang up the stairs two at a time, now – not from keenness but from apprehension. He did not wait to knock at the door but instead strode in. Godfrey was sitting at a small desk, pen in hand. He turned as his brother entered, and placed the pen down carefully. 'Hello, old chap.' he said quietly.

Oliver said nothing at first. He took in Godfrey's appearance inch by inch – from the sheen on the riding-boots to the polished holster-belt to the insignia on the khaki jacket. His cap lay on the table before him, bearing the familiar emblem of the Manchester Regiment. An overwhelming sense of betrayal rose within Oliver. 'What in God's name is the meaning of this?' he demanded furiously. 'Why are you dressed as if… as if you're going back.?' Even as he asked the question he knew the answer.

'Because I *am*, Ollie.' Godfrey's voice was gentle and almost apologetic. ' I can't stay. I *have* to go.'

'It was your chance meeting with that officer from the 16th – Salini – wasn't it? Well, *wasn't* it?'

'In part, yes. But only in part. It was the *last straw,* so to speak. To be quite honest the thought that I've been here under false pretences has been plaguing me for a while now.'

'*False pretences*! With a bullet-wound in the shoulder I could have put my fist into? And with you falling apart before our very eyes?'

'I'm quite over that, now. Thanks to you.'

'You're not over that wound. It's barely half healed.'

'It'll have to do. I'll manage.'

'You're not fit enough to lead a platoon!' Oliver countered angrily.

Godfrey looked up at his brother with hurt in his eyes.

'That was unkind, Ollie, and unworthy. I can lead my men better than many who have never been wounded. I know what it's like to survive there, you see. And the M.O. gave me a clean bill, anyway.'

'I'm sorry for that comment. It was a harsh thing to say. But it doesn't change the *truth* of it. How much longer d'you think you'll *last?*'

Godfrey smiled quietly.

'As long as necessary' he said, almost to himself. 'There's no getting away from it. The snare has already tightened about me. And it gets worse by the day.'

He paused briefly, picked up his cap and scrutinised the badge.

'It's ingenious, isn't it?' he continued. 'A system which almost every man detests, yet can't wait to get back into. I'm no different to the others.'

'But why go back *now?* Before you have to?'
'Because if I don't go *now*... .'
'I see.'

After the headiness of Godfrey's arrival, the atmosphere in Number Seven changed to a more sombre mood, when the reason for his appearance was explained. Somehow Mrs.M. and Dolly had succeeded in producing a magnificent evening dinner, in limited time and with limited materials. Godfrey provided two bottles of claret which he had bought from Yates's, so the meal progressed in an outwardly cheerful vein. But the gaiety was forced, and deceived no-one.

And afterwards as if clinging to the last shreds of normality they went as usual to the Palace Music Hall, where the slapstick and the jokes seemed a little threadbare and the singers just a little off-key.

How do you say goodbye? How do you convey the vitality of the times you spent together, and the emptiness of parting, distilling into speech all that you have cherished, and all that you regret? How do you condense into a few words what a lifetime of brotherhood has meant, and will always mean, to you?

On their return Godfrey joined Oliver in his room, where they sat and smoked awhile in silence, illuminated only by the fire in the hearth whose flames were mirrored in miniature in their eyes. Past was the need to discuss the practicalities of railway connections, and ferry-crossings, and baggage; past, the need for a veneer of affected gaiety, and contrived good-humour; and past, the need for warnings and for caution. One there feared ever more for the future while the other resigned himself to whatever the future might bring.

They knew it was the last evening they would share together, like this; and each wished desperately to find words sufficient for the occasion. But as neither could say anything beyond the merely commonplace or sentimental, each kept silently to his own thoughts until the embers settled in the grate, and the warm glow began at last to fade with the dying-back of the flames.

The scene at Exchange Station was one of organised chaos. Within the hour six troop-trains were scheduled to depart, bound by various routes for Kent and the Channel Ports. Gone now was the levity of eighteen months before. Amidst the demonic hissing of the locomotives mothers and wives and fiancées craned tear-stained faces up to carriage-windows and waved handkerchiefs, and called out in voices breaking with emotion; or clung to their men for a little while longer, imprinting kiss after kiss on embarrassed cheeks and lips. Some partings were cruel – a young soldier thrusting his sobbing mother roughly from him; others degrading, as two young women – both clearly pregnant – fought like cats for the attention of the same aloof corporal; yet most retained a stoical dignity, and in consequence were all the more heartrending to witness. Smiles were forced amidst the tears, as farewells were spoken and looked, while small brothers tussled with their khaki-clad elders who had no time left for play. There was tangible relief on the faces of soldiers who stumbled upon comrades; for before them stood the opportunity to excuse themselves from further leave-taking, and further pain.

Armbanded transport-officers jostled and barked and pointed out carriages to bewildered Tommies who trailed along with shouldered rifles and overloaded knapsacks.

Fusiliers, The East Lancs., The Cheshires, Manchester and Salford 'Pals', Accringtons and even elements of rerouted Liverpools; it seemed that on this Sunday half the world – and certainly every unit and battalion of local regiments – was there, and was bound for the Western Front.

Standing a little distance away from the throng stood Godfrey Rusholme accompanied by his parents and Oliver. He seemed ill-at–ease as he shifted from one booted foot to another; and he patted his gloved hands together as he looked impatiently about him, avoiding the gaze of his mother and father. Conversation between them was desultory. Clarence drew himself up to speak, and launched into a monologue about duty. 'Patriotism is, I needn't remind you, the cornerstone of British society. And it is from the noble sacrifice of our armies which… which…' He faltered, perceiving that the others were doing their best to shut him out. 'Well… I'm sure you know what I mean.' he concluded lamely.

'It's time.' said Godfrey quietly, looking at his wristwatch.

Ida Rusholme smiled cheerfully at him; but she looked visibly shaken, and there was no concealing the wretchedness in her eyes. He stooped to pick up his case and his kitbag. As swiftly as possible the family made their way forwards, turning their gaze away from the countless other farewells taking place along the platform. As they arrived at the foremost carriages, Godfrey checked the details from his warrant against a number chalked on the carriage's side. 'This is it.' He nodded towards Compartment Four.

He made an uncertain movement towards the open door, as if reluctant to proceed now that he was confronted by what was indeed the final step. As he hesitated Ida suddenly flung her arms about his neck and kissed him and hugged him to her repeatedly.

'Godfrey! Oh, Godfrey! ' Her voice was indistinct with grief. 'Take care, my Darling. For yourself,and Pa, and Oliver and me. Do take care!' Godfrey stood there limply and with head bowed, passively yielding to his mother's embrace. As she released him she raised her hand to his cheek, and caressed it as she had so often done when he was a boy. Then she stepped back and averted her sight., lowering the veil from her hat. Clarence offered his hand to his eldest son and shook it repeatedly, as if he would never let it go. 'Well, my boy. I really could not be more proud of you!' he said briskly. 'Good luck, and do your duty.' Godfrey smiled,despite it all. 'I'll do my best, Pa.'

'I know you will. God Bless, my boy! God Bless!'

Godfrey climbed aboard. Oliver followed him with the kitbag, which he stowed in the luggage – rack. He turned to his brother, and squeezed his arm.

'We'll walk together once more, Godfrey, one day. Out over the snow again, maybe When you come home for good '

'Yes. Out over the snow.' Godfrey said simply ' I'll look forward to that day.'

'When it's all over.' Oliver added. There was no reply.Perhaps Godfrey had not heard. Then he said something strange.

'You know, Ollie, I wish I'd had the chance to get to know a girl properly – closely, I mean. The right sort of girl.'

'I'm sure you will, when you come back'

Suddenly they threw their arms about each other.

'Goodbye, dear old lad.!'

'Goodbye, my dearest brother ! Thank you!'

Oliver straightened himself, and playfully punched Godfrey. 'Goodbye.'

He turned resolutely,and with jaw firmly set descended to the platform. He reached for the carriage door and closed it.

The impact of the door echoed in his mind as it would for many long years after,and as it brought home to him the finality of Godfrey's going. And in that moment Oliver felt that he was sealing a tomb. A whistle shrilled, and then another. Yet more doors clattered, and lines of khaki-capped heads emerged from windows along the entire length of the train. There was a rush of steam from the engine; the carriages jolted and clanked in answer, then almost imperceptibly they began to move. At first the crowd was able to walk alongside, waving frantically; and some Tommies leaned dangerously outwards, seizing the moment to touch for the last time the hand or face of a loved one. Then as the train gathered speed those women and men who could began to jog alongside the carriages and then to run, until finally even the fleetest were outpaced, and they sank back, overcome.

Clarence produced a small Union Jack from his coat pocket, and this he proceeded to wave furiously. Oliver stood watching his brother away, his sad white face framed by the open window. He waved back to them one last time; then the train took a curve to the left, and he was gone.

Oliver walked unseeingly along the platform as wraiths of steam shrouded the last carriage of the train. As he turned to look back his last impression was of his father standing tautly upright, still facing in the direction of the vanished Godfrey. Though his arms had fallen to his sides Clarence Rusholme still gripped the Union Jack in his hand; and the only discernible movement was the fluttering of the little flag in the wind.

Chapter Eight

THE BUILDING rose starkly from the treeless meadows which surrounded it. There was no doubt that it had been intended to appear imposing, and in this its architect had clearly succeeded; but the austerity of its design gave it a harsh unforgiving quality. It was a creation of unrelenting straight lines; in the entirety of its construction no softening curve could anywhere be seen. Its walls were composed entirely of brick of a uniform russet colour, and the whole expanse appeared to be quite new. From either side of the central structure with its neo-Classical entrance there ran out two wide lower wings, each set back from the line of the main building, and each consisting of a single storey which reinforced the uncompromising sternness of the middle. Every window was identical, of that heavy sash variety with neat small panes set in rectangular white glazing-bars. All-in-all its outward appearance impressed rather than welcomed; and from every square inch of its fabric it proclaimed itself a public institution. What activity there was seemed to be concentrated around the left wing where a number of army motor-ambulances were parked, and around which small khaki figures of drivers and orderlies could be seen moving back and forth.

Oliver Rusholme walked up the broad gravel driveway; and looked up at the precise rows of blank windows. Still craning his neck as he surveyed the façade rising above him, he climbed the steps of what had only months ago been The Levenham Grammar School for Girls, but which had quietly been commandeered by the Authorities and converted into an offshoot of the 2nd.Western General Hospital in an attempt to accommodate the increasing flow of casualties from the Front.

Entering the vestibule Oliver stepped across to a porter sitting behind a desk. The man looked up slowly from the newspaper he was reading.

'Yes?'

'I have to report to a Dr. McLeish.' he said, holding out the letter which had come to him from the hospital. The porter glanced at it cursorily.

'I 'avent me glasses. Who d'yer want?' came the reply.

'Dr. *Andrew* McLeish. Department E5, it says here; Respiratory Complaints.'

'Ah. An' your name?'

'Rusholme'

The porter screwed up his nose and laboriously unhitched the earpiece from the telephone, joggling the bracket with a fat forefinger.

'' Ello? Is that Mabel? Yes, its Alfred. I'm at the Front Office. Would yer be so good as ter tell Dr. McLeish there's a gent 'ere wantin' to see ' im? Name 'o *Russian.* Ta.' Then his voice was lowered conspiratorially as he closed his chubby fingers round the mouthpiece, '*Yes... an' you too, Ducks. Later, eh? Ta-ra.*'

He replaced the receiver and pointed importantly to a line of bentwood chairs. 'Take a seat over there. 'E'll be down in a minute.'

Oliver did not have to wait that long.

McLeish presented a tall stooping figure whose premature baldness gave him the appearance of one much older than his twenty eight years. Every step he took as he walked across to welcome Oliver spoke of fatigue; but the careworn expression on his face was dispelled the instant he smilingly offered his hand in greeting, his warm Scottish tones putting the newcomer immediately at his ease. As they walked down a passageway the young doctor seemed in a talkative mood, telling Oliver how he himself had graduated from Edinburgh only three years' previously; and having spent a year at a civilian hospital had like Oliver become increasingly concerned about the uncertain fate of so many of the wounded. In consequence he had volunteered for service in a military establishment, and had been posted to Levenham.

'We were set up to deal with all manner of chest-wounds and injuries here' he said as they walked along a polished corridor bustling with VAD nurses '... and still do; but the increased use by the Enemy of poison and lachrymatory gases in all their forms has meant that we've had to extend our knowledge of their effects on the human respiratory system, and develop new expertise and techniques to deal with them *on the hoof* as it were. But the chlorine/phosgene *derivatives* have been the most challenging – and the most terrible, in terms of their effects on the victim.' He looked significantly at Oliver. 'And nomatter *what we do*' he added with heavy emphasis ' we lose too many of them weeks or even months after they were gassed. You think some poor chap's on the mend, one day; but the very next he's relapsed, and all washed up.' They turned a sharp left from the main thoroughfare and into a second corridor. McLeish placed his hand on Oliver's arm. '*Listen*'.

It seemed that from every side came rasping sounds which rose and fell in an odd cadence; one second louder at the left, then another second louder to the right. The sound was remote, passing as it had to through closed doors and solid walls; but there was no mistaking it; for it was the sound of choking – the incessant and unrelenting asphyxiation of many men.

'Are you prepared for all this, Rusholme?' McLeish asked. The quietness of his voice lent emphasis to the question. 'I only ask because whilst you'll be permitted to assist alongside me or my more senior colleagues, you'll of necessity see things which are certainly not for the faint-hearted ... But talking of the faint-hearted,' he said more lightly as he knocked on an adjoining door, 'you're to be ritually grilled by Matron. Sorry, old chap.' The door was opened by a tiny woman. McLeish was not invited in, much to his relief but not to Oliver's.

'You will wait *outside*, if you please, Doctor' Miss Emily Atkinson instructed him; 'I am sure Mr Rusholme can express himself quite adequately, *thank* you.' The door closed, shutting McLeish out, and Oliver in. She motioned him to a chair placed before an imposing desk. 'Kindly sit down.'

A half-hour later Oliver emerged thinking that McLeish's metaphor was apt indeed. He had felt microscopically insignificant as he sat beneath the icy and all-seeing gaze of Miss Atkinson, listening to the code of standards and conduct required of him, and taking to heart the dire consequences of any breach.

In spite of her elfin appearance this lady bore herself with all the imperious authority of a titan; and breezing to and fro before him in her crisply-starched whiteness she expressed in no uncertain terms her reservations about permitting *just anybody* to wander about her hospital at will. She had, she informed him shortly, been swayed only by the personal intervention of Sir William Aplin – a gentleman whom she held in the highest professional regard – and had been prevailed upon by his repeated assurances as to Oliver's qualities; and even then, she was at pains to point out, she had consented only with the greatest reluctance.

'But you must realise, Mr Rusholme, that these circumstances are quite exceptional, and can on no account be perceived as setting a precedent.'

'I understand perfectly, Ma'am.'

'*Matron* will suffice, *thank* you. At the *specific* request of Sir William you will work under the supervision of Dr. McLeish' a raised eyebrow and a significant pause showing the extent of her distaste for this arrangement 'and you will be answerable to him and to any of the Senior Nursing Sisters whom you will encounter periodically. You will do *precisely* whatever is required by them, and will be *directly* answerable through them, to me. Is that clearly understood?'

'Perfectly, Matron.'

'Then good day to you, Mr Rusholme.'

The two stood in McLeish's office, a room whose disorder contrasted unfavourably with the immaculate Miss Atkinson's. It was not merely unkempt – bottles, packages and text-books lay strewn over almost every available surface – but it had about it that odd musty smell which suggested that it was being lived or even slept in.

'I'll leave you with these. Have a read, and see what you make of 'em.'

McLeish opened a drawer and pulled out a heap of cardboard files which he pushed across the table to Oliver.

'Case histories every one, such as they are. When they arrive most are restricted to a page or two of notes – and sometimes they've only been completed by a half –trained orderly. I suppose' he added sardonically 'that's the one advantage of being here; we don't have to do much reading. The flow of patients is pretty well constant, and the Casualty Clearing Stations rarely have time for anything like a detailed diagnosis. It falls to us to find out from scratch what's really wrong when the poor sods end up here. We pick up the worst cases' he said, looking directly at Oliver 'the ones they can't patch up and send back as A1. Some cynics might call us the no-hopers'

He opened the top file and cursorily glanced over the contents.

'You'll need to get acquainted with the beast' he said waving a hand towards the mound ' so I advise you to read as far as you've a stomach for. I'll be back anon.' McLeish slipped out, closing the door quietly behind him.

Oliver picked up the first of the files and began to read.

When McLeish returned an hour later it was to a much chastened Oliver. What the files revealed had shocked him – not merely because of the number and severity of the injuries which they represented but because of the apparent lack of cohesive treatment. Whilst clearly they were doing everything possible for the victims, it was also evident that it was very much done on an arbitrary basis.

'What did you make of 'em?' McLeish asked.

'It's difficult for me to say.'

'Of course it is. Commendably diplomatic, Rusholme. You'd like to say that it looks as though we rely on guesswork for much of the time. And you'd like to say that you suspect we don't know what we're doing. You'd be right on both counts.'

He placed his hand on the top of the pile in a gesture of resignation.

'It's simply down to trial and error. The German chemists are brewing all sorts of muck these days. As if chlorine wasn't bad enough, they've been tinkering with it and some perverted genius has found a way of producing industrial quantities of phosgene. *That* stuff's ten times worse, if anything. And in the absence of antidotes, we're left floundering about in the dark But even the least of them is horrifically cruel, even by the standards of the present inhumanities.'

'Can nothing be done?' Oliver asked.

'We try to ease the symptoms as best we can. Constant irrigation mainly, most particularly of the eyes and any other affected damp areas, where the phosgene can react with water or sweat to produce hydrochloric acid. We can try to wash it away, and apply emollient creams to the accessible areas when we have. Yet whilst the reaction's a slow process, in most cases the damage has been already done by the time they reach us. But that's only external' McLeish continued heatedly ' and the easy part. How the hell do you flush out the respiratory tract? And especially the lungs, if they've already been chemically burnt? There's water in there, too.'

'In the absence of any effective antidotes could the patient be treated as if he were suffering from pneumonia?' Oliver asked tentatively ' and maybe placed on a saline drip, to mitigate any physical shock?'

McLeish looked shrewdly at him. 'Absolutely,old man!' The astuteness of the observation took him aback and he nodded his head slowly in confirmation. '*Absolutely!* As it happens, that's *exactly* what we've been doing! Very perceptive of you to suggest that.'

'It was only an informed guess.'

'Even so... we try to give the victim as much pure oxygen as possible, either by mask or in a tent – supplies to hospitals have improved greatly in this regard – and he must be kept upright at all times to reduce the likelihood of asphyxiation. Many suffer pulmonary edema and simply drown in their own mucus, or suffer heart failure. It's a terrible death, and terrible to witness. And with phosgene, any moderate exertion days after it's been inhaled can result in sudden collapse. You don't necessarily know you've been poisoned at all until then. Clever, isn't it? I think you'll catch on pretty quick, Rusholme; I can see that.'

They agreed that Oliver would attend at the hospital each weekend and during his vacations, though his weekday evenings would be reserved exclusively for his own studies.

'We can't have you failing now, can we?' McLeish smiled 'I rather think your services'll be too much in demand!'

With accommodation reserved solely for the use of staff there was unfortunately no dormitory where Oliver could officially sleep, But McLeish winked, and said there were a few 'funk-holes' dotted about the place, and if he wanted to stay over the Authorities turn would 'turn a blind eye' to it.

'Now I think we need to make a start!' McLeish said briskly. 'I've been asked to keep you under my wing – ease you in gently, as it were. So I think it would be good to start with what we class here as Category C cases – those which have inhaled or ingested less of the toxins, or who were more severely affected but are now gradually on the mend. I'm due to make a ward visit at three, if you'd care to join me.You'll find a white coat on the peg.'

A pair of double doors opened onto the first of the Category C wards. Even as he grasped the doorhandle the young doctor seemed transformed, drawing himself upright by sheer willpower and shrugging off the fatigue which had bowed him. In place of the stoop he seemed to radiate a positive aura of optimism. As they entered the ward they were confronted by three rows of beds – two arranged tightly along either wall with one row down the middle where they were placed end-on to each other. Most of their occupants had been propped bolt upright, supported by pillows – less because of the imminent visit and more to aid laboured breathing – and here and there a patient sat in a chair by his bed.

There must be sixty in here, at least Oliver said to himself. McLeish read his thoughts.

'It's something of a game of numbers, as you can see.' he whispered; then more loudly and cheerfully 'Good afternoon!' All eyes were turned slowly to him' Good afternoon, sir' came the gasped response.There was a clattering of instruments into bowls as nurses hurriedly tidied up the contents of trolleys, while from all sides there arose a constant coughing – the same ubiquitous noise which Oliver had noted before, and which seemed to permeate the building. Then it had been no more than an incessant background which he had been aware of rather than been compelled to hear; now it was distinct and insistent; so that as he looked about him Oliver began to identify particular patients by their sound.

The two young men walked down to the desk of the Ward Sister, who had risen when they had entered. Oliver was introduced, and the reason for his presence there explained. She smiled a welcome, and appeared to be expecting him.

'Well, Sister. And where shall we start this afternoon.?'

Oliver observed McLeish closely as the round of the ward continued; he listened to the depth of concern which the doctor showed for every case which they encountered, and noted his encyclopaedic knowledge of details relating to individual men. For each he had a personal word of encouragement; and each received a gentle pat on the shoulder as they passed along the beds, with 'You're coming along just fine, laddie' or 'you'll soon be as right as rain' And he was well acquainted with their personal details, too. 'Any news yet of your wife, and the bairn?...Aye, that's grand!... '. 'I'm sure your Dad will be alright, there is plenty of work in the pits, nowadays... '. 'I was grieved to hear about your brother – he may yet be a prisoner, you know; keep your hopes up... '

For the first time the severity and magnitude of the injuries was brought home to Oliver as he observed dressings peeled away from burnt faces and bodies, revealing patches of agonising crimson tissue. The patients winced involuntarily from the shock and pain of the examinations despite every effort by McLeish and the nurses to minimise them; but no word of complaint was ever uttered, amidst the coughing. There was esteem in the hollow-cheeked faces which turned to them as they arrived by each bed and gratitude as they watched them away. With each call they made Oliver's respect and liking for this man grew steadily, and he was moved by the depth of McLeish's compassion.

They came to the bedside of a Sergeant Walmsley, whose burnt-out eyes still wore cotton-wool patches – the insignia of his blinding.

'Doctor's here to see you, Tommy ' the Sister said gently, touching his arm. At this the sergeant drew himself proudly up from his chair and saluted smartly in the direction he thought McLeish might be. Tenderly taking him by the hands the doctor guided him back into his seat again, all the time keeping up a light-hearted conversation with the wounded man and Oliver, who was introduced as 'a fine young chap who is shortly to become a doctor, and who has offered to help us here' Walmsley asked if he might shake Oliver's hand, and did so. Then he settled back into his perpetual darkness, smiling and flattered.

'If you continue to do as well as you're doing, Sergeant Walmsley,' McLeish said brightly, 'I think we'll soon be recommending you for transfer to a convalescent home where you can get plenty of sunshine, and get outside a bit.'

'I'd like that, sir.'

'And maybe your wife could come to see you more often.'

'Aye! Maybe she could, sir. That'd be grand!'

'Never a word of complaint or bitterness' McLeish said quietly after they had passed on.

'Does he know the truth about his sight?' Oliver asked.
'About his being permanently blind? Yes, he does.'

'We're investigating various emollient compounds at the moment- in creams,mainly. One idea being a mixture of zinc oxide and fish oil.' McLeish said in a matter-of –fact way 'and there are indications it may be helping, in more than a few cases. *Not this one though*' he whispered as they approached the last patient. Oliver looked down at the bed. The pitiful smallness of the figure lying there was accentuated by the bulk of the contraption supporting the blankets. Oliver caught a glimpse of a shock of black hair crowning the thin little face of a child. 'Not in a *military* hospital, surely?' Oliver said 'How could... ' but he left the sentence unfinished as reality dawned. 'He wasn't a soldier *Surely*?'

' He was – and still is; but they must be making especially tiny uniforms these days, if the Army's sunk so low that they'd take this poor little laddie. He insists he's seventeen, but his mother doesn't. He's barely fifteen; and it's hard to believe that, he's so starved.'

They drew by the bed, and the nurses pulled the screens around. Immediately McLeish's demeanour brightened. 'Well now, Holcroft! Was last night better?' The boy just peeped up at McLeish with ghastly eyes – like a broken rabbit, Oliver reflected later – neither replying nor moving anything other than his stare which fastened on face after face in turn.

'Bill? *Billy*?' the Sister asked softly as she smoothed his forehead with her hand 'Doctor McLeish is asking you a question.'

'Did ye manage to get some sleep last night, Holcroft?' McLeish persisted bluffly. There was no reply, unless it was in the boy's eyes 'Well,well! Never mind!' he continued 'we'll perhaps arrange for a little chat later, eh? Sister!'

'Yes, Doctor.'

Without another word she and a VAD nurse rolled back the covering on the bed-frame.

Billy Holcroft had no pyjama bottoms on. Nor did he have any bandages or dressings, for he could not have worn them. Oliver caught his breath and involuntarily turned away in shock. The boy was watching him and their eyes met for an infinitesimal time. The memory of the fear and despair which his entirely natural lapse evoked in Holcroft would remain with Oliver for the rest of his life.

From the waist down Pte. Billy Holcroft was an unbroken mass of suppurating ulcers. His thighs, his spindly starveling legs, his feet, his pathetically immature genitals; all varied from yellow to dull red like some topography of suffering. There was no skin whatever.; and evil-smelling matter drained onto the rubber sheet and formed into a viscous pool, in which Billy lay.

'You're doing just grand, lad!' lied McLeish. 'We'll have you back with your Mam before you could say *Jack Robinson*. But perhaps a *few* weeks longer yet, I think.'

At that moment Billy Holcroft started to cry. The sound seemed to wrench itself upward from somewhere deep within the boy's ragged frame, and it pierced all who heard it like a dart. The misery in it reawakened much that was recent in Olivers' mind, and he bit hard on his forefinger until he could have cried out himself.

McLeish was instantly at the boy's side 'There, now, Billy! There, now !' he crooned, as if speaking to a little child.' Ye're the brave soldier. There's none braver, I swear.'

It was the first and only time that Oliver would ever see the speaker nearly lose possession of himself. ' No, there's none braver than our brave Billy'.

McLeish regained his composure in action. 'Nurse' he said quietly 'Hurry and bring one ampule of morphine, a syringe, surgical spirit and cotton wool. Quickly, now.' McLeish admistered the drug to Holcroft who fell silent and was released into unconsciousness.

'Sister French. A word with you *promptly,* if you please' The Doctor's tone was one which Oliver had not heard him use before, and it brooked no refusal. Politely McLeish held the doors open for the Senior Sister. She exited stiffly and with a white face.

'Rusholme, old chap. Please excuse us for a moment.Something's cropped up. Hold the fort with Holcroft here, if you'd be so kind.'

Minutes passed. Oliver checked the boy's breathing and pulse. A little fast at first but then came the inevitable slowing. He could hear McLeish's voice through several walls, but while the language was indistinct, the general tenor was not.

The Sister returned first even whiter than before, dabbing her eyes with a dainty handkerchief.Oliver imagined what the topic of McLeish's dressing-down had been.

'Sister?' McLeish reentered the ward. '*This* is the most recent set of notes. I will leave them with you. Move Holcroft into a *single* room in the Category A wards. Room Five is I believe ideal – it became available this morning.There's a large commercial sink in there, and a warm water supply Ensure *immediately* that the sheeting is made self-draining, and that it is changed promptly at hourly intervals. Apply the emollients whilst the effects of the morphine prevail. Employ two VADs to help you with the creams.'

'Yes, Doctor.' Her tone was contrite.

'I will write down a detailed schedule for his treatment, though I have to say I am now very concerned as to the outcome. You must send for his mother immediately. Her name is Maggie… Margaret Holcroft – and her address is 43 Turton Road Bolton, as I recall. The father is dead. But I think it's in the notes.. Do not alarm her unnecessarily, but try to… no,'he said reflecting. 'On second thoughts I'll deal with that'

'As you wish, Doctor.'

'Poor little bugger crawled into a shell-hole for shelter, on some trench-raid.' McLeish said as the two made their way back to the entrance 'but he'd peed himself with fear over and over again. and his trousers were very wet. Anyway, it had been raining. The phosgene lingered, y'see? Wetness- even urine – a sensitive skin, a delicate constitution… .. And now you've got Holcroft, and massive secondary infection. It didn't even have to get him in the lungs. But he got a dose there too, just for good measure.'

'He's dying, isn't he?'

'Yes.'

McLeish looked steadily at Oliver. 'Are you coming back, Rusholme?'

Oliver smiled broadly for the first time. 'Do you really need to ask?'

They agreed that Oliver would present himself at Levenham on the first available Friday evening, and return to Manchester by the early train on Sunday. The local station, though tiny and still very rural, was situated on one of the main southbound lines leading from the City; and enough trains were scheduled to halt there because of its closeness to the old Albert Road junction. From the hospital it was no more than a two-mile level walk over the Cringle Fields, and Oliver found he could cover the distance comfortably in less than half an hour.

The parting from McLeish was mutually warm and sincere; and as they took leave of each other he sensed that not only had the doctor been favourably impressed with him, but had valued his offer of help the more because of the spirit in which it had been made..

Several times his mentor had given him the same piece of advice –*get your head down during the day, if you can; you're sure to be needed during the night.* Oliver could see that there was perhaps some merit in this, as far as it went. It was common knowledge that there was a low point which the sick often reached in the darker hours, and he could think of no other explanation than there would be greater demands made upon all staff in that period; but somehow the emphasis with which McLeish had spoken caused him to be dissatisfied with that explanation. Yet what the underlying reason was, he could not guess.

As he sat in the carriage listening to the rhythmic beat of the wheels Oliver reflected once more on the few hours he had spent at Levenham. The sight of the wounded – brief and sanitised though it had been- had hardened his resolve that he would devote every spare minute to doing what he could for them.

He was drawn to the hospital, dour and institutional though it was. He felt that for him the essence of duty was now more clearly defined; though – or perhaps because – it was the very antithesis of all that the tub-thumping 'jingoists' like his father seemed to epitomise.

His cynical side pointed out almost at once that it was a simplistic view and perhaps even rather naïve; it even pragmatically advised him to keep such thoughts to himself; but the idealist remained in the ascendant. The inmates summoned him with an insistency to which he could never be deaf, and whose whispered call he could never deny. There was a certainty to his perspective on the future, now. And though it was dark indeed, his resolve was like adamant. As he sat there he vowed silently to himself, to Archie McLeish, and to the countless Private Holcrofts and Sergeant Walmsleys that he would fight to treat the effects of war, and never be their cause.

Chapter Nine

IT HAD RAINED incessantly for three days. There had been no downpour, as such; but the drizzle had persisted; and now that every ditch and watercourse was filled to overflowing it was impossible to distinguish the margins separating land from water. In their unmetalled state the crossroads at Suzanne had ceased to be a meaningful thoroughfare, and had degenerated into no more than a few thin strips of semi-liquid mud under the constant traffic of carts and limber-wheels. Everything within spraying-range of the road was daubed in the same dull coffee shade and seemed to have been constructed from one and the same material whether it was a team of horses, a wagon, a cottage or the gate before it.

A half-mile or so from this vital artery lay the village itself. Once it had boasted the conventional French attractions, though on a smaller scale. There had been a pleasant Louis XV chateau with its own leafy drive from the main street. It had possessed a splendid pair of gates, which had always seemed a little too important for the house sitting smugly behind. The British Army had arrived, and it had become for a while Headquarters to a Midland regiment – until it was pointed out that it was located within shooting distance of the Front Line. Withdrawal was prompt and clandestine – the whole entourage decamping in one night.

The combat officers who took over were grateful; but their gratitude was short-lived, as was their residence there. Staff cars sporting red insignia had some days before been spotted by an eagle-eyed German pilot, who reported the coordinates to the heavy artillery. That same night an expert gunlayer calculated range and trajectory.

The first round destroyed the gates but it was the third huge Howitzer shell which put paid to the chateau, and the five junior officers within. Division was most concerned to hear what a close shave it had been for the Staff.

The Front had shifted, and the ruin remained together with that half of the village which was reasonably intact, and there were passable billets here and there if you looked for them. With the stalemate along the Somme and beyond now entering its sixth month the Manchesters – who had not moved laterally more than ten miles all told – had begun to regard this battered cluster of buildings with affection, and as rather uniquely their own.

While the former Hotel de Ville had been appropriated almost at once as 16th.Battalion Headquarters – to the irritation of other battalion commanders – the more junior officers of the companies pulled out of the Line had to take whatever accommodation remained, and it was at the rear of a cobbled courtyard they had found a gaunt building which had *La P-ste* painted on a cartouche above the door. Occupation had been immediate. Now at the top of the steps approaching it there was arranged a line of foul-weather footwear, trench-boots and cutdown trench-waders, all clogged with mud and shedding their reeking load in a stream which percolated down hollows in the stonework. Though it still rained the outer door stood ajar and a cheerful light flowed through and glistened on the setts of the yard beyond.

The main room which had till recently been the only post office in the town was far too lofty for its length, and the narrowness of the walls accentuated the angularities of the ceiling far above; but the new tenants had furnished it with a mixture of youthful verve and imagination. In various knots around the room was distributed a collection of armchairs, the better examples still retaining some upholstery and borrowed either from the wreckage of the chateau or purchased at extortionate prices from the locals. A small group of officers of the 16th. sat round an open fire, smoking and discussing nothing in particular.

Lieutenant Godfrey Rusholme sat within the circle, but remained silent for the time, simply listening. The welcome he had received from the Company and his platoon on his arrival back a week previously had been genuine and warm, but never exuberant except from some awe-struck subalterns who had obviously been fed some sort of tosh about him by the others. He'd never expected or wished his reception to be otherwise. Not because it wasn't the *done thing,* or that there weren't many officers and men who were heartened to see him, apparently so well and back with them; but because experience had taught them repeatedly that it didn't pay to do it. Emotions had to be masked, kept under wraps and within manageable limits. Close friendships were not uncommon but were a dying breed; they lasted only as long as the original men. And once dead, they were only cautiously replaced.

But when Godfrey arrived back, his familiar space had opened for him and he was able to slip back more easily and more naturally into the way of things. That they had been on battalion relief several miles behind the lines was doubly fortunate. It had given him the opportunity to 'catch up' with the 16th. and reacquaint himself with the duties of platoon command. His underlying fear about returning had been precisely that. He seemed to have forgotten so much during the strange other-worldliness of convalescence and home, and had agonised constantly on that long journey back to France about his capabilities.Now an unremitting daily routine of marches, drills, fatigues and even the laying of an extensive series of communication – cables had kept the whole Company hard at it; and despite the discomforts of mud and rain the process had been a positive one as Godfrey and his platoon reforged the old links which bound them to each other. But it had been particularly good to meet Albert Chadderton once more.

The Sergeant had stepped forward briskly on Godfrey's first arrival at the billets; had brought himself smartly to attention and saluted, with a simple 'welcome back, Sir'; but with the military formalities over had shaken Godfrey's hand firmly and the looks which they exchanged spoke of all that they had been through together. And as Godfrey and he took the first roll call it was concluded with a well -meant 'three cheers for Mr. Rusholme!'

'Welcome back, Sir! 'said Chadderton once more, smiling as broadly as his wounded face would allow. 'We're ever so pleased you're back.'

'I'm glad to be' Godfrey said appreciatively 'I'm very glad to be.'

Godfrey leant towards the fireplace and knocked out the contents of his pipe on the irons. As he was refilling it a strongly built officer of about his age entered, threw a streaming trenchcoat in the direction of the coat -rack and without even turning to see where it landed made for the fireplace. 'Bloody French nights.' he grumbled, as he lifted his jacket-flaps to warm his backside. 'Can't bear'em. Somehow the rain's *wetter* here than anywhere else I know. Surprised the local Frogs haven't developed amphibian characteristics.'

A sandy-haired officer by the name of Frank Gartner was slumped in a neighbouring chair. He was attempting to read a crumpled copy of *The Daily Mail* by the light of an oil-lamp and the coal-fire.

'I was very sorry to hear about 'Walt' Houghton' Godfrey said.

'What's that, old man?' Gartner looked up abstractedly from his paper.

'Walt Houghton. I heard whilst I was in Manchester; I bumped into Salini there. He told me all about it.'

'Yes. Bad business. It was while the Krauts were having one of their afternoon '*hates*', apparently.'

'Hates?' Godfrey queried 'What are they?'

'Since you got your Blighty the Kraut has adopted a new tactic. We might be going nowhere fast, the way both sides are dug in, but apparently just to dispel the boredom *he's* taken to giving an absolute battering to a particular coordinate whether or not its of any immediate strategic value- though sometimes its softening-up prior to a raid. Anyway, just before we were relieved – the Tuesday before you got back, in fact – they gave us a pasting along Royton Sap. Four or five ORs were killed, and Tomlinson from the 17th. and a half-dozen ORs wounded. He's been sent back, but they say there's not much hope for him, poor chap.'

'I didn't know him.'

'No, you wouldn't've. He'd only been over a couple of weeks. Anyhow, by way of retaliation our Acting CO… .'

' 'Bertie' Fairclough?'

'Yes, 'Bertie'. Well 'Bertie' decided to let the chaps get their own back, so somewhat unofficially he collected all the available Stokes and Heavy mortar rounds – even begged some from the ordinance dump boys – and sackfuls of rifle –grenades; then he got the 3rd. and 8th. Platoons together with the mortar teams, and with the support of the 18 pdr. batteries at Bazentin – CO's an old chum of his – concentrated *all* that firepower onto a Kraut strongpoint at 'Y' Wood. Gave the place an absolute hammering. Can't say it did any good,actually, but the boys let off a lot of steam. The Krauts retaliated pretty sharpish with H.E. though, and a few of our lads weren't quick enough into the dugouts.'

'I see. Has there been any word about the CO's replacement?'

'Now, that *is* strange! Had you asked barely half-an-hour ago I could have told you nothing. But as I was coming in I met Paddy Curran from the 17th. *He* said, it's pretty hush-hush, but our new CO's *en route* at this *very* moment, and he'll be with us within the next few days. Pretty sparkling character, apparently. *Very* glossy! Requested the Command of the Company from Brigade itself, by all accounts. Got it too. Just like that.'

'Did he, indeed? You didn't hear the name?' There was an odd note in Godfrey's question.

''Fraid not. I'm sure old Pad. would've said, if he'd known.' Gartner looked across quizzically at Godfrey ' Any special reason why you ask?'

'No… no reason particularly.' Seeing that the conversation was at an end Gartner took up his newspaper once more; and Godfrey fell into silent conjecture about the identity of this enigmatic new commander who had specifically asked for 'F' Company – *his* Company. Disquieting thoughts kept occurring to him, and as he banished one another appeared in its stead. The same unthinkable possibility kept rearing up, nomatter how persuasive the arguments against it, and how absurd such an appointment might be.

The weather gradually eased, though the landscape in all directions resembled a series of chill swamps. Travel – even over a mile or two – had if anything become even more difficult; with trucks, carts, limbers, their horses,their mules and their drivers – bogged to the axles or the midriff if they strayed from the relative firmness of the 'corduroy' trackway – a surface of coarse woven matting resembling the withy hurdles used in more peaceful times to corral livestock.

But adverse weather conditions neither influenced nor even entered into the fuddled thinking of British High Command. Incessant rain is a minor inconvenience when one's world is circumscribed by the tapestry- and portrait-hung walls of a royal chateau thirty miles away from the fighting, and one's experience of France has been limited to the elegant boulevards of Paris. Someone decided that the Manchesters had done such a good job laying deep telephone cables that they should continue doing it elsewhere; so Godfrey and his platoon were detailed to cut a trench beside the elongated morass which passed for the Montauban Road. The success of the venture was doubtful from the outset. Each day they would rise an hour before dawn; and after a cold and meagre breakfast they would shoulder their picks and shovels and drums of communication-wire, and after some two hours of slogging through the hinterlands of a war landscape would reach their objective only to find it awash with floodwater or collapsed by the passage of night-traffic. After a week of fruitless effort Godfrey sent a furious note to Headquarters advising them of the impossibility of continuing. Some twenty hours later he received a reply informing him that they had no trace of the original order, and advising him to return his men to their billets accordingly and await further instructions.

This news was received by Godfrey with a mingled sense of rage and relief; and as he handed the scrap of paper to Albert Chadderton the older man scanned its contents without any apparent reaction.

'Well Mr. Godfrey' he said calmly 'it appears we'll not be diggin' ditches tomorrow after all, shall we?' His face remained outwardly expressionless, wearing that inscrutable look which lay somewhere between a smile and a frown, but yet was neither. Godfrey had long since learned to disregard the face and focus immediately on the eyes if he wished to read Chadderton's true feelings. Now the eyes glittered mischievously ' but whether we'll be any drier, sir, now, *there's* a conundrum.'

'I wouldn't go so far as to hope for that,' retorted Godfrey bitterly ' someone at Brigade will have a clever wheeze tucked up his sleeve to guarantee we're not.'

'No doubt, Mr. Godfrey. But the men need the relief, as you know, sir. They can't get dry, not in the stables they're billeted in – there's no heatin' at all – an' the mud soaked into everythin'. Neither the capes nor them boots were any use in keepin' it out.'

'I know, Sergeant. Tell the men I'll be along at 2000 to see how they're managing.'

'Yes, sir'

'And whilst I expect everything to be as shipshape as possible, under the circumstances there will be no inspection.'

'Yes, Mr. Godfrey. I understand, sir. Thank you.' And bringing himself to attention he saluted and left the Orderly Room.

Godfrey was about to depart for the Officers' Mess when the duty corporal handed a sealed packet to him.

'It's a General Order, sir, just come in this minute, for all the officers from the 16th. As you yourself are an officer of the Battalion, would you mind receiving it?'

Godfrey agreed to take it along, and slipping it into the inner pocket of his jacket made his way back along the trickling streets to the comparative cheerfulness of the Mess. Without delay he headed for the narrow corridor which led to the rear of the old post-office where there was a room piled with oddments of old furnishings, domestic and official. Rooting through a pile of broken chairs and other rubbish he grunted with satisfaction when he unearthed what he had been looking for. Before him stood a rusty iron stove of the upright cylindrical kind, complete with a small iron door glazed with orange mica windows.

'Right!' he said with satisfaction. 'Just the ticket!'

After sending a brief message to Chadderton to detail four men to report to the Officers' Mess he went upstairs to the room which he temporarily shared with a fellow officer of the 16th. Carefully he removed his jacket and shirt, and stripped to the waist examined his shoulder-wound with the aid of a couple of shaving-mirrors. It was coming along well enough, he thought, and whilst it would never be pretty at least the discharge had stopped, and it was mainly the consequent lack of mobility which galled him now. He recalled how concerned Oliver had been when he had seen it, and him; and the recollection touched him deeply even yet. But he had difficulty recalling Oliver's face. Godfrey found that his very presence at the Front – or a few miles behind it – had a peculiar bleaching effect when he attempted to remember colours. Most peculiarly this phenomenon seemed to influence his memory for someone's face, and their colour of eyes, or skin or hair. He could have described Oliver to a 'T'; but somehow – despite their closeness – he could not picture him other than as the sepia image which he carried in his wallet, and which he had abstractedly drawn out.

Placing the wallet on one side together with his thoughts of home he filled the washbowl with cold water from the jug. He scrubbed himself vigorously with the unforgiving carbolic soap, then dried himself and fitted a new collar to his shirt. He was making the final adjustments to his belt when there was a smart rap on the door. Four men from his platoon were waiting out in the yard, the messenger informed him, accompanied by Sergeant Chadderton. Godfrey sent instructions for them to meet him by the sheds at the back of the Mess, and he made his way down by a rear stairway. There was no light except that which came from the hurricane-lamps which they carried, and the flames reflected sporadically in the mens' eyes as they stood in the darkness, stamping their feet against the night's coldness and speculating as to what they were needed for.

'You'll find out soon enough; here's the Officer now.' As the door opened they drew themselves immediately to attention at Chadderton's sharp command.

'All here Mr. Rusholme, as instructed. Willis, Lenaghan, Hartopp and Warren.'

'Excellent, Sergeant! Now, I've been giving some thought to the problem of warmth and dryness of the platoon's clothing. I've unearthed a stove which I think will fit the bill quite effectively. It does actually belong to the Officer's Mess, but as it's not being used I've borrowed it for the time we're in these billets.'

'Thank you very much, sir' said Chadderton readily, 'I'm sure the lads'll appreciate it, 'specially on the damper nights.'

'Exactly so. But don't thank me until you've got the blessed thing working. As for fuel, take some of these sacks and *quietly* break up some of the older furniture in the store.'

Five shadowy figures moved the stove and a supply of chair-legs, table-tops, and stools to the platoon's dank billet; its arrival was greeted with near-disbelief, and the whole platoon set about installing the contraption beneath a broken window which would have to serve as a makeshift chimney. There was no way they would have allowed it not to work; and there was sufficient expertise amongst them to ensure that by the time of Lieutenant Rusholme's arrival it was blazing away with such fury that it was impossible to stand within a yard of it and avoid being burnt. Attempting to renovate the stove with boot-polish had been fine in principle but in practice proved less so; for as the polish heated up it began to give off an appalling stench of rancid fat – presumably because it consisted largely of it, the original material having long since been replaced with a cheaper substitute by an opportunistic contractor.

But the stink didn't matter much, if it was a choice between that and the invasive dampness which after an hour or two seemed to penetrate to the very marrow. Whilst the fumes made them wince there wasn't a soldier there who would have had it otherwise. Godfrey had already decided to keep his visit short; but the evil atmosphere caused him to make it even shorter – spending just enough time there to make sure their conditions were a little more tolerable than before. Returning Sergt. Chadderton's salute he bid his platoon good night, and turned away into the darkness.

'Now *there* goes the best bloody officer in t' Regiment ' said one voice.

'Aye, 'e is that' another agreed

Godfrey flopped down into an armchair and fished about for his pipe and tobacco. The movement caused a dull crackling of paper from within his breast pocket and he drew out a sealed packet. At first he was at a loss to explain why it was there at all; then he recalled the orderly's request to communicate the general order to the Battalion. He looked about him and saw 'Bertie' Fairclough holding forth to another officer in the corner. Godfrey approached and handed the packet to him as senior officer present. Fairclough turned the packet over and looked quizzically at Godfrey.

'No ideas at all, Bertie' said Godfrey pursing his lips ' your guess is as good as mine.'

Fairclough slit open the packet and scanned the contents. His eyebrows rose in surprise, but as he read on his looks clouded. Without a word he passed the note to Godfrey.

'So we're to meet him here tomorrow at 0900 and all will be revealed. And the Battalion's to be in readiness for Full Inspection by 1500.'

'A *Full* Inspection?'said an incredulous voice.

'That's what it says here. One imagines they actually mean it. I think we'd better get weaving.'

The contents precipitated a sudden flurry of activity, most particularly from platoon commanders who had most to see to and supervise. No junior officer nor Other Rank of F Company was destined to have much rest that night.

By 0800 the last preparations were in hand. Jackets had been brushed, belts and boots polished by servants and brasses buffed up to a starlike brilliance. Then came the uneasy wait, with the junior subalterns' horseplay creating a schoolboyish atmosphere until warned off by their seniors.

At 0859 a staff car ground into the front yard of *La Poste*. Salini – now returned from leave – shot a look across to Godfrey; but the latter's expression remained impassive as he stared unblinkingly ahead of him.

The door swung open and a number of officers entered. Those of F Company drew themselves to attention.

'At ease, Gentlemen! At ease!' the genial voice of Maurice Gatlin, Battalion Commander, boomed out 'and please feel free to smoke. Without further ado' Gatlin continued 'I'd like to put paid to any further speculation about the successor to the command of F Company. I appreciate that hitherto we might not have done these things quite *by the book* as it were, and perhaps a little too informally. But Staff – and indeed we at Battalion HQ – feel that the present circumstances are sufficiently… .well, extraordinary, to warrant a rather special introduction. Would you step forward, Captain… ?'

As the new Commander stepped forward with head inclined modestly downward, Gatlin launched into a eulogy extolling his achievements while at Staff Headquarters – of the administrative wonders he had accomplished, and of the efficiencies he had brought about. There was however no mention of combat experience.

He had certainly matured with the time spent at 'Staff'. His profile was if anything even sleeker, altogether rounder and more comfortable than it had been. And he exuded a serene yet authoritative confidence. But whilst there was some discreet craning of necks by those curious enough to want to get a better look at the new man, Godfrey did not move other than to fix his gaze on him when he stepped forward from the shadows of the entrance. Godfrey was no longer surprised, although he had told himself a hundred times that even Division would recognise the insanity of such an appointment.

To battlefield command from the abstracted other-worldliness of General Staff, in one fell swoop. But it had been done, and that was that; they would all have to learn to live with it, and with the difficulties that he feared would follow.

The eyes of Captain Gerald Richards Warrington met the unwavering gaze of Lieutenant Godfrey Rusholme, and the newcomer inclined his head slightly in acknowledgement of his old school friend. Godfrey returned the compliment and smiled; but he did not release his new Company Commander from the fixity of his gaze, and for a second or two there as a tension – almost a visual skirmish – between the two. Warrington had the uncomfortable sensation that he was being interrogated – stripped bare- and looked back with a glint of defiance in his eye, while Godfrey searched his face for clues as to the motive which had brought Warrington to this of all places.

Then the new commander was asked to say a few words and promptly did so, launching into a well-rehearsed and polished speech about duty and sacrifice and ultimate victory; and how his arrival there was the fulfilment of a boyhood dream. He said how proud and humbled he was, at receiving such an undeserved honour; and how he would strive to earn the right to lead the splendid officers and men of 'F' Company. It was stirring and persuasive stuff, and almost all of those assembled applauded. Even Godfrey did, for form' sake.

On the one hand it was perhaps a compliment to Godfrey that Warrington had used his influence to gain the command of F Company, of all companies and of all battalions; for they had certainly distinguished themselves in the course of the last terrible year. But then so had countless other units, so that combat distinction was if anything the rule rather than the exception. He could have had his pick, if he'd wanted. And presumably he had, Godfrey reflected.. Movement from Staff and Brigade to Front Line duty was rare enough to make it a red-letter event, if ever there was one. He smiled sardonically when he envisaged the upset it must have caused when Warrington submitted his request, and they realised he was serious.

There was of course every reason to suppose that friendship was the simple motive behind it. Though a year of conflict had turned him into a cynic about many things, there was still enough of Godfrey's straightforwardness of character remaining to prevent his suspecting the existence of any ulterior purpose, and he felt that he should be flattered. Thus he was blind to the possibility that a curious blend of envy and emulation might also have been a factor in Warrington's decision. But on the other hand he could not dismiss his serious misapprehension about the error of the appointment. On his own part there was a complete absence of baser sentiments in his assessment; in fairness he would have applied the same criteria and had the same reservations whosoever the new Company Commander might have been. Had Godfrey but known it his feelings were shared by more than a few of his fellow officers. Those who had withstood the trials of the Front Line knew that if nothing else the new man must be able to demonstrate an impeccable record of practical field command – not only as a means of earning the confidence of his subordinate officers but by showing that he was equipped to deal coolly and objectively with the crises which they daily had to face. And there was that other misgiving which had gnawed away periodically at Godfrey whenever the subject of Warrington had come to mind; the presence – or was it the absence? – of some factor which though indefinable caused him much disquiet.

'… and my first duty as Company Commander..' Warrington continued

'... is to advise you that we have received orders from Division for the Company's return to the Maricourt Sector – a sector which I understand is not unknown to the Battalion. We are to relieve the 18th. and be in place in the Line by 0400 on Thursday. '

Maricourt again? said someone half-audibly *Christ that's only the day after tomorrow.*

Bloody hell muttered another; *the 18th.'s had an absolute mauling, so I've heard.*

'On a personal note' Warrington concluded 'I have to say that I am looking forward with unqualified enthusiasm to this opportunity for F Company to acquit itself with the greatest courage and distinction.'

Most of the junior subalterns listened to Warrington with rapt and eager expressions on their faces; but amongst the more seasoned officers the inclination of heads and the uneasy shifting expressed their doubts with an eloquence equal to the spoken word. They had been there, most of them; and they knew every inch of battered trench and every obstacle in No Man's Land. *Maricourt.* The 16th. had made its intimate acquaintance, and the cost had been a heavy one. A return to it was not an occasion for fine and dignified words, for it was not a fine or dignified place. They would have more willingly faced a similar peril elsewhere, and with greater equanimity. But Maricourt was immovable, and reeked not only of the deaths of anonymous others, but of too many of their own. To pass and repass across the same old places of slaughter somehow reemphasised the loss. And they'd be back there within two days.

As the news was sinking in Warrington made directly for Godfrey and having halted squarely before his old friend, extended his hand. Again their eyes met, and now at close quarters; but this time there was no hint of animosity or rancour. Rusholme was neither churlish nor vindictive by nature, and despite his concerns truly wished Warrington to succeed. He took the outstretched hand immediately, and grasped it firmly. 'Welcome to the 16th., and to F Company.' he said; and he grinned broadly at Warrington, who grinned back.

'Glad to be here, old man. Very glad.'

Chapter Ten

DESULTORY FIRE was being kept up by the field gun batteries situated some few miles beyond Montauban. It mattered little whose guns they were to the lines of gas-caped and heavily-laden infantry packed tightly into the communication – trenches; it only mattered that the fire was not being directed at them. Many infantrymen regarded the artillery as something of a race apart, governed by different rules of engagement. Some thought it a curiously detached job, where your own guns fired over your head and beyond you, for much of the time; whereas the enemy fired directly at you, again for much of the time. That shells sometimes fell short whether through misread coordinates or defective gunnery or charges was just another hazard to be added to the innumerable dangers of Front Line duty.

The usual bottleneck had arisen as the men of the 18th. attempted their withdrawal down the same trenches which contained the relief companies of the 16th. And it was imperative that the whole process be done as silently as possible and in total darkness to avoid giving the Enemy an inkling as to what you were up to.It was at times such as these that the troops – and the Front Line itself- were particularly vulnerable.

'Bloody terrible, up there mate!'

'Buggers at it night an' day'

'We've left the dugout nice an' warm for yer'

'Don't forget to put out t' cat'

Despite your exhaustion it was good to joke at the expense of the Relief, whispering your sardonic comments to the apprehensive platoons as they squeezed mutteringly past you, and feeling the growing sense of release as you made your way back to the rear, and to the comparative comfort of the billets. But the sense of dread grew steadily in your mind as you slithered and shuffled your way blindly back up the Line, led only by remote guides positioned at the head of your platoon.

Godfrey had marshalled his men almost a half-mile behind the Fire Trenches which they were to occupy.There they had loaded themselves like beasts of burden with materials for trench repair, and trench warfare; more shovels, more stakes, more timber, more wire, more small arms ammunition for the rifles and for the Lewis-guns, and more grenades; their new commander had instructed that they provide themselves with an extraordinary number of these things, and Godfrey had wondered why.

The 16th. made their descent into the slough of the communication trenches like latter-day Orpheuses, and into an underworld of slime; mud walls rose upward from a mud floor, and it seemed to many that even the canopy above them was mud. Pressed downwards by the passage of countless overladen boots the duck-boards had subsided into the ooze; already the slop was knee – deep, and they had barely started. Now Lieutenant Rusholme was consulting with his guide – a lance corporal from the sappers – in fierce undertones, as they attempted to decipher the route from a crumpled map with the aid only of a small flashlamp.

The night had closed about them with the consistency of thickest pitch; perpetual raincloud hung over a hundred miles of the Line, extinguishing star-and moonlight alike and making movement seem strangely purposeless and incorporeal. With strenuous effort you shifted your body and your load until you bumped into the man in front, who sometimes cursed you; but still you got no further. And the endless zig-zags and meanderings of the trench disoriented your senses of place and time. You swore you'd been at it a good hour or more; but a glimpse of the luminous dial of your wristwatch seemed to tell you otherwise; Christ, ten minutes only since you'd last looked. You mistrusted the bloody thing. It *had* to be longer than that, surely? and you shook your watch, if you could, and crammed it under your helmet to your ear; but it was still ticking. And yet more of the 18th.'s survivors clawed their way past you with their glinting eyes. Then you heard the man in front stir, and heard the suck of the mud as he lifted his boots, and you were on your way again.

It took F Company upwards of four hours to flounder the three-quarters of a mile to their section of fire – trench. They did not arrive at the allotted time. Constant misreadings of the map and the partial collapse of several sections of the support trench brought about by the previous day's shelling had delayed them by a further two hours, and caused them to reach the Line even as the sludge – coloured dawn was breaking. As the greyness percolated into the trench they were confronted by a sobering sight. The rumours of the mauling which the 18th. had suffered were everywhere borne out, even to the scattering of corpses they had left behind – victims of shellfire in the last minutes before their withdrawal, and which had of necessity been abandoned by their comrades as they withdrew to the rear. Godfrey was considering them abstractedly when he was approached by a white-faced subaltern of the 18th. whose very salute seemed fragile.

'Good-good morning, sir' he faltered. 'Second – Lieutenant Barrett, sir.

B Company, 18th. I'm very glad to see you're here safe and sound. If you'll permit me, sir, I'll take you round this part of the sector, and show you about a bit.' He saw Godfrey's eyes shift momentarily to four corpses nearby which had been left in the same distorted attitudes in which they had died. Barrett moistened his colourless lips with his tongue. 'I – I'm truly sorry about that, Sir. We'd have seen to them before you relieved us, only… only.'

'Never mind, Barrett' Godfrey said quietly. 'But I think we need to sort them out now, don't you?'

Stretchers were dragged out and they had the bodies placed upon them with what decency they could; and the appalling mutilations were hidden beneath empty sandbags and an old gas-cape or two. Then the dead were laid head to toe on one side of the trench, in readiness for their collection by the rearguard of the 18th.as they withdrew, and for their final journey down the Line.

The tour was a swift one indeed. Both officers were for different reasons eager for it to be over as soon as possible; Barrett because at barely nineteen years he'd had enough and was at the end of his reserves of courage and determination; and Godfrey, because although the trenches thereabouts had been remorselessly shelled since his wounding he recognised the basic layout as being much as he remembered it. These practicalities aside, his junior's twitchiness was infectious,and was making him feel ill-at-ease.

His instincts told him that Barrett would be unlucky – particularly unlucky, even for the Western Front. The young man seemed to radiate misfortune and Godfrey imagined that he'd come to a bad end, and was keen for him to be gone. So it was that within a half-hour they gladly parted company from each other at the junction of Ardwick Alley and Soap Street.

Their brief acquaintance would never be renewed, and Barrett and most of his platoon would be dead before the close of the month.

Though they seemed to have multiplied, the dugouts had not improved any. Excavated beneath the enemy side of the trench they descended below the parapet, and their low entrances were mostly curtained –off with a piece of wet sacking hung there not primarily for privacy but as a counter against the initial effects of a gas attack, or to catch fragments of hot shrapnel.

As barriers to either the sacking was relatively ineffective; but as there was nothing else it had to do.

Accompanied by Albert Chadderton Godfrey set about an immediate inspection of these stygian pits. His examination revealed a degree of squalor which was appalling even for that notorious sector though blame for it could hardly be laid before the 18th Battalion. Clearly some efforts had been made to improve the drainage, but all such attempts had clearly proved futile. With the constant rain the deep sumps which had been scraped out beneath the floors had simply filled with liquid mud; and once full, had then overflowed forcing their noisome contents up between the slats in the duckboards.

The dugouts had by now degenerated into little more than subterranean pools of filth, and yet it was into these that the men of F Company were glad enough to scramble and claim a little corner for themselves. And there was always the companionship and the humour, which made conditions even such as these a little more tolerable. Their platoon commander was well aware of the spirit which sustained his men, and amongst their many fine qualities he would perhaps have placed it foremost; yet the simple fact that such conditions were tolerated did not make them any more acceptable. Floundering back to the Officers Dugout – which was better than the common infantryman's only in that it boasted a few sticks of furniture and some camp beds raised out of the mud on wooden blocks – Godfrey sat down to write a blistering note to Battalion Headquarters. Frank Molyneaux, a fellow officer from the 16th.,innocently enquired, *was Godfrey writing a letter home?* But the glower which met his question was answer enough and Molyneaux withdrew discreetly. Godfrey began by protesting in the strongest terms about the conditions he and his men had found awaiting them on their deployment; and concluded by demanding that immediate steps be taken to improve trench drainage and dugout conditions throughout the entire sector. In truth, the remainder of his fellow-officers had found the situation to be little different in their sections of the Line; but Godfrey's intention was to speak for his platoon alone. He knew that his note would be read by Warrington – and there was an unquiet element in him which made him glad that it was so – but foremost in his mind were the shocking conditions which *his* men would have to endure for anything upwards of a month. The problem of the dugouts was a situation which would have to be addressed, one way or another. He read the note through and smiled grimly at the imperious tones in which it had been couched. But he did not change so much as a syllable. Then he dispatched it via a runner to Battalion HQ.

As far as the inspection of the dugouts was concerned all had been investigated with only a single exception. During the sporadic bombardments of the previous week one of these makeshift shelters had been struck by a high explosive round. It had penetrated the earth and corrugated iron roof which afforded poor protection at the best of times, and virtually none in the event of a direct hit. The *whizzbang* had exploded deep inside, bringing down the whole structure onto those sheltering within, and burying them. Despite the frantic efforts of their comrades who set to with picks and shovels all rescue attempts were hopeless. And as a German sniper claimed another victim from the squad of would-be rescuers all further attempts to save those trapped had been abandoned. What had been a shelter for ten had been converted by Fate into their mass grave. Godfrey had looked at the wreckage and sniffed the sour odour of detonated explosive which the ravaged trench-walls seemed to exhale even yet; and in his mind he pictured it all for a moment. Then he turned away from the sight and in clipped tones ordered new revetments to be constructed across the front of the crater, with a new infill of earth behind it. As a tomb it would do as well as any other.

Along the forward trench Godfrey had offered words of encouragement to the strained and haggard faces which were raised to them – faces of men who had not slept for hours almost beyond count, and whose seemingly endless slog to the Front had culminated in yet more harsh labour. Hardly had they bent their backs to their tasks than an enemy shell passed over with a shrieking whistle, detonating somewhere near the reserve trenches. It was followed by two more in rapid succession. This was to be but the opening salvo in a brief but vicious bombardment of their sector, during which shells of various calibres burst upon them as German gunners raked the British Line. Then in the manner of a summer storm, though infinitely more deadly, the bombardment subsided as abruptly as it had begun.

'It's rather like Jerry's sending us a welcome back present isn't it Mr. Godfrey?' Sergeant Chadderton commented drily. 'An' it's as if he's really missed us.'

'Let's hope that he misses us some more' Godfrey retorted. They shook the thin covering of soil from their capes and helmets, and cautiously emerged from the sap where they had taken shelter.

He was summoned to Battalion Headquarters to explain the nature and tone of his complaint. 'What's the meaning of *this?*' demanded a crimson-faced major, as he threw Godfrey's note back at him across the table. Godfrey paid little heed to the blusterings as he mildly received his 'carpeting', though the major made the united displeasure of the senior officers abundantly clear with the colourful epithets he employed. 'And *furthermore*, Rusholme, you're bloody lucky to've got what you *have*.' he concluded 'Now bugger off back to your platoon.' Godfrey brought himself smartly to attention as the major made a loud aside to the adjutant 'Bloody wartime officers!' and as ordered the wartime officer 'buggered off' back to F Company. He had made no headway whatever yet his heart was inexplicably lightened, and as he ploughed his way back he set about planning the improvements necessary for the safety and comfort of his men.

But his ambitions were to be short-lived. If Lieutenant Godfrey Rusholme had fondly thought that the matter was now closed he was seriously mistaken. Within hours he was summoned again – though this time by Warrington – and the purpose was not a carpeting but a search for a volunteer.

Chapter Eleven

OLIVER RUSHOLME stretched out stiffly in the darkness and peered at his wristwatch with bleary eyes. Though it was barely three o'clock on that black and chilly morning he felt a constant movement around him – a series of shiftings, each possessed of an urgent purpose and direction. It must have been these which had caused him to wake. At first he was disoriented – where on earth *was* he? And what were those white things which shone semi-visibly above his head? Then he remembered, and was fully conscious and alert in an instant. The laundry-store – on the Second Floor. By the Category A Wards. Where Archie McLeish had suggested he might sleep, and where he might be most useful. It was curiously quiet in here, on your own, and reasonably comfortable if you didn't mind sleeping on the floor. The piles of ironed linen which stood on the shelves around him and which had caused his momentary confusion, deadened the pervasive sound of the coughing; though here amongst the Cat A cases the coughing was weaker, and therefore somehow worse. He struggled his way up from the mattress McLeish had found for him and kicked the blankets clumsily to one side. Having fumbled around for a match and candle he now dressed in its feeble light, dragging on his trousers,shirt and boots with a total disregard for his appearance; then knotting his tie hurriedly he extinguished the tiny flame and stepped out into the greenish gaslit corridor. He shivered involuntarily, and wrapped his arms around himself to stave off the unseasonal chill. In the distance he saw several uniformed orderlies steering wheeled stretchers in the direction of the rear exit. He decided to follow them. At the same moment McLeish stepped through the doors leading from a stairwell ahead of Oliver. His attention was also attracted by the clattering of the trolleys and at first he did not see the younger man. It was clear from his dishevelled appearance that he too had recently risen, and for a moment he simply stood there, running his fingers through his uncombed hair uncertainly. Then he shook himself almost like a dog, and in his characteristic way drew himself physically upright, breathing deeply in the cold air.

He turned toward Oliver as he heard his steps approaching.

'Rusholme ! Good morning, man! Y'know, I thought that somehow I'd find you here. Well, it's started. The notification came in last night, after you had gone to bed. I didn't want to wake you.'

'What has started?' Oliver was still mystified by these clandestine emergencies '*What*,exactly,has started?'

'The night arrivals.' McLeish said with some heat.'They bring in the worst of the casualties – and the largest number of 'em – by night these days. The poor souls have to be dragged in during the dark hours, like criminals. The government thinks it's better all round, to keep everything as quiet as possible.'

'For whom is it *better all round*, exactly?'

'Ye might call me a cynic, old man; but in my view it's mainly for the Government. Too many casualties, y' see. If the true extent of our losses was widely known – and God knows, it should be – they'd have a few questions to answer, I'm thinking.'

Oliver now saw the reason for the advice; *get your head down during the day, if you can; you're sure to be needed during the night.*

'Of course' McLeish continued 'specialism doesn't matter a jot; it's all hands to the pump when the hospital trains arrive. We've got to be 'jacks of all trades' then.'

They sped along the corridor and down a flight of stairs, their feet clattering on the wooden steps, then on to the rear of the building where the ambulance lorries and their drivers usually sat idle. As they reached the ground floor a draught of cold air caused Oliver to gasp, but it banished any residual sleepiness and honed his senses to razor sharpness. McLeish led the way without lessening his stride. The hubbub of many voices – some shouting, others crying out – grew steadily as they approached.

'*The Admissions Rooms*'.

McLeish turned a sharp left in the direction of the noise. A scene of organised chaos met Oliver as they turned the final bend, with VAD nurses sweeping back and forth amidst lines of grunting medical orderlies bearing loaded stretchers or pushing the wheeled contraptions which he had seen previously. This time each carried a human load, wrapped about in blankets from which bandaged arms, bandaged legs and bandaged heads protruded. Some appeared to be unconscious, as a forearm in ghastly crimson dressings lolled out from the bedding, and bounced up and down as the stretcher and its occupant were shuffled in together. Others were awake, as you could see from the glittering blackness of their eyes as they peered warily about them; and still others groaned or called out faintly. And amidst it all the overpowering smell of disinfectant, urine and faeces.

'Hospital train's in at the station' said McLeish shortly. 'We're to admit some eighty or so, tonight – all severe battlefield cases. We can't tell the numbers precisely until we've seen who's survived the journey, and who hasn't. And it's just pot luck as to what forms their wounds'll take. I just hope that Base Hospital's notes, such as they are, haven't gone adrift… .it's happened before. *Good morning, Ginsberg*!' he said, acknowledging the greeting of another of the gathering group of doctors. 'Have rooms been allocated?'

'You're in Seven, I think' replied the other. 'Leastways, I *was* down for Six, and you're certainly next to me, as I recall.'

'Fine! Seven it is' McLeish exclaimed 'Down to work! Oh, Ginsberg. This is Rusholme, by the way. He's volunteered to assist. Final Year.'

'Ah, yes; I've heard.Welcome, Rusholme' Ginsberg said, offering his hand. 'You certainly choose your times ! But still... 'The little man shrugged and rocked his head 'still, you're going to be needed! Good luck, young man.' Then he turned to McLeish, and added in lowered tones 'Four dead on arrival'.

Oliver thanked Ginsberg, and prepared himself to confront the starkest of realities.

Room Seven was in readiness for the first admission. They entered,blinking under the comparative brilliance of the electric lights, then only a recent addition to the hospital. Fortunately the casualties' notes had not been mislaid, and even before the first of the motor lorries roared away into the dark for their next consignment of wounded a patient was already being wheeled into place. The soldier was an older man of broad build with a face furrowed by protracted suffering; and he lay tautly on his side as if he were incapable of movement in any direction. The nurse drew the blanket gently back from his body. His chest was heavily bandaged, as was the stump of his right arm which had been taken off just below the shoulder. McLeish drew closer to inspect the bloody dressings; and as he did so he assumed the familiar veneer of casual optimism, chatting about this and that while he scanned the notes; and with the doctor's apparent light-heartedness the soldier's tenseness seemed to evaporate.

'So, ye're from the Highlands, are ye?(*scissors, nurse, please*)' he breezed as he laid bare the man's terrible wounds. ' I've been on many a holiday up there. Do ye know Kingussie at all.?'

The soldier nodded 'Aye, sir'

'You *do*? What part do ye hail from?*Nurse, would you pass me the sterile forceps, and the swabs?*. Newtonmore! Well now, there's a coincidence! When I was a bairn I used to walk with my father often on the Glenmore hills and thereabouts, and down by Loch Laggan; indeed, my Grandma lived right in the village. *Mr.Rusholme, would you care to examine the flap of tissue and observe the stitching to the residual arm?* No doubt ye'll recall the place well enough. Anyhow, that's grand!' he beamed after investigating the mass of lacerated and punctured flesh which had once been the wounded man's chest. 'We're done with ye for now, Corporal Donald. Nurse'll get ye all bandaged up and washed, and into a proper bed for a decent sleep.'

'That was caused by a rifle grenade which dropped into Donald's trench' McLeish said when they had withdrawn. 'What did you make of the arm?

'Well, it's not really for me to say... 'Oliver hesitated

'But say it anyway' the other insisted.'What did you make of it?'

'Frankly it seemed to me a shoddy piece of work. Imprecise and random stitching, and superfluous tissue employed in patching the stump. There's a great deal of inflammation in the region of the wound and what looked like peripheral necrosis present in the tissue. It has to be removed.'

'Exactly. That's the price ye pay for letting half-trained orderlies do a job which a doctor should only be allowed to do. Go on.'

'Urgent treatment is needed if the infection already present is to be confined and eradicated.'

'Quite. What about his chest?'

'Well there appear to be multiple wounds present which give greater cause for concern.' Oliver said hesitantly.

'Yes?'

'I understand that such weapons are designed to emit fragments of metal when they explode' he continued with growing conviction 'I'm only guessing, but from what I saw there is the possibility that the chest and rib cage have been punctured in several places. We can't know how deep those wounds are, and the extent to which organs have been affected. We need to explore further. '

'Which is precisely what I intend to do with your assistance, once we've dealt with the rest of the admissions. About that arm' he said, looking sidelong at Oliver. 'Would you care to deal with it?'

Oliver faltered 'But... Doctor McLeish, I'm unqualified. Surely I'm not... ?'

'I've faith in you, laddie, and in what I think ye can do. And I'll be right beside ye.'

Oliver felt a heady surge of anticipation. He had presumed that he would be required to assist in surgery, certainly; but this was a departure for which he had not planned. He was flattered that McLeish's confidence in him was such that he was prepared to allow him this unprecedented opportunity, and suddenly Oliver began to feel the weight of responsibility which had now been unexpectedly thrust upon him.

'I'll do my best, Doctor' he said.

'Good, laddie! Of course. I know ye will.'

They edged their way back through the columns of stretchers which trailed into the hospital from the night beyond, and into Room Seven, where the next of the wounded awaited their attention.

Under McLeish's expert guidance the operation on Corporal Donald's arm went absolutely as they had intended it. Scrubbed-up and dressed in the white gown of a surgeon Oliver wielded the scalpel himself; and though McLeish watched every move minutely he needed to make only the briefest of corrections about this or that as the wound was treated and restitched. He marvelled at the degree of skill and precision which Oliver unconsciously demonstrated, and which would have been a credit to a practitioner of many years' standing. But as he observed the tenderness with which this student worked he saw something else – something which made a lasting impression upon him – for he saw Oliver's fierce compassion for the suffering of others which manifested itself in his unstinting devotion to the cause of healing. During that hour in the operating theatre there were planted the seeds of mutual respect and friendship which would continue until the end of their lives.

Yet the cost of Oliver's commitment to the wounded at Levenham looked likely to be a heavy one. The single-mindedness with which he pursued his work there began to tell on him physically, as his normal robustness began to be eroded by unremitting work – work without respite or relief. Work dominated him utterly. Even the chalice of qualification seemed a vague and indistinct goal when he considered it now. His life in Nelson Place was one of unrelenting study, and the weekends spent at Levenham were sleepless and crisis-strewn. Yet for the world he would not have been anywhere else, nor would have had it any different.

On a Sunday in late May 1916 he was following his usual path across Cringle Fields, en route for the station and for Manchester. During the previous months Oliver had come to be regarded as an integral member of McLeish's little team, and indespensible as an assistant. But the last two days had been particularly gruelling, for there had hardly been a pause in the steady stream of casualties, and it had flowed on through both nights and into the daytime. More rooms in the former school annex had recently to be converted in order to accommodate the anticipated numbers; and wounded could always be found to occupy the new beds within. And somehow the wounds and the gassings became even more terrible, and the Mortuary seemed ever fuller as the War ground on.

It was early evening. A light dew had begun to settle on the long grass which had become slippy underfoot. Oliver looked ahead of him across the wide expanse of farmland and over to a distant hedge through which there was a gap leading onto the Stockport Road. He could make out the opening easily enough, at first. But then it seemed greyer, and a mist clouded his vision. His stride was not as vigorous as it had been only weeks previously, and he faltered and stumbled over small obstacles and tussocks as he walked. He raised his hand to his eyes and rubbed them, but his vision did not clear, and his head swam. He tottered a few more paces, then with a sigh he sank down onto his knees. His hands seemed to have lost all their strength and his bag slipped from his grasp Then he fell headlong, and lay motionless on the ground.

Chapter Twelve

CONSCIOUSNESS returned to him only dimly. He was aware at first of sensations rather than sight, as he felt himself being turned over onto his side., which ached dreadfully; and as he opened his eyes he saw a stout pair of leather gaiters rising above a pair of equally stout boots.

'E's alive alright' said a disembodied voice in soft Lancashire tones.

'Move over, Edwin' said another voice, deeper and older than the first. Slowly and heavily the second man knelt down beside Oliver. 'Eh, lad, ye gav' us a right scare. We thought at first ye was a drunk or a tramp, but we can see now yer neither.'

Oliver looked up into a farmer's weatherbeaten face on which concern was written.

'We'll give ye a hand up. Ye can't lie *here* all day; you'll catch yer death.. *Edwin*?' Oliver heard a movement behind him.

'Edwin, tak' his other arm when we turn 'im.' Gradually Oliver was helped to his feet, but he could not stand unaided, leaning instead for support against the burly chest of the old man. 'Th-thank you' he muttered 'I do apologise… I... I'll be all right now, I think.' The dew had soaked through his tweed suit and drenched him to the skin, and he felt weak and deathly cold.

The horses trotted swiftly along the old Stockport Road with Edwin at the reins and Oliver swathed in travel-rugs beside him. They approached Levenham Station without drawing rein, and on Oliver pointing out that it was his destination Edwin simply smiled.

'Pa told me to take yer all t' way home. Ye might as well settle back sir.'

They drew up outside Nelson Place and as Edwin secured the horses Oliver climbed wearily down from his perch. Almost at once the doors of the house flew open and Mrs Monaghan and Dolly, their faces taut with anxiety, descended the steps. Oliver smiled wanly at their anxious enquiries. He was alright, he said. He'd had a minor accident and was sorry he had not thought to inform them sooner. Kathleen Monaghan's relief turned to indignation, and she was about to deliver a lecture about selfishness when Edwin appeared round the gig, carrying the suitcase.

'Your Mr. Rusholme' s been taken right poorly, Missis' he said; then despite Oliver's attempts to forestall him he told them how he had been found, and the condition in which they had found him. The landlady's anger abated in a second as she held her hand to her mouth in horror. Oliver felt that his thanks to Edwin were hardly adequate; and fumblingly he drew out his purse and offered the young man a sovereign as a token of his gratitude. Edwin flushed red, and politely declined.

'Then at least take my hand' Oliver said, and so they shook on it.

As Oliver was helped up to his room the tears of relief were not confined to Kathleen Monaghan alone.

During the first few days Oliver's condition did not greatly improve. Physical and emotional exhaustion combined with pneumonia-like symptoms to lay him low with a fever, and his recovery was felt to be in the balance. The doctor was called, which prompted some wry comments from Oliver; but as they agreed both as to diagnosis and as to treatment they got along well.

Because of her duties elsewhere Mrs. Monaghan was unable to attend adequately to Oliver's needs, and despite her reservations she was compelled to deputise Dolly Chadderton as his nurse. She could not have made a wiser choice, however; for the devotion which the girl showed in caring for her reluctant patient could not have been had at any price. She would sit by him in the lamplight, watching his sleeping face with her soft eyes; and whenever he stirred and turned there she would be, and it was her image which shaped itself before him as he woke. She attended diligently to his every need, serving at mealtime and coaxing him to eat whenever he tried to refuse; and she jealously guarded these duties as being hers exclusively and as of right.

Oliver forbade them to tell his parents of his illness. Least of all did he want his father there, with his sanctimony and his preaching. He would have liked to see his mother, certainly; but as Clarence would have insisted on accompanying her he decided to do without them both.

By the end of the second week there was a turn for the better – due equally to the care lavished on him by Dolly, and the enforced rest. He received notes from Archie McLeish and several of the other Levenham doctors wishing him well; but most surprisingly he had a warm letter from 'Bill' Aplin himself, who urged him to take every care and not to worry himself overmuch about the Finals. It was easy to say, of course; although physically inactive Oliver was certainly not mentally so; and whilst lying in the semi-darkness he set about planning his revision schedule.

Within a week of his return the unfortunate Dolly had of necessity to become conversant with a medical student's filing- system and notebooks. But she was a quick and eager learner, and would sit beside him as he 'swotted', retrieving this essay from the cabinet, or that folder from the bookshelf. Oliver soon discovered her to be both sharply intelligent and the easiest of companions. As the days passed he found increasing pleasure in explaining quite complex medical points to her – points which she seemed to grasp with relative ease. Partly it was through his love for his subject, and the skill with which he imparted it; but as much if not more was owing to the fact that regardless of what he had to say, Dolly would have hung on his every word.And sometimes he would tell her of his beloved Wales, and Ridland,and the Clwyr; and about the wild creatures there, and the low stone walls with their ivy, and the whitewashed cottages and the fishing-boats and the weed-hung wrecks.And her eyes would mist as she attempted to picture places she had never seen, but which had begun to assume a particular significance for her.

'I think, Dolly, I'll get up properly today!' he said as she drew back the curtains in his room 'I can't bear the thought of lying abed one minute longer than I need.'

'Well it's a lovely day outside' she smiled 'You might want to go out for a walk, pr'aps;Whitworth Park's nice at this time o' year.'

'It sounds like a good idea. I just might do that, Dolly! Now, would you excuse me for a minute or two? I need to shave and get dressed.'

A quarter of an hour later Oliver came downstairs with much of the former spring in his step. His face was pinker and healthier –looking than it had been for a good few months.

'I'll have a dose of nervous exhaustion every so often' he joked with his fellow-students as they noisily welcomed him back into the dining-room; 'it's good for the system!'

Breakfast was finishing as Oliver rose from his chair.He had made his mind up to go for that walk and was regretting inwardly that Dolly could not accompany him when his eyes casually fell on an envelope lying on the sideboard. The crumpled and travelstained paper looked incongruous in such immaculate surroundings.

He recognised the handwriting on it as familiar. It was his own.

He picked it up uncertainly, mystified at first as to why it should be there at all. He knew to whom he'd sent it; to his friend Percy Crossley. It *had* been sent, surely? He distinctly remembered asking Dolly to do it.- and the stamp on the envelope had been franked. So why on Earth was it back here? Possibilities rushed in on him as he read the pencil scribbles. He read them again as he slowly tried to take in their bitter significance, revolving the letter in his fingers as if some rational explanation might present itself somewhere on the reverse; but it did not.

Recipient deceased... recipient deceased... he repeated the phrase in his mind as he scanned the weatherbeaten paper. And nomatter how he read and reread it the meaning came out the same.

Though initially sceptical about what the message conveyed – that Crossley could surely not be dead – he was now in contrast confronted by the terrible and unavoidable certainty. He slit open the flap and pulled out the letter he had written to his friend. He read once more the words of hope and encouragement he had sent – words written whilst his friend yet lived, and now words addressed mutely to a dead man. Words which could never now be read by poor deceased Percy Crossley.

How bloody futile it all was. Never had there been anybody less fitted to be a soldier, yet Crossley had died as one. And now as he thought about *it* and *him*, and reflected on what he'd seen in the hospital, he saw how impossible it would have been for the half-blind Crossley to have survived at all.

Oliver replaced the letter in its envelope. Then he tore the paper in half, slowly and deliberately and almost tenderly; and walking to the fireplace he silently offered the pieces to the flames.

Three weeks later Oliver sat his Final examinations at the School of Medicine. During the silent and agonising interim his frayed nerves told him that every letter which dropped through the door *had* to be the one, but it never was. Then on a sunlit morning in early June an ashen-lipped Dolly Chadderton brought him an envelope bearing the University crest. He hesitated to open it, at first, fearful of the outcome; then casting caution to the winds he tore into it and with shaking hand read the contents.

It was a letter from Sir William Aplin in person, congratulating Oliver in the. warmest terms on the exemplary standard of his papers, and informing him of the unanimous decision of the Board of Examiners to award him a Double First.

'Have you done well, Mr Oliver?' Dolly inquired timidly, 'Is it good news?'

'Yes, Dolly. Quite good. Indeed, it's excellent news!'

The girl beamed up at him, the joy in his eyes mirrored in hers.

He was now Doctor Oliver Rusholme. Percy Crossley would never know, but Oliver felt that if the honour belonged to anyone, it belonged as much to him as to any soul living or dead.

And so he wrote Captain Bonnard, knowing that the old man would understand his meaning, and endorse it.

Chapter Thirteen

HE DID NOT come from a family where religious observance had seemed to matter much.He'd attended the Lutheran Kirche with his parents to celebrate Easter and Christmas, but in his heart had never felt any warmth of commitment to it. It had just not seemed relevant to his life of study and sport and school, though it had retained a traditional presence in the latter's hoary precincts. But there – especially there – it had seemed so integral a part of the school's fabric that it had blended indistinguishably into it. And so from being a ritual of observance it had become little more than a burdensome routine for all, Staff and boys alike. And until the night of the 13th. May 1916. Godfrey Rusholme had almost forgotten how to pray.

He scrambled up a trench ladder and slithered a few feet into the debris of No Mans Land. Slowly he took out his binoculars and from his concealed position trained them on what he thought might be the German Front Line. He could detect nothing in the pitch blackness. No movement, no sound, no light; no life. And he could not see the wire. Warrington had assured him that the previous day's bombardment would cut the wire into manageable pieces and disperse the entanglements, making their task easier.

He *had* provided the batteries with the precise coordinates,he insisted, despite the fact that in the course of the hour-long barrage all the HE shells had landed rather to the left of where the raiding party were expected to penetrate. Godfrey had requested Warrington to come and have a look for himself, almost dragging his senior to the Forward Trench where they had together assessed the net effects of the shelling. Much of the wire – indeed the largest part – was still apparently uncut and intact. But Warrington would have none of it.

'If you look *there* to the right of that mound' he'd insisted, peering through a box periscope ' you'll see that it's clearly thinner-probably no more than a few strands which can easily be dealt with using wire cutters. A few snips and it'll fall away, you'll see.'

But Godfrey had experienced rather more of barbed wire than Warrington, and all he could make out was a greyer patch amidst the rust-coloured masses. He'd remained sceptical.

'For all we know that patch could be an area that the Bosches have freshly wired. It's got that colour about it.'

'Nevertheless, in my judgment it's not an insuperable obstacle. You should get in alright' Warrington said 'and I certainly don't want a bit of cold-footedness to compromise what could turn out to be a raid of exceptional importance – particularly to our understanding of the Enemy's deployments.'

Godfrey rounded furiously on Warrington.

'What exactly d'you mean by *cold footedness?* What are you hinting at? I insist you explain!'

'I certainly didn't mean to insinuate that you *yourself* were 'windy'' Warrington replied, reddening 'and I apologise if it came out like that. But I feel that the proposed raid has not received the *unqualified* support of all officers in the Company – the support it deserves. It's a bold and daring action, and I'm honoured that Battalion has entrusted us of all the Companies with the task. I'm frankly disappointed that you don't seem to see it that way too.'

'As for the *honour* ' Godfrey retorted bitterly 'there'd be a damn' sight more honour in it if we knew we stood a fair chance of getting *out* in one piece as well as getting in.'

'Well, if you didn't wish to take part in the Show, why did you volunteer for it?

'Do I really need to explain that to you? I shouldn't have to.'

'No. Quite. You don't have to. Look here, let's not fall out over this. Do you really want to get out of it? I'll arrange it, if you wish.'

'You know full well I don't. It's just that I have reservations, that's all.'

'Naturally you do, Rusholme. We all have' Warrington said equably. 'But I can assure you that it is planned down to the last detail. Artillery will cover your retreat as the signal is given. Make the Jerries get their heads down as you're on your way home. It can't fail.'

Godfrey made no reply; but saluting his superior was about to turn back down the trench in order to make sure all was in readiness when Warrington added 'and I've given Battalion my word. They're setting great store by this. Remember, Rusholme, the priority is *prisoners*.'

Zero Hour for the 'Show' was imminent. He shuffled himself slowly backward and blindly fished around for the rungs of the ladder with his feet. Hands grasped his legs firmly and guided them onto the timber. Sergeant Chadderton was awaiting him as he arrived at the bottom. 'Did you *see* anythin', Mr Godfrey?' he whispered.

'It's like pitch out there' came the terse reply. 'We can only hope it stays that way as long as possible to give us something of a chance.'

They made their way along the forward trench to the Assembly Point. There they met with the spectral shadows of the 7th.Platoon who with the officers and selected men of the 2nd.,3rd. and 8th.would be mounting the raid – a combined force of some eighty, all told. Each had in the preceding days familiarised himself with details of the route he had to follow to the German front line, and with the tasks he had to accomplish. It had been decided by Battalion that an enemy outpost amidst the smashed stumps of 'Y' Wood was to be the raid's target. Though barely a hundred yards away at that point it was strewn with obstacles apart from the wire, and to get lost or tangled up in it was the road to certain disaster. And it was also uncomfortably close to a heavily defended concrete strongpoint.

Godfrey had ordered the men to be issued their last tot of rum. Now he passed along the lines of waiting troops, flashing his torch briefly on each as he and Chadderton made the final checks. Though it was a chilly night for May, beads of sweat glistened on the sombre faces. Someone was tapping his fingernails nervously against a metal object.

'Stop that racket, whoever it is!' The tapping ceased.

'Worrall – did you take that extra sack of bombs?'

'All 'ere, sir.'

'Are the fuses in?'

'Yes, sir'

'You men there – with Cpl. Duncombe – have you remembered the cutters?

'Yes, sir.'

'How many?'

'Six in all, sir.'

He realised he had whispered the same questions a dozen times.

Am I getting windy? he asked himself. Time would tell. He peered at the luminous hands on his wristwatch; 0325 precisely. Five minutes to the off. He thought of the meticulous planning he had put into it, once the fate of his platoon had been decided by the Higher Powers. The issue of compasses, service revolvers, grenades, shortened bayonets for hand-to-hand combat should it come to it, and manacles for the securing of any prisoners; all had been taken care of. The equipment they would carry was minimal. No rifles,no greatcoats,nothing which might impede the attack; and no insignia to be worn which might prove useful to the enemy when British captives or bodies were searched. The rules were elementary; simply capture or kill, and get out of it with your life.

Some of the men carried axes, others roughly fashioned trench -clubs which in their appearance closely resembled the mace of medieval warfare.

They were hideous weapons, usually fashioned by the men themselves from a chairleg or similar object through the end of which were driven sharpened steel spikes. Godfrey had shivered involuntarily when he first saw one, for of all the savageries of the Great War this thing seemed in its barbaric simplicity to epitomise the very worst.

Since then he had witnessed its usefulness more than once; but he would never cease to regard it as a vestige of Dark Age brutality, and a symbol of how little mankind had progressed.

He patted his pocket for the Verey pistol and flares. A green was already loaded ready to signal their withdrawal after the raid.

He checked his watch again. 0328. '*Sergeant*' he whispered '*move the men to the firestep Check the ladders are in position.*'

'Aye, Sir'

'Good luck, Sergeant.'

'Thank you. An' you too, Mr. Godfrey.'

Chadderton moved up the line of uneasily shifting troops.

'You 'eard Mr. Rusholme. Absolute silence, or I'll skin yer when we get back.'

Lieutenant Salini was to take the left flank with his 2nd Platoon, Gartner the centre with the 8th. while Godfrey and a nineteen year old subaltern Collings would maintain the right flank with the 7th.and 3rd. respectively. He was confident enough of Salini and Gartner; both had been around for far longer than might have been expected, and both had been at the sharp end of trench raids before; but Collings … a fresh-faced boy hardly out of school and the OTC. He'd only been with the Battalion four weeks and still suffered from that naïve idealism which drove him to prove himself. And to whom? Godfrey wondered. To admiring parents ignorant of the appalling realities of trench warfare, and more terrible still, of the trench raid? Or to some impressionable girl smitten with the subaltern's dashing uniform, brand – new from the tailors? Godfrey was increasingly apprehensive about him. The boy had been the first to volunteer for the raid, and he was shocked to hear that Warrington had approved wholeheartedly of Collings' participation. With a chill of foreboding he recalled his last words to the young man '*Hold your men back and stay as close as you can to me. Don't rush the objective. Go cautiously … '*

Go cautiously. But would he? Little in standard officer training could have equipped him for what they would soon all have to face. And the presence of Collings added yet another burden to Godfrey's already troubled mind.

The hands of his watch moved inexorably. 0329 … 0330.

'Pass the message. *Remember the gaps*.The sooner we're in, the sooner we're back.Double rum for every man when we're done. Best of luck to you all.'

All along the trench there was whispered movement as shapes of men rose against the night horizon. Now out of the trench and in the open the wind felt fresher – almost pleasant compared to the staleness and stink they'd left behind. But only a madman or one bent on suicide would have willingly exchanged it.

'Keep low and follow me as best you can.' The cutters went feverishly to work to create gaps in the British entanglements which lay before them. Godfrey drew out his revolver as he made his way through; and stooping almost double, led his men into No Man's Land.

But where was Collings and the 3rd.? Almost as soon as they had risen to the attack he had been swallowed by the darkness and now there was no trace of him or his platoon. Anger rose momentarily within Godfrey. The kid had not listened to him, had paid no attention to what he'd said. It was just as he'd suspected – the bloody idiot had gone racing off into God knows what, and with his men. It was more than he could do, to have to nursemaid some schoolboy who still thought this was all a jolly jaunt. But as swiftly as his anger had flared, it died. He had his own men's safety to think about, let alone the job they had to do. He shifted his revolver to his left hand, and wiping the sweat from his right, dismissed all thought of Collings from his mind for the time.

It seemed to take an eternity, that creeping forward from shell-hole to shell-hole, that stumbling over invisible snags – some hard and metallic, others revoltingly soft – an eternity of listening pauses and fearful hesitations until they reached the German wire. It was pretty well where he'd expected it to be, and as he had feared it was largely unbroken. Gingerly he felt his way along the rusting coils. There was nothing. No way through at any point, apparently. He jumped nervously as a hand tapped him on the shoulder.

'This way, sir.' came a whisper ' There's a gap, we reckon, twenty yards up from 'ere.'

It lay where they had noticed the greyer patch, and it appeared that Warrington had been right. The whole area was newly wired, certainly; but the Germans had inexplicably left a narrow funnel-shaped alley between the half-visible mounds which was quite free of the stuff. Godfrey checked the orientation by his compass; the gap seemed to lead directly toward the enemy line. It was all too easy; and deeply suspicious of this apparently heaven-sent opportunity he posted their two Lewis-guns in craters directly to the left and rear, to provide covering fire for their retreat.

They crept forwards once more until they were within ten yards of the enemy trench. There he signalled them to halt and listen.

At first they heard nothing but the wind playing in the entanglements behind them. Then a muffled cough reached their ears, and someone spoke. A faint glow of light illuminated the parapet briefly as a cigarette was lit by an unseen sentry. Still their presence had not been noticed The wind shifted slightly, bringing to their noses the savour of frying bacon. It was the most homely and oddly comforting of smells, yet most bizarre in their present circumstances. Here they were on the brink of a bloody surprise attack on an Enemy who was cooking his rations only yards in front of them. Had any vestige of decency remained in that conflict it would have seemed despicable to proceed. But on a raid such sentiments had to be dismissed from your mind, for they could cost you dear. At that moment the prevalent feeling amongst the platoon members was relief that the Bosches were evidently not expecting them.

As they arrived and crouched waiting, Godfrey looked once more at his watch; 0339. Collings *must* now be in position, as should Salini and Garten. As the minute hand shifted he stood upright and lifted his arm in readiness to signal. 0340. The 7th. stood likewise, and as Lieutenant Godfrey Rusholme's arm descended they moved forwards as one man toward the enemy trench.

Godfrey's boots clattered onto dry timber flooring and he cursed himself for the hellish racket he was making. Two German soldiers were stooped over a small brazier of coals, on which a mess-tin was balanced. One was seeing to the bacon whilst the other watched appreciatively. A third – the cigarette- smoker – was standing on the firestep by the loophole, but was clearly more attracted by the food than by his sentry-duties. All three turned aghast to Godfrey as he confronted them. The sentry tried to raise his rifle to fire but in a second Godfrey was on him, striking him repeatedly in his face and neck with the handle of his revolver. As the German dropped his rifle and attempted to ward off the blows Private Willis drove a bayonet through his jacket and into his chest. The German went limp and slumped to the floor; and as Willis pulled out the blade it was followed by a spurt of dark arterial blood. The pan of bacon and the brazier was kicked over, as others of the platoon sped off to investigate the trench and try to secure it. Eyes round with horror and fear, the two remaining Germans stood with their backs pressed hard against the wall of the trench and with their hands on their heads in token of surrender. All was confusion as the dim light afforded by the coals was scattered, and as the attackers floundered about with only torches to aid them. Without warning a low door of a dugout which none had noticed opened, and an unhelmeted enemy soldier stepped cautiously out.

'Albert?' he called out 'Albert? *Was ist los*? *Albert*!' But as he peered out one of the attackers dragged him upward by his shirt; then illuminated by the red light of the dugout struck him a terrible sideways blow with a club. The German groaned something amidst the blood, then quivered and lay still. Suddenly two or three small canisters with handles attached were hurled out from the door.

'Bombs! Watch for them fuckin' bombs!'

Then came a succession of blinding flashes accompanied by earsplitting detonations. Godfrey was hurled backwards and momentarly winded by the impact of Willis' body against him. As he regained himself he flashed a lamp on the soldier's remains. The front of his body was still smouldering from the blast, and Willis' face had been torn clean away from his skull as far back as his ears. Godfrey pulled himself free of the corpse and stepped over it. The alarm had well and truly been given, now. Their number was up.

'*Take the prisoners and get out quick* !' he roared. But small arms and some machine-gun fire had broken out along the line, and none could hear him. 'Bombs! *Bomb the bloody dugout*!' he shouted but too late. Four Germans rushed out of the entrance, wielding short trench-swords and pistols. There was a number of sharp reports and someone from the 7th.screamed in agony and fell forward, shot through the body. The man lay on the duckboards writhing like some reptile. Godfrey made for the nearest German and struck at him with his trench-dagger,but his opponent parried the blow with his bayonet and inflicted a deep wound in Godfrey's forearm. He winced and gritted his teeth at the pain, then lunged forward with all his body-weight, catching his opponent off-guard. The German staggered and gave Godfrey sufficient time to drive his knife into the soft part of the man's stomach. He drove the blade in again. And again. The German clutched at Godfrey – not now out of hostility but for physical support. He thrust the German from him, whereupon the man doubled up in misery retching and vomiting blood. He raised his eyes slowly and painfully to Godfrey; then he dropped them once more, and groaned. Godfrey levelled his revolver and shot him.

All along the trench the raid was going horribly wrong. Though Garten's platoon had penetrated the enemy line, bombing two dugouts and taking several prisoners the conflict had grown in intensity. In the flickering bluish light of exploding bombs men of the 16th. found themselves trapped – hemmed in on three sides by vastly superior enemy numbers which were steadily closing in upon them now that the alarm had been raised and the element of surprise had been lost. And now they were fighting for their very lives, with a scrambled retreat across the open space of No Man's Land their only way out. Communications had almost immediately broken down as German counter-attacks successfully cut off access from one part of the trench to the next.

Where Collings was, God only knew.

Shouts and explosions were peppered by the crackling of small-arms fire, with heavier bursts from machine-guns rattling and pinging across the barbed wire in front. Amidst a rain of bullets Chadderton appeared round the corner of a sap driving another German before him – a heavy set man bearing the insignia of an officer. Both were covered in blood – their own, and that of others.

'Ere's another, sir' Chadderton said grimly 'another bastard Hun for t' bag.'

'Right. That's three. We've done enough. Pass on the order for withdrawal.' The prisoners' hands were manacled behind them and they were shunted down the trench to where a ladder had been propped against the parapet. Some of the 7th. who had survived now began to gather in that section, while others further along held off the counter-attacks by hurling bombs over and around the bend in the trench. Then with dull thuds rifle-grenades began to drop among them, bouncing and rattling across the floor-planking. The first was kicked down a sap by a private called Bradbury, where it blew up with a crump, showering earth into the air. Lenaghan picked another up and tried to pitch it over the parapet but his action, though brave, was just a fraction too late. A flash, a detonation and a cry; and Godfrey watched appalled as Lenaghan was blown to pieces before his eyes, his gorge rising in his throat as he was spattered head to foot with something warm. Then yet another detonation, and a searing heat struck him like a whiplash across both legs. He looked down at his boots, which he could see even in the half – light were perforated with shrapnel-holes. And two more of the survivors were down now, with their Lance-Corporal bending over them. Pickersgill had caught the blast in the face and was shrieking over and over again ' I can't see! Help me, Georgie ! Oh, God, I can't see!' while Kealy who had lost his left hand was rocking back and forth, trying to stem the flow of blood by cradling the tattered remains of his own wrist.

'*Get a field dressing on it quick! Staunch it* !' Godfrey bawled amidst the din ' We'll take them with us. We're getting out !' As he spoke he fired the

Verey pistol and the flare ascended and burst over the scene of horror. Not one man waited for it to drop, but instead climbed upward as quickly as his wounds allowed, illuminated by the greenish light. Kealy and Pickergill were guided up the steps of one ladder and had attained the top of the parapet when a hidden German machine –gun – cunningly trained on the gap in the wire- opened up, raking the area of the parapet from a position no more than thirty yards away. Kealy was dragged downward in the nick of time, but Pickersgill remained bemusedly upright. The blinded man's shrieks could be heard even above the rattling of the gun, as he staggered this way and that. Despite his guide's frantic attempts to pull him down it was too late for them both The shrieking suddenly ceased as the two fell riddled and lifeless only yards in front of where the remainder of the 7th. huddled with their prisoners.

It was fortunate that Godfrey had posted the Lewis-teams where he had; for their presence was in turn unsuspected by the German machine-gunners. In the dark the flashes from their weapon had advertised its position as surely as if it had been lit up. Now the Lewis –guns concealed in the shell-crater were trained in turn on the aperture through which the enemy was firing. In a few seconds the gun was silenced, its crew wounded or dead. But the firing also gave Godfrey and his platoon a beacon which led them to the gap in the wire. Crawling and stumbling they made their way back by the same shell-holes and craters, waiting for lulls in the enemy fire.Godfrey mentally counted the men in as they dropped gratefully into a deeper bowl-shaped cavity.Seventeen out of the thirty who had started barely a half-hour before. He hoped to God there were others still alive elsewhere, separated from the main body but making their own way back And the three prisoners were in almost as bad a state as their captors. Two were terrified, and eager only to get the protracted nightmare over with. They were pitifully compliant as they nursed their own wounds, obeying their captors' every instruction and gesture as best they could. But the third German – the officer – glowered defiantly back as they attempted to dodge the enemy fire by swift movement from hole to hole. It seemed to them that he was purposely trailing behind, moving sluggishly with the intention of impeding their retreat. And the situation was getting more desperate by the minute. Each time they broke cover to hobble onward he had to be dragged reluctantly to his feet though his legs appeared to be unwounded, and the only means of steering him was by pulling him along by the rope which tethered him. In spite of the desperate blows and kicks of his guards he maintained the same shambling gait, and the same expression of hatred for his captors. He was rapidly becoming a liability.

Godfrey crawled to the rim of the crater and peered over. Intense fighting was still taking place further across where the platoons of Salini, Garten and Collings were engaged. He watched as crackling gunfire dispelled the night with tiny stabs of lightning, with here and there the vicious accompaniment of exploding grenades. *Poor sods* he thought. *Poor bloody sods.*

There was need now for even greater haste. The Germans understood well what the purpose of the raid had been and would take every measure necessary nomatter how desperate to prevent the prisoners from falling into British hands. He knew that the coordinates for the sector would at that very moment be winging their way to the enemy batteries, and it would only be a matter of time before the bombardment began in earnest. And then there would be the British barrage to add to it.

He scrambled downwards and ordered them to be ready for their next move. But the German officer would not budge. He lay there, scowling at his captors and refusing to get to his feet regardless of the blows which rained upon him. He was a very large man, and Godfrey was not prepared to endanger the lives of the two soldiers detailed to guard him by ordering them to stand upright and haul him to his feet. Precious time was being wasted in this grim charade. Suddenly the man began to shout at the top of his voice. *'Hilfe! Hilfe mich! Ich bin ein Gefangene! Hilfe'*

Chadderton clapped his hands over the man's mouth to try to stifle the cries, but the German flung him off and continued to bellow.

'The bugger's goin' to give our position away !' growled Chadderton ' you could 'ear the swine in Paris!'

Godfrey drew his revolver. The German stopped his shouting as he looked at the weapon, and considered Godfrey coldly.

'You cannot shoot me'.His English was refined and perfect. 'You came for prisoners, did you not? I am only of use to you alive. Those two over there – what do they know?' his tone was supercilious, sneering. 'What *do* they know? You would be unwise to act hastily.'

'You overestimate your importance ' replied Godfrey in German, imitating the other's tone. 'Glauben sie das sie sind mehr wichtig als ein Leben von meine Soldaten?' *Do you believe that you are really more important than the life of one of my soldiers?*

A look of surprise crossed the German's face at the reply. Godfrey cocked the revolver and, arm outstretched, aimed it steadily at the man's forehead. 'Stehe jetzt! Oder ich habe keine Alternative. *I will kill you'* The German looked into Godfrey's eyes and saw that he was in deadly earnest.

His resolve wavered, but still he did not move. '*Stehe! Jetzt!*' came the sharp command once more. The German prided himself on being an astute judge of character; and he saw that with this British officer there would not be a third time. In a moment the German's defiance crumbled and he struggled reluctantly to his feet once more.

Their return through the British wire proved to be almost as hazardous as their negotiation of the enemy entanglements. The gaps made earlier by their own cutters had of necessity been narrow, and though coloured markers had been left they were almost invisible in the murk except when the searcher was within a foot or two of them. And worse, their wire cutting gear had been abandoned in the fighting. Godfrey realised that one man could accomplish more – and less conspicuously – than the whole platoon. It was not a job he relished, but equally not a job he was prepared to order another man to do. Though his wounds still throbbed terribly, though he could feel the blood squelching in his boots, the bitter choice was at least made for him; stay put and await the dawn, and the imminent barrage – and if they survived that, they would have to run the gauntlet of the enemy snipers when they finally made a move. Or be prepared to search blindly in the dark for the gaps, with all the risks that it entailed. Even as he considered them he decided that the former was no option. Leaving Chadderton sheltering with the remainder in a shell-hole he slipped over the edge and crept forward cat-like in the dark, watching for the tell-tale glistening of water drops on the wire. It wasn't hard to find. The unbroken belts ran parallel to their hiding-place, and within only a few yards. Godfrey was feeling his way along it when a distant enemy machine gun commenced firing, traversing the immediate area with steady sweeps. Clearly the gunners had orders to maintain a constant fire, though by the way it was being done it seemed they had little heart for it. Yet the regularity of their shooting helped him, for he was able to conduct the search in phases. As the bullets struck the rusting masses some ricocheted off metallically and it was not difficult for Godfrey to gauge when the stream of bullets was approaching. Then he would almost claw himself into the ground as they passed barely inches above him. Their closeness caused him to remember his previous wounding, and once more he became conscious of his shoulder, involuntarily turning it so that it lay furthest from harm. As the deadly stream passed over he would cautiously rise to his knees and continue his furtive searching. Inch by painstaking inch he groped his way along, but still there was no gap.

He was convinced that they could not possibly have gone so far over and was on the point of turning around when a cloth tape fluttered limply against his hand. Bringing his eyes close to it he could make out its colour; red. With renewed hope he searched on,and in a second or two had found the corresponding marker.

Chapter Fourteen

THE PRISONERS had been marched stumbling away to the rear. With his eyes closed Godfrey stood leaning against the wall of the Reserve Trench. A lit Woodbine hung from his mouth though he did not make any attempt to draw on it, its end glowing red at each intake of his breath. All the platoon – at least, those who'd survived the raid – had been dispatched to the Forward Dressing Stations where their wounds would be assessed and they would either be patched up and sent back, or in the more serious cases, be ordered down the line to hospital. He knew he ought to be going down to the FDS himself; but the prospect of taking his boots off, though his calves and feet hurt abominably, was one he could not face just then. And he had a foreboding that, though he and the remnants of his platoon were back, the matter of the raid was far from being settled. Slowly and with growing apprehension he made his way once more to the Forward Trench – a place most feared yet which he and his men had gratefully regained barely five minutes earlier.

An atmosphere of nervous inactivity pervaded there. Beside the posted sentries a few of the reserves from the 2nd.3rd. and 8th. platoons were loitering about. The feeling was one of profound unease.

'Have Mr. Garten, Mr. Salini or Mr.Collings got back?' Godfrey read on the face of a corporal what his answer would be. *'Have they got back?'*

'No, sir. None of 'em. That's what we're waitin' for, sir. They're still out there. But it's good to see *you* back, Mr.Rusholme.'

Sudden anxiety for those doomed officers and men together with an overwhelming remorse for his anger towards Collings combined to goad him into action. Despite his wounds he could not bear to wait about there as all the others seemed to be doing. While the sentries watched in disbelief he seized a ladder; and ramming it against the trench wall he climbed once more into No Man's Land just as the German artillery opened their retaliatory bombardment in hellish earnest.

Entirely alone and lying exposed on this strip of pulverised earth Godfrey took stock of the insane position he had put himself in. Common sense told him there had been no need for it. Was it simply a stupid act of bravado in the same self-seeking vein which he had condemned in Collings? He had done all and more than was expected of him in the raid, and with the few stragglers who had made their way back separately he had lost fewer than eight of the thirty men he had led in. He could still turn back. For once no-one could censure, no-one could indict; he had gone over the top a second time, and out of his own free will. There was still time – time to crawl back, time to find a dugout, time to get to the FDS and get his arm and legs fixed. He lay there as the shells howled and burst about him. Time till then had been governed by the passage of the hands on his wristwatch. Time, he saw then as a blinding truth, was no more than the invention of Man to mark his passage from life, to death. It was the creation of a mind preoccupied with imposing a logical framework upon the illogical. When he looked at it in that light, Time did not matter any more for him. In contrast to the fear of only a hour before he found to his astonishment that he could view his position with serenity and calmness. Here he bore no responsibility for the lives of others, but only for his own. And he valued his life at nought.

But then there was the poor innocent Collings. Godfrey had known and feared what the unfortunate Collings could not know, and lacked sufficient experience to fear. He could not dismiss him from his conscience and abandon him to his fate. Godfrey was a pragmatist, and in all likelihood Collings was already dead, and his platoon with him. But despite it all he *had* to know. And he had to be there, come what may.

Collings had not followed him through the gap which the 7th. had used. Yet they had got through the wire somehow, and attained their objectives along the enemy trench as the ferocity of the fighting seemed to confirm. But as yet it was impossible for Godfrey to move a step further out of the hole which sheltered him. And as he lay there the storm of the enemy bombardment broke in fury on No Man's Land. He dragged a sheet of corrugated iron over him like a harsh counterpane, and drew it over his head- not for the feeble protection it afforded but because it gave the illusion of shelter, while the tornado of fire and steel searched for the raiding party and its prisoners. The magnitude of it overwhelmed him; it was hellishly impressive, all that murderous power trained on one spot on the planet's face. How many of the enemy's artillery were engaged, he could not guess; but huddled beneath his makeshift shelter he was determined to defy them all.

It afforded him a bitter satisfaction that all this was because of what *they* had done. And still the shelling mounted until it seemed to howl with one sustained demonic voice. The sour fumes of the detonations blew in low white columns across the tormented earth, choking him; and he coughed and heaved for air.

Half-stunned he laboriously pushed away the sheeting. He'd

disregarded his wounds while the bombardment was at its height; but now with its cessation they ached anew, and doubly. His feet felt swollen to twice their size, and the knife-wound in his arm throbbed constantly. Yet it was these and other unseen pains which impelled him forward. He rose with difficulty, and limped back toward the German lines.

Though the light had improved with the dawn, the visibility had not. He immediately saw an advantage in this; for whilst the fumes from the reeking shell-craters obscured his sight of No Mans Land, they also rendered him invisible to the enemy. And there was the double blessing of a clinging mist.

Some machine–gun fire stuttered away to the left, where he suspected the German strongpoint to be; and he stooped instinctively. But it died away as it had started, leaving a sepulchral quiet in its place. And everywhere now as he looked about him there were bodies, thrown back or slumped forward or mutilated beyond recognition by shrapnel. Some lay singly while others crouched in small huddles just as they had been caught in the enfilading fire of the enemy's guns.

He turned one over in the hope of identifying whose platoon it was. The dead eyes which stared up at him were those of Chappell, the sergeant of the 3rd. – Collings' Platoon. Slowly he release the man's shoulder and the body rolled limply back down again.

He paused by a deep crater in which five or six corpses lay. He considered them unemotionally for a moment, and was about to move on when one and then another of them stirred. He heard the clicking of a revolver mechanism, and turned just in time to see the weapon being levelled at him.

'It's one of our officers – *it's Mr Rusholme*' someone croaked 'Fer Christ's sake put that bloody gun down.' But the revolver remained levelled at him, as if the soldier who held it expected only hostility,and could not believe that the figure gazing down at him was a friend. The one who had spoken extended his hand cautiously and removed the gun from the soldier's grasp. He offered no resistance as he was deprived of it, but continued to peer ahead of him with unseeing eyes. Godfrey struggled down to them, trying to avoid treading on the bodies, and the pool of stagnant water at the bottom which was reddening with blood.

'Which platoon are you.?' There was no immediate answer.

'*I said, which platoon are you?*' Godfrey took hold of the other by the arm. He shook him roughly, and the soldier winced.

'I'm sorry. Are you from Mr. Collings' platoon? *Are you from the 3rd.*?'

'I'm not. But '*e* was, though.' The soldier looked across to his companion who had not altered his posture nor the fixity of his stare. 'I was with the 2nd. With Mr Salini.' Godfrey felt a sickening chill as he noted the soldier's use of the past tense. *Was*.

'What are your names?'

'Shaw, sir. An' Willmott.'

'Where *are* the platoons, Shaw? And where are Mr. Collings, and Mr. Salini, and Mr. Garten?'

'Didn't you see the boys, sir? On the way across? They're all about 'ere – most of 'em, any road. Rest of 'em are in t' Jerry trench. That's where we left 'em.'

'*And your officers. Where are they*?' Shaw turned his head almost languidly and nodded in the direction of the German wire entanglements. 'There, sir.'

'All three of them?'

'All three of 'em.'

Godfrey recoiled as if from a physical blow. 'Shaw, you *must* tell me what happened.' His voice was altered from that of a commander to one who pleaded. The man turned his face to him with eyes that had witnessed nightmares.

'It were terrible, Mr Rusholme. Terrible. We got lost as soon as we'd gone into No Man's Land, and we ended up bumpin' into the 2nd. and Mr Salini. He weren't too pleased, neither.'

'It's what I feared' Godfrey muttered to himself. 'Go on, Shaw.'

'Well, we got through the wire alright in the end – though it weren't cut by the barrage like we'd expected. We 'ad to go at it ourselves, y 'see? An' it took us longer than we'd bargained for.

Anyway, when we got to Jerry's fire trench he gave it us hot. A lot o' our chaps… .well, we took a couple o' prisoners, but then Jerry counter-attacked… .' Shaw paused, staring ahead as he struggled with scenes too appalling to recount. 'Well, 'e came at us all at once, from both sides an' over the top. We held 'im off as long as we could, but it weren't no use…… '

'And then?'

'Then Mr. Salini ordered the retreat, an' said he'd cover us as we withdrew. But Mr.Collings couldn't find the gaps we'd cut in the wire, an' when Jerry opened up on us from that strongpoint well… he got upset, sir.'

'What d'you mean *upset?*'

Shaw's reply was reluctant. 'Upset, sir. He ran about, tearin' at the wire, an' screamin' out loud. He just screamed an' screamed sir. An' as 'e tried to push 'is way through, he got caught up. Then'e was hit, but not bad, not at first. Mr. Salini saw it as he was withdrawin' himself, an' went over to try to get Mr. Collings off, but then 'e was hit too, but bad. An' then Mr. Garten… '

'Mr. Garten, *too*?'

'Mr.Collings… he… kept up that screamin, all the time… an' he was writhin' about in the wire, an' getting' more caught-up the more he did it. An' then Mr. Garten rushed in, an' pulled at'im frantic, like 'e was 'is own brother. Then Jerry… ' Shaw paused to regain his composure. ' They're up there now, Mr.Rusholme.' and his voice broke with emotion ' Oh, sir. It was awful to see… awful.'

'How did you get to here?'

'Sergeant Chappell saw how it was, an' shouted *'c'mon lads! We'll get out, yet!* An' *he'd* remembered where the gaps were, so he led us through. But Jerry put up flares, an' we got lit up. Then the buggers finished the job.'

So that was how it had ended. Three out of four platoons decimated, and their officers with them. Why, he asked himself, had *he* survived, when the others had not?

'Over there, you say?'

'Over there, sir.'

Godfrey crawled to the side of the crater facing the enemy.

'You're not goin' over, sir, surely?' Shaw's voice was filled now with alarm. ' There's nowt you can do for ' em. Sir! Don't go!'

But Godfrey had already gone. Taking advantage of the fog he moved along the belt of wire indicated previously by Shaw. It was an easy route to follow, for a broken line of corpses continued onward, hedged in by the cruel wire, and pointing like ghastly signposts to where his brother officers had died. Suddenly he came upon them, as the fog shrouding the scene shifted a little.

To one side hung Salini. His body was spreadeagled backward in the wire as if he was resting there, his face unmarked and strangely peaceful, appearing to all the world as if he were sleeping. Until one looked for his legs, which had been severed completely at the thighs by the intense machine-gunfire, and which now lay a few yards off in a bloody heap. Beyond him was Garten, his fists still clutching in his death throes at the tattered jacket of the doomed Collings, as he struggled in his final seconds of life to free the youth. And then there was Collings. The expression on the poor dead face was terrible beyond anything Godfrey had ever seen, and it harrowed him to his very soul. He had seen fear before, but that face seemed to encompass all the terrors that could ever be. Godfrey could not bear to look any longer and he turned away for a moment, roughly wiping his face with his sleeve. Of all the losses, appalling though they were individually, this had to be the worst; for it was so unnecessary, and so utterly pointless. He resolved he would not leave them thus, as a spectacle for the enemy or as carrion for rats. He gently prized Garten's dead fingers away but the claws of the barbed wire refused obstinately to yield up their victim. This, together with the ungainly angle in which Collings lay made shifting the body an impossible task for a wounded and spent man. Godfrey pulled feebly but only succeeded in causing the heaped coils to shift like a giant spring. The Germans had hung tin cans and other metallic objects from the wire for just this eventuality; and now Godfrey heard a distinct clanging a few yards away. Almost immediately sporadic rifle-shots broke out; then a machine-gun began to traverse the area, rattling blindly into the blanket of mist. Bullets began to sing off the wire not far from him.

Leaving them hanging there was somehow the worst of it; and Godfrey would not forgive himself for what he believed was his failure of his comrades. So began his second and most agonising retreat from No Man's Land that day.

'We must get back to our lines while the mist holds.' He had by some miracle or other avoided the enemy fire, though it had at times come very close. Now he faced Shaw and Willmott once more. The Germans were probably as exhausted as their enemies, and gradually the firing had dwindled to the occasional crack of a rifle.

'Can't, sir. Me leg's shot quite through. I think it's broke. You go back, sir. We'll be alright.'

'Nonsense. What about Willmott?'

'Shell-shock, sir. I don't think 'e knows *where* 'e is.'

Godfrey stood and dragged the lost Willmott to his feet. Then hauling Shaw up and over the edge of the crater, he motioned Willmott to support the wounded man under one arm while he took the other. And thus they struggled the sixty miserable yards to the British Forward Trench.

Chapter Fifteen

IN SPITE OF his protests Godfrey was ordered to report to the Base Hospital to have the bayonet-wound cauterised and stitched, and have his legs looked at. Though a dozen shrapnel – splinters were removed, more had to be left either because of their nearness to an artery or simply because they could not be found. The Medical Officer had offered the opinion that as the injuries were hardly minor he might swing it as a 'Blighty' – would Godfrey like to have a few weeks at home in England? It wouldn't be difficult, given what he'd heard about Godfrey's conduct of the raid. All the Battalion was buzzing about it, he said. And if the rumours were true, Lieutenant Rusholme was up for a 'gong'. Godfrey turned over and faced the wall. All the time he lay there in the clinical quiet scenes from that terrible raid rose before him – even when awake, and with eyes fully open. He thought he saw bodies strewn across the floor, blood on the white uniforms which fussed around him, and loops of barbed wire in the corridors. And worst of all he saw men caught inextricably on wire which jerked and moved as if it had a malevolent will of its own. He would blink hard, and the visions would gradually fade. He thought he was going mad, and he resolved to get out of there as soon as possible.

Within a few days of the operations he discharged himself. Walking was not easy, but he persuaded the MO to certify him as fit and ready to return to Front- Line Duty. The MO shook his head uncomprehendingly, but signed the papers anyway.

He had been visited by Warrington, who passed on Helene's warmest wishes to him. Godfrey thought this a bit odd, since he himself had received nothing from his sister for some time, and news of his wounding could hardly have reached London in the intervening days. Warrington congratulated him heartily on the resounding success of the 'show'. Brigade were delighted with the outcome, and the prisoner brought in had proved to be of incalculable value. Yes, their losses had been heavy, and the deaths of their fellow officers were to be deeply regretted. And he was very sorry about Godfrey's wounds. But given the nature of raids losses had of course to be expected, and must be balanced against the great advantages gained.

It had been a splendid action, all in all, and the Battalion had distinguished itself. He'd heard *that* from the Brigadier in person.

Warrington congratulated Godfrey once more, and left. But not before he had whispered confidentially *the Big Push is definitely on. We're to know before the week's out.*

Had there been no other reason, Godfrey would have discharged himself and returned to the 16th as soon as he was able.

Within five days of his wounding he was back with the 7th. platoon, who had been pulled out of the Line with the remainder of F Company. The reserves of the three ill-fated platoons had played no part in the raid, and had therefore remained unscathed. But with the deaths of Salini, Garten and Collings they were effectively leaderless with not one officer between them, and only one surviving sergeant who with a mere ten men had somehow found his own way back. Godfrey was detailed to take all four platoons to the rear, where they were to await replacements for the officers and other ranks killed or wounded. It was a profoundly gloomy period, this filling of gaps in the ranks. When not seeing to the replacements and the wellbeing of the platoons he took to walking alone in the worn-out countryside thereabouts. He persuaded himself that he needed to get away from the asphyxiating climate of the Officers' Mess; but he found the walks unsatisfying because from being purposeful rambles they invariably degenerated into aimless wanderings. And once more the visions returned to plague him. This self-scourging was relentless as he blamed himself directly for Collings' death, and indirectly for the deaths of Salini and Garten. Had he intervened more forcefully on Collings' behalf when Warrington was still seeking volunteers for the raid, the youth might never have been allowed to take part. Then he and his platoon might never have become lost, and Salini and Garten might never had died trying to save him. Or so he told himself a hundred times a day. In the absence of any close friend to whom he could unburden his soul and gain an objective and rational opinion these grossly distorted judgements about himself grew in his fevered mind, feeding the conviction that he of all of them should have died that night.

The preparations for the long-awaited *Big Push* were ironically to be Godfrey's saving grace – at least for his immediate sanity; for the planning behind it was certainly immense both in its volume and its detail, and would require the total commitment of all front-line officers and Staff. This brainchild of Field Marshall Douglas Haig, they were told at Battalion Headquarters, would prove to be the ultimate blow which would crush the Enemy in one; would effectively neutralise his armies in the field and enable the Allies to sweep through the remnants of the German defences and head for Berlin and Ultimate Victory over the Kaiser. It was just what everyone had been waiting for, and now they were on the brink of it. Some of the Senior staff said they felt proud and even privileged to be playing a part – however small. It all sounded quite splendid, particularly as the Top Brass assured the field commanders that it simply could not fail.

Godfrey sat listening impassively to the eulogies about the Plan as Warrington addressed the Platoon commanders. It occurred to Godfrey that the ones who sat forward in their seats with eager faces were invariably the replacements, mostly fresh from Officer Training. As far as he was concerned he had heard a lot of it before. To him these young men resembled Collings too much, with their scrubbed pinkness, their school banter and the light of battle in their eyes; so he didn't stick around in the Mess more than he had to. There were few left there that he knew now, anyway. And they were growing fewer. To the youthful draft he appeared a sour and embittered older officer whom it was advisable not to cross; they would not have believed that he was barely six years' older than the youngest of them.

Warrington informed them that a full – sized replica of the Battalion's objectives was at that moment in the course of completion in open country some miles to the rear at Briquemesnil. It was accurate down to the finest detail, he said with some pride, and every feature which the attacking force of Manchesters would encounter was represented – down to the last building, trench and fortification. The platoons would be drilled in what was expected of them – where they must cross, which strongpoints to assault, and which to hold. They might expect some pockets of resistance from the remnants of the German defenders, and with this in mind training would be given in the layout of the streets and alleys of the objective, which lay some two miles behind enemy lines. Every officer and man would have his tasks set out for him, and to which he should dedicate himself single-mindedly. High Command were brimming with optimism about the outcome which, Warrington assured them, could only be that of a complete and crushing defeat for the Enemy. More significant and sinister was the order that all NCOs were to be instructed in fullest detail as to the tasks specifically allotted to their platoon, so that in the event of officer casualties the NCOs could themselves assume command. The name of their objective? He didn't think mentioning it would matter too much, seeing that they would know about it soon enough anyway.

It was to be the village of Montauban – within a stonesthrow of the River Somme.

At the conclusion of the meeting Warrington motioned for Godfrey to stay behind.

'Good to see you about on your pins again, old man' he breezed. 'How are your wounds coming along?'

'Very well, actually. I hardly notice them' Godfrey lied 'Thank you for asking.'

'Think nothing of it, Rusholme' Warrington continued 'we can't have you laid up while the whole Battalion's *girding its loins* so to speak.'

'My thoughts exactly.'

'We'll need your brand of level-headed courage if the going gets a little rough. I said precisely that to the CO just this morning.'

Godfrey thanked him again.

'Actually, Rusholme, I'm in a bit of a sticky corner, and I wondered if you'd help me out.'

'If I can.'

'Well, you see, old chap, it's these letters of condolence. To the families of Cansini, Garten and Collins.'

'Coll*ings*'

'Quite. They're so damned difficult to write. I – I didn't *know* them as well as you did, old boy. I wondered if you've any ideas, that's all.'

'You haven't *written* them yet?' Godfrey was appalled. 'Why ask me?' he returned with some bitterness. 'You were their Commanding Officer. I can appreciate that the job is distressing in the extreme, but it's in the line of duty that we sometimes have to do it. *You* must write their letters, as I have had to for my own platoon.' Godfrey would not allow Warrington any easy way out. He'd sought battlefield command; well, this was a tragic but inseparable part of it. While some wrote such letters to a formula, there was scant decency in it. And he would not provide Warrington with any acceptable form of words. 'No. I'm sorry. I can't help you in this. It's something you must do personally.'

Warrington shrugged. 'Oh well' he said 'just thought I'd ask. I'd better get down to it, I suppose.'

But on his return to the dugout Godfrey took out his writing- case and three envelopes. He couldn't depend on Warrington to say what needed to be said to the grieving families of his dead brother-officers.

'Incidentally' Warrington had concluded 'I'm taking a spot of leave – it *is* due to me, you know ' he said defensively 'so if there's anything you want to be taken back, letter or parcel, I can arrange to have it delivered for you.' Godfrey declined the offer.

Before the week was out the 16th.Manchesters received orders to transfer from their billets to the railhead. From there the whole Battalion was marched to Briquemesnil, where their training for the Great Offensive was to begin in earnest.

Chapter Sixteen

THE WEEK following the award of his degree was one of almost unbroken celebration for Oliver.

In addition to the boozy trips round Manchester masterminded by Pottinger,warm letters of congratulation began to arrive from the expected quarters – one in the unsteady hand of Captain Bonnard, another from Helene, and yet another from Archie McLeish and from colleagues at the Hospital; but less expected were the ones from his old Headmaster Mr. Swan, and from his parents. Penned by Ida on behalf of them both she expressed their considerable satisfaction at the honour Oliver had brought upon himself and upon the family.

He read the letter through many times, and came to the unavoidable conclusion that the author of the congratulatory part was his mother, whereas that of the closing eulogy to Godfrey and his accomplishments was clearly his father. But Ida's voice rang out loudly in the closing words

When will you come to visit us, my Darling? for we miss you dreadfully and it has been too long since we have seen you.

Oliver felt guilty at his avoidance of Desbury, and decided that the gentle reproof contained in his mother's lines was just. He decided there and then he would visit the next weekend.

A secret party had been arranged by Oliver's fellow students at Nelson Place with the connivance of Mrs.Monaghan. She and Dolly spent many extra hours in the kitchen and scullery baking the mounds of pies and cakes which the landlady knew from experience would last only a short time once the Medical Gentlemen were let loose on them; and bottles of adequate French wine appeared mysteriously from one of Wilfred Hallett's shady sources.

During the evening of the surprise party Oliver had been reading quietly in his rooms when the dinner gong received a vigorous pounding from Dolly. Thinking nothing more of it than she was a little later than usual he made his way down the stairs to the dining room. Grasping the doorknob he strolled casually in,only to be met by the cheers of his fellow residents. He looked around him, speechless.

He took in the long mahogany table which was heaped almost to collapsing, took in the crystal glasses which twinkled in the lamplight, and the gleaming bottles. Only slowly did it dawn on him that all this had been done in *his* honour. Pottinger and Hallett guided him to the head of the table where a carver-chair had been draped with ribbons and a Union Jack.

The meal went with a swing, and cheered by the wine someone yelled 'Speech!' Then others joined in. ' C'mon Rusholme!. Give us a speech!'

Oliver declined at first; but when it became clear that he had no alternative, he embarked on a vote of thanks to all his friends and colleagues, '*and most particularly Mrs. Monaghan for putting up with me for so long, in sickness and in health…* '

'You're not married to her yet, old man' Hallett chipped in

'… *and for this splendid feast!'* Oliver concluded. He raised his glass to Mrs.M who blushingly accepted the toast, and there were more cheers. He had just finished and was about to sit down when he glimpsed a movement outside the door. A slight shadow passed across the light in the hall, and then was gone. It could only have been Dolly Chadderton, who must have been listening beyond the doorway. Dolly! *You bloody heartless fool, Rusholme! Here you've been chattering on regardless, thanking everybody but the one person who helped you through more than anyone else!* Oliver cursed himself for his thoughtlessness. Excusing himself from the table he slipped out of the room and headed for the kitchen. He knocked on the door. There was no answer. He knocked again, and more urgently. Still nothing.

At that moment all else was secondary to his burning desire to say… to say what, precisely? *Thank you*? It sounded so effete, given what he *had* to say – what he yearned to say – to this girl who had been his support throughout his illness, who had been beside him day and night.

He let himself into the kitchen. It was empty. She was not there.

He looked to the scullery door. It was closed. He crossed to it in a few strides and paused, listening. From within he could hear the clattering of crockery being washed in the stone trough, and a girl's voice singing -or trying her best to sing – amidst weeping. Oliver gently opened the door. 'Dolly?'

She turned her face away from him, wiped her eyes with her pinafore, and continued with her washing.

'Dolly. Can you ever forgive me for my ingratitude, and my unkindness?' She did not pause in her work, but inclined her head to the task as if she had heard not a word of his apology. He stepped forward, still closer to her – so close that he could see the individual wisps of hair which had strayed from the rest. He noticed the scrap of lilac ribbon which held it, and was struck by the graceful curve of her neck.

'Dolly! Will you listen to me, please? *Please* turn round.'

The movement of her arms ceased, but still she did not turn. 'There is no-one in this world I would less willingly hurt than you.' he continued. 'Nobody ever cared for me as you did. You have been my good friend, Dolly. Please say you forgive me.'

Her breathing came fitfully, as she fought to control her sobs. In her turn she too damned herself for her naïve self-delusion Her tears were less for the slighting she had suffered than for what she saw now was the hopelessness of her love for this man, whose social status was – and always would be – unattainably higher than hers. A cheap little serving-girl on shillings a week – what trick of the light had made her aspire to the impossible, and cause her to assume that she could be someone whom she now saw in her misery she could never be.

She raised her head to peer unseeingly through the tiny window which lit the scullery. Her hands still rested in the soapy water, and still she would not turn to him. Oliver came beside her and reached into the suds for her hands. They were surprisingly small – he had never touched them before – and slowly he drew them upwards and out, enfolding them in his own. Then in a moment of impulse he raised them to his lips and gently kissed them, wet as they were. Only then did she turn to him, her eyes red-rimmed and lustrous with tears. The sight of her face cut him more than any word could have done.

'Forgive me,Dolly! Say you do.'

'What can *I* say, sir? Who am I, to forgive you?'

'Dolly! Don't call me *sir*. You know my name, well enough.'

'Don't trifle with me, sir. Please don't. Go now. '

Oliver was about to say something, but thinking better of it took a step backwards and remained silent; then bowing to her, he left the scullery.

A week later Oliver returned from Manchester to find that Dolly Chadderton the serving-maid had unexpectedly handed in her notice with immediate effect, and had left Nelson Place to return to her mother's. She had not even said goodbye to him. Mrs. Monaghan was quite put out, and said she thought the girl had had more about her, but obviously she'd been wrong. Oliver caught the landlady looking strangely at him once or twice; but she said nothing further on the matter.

Oliver's first impulse was to take the next available train to Desbury and seek Dolly out. Once there he would put things right between them. But he immediately saw the error in such a course of action. The girl had gone away to escape from Nelson Place, and principally – or so he believed– from him. He had been guided by his own feelings in the matter – feelings to which he had hitherto been a complete stranger. Lack of experience had led him to misread the signs, he told himself; what had been her simple acts of kindness had been misinterpreted by him as something stronger, something entirely different from mere duty.

He cursed himself for his impulsive behaviour in the scullery. She probably believed he had wanted to take advantage of her, and he felt that his apparent indifference at other times could only have supported this impression. Because she was poor and a servant did not give him the right to treat her any differently than if she'd been a Countess. In Oliver's code to do so would have been beneath contempt. But whilst he was desperate to correct the misunderstanding he had no choice but to let her go, and live with his aching heart.

Blinded by his own self –disparagement he was quite unable to see that the girl was deeply and irretrievably in love with him.

His concern for his brother was to prove another dark shadow in the sunlight of his success. Oliver had more time to read the papers now; and he voraciously consumed every piece of news, trying to glean any hints as to the real situation on the Western Front from the welter of jingoistic optimisms and half-truths pumped out by the Press. Here and there rational and articulate voices were being raised in opposition to the continuing War. A few of the most courageous, of the calibre of Lady Ottoline Morrell, dared to challenge the Establishment's bloodlust via Letters to the Editor; but she and her group of protestors were clearly only a tiny minority – a minority increasingly marginalised by being branded at best as unbalanced and at worst as downright traitors. Oliver winced as he read the vitriol which flowed in the wake of every letter. Nevertheless he got an impression albeit faint that all was not going quite as well as might be expected. And always there were the seemingly endless Casualty Lists.

He had not assisted at Levenham for a good many weeks, and had not returned there since his illness. But the place, the patients and McLeish were never far from his thoughts. Now he resolved to go back as soon as practicable and do what he could to help before receiving his first placement. He had requested a posting to Levenham but the powers-that-be had brusquely informed him that it was entirely out of the question. The decision was not his to make, the officious little man behind the desk informed him; he could not pick-and-choose, and would have to wait and see. The most he could hope for was a place in one of Manchester's larger hospitals – but even that could by no means be guaranteed. So Oliver sat and waited for the administrative wheels to grind into motion.

Increasingly he felt the need for a change – felt the need to move his focus physically away from Nelson Place, where he had spent close on five years and where he now felt very alone. Each time he crossed the landing his glance would wander involuntarily to the narrow flight of stairs leading upward to the attic room which had once been Dolly Chadderton's home, and which now was just an empty and hollow space above him. Everything about the house now served in one way or another to remind him of her – the opening and closing of the dining-room door; light footsteps on the stairs, the echoing of a female voice from the kitchen; and with each reminder he would always feel a lump in his throat as the image of her face and her slight figure rose before him. He had to escape from the pain of her leaving which stung him every hour he was there. Others of the 'Medical Gentlemen' had already departed or were about to depart, to go their separate ways. Pottinger had taken up his post at Leeds Infirmary some two weeks' previously,and Wilfred Hallett was due to go to down to Barnet in London in the course of the next few days. Packed boxes and roped-up trunks had already begun to appear outside his rooms.

Having decisively failed his Final Year the future for George Gilbank had appeared less certain until the evening before Hallett's farewell party. From the manner of the knock on his door Oliver had no doubt who was outside.

'Come on in, Gilbank.' Oliver offered him a seat and his guest perched himself on the edge with a curiously animated expression on his face.

'I hope you don't mind, Rusholme' he began 'but after the mess–up in my exams, I 've been thinking hard.'

'You're going to retake, of course?'

'Well, that's what I'd really welcome your opinion about, old chap. Y'see, I don't really think I'm cut out for the medical exam side of things. Find 'em ruddy difficult, actually!' he added, smiling ruefully at his own shortcomings. Oliver had known just how much of a struggle his medical studies had been for the kindly Gilbank. He had always had a soft spot for this ineffectual young man, and had sympathised with his problems; but did not see the necessity of his having to give up his hopes of qualification entirely.

'You *are* going to retake, surely, after all those years of work?'

'Well, I've had a few ideas on the subject. I thought I might do something a little different for a while.'

'Go on.'

'I wondered about the possibility of joining up' he said simply.

His words struck a chill note in Oliver's ears.

'No! Don't even consider it. The army's losses are terrible. Even the Government can't cover them up. We're losing thousands a week! And I fear it could get even worse. They're all talking about another Offensive somewhere along the Western Front, more massive than anything they've attempted up to now. People are saying it'll end the War quickly, but it still makes me feel uneasy. George, you mustn't do it.'

Gilbank looked rather abashed. 'I thought your brother Godfrey was in the army.'

'He is, and I wish to God he wasn't. You don't know the half of what he's been through. Do reconsider!.'

'I can't.'

'Why on Earth not?'

'I've already done it.'

Oliver made no reply.

'I've joined up, Rusholme. Not as a soldier. I couldn't do that. But they thought my skills would come in particularly handy as an orderly or a stretcher-bearer. You know, patch 'em up on the battlefield and bring'em back in safe and sound.'

Gilbank's innocence mortified Oliver. What yarns had been spun to get him to sign his life away?

'You fool, George! You don't know the first thing about it! About what you've let yourself in for. *Patch'em up... bring'em back safe and sound!* Is that what they told you?' Oliver looked at his friend and his eyes narrowed as he repeated the question. 'Is *that* what they told you?'

'Yes. Well, more or less.'

Oliver saw there was no point in trying to dissuade him;they had gone past the point where argument could serve any useful purpose. Now even if George Gilbank were to have second thoughts, it was immaterial. Oliver knew enough about the Army and its ways to recognise that his friend was as trapped as a rabbit in a snare. There could be no undoing it now.

'Aren't you going to wish me luck?' Gilbank asked in a crestfallen voice. The childlike nature and the naïve simplicity of his friend touched Oliver deeply. He took Gilbank's hand and shook it firmly, forcing a smile.

'Of course I am! I wish you the very best! I'm sure you'll do splendidly. They're lucky to have you.'

'It's jolly decent of you to say so.'

'I mean it, old chap.'

The three remaining residents of Nelson Place dined out on the Tuesday evening prior to Gilbank's departure. Oliver and Hallett went 'dutch' on the meal at the *Royal Hotel* in Piccadilly –a rather more flashy restaurant than any of them was accustomed to; but there was a general feeling that as the circumstances were out of the ordinary, something special was called for.

But despite the brilliant surroundings and the fawning attentions of the waiters there was something missing from the company and from their conversation. There was an artificiality about it, and their good humour seemed contrived to blot out disquieting thoughts. There was a dearth of the usual banter and jokes – tasteful or otherwise – and the evening was brought to a dispirited and lacklustre close.

Next day Oliver bid farewell to Gilbank. Once more they shook hands; then he watched his friend shoulder his bag and stride resolutely off and away down Nelson Street. Gilbank reached the junction with Oxford Road, and paused. Taking off his cap he waved it cheerily.

Then he was gone, leaving Oliver to stand for a while contemplating the empty pavement. With a leaden heart he made his way back up into the hallway which echoed to his footsteps. Oliver was the last of the group who had come together all those years before –years of friendship which had passed so swiftly for him, and whose passing he now almost mourned. With the departure of Hallett and Gilbank Nelson Place represented only the facade of what it once had been to him. Suddenly the urge to leave became irresistible. He would visit Desbury for a day or two, and see his parents and Alice; then before returning to Levenham he would go on to Forydd and the Clwyr.

As he thought about the river a nostalgia for the sigh of the wind, for the sundappled waters and for the blue mountains overwhelmed him. He longed to look again on the old familiar places, feeling a need as fundamental as life itself to breathe the Flintshire air once more; and the Vale of the Clwyr was his lung. His spirits rose even as he formulated his plans. He would make for Wales after his long absence from it, and would spend a few days there to revive his inner self. And he knew he would be the better for it.He wrote a brief note to Captain Bonnard telling him of his intentions, and expressing the hope that his old friend would be there. Then he collected together a few things in his old travelling- bag, and planned his departure for the next day.

On the following morning he received a letter from a Dr.Samuel Neary notifying Dr. Oliver Rusholme that he was to take up his first appointment as registrar at the New Heath Hospital. Should he require it, suitable accommodation nearby would be found for him. The relative closeness of New Heath to Nelson Place did not tempt Oliver to stay put in his rooms. Indeed, had the hospital been across the street he would still have found it imperative to move. Without hesitation he replied to Dr. Neary by return of post accepting the offer both of the position and the lodgings. And within the hour he had handed his notice in to Mrs. Monaghan. Of all her Gentlemen Oliver was the one she was most reluctant to lose; she had developed a high regard for this quiet, unpretentious and deeply studious young man and it was not business considerations which caused her to ask him to reconsider. But despite his regret at hurting the feelings of the big-hearted Irishwoman he knew he had to go, and when she asked him whether there was any other reason for his leaving he replied simply in the negative, and reassured her that she had done all and more than anyone in his position could ask. Then he returned to his rooms and began to pack in earnest. While filling his boxes and trunks he mulled over the contents of Dr. Neary's letter, and looked forward with growing anticipation to the day which would mark the *debut* of his professional medical career. It would prove to be a memorable day not only for Oliver Rusholme but also for millions of young men then at war in Europe, a day which would be perpetuated in the collective consciousness of future generations as being amongst the most infamous, and as the most catastrophic, in British history.

Oliver pulled out the letter from his pocket and considered it again, and for the tenth time.

He read the date once more, as if to be certain of it.

It was to be a Saturday; the First of July 1916.

Chapter Seventeen

THE TREES lining the driveway looked taller and more imposing than he remembered them. The last time he had seen them they were sparse and wintry; now resplendently in full leaf they had shed their austerity and assumed a constantly-moving mantle of green. Their size seemed to dwarf the house which they framed, diminishing its proportions and somehow its significance. It had been far less than a year, but so much had occurred to Oliver in the interim – and Millwain Place and its occupants had figured so infrequently in his thoughts – that an age seemed to distance himself from the youth who had passed between those selfsame trees only months earlier.

He pulled on the doorbell – the electric version was still disconnected – and listened for the familiar movements of Alice from her kitchen. She came, but approached more slowly than she had once done; the purposeful bustle was gone and her every effort appeared laboured. She still muttered to herself, as always; and as she stood fumbling with the lock Oliver could not restrain a smile as fragments of her repartee came through the door to him. Apparently it was the locksmith and the dairyman's boy who this time had jointly incurred her wrath.

' Blast this 'andle... it won't turn proper... Morrison's not fixed it at all, like he said 'e had... ' she groused '... an' if it's Williams' boy for t' money I'll give 'im what for. I've said a hundred times to use t' back way.'

The door slowly opened and Alice's thunderous expression melted into one of delight when she beheld her Oliver on the threshold.

'Master Oliver!... or rather, shouldn't I say *Doctor Rusholme*?' she beamed.

'No you shouldn't! And I'm still your Oliver,' he said, hugging the old lady to him.

'You're right posh, now, lad' Alice said, catching her breath. 'Up amongst the top-nobs, like I knew you would be all along!'

'I've a long way to go before I'm *that*!' he laughed 'and it's wonderful to see you again, Alice.'

She wiped her eyes with a corner of her pinafore. 'You've done t'family grand, lad ! There's nobody more proud of you than me – except,of course, your Ma and Pa.' she added

'Are they in?'

'Your Ma certainly is – she's expectin' you. Your Pa has had to go into town with George – important business that can't wait, 'e said; but 'e'll be back by the five o'clock train. He was sorry he would miss you arrivin' home.'

The parlour door opened and Ida stood there. She strode across to him and without a word enfolded him in her arms. 'Welcome home, my Darling' she said 'Welcome home, and well done.'

It was clear from the indistinctness of her voice that she was crying, and Oliver felt discomfited by this outrush of emotion. Gently she released him and holding him at arms' length regarded him through moist eyes. 'Well, Oliver. You've achieved everything. You've done magnificently on your own initiative and ability, and with little support. '

'I wouldn't say that, Ma. I couldn't have done it without your generous allowance to me.'

'You know what I mean, Oliver.'

'Well. Let's put that all behind us, shall we? I don't think it's worth talking about.'

'No, it's not 'she said, then added 'your Pa's as pleased as I am, you know.'

They had tea together in the lounge. Alice insisted that she and not the maid should wait upon them, though her efforts were hampered by her *rheumatics* and Oliver saw that her every movement was now painfully slow. The conversation was light and breezy at first, with Ida listening eagerly to all Oliver had to say, and laughing out loud at his anecdotes about his years at medical school. It was strange to be sitting there, recounting it all to her. He had been home before, but somehow the circumstances had never seemed appropriate for their telling. And even now as they talked his mother appeared to be withholding something which he suspected related to Helene, who was still in London. When he asked her directly what it was she was coyly evasive, telling him that he would have to wait for his Pa to get back from the office- she was sworn to secrecy until then. Oliver did not press her further, and decided to let the mystery be for the time being.

Inevitably the subject turned to Godfrey, and their shared concern about him. Little had been heard for some weeks other than a string of meaningless Field Post Cards from the Front; but at least they could look on the bright side, Oliver said; at least they showed he was still alive, and unwounded. By unspoken agreement they passed from Godfrey to other less distressing territory;no more could constructively be said about him that was not mere speculation; and Ida felt that the afternoon belonged for once to Oliver.

And the afternoon went with a swing with just the two of them there, Ida discovering in her youngest son a fierce individuality which hitherto she had not suspected, underpinned by a quiet resolve to use his skills for the benefit of others before himself.

She smiled inwardly at what she assumed to be his youthful idealism; but it touched her, nonetheless. And Oliver found in Ida a considerate and thoughtful confidante who listened to his views, debated them and where appropriate applauded them. He was pleased and proud to tell her about his position at New Heath; yes, it was located amidst one of the poorest districts of the city, and yes, disease and malnutrition were rife in that quarter, so he'd heard. But it was the sort of beginning he wanted, one which would furnish many opportunities for him to prove himself.

In her turn she talked to him of philosophy and the Arts, and was surprised and pleased to find that he still attended the Halle Orchestral Concerts, when time allowed. Through their interests and their ideals each explored the person the other had become during the missing years, setting in train a process of mutual rediscovery during the two delightful hours they spent together.

Not once did he hint at the tangled mess his heart was in, though Ida intuitively sensed that there was something which he was withholding from her. When she asked was he walking out with anyone? he truthfully replied that he was not; but her intuition read the shadow which fleetingly passed across his face as he said it, and she squeezed his arm reassuringly.

With the ringing of the doorbell the positive tenor of the afternoon dissolved in an instant. Oliver had been expecting his father to arrive from the station at any time; there was nothing odd in that, and he had prepared himself for their meeting. But though he told himself a hundred times that his qualms were irrational he was nonetheless ill-at-ease. It was hard for him to change the habit of a lifetime when he had been conditioned to expect indifference or worse from Clarence.

Oliver listened as the maid answered the door, and froze involuntarily as he recognised his father's terse greeting. He listened as Betty helped him take off his coat and hat, and heard the clicking of the hanger as it was placed on the cloakroom rail. He heard his father's precise step as he approached the door and watched apprehensively as the doorhandle turned, as he had done when he was a schoolboy.

He rose abruptly from his seat beside his mother as if he had been caught in an unseemly act, and Ida's glance flew anxiously between the two of them. Clarence appeared to be preoccupied with the time, continuing to frown downwards at his pocketwatch and only raising his eyes to the horizontal as if it were an afterthought. He took in the scene which greeted him – Oliver stiffly upright, and attempting a smile; and his wife seated forwards on a sofa, also smiling disarmingly. He wondered what they had been discussing in his absence. He stopped in the middle of the room and pulled crisply at his shirt-cuffs so that they protruded from the sleeves of his jacket.

'Ah, Oliver. Good to see you after so long a period ' he said cordially, but Oliver felt there was an oblique note of censure there. Clarence extended his hand. 'Well, how have you been getting along?' he asked. 'Your Mama and I were most gratified by the excellent results which you achieved in your Finals – weren't we, my dear?'

Ida nodded beamingly.

'I've been managing quite well thank you, Pa.' Oliver replied. 'And thank you for your letter.'

'Have you received any indication as to where they might place you? I do not need remind you of course that it is imperative that you secure the *right* sort of post – the sort of post which will bring you to the notice of the *right* sort of people.' He paused, obviously pleased with his verbal dexterity.

'Of course, Pa. That is, I'm sure you're right.'

'Naturally, with what you have, *consultancy* would certainly not be out of the question, allowing for the passage of a few years *to get your feet under the table*, as they say, and make your mark in some sort of specialism. Several, I hear, are *most* lucrative. Time to build up a decent rapport. And one cannot overestimate the social advantages which might be gained. ' He was clearly in an affable frame of mind, for once, as he warmed to his subject. On the whole Oliver found this apparent change in his father's attitude towards him more difficult to manage than Clarence's habitual contempt.

He sensed enough to know that this was no hand of friendship, and he was not going to allow himself to be manipulated for the purposes of Clarence's vicarious ambition at this late stage. He had been emotionally independent of his father for too long, and to inform him of his real intentions would only serve to create friction which he wished to sidestep primarily for his mother's sake. He decided to lie about his post at New Heath.

'Have you had any indication yet?' Clarence repeated.

'No, Pa. But I'm sure I shall.'

Ida shot him a glance. It was not entirely reproachful for she thought she understood why Oliver had lied; but, like him, she despised untruthfulness.

'I have to say I'm rather surprised' Clarence retorted archly, 'when one hears of the shortages of doctors because of the War.'

'I'm sure something will turn up for Oliver before long' Ida intervened 'and he's been working at a hospital for wounded soldiers, haven't you?' Oliver nodded.

'Yes. Yes. Very laudable. But you need to have your future planned.'

But not by you Oliver thought. *Those days are over for ever.*

'Of course, Pa.' he said.

Why had he come back at all? he asked himself. He was standing before the wardrobe mirror in his old bedroom., gazing at his reflection. It was the same mirror in which he had admired his new cricket persona many years before, and he recalled the incident with a mixture of pleasure and embarrassment. He considered his image now, and made a mental comparison between the man who returned his gaze and that long-gone boy. Living in that house under the regime of his father he had been shown precious little to admire in himself, had been taught to value and applaud qualities in others which others rarely acknowledged in him. His father hadn't changed, except visually. It would have been too much to expect, and too much to hope for.

Clarence was even more dried-up, more withered inside as well as out, and in a dimension new to Oliver, he saw the extent of his father's avarice.

Why *had* he come back? He rummaged in the wardrobe and produced his cricket-bat, the only one he had ever owned. He ran his palm along the face of the wood. It was still in good condition. He thought of his mother buying it for him. She'd cared then, just as she cared now. He took a swing with the bat. It was too short for him, but no matter.

He understood now how difficult life must have been for his mother, when it came to him and his father, and maintaining a sort of peace between them.He knew then why he'd come back.

Dinner was nearly over, and despite the overcooking of one or two items, it had on the whole been a good meal. Clarence was in a talkative mood, though his conversation had focused largely on the War in general and on Godfrey in particular. Oliver was about to raise the subject of Helene for the second time that day when with a conspiratorial air his mother leaned over to Clarence 'Shall you tell him, dear, or shall I?' Her husband rose from his chair rather pompously and walked round the table to Ida.

'You know that Captain Warrington was and is a particularly close friend of your brother Godfrey?'

'Yes, Pa.?'

'And that over the last few years he has become a frequent and welcome visitor to our house.'

Oliver inclined his head.

'Well it seems that he has inadvertently made the acquaintance of your sister Helene. And... *ahem...* whilst your Mamma and I cannot say we approve *wholeheartedly* of the way it was done, it appears that they have come to an understanding.'

So after all this time it was still going on! Oliver was taken completely aback. He'd known ever since that night by the stile that there had been something between them, but had assumed that it had fizzled out years before. He smiled to himself. They'd certainly managed to keep their affair well hidden!

'Captain Warrington recently took some well – deserved leave from his duties at the Front' Clarence continued ' and came expressly to see me last week. In short, he asked for my permission to marry your sister. Permission which, after due consideration, I was pleased to grant. Their engagement will be announced formally this week, though owing to some pressing matters of his command Captain Warrington has had to return to France.' Oliver made no comment. 'You don't seem surprised ' said his father.

'I suppose I'm not, really.'

'Why not?' Clarence's tone was fast becoming unpleasant. 'Why not? *Did you know*?'

'One can have one's suspicions, certainly' Oliver said mildly.

'*Suspicions!* You knew, and we did not! Did you not feel it might be appropriate to inform your parents of your *suspicions?'*

'Clarence, *please...* ' Ida looked from one to the other with growing alarm. It seemed that her husband was hell-bent on provoking Oliver, even now.

'I don't feel bound to report every bit of tittle-tattle to *you,* or to anyone else for that matter' Oliver retorted heatedly 'and as far as I'm concerned, it *doesn't* concern me. Nor, for that matter, should it concern anyone else.'

Clarence turned white, then crimson.

'If this is how you treat your parents... ' he began, but Oliver forestalled any further confrontation. Rising decisively from his seat he thanked them for their hospitality, and stated simply that he would be leaving as soon as he was able.

He still had some of the anger of the previous evening's debacle to burn off, and despite Ida's pitiful attempts to prevail upon him to stay, quit the house early the following morning. Whilst he had initially intended to take the most direct route to the Hospital his heart caused him to make a brief diversion through Desbury Village. Passing along the opposite side of the near-deserted highway by *The Red Hen* he halted, consulting the contents of his pocket-book as if his life depended on it while secretly glancing across at the neat little cottage where Dolly lived.Other than himself the only moving objects on the landscape were that of a waggoner and his team of draft-horses which cast long grey shadows in the early sun, and whose harness their master was adjusting in a leisurely way. As he tugged and slackened the man kept up a cheerful monologue to his animals who nudged him affectionately. Oliver came alongside and the waggoner nodded affably to the lovelorn young man, wishing him a hearty good morning. Oliver returned the greeting.

The older man looked him up and down enquiringly then turned back to his duties with the horses. Uncomfortably Oliver realised that he could not loiter in the street without exciting suspicion, and as the blue–painted door seemed destined to remain shut he retraced his steps through the village. Diving down an obscure track he cut across- country using lanes and pathways which he could have negotiated blindfold.His route brought him to a sharp bend in the river where over the centuries the waters had cut a channel through the lush meadows. At this point in its course it had come up against some unyielding obstacle beneath the earth which had caused it to perform a u-turn, doubling back on itself until like a living thing it had found a means of escape through the gentler soils of the lower valley.

Oliver paused to watch a small bird investigating an ancient willow which overhung the apex of the bend. Some branches had subsided entirely into the flow and though washed constantly by the river still sprouted lithe young shoots. The tree looked mighty, and very old; and the little bird hopped and fluttered amidst its boughs for a few seconds; then finding nothing which interested him, was gone again in the twinkling of an eye.

Oliver shook himself from his reverie and strode on, his boots stirring up clouds of tiny insects which gyrated about him as he walked. He loosely followed the river's course until he saw, smoke-blue in the morning haze, the silhouette of a copse. This he made for directly; and weaving his way through the hedgerow which fronted it, he arrived where he had intended. Lifting a leg smartly over a wooden fence he dropped onto the hard earth surface of the Parrs Wood Road.

A quarter of an hour's stiff walking brought him to the marshy woodlands of Green End with its perpetual springs,its moss-grown stumps and its fungi; and another twenty minutes saw him turning into the driveway which led to the austere frontage of Levenham Hospital. Oliver surveyed the scene in amazement. What had once been the school playing-field now resembled an army camp with regimented lines of timber huts intersected by concrete paths.

The walk had reinvigorated him more than he had expected, and he entered the double doors with little trace of the previous night's rancour in his heart. He was greeted effusively by Archie McLeish and a few of the other doctors who had heard of his success. In his last letter McLeish had accepted Oliver's offer of assistance with alacrity and, subject to the approval of the Hospital Authorities, lost no time in employing his friend as his temporary surgical assistant for the few days he could be with them. Though the flow of casualties had not abated with the summer months,McLeish said, the good news was that their numbers had not materially increased. But the urgency with which temporary wards had been erected – the same timber buildings which now covered the former sports field- was he thought far more disquieting.

'Though I've had no firm information, the current rumour is that something big's going to come off in the near future. Some say it's the *Big Push*, but I wouldn't know about that. What I *do* know is that on the face of it the Powers–that–Be are expecting unprecedented casualties – why else would they go to all this trouble?'

Having stowed his baggage in the linen- cupboard Oliver joined McLeish for the morning's rounds of the gas cases. It was the first time he had donned a white coat since qualifying, and even for one so unpretentious as Oliver it was a heady moment when his fellow doctor introduced him to the patients. Though the individuals he had first encountered there had long since gone – to their homes, or to sanatoria, or to their graves – the symptoms and the suffering were no different.

'This is my friend and colleague Dr. Rusholme, who has kindly offered to join us for a few days. Ye'd better look out, chaps, now there's two of us to contend with!' Some weak laughter rose amidst the incessant coughing, and wan faces turned respectfully to them both. Oliver was back where he needed to be.

Chapter Eighteen

AS THE Holyhead Boat-Train sped through Cheshire and on into Flintshire he sat forward in his seat with all the eagerness of his schoolboy years – an eagerness which he did not bother to disguise.He had even shut his eyes firmly and tried to guess when they had crossed into Wales, as he had done as a child.Wisps of steam from the engine were caught by the sun as they curled around his carriage window, and as the meadows gave way once more to the steep grey valleys with their crags and little sheep-pastures each seemed to proclaim their welcome to him.

Oliver climbed down from the trap which had carried him to Ridland. He paid and tipped the driver who doffed his cap to him, then retrieved his travelling-bag and took in his surroundings – the hoary old bridge, the irregular roofs of the little Welsh cottages jostling with each other for a frontage to the road, and the crumbling bastions of the castle. The late afternoon sun seemed to cast shadows of a particular definition, where the demarcation between light and dark was especially pronounced, all that was not sunlit being thrown into deepest shade.

Everything was as he had hoped and expected it would be, and shouldering his bag he went down to the familiar stile. As he strolled alongside the Clwyr the spirit of the river flowed back into him like a current, inexorably and irresistibly. Sheep scattered before him as he made his way to the distant cottage whose shape he could just make out, and from whose chimney rose a bluish plume of woodsmoke. Captain Bonnard was at home, and the fire was lit.

The old man had been his major protagonist. And now the one who had championed his cause and who had never lost faith in the boy felt entirely vindicated as he beheld the man. He shook Oliver's hand repeatedly even as he stood on the threshold, welcoming him as if he had been a long lost son.

'Well, Oliver! Well! Well!' was all the Captain could say at first.With the kettle singing on the hob he eagerly consumed all of Oliver's news, with a quickening of the eye when he heard once more of his former pupil's triumph in his Finals and with a shake of the head when told of Godfrey, and the casualties, and Levenham. He picked up a copy of *The Times* and waved it in the air.

'There's more to come yet, mark my words!' he said.

Not much had changed. The old man seemed a little more grizzled and a little less robust; but he still strode around the cottage and its precincts with the same uprightness in his bearing and firmness of step. And Oliver noticed that the pair of framed photographs – the sepia images of the beautiful Victorian lady and the young officer in the Boer War uniform – had been restored to their original places on the dresser shelf. Still the lady's eyes seemed to follow him just as they had done when he had seen them first, though her smile now appeared to be directed at him, almost as though she appreciated his being there. And the young soldier still gazed over and beyond him, and away into the far distance.

The season was over for the spring salmon, the Captain said, and there were hardly any sea-trout to be had; nonetheless there were quite a few nice brown-trout holed up around the gravel shoals at the top of the beat. He's had one or two to a *Wickham's Fancy* but they were fickle, taking the fly short and warily.

'But *best* of all,' he continued ' there's a terrific run of 'flatties' down in the estuary.' He licked his lips in anticipation. 'D'you know, Oliver, there's nothing I'd rather have grace a plate than a whole dab or a fresh flounder. Salmon and trout are fine; but the *flatfish*... they have a quality all their own. And they're shoulder-to -shoulder, down there' he smiled dryly. 'You could walk across the river on their backs! Still,' he added wistfully ' lemons are unknown in this neck of the woods... and plaice ought *always* to be served with a slice of lemon!'

Rising before first light they climbed down from the jetty into the old boat, gliding downstream with the current. In the spreading seapool bordered by the wrecks they tied up, hard against one of the jutting ribs. With the soothing lap of the water beneath them the fishing was easy; and as the Captain had said, the fish were plentiful and large. Taking sufficient for their evening meal the rest were released and they fished on for the sport alone until the turning of the tide, when they pulled back upriver to where the old jetty extended its arm to them once more.

They sat opposite each other, with the glowing fire between them. Like the meal, the week had been singularly enjoyable. Whilst they had renewed their old acquaintance Oliver felt that he had gained something more significant during the few days he had spent there. Rebuffed once more by his father's abrasiveness he had found a generous and considerate substitute in the old man. Oliver had long felt affection and regard for his former teacher, but he now sensed that in a way each had by unspoken agreement adopted the other. During the week the Captain had called him Edward several times; and whilst it was no more than a slip of the tongue it had given Oliver cause to wonder not whether but how the name and the sepia photograph were linked.

The Captain rose to fetch two glasses from the dresser and was about to reach for the whisky when he paused and picked up the photograph of the soldier. He looked silently at it and turned to Oliver as if to say something, but then evidently thinking better of it replaced the picture in its original position. He gave out an almost inaudible sigh, and returned to his chair.

'I'm afraid, Captain, that I must leave tomorrow' Oliver said.

'Of course you must, old chap.'

'I've enjoyed my visit immensely, as always. I'm very grateful for your hospitality.'

'You've been fine company for an old man; it's always a pleasure to see you here.'

'I'll come back whenever I can – though I can't say exactly. I don't know what leave I shall be entitled to.'

'We live in troubled times, my boy. You have your new duties to attend to, and I have no doubt there are many who will live to be grateful for your commitment.'

He fell silent for while, then continued haltingly, as if making a confession.

' I'm very proud of you, you know. I could not have asked for more had you been… well, my own son. But promise me one thing. Promise that you will never take… never take *unwarranted* risks. Too many fine young chaps such as yourself have come to grief in the last year or two. '

'Oh, I don't intend to! I think I'll find my work is cut out for me when I start at New Heath.'

'Exactly! Your skills are those of a doctor, and they're a rare gift. We all of us hear the summons in times of war, to do our duty as we see it. If only I was thirty years younger! But you can serve too, Oliver, and nobly. Each to his own. Work your magic for the wounded and the sick. Don't let a rash decision be a cause of lasting regret.'

Early next morning Oliver set out for Ridland on the first leg of his journey to Manchester. As he said goodbye to Captain Bonnard the old man pressed his hand as if unwilling to release it, and once more reminded him of his promise.

'Do your very best, my boy. There are those who sell their souls, others their very lives, in pursuit of a goal. You need do neither.'

The friends walked together through the neighbouring pasture, to the end of the path. There they parted. As Oliver strode down to the stile he turned once more and saw the Captain waving farewell. He waved back, then vaulting the stile he was lost to view.

Chapter Nineteen

90th.INFANTRY BRIGADE OPERATION ORDER NO.23
BY
BRIGADIER GENERAL C.J.STEAVENSON C.M.G
25 – 6 – 16

Reference Map : MONTAUBAN (57d S.E., 57c S.W.)
On a date which will be communicated later and at 60 minutes after Zero on that date, the 90th.Infantry Brigade will leave their ASSEMBLY TRENCHES S. of CAMBRIDGE COPSE and attack the German position at MONTAUBAN…
On the night previous to the attack the Brigade will march to ASSEMBLY TRENCHES shown in the plan and take up its position where the road running N. to MONTAUBAN cuts the W. end of GLATZ REDOUBT…
The 16th. Battalion Manchester Regiment will attack with its left on the E. edge of TALUS BOISE and its right on the left of the 17th. Battalion with whom it will keep in continuous touch…
400 Trench bridges and 400 trench ladders will be issued…
At 30 minutes these will be placed in position in the trenches at the rate of 3 per 2 sections…
Prior to the attack the troops occupying ASSEMBLY TRENCHES should cut steps in the side of the trenches to facilitate climbing out…

Godfrey Rusholme read the Order again,smoothing it out on the table with his left hand as with his right he positioned an oil-lamp to make out every detail. As he finished reading the Order he turned once more to the map and scrutinised it as he had a dozen times before that day, feeling his way mentally across each inch of ground which lay between Cambridge Copse and their ultimate objective, the battered ruins of Montauban.

First, cross No Mans Land and penetrate the enemy entanglements to Brick Point and Valley Trench, the German front line… and from there to Alt Trench and to its right the Glatz Redoubt. He tapped the spot thoughtfully with his forefinger and speculated darkly on what the outcome might be if the artillery *didn't* give it a pasting sufficient to knock out its defenders. If there were enough of the Bosches left to man a few machine-guns it could be all up with the 16th. He had an icy presentiment that if the Redoubt was still held when the assault went in, the Manchesters might well be caught 'between the hammer and the anvil', between the enfilading fire from both Alt Trench and Glatz. He considered the cunning with which the enemy had prepared his defences, and his ground. The Bosches were old hands at it, he admitted grudgingly, and the obstacles were formidable in the extreme. He'd heard the confident assertions issuing from Brigade and the batteries as to how the preliminary barrage would obliterate all enemy resistance between them and their objective;yet from bitter experience he had seen the shortcomings of even the most brilliant plans when the time came to put them into practice. But he saw also there was not a damned thing he could do about it, other than to put his trust in Fate and the artillery. And perhaps he'd got it all wrong; perhaps he *was* being unduly pessimistic. Certainly as far as his fellow officers went his views placed him in a small minority.Talk in the Mess was bullish in the extreme, with speculation rife as to whether the War could be over by the following Christmas.All that was needed was the crucial breakthrough, which the Big Push was intended to provide.

He unbent himself stiffly from the table – his legs and arm still ached mercilessly – and listened to the roar of the barrage which ebbed and flowed above him, behind him and before him – ebbed and flowed unceasingly with one combined and hellish voice.He recalled that night bombardment which he had watched from the convent, and the corrugated iron which had sheltered him in No Man's Land. It seemed very long ago.

He stooped again over the map, and continued to follow the 16th.'s intended line of attack. *Past Train Alley and over the railway cutting... five hundred yards. Then another five hundred of sloping ground alongside Nord Alley, to a frontal attack on Southern Trench.*

At that point they would be within two hundred yards of Montauban. Having taken the village, they were to advance beyond it and assault the German trench known as Montauban Alley.

All told, the Order required them to cross almost two miles of enemy territory. And as each man would be carrying some seventy pounds of kit – ammunition, wire, pickets, bombs – they would be overburdened from the word go.

Godfrey lit yet another Woodbine, and gazed out through the shattered windows of Battalion HQ. The radiant blueness of the sky made the thing seem incongruous, and less threatening. He knew the idea was absurd, but the prospect of dying on such a day seemed oddly more remote, despite the fact that in the clear air the attacking lines would provide much better targets. And of course there had been the asinine decision from 'up top' to issue the trench ladders and bridges days before. Of new unpainted pine, hardly any attempt had been made to camouflage them. Stacked in huge piles behind the Reserve Trenches they could hardly have been missed by the overflying German pilots. *We might as well have put an advert in the local paper* someone in Godfrey's platoon muttered. Though he had agreed entirely with the sentiments he'd still reprimanded the offender.

The door behind him opened, and he turned slowly to find Warrington contemplating him.

'Good afternoon, old man' he said companionably 'been reading over the Order, have you?'

Godfrey nodded, pursing his lips.

'It'll be magnificent, mark my words' Warrington continued 'perhaps the best opportunity the 16th. will ever get to show its mettle.'

'Do you really think so?'

'I don't see how it can be otherwise. To think of hundreds of thousands of our troops rising as one from our trenches where we've been rotting for nearly two years, and moving against the Huns in a huge unstoppable wave. And they'll be led by such as us.'

'You don't still believe all that stuff, do you?' Godfrey's tone was not intended to be ironic, though it sounded it..

'And why not?' Warrington countered 'Why so sceptical? The whole show's been planned down to the last detail; every contingency has been allowed – and compensated – for.'

'Except for the Enemy. Unfortunately he's the one *loose cannon,* to coin an unfortunate phrase. It's rather difficult to plan for what he will or will not do.'

'What's left of him after the barrage. I think we'll have little more than a sweeping-up job.'

'I sincerely hope you're right. Don't forget the reports we've had from raids further down the line. About the depth and extent of the Enemy's shelters. One of the raiding parties actually got lost in their tunnels.'

'*If* such defences exist at all in this sector –which I rather doubt – it will be a simple matter to seal 'em up as we sweep over.'

In contrast to Godfrey, Warrington was becoming steadily more animated by the prospect of the impending offensive.

'Will it' said Godfrey dully. There was an uncomfortable pause. Warrington stepped across to the table, and absently fingered Order No.23.

'I'll be leading the Company' he said simply, turning to Godfrey. 'It's what

I left Staff for. It's the sole reason I'm here. I wouldn't miss it for the world.'

Godfrey looked at him. It was not Warrington's assertion itself which perplexed him but the way in which it had been put, for it sounded curiously childlike. It was almost as if the speaker was delighted that he had found a way to please, a way to prove himself to others, and would not be deflected from his purpose.

'I've come to tell you something else' Warrington said, reddening.

'Yes?'

'Well, it's like *this*. I don't know if you've noticed – or whether she's told you, for that matter. But Helene – your sister – and I… well actually we've been seeing quite a lot of each other, lately. And… well, I've seen your Ma and Pa and asked for her hand.' Warrington moistened his dry lips. 'They're pretty made up with the idea, anyhow. And Helene's accepted me.'

Godfrey felt nothing. The thought occurred to him that it had all been going on behind his back, but still he felt nothing. The prospect of having Warrington as a brother-in -law left him unmoved; neither for nor against; and he viewed the news with utter indifference.

The man before you has been your friend since childhood he reminded himself; *you ought to be delighted..*

Mechanically he offered Warrington his hand and congratulated him. It was the thing to do, the routine through which one had to go.

He knew he should react positively at such a time, and felt boorish that he did not. He had no opinion one way or the other in a matter which seemed utterly remote, relating to people immeasurably distant from him. Considering them in this way was like looking at them down an inverted telescope; they seemed diminished, their features blurred and indistinct. And as for the future – if there was to be one – what of that? The die was loaded against them – all of those who wore that uniform and who faced the terrible uncertainties of a great battle still to be fought. To link yourself emotionally with anyone – whether it was your sister or someone else's – seemed foolhardy and fatuously optimistic.

'I'm very happy for you both' he said, forcing a smile. 'Very happy.'

Later Godfrey found himself before the billets once more, gazing at the night horizon. It glowed patchily with ember-like hues as the bombardment grew steadily in intensity, and it obscured his further vision, preventing him from seeing any future beyond – a scarlet rim which seemed to encompass the whole of the tangible world within the mouth of a volcano.

Ten thousand guns, some said, ranged over a twenty mile front. The biggest concentration of artillery firepower in history, said others; a gun every four yards., and eleven hundred rounds per gun. *For twenty miles.* It hardly seemed possible, except that the combined roar testified to it.

On the one hand it was reassuring to know that so much attention was being given to obliterating the enemy; but on the other there was no better way of publishing your intentions to him.

As he stood listening the very earth seemed agitated, simmering with uneasy motion. The shiftings of countless thousands of men, their breathing and the pulse of their blood in their veins seemed to fill his mind and consciousness. And the entire planet pounded and echoed to their regimented movements as the Battalions drew ever closer to the onset, and Zero Hour. And above it all the tornado of the bombardment rose to ever greater heights.

He was possessed now by that same serenity which had sustained him when trapped in No Man's Land – a serenity borne of resignation and even indifference to his ultimate fate. He found he could not struggle against it, nor had the willpower to do so any longer.

The prospect of the imminent battle was for him unromantic in the extreme; and burdened as he was with innumerable details he could only contemplate the immediate present, leaving the shadows of whatever future there might be, to themselves. He saw that there was little more that could be done, now. His fate was sealed, one way or the other. He'd either perish in the coming fight, or live through it. He cared little which it was to be, and viewed the prospect of either outcome with indifference. The only fear which possessed him was that he might be disabled in some way – oh, he'd seen them in their wheelchairs at Amiens and at home, dressed in their hateful blue suits, being pushed here and there by pretty nurses while their heads lolled about and their mouths drooled. And he'd watched the wretch with his arm and leg missing trying pathetically to get himself around..No; it wasn't for him. He'd have death in preference to *that*, any day. And if it came to it, he'd do the job himself.

Yet there were still the men of his platoon. They looked to him as their guide, their leader and their commander. Without flattering himself he knew they all thought highly of him – a respect and affection which he doubted he deserved. He believed with a passion that irrespective of his apathy towards himself he had a moral duty to see them through it and to the end as long as he drew breath.

He turned away and reentered the billet. Lighting an oil-lamp he took some paper and envelopes from his box and began to write. Then having completed the task he sealed the letters and placed them together in one larger packet which he endorsed hurriedly. Opening his box he laid it uppermost by the side of the photographs of his family, and Oliver. He closed the lid firmly and inserted his key, but then decided against it, and removed the key once more.

Events seemed now to march on apace. Earlier in the day artillery reports had come through stating that:

all wire entanglements have been cut in the front line before Montauban and cutting is progressing satisfactorily on the second and third lines…

Then the weather closed in against them. The whole of the 16th. and all other Battalions were ordered to withdraw from the 'jumping off' trenches and once more Godfrey trudged back with his platoon to their soaked and mud-spattered tents where they marked away the hours with further drill, cleaning already clean rifles and bayonets, and the writing of letters home. The British High Command decided that there would have to be a forty-eight hour postponement of the assault – from the 28th.June to the 1st.July.

The massing of troops for the Big Push culminated in the Assembly Trenches where they stood and waited to move up, some the prey of every imaginable fear while others seemed almost in a celebratory mood, excited and eager at the prospect of being amongst the first to 'kick off' in what they believed would be the greatest and most decisive battle of their times.

Lieutenant Godfrey Rusholme stood with his platoon in a trench directly in front of Cambridge Copse – a collection of blasted stumps which had once been woodland. He squinted at his watch. 0430. They had been standing in the forward trenches for three hours already, smoking the time away nervously and so closely packed together that there was simply no room to sit down. Godfrey's wounded legs ached, and he stamped his feet to try to restore some life into them. Though seemingly endless, the night had passed uneventfully with only a few sporadic attempts by the Enemy to shell the British lines. The air was chill, but free of the rain which had plagued them the previous day; and the early morning sky pulsed even yet with starlight. He wondered how far away some of them really were, for in the clearness it seemed as though all he had to do was reach out to gather them in. He smiled inwardly at the childish fancy and brought his thoughts and his sight back to earth, and scanned the indistinct lumps which were his men. As always Sergeant Chadderton was seeing to this matter or that, making sure of the strapping on the loaded packs, checking the ammunition and weapons and identification–flashes of the youngest and the most inexperienced, and keeping up a gruff banter with Corporal Sam Fernihough.

Food had been both poor and scarce due to the postponement of the attack, but the NCOs had managed 'to rustle up a Dixie' from somewhere, dragging it back with great difficulty to where the company was assembled; and at least the men had a mug of hot soup to drink while awaiting the dawn. Godfrey watched as it was distributed, and the paternal way in which his family's former handyman saw to the needs of the newest conscripts; they would need careful guidance,which he knew they would receive from Chadderton. He watched as he moved amongst the platoon, his every action crisp and purposeful. Albert seemed the very antithesis of fear, his stolid three-dimensional presence bringing calm and reassurance to the most fearful. With the Sergeant and Mr. Rusholme beside them, they'd be all right. *They'd* see to it, if anyone could

Godfrey knew he could never have got so far without Albert; *he* was the cohesive factor in the platoon moreso even than his officer, who now looked across to his comrade in arms with a mixture of affection and respect. The man's courage, resolve and unbounded initiative had been an object-lesson to Godfrey. He was proud to call Albert his friend; and it gladdened him to know that they would be going over the top together.

At 0630 precisely a dull rumbling from the rear proclaimed the onset of the final bombardment, as a preliminary to the attack by the first wave. The Manchesters were positioned so far forward that the detonation of thousands of high-explosive shells no more than two hundred yards from where they crouched caused an aftershock which struck them like a body-blow. Conversation was impossible amidst the din as men held their hands to their ears and apprehensive looks were exchanged between those who not an hour since had been the most optimistic and buoyant. There was real fear in many eyes now.

At 0715 the artillery suddenly fell silent. Men shuffled nervously, wiping their faces or hands against sleeves. With a dull crump which seemed to issue from the bowels of the earth Stokes Mortars opened up, hurling their projectiles near vertically to drop and burst with a monstrous roar in the German forward positions. Men accustomed to explosive violence gasped, appalled at the inferno which had been unleashed before them, doubting that anything living – whether enemy or friend – could withstand such a holocaust.

And as the hands of countless wristwatches crept to 0725 the order was given to raise the ladders. Heedless of the splinters they seized the ramshackle things and thrust them up against the trench walls.

At 0728 Godfrey yelled his last orders to the line of ashen faces.

'*Remember, 7th.Platoon! Do not stop for the wounded – ours or theirs! Take no prisoners, and do not spare the enemy! Stay close to me, and keep to formation. Good luck to you all, men. Let's show them what the Manchesters can do!*' He looked again at his watch. Drawing a whistle from his breast-pocket he held it poised before his lips.

'*Fix bayonets!*'

Hands fumbled as the weapons were clattered noisily into place. Chadderton ran a practiced eye along the line.

'All ready, Mr. Rusholme!' His cool blue gaze lighted on Godfrey, and they exchanged glances.Albert Chadderton nodded to him and Godfrey nodded back, and smiled – a wistful smile which embodied so much. He extended his hand, and Albert Chadderton took it.

'Once more, Albert, good luck.' Then he added 'let's hope this is for the last time.'

'Aye, sir. Let's hope it is. And good luck to you, Mr.Godfrey.'

At that moment it seemed the whole Front had been struck by an earthquake. The ground trembled, and trickles of soil ran down from the parapet. A distant column of smoke and debris rose almost leisurely into the higher airs, clouding the sun as it expanded and lowered over the field of battle like some terrible incubus. The violence of it appalled even the hardest, as the eyes of countless thousands turned in horror towards it.

A hundred tons of ammonal had been detonated beneath the German lines.

'*Ready!*' Godfrey drew breath and put the whistle to his lips.0729… 0729… 0729… 0730.

From all along the trench came the dreaded sound which prefaced every attack.

'*7th.Platoon! Advance!*'

Loaded –down forms clustered and cursed at the base of every ladder as streams of young Manchester men flowed upward, over the top and into No Man's Land.

The Battle of the Somme had begun.

Chapter Twenty

THE SCENE WHICH met them as they emerged into the light defied all description. It was the topography of a nightmare, for the artillery had reduced every solid thing to powder, with craters left by the heavier howitzer shells the only recognisable features. Walking forward in formation was hard going, as the surface seemed to slip away beneath their boots. The gunners had certainly put paid to the enemy entanglements which had been torn into countless shards of barbed wire; and the few remaining clumps could be bypassed easily enough. Yet barely thirty yards into this lunar hell Godfrey's men start to fall, some dropping like lead while others twisted and turned or doubled up, clawing at their tunics with desperate fingers as they were hit in the chest and stomach. Machine –gun bullets sang around and past the bunched survivors, and still they pressed on past their fallen.

The enemy was alive, and active; the much vaunted bombardment had not done for him.

'Keep the line! Keep to formation!'

Godfrey's mind and sight were fixed on the further rise which was Montauban. And men were falling all about him, as German gunners on the distant ridge swept the lines of the Manchesters with a terrible and relentless fire.

'*Maintain the line... Close up... Keep to formation!'*

The man to his left sighed and fell backward with a small black hole in his forehead.

'*Close up!*

The next man stumbled as if he had tripped, tottered a few paces then sank down onto his knees with his head lolling.

'*Keep to formation!'*

It was nothing more than mechanical repetition now; Godfrey heard his voice doing it all for him.

He glanced to his right and left, in desperation.He could see no further than a few hundred yards in either direction, but all along the advancing lines of the 16th. little khaki-clad shapes were crumpling up or dropping leadenly to the ground. From his right came a scream as the seventeen year-old Arthur Picknell was struck in the neck, and he kicked and cried out in his death throes as he fell.

'*Maintain the line... Keep to... agh... oh God...* ' Something red hot burned into his face. The brute force of the blow spun him round and floored him for a moment. Lying there half conscious he raised his hand hesitantly to his cheek and drew it back, gazing at it blearily. It was running with blood.

Seeing Godfrey fall, Chadderton's first reaction was to go to the aid of his officer and friend; but as far as he could make out he was possibly the most senior NCO remaining in that section.

The order remained; *do not stop for the wounded...* and the order extended to them all. With a wrench which tore at his heart he yelled to the remains of the platoon.

'*Mr. Rusholme's out of it, lads. Take your orders from me.*'

And Albert Chadderton reluctantly took command of the 7th.

But Godfrey was not out of it. Breathing more evenly he managed to compose himself, and with a supreme effort he slowly rose to his feet. Bullets still pattered around him, throwing up little puffs of earth. His head swam and he took a moment or two to collect his thoughts; then raising his eyes he fixed on the middle distance and the rise where the machine guns were, and staggered forward.

At first he lurched along like a drunken man but as he progressed the momentum seemed to revitalise him, returning strength to his legs which the rest of his body had briefly lost. Indifferent to the wound in his face he was jogging now, and closing rapidly on his platoon some thirty yards ahead. They were making heavy weather of it, he could see that. The ground was peppered with casualties. Every few yards lay the khaki body of this or that man all of whom were known to him, some in the ghastly attitudes in which they had died while others who still lived feebly attempted to crawl out of the line of fire. Alfred Pearce even looked up at him as he passed, and raised a weak hand of acknowledgement.

He was amidst the 7th. now; and as he entered their ranks he shouted '*I'm not dead yet, lads! Let's give the bastards what for!*'

Chadderton turned with an expression of triumph as he heard Godfrey's voice, but winced involuntarily when he saw what had happened to his face.

'Let's level the score!' As Godfrey passed through them they in turn broke into a run despite their heavy packs; and within seconds they were dropping into a featureless recess which crossed the line of their advance.

They had reached the first of their objectives. The 7th. had attained Valley Trench.

But the Germans had withdrawn long before, leaving only the tattered remains of their equipment, their weapons and their comrades. The dead lay everywhere, just as the bombardment had caught them. Horribly disfigured or even dismembered, they lay partly buried by successive shell-blasts. Of the living enemy there was no trace. As the remnants of his platoon piled in beside him Godfrey motioned to them to stay low, for the trench was –at barely four feet deep- perilously shallow and the top was raked intermittently by bursts of machine-gun fire. He was making a quick count of heads as Chadderton and a few stragglers stumbled and slithered down to join them.

Forty-two, all told. That made eighteen casualties in the first three hundred yards. At that rate there wouldn't be a man left after the first half-mile.

The trench was the key, he realised that in an instant. Maybe it was impossible to move forward, but they could most certainly use the enemy's trench system, battered though it was, to their own advantage. He pulled a map from his breast pocket, and with his cuff wiped away his own blood which trickled down onto it. There *was* a way out, and if it was even remotely intact it would take them to their objective.

'Sergeant Chadderton!'

Albert scrambled across to him.

'You should withdraw, sir' he said quietly as he approached, looking narrowly at the ghastly wound in Godfrey's face. 'Nobody would think anything the worse of you for it. There's enough left of us to do t' job.'

Godfrey behaved as if he had not heard, but grasping the map in his clenched fist pointed repeatedly at a zig-zagged line which indicated the course of the Valley Trench

'Look here! Look!' he said almost ecstatically 'if we head west along here for about two hundred or so yards it'll bring us to a dog-leg in the trench. This was photographed only a week ago. The Bosches have cut a communication-trench at right-angles to us! If it's in no worse a state than this one it might give us sufficient cover. What do you think?'

'Seein' that you're stayin' on with us,sir,' Albert replied phlegmatically 'we can do nowt less than give it a try. We're sittin'ducks here, so its forward, sideways or back.'

'Tell them to get those bloody things off' Godfrey said, nodding at the enormous loads of gear strapped to the mens' backs 'and carry only what is absolutely necessary. The Lewis gun must come, and all the ammunition, and bombs. Each man to carry his own water-canister – you know the form. What we *don't* need is to offer the Bosches an easy target, and let them know where we're coming from.'

They willingly offloaded their packs. Now shorn of the Quasimodo – like humps they were immediately more agile, more able to inch along unseen and more prepared for the combat yet to come.

Together with a few stragglers from the 3rd. and 6th. platoons – who had if anything suffered even worse than the 7th. – they set off along the derelict trench, stooping low beneath the horizon and crawling like reptiles over the sections where the bombardment had been at its most intense, and where the hollow was reduced to barely waist height. Because of the number of enemy dead the task was rendered doubly horrible and sometimes there was no alternative to slithering over piles of German corpses, but it had to be done.

They had covered perhaps a hundred yards when without warning a salvo of 'whizzbangs' exploded around them. Perhaps they had been spotted by an enemy observer, or perhaps the shells had been fired randomly on the assumption that *some* British must have reached the old forward trench by that time. Whatever the reason, all except one landed beyond the platoon and detonated safely, but that one rogue shell found its way to a soft target, bursting directly amongst the line of crawling troops.

The carnage was terrible. Amidst the cries and as the choking fumes cleared Godfrey could see how bodies had been tossed about like so many rag dolls, broken and lifeless and grotesque.

Of the eight dead, two could not be found anywhere; whether they had been blown over the parapet or whether they had simply been blown to bits would never be known. But now the ghastly job of clearing away their dead fell to the living– six comrades mutilated utterly beyond recognition and whose remains had now to be shovelled to one side to allow the ones behind to progress. Godfrey crept back to see to the others – three of whom had been so severely wounded by shrapnel that they could not possibly last the hour. Leaving them with two men with leg wounds to provide as best they could for their final needs, the dwindling column once more set itself in motion.

Even though they had expected it to be where the map indicated, it was a shock to come upon it so suddenly, and to find it in such good condition. How successive barrages had contrived to miss this small corner of the enemy's network was a mystery. But as the communication-trench yawned open to their right, descending downward to full depth, few there spared the time to consider how or why it had survived intact; their only sense being one of temporary relief, and gratitude for a respite from the horrors of that crawl. Godfrey motioned them to silence – for even with the constant shelling, sounds could be funnelled some distance along a trench.

They formed up in the shadow of the revetted walls, and Godfrey whispered his plan of attack. From the almost constant rattling of heavy automatic fire and from the whistling of bullets above them it seemed that they were not far from an enemy machine-gun emplacement – one of the many still enfilading the attacking Manchesters. Chadderton fished in his tunic pocket and produced a ladies'compact- mirror bound with wire, which he attached to the tip of his bayonet. Gingerly he raised it a few inches above the parapet and peered cautiously up into it. At first he could make nothing out, but by slowly rotating and tilting his rifle he began to gain a clearer impression of what lay beyond.

'The Bosche gun's there, right enough, Mr. Rusholme. Positioned about thirty yards to th'east of us, give or take a bit.'

He handed the makeshift periscope across to Godfrey, who seized it like a man possessed.

'*I see him now, Sergeant*. You're quite right. He's dug in very low, and it looks as if he's safe within a concrete embrasure. We can only take him from the rear. We'll use this trench to provide us with cover.'

Again they moved stealthily forward, halting with backs pressed against the wall as they approached each bend in the trench. With rifles loaded and levelled they waited with pulses racing as the mirror was employed once more. This procedure was repeated every ten yards until the sound of the gun and the direction of the bullets indicated that the enemy was slightly behind them. Godfrey climbed up some splintered planks and squinted through a small gap in the sandbagging.

'A few more yards and we're dead right' he whispered. 'I need two men to sort that Bosche gun out.' It was a request he detested himself for having to make – to ask men either to endanger their lives by volunteering in this way, or to cause shame to otherwise brave men who might have to refuse. He would have willingly done the job himself, and Albert would have gone with him, he knew; but that was the price of command. He must risk neither himself nor his senior NCO when there were alternatives.

A number of hands went up. Godfrey ignored the youthful ones, and instead chose Lance-Corporal Tom Hathersage from Ardwick – a hard-fighting man and one of the dwindling number of his original platoon – and Private Charlie Pawson – ruthless despite his reputation as battalion comedian.

'What exactly d'yer want doin' sir?'

'Leave everything behind. Take my revolver – and two Mills bombs each. Work your way slowly round the back of the enemy gun position. Keep as flat as your hat. Understood? We'll set up the Lewis gun should you need covering fire.' He handed the revolver to Hathersage who opened it and coolly checked the chamber, then closed it again with a practiced flick.

'I think there's a hollow to the rear of the gun position – possibly a shell-crater' said Godfrey;' get to it as quickly as you can. From there you should be able to get a better idea. Don't make a move until you're sure of the ground.Use bombs.Two at a time.When the job's done, get out fast. '

'Right, sir.We'd better be off then' Pawson said.

'Good luck, both of you.'

The others gave a leg-up to the two attackers who slid like cats over a ledge where the revetment was lowest. Pulling themselves along on their stomachs they disappeared inch by inch- first their bodies then their legs then their boots, until finally they were gone.

While Albert Chadderton deployed men to guard either end of the trench Godfrey took up the mirror and watched intently. His choice of Hathersage and Pawson – though hardly an enviable one to have to make – was nonetheless wise. *Somebody* had to do the dirty work, and it had fallen to these two. They were both of that sort to whom violence came easily, and before the war each had been well known to the Collyhurst police as bar-room brawlers, Hathersage having served a term in the notorious Strangeways Prison for a knifing. Godfrey's distaste for them as individuals had not influenced his decision other than knowing that they would not hesitate, would not give a second thought to the killings that they must commit. He knew their characters well enough and had himself witnessed what they were capable of; he knew they would act without compunction and without hesitation. But that was what they were there for; a Western Front battlefield was no place for moral sensitivity. And if any could do the job and survive, it was Hathersage and Pawson.

The scrap of mirror afforded a poor view of what was going on, and at first he could make out nothing whatever. But as his sight became accustomed to the jolting of the glass he was heartened to see a slight movement just a few yards to the rear of the German position.

Still the gun traversed, maintaining a slow sweeping fire over the top of the trench. Screwing up his eyes he focused on the spot. His pulse thrashed in his temples as he saw two shapes slip furtively over the last obstacle and drop into the crater behind. It was surprising that the Germans in the rearward defences had not seen the two – perhaps the smoke of a renewed bombardment had unsighted them; but now the attackers were within feet of their target, and Godfrey mentally rehearsed the drill...

lie on your opposite side to your throwing-arm... withdraw the pin... count and throw with arm outstretched...

Even as he envisioned their actions he heard two dull thuds, followed after a few seconds by two more, and an unearthly howl. Then came another fitful burst of machine-gun fire, and suddenly the gun fell silent. Two revolver-shots cracked in rapid succession, unmistakeable despite the surrounding din.. Godfrey and Albert exchanged knowing glances, in which there was an element of triumph. *They've done it! They've knocked the gun out.*

'Sergeant! Prepare the men to move off as soon as Pawson and Hathersage return. The Bosches will know soon enough what's happened and it'll only take them a minute or two to call in their artillery. They' ll paste this whole sector, so we'd better look sharp.'

Heedless of the risk Godfrey climbed up the parapet and peered through the gap. The shadowy figures of the two men could be seen weaving and ducking from hole to hole, trying to avoid an enemy sniper who fired steadily at their fleeing forms and who missed by a hairsbreadth each time. They had ten yards to go, now... five yards... two... they were on the brink of the parapet... Hathersage crashed back down amongst them, grinning from ear to ear. Pawson did not follow. Indifferent to the danger Godfrey levered himself up somehow.

Pawson was lying there looking straight at him. Or at least the expression in the glaring eyes suggested that they were.

'Pawson! *Pawson!*'

Then Godfrey noticed the little round hole in the man's temple.

They were making excellent progress and were a good hundred yards closer to the German lines when the enemy barrage broke in full fury on the sector. The enemy's range was good and his gun-laying excellent as salvo after salvo was directed toward his own trench; certainly the battering it received during the minutes the platoon waited flinching for it to lift would have done for them all had they stayed put. Yet oddly the section in which they sheltered now remained unshelled, and not a man was harmed.

'Bosche gunners are losin' their touch!' Private Aldcroft smirked.

'No, they're not lad' muttered Albert. 'They're no fools.' He frowned. '*No, they're not goin' to shell their own men...*'

Godfrey had had similar misgivings. Ordering bombers forward he motioned the rest to withdraw a few yards and crouch down to offer as small a target as possible as they levelled their rifles along the trench, in readiness. Pins were pulled from a couple of Mills grenades and having lobbed them over the top, the bombers sped back to rejoin the main group.

They listened intently, hardly drawing breath. Two muffled detonations in quick succession were followed by a shriek of pain – an animal sound, terrible to hear- which for some oddly disconnected reason reminded Godfrey of a wounded fox he had once seen shot. Then a black object with a handle attached dropped some ten yards ahead of them, followed by another.

Down! Get down!' The flash and blast of the exploding grenades momentarily winded them, but the effect was otherwise negligible. There was a deathly pause as earth and splinters of wood showered down. Then as if from nowhere a group of tall figures in *feldgrau* rounded the bend in the trench at a run, wielding rifles with bayonets fixed. Briefly disoriented by the pall of smoke which still lingered they did not at first catch sight of the 7th.who as one fired into them as they advanced. German voices cried out in fear and dismay as they dropped to a man before the fusillade, killed outright or wounded, and as Godfrey dashed towards the carnage he fired point blank into them as he approached. Though it seemed to him to take an age to cover the ten or so yards he in truth accomplished it in seconds.

The first of the wounded he shot dead; but another, a heavily- built man, lay on his side, his fingers weakly clutching and unclutching at the trench floor.

Godfrey found he could not pull the trigger.

The man's helmet had fallen off, and beneath his greying hair Godfrey was confronted by a simple country face – the face of a farmer, a not unkindly face whose deep-scored lines and weatherbeaten complexion suggested that he had withstood many a storm. Now distorted with pain it strained silently up toward him, resignation and acceptance reflected in the steel blue eyes. There was no note of accusation, nor even of hatred or hostility in them. Just a silent plea; *do it now! Finish me, but make it quick! Do it!*

That look cut deeply into Godfrey as he stood over his helpless enemy, and it struck a familiar and terrible chord in his soul. For a moment he and this middle aged German, who should not have been there – who *would* not have been there but for dreadful circumstance – understood each other, and shared in a common defeat. It was not compassion which stayed his hand, but an overwhelming sense of the bloody uselessness of it all.

And Godfrey could not do it. The loss of the helmet, the grey hair and the weatherbeaten face combined to rehumanise his enemy into nothing more or less than a man. At that untimely moment he felt an affinity with one who knew suffering even as he did. The German soldier saw the hesitation, saw the reluctance and revulsion in the British officer's face; and as the revolver drooped in Godfrey's hand the German sank back, and closed his eyes.

There were no others. Clearly a small detachment had been sent to deal with what was felt could only be a minor incursion.

As the 7th.reformed and made their way up the trench they heard the dull thud as the wounded German detonated one of his own bombs against himself.

They had advanced barely fifty yards before discovering that the communication trench was effectively blocked against them.The Enemy had not left it all to chance but had constructed a wall of razor-wire and stakes to prevent any British movement beyond that point.The obstacle as it presented itself was insurmountable. Even if they'd brought cutters – abandoned long before – it would have taken a good half-hour to dismantle. And that was assuming the enemy was deaf as well as blind.The prospect of attempting to penetrate it under fire was too awful to contemplate There was nothing for it – retreat, or quit the trench entirely. Guessing that the Germans would keep a close watch on possible exit routes in the immediate vicinity Godfrey ordered the 7th. to draw back to where they had encountered the enemy infantry. Piling some smashed timber against the revetment they constructed a makeshift platform from which they could climb up to ground level once more. Godfrey led off from the front. Scrambling over a morass of churned up earth and wire he dropped into a crater several yards deep, followed by the survivors of the 7th. who leapt across the space in a couple of bounds. Exposed in No Man's Land once more they would have provided a soft target for the enemy machine gunners had not Pawson and Hathersage dealt with the threat. Godfrey was suspicious as to why the Germans were apparently making no attempts to reuse the gun; the team after all could easily be replaced. He peered gingerly over the rim of the crater. Firing had died down in their vicinity and it was obvious that the machine gun was still silent.

'It'll not be firin' again, Mr Rusholme' Albert said, divining his officer's thoughts 'leastways, not for a good while. Hathersage pinched some o't' mechanism, and chucked it away. He smashed the rest.' He knew that it was something that he himself should have checked out; but nevertheless Godfrey smiled grimly at the news, and as broadly as his mutilated cheek would allow.

The position was now a little more hopeful than it had been. Running diagonally from where they crouched there was a natural hollow which, though eroded by constant shelling, might still afford them cover. And most hopefully of all, it led roughly in the direction of Montauban. Stooping low Godfrey and the 7th. platoon moved furtively across into what must once have been a sunken trackway. This carried them out of sight of the enemy a good half-mile further toward their objective, and when it finally gave out entirely they could make out before them the battered remains of the village.

The Germans had clearly decided to hold Montauban as a strongpoint, for now concentrated rifle- and machine-gunfire poured down upon the Manchesters from the ruins. Contrary to the intention of driving the enemy out the British barrage had created ideal conditions for defence, with mounds of masonry and half-collapsed walls providing loopholes through which the German infantry could fire.

Yet despite the lethal ferocity of the defence, and despite the loss of almost half the battalion since they had quit their assembly trenches, the survivors of the 16th. Manchesters rose to press home the final attack. Further along the line of advance Godfrey could see that already some scattered units had reached the ruined outskirts of Montauban and the crackle of answering rifle-fire confirmed that they were already engaged in heavy fighting.

Someone had the presence of mind to call in the Stokes Mortars which in minutes laid down a screening barrage of smoke. This gave the 7th. Platoon the chance to move forward with greater confidence; and as Godfrey climbed from the crater his men scrambled up behind him as one, cloaked by the dense white clouds. Effectively blind, the enemy gunners frantically increased the arc of their fire. Still the Manchesters continued to fall as they moved forward, but less frequently now as many bullets went wide of their invisible marks. All the Germans could do was rake the areas where they had last seen the advancing British, but their efforts became wilder and more panic-stricken..

A light breeze sprung up from nowhere and it shifted the fog, alternately condensing it here or thinning it there; and they would occasionally glimpse knots of khaki- clad figures moving purposefully towards them. But as they took aim the floating mass would close once more and their targets would be absorbed back into the mist.

Against all the rules Godfrey now ordered his platoon to bunch more closely together, seeing at once that the pathetically few men he had left could easily be disoriented in that fog, and become lost. And if they were to mount any sort of assault at all, it would have to be cohesive, and together. *This way,* he thought, *at least a few of us should survive.*

Detailing Albert to follow up at the other extremity of the platoon Godfrey led the 7th. forward into Montauban.And even as they crept warily into the first of the rubble-strewn streets the muffled crump of high explosives signalled the assault on Glatz Redoubt on their far right, abandoned now by all except the dying and the dead.

'*Still! Lie absolutely still!*' Godfrey motioned furiously with his left hand. They had pushed through the village and though engaged in a running firefight with a group of retreating Germans had now penetrated almost to its furthermost edge. The devastation had been total, for not a single recognisable structure remained; and the slaughter on both sides was appalling beyond description. Corpses lay everywhere, in every posture imaginable and unimaginable, in places so closely packed that it was impossible not to step on them. British and German, some lying almost leisurely as if asleep, others twisted and bent in death, and still others grappling with dead fists and fingers at their motionless adversaries. And those still living crawled or cried to him for help as they clutched their wounds.

Godfrey felt numbed, emotionally anaesthetised by the horror, the only sensation a constant throbbing of his mangled cheek As he'd peered at the grey faces and into the dark eye-sockets of the twenty aged youths remaining from his platoon words of Marlowe occurred inexplicably to him;

'Why, this is Hell, nor am I out of it… '

They were in an earthly Hell, all right; one of their own making… and it seemed to him then that they were at the world's end, the dross of a species cast aside by humanity and left to its own bloody devices.

The 7th. lay huddled in the pulverised remains of someone's house. Men sat or crouched inertly, their empty gaze fixed on the void behind them. After the briefest of respites they were to move on again, and renew their attack beyond the ruins, for having consolidated their hold on the village the Order of the Day required them to advance to assault the enemy's trench system known as Montauban Alley.

Men bowed to the inevitable.. If *he*'d missed them so far, he's make sure of it *this* time; their numbers were up, all right.

As if carrying the heaviest of burdens Godfrey rose weakly from the smashed brickwork on which he had been sitting. He was mechanically adjusting his belt as Albert tugged his arm urgently.

'*There's movement, sir*' he whispered '*just behind that wall. Sure as eggs are eggs.*'

He pointed to the ruins of a barn some twenty yards distant.

'What was it?' Godfrey never disregarded such warnings, and least of all from Albert. 'What did you see?'

'Nowt definite, Mr. Godfrey. Just a little flash o' somethin' metal. Could just o' been a buckle, but you never know.'

'No, you don't. One of our chaps?'

'But why there, and why so tricky-like?'

'Get two of the men to check it out, would you?' he said as he scanned the faces for likely volunteers. But they looked so jaded that he couldn't ask even that small thing of them. 'On second thoughts, Sergeant, I'll go. It'll give them a few more minutes, and we all need that.'

'I'll come with you, sir.'

Quite inexplicably Godfrey felt unwilling to agree. At any other time, and in any other place he would have given it no thought, and accepted the offer without demur. It was basic commonsense, after all. But now he felt an odd reluctance to have Albert accompany him on this most insignificant and routine of duties. 'I'll go alone. But thank you.'

Albert looked uneasily at him. 'Fair enough, sir.'

Godfrey picked his way through the rubble and entered the ruin. He looked about him. Nothing. To the left lay what had perhaps been a milking parlour, its whitewashed stalls broken and cast about like giant playing-cards. He walked slowly toward them. Again nothing other than a pile of stained clothing in the corner. As he stooped to examine them he spotted a movement from the corner of his eye. Spinning round he caught a glimpse of a grey-clad figure hardly ten paces away. Its jacket flapped open, revealing an upper chest swathed in bloodsoaked bandages. The spectre tottered forward, and the rifle and bayonet it was holding was levelled directly at him. Godfrey heard the trigger click, and braced himself for the impact; but there was no report.

He saw the man struggle desperately with the bolt. He heard it slam to, and there was another click; yet still no report. With maddened eyes the German lurched toward the enemy officer, wielding the bayonet. Godfrey watched almost indifferently as he approached, and as the wan sunlight reflected along the weapon's cutting edge.

He did not attempt to move. He did not have the will to parry or resist and he waited resignedly for the blade to strike home. And it did, deep into living flesh; yet it was not Godfrey Rusholme who took the blow. Another had slipped quietly in beside him, and in a split second had placed himself between his officer and the attacker in an attempt to ward him off. Albert Chadderton received the thrust full in the stomach.

Like a bystander in a horror show Godfrey watched as his friend staggered a few feet, then buckled and fell sideways to the floor.

'What have you done? *What have you done?'*

Was Godfrey crying out to the German, or to Albert? Or was his anguish directed to anyone who might hear and have an answer? The voice of accusation echoed amidst the ruins, then fell like lead.

The German soldier released his grip on the rifle and staggered backwards with eyes bulging like a crazy man, brushing frantically at his tattered tunic as if attempting to sweep away the evidence of a ghastly act. He retreated to the doorway with a bewildered expression as he stared at his two enemies, one now stooping over the other. Then he was gone.

Godfrey gently turned his friend; and grasping the rifle slowly drew out the bayonet. There was a spurt of dark blood, but the wounded man made no sign. Taking off his jacket he rolled it and placed it beneath Albert's head to try to give what comfort he could.

'Cheer up, old chap!' he said, in a vain attempt to sound optimistic ' you've a Blighty one, Albert! Think! You'll be home before you know it… *Help! Wounded man! Help!'* he shouted out in desperation *'Stretcher bearers! Find the stretcher-bearers!'* Some of the platoon came running, but all they could do was stand appalled and watch as Albert Chadderton's life ebbed away before them.

This loss was to them as bad as any that could be imagined. *The* sergeant. *Their* indomitable, indefatigable sergeant, cut down in a moment's mindless violence. It was all so pitifully, bloody pointless.

'Cheer up, old chap! Help's coming.' Albert Chadderton stirred slightly and opened his eyes. 'Don't worry. You're going to be all right.' Godfrey said.

'I don't think so, sir' Albert sounded so remote, as though he were speaking to them from an immense distance. Godfrey bent his head to hear the rest.

'I've always wanted to tell you this… an' it looks as though I can, now… I always thought you were a grand pair… both you and Master Oliver… I've always been right fond of you ever since you was little lads… an' if I'd had a son… I would've wanted him to be like you.' His whole frame shuddered and he fell silent for a moment.

When he continued his voice was barely a whisper '… *will you tell them at home what really happened an' say I'm sorry, to Betty?… I wrote a letter to 'em but didn't post it… will you do that for me…* ?' He did not speak again.

Godfrey squeezed his friend's hand as he died. 'Of course I will, dear old chap… 'he said indistinctly 'Of course I will.'

Godfrey released Albert's hand and placed it reverently across the body. Then waving away the rest of the 7th. platoon he removed the stark identification disc and put it in his pocket. He laid him out as decently as he could and placed his helmet and his pack beside him; then he covered the whole with a discarded gas cape.

The face which looked across at the German trench was cold, and ashen. Whilst he had felt deadened before, his grief had only been suspended, held in abeyance whilst his emotions lay dormant. Now the full weight of tragedy had borne itself down upon him once more, and he felt himself in turmoil. He had believed it could get no worse, and had performed his duties like an automaton; but now he saw that it was not so. He wanted to weep for Albert, for his friend, but could not. The pain stayed aridly within. There would be no release from it all, he felt, but one.

He looked at his wristwatch. It was 10. 30 am. Three hours. *Just three bloody hours.*

Emerging from their cover the battle-weary survivors of the 16th. Manchesters took by storm their final objective of Montauban Alley. In some places the Germans appeared to have withdrawn from their defences, leaving the British to overrun the trench line almost unopposed. But in others they had concentrated all their resources of men and weaponry, creating strongpoints which poured a terrible hail of fire onto the advancing infantry. Entire companies which had endured the shrapnel of No Man's Land, the nightmare of Glatz Redoubt and the withering firefights in the village now finally succumbed to the combined effects of machine-gun and rifle, and fell almost to the very last man. On his way in Godfrey had overtaken the remnants of the 2nd. and 5th. platoons, all of whose officers and NCOs were dead or missing. These stunned, leaderless men he now accepted into the ranks of the 7th.; and together, as if risking all on the last throw of the dice, they made for the point where the fighting was at its worst, for there they knew the enemy would be.

Godfrey sat on a discarded German ammunition-box. Beyond him a sentry stood on a newly- cut firestep and peered over the parapet which now faced northward instead of south. He gazed out over the new No Man's Land whilst ant-like figures of stretcher-bearers and orderlies picked their way amongst the wounded and the dead strewn across the old.

A mile and a half of pulverised, bloodied earth which had cost the lives or the health or the minds of countless thousands in the months which the Manchesters had contested for it. It didn't look much, yet it had been bought at an appalling price.

The young sentry glanced briefly down at the officer with the wounded face. He only knew him vaguely and by sight; and now he was barely recognisable. It was Mr. Rusholme, the officer of the 7th. under whose command he'd come when all his pals and his own CO had gone down. He wondered why he'd not withdrawn before now, for his face was a right old mess. And Godfrey sat on unmoving, enmeshed in his own thoughts. He did not even notice for some time that the stub of his Woodbine had burned down to his fingers. His mind constantly reworked the events of the day. And a persistent voice – his own – heaped recriminations upon him.

'If only you had followed a different course… had led them better… mightn't more have made it… ? If only you had acted differently… '. He felt deadened to all else but his grief, and the shock of the losses – *his* losses- and his misery yawned before him like some stygian crater.

He did not think of the families, the parents, the wives,the sweethearts. He could not – not just yet. Otherwise it would have driven him completely mad. And still the finger of guilt pointed accusingly at him; and the voice said ' *Oh, you led them, all right; but to what end? Why should you survive, when they could not… ? Why did you live beyond your men and your usefulness?* And he could offer no answer.

He reworked over and again in his mind how together they'd rushed the final German defences and how the heavy machine-gun had cut the last of those he'd led, to pieces. How he'd grappled with the very barrel of the thing which had done such murder, and how its crew had recoiled in horror from him, and had attempted to escape; and he shuddered when he remembered how he'd killed like a thing demented – again and again and again.

It hadn't stopped there. He'd lost count of how many. The trench behind was still heaped with his victims and he didn't want to know.They'd had families too, no doubt. But he'd leave that to another time… .

He was roused by a voice which sounded vaguely familiar, but the tones seemed changed.

'Lieutenant Rusholme… *Godfrey...? Is that you*?' The enquiry sounded empty, flat, leaden. He raised his eyes to the speaker. Before him stood Gerald Warrington. His right arm and shoulder were heavily bandaged and his trousers were bloodstained. He had lost his helmet somewhere.

'*Godfrey*?' His voice was a little more animated now.

Godfrey nodded, for speaking was difficult.

'You made it, old man. I'm very glad. So *very* glad. It was hard going wasn't it?'

Godfrey nodded again.

'I don't know what I feel... the Company, and all... there isn't much left of it, you know.'

'No. I don't suppose there is.' Godfrey said at last.

'We'll find out at Roll Call... maybe tomorrow. Or the day after.'

'What is there to find out, Warrington? The whole thing's a game of bloody numbers, after all. We kill more of them, or they kill more of us. It's simple.'

'I... I can hardly face the prospect of it... to be quite honest. I think that'll be the worst part, somehow.'

Godfrey looked at Warrington and saw how profoundly he'd been changed. 'War's never as you think it'll be, is it?' he said.

'It was magnificent, the way the men went at it. I'd never seen anything like it before. Not like that. But it was terrible, just the same.' He put his hand to his forehead, then regained his composure. 'We've been ordered to withdraw, immediately. We're to hand over to another company from the Reserve. Whilst there's a lull. The Bosches are expected to counter-attack soon.'

'Can't we stay?' Godfrey's tone was almost pleading.

'No, old chap. We can't. And I'm afraid we're neither of us much good as we are.'

Then he added, almost as if form form's sake 'All our objectives have been achieved. They're delighted with the Manchesters.'

With a group of walking wounded the two started on their slow and limping road back to the old British front line. Sometimes supporting others and sometimes receiving support, they stumbled back from Montauban Alley to the village itself. As they passed through the ruins Godfrey halted, looking through narrowed eyes to the place where Albert had been killed.

'I wish to stop a moment. Bear with me, Warrington.'

The column of wounded shuffled onward and past, as Godfrey made his way into the barn to bid a last farewell to his friend. But the body was gone, removed already to the rear by one of the endless line of orderlies. All that could be found to testify to his ever having been there was a crimson patch which was slowly congealing on the ground. Godfrey apprehensively called a passing orderly over to him.

'I am looking for a man who was lying here. Do you know where the body has been taken?'

The orderly brought himself to attention and saluted. 'No sir. Haven't seen anythin' '

'Who might have removed it?'

'Well, this lot was all cleared by the RAMC boys. All the stiffs are being taken to the rear, for burial.' The orderly could say little more. 'If you want to find whoever it was, they're pilin' 'em up by the Reserve Trenches' he added helpfully 'I'd look there if I was you, sir. You can't miss'em.'

Godfrey turned with an expression of frustrated anger.

'I'm so sorry, old chap' Warrington said, genuinely sympathetic 'Who was it? Some particular friend?'

'My sergeant. And yes, he was.'

'Not *Chadderton,* surely?'

'Chadderton. *Albert* Chadderton,' Godfrey replied hollowly, placing particular emphasis on the Christian name. And he told how Albert Chadderton had given his life for him.

Quitting the ruins the two men resumed their pain-filled journey back. Warrington gazed about him in horror as they passed through scenes of unbridled chaos and tragedy, where the corpses of half the 16th. Battalion still lay. As he walked the enormity of the losses they had suffered was brought home to him, and he found it impossible to speak.

As they returned to Cambridge Copse and their old front line a series of distant explosions signalled that the enemy bombardment of what was left of Montauban and the Alley trench had been unleashed at last.

Warrington was dispatched to a Forward Dressing Station to have his wounds assessed, but Godfrey would not go until he had at least made an attempt to find where Albert's body had been taken.

An orderly pointed across to an area where there was considerable activity, and he could see a swarm of distant brown figures labouring with many limp burdens. With a terrible sense of urgency Godfrey made straight for them, as quickly as his wounds would allow.

He had witnessed horrors almost beyond count – sights which had seared his mind and memory irreparably. But nothing in his previous experiences could have prepared him for the scene which now confronted him.

In a low cavity in the landscape just to the rear of the Support Trench they were rummaging through the British dead who lay piled in vast heaps. When they had stripped them of all reusable equipment – helmets, buckles, even their boots if they weren't too knocked about, and all other property belonging to His Majesty's Army – they carried or dragged the corpses to the adjoining trench, into which they were then unceremoniously dumped.

In places the trench was already nearly full, and from the seemingly endless lines of bodies still being brought in on stretchers from the battlefield and from the many dressing-stations there was no doubt that they would run out of space sooner rather than later. At once Godfrey realised the near impossibility of discovering Albert's body amongst so many; for in places they were piled ten deep, like so many khaki and crimson sacks

Still he continued to wander aimlessly though this huge charnel-house, peering about him at the indifferent dead. And as he looked about him, the fury in his head seemed to erupt and he began to shriek out at the top of his voice *'Oh Christ... oh Christ... oh bloody Christ... '* And the wound in his face seemed to burn as if hot sulphur was in it.

A hand took him by the arm. The gesture was surprisingly gentle and compassionate, and it steered him away from the sight. He yielded passively, but as he went he kept looking back over his shoulder, at the terrible mounds.

The medical orderly saw him to the dressing-station where he was seated with a few other officers, some way apart from the trailing lines of other ranks – the euphemistically named 'walking wounded.' There he was found by Warrington, who was having his field dressings removed. The air was heavy with the smell of disinfectant and blood, but there was a strange and unearthly silence – as if the wounded had gone beyond the power to cry out in their wretchedness. Godfrey looked at them, considering the lost grey faces.

For the first time since he had been shot he gave thought to his wound, and tried to feel the injury. He had seen the expressions of the others as he had been brought in, and their looks had said much. His fingers lighted on where his cheek had been but the flesh was torn and distorted. No, he could not live with the prospect of endless echoing hospital wards, and the expressions of pity; and he speculated on how people would recoil from his appearance, and he heard their whispers.

But most of all he could no longer confront the letters – the heartbroken enquiries he would receive, and the interminable stream of letters he would have to write. What answers had he to offer? And what comfort? How could he justify *his* survival to the loved ones of the men who had perished? Men who had placed what faith they had left, in him? He had read it in their eyes. He did not believe that he deserved better or more than they. He would have liked to put *that* in his letters – the admission of his own failure – and he might have done it too, save that he would not add to others' pain by burdening them with his own. It was not for him to expiate his sins in such a way.

He truly wished he had died with his men.

He rose unsteadily to his feet, and made some excuse. A motive force he did not understand but which he could not resist led him slowly to an earth bank in front of the dressing station. He climbed it, and looked far out across the Somme.

Friedrich Emmler of the 6th.Bavarian RAR had been having trouble on and off all day with his bloody machine-gun. One minute it'd be rattling away ten to the dozen, the next it would jam up solid. He'd cleaned and oiled the mechanism more than a few times, but right in the middle of the Tommies' last attack it had packed up yet again – this time particularly dangerously because the wave had got within twenty metres before they were finished off by an enfilading gun. It had been too close for comfort, and he would make sure it wasn't repeated – if only to avoid being put on a charge by his company commander who'd blisteringly accused him of neglect.

Emmler thought he'd try a new belt of ammunition – the cloth on the last one had looked a bit fuzzy along the leading edge. Closing the breech he levelled the gun at nothing in particular, and wound off a few trial shots. Then- wouldn't you know it – the gun jammed yet again. Emmler kicked the barrel in ill-temper and reaching for his toolkit, set about stripping it down once more.

Of the three bullets Emmler fired,two ploughed harmlessly into soft earth not a hundred metres ahead of his position. The third would have done the same, had it not been for a large piece of shrapnel from a howitzer-round which lay nearby. The bullet struck the immovable iron and glanced off, ricochetting across the old battlefield and winging swiftly upwards and away over the remains of wire entanglements, lines of old trenches and the stumps of ruined woods.

Two miles into its fateful journey it began its descent.

It struck Godfrey in the chest, just below his tunic pocket. And there was enough of its malevolent energy remaining to cause it to penetrate, and lodge itself near his heart.

Warrington saw him fall, and tearing himself free from the orderlies he ran to the spot. Hands steeped in blood he tried frantically to staunch the flow from the wound; but all he could do was to hold his palm against the puncture. And still the blood flowed, trickling out between his fingers. Then raising his hand Godfrey grasped Warrington's lapel in his clenched fist. He gazed with a fierce intensity at his old friend, and he shook his head.

Slowly he relaxed his grip and laid back again on the ground. And almost imperceptibly he shook his head once more; not at Warrington, but at the world.

Freed by the bullet Godfrey's weary soul took flight, and quit the battlefield and the Somme and France, forever.

Chapter Twenty One

THE WEATHER was something of a rarity in Manchester. A hot mugginess which had overhung the city during the preceding days had gone entirely,and lumpy grey clouds now scattered before a freshening breeze from the west. A July sun which would have been more at home in an Italian sky beamed onto the city. It illuminated the narrow warrens of New Heath's streets and alleyways, penetrating the sootiest corners of backyards and bathing everything it touched in a new light. The old cattle market which spanned out at the junction of three ancient roads seemed to open its odd triangular shape up to the embrace of the sun; and windows in old townhouses which bordered the thoroughfare shone with a hundred different facets. Tethered horses stamped here and there on the cobbles as smoke –blackened sparrows argued noisily in the eaves; and all in all it was as though a little corner of the grimy city had for a brief moment abandoned its industry, and assumed the rural ambience of an earlier time.

One of these narrow side streets sloped downwards onto a towpath bordering the sluggish waters of the Rochdale Canal. In places it was hemmed in by the walls of towering cotton mills built on either bank; and in such gloomy spots the current flowed in perpetual shadow; but in others where industry had intruded to a lesser degree there was space and light enough for grass to sprout between the cobbles, and even for the occasional tree to take root. As a retreat and a recreational spot it came a poor second to the far blue Pennines, whose heathery wastelands and moors could be seen from the upper floors of the mills; but for those who sought a little quiet simply to think and could spare neither time nor money to get there it was the best that the district could offer. Popular with courting couples, the canal's grassy banks and reed-fringed margins offered solitude from the crowded streets. And for those with aching hearts it was a place to be alone.

It was for this reason that Dr.Oliver Rusholme had made his way there. Seated on the beam of a lock-gate he felt the warmth of the sun on his back, but did not appreciate it much. Try as he might, he could not free himself from his thoughts about Dolly Chadderton. Memories of her filled every moment of his leisure like some sad refrain; the image of her blonde hair, her piercing blue eyes and her slender shape rose before him constantly and even when asleep he dreamed of her over and again. He would rise early and unrefreshed, and doggedly immerse himself in his work. If an extra duty was required or a colleague absent, Rusholme would never refuse.

He always seemed to be about the place – attending in this ward or at that clinic – but while his commitment and his talent were respected by his fellow-doctors he was fast getting the reputation of being an 'all-work-no-play jonny', and thoroughly dull. He did not accompany them on their jaunts around Manchester, and as he had declined their invitations once or twice they did not bother to ask him a third time.

Underlying it all there was the constant worry about Godfrey. Though the occasional letter had come from France, they had become increasingly superficial. They did not represent the brother he knew, but instead seemed anodyne and penned for form's sake only. Some momentous event was imminent, he could read that between the platitudes; but as to what that event would be he could only guess; and he would not ask. Then the news of the great offensive on the Somme broke, with speculation rife as to the probability of the long- awaited breakthrough.

The Enemy Broken... Fleeing Our Guns... Huge Gains Made... Our Armies Advancing on all Fronts... Casualties Believed Acceptably Light... so the headlines ran, though detail was disconcertingly absent. Dismissing it as no more than tub-thumping rhetoric which was as full of hyperbole as it was barren of fact, Oliver had turned for enlightenment to *The Manchester Guardian*. But whilst its reporting was more objective and measured, there was still a dearth of information as to what precisely was happening, and just how successful the offensive had really been. Oliver saw well enough that his brother must have been preoccupied with countless final details, and that this consideration alone might explain the cessation of his letters. Certainly most passers-by in the street seemed buoyantly optimistic, seemed in a celebratory frame of mind as if the war was virtually won, all bar the shouting. But at the same time there was a tense undercurrent as though while they outwardly rejoiced they simultaneously harboured fears for someone out there.

Oliver absently flicked a small stone into the depths of the lock and as he listened to its fall he considered his life and his duties at the Hospital. In one sense he had never experienced such fulfilment as he enjoyed now; the ailing and the sick were a magnet to him, and the enduring challenge was to ease their suffering and cure them if it lay within his power. But whilst he might relieve the pain of others there was no apparent remedy to ease the ache in his heart. For many of his contemporaries the prospect of working long hours for relatively little pay in the free clinics where of necessity the poor and the near destitute sought help would have appalled them. They would have spurned just such a job as Oliver did now, would have regarded it as being utterly beneath contempt. And they would have continued to wax fat on the fees of the self-indulgent and the hypochondriac, and have pandered to their clients' whims and fancies. As was his way, Oliver failed utterly to notice the regard in which he was held by the poor of New Heath. He was the young man who always had time and always listened. That he had set aside the customary aloofness of the doctor and spoke to them civilly and compassionately did not reduce him in their eyes, but instead elevated him to almost saintly status. He noticed that if he came across his patients in the street they would step off the pavement for him, the men doffing their hats and the women even curtseying to him. It made him feel profoundly uncomfortable at first; then he rationalised it by pointing out that this was their way of showing respect to a doctor – any doctor. He did not hear what they said of him as he passed. Though he had been at the hospital barely a few weeks he was already well on the road to earning a permanent place in their affections.

Back in the echoing lodging house where he now lived the maid brought him a letter. It was from Wilfred Hallett, whom he had not seen since his departure for London. He would be in Manchester that very weekend, he said, with the intention of looking-up his old crony and comparing notes. And what about a jolly night *on the tiles*? Seemed a pity to waste the train fare…

In spite of Oliver's pleasure at hearing from his waspish old friend, his first instinct was to turn down the offer, to cry off on the pretext that he had an evening duty to do (he had already volunteered himself for the Saturday night, a most unpopular roster when the brawlers were carted in). He wrote the reply, cordially negative, and had sealed it in its envelope when he caught sight of himself in the shaving-mirror. He looked again. In his face he was alarmed to see signs which had presaged his earlier breakdown. His eyes were dark-rimmed and tired, his brow lined and his mouth tense. He swept his hand through his hair. It felt distinctly greasy. He looked a mess. In an instant he changed his mind. He would spruce himself up, and he *would* go out with Hallett.He crumpled up his reply and dropped it into the paper-basket; then sat down and swiftly penned another.

As the 7.30 from London hissed into Manchester Victoria Hallett stepped down from the carriage without waiting for the train to stop. He looked about him with the air of a baronet surveying his estates; but as he caught sight of Oliver his face lit up and any hint of superiority was dispelled in a second. Waving furiously to each other from opposite ends of the platform they met and shook hands warmly – not because of any long absence, for it had only been a month or so since they had last met – but because each had been changed by the intensity of a shared experience which made them part of an exclusive fraternity.

Hallett certainly looked every bit the medical man, dapper in a dove grey suit of impeccable cut and sporting a silk tie and spats. Oliver had been a little more conservative in his dress, and a little less showy. But for all that the two friends looked an impressive foil to each other as they strolled out of the station and down the bustling Hunt's Bank to Fennel Street and *The Shambles*, where they proposed to have supper together.

Meeting up with Hallett again refreshed Oliver tremendously, as they talked and laughed about eccentric patients they had encountered, about starchy matrons and ward-sisters and about the shortage of decent accommodation. It was only after paying a visit to a music hall whose prices were now first rate even if the performers were distinctly second, and where more khaki cavorted on the stage than off it, that Hallett referred to the old days at Nelson Place.

On their return to the station Oliver had hoped the evening might pass without so much as a reference to them, and for his part he had studiously avoided even hinting in that direction. But he had hoped in vain. In a moment the melancholy which the evening had gone so far to dispel, was back with a vengeance. At first Hallett did not observe the effect the subject had on his friend as he barged on regardless about their years there. But Oliver's silence and the expression on his face caused him to pause.

'My word, I hope I didn't say anything to offend?' he asked concernedly. 'If I have, I'm most terribly sorry… '

'No, Hallett. Nothing you've said. It's nothing' he said lightly, trying to force a smile. But Hallett was not easily fooled. He looked at his friend searchingly. 'Excuse me for contradicting you, old man, but I think there *is* something. You look as if you'd lost a fiver.'

'Do I? I'm sorry, Hallett. It's nothing you've said, really.'

'What was it, then?' Hallett persisted. 'You know how damnably curious I am about people's doings, and what-not. Do tell.'

'There's nothing *to* tell. Sadly.'

'Gosh, there's something *really* wrong, isn't there? Well?' He looked more searchingly still at Oliver. 'Well?' He racked his sharp brains for a clue, since it appeared that his friend was unwilling or unable to unburden himself. 'It wouldn't be an affair of the heart, would it?'

This was something of a stab in the dark, but at Oliver's reaction Hallett began rapidly to examine certain possibilities; and there was one which stood out prominently amidst all others, impossible though it might be to contemplate.

'It surely wasn't that little serving-maid – what's her name… Dolly? I recall you turning a trifle mushy whenever she walked in.' Oliver did not reply. 'My goodness ! I see it was – and still is, by the look of it. What *have* you been up to, old chap?' But though Hallett was spot on as to the other person involved, he was way off the mark as to the cause. 'I say, you weren't tempted to fish where you shouldn't, were you? Because if… '

Oliver caught the drift of Hallett's meaning 'No I *certainly* was not' he retorted furiously. 'I would never consider such a thing! I'm disappointed that you should think I might. I thought we were friends'.

Though Hallett was possessed of a sardonic nature he could also show compassion if the right chord in his feelings was struck. He saw now how it was with Oliver. 'And so we are' he replied in a kinder tone 'You're in deep, aren't you, old chap?'

Oliver just nodded his head.

'I must say, I'm rather surprised. How did your Ma and Pa take it?'

'They don't know, and they never will. I don't intend to tell them.'

'Would they think it a suitable relationship –an *appropriate* one, for someone in your position?'

Oliver knew what Hallett was driving at and he bridled once more.

'Frankly I couldn't care less what they'd think. It doesn't matter to me one jot.'

'I see.' A silence fell between them for a minute or two. 'What does the young woman think about it?'

'She doesn't. I haven't mentioned my feelings to her. I don't know if she thinks of me at all.'

'Then my advice to you, Rusholme, is to let the passage of Time do it for you. It's a great healer, as they say. If there's nothing you can do about it, try to forget her.'

Then Oliver wretchedly told it all.

Hallett looked seriously at him as he concluded

'I don't know what to do for the best.' Oliver said heavily.

'Then though it sounds rather lame, I'd do nothing. I don't think you've anything to chastise yourself for. You seem to have behaved decently, albeit a little unwisely. These things do happen' he said resignedly. ' Just await events, and see how they work out. Who knows what's just around the corner? The chance you're hoping for might arise when you least expect it.'

Hallett did not know then how portentous his advice to Oliver would prove. And as one bid farewell to the other, neither of the young men could possibly suspect that tragedy would bring about what Oliver had longed for.

He was glad of Hallett's visit, and on reflection was grateful to his abrasive friend for allowing their evening to conclude the way it had. He felt a profound sense of relief to have unburdened to someone, and while his difficulty was hardly any closer to being resolved, felt more able to face up to it, and even put it in perspective.

He continued to attend long hours at the hospital, and with little rest. As for his lodgings they were just that, and no more; there was none of the conviviality which had marked out Nelson Place. His landlady was an unsmiling, pinched little woman who begrudged extra butter, and measured the meat. She worked to the minimum, to maximise her gain. Not that Oliver cared much, either way. For him it was just another staging-post on a long road to God only knew where.

Chapter Twenty Two

HE WAS returning to his lodgings after a long and trying night duty. Running his hand over his chin he realised he certainly needed a shave, and decided to request some hot water from the kitchen, if it was not too much trouble. It was that time in the early morning when the mill-hands should have already entered the iron gates of the great cotton-palaces, and the looms be working flat out. So it surprised him to see numbers of women of all ages – many identifiable as likely spinners or weavers from their clogs and heavy shawls – clustered about here and there with haggard faces, or heading in one particular direction and with one common purpose. There was an atmosphere of foreboding in the air– an indefinable sense that something terrible had occurred –which hung about the streets down which he walked.

It fuelled his own anxiety about Godfrey and he called to one of the crowd, a man whom he recognised as a porter at the hospital.

'Macklin? What's happened? Why are all these people about at this time?' The man touched the peak of his cap to Oliver.

'The news has just come through, sir. They've posted t'casualty figures, wi' names an' all. It's very bad, sir. There's pages an' pages of 'em, stuck up on the notice-board over yonder.' The man pointed to the wall of a council office where a crowd was gathering.

'It looks like the *Pals* have copped it ' Macklin added tersely as Oliver turned to join the hurrying women. 'There's 'alf the Regiment on them sheets.' Oliver felt a chill run through him as he was jostled by those struggling to get a sight of the dreaded Lists. He wanted to push himself, such was his fear for his brother and his conviction that somehow he would discover the worst; but pity for those around him caused him to hold back. He was not a small man, and it seemed base to elbow his way forward at the cost of such people as surrounded him. He caught a brief glimpse of outspread newspaper pages which had been attached with drawing pins to a wooden board. There hadn't been enough space to contain them all, so the extra papers had been fixed to the brickwork with parcel-tape.

'*Make way, there*!' someone shouted from the front of the ruck. 'Make way! There's someone who's been took bad.' A stout woman of middle age was half carried half dragged through the throng. Her face had the pallor of death about it, her lips a pale grey.

'Her two eldest lads, who volunteered on t' same day. They're posted as killed, the pair of 'em' another woman explained to anyone who would listen. 'an' now she's been took bad wi't' shock. She just swooned away when she read it; just swooned away.' The pressure from the outer edge of the crowd intensified still further at this, while from amidst the crush of families and friends there came cries of anguish, and suppressed sobbing, rising and falling in a cadence of sorrow.

Desperate though he was to know the worst Oliver could not face learning it under such circumstances. Slowly he extricated himself from the scene, though it cut him to the heart to have to do so. Slowly he walked back towards the hospital entrance where there was a newsstand, and there he bought a copy of the paper from the vendor. He read the headlines;

England's Bravest

Considerable Lancashire Losses

MANCHESTER'S PRIDE IN HER 'PALS'

Without reading further he folded it up deliberately,and made his way back to the hospital where he hurriedly collected a few basic medical items and put them in a bag. In it he also placed the newspaper, still folded and unread. Then with his heart in the grip of a dreadful foreboding he walked purposefully back to the crowd whose numbers had swollen in the few minutes he had been absent, a crowd now near- frantic with anxiety.Shawls clasped tightly by labour-worn hands framed eyes from which hope had fled; and knots of women gathered here and there around one who had discovered she was bereaved, robbed of son or brother or husband, proffering a supporting arm or a shoulder to weep on, and hide their tears from the gaze of the world. Oliver turned to those for whom the blow had been too much and who, in a state of collapse, now sat on the pavement or leant against a wall. He bent to them, and offered what treatment he could for grief.

'It's that new doctor from th'hospital' someone said in hushed tones 'the one whose brother were an officer. Y'know… it says so on t' List.'

'Perhaps he hasn't found out yet, poor lad.'

'Don't say nowt about it.'

'No.'

But Oliver did not need to search the Lists to know the terrible inevitable truth. He knew and understood too much about Godfrey to hope for any other outcome. And he shared in their agony as individuals and as a community, burying his heartache for a while beneath his duties.

He sat motionless on his bed, his sight fixed unseeingly on the fireless grate. The newspaper was open now, and lay beside him. On the fourth page of casualties notified from the Somme there was an entry which had been accorded the honour of its own box, in recognition of the rank of the deceased.

A Fine Sportsman and Noted University Bat

The death from wounds of Lieutenant Godfrey Clark Rusholme of the 16th. Battalion and the eldest son of Clarence Rusholme Esq. senior partner of the eminent Manchester law firm of Rusholme Standish and Co. has been notified to his immediate family. A former pupil of Hugh William's School, he was exceptional both as a batsman and in the academic field. As a recent graduate of Goldring College Oxford, he was expected to pursue a career in the law.

His brother is understood to be a doctor practising at one of the City's hospitals.

Oliver ran his fingers though his hair again and again. He felt nothing, saw nothing. The news, though long expected, had nevertheless struck him a near-mortal blow. He could not think of the immediate past nor endure any recollection of his dead brother at that moment; and he could not face up to how he would mourn him. He would have to consign all that to a bleak future, if he were to avoid the impending and inevitable devastation of himself. For the moment he would hold tightly onto the present; for as far as he could see it was his only liferaft.

Rising like an automaton he made his way to the door, passed down the stairs with a rigid gait and left the lodging house. Making his way down to the canal he crossed the old stone bridge where the towpath switched banks; and turning left strode blindly along by the waterside. His limbs seemed detached from his conscious mind, bearing him away as his distracted thoughts turned inward upon themselves. How long he walked he did not know, but he did not pause in his stride until Manchester and its suburbs had given way to the sparse moorlands which rose above Middleton. How he found himself to be there, and why, he hardly knew. The empty landscape which confronted him was alien, and unknown; he felt a stranger there, and as his eyes followed the dark ribbon of the canal onwards until it became obscured by the fold of the next treeless slope, he felt profoundly lost. He sat down by a hedge of stunted thorn-bushes, and buried his head in his hands.

He was roused from his blackness by the remote sound of a horse's hooves. The metallic chink of the creature's harness as it strained under its load seemed as foreign and as incongruous in that place as he was, and as the rhythmic plodding drew closer he raised his head to see what it was that approached. Rounding a gentle bend of the canal came a draft – horse and its barge. As the mare's muscular shoulders leaned forward with her effort, two little boys whose cast of chin and brow confirmed them to be brothers tripped along lightfootedly beside their charge. Along her harness were ranged small brass bells which tinkled musically with each shift of her chest, and from time to time the boys chimed in with words of encouragement.

'*Easy-go, Daisy! Good girl! Easy-go*!' and the horse though blinkered would turn her great head to catch a glimpse of her diminutive masters. The barge was heavily laden with a cargo of coal bound for the city, and the waters lapped dangerously close to her topsides leaving only an inch or two to spare. The vessel's bright decorations shone out incongruously like a fairground ride amidst the dour heathland, and as it slipped past Oliver the bargee standing by the tiller looked over at him with some curiosity.

'Good mornin', sir' he said politely, raising his cap above a tanned face. The pretty woman who sat beside him hurriedly closed her blouse on a bared breast at which her baby was suckling, and flushing pinkly, looked away in her embarrassment. Oliver returned the bargee's greeting hollowly.

As the barge and its attendant sounds began to diminish in the distance, and as the sighing wind closed about him once more, a sudden loneliness welled up within him, and a desire to return to the city and to its people and all that the return entailed. For some obscure reason he did not wish to let the barge out of his sight; perhaps its slow disappearance in some way emphasised his isolation; perhaps the cohesion of that little family represented what he would regret most, now Godfrey was gone.

Stiffly he rose to his feet and with the vessel and its family still in sight he followed, keeping to the same easy pace as the horse but maintaining a decent distance from them. And the long walk back to New Heath calmed him, and made him more ready for what was to come.

On his return to his room he collapsed on his bed fully clothed and immediately fell into a deep sleep, having had no rest for almost thirty hours.

An insistent knocking at the front door roused him from dark dreams. He looked blearily at the time. 10.30. Was it a.m. or p.m? In his disoriented and still exhausted state he could not be sure.

The caller was a boy bearing a telegram. It was addressed to Dr. Rusholme.

Dear Oliver.

You will have heard the most terrible news concerning our dear Godfrey. You must come home at once. Please do not delay. There is more I have to tell you. In sorrow Your Mama.

Pausing only to throw a few necessities into a small case Oliver sped down to the hospital. His colleagues received him with many expressions of sympathy and offers of support; without demur they agreed to cover for him until better circumstances enabled him to return. Sprinting to the station he caught the 10. 55, and within the hour was walking with a sinking heart through Desbury.

On entering the middle of the village he took the trouble to pass on the side of the road which was opposite to that on which the Chadderton's cottage stood. If Dolly was at home he did not wish to distress her further by his presence nearby, and he did not want to face being in such close proximity to her. But despite his wretchedness he could not prevent himself from looking in that direction, and he was disturbed to see a group of people- both men and women – gathered around the open front door and conversing in hushed tones.

He paused at the entrance to the driveway leading to Millwain Place. It was all too familiar, and he caught his breath. Now the recollections came in upon him thick and fast and remorselessly, try to disregard them though he might. He saw the snow once more, and Godfrey dressed in his walking-clothes; and the figure seemed to turn and smile wistfully back to him over its shoulder. There was such a depth of sadness in that smile. But still Oliver found himself unable to weep. With an act of physical will he forced himself to negotiate the driveway, every grating step upon the gravel taking him closer to a mother who needed him, and a father from whom he was estranged.

He approached and looked up. In every window the curtains were closed, as if the very house were itself blind with grief; and fixed to the door was a small wreath of laurel wound about with black ribbons. Ever after Oliver would associate the glossy leaves with tragedy and turn his face away from them involuntarily, as he did now.

He paused on the threshold before ringing the bell, and listened. There was an absolute and deathly silence in the house – the hush of mourning. Nothing stirred, as those within seemed benumbed.

He rang again.

He did not know how he coped with their reception of him. Alice, seeing him there before her as she answered the door broke down entirely, wringing her arthritic fingers and repeating over and again amidst her sobs ' poor Master Godfrey… me heart's quite broke… poor dear Master Godfrey… '

He put his arm round her and gave her a reassuring hug.

'Bless you, Master Oliver for comin' so quick. Your Pa took the wicked news very bad, when the telegram came, an' the doctor's been to both of 'em. God knows but they need you here… '

The study door opened silently and Ida Rusholme came out. He was appalled at the change, for he would hardly have recognised his mother from the handsome middle aged woman she had been only months before. Dressed entirely in black which accentuated the pallor of her face, her eyes were now sunken and red. She had drawn her hair back and had pinned it ruthlessly behind her head; the outlines of her cheekbones and her skull were now clearly visible and the overall impression was one of sudden ageing. With her gaze fixed solemnly upon him she approached and put her arms around his neck without uttering a word; then inclining her head she rested it against his shoulder.

'I've come, Ma' Oliver said simply.

They stood together in that position for a little while. Then a low moan came from her lips and her whole body shook.

'Let's go through, Ma. Let's sit down together, shall we? There's no point in staying here. Then we can talk.'

He led her back into the study, and closed the door quietly. The room was in semi-darkness because of the closed curtains. Oliver led Ida to a sofa and he sat by her side, holding her hands in both of his. How thin they suddenly seemed, and how cold. They were as chilly as ice. He rubbed them a little, to try to restore some of their life and warmth.

'The telegram…' she began suddenly 'the telegram arrived early yesterday.' She halted, fighting to regain her composure. 'It was sent from The War Office. It told us only… only... '

'I know what it said, Ma. Try not to distress yourself too much.'

'It's as if a light has gone out of our lives, Oliver.'

'I know.'

'You loved him dearly, didn't you?'

'You know I did, Ma.'

'And he loved you with all his heart. He told me, in so many words, the last time he was on leave. He called you the finest of brothers. He said no man could ask for a better… '

She broke off as her tears flowed and her voice became indistinct. Oliver rocked her to and fro, just as she had done with him when he was a child.

'I knew his worth, Ma.' Oliver said ' I knew his worth.'

'Your Papa' she went on ' your poor Papa has taken it dreadfully. He became very ill only a few minutes after we received the telegram. He started to choke and could not breathe. I didn't know what to do, and Alice helped me a great deal. Dr. Harbin came as quickly as he could. He says that your Papa has had a stroke, brought on by the shock.'

Though distant from his father and though there was a dearth of affection between the two, this further piece of bad news appalled him nonetheless. 'Where is he, Mama? I must go to see him.'

'He is in his room. He is not able to sit up, but has to be propped upright to assist his breathing, so Dr. Harbin says.'

'And Helene? Does she know?'

' I sent a telegram to her. She wired back at once to say that she will come as soon as she is able. She tells us that Gerald Warrington was badly wounded on the same day as..as..Godfrey was… and she wishes to be there for him when he is brought back.'

Oliver knocked gently on his father's door. There was no answer. He knocked again, and it was opened to him by a nurse clad in sepulchral white. 'I have come to see my father.'

She silently ushered him in. At first he could not make out where in the bed his father was. He saw the counterpane and the pillows but nothing else besides. The room smelt familiarly of medicines and hygiene and was chokingly warm. He approached and peered downwards onto the pillow. The bed seemed too big for the shrivelled human frame which lay within it.

'Pa?' he said gently 'Pa, its Oliver.' His father had sunk between the pillows so as to be almost swallowed by them, and only the thin wisps of his hair were immediately visible.

There was no movement or sound to signify that his father had heard him, or was even conscious. Ida approached silently and stood beside her son.

'Clarence' she said gently 'Oliver's here. He's come to see you.'

There was a slight movement which showed him to be still alive, but nothing more.

Ida repeated her words. This time there was a gurgling sound as if his father was attempting to say something. Ida turned on the sidelamp whose soft glow enabled them to see Clarence better. His eyes were open, but they did not seem to be focused on anything. His mouth began to work, gasping and opening and shutting like a fish; but only incoherent sounds came out.

'It's Oliver, Pa. I've come as you wanted. I'm here, Pa.'

The mouth continued to open and close; then with a supreme effort Clarence brought his left hand from beneath the counterpane. It dropped down heavily as if the labour had exhausted him. Clasped within his bony fingers there was a crumpled piece of paper. Clarence's eyes slowly shifted till his gaze fell on Oliver. Once more the mouth began to work, and the fingers uncurled. Perceiving that his father wanted him to take the paper he carefully removed it, and smoothed it out a little against his knee.

It was the telegram. Oliver read the formularised expression of sympathy, and how His Majesty deeply regretted the death of a man of whose existence he was absolutely ignorant. A choking noise, almost like a sob, came from his father's throat. Oliver looked in to the lost eyes and saw the utter desolation there. He folded up the piece of paper once more and placed it back into Clarence's hand. The fingers suddenly gripped it with alarming force, as if by doing so they might distil from it the last living essence of the son whose dead name was printed there. Oliver put his hand tenderly on that of his father's. The old man shuddered, and made as if to draw it away.

'Don't worry Pa. I'm very sorry' said Oliver 'We all loved Godfrey. You most of all.'

Oliver was sitting beside his mother in the study once more. Phoebe had brought in the tea, but they had sipped it from habit only, tasting nothing.

'You know that the prognosis for your Papa is... is very poor, Oliver?'

'Yes. I doubt that he will recover.'

'This dreadful, monstrous war!' Ida burst out suddenly 'Oh, if only those politicians who so blithely send others' boys out to die knew what wretchedness... what misery they cause! No act however base is less... less deserving of forgiveness. But they sleep soundly in their beds! And will they go themselves? Not *them*... ! Oh no, not them! They hide behind their 'patriotism' and their political duties!'

Oliver put his arms around his mother in a vain bid to calm her, and held her as she wept and raged against those whom she held responsible for the death of her son.

She quietened after a while, and even smiled wistfully through her tears. 'Others suffer even as we do, Oliver,' she said.

'I'm sure there are many who do at this moment.'

'Do you remember Albert?'

'Of course, Mama.' The mentioning of Albert's name in the context of their conversation sent a chill of foreboding though Oliver.

'Did you know he was *Godfrey's* platoon sergeant?'

'I did. Godfrey thought the world of him; he told me he was the bravest man he'd ever met.'

'Our dairyman – who comes from the village – told Alice that the Chaddertons have received a telegram too. Albert was killed on the same day.'

Oliver's head spun. This was tragedy heaped on tragedy. Now the sombre group of people outside the Chadderton's was explained.

Just as once before, he could have kicked himself for his obtuseness; now his heart beat for another bereaved family, a member of which, he now realised, mattered to him more than any living person.

What of *her?* What of Dolly? Even now the girl would be going through all that he and his family were suffering. In a confusion of thoughts and emotions he resolved to do what he had vowed he would never do; he *must* visit the Chaddertons and offer what sympathy and support he could.

His motives were irreproachable; had it been for selfish reasons – under a pretext of visiting them in their distress to fulfil his desire to see the girl once more – he would have despised himself and could not have gone through with it. But his concern was for the girl he loved. Even if he did not see her, he would not rest until he was sure she was all right, and that the family wanted for nothing.

He told his mother of his intentions, and composing herself sufficiently she wrote a letter to the widowed Mrs. Chadderton, including in it two five-pound banknotes *as a mark of our esteem for Albert, and in the hope that it may go some way to alleviating any difficulties which might arise through your sad loss.*

The evening was mild, and warm, and peaceful. Hardly a leaf stirred on the oaks bordering the road to Desbury. Far above him – infinitely far, so it seemed – a scattering of milky clouds moved serenely across the sky. It occurred to him that those same clouds might have passed over France, and the Somme.

With a determined step he walked the same route he had taken earlier that day, and was soon standing before the maroon front door of the Chadderton's cottage. The brass knocker had been muffled with a piece of flannel and, as at Milwain Place, the curtains were closed. Timidly his hand rose, and he knocked softly, his pulse racing and pounding in his ears.

Am I wrong to be doing this? he had asked of himself a dozen times on the way down; but though he still harboured doubts, they did not seem to carry weight sufficient to counter what he was now doing.

There was no answer, so he tried again. A sound came from within, and someone spoke quietly. The latch rattled on the inside of the door, and slowly it swung open. The figure standing before him was that of a heavy-set man with a broad bearded face. Oliver thought he noticed a vague similarity between him and Albert – the same smooth sweep of the forehead, the same fine nose and brow.

'Can I help you, sir?' the man enquired politely. Oliver took off his hat.

'Would you… would you be so kind as to tell Mrs. Chadderton… that Oliver – Oliver Rusholme – would like to speak to her for a moment? I have a letter for her from my mother.'

'Would that be Mrs.Rusholme, up at the Place?'

'Yes.'

'I'll tell her,sir; but you must expect her to say she cannot see you, since… well, I'm sure you know all, sir. Would you kindly step this way?' Oliver seemed to step across the gulf of a lifetime as he was ushered into the little front parlour, now darkened like the house from which he had come. 'Will you excuse this, sir?' the man asked deferentially 'only it's my sister-in-law's wish that the curtains should remain closed, for now.'

'Are you Albert's brother?'

'Yes, sir. I was.'

The man fetched an oil-lamp and showed Oliver to a chair – the same chair on which he had perched as a little boy long ago, when he and Godfrey had visited with a message for Albert. In the sombre half-light Oliver pictured his brother there, recalling fondly his easy grace and the warmth of the bond between them. He swallowed hard. Godfrey was not the reason he was there.

The faintest movement of a dress-hem brushing on the flagstones caused him to look up. Mrs. Chadderton had entered almost silently and now stood before him. Her face seemed expressionless at first glance– calm and cold; but as he looked at her again he saw that what he had mistaken for frigidity was in fact a study in supreme self-control, the eyes in her taut face infinitely and inexpressibly sad. Oliver marvelled at the dignity which Albert's widow now possessed.

'Thank you for coming to see us, Doctor Rusholme' she said. The crepe of her black dress rustled as she seated herself opposite him.

'I… I have brought you a letter from my mother, Mrs. Chadderton. She said that you need make no reply.' He drew out the envelope and handed it to her.

Almost reluctantly she took it from him.

'Thank Mrs. Rusholme for me, Doctor' she said ' and say how deeply grieved we all were when we heard of your own poor brother. My husband…' she halted, almost overwhelmed, then mastered herself, speaking distinctly and very quietly 'my husband, my dear Albert, said he was the best officer any man could have. The bravest and the best. An' he always said Mr. Godfrey was a true gentleman, even as a young lad.'

'He was, Mrs Chadderton.'

'And he said much the same o' you, too.' Suddenly from its previous tautness her head sank limply onto her breast and she started to cry quietly for an irreparable loss, a cry all the more expressive because of its simplicity. The sound cut Oliver to the marrow and he averted his sight. How could he feel the pain of others, and yet still not weep for his own?

Regaining her self possession as swiftly as she had lost it, she drew herself upright.

'Please excuse me, Doctor Rusholme. I'm not myself, I'm sure you'll understand. Thank you for your kindness in coming.' With that she stood once more and turning stiffly left the room. He had not had time to speak of his own regret nor express his sympathy. Nor had he even asked about Dolly.

He sat alone in the half-light for several minutes. No one seemed to be coming and with a heaving heart he rose to see himself out. He picked up his hat and was about to open the parlour door when it seemed to open by itself and the slender figure of a young woman entered. There could be no doubt as to who it was. Oliver stared, almost in disbelief. Though he had come for the best of reasons he could not remove his gaze from her. The sepia light of the oil-lamp added lustre to her tear-filled eyes, and stroked her hair with gold; and as she stood there before him he swore to himself that he had never beheld anyone so beautiful, nor anyone that he would ever love so much.

They stood facing each other for an uncomfortable moment, each uncertain as to what to do or say next.

'How are you, Dolly?' *God, the words seemed so lame* ' I… I came to see your mother..and especially you… I wanted to tell you how sorry I am – how deeply sorry – about your Pa.

He was a very fine man. We are all deeply grieved by the news.'

'Thank you.'

'And if there is any way in which I can help – anything at all – just say the word, and I'll do my utmost.' Oliver's voice deepened with emotion.

'You're very kind, sir' she said emptily.

She did not move from the door but remained standing there as if prepared to retreat at any moment..

He took a step toward her. 'Dolly, please hear me out. I'm sorry that the circumstances are so terrible, and I wouldn't for the world broach it. But whatever you might think of me, and in spite of the contempt or dislike you might feel, please believe me that I never once intended to mislead you, or trifle with you.'

He paused, then added with depth of feeling 'The last thing I would ever want would be to hurt you.'

She remained silent for a while. 'I thought at first you did mean to do those things, Dr. Rusholme. An' it made me feel very sad that you would've. But I have come to see now that… I was wrong. I don't believe you would ever act so.' Stunned with grief as she was, the girl sought to decipher what this man whom she loved and who stood so penitently before her was really saying.

Yet still she forcibly suppressed all hope, for what grounds had she to hope at all? Her pragmatic side reminded her that he had come there for the very reasons he had given – to say sorry about her poor Pa, and apologise for the offence he believed he had given. She knew him well enough to know that would be his way, and loved him still more for it. Yet the sanguine side of her intuitively detected something else, an element which seemed to run parallel to his sympathy and his regret, both of which she knew were genuine. Again she did her best to deny it, and dismissed the thought once more; yet he continued to speak to her in the same vein.She now began seriously to doubt her own judgment.

'Dolly, dear Dolly. Will you say you forgive me? I can't go on without… '

Without what? What can't you go on without? Please say it, my darling Mr. Oliver! the words almost escaped from her as hope overcame scepticism, and welled up within her once more.

'I can't go on without you knowing… *that I meant no offence*' he concluded.

The words he so yearned to say stuck drily in his throat; it was so tasteless to utter them there, to declare his love at a time of mutual misfortune. Yet if not now, then when, if ever? And would such a declaration compound the tragedy? If she cared nothing for him it might well do so, and he did not wish to take advantage of her vulnerability. But at that moment of hesitation the unseen electricity which sometimes passes between lovers linked their hearts and their hopes and gave Oliver the impetus which pushed him beyond indecision..

'There's something I must tell you, though the circumstances are so very wrong that I find it doubly hard to say… I fear that I may offend you again if… '

'Yes?'

'Dolly… when you left Nelson Place, and without saying goodbye… I realised that your friendship meant far more to me than I had suspected… in fact I've not been able to… oh Dolly, do you think you could ever care for me, even a little?'

She did not need to answer in the affirmative, for her eyes soft with love for this gentle kindly brilliant man said it all. But she spoke nevertheless.

'Can you ask, Mr Oliver? Can you even ask? Did you never *know*?'

Joy and hope combined in him in an instant. ' Dolly, I didn't ever suspect it for a minute!

'Then you were silly.' Despite her cares and her sadness she smiled a little.

'I know I was! Dolly, I care for *you* a great deal. I love you very very much.'

These were words which she had contemplated in her dreams a thousand times – words which she had imagined being spoken but had never hoped to hear. And now he had said them. She did not reply at first, as if weighing their significance for a moment. Then she lifted her face to his, and looked into his eyes.

'An' I love you too, Mr Oliver.' she said gravely ' With all my heart, I do. I have always done, I think, ever since we first met, when you came to see my Pa. I've *always* loved you.' Even as she mentioned Albert the reason for their being there at that time rose before them both like a grey mist. Her shoulders began to shake as the tears rolled down her face. Oliver hesitantly reached out and touched her cheek. She inclined her head into his hand, feeling the great love in his caress. Without another word he enfolded her in his arms and held her closely to him, kissing her head tenderly and stroking her hair until her wretchedness had subsided a little.

Tragedy was common to them both; and though their love affair had begun in the shadow of it now at least they would be able to share their burden together.

Chapter Twenty Three

A WHITE BEARDED figure slowly climbed down from the trap which had carried him from the station. Drawing out a worn leather purse he paid the driver who tipped his hat to him as he clicked the horse away. The man looked about him with the uncertain gaze of the elderly, taking in surroundings which were unfamiliar to him It was evident from his bearing that he had once cut an impressive figure; the barrel-chest was still there, as were the broad square – set shoulders. But these were now bowed with age, and the impression was of one who seemed careworn and tired of life. And though the day was a warm one he still wore a scarf and a heavy woollen overcoat as if he were perpetually cold.

The visitor turned a drawn face towards the house which lay partly shrouded by trees; and leaning on a walking-stick began laboriously to make his way over the gravel, looking neither to his left nor his right but keeping his eyes fixed resolutely ahead of him. Having negotiated the driveway he began to climb the sandstone steps, one at a time and heavily, pausing halfway to get his breath.

He contemplated the black wreath which hung there as he stood before the door, and shook his head.Phoebe politely took his visiting-card and his coat, and ushered him through to the study, where he gratefully sank into a chair.

'There's a gentleman to see you Ma'am' she said, offering Ida Rusholme the card. She took it up and read it with some surprise, then passed it across to Oliver who sat beside her.

'Please inform the gentleman that we will be along directly, Phoebe. And would you kindly arrange for tea?'

Oliver stood and offered his mother his arm. She had become visibly weaker of late, and only with difficulty could be persuaded to eat even the smallest amount. Supported by her son Ida made her way into the study, where the visitor made an effort to rise as they entered.

'Captain Bonnard! It is very kind of you to come' she said 'And so far… from Wales, was it not?'

'Indeed, Madam, from Wales. But it was no trouble, I assure you. On the contrary the weather was fine and my journey..well, would otherwise have been pleasurable enough had it not been for… for the purpose of my visit.'

He faltered, then continued. 'Oliver and I have enjoyed a warm and regular correspondence as you will know, and whilst I am gratified to see that he is here with you, it was to express my sympathy to you personally that I have come. Forgive me for intruding upon you in your time of grief ' he said, perceiving how his allusion to Godfrey' death had caused what colour there was in Ida Rusholme's cheeks to drain away entirely.

'Captain' she said 'the pain of our loss is almost unbearable; but despite it all I appreciate deeply that you have come so far, and put yourself to such trouble.'

'There are sentiments which a letter cannot convey, Madam. When Oliver told me of your sad news I wished most particularly to see you in person. I have heard about your husband's illness, and am deeply sorry for it. Believe me, Madam, I know and understand a little of what you are now suffering.' He turned to Oliver.'You recall that when you first came to the cottage long ago there were two portraits resting upon the dresser?'

'I do, Captain.'

'And that I rather rudely shut them away when you looked at them?'

'It was not rudeness, Captain' Oliver replied ' and I never considered it so. I realised then how important the people in the photographs must be to you, and it was not for me to pry into something which was no business of mine.'

'You did not pry, old chap. It's natural enough for a lad to want to look about him – take in the lie of the land, so to speak' he said with forced bluffness. 'and it's partly to do with them that I have come today.'

'I recall the photographs – those of a young lady, and a soldier.'

'That lady… was my wife ' Bonnard said simply 'for a while... for a short while. My darling Emmie. It's a very good likeness of her.'

'She was very beautiful' said Oliver.

'Yes, she was… oh, she was!' The old man spoke with the passion of long departed youth. 'It was taken a little before... well. In 1876 my regiment was posted to Calcutta. The climate did not agree with her, poor Emmie. During that summer – which was intolerably hot – there were the usual outbreaks of cholera, and she succumbed. There was nothing I or the surgeon could do. She passed away in the July.'

The significance of the date was not lost on them.

'And the soldier,' continued the Captain, 'was my only son. His name was Edward – we named him after the Prince of Wales; that was the last picture of him. He had it made for me just before his embarkation with his regiment for South Africa and the war with the Boers.' He looked away as if recalling his last parting with Edward once more, and in his moist eyes there was that same remote light which Oliver had noticed when he had seen the photograph as a boy – an abstracted gaze back in time to places and events which lived only in the fond memories of an old man.

'We fished together on the high rivers of the hills, in the snow-waters, up beyond Delhi. Never missed the season… every spring we'd be off, just the two of us and the bearers. And we'd pitch camp, and live like lords. There were trout and mahseer the size of dogs… They were good days.'

'The rod and reel you gave to me… ?'said Oliver.

'Were his… were Edward's. He would have wanted you to have them.'

'You were very kind. I never thought… '

'Sometimes it pays not to think too much, old chap. He died gallantly, so they told me. Before Mafeking. He was my only boy… my only boy.'

The old man cleared his throat, and took a sip of tea. 'There was a girl, as well. Emmie quite doted on her, but we lost her in infancy. My wife took it very hard. I had a picture of her, too; but it was mislaid when I returned to England.'

'Captain Bonnard… I'm so deeply sorry.' Ida placed her hand on his gnarled old fist.

'Ach! We live in grim times, Madam' the old man grunted ' grim times. I do not think I have told a living soul about them, until today. And I appreciate your discretion and your kindness. But I came seeking neither sympathy nor anything like it. What I wish you to know is that you are not alone in your loss. There are many now who feel as you do, and understand too well what it means. Others continue to suffer far worse than we, but they hold on nevertheless, and manage as best they can. Day by day, Madam. It's an uphill struggle, but one ultimately reaches the top. And learns to live with the hand that Fate has dealt us.'

'I find it very hard, Captain. Impossibly so. And my husband is now gravely ill as a consequence. I do not know where it will end.'

The old man agreed to have lunch with them, but politely declined Ida's offer of accommodation for the night in one of their guest rooms. Wales called, he said, and he could sleep nowhere else; so after a respectful interval he took his leave. Oliver harnessed up their pony himself as almost all grooms, stable-lads and similar of military age had joined up, as volunteers or as conscripts; and now the family had to share the services of one young village lad with some distant neighbours. Oliver took on the task of driving himself, edging the little trap though the lanes on their slow way down to Desbury Station.

While they drove they talked, at first about things they shared in common – the Clwyr and Ridland in particular – but their conversation shifted inevitably to the War, and to Godfrey.

'I had come with the intention of speaking more fully about the high regard in which your brother was held by all at the School.' Bonnard said 'but I saw at once my error, and how the slightest mention of it at this time would only serve to distress your mother still further; it was obtuse of me not to think of it in that light.'

'It was very kind of you to have come at all, and to travel the distance you did' Oliver replied 'I know that my mother is very grateful, and was deeply moved by your consideration.' A silence fell between them, broken only by the trap's rhythmic creak and the steady plod of the horse, as each became lost in his own thoughts.

Suddenly Captain Bonnard spoke in an artificially bright tone much at odds with his feelings 'Though I'm very remote where I am, I keep in touch with past colleagues when I can, and pop in to see them if I'm ever up that way, which isn't very often.'

Then his voice changed again. 'The old School's suffered rather terribly, you know. I dropped by, to see a few old chums. The place seems devastated by the recent news, though they're trying to put a brave face on it. You knew about Mr. Crossley?'

'Yes. I heard.'

'Well since poor Crossley they've lost Mr. Donnelly, the maths man, Mr.Rollings of history– you'll remember him, always sported an Edinburgh tie and rode a bicycle – and Mr. Barrow of classics, though he wasn't with us very long. Besides that, the toll amongst the boys has been unspeakably heavy. Mr. Swan himself told me that of boys past and present, forty-seven have so far laid down their lives – including your brother Godfrey. They're of course very proud of them, and what they have done for their country; but one cannot help wondering sometimes… ' he reflected 'Your brother was of the finest sort, you know. Mr.Swan has written a personal letter to your parents to offer his condolences… he was particularly affected by Godfrey's death… said he could never recall the School producing a better pace bowler, and that we'd all be the poorer for his loss… ' the old man seemed to be speaking more to himself now than to Oliver;

'Yes, we'll certainly be the poorer'.

As the little old train ground to a halt Oliver helped the Captain into the compartment, and they bade a sad farewell to each other.

'Do make the time to come across to Ridland when it's convenient' the old man said 'and remember, whilst it is noble to serve your country bearing arms, it is equally noble to serve her as you do. There is no point in risking all as so many have done. You are doing far more good as you are.'

'I don't think I'll be volunteering just yet,' Oliver reassured him 'if ever; I fear I would make a very poor soldier indeed. I know where my duty lies.' His assertion was categorical enough; but there was something in the way it was said – just the faintest inflexion which hinted at uncertainty – that alerted Bonnard to an unthinkable possibility

'Even so, never falter in your resolve,' he said emphatically, leaning through the open window. 'Our Country needs your talents, which I fear will be in increasing demand before this terrible business is over. Goodbye, Oliver.'

They shook hands warmly; then with a hiss the engine clanked into motion,and gathering speed rattled away into the afternoon.

Oliver walked slowly back to where the pony and trap awaited him, reflecting wistfully that he had never had a truer friend than Captain Bonnard.

Oliver was torn between the obligation he felt to be with his family and the conflicting call of his professional duties at New Heath. There was little he could do for his father – he saw at once that Dr.Harbin had done everything possible, and that Clarence was being well nursed. There was no doubt that his mother needed him there, but he found the atmosphere emotionally asphyxiating, and nomatter how guilty he felt he needed to escape it.

They had agreed to meet on the following evening, along the obscure path which wound upwards into the woodland behind the basket-weavers' cottage. There in the shade of a gnarled oak tree Oliver counted the minutes away with rapidly beating heart, striding back and forth with all the fevered impatience of the lover. His passion accentuated every sound; the blackbirds seemed to roar their evening song with uncommon power and he felt he could make out every wingbeat of a chaffinch as it flew by him. He turned sharply as he thought he heard a slight step further down the path. Squinting between the leaves and the heavy sycamore and chestnut boughs he could make out nothing, but suddenly there she was, no more than twenty paces from him, picking her way gingerly over the stones.

She was dressed simply in the black of mourning. Abandoning his cover he made his way down to her; and as she raised her face she smiled up to him in the way she had done when she had nursed him. The smile was full, and he wondered then why he had never noticed the love for him that radiated from it. Once again she was in his arms and they kissed deeply and long; then whilst she rested there she whispered closely to him, and he to her. Though she wore no perfume her hair was fragrant with cleanness, and as Oliver looked down onto her head as she lay against his chest he could not have imagined that the world could contain so complete a joy. While they held each other he put to her an idea which had occurred to him as eminently sensible and one which would serve everyone's purpose without resorting to deceit, which he despised; Dolly had earlier told him that she had only been able to secure employment in the local dairy, and that only on a casual basis. Oliver took the plunge.

'Dolly, would you consider working for my mother at Millwain Place? Not as a servant but as a sort of housekeeping assistant?'

She pushed him off and looked up at him in alarm. 'I don't want to be *kept*, Oliver!' she said archly.

'My darling, you wouldn't be! Alice is really very infirm these days and can barely manage to cook let alone do anything else; and some of her domestic duties are becoming too much even with Phoebe's help now that my father is gravely ill… '

'I don't know' she said doubtfully. ' It seems a bit dishonest, somehow. I mean, we'll want to see each other, won't we? I don't like the idea of deceiving Mrs. Rusholme nor anyone else as to the reason I've gone there.'

'There's no deceit in it. We have a secret which we will keep to ourselves. Where is the wrong in loving someone with all your heart who happens to work for your parents?'

She placed her little hand in his, and he squeezed it.

'I'm still unhappy about it' she said with surprising firmness. 'and we can't tell anyone what we feel… '

'I *have* told someone about us' Oliver countered sheepishly 'and if he knew what I've proposed I'm sure he would see the sense in it. Look, Dolly, was there anything wrong in your loving me while we lived at Nelson Place? Or in me loving you, for that matter? It wasn't *that* which decided you to leave, was it?'

'No… '

'And I'll be coming down from Manchester every week-end to visit my mother and father. You might want to work then, if you wished, and I could offer to see you safely home. *That* wouldn't be dishonest, now would it?'

'Well, it depends on what you did, Oliver! A gentleman shouldn't kiss the girl he's escorting, now should he?' Despite herself she giggled.

Linking arms they slowly walked the path up to the higher meadows, beneath honeysuckles whose saffron fingers caressed the couple as they passed; and as they strolled he pointed out how everyone would stand to gain from the arrangement and how his mother would certainly be guided by him. Dolly could live at home with her own mother where she was equally needed, he suggested; this occurred to her as quite reasonable and she began to warm to the idea – for the mile or so walk to Millwain Place would not be a major problem. By the end of their prolonged parting Dolly had been won over.

'You see, Ma, I went to call on them with your letter,' he told Ida, 'and to offer my sympathy, and I met Dolly there. She tells me she has only had casual employment since coming back to Desbury, and she wishes to stay at home to comfort her own mother and to support her family as best she can. But she'll be an invaluable help to you all here, and by paying her a regular wage it will add considerably to any widow's allowance which Mrs. Chadderton might get- and I doubt it'll be much.'

'Well, you seem to know her better than I, Oliver. On the few occasions that I've met her she appeared to be a smart and presentable young woman. And clearly we are in need of additional help, in all sorts of ways since your poor Pa fell so ill.' Ida turned her sorrowful gaze to Oliver. 'You do as you see fit, my darling,' she added 'You can manage these things far better than I. Would you mind terribly if I left it all to you?'

'Absolutely not, Ma. I'll see to it at once' The enthusiasm in his voice was only thinly disguised.

'And will you speak with Mrs. Chadderton as to the terms under which she would be agreeable for Dolly to work here?'

'Certainly, Ma.'

His constant activity, his preoccupation with the wellbeing of his own family and of the Chaddertons – and most of all his abiding love for Dolly – postponed rather than diminished the need to acknowledge his own grief about Godfrey's death, and seek release for it. He focused on the immediate, now – for it was the issues of the present which made constant demands upon his physical and emotional resources. He knew he would have to confront the full and terrible reality of his loss in the future; but he resolved to avoid such a confrontation for now, and deal with it in his own way and in his own time, and apart from the rest of them. Dolly was the only one who, though still inwardly grieving, had not allowed it to prostrate her. She, like her lover, could not permit herself to succumb. And like Oliver, she saw that much depended upon her remaining as composed and as collected as possible, buoyed up but not distracted by their deepening love for each other.

Lighter of foot Oliver went down to the village and to the Chadderton's that morning, with more than a valid reason for calling at the home of the girl who occupied so much of his thought.

He was admitted and again shown to the parlour where Mrs. Chadderton soon came to him. She heard him in silence, nodding gravely to everything that Oliver proposed on Ida's behalf, and on Dolly's. Her wages would be generous – almost double what a domestic servant might expect to earn elsewhere – but Oliver had suggested to Ida that as she had fully intended to pay the Chaddertons an allowance, this might be a way to do it without offending the family's sensitivity at having to accept charity.

'Thank you, Dr. Rusholme.' Mrs. Chadderton said 'and thank your mother very much for her kindness… .and for the letter, and what she put in it.'

'Are the terms satisfactory, Mrs. Chadderton? Do you feel you can agree?'

'Yes… yes of course, sir… it's very generous, I'm sure… an' my daughter will be happy to work as hard as she can.' Oliver extended his hand and she hesitantly took it in her own. He noticed how cold and deathlike it was, and how like his mother's.

Shortly before Oliver's necessary return to Manchester his mother received a letter from Helene in London. Tersely written, it was quite at odds with her customary exuberance – yet it was the more eloquent for the strain and worry which were communicated in every line. She deeply regretted what had happened to Papa, she said, but she hoped they would see that she could not possibly leave Gerald Warrington in his present condition. She did not have words sufficient to speak of her feelings about Godfrey; she hoped they would understand. Gerald's wounds were worse than the doctors had first thought; his arm and chest were still very bad, and an infection in them had caused a fever from which he was only slowly recovering. He needed her there, though she felt split in two by her duty to her family. Gerald had told her he had been with Godfrey at the end, and despite still suffering terribly from the shock he was fretting that he must write to the Rusholmes, though the doctors had expressly forbidden it in his weak state. When Gerald was better she would try to take a little time off to come to Desbury, and visit them.

She ended the letter with her love to them all. The ink was smudged.

On the Sunday evening two figures stood in a close embrace at the furthest end of Desbury Station. The platform was otherwise deserted except for the churlish old porter who shuffled about with a broom, muttering constantly to himself. The young lovers exchanged tender words amidst the kisses; and then with the arrival of the Manchester train came the time for parting. Oliver stooped to Dolly and kissed her forehead, her cheek and her lips one more time, and she in her turn raised her small hand to his face and caressed it. He stepped aboard and the door closed with a metallic click. Instantly the window was down and Oliver leaned out as on tiptoe she stretched up to him. One more kiss, and the train began to move. 'Next weekend, Dolly!'

'Next weekend, Sweetheart!'

The Manchester streets resounded emptily in the greyness of the twilight as Oliver walked back to his lodgings. That complex of emotions from which he had suffered and which he had held in abeyance whilst with Dolly now surged in upon him anew. There was his work, of course – he took no issue with that, for he looked forward unreservedly to taking up his duties at New Heath once more; but there was the loneliness of his hours at the lodgings; and what little leisure time he had, he feared.For then he knew that the darker thoughts would rise before him, try to suppress them though he might. So far they had been compartmentalised and isolated; but his attempts to neutralise them were temporary at best. He knew that the time was fast approaching when he must confront the reality of what had happened to his brother.

Events were so to fall out that he had not long to wait.

Chapter Twenty Four

HE DID NOT notice the letter, at first.

On entering his rooms he laid his bag down at the foot of the bed, and sat down heavily in the sole armchair.He remained there motionlessly, turning over in his thoughts the events of the previous week until every object in the sparsely furnished room seemed a shadow, and when only the outline reminded him of its form. He looked down at his hands, and raised them slowly before his face.They too seemed shapeless, dark and incorporeal. He had seen death before, in the wards and in the mortuary; and he wondered if it was like this when it came. His thoughts once more turned to Godfrey, but despite the sharpness of recollection it still did not seem to him that he grieved.

The misery was still bottled up within, almost beyond reach of his conscious mind. What the catalyst was which could release it he did not know. He had wanted to visit Godfrey's room, to be alone in it with the commonplace things which his brother had owned and used, and which had absorbed something of his character and soul; but Ida had locked the door and refused access to everybody – even to Oliver.

He rose to look for a box of matches with which to light the gas-lamps and was fumbling for them on the washstand when his fingers brushed against a thin packet propped alongside the water-jug. It fell to the floor noiselessly, and he paid it little attention.The matches found, soon the room was tolerably lit, though the greenness of the flame was accentuated still further by the drab olive wash on the walls. Then he noticed what had dropped, and picked it up. It was a letter.

He turned it to examine the postmark, but his eyes never got beyond the address.

It was directed to him, and the handwriting was Godfrey's.

With quaking hands he slit open the envelope, and drew out the sheets of paper within.

To be delivered in the event of my death.

Dear Old Lad

If you receive this you will know that I have passed beyond all earthly troubles and that for me the war is finished at last. Do not despair too much for I am glad for it; but sorry – so very sorry- that my release will in turn be a source of pain to those for whom I care so deeply. It is for you, Oliver, to go on with life and take all that it has to offer, fulfilling what I have long believed will be a great destiny.

I often think about the times we spent together rambling, the byways we got to know and the distant hills we looked to; those memories were always a great source of comfort to me when times got rough. I recall that long walk in the snow- last March, I think it was- but it seems a century ago, somehow. I was very black then, wasn't I? and must have been poor company indeed. I am sorry it should have been so, and wish our last walk together had been different; but I hope you can draw some comfort from knowing that at last I have achieved an inner calm- curiously, perhaps, in the light of what I soon must do.

I am at peace now, and as tranquil in myself as I have ever been. I wish you every good thing that the world has to offer, and a long and happy life. Make the most of it, my dearest brother and my dearest friend. Had I lived we should have had some grand times together.

Farewell old chap, until we meet once more on the longest path of all.
Your loving and devoted
Godfrey

And the floodgates of grief, so long pent up, opened for Oliver at last.

Chapter 1

THE YEAR 1916 ground at last to its bloody end. Decimated by the long months on the Somme, where one battle seemed to follow close upon another with genocidal regularity and with barely a pause even to count the dead, the Manchester Pals Battalions withdrew to regroup and retrain those hundreds of conscripts drafted in to fill the eloquent gaps. Few of the officers and men of the battalions had survived unscathed – or indeed at all – to see in the New Year of 1917. At Delville Wood, Festubert and Transloy Ridge young Manchester men had paid appallingly over and again for each ill-judged attack. A thousand would fall on the last day of July 1916 alone during the assault on Guillemont; yet the offensives were pressed home relentlessly throughout August September and October. It was the stuff of nightmares, and in one's wildest imaginings it could get no worse as the October deluges transformed hard-packed summer clays into a foul quagmire.

But then with the New Year came Croissilles and Bullecourt; and on the 9th. April, the Battle of Arras was launched in all its fury. It was then that the Manchesters – in common with so many other Battalions and Regiments – came up against the near-insuperable obstacle of the Hindenburg Line, a complex system of strongpoints, trenches and deep shelters constructed of concrete and steel, and fronted by barbed wire entanglements in places a hundred feet thick. Behind these were the machine-guns, and behind them, the German artillery.

But in all this Gerald Warrington would play no part. The wounds in his chest and arm had healed only slowly, and severe infection had weakened him. So it was that Helene had been unable to pay more than a few fleeting visits to Desbury, and only then after her fiancé had been declared to be out of immediate danger.

Though Clarence Rusholme's stroke had been expected to be the end of him, it was not. Defying medical opinion in which his surviving son shared he began to rally a little, and by the December was able to hold a reasonable conversation though his impairment had turned him peevish and even more quarrelsome.

Very possibly the underlying cause of the improvement had been the posthumous award of the Military Cross to Godfrey. Ida had received the news almost indifferently, for she had little use for medals and awards when they had been bought at so high a price; but she knew enough of her husband's nature to see that it might do him far more good than any of the medications which had so far failed to improve his condition. So she had taken the War Office missal together with the copy of *The London Gazette* up to him. At first he did not respond, but by cajoling and reading extracts from the citation – though it cut her to the heart – she succeeded in awakening some glimmer of interest in him. He reached out a shaking hand and she placed the *Gazette* into it. He gazed at the print blearily, but evidently could make nothing out.

'Shall I read it to you in full, Dear?' she asked. He nodded.

'Read it… read' he faltered. They were the first words he had uttered since the stroke.

'***Military Cross. To Lieutenant Rusholme, Godfrey Clark.***

For conspicuous gallantry and devotion to duty. On the night of 13th May 1916 he displayed great coolness and initiative when engaged in a raid on enemy positions in the vicinity of Montauban. With a complete disregard for his own safety he led his men into an enemy trench and despite fierce and sustained resistance succeeded in capturing several prisoners who later furnished invaluable information as to enemy dispositions. Having returned from the raid and despite being wounded he then proceeded back to the scene of battle in order to ascertain the fate of fellow officers and their platoons.

He clasped the newspaper to his chest, and breathed rather than said 'Godfrey… Godfrey, my son… '

The citation – and the subsequent arrival of the Cross in its silk-lined case – proved to be the turning-point for Clarence Rusholme. Like a jealous child he gathered the medal to him; and it was as though the fierce love he bore for his dead son and the loyalty he owed to his name rejuvenated his failing mind in some strange way, giving it a new momentum and him a new lease of life which none expected.

But with it came a growing intolerance towards his immediate family, and he became fond of berating his wife and his younger son before anyone who happened to visit him, humiliating them with bitter sarcasm and offensive comments if they were present. Oliver did his best to assure his mother that such behaviour could well be expected from a stroke-victim, and that she should not allow herself to be unduly distressed by it all. But because of the embarrassment caused to the wellwishers who out of politeness had to sit and listen to such stuff, they soon gave up visiting him at all; and then it was they who in their turn became the target of his poisonous tongue.

He had never been a popular man even when in his prime, classifying the large majority of those he knew as acquaintances rather than genuine friends. Now that he was permanently incapacitated and unable to venture out beyond his own grounds his business and legal associates soon saw the way the wind blew, and began to discuss amongst themselves how he was to be replaced.

Gerald Warrington sat before a desk in the officers' convalescent hospital, much as almost a year before Godfrey Rusholme had done when writing to the widow of Private Tom Formby.

He gazed at the sheet of paper which lay in front of him; it was his fourth attempt at it, and still the words would not come. So far they were all too bland and stereotyped somehow, for none had struck an acceptable balance between what he had witnessed on that most terrible of days, and what he needed to say to the Rusholmes about the death of their son,his closest friend. He felt an uneasy sense of guilt that Godfrey had been right in his appraisal of the war, and of their part in it. Certainly they had both paid a bitter price for initial idealism, though Godfrey's had been the ultimate one; and most disquieting of all, he still wondered at his friend's motives during the last minutes of his life.

He slowly picked up his pen and began once more.

Dear Mr. and Mrs Rusholme, and Oliver.

I had never thought I would have to write such a letter as this, to tell you how Godfrey – whom I counted as my dearest friend –died. You will, no doubt, have heard from the newspapers of the immensity of our endeavours on that day. The assault in which our Battalion was engaged was of vital importance to the course of the war, and in bringing about a speedy and victorious conclusion to it. Godfrey had been in the foremost ranks of the attackers, leading his men with great dash and distinction, and was instrumental in the capture of several of the enemy's strongpoints. We had reached our objective and with characteristic spirit he rallied a group of survivors from other platoons whom he then led in a frontal attack on the most heavily defended section of the enemy's line. The outcome had been in the balance until that moment, but I must say that Godfrey's initiative turned it in our favour.

We had withdrawn after the action in order to regroup and were in a Forward Dressing Station when Godfrey decided to 'take a last look' at the field when he was hit. You may take comfort from the fact that he died almost instantly, and without pain; I was beside him at the time.

I have to tell you that our attack was a resounding success despite the heavy losses we suffered; and you may rest assured that Godfrey died in the knowledge of having done his duty to the last, and without regret. Had he lived to old age he would never have accomplished anything finer than he did on the 1st.July. The honour which he was awarded posthumously must stand as a small acknowledgement of his constancy and his fortitude in this as in previous actions.

As a platoon commander he was of the finest sort – selfless, brave and always concerned for the wellbeing of his men who, even as I, mourn his loss deeply.

I will always be proud to have called him my friend.

Once more, please accept my heartfelt sympathy

Gerald Warrington

The letter was duly posted, and was received at Millwain Place the following day.

As for Oliver, he once more became a regular weekend visitor to his old home, seeing to his mother's wellbeing and dealing with any day-to-day problems which might have arisen during the previous week. He would dutifully visit his father and sit with him until he was curtly dismissed, which was often not long after his arrival. But Ida appreciated his presence and fussed around him, as though in a bid to make amends to one who had been neglected and ill-used. Now the whole household tended to look to him for advice and approval, as if he were master there- which he in fact was, in all but name; for his cool head made the organising of his mother's affairs an easy task.

Yet his hidden joy was in the frequent chance meetings with Dolly as she went about the house on her various chores, and the fleeting caress of hand against hand as they passed. Occasionally they would steal a moment when certain of privacy, to exchange a swift kiss; but such moments were infrequent and it was his pretext of seeing her home on the Saturday and Sunday evenings which supplied the rare opportunity, when they would walk the lonely path down to the village, entwined in each others' arms.

By working even longer hours and undertaking less popular duties during the week Oliver had secured a greater part of the week-end as free time. He had made no mention of his parents' situation nor of Godfrey' death for he did not wish to benefit by taking advantage of others' sympathy, and it would have seemed dishonourable, somehow. Instead he had put his case simply, saying that he had obligations to a young lady. The Authorities winked knowingly and granted his request, well aware what an asset this gifted young doctor was to their hospital. Though the hours were long and arduous Oliver was sustained by the prospect of Friday evening. Physically tired out though he might have been at times, he no longer suffered the debilitating bouts of mental fatigue which had plagued him; instead there was a lightness in his step as he strode down to Exchange to await impatiently the Desbury train, followed by the endless stops and starts at suburban stations – it had to be the slowest train in the North – and then the breathless sprint from the station to the House just in time to catch Dolly as she finished her work, and the delight of seeing her home. If he were delayed for a few minutes she would always have a unfinished job or two which she busied herself with, until with beating heart she heard the doorbell ring and she would open to him.

Thus the year of 1917 wore away as they lived from week-end to week-end. Life for the two lovers was bittersweet, for the mutual joy which flowed from their relationship was always tempered by the shades of Godfrey and Albert. But their resilience was strengthened by the momentum with which their love grew, and it invested them with the emotional resources to support each other and those in their immediate families who were less fortunate than they.

Ida's female intuition had not been blunted by her grief, and the fact that Oliver was her sole surviving son had if anything made her even more receptive to subtle shifts in his mood. Of late she had begun to notice a profound change in him. Despite all he smiled more, was more forthcoming in conversation, and had an altogether less chastened manner; then there was the flushed and eager expression when he arrived on Friday evenings, and Dolly's increased bustling and tidying. Ida noticed how she always contrived to be in the vicinity of the hall when Oliver's arrival was imminent, and she listened to Dolly's tripping footsteps as the door was answered. She saw too how, if the girl entered while she and Oliver were sitting together, her son's gaze was drawn inexorably to the slim little figure and face and lingered there, and how Oliver always insisted upon walking her home.

Ida was no stranger to the heady fragrance of love which seemed to emanate from the very walls when the two were in the same room, and she was in no doubt as to how matters lay between them.

Ida was not pleased by what she saw, and decided to confront her son about it on his next visit.

'One cannot help but notice, Oliver, that you seem to be on quite friendly terms with the Chaddertons' she said, introducing the subject casually ' I am very happy that you are; they are such a pleasant, hardworking family. They have always served us faithfully. And Dolly has been most satisfactory. It was wise of you to recommend the arrangement.'

'I'm very glad, Ma.' Oliver replied, smiling. 'Yes, they are kind and genuine people.' But even as he spoke, he began to wonder why his mother had broached the subject 'Why do you ask?'

'Oh, no reason in particular. Only… I had a faint idea that perhaps… but I'm sure I'm wrong, and that I've no reason to be concerned… '

The smile faded, and Oliver's brow knitted grimly.

'Concerned about *what,* precisely? What concerns do you have?' he demanded sharply.

She looked at him with a pained expression. 'I am surprised and hurt that you assume such a tone with me, Oliver' she said affrontedly ' I did not expect to be *interrogated..*'

'Nevertheless you are implying *something,* Mother, are you not?'

Ida now became defensive ' I was not implying anything, exactly.'

'Forgive me, Mother, but I think you were. You were wondering if there was an understanding between Dolly Chadderton and me, weren't you?'

'Well… I *had* noticed, as I'm sure many others must have, that… '

'Since you ask, Ma, there is. I am very attached to Dolly, and she to me. If it lies at all in my power I intend to marry her one day, if she'll have me.'

'If she will have *you,* Oliver? *She* have *you?* Think, oh think what you're *saying*, my Darling!' she implored him. ' She's a most pleasant girl, certainly, but she's only…

'Only *what*? Were you going to say she's only a servant, Mother? A 'skivvy'?'

'Please don't use such coarse words, Oliver. But if you must have it so… well, yes. She is a domestic servant, after all… I only want the best for you, my Darling.Such people are not of our *class*, Oliver.'

'And what *is* our class, Mother?'

'Don't be deliberately obtuse. It ill becomes you. You know perfectly well what I mean. The Chaddertons are of the labouring classes, Oliver. Don't, my Darling, throw yourself away in a liaison which can never come to good. You cannot be part of her world any more than she can be part of yours. Undoubtedly she is a fine girl as far as it goes… but *consider!* You'll be caught in some sort of limbo, if you do marry. Where would you live, and what would your friends think?'

'If it comes to it, Mother' Oliver said bitterly ' I'd rather live amongst the poor and disadvantaged than live a lie and in unhappiness. And as far as my friends are concerned, if they abandoned our friendship because of my feelings for a respectable, decent and lovely girl then I wouldn't wish to count them as *my* friends any longer.'

'You may not think so now, but you will regret this rashness. Put it down to experience, Oliver – young men will do these things, and it's not a black mark against them – but see it for what it is, a transient flirtation. Nothing more.'

Oliver looked coldly at her. 'Mother, you are a hypocrite.'

'Oliver!'

'You brought us up quite rightly to behave fairly and decently towards 'such people' yet your egalitarian principles don't stretch quite as far as liking or even loving them.'

'I didn't expect you to marry one. That was not my meaning.'

'Yet we hear that the father of one *such person* willingly gave his life for Godfrey,and it was Godfrey who said of him that he was the bravest man he'd ever met, and the finest. How do you reconcile *that* with your view of the 'lower orders'?'

'It is quite uncalled for that you speak to me in this fashion, Oliver! I am your mother, after all' Ida was becoming increasingly defensive.

'But you invited it ! I did not broach the subject. And I have as much a right to happiness as anyone else.'

'Nobody would deny you that, my dear. I just cannot see how you could ever be truly happy.'

'Like *you,* Mother? With Pa? Was *yours* so acceptable a marriage in the eyes of all your friends and family? After all, you're a *Bosche*!' As soon as the bitter words were out of his mouth he regretted them, could have torn out his own tongue. At once he was beside his mother as her eyes brimmed with tears. 'Oh, Ma! Forgive me.! It was a terrible and an uncalled–for thing to say. I don't know what possessed me. I didn't mean it, truly.'

'Yes, you did, Oliver' Ida said through her tears. She reflected quietly for a moment.' And though it was harsh of you' she added 'you were right.'

She considered his face in which love for this girl was mingled with solicitude for her. 'We are none of us our proper selves, Oliver. The terrible times we live in have made sure of that.'

'They're changing, mother. When this war is over I cannot think that anything will be the same, so much has been infected and ruined by it. We have to hang on tight to what certainties are left us.'

'Your feelings for Dolly Chadderton?'

'Yes, Ma… .I consider that a certainty, amongst other things.'

'And as for Dolly… how does she regard you?'

'She was unsure, at first. Not of her feelings, but as to whether our relationship was appropriate.'

'She is a wise girl.'

'But she sees it now in the same way as I do.'

'I cannot deny I am disappointed in your choice, Oliver. I had hoped you would make a more suitable match.' She paused for a moment 'but if it is your express wish to marry this girl- and I read it in your face that it is- then I will not try to hinder you.'

'Ma, would you give us your blessing?'

Ida looked down at her wedding ring as she slowly revolved it on her finger, as if recollecting the vows made by an older man to a young girl long before, when he had placed the ring there.

She reached out and took Oliver's hand in hers. 'I am disappointed in what you have decided upon; nevertheless I do give you my blessing, my Darling.'

By mutual agreement they decided to keep the matter to themselves and make no mention of it to Clarence.

Chapter Two

HELENE'S RETURN to Millwain Place lacked the zest and the colour of the pre-war days – for the time she had spent with Warrington since his wounding and slow return from France had dulled something in her. She no longer sparkled as she had once done, and she appeared dispirited. Now she only smiled where once she would have laughed out loud and she habitually wore a preoccupied expression. Her eyes – once the most beautiful feature of a beautiful face – seemed tired and perpetually anxious, and she looked downwards more often now.

She came alone – for she confided in her mother that even when convalescing in Weymouth, Warrington had been been profoundly uneasy with himself. In a bid to dispel his darkness they had taken long walks together, along the beaches, up through the town and out into the country; but whilst enabling him to regain something of his former physical vigour it left his mind untouched and unrefreshed; and his introspection persisted like a toxic cloud. The blithe self-confident young man she had known before the war and who had so entranced her was far away, lost in contemplation of landscapes, events and people of whom she could have no conception. She felt isolated from him, excluded from a significant part of his life in which she played no active part.

After the affection of their first greeting the times which they passed in each other's company had become by degrees more strained By sheer strength of will she would drag him out of the gloom which was engulfing him. He would make all the effort he could, and would rise from it for a while almost as though rising above a mist; but within the hour he would succumb once more as the dark shutters of his thoughts closed tightly on the outer world.

The uncertainties to which he fell prey became more palpable to him with each day of enforced recuperation. He was grateful for all that people did and much that they said by way of encouragement, but no longer basked in the adulation of the well-meaning 'Blighter'. He did not look for their respect, nor value it. The regard in which he was held by those with whom he had shared the suffering of Montauban's trenches- and who understood – was what mattered to Gerald Warrington. The admiring glances which they drew as the couple walked the sunny Dorset streets did not gratify him but only added to his discomfiture and sense of guilt that he should be there at all while his fellow-officers and men confronted God knew what on a daily or even hourly basis. He felt a fraud, and cheap.

He took to corresponding with Brigade Headquarters, asking at first for a general picture of how the 16th. was doing. The replies he received were desultory and non-committal, saying nothing that he could not have gleaned from the newspapers. This unsettled him even more and he became irritable and snappish with tram-conductors, waiters and even with Helene. Had he known it, the path he was now following was the same trodden by his dead friend Godfrey Rusholme.

Confidentially he applied for a medical examination to confirm his fitness for return to active service and to his command; and as with Godfrey, the M.O. shook his head and tutted, but signed the papers nonetheless.

She was not surprised when he told her of his intention to return to France. She did not try to dissuade him, for she read his heart and mind well enough to know that any such attempt would have been fruitless; it would have been a source of conflict between them and would only have added to their pain. And Helene's intention was that their last days together should be worthy of remembrance.

On his receipt of a letter informing him of the date of his embarkation a burden seemed to lift from Warrington's shoulders. He was once again almost the man Helene remembered and loved – bright, engaging and witty, and once more he doted on her. Though the blackness still persisted he was better equipped to deal with it and banish it to a more obscure recess in his mind. The days passed quickly and Weymouth seemed a new place in their eyes, the late June sunlight brighter and more vivid as every object and building seemed to stand out with a greater definition and clarity; and Helene and Gerald Warrington found their love for each other again as they explored the sundappled lanes and byways of the old town, stepping gingerly round drying nets and piled lobster -pots. There they found their way to a little cottage where an ancient woman called them *dearies* and served them with tea and cream and strawberry jam and hot scones. They thanked her and kissed across the table and looked long into each others' eyes,as they had once done.

The day before his departure was particularly hot. They spent it in a whirl, taking a boatride around the harbour and barely concealing their fun as they watched the old ferryman's distorted expression as he grunted at the oars.

Then lunch behind the fine Georgian façade of the *Royal*, and a visit to a small gallery advertising *seascapes.* In the afternoon they walked halfway to Portland which stood out blindingly white against the almost Mediterranean blue. And in the slow crimson rays of the dusk they made their way arm in arm back to Helene's lodgings. Just out of sight of its bow windows they halted clinging to each other as if the realisation which they had postponed for so long had ultimately come upon them. Their time together had run its course. How long they stood there, locked in a wordless embrace which neither wished to sever, they did not know. But at its conclusion the sun was already in its long decline into the West, burning its way into a blood-red sea. Their shadows had lengthened and the outlines of the two lovers seemed attenuated and unreal.

'Good-night my darling.'

'Good-night, sweetheart.'

Hesitantly Warrington turned to go back to his clinical white room at the convalescent home. Helene stood on the warm pavement watching him go. Something about his step seemed too conclusive; and for the moment she refused steadfastly to acknowledge the finality of their parting, though intuition told her it might be for ever.

Her feelings for this man rose precipitously in a tide of love, of grief and of desire. She could not let him go, just like that.

She wiped her brimming eyes with her handkerchief, torn between what the code of her middle-class upbringing said was correct and decent and what she longed for, and knew in her aching heart was right.

'Gerald!' Suddenly she heard her own voice calling to him and she put her hand to her lips almost as if to stifle her own impetuosity. As her breast rose and fell with her racing pulse, Warrington stopped and turned. Though now barely a shadow in the twilight she knew he was looking back at her. In a second her feet seemed to take flight and she was caught up in his embrace once more.

'Gerald,' she said indistinctly ' Gerald, please don't go my darling; at least not yet. '

'I won't, if you wish me not to.'

'Gerald... .' she sobbed ' will you... stay? Don't go! Will you love me... ? Please?'

He had never seen a woman's body before. Now as she lay naked beside him on the bed he was amazed that anyone could be so beautiful. Gently he replaced a lock of her dark hair which had fallen across her forehead, and kissed her once more, as he had done a thousand times during that long heavenly night as they made love.

She opened her eyes and looked at him and smiled. Barely touching her, he caressed her breasts- first one and then the other – marvelling at their softness and their perfection. Then downwards his hand followed the contours of her waist and her buttocks, and the smoothness of her legs, and between them. She snuggled closer to him, and he held her there. So they lay until the first light filtered through the curtains, announcing the dawn of the last of all their days together.

As they made their passionate farewells on Weymouth Station she knew why she had acted thus on their previous evening, and as she waved him goodbye she regretted nothing – not a moment of what they had shared together. Now as the train bore away the only man she had loved in this way, and knew too she could ever love, a terrible foreboding overcame her and she sank down on a bench, and wept.

A porter's kindly enquiry roused her ' Are you all right, Miss? Would you like a cup o' tea?'

'No. But... but thank you for asking.' She stood, and drew herself upright. Then with a determined step she returned to her lodgings where she packed her bags. Calling a cab she returned directly to the station, and bought a ticket for Manchester.

She stayed a month at Millwain Place, living her life in her letters to Warrington and in his letters to her, and only existing in between. Then they stopped coming, as she had suspected and feared they would. A terrible silence possessed her every hour, waking or sleeping; she was on the edge of a precipice, and she awaited the inevitable fall with dread.

A letter arrived addressed to her, written in an unknown hand.

It bore the stamp of a Field Post Office in France. Ida took it from Phoebe and brought it up to Helene in person.

She read her mother's face before she read the letter. Her drawn countenance, her apprehensive eyes, her bloodless lips, said enough.

'Would you leave me for a moment, please, mother?' Ida silently closed the door behind her, but waited awhile on the landing, knowing she would be needed.

The gasp of misery which escaped from Helene's lips as she read was sufficient for Ida to enter unannounced. In a second she had her arms around her, comforting her daughter whose shoulders heaved and fell in tearing sobs.

The letter lay open beside her on the bed.

Helene reached for it with a trembling hand, and passed it to her mother. Ida scanned it quickly, taking in enough to confirm beyond doubt what its contents related to.

Deeply regret... Captain Warrington... when gallantly leading... seen to fall... adverse conditions... Ypres Salient, and at Passchendaele... ... could not be found despite exhaustive searches... bravest of officers... finest company commander... only and unavoidable conclusion... missing, believed killed.

And it was signed, with deepest sympathy,

Wilfrith Elstob, O.C.16th. Battalion, Manchester Regiment.

Thus Gerald Warrington became one more insignificant statistic to add to the 77,000 others wounded or killed at Ypres in the first four catastrophic days of August 1917. Of the few whose bodies were later fortunate enough to be found and identified, Warrington was not to be amongst them.

In the following days, when the tragic news was not new, Ida would read the letter again and wonder fleetingly at the strangeness of the name of the signatory. It would not be the last time she would hear it, for it was a name which in later years would become synonymous with coolness of command, with unstinting self-sacrifice and with unparalleled heroism. And it was a name which would be associated with an illustrious predecessor, as one capable of drawing the elusive qualities of loyalty and reverence from one's men; men who would hold out when all was lost, because of their devotion to their commanding officer, and their absolute faith in him.

And in the whole appalling history of the Great War, if any one man possessed the *Nelson Touch*, it was Elstob.

Chapter Three

THE EFFECT OF her lover's death on Helene was terrible to witness. She would not eat and became reclusive, shutting herself away from the outer world in the confines of her rooms. There she would sit the day long in a chair, her hands folded on her lap or gazing from her window down to the end of the garden, where the stile was. She would not read, and was reluctant to talk to anyone but Ida.

Both mother and daughter seemed to have aged many years in the course of only a few months. Whilst Ida's hair was still dark at its ends, it passed through every shade of grey until, at her scalp, it was now utterly white – as if a harsh passage from youth to age was reflected in her long tresses.

And Helene seemed to wear away visibly. Her lack of appetite caused her to lose the roundness of her face, which became angular and thin; and the veins stood out bluely in her temples and in her waxen hands. Her lustreless eyes peered around at the surroundings of her self-imposed exile, but they saw little and seemed to comprehend even less. She could not tolerate anyone in her room for more than a few minutes and became agitated if cleaning needed to be done.

At first Phoebe was instructed to attend to her needs for Ida did not think it appropriate for Dolly to do so. But there were occasions when Phoebe was unavoidably engaged on other duties and the lot of clearing the uneaten meals, tidying the room or changing the bed-linen fell to Dolly.

Helene was completely indifferent as to who Dolly was; she was only vaguely conscious of a figure clad in the black-and –white of a maid who came and went with things, and she paid the girl no heed. She did not wish to know her, and at first did not make any effort to find out.

'Excuse me, Miss Helene? ' Dolly had knocked several times, but as she had received no permission to enter she cautiously opened the door to Helene's room and put her head round it.

'Can I come in, Miss? I've brought you a glass of milk to drink.'

Helene sat in the usual chair, her shoulders wrapped in a shawl despite the warmness of the day. Without turning her head she raised her hand listlessly and motioned towards a side-table.

Dolly placed the tray and its contents down. Helene turned to look at the glass. 'I don't want it'.

'Well, Miss, your mother said that Dr. Halpin has prescribed it to build you up. Perhaps you should try to drink a little.'

With alarming speed Helene rounded on Dolly.

'What gives you the right to say what I should or should not do, I'd like to know!' Her eyes flashed passionately, and Dolly stepped backwards in fright. 'And who *are* you, anyway?' Helene continued 'Well? Answer me!'

'Just someone from the village' Dolly said apologetically 'Mrs Rusholme engaged me to help Alice and Phoebe with some of the... '

'I don't want to hear your life story' Helene interrupted waspishly ' If you want to help, take it away and don't bring me any more.' She saw Dolly's hesitation '*Take it away, I said!*' she shrieked '*Can't anyone understand?*'

Dolly picked up the tray. 'As you wish, Miss.'

On quitting the room she heard Helene break down into convulsive weeping. Despite the ill-treatment she had received at her hands, Dolly's heart went out her nonetheless, and she yearned to help a fellow soul who was clearly in such misery. But the opportunity did not arise for some considerable time.

In the interim whenever their paths happened occasionally to cross Helene would pierce her with a stony glare, as if Dolly were the root cause of all her troubles. This aloofness was one manifestation of her enduring grief for Gerald Warrington and for Godfrey – and of her complete inability to come to terms with it. And as for poor Dolly Chadderton, though resourceful and resilient to a fault, she was at a loss to understand what she had done to incur the dislike of a woman she had grown to admire from Oliver's accounts of her, and was deeply wounded by the slights and coldness. She drew some comfort from the belief that Helene was not herself; but the perception that she was regarded as a faceless, anonymous domestic servant still hurt and demeaned her. Out of her love for Oliver she resolved to say nothing to anyone about it.

On the few occasions that Helene felt well enough to see Oliver he was shocked by the change which had come over her. Lack of nourishment had meant that the previous shapeliness of her figure had gone. Now she was wasted to nothing, a mere shadow of her former self. She dressed sombrely in grey or black, but as the clothes she wore had been tailored for a fuller, healthier woman they now hung from her attenuated frame like an ill-fitting shroud. Nothing he could do or say would induce her to eat more than the necessities for basic survival, and he now feared she was not even eating that, despite Alice's efforts to prepare the dishes of which she had once been so fond.

She now began to refuse point blank to leave the house even to enter the garden, and it was this last which convinced him that if the family was to avoid a third tragedy urgent specialist help must be sought.

Dr. Halpin – whose visits to Millwain Place had now become an almost daily event – concurred; he freely admitted to being confounded by her condition, offering no diagnosis other than the old aphorism that Helene had simply lost the will to live, and was dying of a broken heart.

The specialist spent several hours with Helene, attempting to elicit a response from her and tease out the underlying factors in her depression. A change of scene was prescribed, with as much vigorous activity as the patient could manage in her delicate state. Helene had at first resisted all attempts to persuade her to leave Millwain Place, and had become tearful almost to the point of hysteria. But after a period of calmer reflection she had passively allowed them to make the arrangements. An additional nurse had been hired to attend to Clarence, and as he for once raised no objection the plans were laid. The very next day a motor cab took mother and daughter together with some hastily packed cases containing a change of clothes, easels and paint to Altrincham where they caught the train to North Wales, and thence to Llandudno.

As far as painting was concerned the visit was only a limited success, as Helene at first could hardly summon the strength to walk down as far as the sea-front. But by degrees her spirits rallied in the warm autumn sunshine and gradually she began to look about her more, and was even persuaded to take in the view of the Great Orme from the sea.

A boatman was hired from one of the many lounging on the beach thereabouts, and for a modest sum the man agreed to take them out as far as the rocky sea-cliffs; but no sooner had they embarked and the man began to pull strongly at the oars than Helene turned deathly pale, and begged her mother that they should return as quickly as possible. Ida could not believe it was seasickness, for the water in the bay was glassy smooth; but Helene's distress was so genuine that she asked the boatman to turn back immediately. This he did, laboriously bringing the boat about with a shake of his head at the oddities of the English visitors.

Helped on to the sand Helene strove to regain her composure; it had been a touch of queasiness, she told Ida, and she would be all right soon. Ida doubted the truth of it, but did not press her any further. The gentle rocking of the boat, the creak of the oars in the rowlocks and the smell of tarred planks had combined to remind Helene of Weymouth, and an earlier trip she had made with someone she mourned for. The event was still too close for recollection, and the pain too recent; the memory had taken her unawares, and it had simply been too much to bear at that time.

So they confined their holiday to walking leisurely beneath the wrought-iron arcades of the neat resort, and taking tea in a little café-restaurant they had found.

If by chance she caught sight of an officer in uniform – for there were many on convalescent leave – she would avert her gaze to avoid others' noticing the tears which started in her eyes too readily, and once more she would succumb to that introspective mood into which her mother was so fearful of intruding.

A week passed, and then another. At last it seemed that the change was beginning to do Helen some good. She had started to eat a little more, smiled a little more often; and even sent a postcard to her old friend Dulcie Grady. By the same post Ida despatched an optimistic letter to Oliver, saying how much better his sister was, and how they hoped to return by the end of the following week; would he arrange for their rooms to be made ready, and for a motor-taxi to be at the station to meet them?

Their arrival back was awaited warmly by all the household but one. When told of their intended return Dolly was seized with anxiety as to how Helene would receive her. She resolved to keep out of the way as much as possible, but it so happened that Phoebe inconveniently took the afternoon off to visit her mother, and as Alice was suffering badly from her rheumatism it fell to Dolly to answer the the doorbell.

'Good evening Madam, and Miss Helene' Dolly said as she smilingly opened to them 'I hope you had a nice holiday?'

The rebuff she had feared was not long in coming. For reasons Helene did not understand herself she looked down disdainfully at the girl; she couldn't restrain the impulse to be hurtful and unpleasant. 'And what's it to you if we did or did not?' she snapped.

'*Helene*!' Ida looked at her daughter in disbelief, then to Dolly whose eyes were brimming. 'Yes, Dolly, we did, and thank you for asking' she said, forcing a smile.

Helen made her way up to her room, and shut herself away for the remainder of that evening.

After visiting her husband Ida Rusholme called Dolly to the study and asked the girl to take a seat beside her. Dolly timidly complied.

'I must apologise for the way in which Miss Helene spoke to you just now,' she began 'I really don't know what caused her to conduct herself in such a fashion'

'You don't need to, Madam; you don't need to say anything.'

'No, Dolly. I think I most certainly do. She had no right to reply to your enquiry so. All I can say is that… well, Miss Helene has been very distressed, as you know. Things of late have been very upsetting for her – as I realise they have for you, too – and she has so far found the loss of Captain Warrington almost impossible to bear – he was a close family friend, and particularly of… of Mr. Godfrey. We miss them both dreadfully.'

'I understand, Madam. I'm sure that when she is better she will feel differently.'

'I'm sure she will, Dolly. Thank you for being so understanding.'

The girl rose to go, and Ida Rusholme watched her away as she left the room. She admired Dolly's quiet dignity and her self-effacing manner, and to her surprise found herself admitting that she was rather fond of her.

Ida made her way up to Helene's room and walked in without knocking. Her daughter was standing by the window, gazing out into the distance. She did not turn as her mother entered, as if she knew who it would be and had expected her.

'I think we need to have a talk, you and I.'

'Do we,Mama?

'You cannot continue as you are.'

'I..I do not follow you.'

'I think you do, Helene. We all of us understand how you must feel.'

'I doubt it!' she replied bitterly.

'Nevertheless… whilst it is appropriate that you should feel as you do, it is unfair of you to vent your unhappiness on another.'

'She's only a *domestic*, for goodness sake!'

Ida remained calm. 'Yes, indeed. *Only* a domestic. Do you know who she is?'

'Why should I?'

'Have you even troubled to find out her name?'

'I've never had cause to.'

'Now I think you do have cause, and I'll tell you. It's Dolly. Dolly Chadderton.'

'Well?' But even as Helene spoke the name began to strike a familiar chord in her memory.'*Chadderton…* ?' she said, but less assuredly this time.' *Albert* Chadderton? Is she… ?'

'His daughter? Yes, she is; she's the daughter of the man who gave his life to protect Godfrey's. For a number of reasons we have cause to value Dolly, and make her welcome in this house.'

Helene turned to face her mother. 'Oh, Ma, I'm so wretched! So wretched!'

Ida came to her and put her arms around her as Helene's tears fell; but now the tears of self-pity were mingled with those of remorse.

Some days later it was necessary for Dolly to visit Helene's room on some insignificant errand. It was not a place that Dolly wished to be – in fact she could hardly imagine anywhere worse, and trembled at the prospect of being the butt of more sarcasm. The ill-usage she had received at Helene's hands had made her fearful of another encounter with her volatile and unpredictable young mistress;the last snub had hurt her deeply, and she wanted to avoid its repetition at all costs. Now she did everything in her power to avoid any chance meeting with Helene; and her heart had sunk that morning when Alice asked Dolly to take something upstairs to her.

She tapped meekly on the door.

'Come in.' This time the response was immediate. As she entered Helene was seated by the window, as usual; but instead of maintaining her gaze on the far distance she turned to her.

'Yes, Dolly?' Her tone was very different from what it had been; and whilst the change surprised her Dolly was not that easily won over.

'I've brought you your tray, Miss'

'Thank you very much. Put it on the side table, would you?... Just there… .thank you' The grateful – almost friendly – note in Helene's voice persisted. Dolly was nonplussed as to the sea-change which had come over her. She'd heard from Alice when pouring out her heart to her that Helene always had been spoilt and mercurial, but she could no more easily account for the difference in her reception than if, having entered a tigress's den she had encountered a kitten.

'Will there be anything else, Miss?'

'No… no thank you, Dolly.' The girl turned and was about to leave the room when Helene called her back. 'Dolly?' Both young women seemed faintly ill at ease at this now frequent use of a name which had hitherto been studiously ignored by one of them.

'Yes, Miss?'

'Would you… would you come back in for a moment… please?'

Dolly quietly closed the door behind her.

'Please sit down.'

Dolly walked to a chair directly opposite to where Helene was seated.

'I wish to say how sorry I am that… that I have behaved the way I have towards you, Dolly.' Helene's look was downcast and she spoke in a voice whose subdued tone contrasted with the sardonic sharpness of only hours before. 'Though it's certainly no excuse' she continued 'I ask you to understand that I've not been myself… due to my circumstances.'

'I understand perfectly, Miss. You don't have to say anything.' Dolly's voice was charged with emotion 'You *really* don't. Recently so many awful things have happened to people, no one can see anything clearly any more.'

'I know that you have suffered as much as I have. Mama told me about your Pa… and what he did for my brother. And C-Captain Warrington said the same too… about how brave your Pa was, and how noble. He told me, over and again… h-he told me… ' Helene could not finish.

The girls looked at each other through their tears. Both rose on an impulse and hugged each other, and cried together, then dried their eyes, and smiled a little. And as they parted shaking hands, Helene stooped to Dolly's cheek, and kissed it. 'Let us start afresh, shall we, Dolly? I think we could be friends, you and I.'

'I think so too, Miss Helene. Oh, I really hope we can be!'

Though in after days Helene would never cease to mourn her lost lover, her sadness assumed a more melancholy cast in which bitterness no longer played a part. So began a gradual healing process which first manifested itself in her efforts to make amends to Dolly for her treatment of her, and the beginning of a quiet friendship in which mutual respect and even affection would figure- a friendship which would support them through still darker times to come, and would endure to the end of their lives.

A few weeks later the house received a much needed visit from Dulcie Grady. She had been promising – or rather threatening, as she termed it – to come across from the military hospital on the Wirral where she was serving as a VAD nurse. The depressive sobriety of Millwain Place was banished at the instant of her arrival – not because she came with a light heart, for she did not, knowing well what the Rusholmes had suffered – but because it was impossible not to feel one's spirits rise as she struggled through the door with her bags and baggage, accompanied by a grinning cabbie. A few minutes in her presence was all that was necessary to set her companions smiling, and her goodwill and good spirits diffused themselves about the house like nitrous oxide. She did not come with levity in mind, and certainly not to entertain; but her very presence refreshed all who met her.

Though the weather was rainy Dulcie persuaded Helene to go for a walk, astutely reading how the climate of the house had adversely affected her friend. Arm in arm and locked in deep conversation they were gone for hours, and returned with Helene smiling more readily and with something of her erstwhile beauty restored.

Dulcie worked in a sanatorium for soldiers permanently disabled either by blinding or by loss of limbs, or both. The place was full, and there wasn't a bed to be had. Though so much was hopeless, Dulcie exuded hope. Less than proficient in some things, in others she must undoubtedly have been the cornerstone of some of those unfortunate men's recoveries. Not that she ever said as much; that evening over dinner Dulcie told tales of the Hospital and of her failings there – self-deprecating stories which were intended to make the hearer smile, rather than laugh.

At the end of the week Helene told her mother of her intention to follow in Dulcie's footsteps and enrol for training as a VAD nurse herself. Though Clarence cavilled about it Ida had no reservations whatsoever. Within days of Dulcie's return to the Wirral Helene received a letter inviting her to interview in Manchester. She was accepted and before the month was out had left Millwain place once more, to commence her initial training.

Chapter Four

THE LONG savage summer of 1917 wore its way into a dour autumn, with almost daily dispatches from the Western Front in which the worsening news and the catastrophic casualty figures could not be glossed over or suppressed despite the skill of the newspaper propagandists.

Whilst Oliver was still engaged in his general duties at New Heath Hospital he noticed an increasing number of army veterans amongst his day-patients.Discharged as 'Unfit for further military service' and cast off by a grateful country to eke out what life remained to them on a pittance, these thin men could be found in almost any hospital queue, and were easily distinguishable by their sallow ill faces, their proud military bearing which persisted even yet, and boots which despite their worn-out soles glittered like patent leather. Unhealed wounds, trenchfoot, gassing and emphysema, surgery gone wrong, amputations… they were now the daily fare of Dr. Oliver Rusholme and his colleagues. His unease grew with every report of severely wounded men whose journey even as far as the Forward Dressing Station might take a full six hours because of the waterlogged Passchendaele clay. *Six hours* for the stretcher-bearers to cover barely a mile or so. And so many died in misery on that mud-spattered crawl. Increasingly he began to ask himself whether he might not be better employed in saving life if he were elsewhere than in England. But of course he had obligations; to his mother, and still to his father; but most of all, to Dolly. How would she take it… .and how could he bear to be parted from her, and lose even a weekend? Then his conscience would prick him, and remind him of the Other Ranks on the Western Front, most of whom had had no home leave for a more than a year, and of the countless thousands who would now never go home… but then he would shrug off the thoughts and reassure himself that he was still doing his duty, and to the best of his ability.

Christmas Eve 1917 found Oliver on a twilit Deansgate having spent the afternoon on a protracted shopping trip – a novel experience for him. He felt pretty satisfied with himself, for the last purchase had been something very special indeed, and after a great deal of indecision he had now completed it.

He stuffed the little package safely into his inner pocket and was heading to the tram and his lodgings when his way was suddenly barred by a thinly dressed young woman. She stepped out before him – seemingly from out of nowhere- and planted herself squarely in his path.

'Excuse me' he said as he tried to negotiate his way around her, but she adroitly tripped across his path again and once more blocked his progress. 'Goin'home are you?' she said. Her tone was most unpleasant, and the corner of her mouth turned contemptuously.'Done our bit for King an' Country today, have we?'

'Miss' Oliver began 'I don't know you, and what I do is my own affair. Please step aside and let me pass.'

'Oh, with *pleasure,* sir. You sleep safe an' sound in your bed tonight. There's a lot that's better than you who won't.'

She rummaged in a little bag she carried, and pushed something into his breast pocket. 'Here's an early Christmas present for you. It'll suit you just fine.'Then she was gone.

Oliver fished into his pocket to find out what it was she had pushed in there. His fingers closed on something light and soft. Withdrawing his hand he saw that he held a white chicken-feather.

He had vowed he would never surrender to the coercion of war propagandists of whatever complexion. But the girl with the bag of white feathers had in her crude way added one last intolerable straw to a mountain of pressures, some more subtle than others but all combining with one unrelenting and almost irresistible force.He heard again Godfrey's words in that letter of long ago, and they gave him pause to rethink his decision once more as he stood on the icy pavement before the Recruiting Office at Ardwick Barracks.

'... you haven't given in and enlisted, have you? Remember what I said, and don't yield to mindless sentiment. You will do far more good where you are... '

He knew the wisdom of those words, for he knew the bitter price that the writer had paid for them. But despite their clear sense he chose to disregard them – not from blind patriotism nor even from a desire to serve his country, but from altruism- the simple belief that he could save life which might otherwise be lost. There seemed no other way open to him than the course he had reluctantly chosen to follow.

Had he but known it, the girl with the feathers had merely provided the last push to an already moving mass. He saw the chasm yawning before him, and grasping the doorhandle of the Recruiting Office drove himself over the brink.

Those within welcomed him with open arms. The corpulent sergeant who struggled up from his chair as he entered could hardly believe his good luck. Trade had been very slack in the weeks preceding Christmas; and though conscription had, as the Punch cartoon put it, resharpened the swords of the Allies, volunteers of the calibre of Dr. Oliver Rusholme were becoming harder to find.

He made it quite clear to them that his purpose in joining up was to serve exclusively as a medical officer – there should be no question of his participating in combat. The experience he had gained while at Levenham and at New Heath was impressive, and he emphasised his usefulness as a casualty doctor. His only request was that he be allowed to join the 16th. Battalion, as his brother and as Gerald Warrington had done. The officer behind the desk agreed to make every effort on his behalf, and advised him that he would be hearing from the War Office in early course. He shook Oliver's hand warmly, and congratulated him on his patriotism as he showed him to the door.

The die was cast for Oliver Rusholme.

Christmas at Millwain Place was a time of sad reflection. Helene was able to secure a few days' leave from her training hospital and seemed reinvigorated by the prospect of work which lay before her, and Oliver had made a point of being there too. A fir tree had been bought and decorated by Ida, but its presence in the house seemed incongruous, emphasising as it did the carefree days before the War when the family had reason to celebrate something. Now the memory of Godfrey and Gerald Warrington cast a cloud over the preparations, which all felt were an unwelcome necessity which had to be got through somehow.

Conversation was contrived and affectedly light, and discussion about the War and what it had cost them was avoided scrupulously. Oliver tried his best at superficial chat, but it was a poor attempt. Even with their thoughts elsewhere those in the house felt him to be particularly remote from them, and in the few snatched minutes which Dolly and he were able to salvage for themselves the girl noticed his abstraction, and wondered at it. And well she might, for though he had postponed informing his family – and in particular Dolly – of his enlistment until the New Year, his mind dwelt constantly on how to tell them, for he feared the distress it would cause.

New Year's Day came and went with little to mark it in the Rusholme household. It seemed that though they had gathered, noone knew exactly why. Oliver took himself off on a frosty walk, avoiding as much as he could the old routes along which he and Godfrey had rambled together. Encountering this stile or that curve in the path, he would purposely give it a wide berth as the pain of recollection caused him to recoil almost physically from it.

With each step he took he deliberated on what he had done and how best to tell them.

His return path led him through Desbury, and on an impulse he knocked at the Chadderton's door. He was now a fairly frequent visitor, using the pretext of calling on business to do with Millwain Place as a valid enough reason, and for seeing Dolly. Today he intended to call with a small packet for Mrs. Chadderton which his mother had sent.

Dolly answered the door; she knew his knock by now, and was expecting him. They greeted each other formally on the doorstep – there were a few villagers about – and she showed him into the parlour where in an instant they were in each others' arms, kissing long and deep. Then she thrust him away from her, her eyes shining.

'No, Oliver!' she panted, wriggling free of his grip. 'Ma and Tom are in the kitchen, an' they'll notice if I'm too long!' She glanced back over her shoulder at him then tripped from the room and into the hallway where she swiftly tidied her hair before telling her Ma who their guest was.

A minute or two later Mrs. Chadderton entered, bringing with her a tray loaded with cups, saucers and mince-pies.

'It's right kind of you to come to see us, Dr. Rusholme' she said warmly. Oliver noticed that the outward signs of grieving now seemed less apparent, though in her as in his own mother the marks of sudden ageing had become more pronounced.

They talked about general things at first – but then the subject shifted to how happy Dolly was with her work at the Place, and how they all hoped his mother and sister were getting over their double loss.

'Will you be staying at the Hospital, sir?' Mrs. Chadderton asked suddenly.

'Well, yes… and no.' He hated untruths, and here he was cornered into telling one. 'I won't be there for very much longer – not at New Heath, anyway.'

'Will you be staying in Manchester?'

'Well at first, yes. But… look, Mrs. Chadderton… I've come to tell you… I don't know how to put it, but… ' He fell into an uneasy silence. Mrs. Chadderton looked long at him.

'You've joined up, haven't you ' she said levelly. It was less of a question than a statement.

'How did you know?'

'Because when my late husband – Albert – did it, he had much the same difficulty in sayin' it as you have. Forgive me, Dr. Rusholme.' Oliver said nothing.'You'll no doubt be telling Dolly?'

'Yes.' He looked into Mrs. Chadderton's careworn face. In the manner of one confessing far more than his words represented he continued ' It was my main reason for coming here today. You see, I wanted her to know before anyone else – even my mother.'

'She cares a great deal about you, Doctor. It will upset her a lot.'

'Has she told you about… about our understanding?'

'No. She's not said anything. But I'm her mother, and I couldn't help noticing.'

'I love her, Mrs. Chadderton.' He was shocked at the simple forthrightness of his own admission, and wondered how she would take it.

'I'm glad to hear you say that. She's very precious to me, now as always.' She stood up, and smiled at him wanly. 'There's no changin' young mens' minds when they're made up. Please look after yourself, lad, an' come back. It'd quite break her heart if you didn't.'

She made her way slowly to the door. 'I'll send Dolly in to you, Doctor Rusholme. I think you need to tell her now.'

The smile on Dolly's face faded as she entered the room. Her mother had told her that Oliver wanted to see her about something important, but had said no more than that. What the something could be, she had no idea; but she read much from her lover's clouded expression.

'Well, Oliver?'

'I've joined the army as a Medical Officer.'

At first she remained silent, looking at him incomprehendingly.

'The army… ?' She must have misheard him. 'The *army*?' Gradually the significance sunk home. 'How *can* you… after all that's happened… to my Pa, to your brother, to Miss Helene's fiancé… '

'No, Dolly… don't… ' he put his hand on her arm but she shrugged it away fiercely.

'Don't… *touch* me, Oliver! I thought you cared enough about me never to want to… do any such thing!

'My darling, I do care desperately about you. It's just that… I *have* to go. I could never live with myself if I thought that I could have helped to save one life… just *one,* yet had done nothing. I know you must think me unfeeling and self-centred, but I'm going despite my desire to stay home safe with you. *That* would be more selfish, in a way.'

'And if you don't come back? What then? What *then*… .?'

She started to cry, and he again reached out to touch her, longing to reassure her, cradle her in his arms as if they would never be parted. But again she shrank away from him.

He quietly left the parlour, and tapped on the kitchen door. Mrs. Chadderton opened to him.

'Have you told her?'

Oliver nodded. 'She's very distressed about it… .I think I should go.'

Mrs. Chadderton did not press him to stay, but looked past him towards the parlour.

'I'll go in to her, Dr. Rusholme' she said tonelessly. 'Good day to you, sir. And thank you for coming.'

He doffed his cap to her as she showed him out, and the front door clicked to behind him.

With a heavy and an aching heart he turned and began to make his way homeward. The day was bitingly cold, and he wrapped his scarf around his neck tightly to keep out the chill. Desbury's main street was quiet, with only a scattering of small boys playing football in spite of the weather. They had removed their jackets and mufflers which now served as goal-posts. When a solitary brewer's dray wished to pass through them the match was temporarily suspended, goal-posts removed and replaced behind the lumbering waggon in a second; and once more the street rang to the voices as the game was resumed. As Oliver listened to their carefree shouts and watched their animated faces events from his own boyhood sprang up before him and tears pricked his eyes. Crossing the main thoroughfare he was on the point of taking the path by the basket-weavers' cottage when he heard rapid footsteps behind him. He turned and there was Dolly, without coat or hat, approaching him. Both stopped dead in their tracks within a few feet of each other.

'I didn't want you to go… not like that' she said, her breast rising and falling 'Oh, Oliver! Can't I get you to change your mind? It's not too late, is it?'

He came slowly up to her, and took her hand gently.

'It *is* too late, Dolly' he said 'and I couldn't go back on it now, even if I wanted to.' He took off his walking-jacket and wrapped her in it. 'You were silly to come out just as you were' he scolded her 'you'll catch a chill.'

'Do you think that matters to me?' she said, looking up at him with eyes brimming. 'How can I think about coats and things when… when you'll be going away?'

'You must look after yourself. And I'll be back. You'll see.'

And heedless of the gaze of the little boys he put his arm round her shoulders as they walked in a close embrace along the old coach-road and down the hill beneath the overarching boughs of the elms.

They walked without speaking, skirting cart-ruts which reflected the last of the sun in tongues of watery gold.

Suddenly Oliver turned to face her:

'I have something for you' he said, blushing redly. 'I've kept it with me all the time, in case the right occasion might come along.' He fumbled in his pocket and produced a tiny box of dark blue leather.He considered it for a moment then closed his fist about it and stood squarely in front of her. 'I'm not very good at this. I don't know the right words, and it *isn't* the right occasion. But, Dolly? Will you marry me?'

She did not answer immediately. Then almost inaudibly said 'When?'

'When I come back. Finally. In the Spring perhaps, when the bluebells are out.' He drew a deep breath. ' I… I know I'm not what every girl would want… I'm forgetful, and thoughtless, and… '

She placed her fingers tenderly on his lips.

'Oh, Oliver! But why *now,* of all times? Don't you know my answer?'

'Is it yes?' he said looking at her hopefully.

'It is.'

'Then,will you wear this for me?' He offered her the box. Carefully she lifted the lid to reveal a ring set with a single ruby which seemed to glow in the dusk like a deep red coal.

'It's beautiful' she whispered. 'I've never had anything so lovely.'

'It's yours, if you'll have me.'

The news of his enlistment broke like a storm over the Rusholme household.Ida 's worst imaginings had come to pass. Her sole remaining son would soon be gone, soon be a part of that same ruthless machine which had consumed Godfrey and Gerald and Albert and innumerable others. Oliver's assurances that he would not need to venture into the firing line brought little comfort; for the prospect of seeing him clad in a khaki uniform was in itself anathema to her.

She could understand his motives, she said; but did he not feel he had duties to those at home, too? Did he not feel that he owed his parents something? And what of his patients at New Heath? Did he possess no moral scruples whatsoever, that he could blithely walk away from them, fired by well-meaning but misguided boy-scoutish principles?

She resorted to every strategy – cajoling, threatening, pleading, even abusing – in a vain attempt to get him to renege on his decision. But it was pointless.

Alice shook her old head sorrowfully when she heard the news, and regretted that she'd lived to see such times. As for Clarence, he said little.

Only Archie McLeish understood, though he did not applaud the decision. On a flying visit to Levenham to visit his old friend Oliver told him what he had done. McLeish nodded his head and evinced no surprise

'The War can't last much longer, Rusholme' he said 'so you'd be well advised to do your best to survive it to the end. Keep your head down, and avoid any heroics.' Then he grasped Oliver's hand, and shook it warmly. ' But good luck, laddie! Good luck!'

On the Tuesday following his return to New Heath Oliver received a packet containing a Travel Warrant and orders directing him to report for preliminary training at Stoke in Staffordshire.

The parting from Dolly was bitter in the extreme. His last recollection was of her standing alone on the platform at Exchange Station, a pale little figure waving a handkerchief. How strange it all was, he thought; for two years before he had stood where Dolly was now and bid his last farewell to Godfrey, just as she now waved frantically to him as he leant from the carriage window.

It occurred to him then that the world had turned full circle, and that Fate was inexorably bearing him away along some predestined path. Where it would ultimately lead he could not guess; but on the 18th. February with his training hardly begun he received his embarkation orders for France. There he was to report to Number 4 Field Hospital, in the vicinity of St Quentin.

His request for a forty-eight hour furlough to visit Dolly and his parents one last time was denied.

Chapter Five

THE REVOLUTION had largely put paid to the Russian army as an effective fighting force and its opposition to the Germans on the Eastern Front had fallen away to nothing.

Now the attention of the Russian infantrymen shifted from the foreign aggressor to the civil strife with which their own Empire was convulsed. Half-starved, they simply left their trenches in thousands and made for home, demoralised by the immense losses and their unremitting suffering. For all practical purposes the war in the East was lost.

In the spring of 1918 the German High Command found themselves in the enviable position of having available a number of divisions from the Russian war with which to reinforce their western armies by over a hundred thousand men – many of them battle – hardened troops. Almost simultaneously a contraction in the French sectors had compelled the British to extend their own lines but with hardly any increase in the numbers of their own forces

The Germans knew they had immense numerical superiority over the Allies, and they intended to exploit it. Such deployments could not be concealed from overflying aircraft, and time and again the concentrations were confirmed by returning pilots. It was only a matter of time before the colossal armies massed against the British were unleashed.

In an attempt to counter this growing menace defensive strongpoints honeycombed with deep trenches and encircled by barbed wire entanglements – in places almost sixty feet thick- were hurriedly constructed; and it was here that the British dug in to await the imminent assault.

Each strongpoint had been so located as to command a field of fire over the lower lands between them- a space set aside as the killing-ground for the heavy artillery ranged behind what was termed 'the Battle Zone'. In terms of Great War military thinking it was a sound enough idea assuming that the defenders' vision was not obscured by one of the frequent fogs which bedevilled the Valley of the Somme. But should such a fog occur they would be effectively blind to the activities of the enemy, and would themselves be open to attack and encirclement from all sides.

One such strongpoint had been constructed on a rise in the ground to the southwest of the German occupied town of St. Quentin – a quiet place before 1914 whose main claim to fame had been its magnificent Gothic cathedral. Now roofless and a ruin,it had fallen victim to the sustained artillery bombardments intended to disrupt the concentrations of enemy troops in the town. Its shrapnel-torn walls could still clearly be seen from the little hill marked in square 21 of the map now held by Second Lieutenant Oliver Rusholme.

He looked at the map once more, and turning it read the name given to the redoubt by the British; *Manchester Hill.*

He scanned the distant strongpoint with a borrowed pair of binoculars.There was little he could make out other than mounds of earth from the newly-dug trench network and the ominous tangles of wire which enclosed the Hill on all sides. His eyes dropped to the Brown Quarry cut like a scar into its southwesterly flank. Of the defenders he could see nothing, though from time to time groups of men would disappear down the reserve and support trenches furtively carrying heavy rectangular boxes and other burdens which he assumed contained weapons or ammunition.There was little doubt as to where they were heading.

He surveyed the battered landscape lying to the right and left. There was something remaining of the greenness of spring, though war had brought down its iron fist upon the little fields and farmsteads lying in the valleys to either side. Blasted by high explosive the tiles on remote cottage roofs hung drunkenly awry on the timbers or were missing entirely, and though still bravely cloaked in young leaves, many trees possessed a haggard and dishevelled appearance with broken limbs and ugly gouges showing white against their bark.

He had never before looked upon such a landscape as this, yet he felt nonetheless it was strangely familiar. It seemed to him that he was as well acquainted with its shell-craters, the constant rumble of its artillery and the sharp odours of cordite and decay as he was with the sights, sounds and smells of Millwain Place.

It was a landscape which he had never expected to see- had vowed he *would* never see- and yet now it lay spread out like some monstrous stage barely a mile or two distant. The Western Front had acted with an evil magnetism on the young men of many nations. How many had sworn as he had to parent, lover, family – and yet knowing its horrors had broken their word and had inexorably been drawn to it? Many had ended up there through compulsion while others, swept along by the collective irrationality of friendship had preempted conscription and had volunteered together. Oliver Rusholme had been subject to neither influence yet had fetched up at this world's end nevertheless.

It had been his altruistic sense of duty which had borne him away to this, he assured himself... yet there was another more subtle factor at play, now that he had time to consider what he had done more objectively. He found himself no stranger to this place for he had absorbed something from his long conversations with Godfrey, and from his brother's letters. The factor was elusive and enigmatic; but he now knew that despite his hatred of this war he had been impelled by a desire to see and experience for himself the circumstances which had so changed his brother, and which had cost him his life.

He had borne witness to the consequences in the torn limbs, the scalded lungs and the tormented minds; but whilst the suffering had been immediate, its cause had been remote. Now he was at its epicentre, the wellhead of all this misery; now he could confront its brutal realities, and on his own terms. It was an awakening for him, an opening upon new pespectives of understanding and even of consiousness. He regretted the distress he had caused to those whom he loved; but despite it, despite the grotesqueness and the horror which he was about to witness-even despite his aching heart – he could no more have remained apart from it all. He had to be there, to do what he could and experience it, at the end.

And now as he looked across the wastes of No Man's Land, barren of all things which made life ordinary and real and tolerable he sensed for the first time the ominous lull which presaged the unleashing of a terrible conflict. Men spoke in hushed tones and exchanged apprehensive looks though not a word was said about the impending battle. They knew their lines were stretched to breaking-point, and that there were no reserves. The strongpoints had to hold – Manchester Hill *had* to hold – or it was all up with them. And its garrison was made up solely of men from the 16th. Battalion.

'*Here we fight and here we die.*' The commanding officer of the little force had expressed himself with the harsh simplicity which their dire situation warranted. Characteristically Wilfrith Elstob had declined the option available to senior officers to direct the defence from Battalion Headquarters; instead he had resolved to stay with the men he had ordered to the Hill, and effectively doomed; the men of 'D' Company – *his* men. In a quaint gesture more befitting an earlier age he ordered the Regimental Band to play the defenders onto the Hill, then ordered the musicians to withdraw to comparative safety, saying to a friend as he watched them away 'those are the only fellows who'll come out alive.'

Oliver Rusholme made his way back over beaten earth now sticky with the recent rains and the passage of countless booted feet.

As assistant to the 16th.'s Medical Officer Captain H.W Walker he had been detailed to one of several Forward Dressing Stations located to the rear of the Battle Zone – a vast open area some mile and a half back from the redoubts. The whole had been strung with barbed wire like a net with the sole purpose of slowing the forthcoming offensive until the field – and heavy-artillery batteries could be brought to bear on German concentrations enmeshed within. It represented the military mind at its most cunning and most ruthless and had been conceived by those whose monstrous brainchild it was to be an arena for mass slaughter; and the almost certain annihilation of the strongpoints' defenders was in their view a risk worth taking. When Walker had seen how the dispositions lay and had realised the implications for the garrison on Manchester Hill he had volunteered immediately to join them. Elstob had accepted, though reluctantly.

Beneath the sagging canvas shanties fronting the dugout which constituted his post Oliver now busied himself with innumerable small tasks in readiness for the imminent attack. Orderlies ran here and there with the impedimenta of a field station- boxes of dressings, bottles of iodine, sterilisers, bandages, tourniquets- and though he had checked supplies or the treatment areas twice or three times at least, he checked them yet again.

Minutes became hours which congealed into days, and still little happened. For more than sixty hours the garrisons sat it out in their strongpoints, and still the Germans made no move. Nerves were stretched almost to breaking point, with only an occasional man carried in by the stretcher-bearers, or limping there under his own steam. All were sniper-woundings, and all but one relatively minor.

'Jerry's gettin' slack!' one bearer observed sardonically to a boy private from the adjoining 17th. Battalion who was carted in with a bullet in his leg 'but never mind, mate; it's a perfect little 'ole'. The soldier painfully hauled himself upright to look at it. 'An' I'll tell yer *what*' the bearer confided knowingly 'there's blokes round here would give yer all of five pound for that.'

'I don't think I'd want to sell it' the lad grinned, in spite of his pain 'how long d'you think I might get convalescent?'

'Depends on how quick it heals, but I wouldn't reckon on less than six weeks.'

'Six weeks!'

'Aye, but I wouldn't bank on gettin' sent 'ome. I doubt if it's a blighty. They'll sort you out in Rouen, most like.'

The soldier's face fell visibly as the orderly set about cleaning the wound.

'*Rouen?*'

'Aye, Rouen. But there's lots o' nice Frenchie lassies in the shops an' streets an' round abouts.'

At this the soldier brightened. Oliver smiled despite himself as he examined the leg..

'Then that's not so bad,is it, sir?' asked the boy.

'No, it's certainly not. It's splendid, from what I hear.' Oliver replied ' Anaesthetise him, corporal.'

And within a few minutes the bullet had been deftly removed.

Oliver glanced furtively at his wristwatch; 1900 hours,on the 20th. March; but he could not recall what day of the week it was. Niceties as to whether it was a Thursday or a Friday didn't seem to matter at all. Oil lamps had already been lit for some hours to try to dispel the murk in the dugout. The surgical tables on which incoming casualties from the Redoubt would be examined now stood empty, their surfaces luridly reflecting the orange-red lamplight. Orderlies stood here and there outside the Dressing Station with nothing to do but smoke one Woodbine after another, and the tips of their cigarettes glowed like rubies in the dusk

Someone coughed loudly amongst a group standing at the further end of the cleared area, and the noise seemed intrusive in the unnatural quiet.Even the perpetual rumble of the artillery seemed more remote than usual, as if it were masked by some element which had the power to stifle sound.There was a dank chill in the air and Oliver was surprised to see that everything – the angular masses of crates, the tangles of wire fronting them and the piled stretchers at the rear- were now beaded with a heavy dew. He breathed in deeply and thought he noticed a faint sickly odour which stood out from the other smells he had already become accustomed to. His eyes seemed to smart a little, and he took out his handkerchief and wiped them

'It's phosgene, sir,or mustard gas, if that's what you're wonderin'' said a voice noncommittally. Oliver called the speaker over to him.The orderly to whom he had spoken approached Oliver briskly, brought himself to attention and saluted. He looked levelly at the young medical officer.

'You said *phosgene*, Burton.' Oliver was no stranger to poison gas; he had learned much at Levenham and elsewhere and what he had seen had made a lasting impression upon him.'Which side's using it – ours or theirs?'

'Well, sir, from what I heard when I came up this mornin', the gas projectors 'ave been ordered up the saps beyond the forward positions.

They've been lettin' it off in the wind. They expected a southerly which would have carried it into Quentin yonder.' Burton jerked a thumb in the direction of the invisible ruins. 'Chaps I talked to reckon there's regiments o' Jerries massin' in the old town, so it's likely Command thought it might be a good idea to give' em a whiff.'

Oliver had so far succeeded in masking his growing apprehension with an outward show of calm. Now the impending conflict menaced with an almost tangible force, seeming to lower just beyond the horizon, invisible to the naked eye yet radiating its own particular energy, its own form of malice independent of those who were its agents. All were about to be caught up in it as participants whether they were friend or foe; he sensed, as many did that night, a shifting presence – incalculably huge- which was poised to strike at them from not three miles away. He was on the brink of a conflict soon to be unleashed, and he recalled his childish dread when peering over the teetering edge of a Welsh quarry. In his mind's eye he saw once more the knives of slate uplifted towards him, and again he shuddered involuntarily as the stones seemed to challenge him to make the next – and final- step. Then he had withdrawn, crawling backwards from the brink with sweat beading his forehead. But now no retreat was possible, even if he'd wanted it. So he held on to the edge.

The night of the 20th. March passed heavily, but with little happening other than a sustained shelling of known German positions. It was curious how the remote mutterings of the guns seemed to enhance rather than dispel the silence, as muted voices in a cathedral emphasise its stillness. Ill at ease and with nothing to do Oliver made his way back from his post, picking his way carefully along a support trench which ran roughly parallel to the Battle Zone.

A young officer from the 17th. – a second lieutenant like himself – had just emerged from a dugout and was drawing his trench-coat on against the icy dampness which seemed to penetrate every layer of clothing. He looked up at Oliver's approach, and smiled a greeting.

'Hullo, Rusholme.'

'Good evening, Wallace.'

'Taking a constitutional?'

'Yes, of sorts. It's confoundedly quiet at the F.D.S.'

'It is for now, maybe. But if this murk persists let alone increases I fancy it'll hot up pretty quick.'

Wallace nodded his head upwards at the mist which even in the dim light of the dawn could be seen swirling slowly over the trench.

'Observation posts'll be as blind as bats in this. I've already had a look up top. You can't see twenty feet. Just the stuff the Bosches have been praying for. Black as your hat, and with poor visibility.'

'I suppose they'll take advantage of it, won't they?'Oliver said pensively. 'It seems to me they can't keep their forces cooped up any longer.'

'Quite. *Cooped up* is what they are, all right. Intelligence suggests that we're up against the German Second, Seventh and Eighteenth Armies.On a front of less than thirty miles, all told.'

Oliver whistled.'*Three* armies? Good God !'

'Yes, I think we're all going to need some Divine Intervention before the day's out.' Wallace said sardonically ' You'll observe that we're spread rather thin.'

'I don't have a military mind.That sort of thinking's foreign to me' Oliver admitted.

'It's right you shouldn't have, old chap. Best stick to what you know. You'll be more use before this day's out than any of us blessed with *military minds*.'

They fell silent for a while,listening to the incessant rumble of the artillery.Then Oliver said pensively 'Do you think they have a chance?'

'Who?'

'The chaps on Manchester Hill.The 16th. Do they have a chance?'

'If this muck shifts, some. If it doesn't? None worth speaking of.Your Old Man – Colonel Elstob – knows the odds better than most. I can't for the life of me think why he's decided to 'hold the fort' himself. Still, I admire his spirit, and I think we can understand why he's there. From what my CO says it's pretty well what you'd expect from the man.'

'He's set up Battalion HQ in bunkers in the Brown Quarry, together with the First Aid Post. They face this way. You can just make out the Quarry from the Ivry Alley Trench.'

'I know.They're to fire red smoke when things get really rough.When that goes up the artillery have orders to plaster the whole area between Manchester Hill and Round Hill. We're watching for it constantly. But there's not a lot that the 17th. can do, when the assault finally comes. Other than hold, that is.'

Oliver declined the offer of a mug of coffee. Shaking hands they bid each other farewell and good fortune and turned back to their posts.

Even as Oliver was making his way to the Dressing Station the call went out to 'stand to'. Men emerged from dugouts at a run; and the trench which only fifteen minutes before had been empty save for the sentries now rattled with weapons and ammunition- boxes while every face he passed wore the same taut expression. With the worsening situation and with the crisis now almost upon them Battalion commanders had not waited for Brigade Headquarters to react, but had taken it upon themselves to order their companies to their battle stations in readiness.

Almost simultaneously the German artillery batteries opened up from their positions behind St.Quentin, dropping a hail of poison gas shells on their British counterparts. And under cover of the dense belts of fog thousands of enemy infantrymen now began to work their way forward along the valleys from St. Quentin, their movements rendered invisible to the defenders. The sodden atmosphere nullified sound and sight alike, and it was as if each man was shrouded in his own grey world where he waited and listened and strained his eyes for a glimpse of an unseen enemy.

The time was 0448. The Battle for Manchester Hill had begun in deadly earnest.

Chapter Six

FROM WALL to mud wall the Forward Dressing Station was filled to capacity with the wounded and dying. Oliver had been reluctant to endanger any man by placing him outside in the adjoining trench and thus beyond the tenuous protection afforded by the dugout. But there had been nothing for it, and there was no space left. Those already dead had now to be removed as swiftly as possible to the open area where the stretchers had earlier been stacked,and there piled one on top of the other like so many soft and yielding logs- each tragic heap an indictment in Oliver's eyes of his own failure. And now the worst choice of all confronted him, for he had to decide between those who could be helped and those who, in the judgement of a snatched minute or two, could not. It was crude and callous, to deliberate like God over those who should be given a chance for life and those who had gone beyond it; yet space and treatment could only be provided for the casualties who might still survive.

Oliver had stooped to examine a sergeant whose torso seemed more wounds than flesh yet who still clung to life by a thread despite it all. He motioned with his head to an orderly who interpreted the signal. The man followed every movement with frantic eyes and now, as the stretcher was hoisted up he fixed his agonised stare on Oliver and wordlessly reached out as if for reassurance. Oliver grasped the man's bloodied hand in his own and walked beside him as he was carried out to the adjoining trench. The orderlies were about to lift him onto the sodden earth when Oliver signalled them to stop. 'Leave him awhile' he said softly ' and fetch me morphine and a syringe.'

He administered a massive dose of the drug and the effects were almost immediate. Slowly the eyes ceased to focus on Oliver, and then closed. A sigh like the passing of the soul came from the man's battered lips, and Oliver gently released the dead fingers from his own. 'You can take the stretcher now' he said dully to the orderlies.'It's done with.'

And still a seemingly endless trail of stretcher-bearers lurched in with their blood-soaked loads, or walking-wounded limped in alone or in wretched groups. Sometimes a man would stagger in with a comrade slung over his back or shoulders; and all – every man – needed Oliver's attention.

As wounds were dressed he dispatched as many as possible back down the line to the comparative safety of the rear, but there was still the gauntlet of the German artillery to run, and high explosive shells were detonating more frequently and more closely to the Dressing Station. And even the stretcher-bearers now began to fall victim to the shrapnel and the increasing rifle-fire coming from the valley.

The conditions in which he was obliged to work were nightmarish and their situation beyond his worst imaginings as Oliver attempted to staunch appalling wounds, apply makeshift splints to smashed limbs or tie-off arteries where legs or arms had been severed.And all of it was accomplished in a foul, mud and blood-spattered cavity in the ground. He worked like a man possessed, and with the furious energy of two; he worked without pause and without sparing a thought for himself, for his own discomforts or for his own exhaustion.

At one moment he would be offering words of encouragement to a man whose fingers had been blown off; while at another he would be extracting grenade splinters from another's back or elsewhere be attending to the scalded eyes of a gas-victim. Meanwhile the stream of misery flowing into the FDS had swelled almost to a tide.

All around Manchester Hill the battle was now raging. The whole of the 16th – its numbers reduced to less than seven hundred officers and men, all told – now faced the combined might of the German 50th. Division – three full regiments of storm troopers who outnumbered the beleaguered 16th. by almost fifteen to one.

Then, inexplicably at first, the flow of casualties coming down the line from the direction of Manchester Hill dwindled to a trickle, then stopped completely. For the first time in hours Oliver was able to draw breath and take stock of the situation. There was no doubt that the battle was still at its height, for the roar of the artillery bombardment and the crackle of rifle and Lewis gunfire was constant, and deafeningly near; yet the numbers of wounded arriving in the FDS had declined to nothing. Oliver turned to a corporal from the 16th. who had been one of the last to come in. The man sat on the ground, cradling a smashed forearm.He raised his grey face slowly to Oliver at his approach and considered him with agonised eyes.

'Have you come from the Redoubt?'

'Yes, sir.'

'What is the position there?' Oliver pressed him '*Are they managing to hold*?'

For answer the man shook his head. 'Barely, sir. There was hardly anyone unwounded when I left 'em. That, or dead. They've not much ammunition, an' the medical supplies have almost run out.'

'Who told you that?'

'Colonel Elstob's withdrawn to the edge of the Quarry an' what's left are makin' a stand there. I got *this*' he said, indicating his wounded arm ' as we were pullin' back The colonel sent me down to the Aid Post which Mr.Walker's got dug in at the bankin'. They've nowt left, to speak of. No bandages, no morphine. Nowt. Me an' a few other wounded managed to get away before the Jerries came down Havre Trench an'cut us off completely.'

'They're totally encircled by the Germans?'

'There's no way in nor out.' The soldier's voice was quiet, almost matter of fact. 'It's all up wi' em, sir.'

Oliver met the news with trepidation. He had always felt a particular affinity with the 16th. Battalion – even a sense of loyalty towards it. Much was undoubtedly due to Godfrey and the bond which had united him with his fellow officers and men;it was a bond about which his brother had spoken most feelingly, and it had proved to be a cohesive factor which had endured even to his death. Though Oliver had learned much about the Battalion and felt that he understood its spirit of comradeship he was still a comparative stranger to it as a fraternal entity – there had been no time to establish friendships with any of his fellow officers independently of his brother. Though he had hitherto only been only a spectator- experiencing it indirectly through Godfrey – Oliver now felt the bond to have been renewed, directly between the Battalion and him. In the desperate straits in which they found themselves he knew beyond all things that if ever there was a time to take action, it was now.

But to desert his post and his duties to the wounded was an athema to him. There was little else he could do for the present but attend to their needs and chafe on the thought that other brave men were trapped and dying for want of medical supplies and aid- and only two wretched miles distant. Yet the opportunity which he sought was to arise entirely by chance.

A general withdrawal was ordered from the forward positions in the Battle Zone – an order to fall back to the second line of defence in a bid to draw the enemy columns into the trap laid for them, and consolidate the tattered remnants of the British forces. That the manoeuvre was to prove futile and costly in the extreme would only later become apparent, but for now it meant Oliver's enforced abandonment of the Forward Dressing Station and the evacuation of all personnel and casualties to safer positions in the rear.

As for the dead, they were left where they lay, in their silent and accusing heaps.

So began the long and agonising trek of stretchers and walking wounded through the devastation of the Battle Zone. Keeping within the communication-trenches where they still existed Oliver led his charges slowly and by a tortuous route back in the direction of Savy, picking his way through the carnage wrought by the unrelenting artillery bombardment. For the wounded the trip was one of sustained misery as they sought the scant cover afforded by what remained of the trench. And as shells burst around them still more fell victim to shrapnel as they dragged themselves along, with stretcher-bearers and orderlies adding in their turn to the ever-growing number of casualties.

By mid-morning the column had reached the rearward lines; and those who had survived were dispatched to clearing station and hospital. Oliver accompanied them as far as he was able, and having satisfied himself that they were receiving care he took his leave. Without pausing for rest or refreshment he made his way to the 17th. Battalion Headquarters which he discovered in a ruined farmhouse on the outskirts of Savy. The building –once a substantial structure – was as a result of successive shelling now hardly recognisable, its formerly stout stone walls disfigured by shell-splinters. A little of the roof remained, however; and Oliver was informed that it was beneath this makeshift shelter that the Battalion Commander could be found. Stepping through the wreckage of the garden Oliver made his way into what had once been the kitchen.

On the far side was a heavy deal table surrounded by a variety of odd chairs. Officers stood about in clusters, some speaking animatedly but in hushed tones while others stroked chins or frowned pensively as they listened; the atmosphere was one of all-pervading gloom. Heads turned to look at Oliver as he entered, his uniform still spattered and smeared with blood. He realised suddenly what a ghastly spectacle he must seem even in that place of war, but dismissed the thought even as it occurred. Time was of the essence, and the niceties of washing would have to wait.

He looked about him, searching the gathering for the most senior officer. An older man wearing the insignia of a major stood poring over a large-scale map of St. Quentin. Upon it were fixed a number of broad crimson arrows-some straight, others curving sinuously – and all without exception tended ominously wesward through the Battle Zone and toward the British lines. Even on the most cursory observation the implications were obvious.

'Fall back... to *here*' the major was indicating with his finger to a captain 'and you can consolidate with 8th. Company and Halliwell at *this* point... just here.' The captain gave a cursory salute, turned and strode to the door without giving the visitor a second glance.

Oliver approached and drew himself to attention before the major whose fingers splayed out across the arrows as though attempting to contain them. He wore a tartan muffler about his neck, and the loose end of it seemed to annoy him for he brushed it away irritably from the map.

He reached toward an ashtray and stubbed out his cigarette while Oliver saluted him. ' Second Lieutenant Rusholme, sir.16th. Battalion. I've been acting as assistant to Captain Walker, our MO. '

'16th.Battalion. Indeed! Been in the thick of things by the look of it, haven't you Lieutenant? Are you wounded?' There was a coldness in the commander's tone as he considered the bloodied figure standing to attention before him.

'No, sir.'

'Forgive me for thinking you were, but your appearance… why have you felt it necessary to report to me here?'

'Well, sir, the FDS have been withdrawn to the rear. My post was amongst them.And there's little further need for it since… '

'Since Manchester Hill was cut off?' Immediately the major's demeanour altered, and other officers turned to listen.'We've been watching the progress– or rather the lack of it – quite intently, from here.You must have been pretty well the nearest to the Hill, if I understand correctly.Just how bad is it?'

'Very bad indeed, sir. Our FDS alone dealt with well over a hundred critical casualties.And there are probably as many dead.'

The muscles in the major's cheeks contracted 'You know better than most the dire position that Colonel Elstob and the 16th. are in.'

'I can imagine it,sir.'

'Well, I can tell you that the Bosche have succeeded in finding and cutting *all* the telegraph and telephone wires between the 16th. and us.The lines were buried deep, but somehow the bastards have got to'em. So now we have no communication whatsoever with the Redoubt.'

Oliver had understood that the outlook for the 16th. was a bleak one; but he saw now that the situation was infinitely more grave than he had assumed.'Isn't there *anything* we can do, sir?'

'Short of breaking through to them with men we simply haven't got and holding off upwards of ten thousand enemy, no there isn't.'

'They're running low on supplies, sir. Particularly medical.'

'I imagine they must be, poor buggers.'

'I'll take some in to them, sir' Oliver said simply.'It's got to be worth the attempt. I can't just wait on events here and do nothing.'

Perhaps the significance of what Oliver was proposing did not register fully with the major. He looked narrowly at him.

'*What*? What was that you said?' he queried.

'They're in desperate need, sir. Captain Walker is bound to be hard pressed – that's if he's... well, if he's still in a position to continue; and I could at least take in some basic stuff, and do what I could when I got to them.'

'*If* you ever got to them ! ' the major retorted. ' How long exactly have you been a member of His Majesty's Armed Forces, Lieutenant?'

Oliver reddened. ' A month, sir.'

'And before that?'

'A doctor.'

The major shook his head and sighed.'Forget it. You're a medical officer. In terms of the impossible military situation prevailing there you simply don't understand – couldn't even begin to *conceive* – what you'd be taking on. This isn't the time for some boy-scout heroics, and it's certainly no training – camp exercise back in Blighty.'

'I didn't assume it was, sir.' Oliver retorted, bristling ' and as far as heroics are concerned, *boy scout* or otherwise, I can assure you that nothing is further from my mind. My concern – my sole concern – is for the remainder of the 16th. who are trapped and beyond all aid.'

'Young man ' the major said with controlled emphasis. 'Do you really believe we are indifferent to the fix they're in? Let me correct your misconception that you somehow enjoy the monopoly of concern for the 16th. You don't. Do you think that we wouldn't have taken steps to relieve them if there had been the slightest of chances – *any* chance at all? We've explored every possibility, and of those men who volunteered to try to break through not one succeeded. Not *one!*'

'I apologise, sir, if I gave that impression ' Oliver said, abashed. 'I have reasons of my own for wanting to help the 16th.'

'I'm sure you have. We all have reasons – some more pressing than others, perhaps. But that's not the point. '

Impelled by a dread sense of urgency and throwing caution to the winds Oliver attempted one last time to convince his superior. 'Sir, *won't* you reconsider? At *least* let me try.' He was almost pleading now.

'If I were to agree I'd be consenting to your suicide... Look, I understand your motives, laddie,' the tone was less abrupt and there was a hint of irresolution, 'and I can hazard a guess as to why you're here at all. You don't have to be a genius to know what's at stake.'

He glanced through the shattered window toward the Hill. 'You'd best stick around here,' he said quietly, 'you're sure to be needed before long.' As an afterthought he said 'when did you last eat?'

'Only yesterday, sir, I think. '

'Find yourself something. And see if you can't clean yourself up a little.'

He was looking about him in an attempt to get his bearings when he heard a familiar voice calling his name. Turning he saw Wallace striding towards him.

'Look, Rusholme' he began without preamble ' I heard what you said in there to the Old Man. I think it was damn' decent of you to volunteer as you did. I'm sure he respects your gesture, although he didn't say as much. We are all of us pretty well 'backs to the wall', as you can imagine. It might explain his attitude more if you knew that his own son is amongst the 16th. He's trapped on Manchester Hill.'

Oliver's first reaction was to stay put, for it was clear that wherever he was he'd be needed. Though the flow of the 16th.'s casualties had entirely stopped there were still innumerable wounded waiting behind the Battle Zone for their journey down the line. His skills would undoubtedly be in demand there. But there were other doctors besides him, other medical orderlies, and adequate supplies, and hospitals He saw ever more clearly that his duties lay along divergent paths, and the decision as to which to follow troubled him constantly.

Beyond all aid... the phrase slipped off the tongue easily enough. Was that how one said it when consigning eight hundred men to death? The ghastly significance of it grew steadily upon him as it reverberated in his thoughts; and the finality and the hopelessness of it made him feel physically sick.

But open defiance of an order? That's what it might well amount to, and many would see it that way. Though unschooled in military matters Oliver knew enough to recognise what such an act could entail. He'd heard rumours of the courts-martial of officers – rumours which circulated despite the Authorities' attempts to suppress them. It was not the potential punishment which caused him to hesitate, nor even the disgrace of it, but the certain knowledge that the CO of the 17th. understood the situation far better than he. On its own this would have been enough to cause him to dismiss the thought from his mind; it was not his part to question the wisdom or otherwise of a superior officer's order. Again his logical side reminded himself that his duties lay here, amidst the wounded behind the lines; alive he was of use to them, but dead he was of use to neither man nor beast. But if the outlook for these wounded was grim, how much grimmer for the beleaguered defenders of Manchester Hill?

And then came the insistent voice which reminded him of the reason for his being there at all. Despite the risks – and they were appalling in the extreme – he could not be a bystander, a passive observer to an unfolding tragedy. Not when he knew where the need would be greatest. Every detonation on the Hill drove home the terrible message, reinforcing through fire and shrapnel the conviction that for him and for many the die was already cast; but with that realisation he broke out in a cold sweat.

And had the major been giving an order, or merely expressing an opinion? Any regular soldier would have put him right at once, on that score. But Oliver Rusholme was not a regular soldier and he persuaded himself of its ambiguity. He did not seek too hard for clarification, for he feared the answer.

He looked once more toward the Hill, now revealed only by the fires erupting through the fogs which shrouded it, and thought again as he had a hundred times that day of the wounded and the trapped and the dying. Each explosion caused him to wince inwardly, yet with each his resolve hardened. His rational side screamed against the manifest absurdity of it, and at the slim chance of success, or even of survival. But he knew he could never confront his future self if he were to remain inactive. *Beyond all aid… beyond all aid.* The path he followed now would be a defining point in his war, and probably that of many others both known and unknown to him.

He turned on his heel and with redoubled purpose slipped away toward the forward positions.

Chapter Seven

IN THE sodden half-light of that same evening an indistinct figure could be seen flitting back and forth between the most easterly of the 17th. Battalion's medical posts. Plumes of acrid smoke and mist wafted almost leisurely across the smashed parapet and for a brief while shrouded the Battle Zone – a scene of utter devastation now held in its entirety by the German infantry. The rumble of the artillery still continued unabated as it had done for hours almost beyond count, with the horizon around Manchester Hill lit redly from time to time by the detonation of howitzer shells, the scarlet tongues of flame and the darkness which they pierced combining to produce an unworldly effect more akin to an Hieronymus Bosch nightmare

The pathetic smallness of the target – disproportionately small as a focus for so much unbridled fury- moved him to anger that men should have to withstand so much. Yet the unceasing bombardment told eloquently enough that the defence of the Hill still held, God only knew how.

Each explosion seemed to galvanise the figure into ever swifter motion, as if the vibration translated itself from the tormented earth to him and spurred him to still greater effort. He hastily finished packing the bottles, packages and other equipment he had collected into a large ammunition box and lashed down the lid securely with a piece of cordage. Then as an afterthought he reopened it once more and taking five Cadbury's chocolate bars – a gift out of his last parcel from home- from his gas-mask case, placed them into it

He tried lifting it. '*Christ!*' He hadn't bargained for this makeshift medical chest being quite so heavy. He tried it once more and having heaved it onto his shoulder this time succeeded in staggering a few yards with it. The weight was crushing, however, and he wondered how long it would take him to cover the two miles to Manchester Hill. 'Well, there's nothing for it' he said to himself. 'I can't leave anything out now.'

Oliver Rusholme steeled himself to drag the box the whole distance and had hauled it beyond the last dugout. The 17th. had been stood to for much of the day and were now engaged in fighting a vicious rearguard action to repel probing attacks by the Germans. Already sections of the reserve lines had been overwhelmed and it looked as though a counter-attack by the 17th. had failed to regain any of the ground lost. Time was very much against Oliver not being captured or killed even before he had managed to set out.

He had responded to a sentry's challenge when he became aware of someone standing in the shadow to his left. He wheeled round suddenly, alarmed. 'Who is it? Who are you?' His first thought was that his intentions had been discovered, that his open defiance of orders would result in his arrest and the failure of his plan to get through to the Redoubt. He would blithely hand himself in to the Authorities for them to Court-Martial him as they wished, *after* the attempt – once he believed that he had done all in his power to bring some relief to the defenders. He could live with that knowledge – or die with it.

'Who *are* you? Step forward.'

Oliver felt a palpable sense of relief as the heavy-set frame of Tom Burton – the orderly from the 16th. who had proved his worth earlier in the day – emerged from the shadow.

'Excuse me, Mr. Rusholme. I didn't mean to startle you.'

'What are you doing here,Burton?' Oliver's tone was crisp and to the point. He had no time to waste providing explanations.

'I was at the 17th.FDS as you were, sir. I saw that you were packin' some things, and it occurred to me that you might be thinkin' of getting' through to the lads over yonder.'

'Well?' There was no point in denying it. Was the whole battalion aware of his plan? As if divining Oliver's thoughts Burton added 'It's still a secret, sir. No-one knows but me.'

Oliver turned on his torch briefly. Burton was transformed from the orderly into a soldier with steel helmet and rifle. 'Are you armed, sir?' The manner in which Burton asked the question suggested that he already knew the answer. 'No? Then you must wear this, Mr.Rusholme.' He provided Oliver with a helmet ' and carry *this* too.' He handed him a service revolver. Oliver took it reluctantly.' Stuff it under your belt, sir.'

'Why are you dressed like that?' Oliver asked.

'You might need some 'elp, sir,' he said simply, 'an' I've got pals on the Hill too.'

'You can't come, I'm afraid. You would be acting without orders. As for me... I have to do it.'

'Of course you'ave to, sir,'

'And if you came with me it's basically desertion. They'd court-martial you, find you guilty and have you shot for it.'

'Desertin' *towards* the Enemy? Now there's a thought! Even so, sir. I'll take my chances on it, if you'll let me come. Besides, the crate there looks to be heavy; I doubt you'd get very far with it.'

Oliver's resolve wavered. What the orderly said was practical commonsense.

'Then we'd better get moving,' Oliver said. He paused for a moment, and offered the other his hand. 'Thank you, Burton.'

Their chances of getting through the German siege were poor at best; but once committed to their undertaking neither would have given a second thought to turning back.

As they braced themselves and were swallowed in the gloom of the communication trench Oliver drew the revolver from his belt and let it fall into the mud.

For hour upon hour the two stumbled and slithered their way forward, wordlessly negotiating every twist and turn of the trench where it still was passable, and scrambling up beyond the parapet where shelling had caused it to collapse. These were till then the hardest periods and the most dangerous, for the whole expanse beyond the trench was periodically illuminated by flares sent up from the British lines to detect hostile movements being attempted under the mantle of darkness. But equally they served to light up the efforts of the two men as they dragged the crate and its precious contents onwards. Several times they were caught in the open as a flare burst above them and they would freeze like statues as it slowly descended, casting their exaggerated shadows on the earth behind. As the flame sputtered and died away they would be galvanised into action once more, pulling and coaxing the thing forward inch by inch until an unbroken section of the trench could be regained. Then one would drop downward again and steady himself as the other lowered the burden to him. This climbing and dropping became a deadly routine within which only they and the reeking walls of the trench gradually seemed to have substance. All else – their loves, their homes, their other lives – seemed infinitely remote and irrelevant now. Driven by an increasing sense of urgency, they disregarded the fatigue which would otherwise have overwhelmed them. Each knew without uttering a word that time rather than the Germans was their greatest enemy.

On its descent the weight of the box seemed multiplied tenfold; as it slipped between their hands they would clutch at it desperately to slow its fall and protect the fragile contents. Splinters from the unplaned timber would catch on their fingers, lacerating them; yet they paid them little heed other than stifling curses. Their only beacon remained the hellish light arising from the bombardment of the Redoubt; and painfully slow though their progress was, they could see that their efforts were bringing them steadily nearer.

They had reached a point where the trench had simply ceased to exist as a means of protection. There they paused for breath and to take stock of their position.Hit directly by a huge shell some time before, all that remained was a crater which-though shallow- was many yards in diameter. In the dwindling light of a flare they could see that the cavity was now half-filled with water, which glistened dully in the bluish light. Both knew that they were close to the German lines, if not already behind them; and now they had to negotiate this, and in open ground too. The two men crouched down low behind the crumbling remains of the trench-wall. Shrouded by the darkness they waited for the next flare to be fired.

'I'll go first, sir, if you're agreeable,' Burton whispered, 'since I've been at the Front a bit longer than you.'

'How long, Burton?' It seemed a crazily inappropriate thing to ask at that juncture; but Oliver felt that he needed to know something about this man who was so willingly risking his life.

'Since 1915, March, to be precise.'

'Three years… you've been through a lot. Did… did you know… ?'

'Your brother, sir?'Burton forestalled him. 'Oh, aye. We all knew Mr. Rusholme, in the Battalion. We was very glad to hear that you'd come to us – leastways, the few of us who were left from the old lot. Glad, an' sad too. '

'I'm very glad – and proud – to be with the 16th. But I'm sorry for the way things have turned out, for you all.'

'Well, we've been through some pretty rough times, it's true. There isn't many left of the original Pals, when you look at the Battalion. Nomore than a couple o' dozen, I should think. Still, sir, the war's got to come to an end sometime… Shall we make a move, now?'

Another flare hissed up from behind them and burst overhead with a dull thump. In its light they could clearly distinguish the mound of soft earth thrown up around the crater's edge.

'We'll make our way around it, sir, after the flare. Try to remember where the edge is an' give it a wide berth. An' watch yer footin'; that stuff's soft and like powder. If yer slip you'll go straight down into *that*' he pointed at the stagnant pool 'an' it'll be nigh on impossible to haul you out.'

The flare dropped languidly, crackled and went out. They paused to allow their eyesight to readjust to the darkness once more; then grasping his rifle with one hand and the furthermost strap on the box with the other Burton stood upright and braced himself to move off. Oliver took hold of the rear strap and followed. Gingerly the two felt their way round the rim of the crater, shuffling forward with the uncertain steps of blind men. From time to time Burton stooped to throw a handful of earth to the right of him, and listened for the sound of it hitting water.

Inching their way forward by degrees they successfully negotiated the perimeter and began to feel their way toward the spot where they knew that the trench continued. They had almost attained its cover when a deafening burst of gunfire pierced the darkness. In a split second all was alive with streaking white lights, and Oliver felt the sensation of red-hot metal scudding within an inch of his face. The box crashed to the ground and with it, Burton. The firing ceased as abruptly as it had started. In an instant and disregarding his own safety Oliver had rummaged for his flashlamp and turned it onto the fallen man's face. The expression on it seemed perplexed; but the eyes which looked at him saw nothing as they gazed fixedly upward and far away. Oliver removed Burton's punctured helmet and turned his companion's head gently with his hand. There was a small hole where the bullet had entered, and half his skull was missing where it had left.

Oliver had seen death before, in many forms; and almost always it had been slow – a process for which the observer could be readied, prepared, steeled against the inevitability. This death was utterly different. It had come unannounced like a thief in the night, and in a cruel instant had robbed an ordinary decent man of all he had.

'*You bloody bastards! You bloody murdering bastards!*' Oliver shouted, raging at the dark and cursing those who killed blindly and anonymously within it. '*Damn you! Damn you all to hell!*'

Who the invisible gunners were would never be known. They did not open fire again. There was no response to his bitter cries other than the hollow detonation of one more shell on Manchester Hill.

Another long hour had passed, and with it the first light of dawn began to seep redly across the scarred fields south of St Quentin. Daylight brought no warmth as it lit the Battle Zone, infiltrating the stark ruins of woods and glancing sullenly from the pools which pock-marked every devastated road and byway. It glowered through tangles of wire which trailed off into the horizon like barbed steel reptiles, and finally it percolated to the bottom of the trench where Oliver Rusholme crouched. Beside him rested the box – the precious box, whose movement thus far had cost so much. How he had shifted it now that Burton was dead was clear from parallel drag- marks scored deeply into the trench's muddy bottom. Physical exhaustion had compelled him to take a few minutes' respite from his labour; and as he sat there gazing balefully at the box he half-listened to the rumble of the bombardment and the insistent tapping of machine gunfire which punctuated it. It seemed to him that the cacophony never ceased; it was a constant and unrelenting presence, so constant and so unrelenting that one could almost learn to exist with it and even to disregard it, – just as one in a normal world might shut out the background murmur of insects in a garden, or the eternal surf on a beach. He shrugged himself awake, though he had not slept, and stiffly drew himself upright.

At that moment his glance fell on a coil of rope hanging from the shattered revetment. It gave him an idea. Pulling out his pocket-knife he fashioned a crude harness from it, one end of which he attached to the box's handle, and the other end of which he looped over his shoulder. He braced himself against the load and the contraption seemed to work admirably. He smiled inwardly as he recalled a picture he had seen in an illustrated newspaper some years before – showing how on Scott's South Pole expedition the team had been ultimately compelled to manhaul their sledges; perhaps it was that of which he had subconsciously been reminded. But now instead of snow, it was viscous mud. He wondered which was worse.

Once more he set off, ironically drawing encouragement from the fact that the bombardment still continued, and that it was now very near.

The condition of the trench was, however, steadily worsening.

The closer the Redoubt, the more intense the shelling had been. And increasingly apparent was evidence of the fate of so many of the Manchesters, with their khaki bodies scattered seemingly everywhere,in every grotesque attitude of death.

Even with the aid of his harness Oliver's progress was now reduced to barely a snail's pace as he slithered and scrambled over the ravaged earth. Sometimes he would drag the box upwards by its rope, while at other times it would be sucked into the sticky morass and he would have to put his shoulder to it in order to get it to move at all. But inch by inch, foot by foot, he moved closer to Manchester Hill. Only when it rose before him so closely that he felt he could simply walk across to it, only when with his naked eye he could make out the Brown Quarry amidst the smoke of battle, did the fatuous impossibility of what he had set out to do first occur to him. So far – and miraculously – he had succeeded in evading capture or shooting by the many German infantry which now patrolled the territory-though how he had done it he could not guess. Perhaps it was the lone midnight forays of his boyhood which had equipped him to navigate unseen and in the dark. But Providence had certainly played a significant part. Now within a quarter of a mile of the Hill he realised with chill foreboding that the luck he had depended upon must by now have long run out, and his chances of getting any further were negligible. But logic figured small in his plans; and he resolved stolidly to press on regardless of the odds against his survival as he tried to slip through to the Redoubt.

Once more he pulled himself to his feet and summoning his last reserves of strength began to drag his burden away.

It was then that he became aware that he was not alone in the trench. Even as he turned he was felled by a massive blow to the head.

Chapter Eight

HE WAS choking on the mud into which he had fallen, and which now filled his mouth and nose. He retched violently as he regained consciousness, spitting and coughing in an attempt to breathe. Water was splashed into his face and as he opened his eyes he became aware that the figures who stood over him were speaking in German.

'Was he armed?' asked a voice. The speaker's accent was refined, and cultured, and distinctly that of a Berliner.

'No, *Oberlieutnant.* Nothin' at all except 'is pocket-knife sir.' The other spoke in the flatter Northern tones of *Platdeutsch.*

'No weapon *at all?'* The refined voice expressed surprise. 'Did you search him, corporal?'

'We did that, sir. He had nothin'on 'im. We found 'im just draggin' this 'ere box along the trench. Litowski fetched 'im one with 'is rifle-butt an 'e dropped like a sandbag. 'Course,' the corporal added, wagging his finger toward the box 'there might be ammunition or bombs in it.'

'Did you open it? Examine the contents?'

'No… no we didn't, sir.'

There was a sharp exhalation of breath, and the sound of the lashings being cut from around the box. Oliver's head hurt appallingly where he had been struck, but despite it he tried desperately to raise himself from the floor of the trench. '*Stay put*!' said another rougher voice.

'No,' said the officer 'let him up. If you've done your job properly, Kassmann, he won't be a threat.'

Oliver staggered uncertainly to his feet, and wiped the mud from his face and mouth. Five or six men dressed in *Feldgrau* stood looking at him with the same dull shellshocked eyes he had seen in the Dressing Stations.

The officer had opened the lid of the box and was lifting out the contents.

'Please… please be careful!' Oliver said in German. '*Vorsicht, bitte*!'

The man turned his head, and looked coolly at him. 'Why? Who *are* you, exactly? What are you doing here?'

'I am a British medical officer. That is all I wish to say.'

'Yes. I can see you are.' The officer replaced the packets of bandages and the bottles with meticulous care. 'You are certainly no soldier.' The German looked searchingly at his prisoner as though trying to assess his motives.

'No-one but an angel or a madman would attempt to break *into* that funeral pyre over there.' He nodded towards Manchester Hill.

'I can assure you that I am not the former' Oliver said.

'But I doubt equally that you are the latter.Why do you wish so much to reach them? They are lost – *done for,*as you say – all of them, to a man. As fellow soldiers we have called for their surrender but depite the hopelessness of their position they have refused.'

Called for their surrender and they refused… Oliver involuntarily looked across the battered strip of earth which was all that separated him from the heroic remnants of the 16th. Hardly fifty yards. Even now they were trapped and dying; and he realised that the very reason for his enlistment, for his being there at all, had been confounded; he had got close- within a whisker – and now when his objective was so near that he felt he could almost reach across to it and touch it, circumstance had so fallen out that he would be fated never to reach those who needed his help. The German read the desperation in Oliver's face. 'It is finished for them' he said quietly 'and they must know it.' There was a note of respect and even of sympathy in the young officer's voice. 'Your comrades have done all and more that duty demanded of them'.

'Perhaps, *Oberlieutnant,* they have no alternative?' Oliver said in German 'Perhaps they believe they must see it through to the end. *Despite the hopelessness of their position*, as you put it. As a soldier you will understand that.'

Each contemplated the other for a moment; and as their eyes met they were aware of something shared,something oddly familiar and common to them both. Was it a consensus of similar minds, or the meeting in adversity of kindred spirits? These factors had a part to play, certainly; but there was another element – far deeper and more enduring – whose existence neither young man at that moment suspected.

'Herr Doctor,it can only be a matter of an hour or two at most.' The German spoke now not as a gaoler to a prisoner but simply as one man arguing his case to another – one whom he clearly respected.

'If you had succeeded in your misguided intentions you would have died on that hill, or been captured. Where would the gain be in that?'

'One has to try. It's all one can do. You and I share a common sense of duty *Oberlieutnant,* and I suspect that the principles by which you act and to which you hold are essentially little different from mine. '

The officer turned aside for a moment, as if weighing Oliver's words.

'I regret deeply having to send you down the line, to some wretched prison-camp.'

'Then why do it? What threat can I be to you, or to anybody?'

'You are technically still the Enemy.'

'Am I? I see no enemies here.' Directly he wondered why he'd said it. The words had been spontaneous; but as he looked at the lost faces of the German infantrymen he felt with certainty that he was right; it was an incontrovertible truth.

'I could be shot for what I just said' he added simply.

'I'm sure you will be, before long'.

What harm could it do, merely to defer the inevitable? The two young men looked long at each other. The German spoke again, articulating his words slowly and with emphasis in a vain bid to mask a growing indecision.

'I do not wish to send you to your death. Were I to agree to your release you *would* die'

'I undertook the risk willingly.' Oliver persisted ' and I will stand by it. It should not be on your conscience. It was – and is – *my* decision.'

'Have I your word that you will not bear arms against us?'

'You know you have it.'

The German officer called forward two of his platoon.

'Ekhardt and Schmidt… carry the British doctor's box down as far as the next sap… do not expose yourself to unnecessary danger, but ensure that he is as close to his own lines as possible. I will order the company to hold fire whilst he gets clear.'

Oliver turned to the German.

'Thank you for what you have done. I… I do not even know your name. Mine is Oliver Rusholme. What is yours?' Yet even as he asked the question Oliver sensed that he knew what the answer would be. He held out his hand, and the other took it. A flicker of recognition passed across the German's face.

'Farewell, Herr Doctor Rusholme,' he said. 'Mine is Otto Bauer.'

The cousins stood as nominal enemies in the No Man's Land of history; two young men with a common ancestry whose paths had, in the fortunes of that most terrible of wars, inadvertently crossed. Nothing was said of the family ties which bound them, nor anything of themselves. The *Redoubt of Time* in which they met was no place for small-talk and pleasantries, for each knew that there was much which had to be left unsaid. And somehow, all that was necessary and fundamental had already passed between them. Fate had decreed that they should meet; and their hands now clasped in friendship.

'Good luck, Oliver.'

'Good luck, Otto.'

'Goodbye.'

They would not meet again, in this life; for by the end of that most tragic of days one would be a prisoner of war; and the other, dead.

Chapter Nine

THE BROWN QUARRY was a hole gouged deep into the southern flank of Manchester Hill. Barely two hundred yards across at its widest extent it had remained unnamed and anonymous even to the French in the more fortunate days before the outbreak of war; but its significance as a strategic point had brought it to the attention of the British High Command. It had to be immediately identifiable, and so it was labelled simply for what it was, the mapmakers lacking for once their usual flair for the naming of places of grisly repute.

For years beyond count local people – farmers, masons, roadbuilders- had scraped and cut into it as a free and readily available supply of stone; now their efforts could be clearly seen in the steep slopes which loosely formed three of the quarry's four sides.The southerly side – that which led away from the Hill itself -inclined more gently down to the St Quentin-Savy road. What remained of this once busy thoroughfare had now been cut by several trenches and it was along the easternmost of these – the Havre Trench – that Oliver had made his way with his precious box.

Throughout the course of the previous day and night repeated German attacks of increasing ferocity had overwhelmed the outer defences, pushing the defenders back from pockets where they still clung on bravely and compelling the Manchesters to retreat to the brow of the Hill itself. Their wounded they had carried or dragged with them; their dead they had been forced to leave behind.

The three sides of the Quarry had been honeycombed with dugouts and foxholes hurriedly scraped into the steep rubble-strewn banks – wretched cover under the best of circumstances, and now providing minimal shelter from the storm which mounted to ever more terrible heights around them.

The number of casualties suffered by the 16th. appalled even Oliver; space for the severely wounded in the two deeper dugouts occupied by the Dressing Station had long since run out, as had the stretchers; and now men were left to lie out in the open on a blanket, if there was one, and on bare stones if there was not. It was round the gaping mouths of the dugouts that Oliver and Captain Walker attempted miracles of surgery amidst the rocks and the drifting dust and the shell-splinters.

When Oliver had first presented himself to his senior, Walker seemed overwhelmed by the scale of what he'd had to do, and alone, and with so little hope; but the unexpectedness of his junior's appearance with desperately needed supplies had given him fresh heart. In spite of multiple splinter-wounds – wounds which he had feebly tried to dress himself – he set to with renewed determination now that Oliver was working beside him.

As if provoked by the 16th.'s tenacity the enemy's bombardment of the Quarry now mounted to an unprecedented fury, and it seemed to the stunned defenders that every German artillery-piece in the sector – every gun whether light or heavy- had been directed to bear down upon their insignificant spot on the map.

High explosive shells raked the slopes from every side, slowly probing every fissure with malign fingers and bursting in salvo after salvo with an almost unbroken roar. Men were winded by the detonations almost as though they had been physically struck,while those unfortunates gathered below could only crouch and cover their ears and eyes.

A pall of chemical smoke gathered above the crater, its bitter reek causing those trapped there to gasp and heave for air, and drifting wisps clad the furthermost extremities in a sulphur- yellow haze.

How the Manchesters continued to function in any way as a fighting force amidst the gehenna of the Brown Quarry was beyond all comprehension; but in defiance of adversity small pockets of men clung desperately to their positions at the rim as they kept up a steady rifle-fire on the enemy infantry – an enemy who had now to all effects overrun Manchester Hill and who now advanced slowly but inexorably toward the Quarry where the survivors of the 16th. now made their last stand. To add to their misery rifle-grenades began to drop down through the cloud like evil fruit which rattled on the stones before detonating amongst them with an earsplitting crack. The cacophony rose to one unbroken destructive howl. *This can't last* Oliver thought to himself amidst the din; *it can't go on like this! It's too much to ask of flesh and blood to withstand.*

From where he crouched over the wounded he could see men scurrying between cover around the Quarry's rim. When hit a man would – if he still lived – slither downwards grasping desperately at the shower of stones which he brought down with him in his descent; or if killed, would slump forward or back, jerking in his death-throes, then fall until his body was snagged by some boulder or other obstruction, where it would hang limply like some ghastly rag. The carnage unfolded about Oliver like a monstrous drama in which he as a shellshocked bystander had little part – a drama of massacre set in a theatre blasted from the unforgiving rock. He had never imagined it would end like this, and for a moment his mind turned to Dolly, and the sudden and sickening thought that he would probably never see her again; then the regret came fast upon it, with bitter scalding tears which burnt his eyes. He wondered how she would receive the news, and who would have the courage to tell her; and how his parents would read that bloody, formal telegram… and Alice, and Captain Bonnard. He had suffered for Godfrey's death, and had witnessed all that it had done to his own family – the inward collapse of so much that mattered, in the aftermath of it. He had got himself into all this, and for the first time self recrimination caused him to question his own ideals and then curse them for the pass which he believed they had brought him to.

By an effort of will he dragged himself back into the nightmare of the present. He turned once more to the man lying at his side; and delving into his box rummaged amongst its depleted contents. He had retrieved the last bottle of iodine and a roll of bandage and was doing what he could for the soldier's many wounds when he became aware that someone was standing over him.

That someone had interposed himself between the light and the ground where Oliver worked, but it was not the loss of the light only which made him conscious that he was being observed. He craned round to see who it was. At first he could not distinguish the figure's rank, but the exceptional height and breadth of shoulder suggested he was a man of imposing stature.

'I'm so sorry, old chap. I didn't mean to get in your way.'

The voice was quietly apologetic, as if the speaker were some casual observer watching an artist at his work, yet despite the din of the bombardment Oliver found that he could hear every word with remarkable clarity.

'Are you by any chance the M.O. that everyone's buzzing about- the one who broke through the Bosche lines to bring us supplies?' the voice said. Oliver noticed it was of that rare sort which commands the immediate attention and respect of the hearer.

'My name is Oliver Rusholme, sir. I'm not an MO; I'm only a second lieutenant. And I didn't break through the German lines – they gave me safe passage onto the Hill, together with my supplies.'

'Did they indeed! Well, well! There's honour yet in this world.And decency too, I suppose, even amongst the Bosche. But however you arrived, well done, old chap! It was deuced plucky of you to have attempted any such thing – and we need your assistance here desperately – but I'm sure you know that.'

There was a straightforward and impressive humanity about this man, and from the few brief moments he was to share in his company Oliver judged him to have an inherently generous and kindly soul. In those few moments he in his turn felt curiously reinvigorated by his presence, as if the man had discovered hitherto unknown resources in him which could now be tapped.

'Thank you sir. I'll do all I can. I'm sorry, sir, but who *are* you?'

'I didn't say, did I?' the figure said, shifting out of the light. 'Remiss of me! The name's Elstob.'

For the first time Oliver caught a glimpse of the man's face- warmly smiling down at him despite a neck-wound which still bled through the rag tied around it.

'Lieutenant – Colonel Elstob! I apologise, sir. I didn't recognise you.'

'Nor should you. old chap. I doubt one could recognise one's own mother in all this muck. Yes, for my pains, the C. O. of what's left of Manchester Hill.'

Oliver made an effort to rise but Elstob motioned him to stay.

'You attend to Pooley, there. Stand when you've a moment.' Oliver bent again to his task. He had done all he could for the soldier and was crawling to another who lay nearby when he turned and almost as an afterthought, said 'Colonel Elstob,sir. When will they... '

'... call a halt, were you going to ask?' Elstob did not answer immediately but looked out beyond the Quarry's edge as if trying to read something of the future from it. Then he turned once more to Oliver and considered him with eyes infinitely sad. 'When it's done, old chap,' he said.

Elstob paused for a moment and scanned the Quarry, where khaki-clad heaps made for a scene of indescribable horror. When he spoke again he seemed abstracted, as if he were talking more to himself than to Oliver. 'We hold until relieved, you see. Until the end... though God knows when... I doubt it will be long in coming, but we will not contemplate surrender.' There was a terrible and chilling finality in his words. 'I do not think there will be any relief,' he muttered. 'There are no reserves, you see. There isn't the time'

'Colonel,' Captain Walker interjected, 'will you at least let me examine you – even briefly? I may be able to do something to make your wounds a little less painful – and with the supplies which Rusholme has brought... '

'No... no, thank you. Don't fuss. They are only scratches; I've had worse playing rugger. Devote your time and what medicines you have to the men. See to them first – but thank you, nonetheless! And you, Rusholme ' he said, turning one last time to Oliver 'I appreciate deeply what you did in coming to us in our hour of need. It was most gallant of you… I have to return now to our outer positions, such as they are, and see what the Bosches have been up to in my absence. If you'll excuse me… '

With that he returned their salute, and was gone.

'Rugger, indeed!Scratches?' Walker frowned over to Oliver. 'Do you realise what he terms *scratches*? Shrapnel – punctures in his chest and thigh, and a bullet wound in the neck. One ought to have been enough to knock down a horse, but not him! Not our Uncle Wilf!'

Even as he spoke Elstob was making his way back up the pulverised slope, using what precarious footholds the rubble afforded and at times crawling upwards on all fours. Stooping as he attained the quarry's edge he skirted a mass of barbed wire which had been dislodged by an enemy mortar-round and dropped into what had once been a deep trench. Remorseless bombardment by the German artillery had reduced its walls to barely half its original height; but its shallowness was not due to this alone. At first glance it seemed to be covered thickly in khaki cloth, yielding and soft and flecked here and there with red. Then one looked again, and realised that it was carpeted end to end with the dead. Elstob took a moment to consider them; silent, distorted, unmoving; those for whom surrender had never been an option. And as he did so a breath of wind ruffled the fair hair of one lying at his feet – a lad barely out of his teens – and as it played with its unseen fingers about the boy's brow it seemed to invest his body with life again. Almost with the tenderness of a father to a sleeping son Elstob touched the dead boy's shoulder; then gently withdrew his hand as if to avoid waking him.

'They've worked their way round both sides of us, as far as we can make out – though frankly, sir, the situation's so fluid that it changes from one minute to the next.'

The officer, whose thin face was accentuated by a heavy black moustache, now shouted even louder to Elstob to make himself heard above the din 'and there's no end to them; they simply keep on coming. I think, sir, we're up against a whole Bosche division.'

'I don't think that's far from the truth' Elstob replied. 'Captain Sharples. How many of our chaps up here are still able to fight?'

'At the last count, some sixty or so; but since you went down to the Quarry the Enemy mounted the devil of an attack on Nos.5 and 6 Posts and their Bomb-stops. They couldn't have held out.'

'You've lost all contact with them.'

Sharples looked crestfallen. 'Yes, sir.'

'Never mind, Norman; it can't be helped. How many missing?'

'Eighteen, including Lieutenant Keeling.'

'Then we're down to barely forty, all told' Elstob said simply. 'It will have to do.'

'Are there no men left down below, sir?'

'None but the wounded. What of the ammunition?'

'Running very low. Mills bombs,.303 and Lewis.'

'Have you stripped the wounded – and the dead?'

'Yes sir.'

'Then I'll fetch some.'

Sharples looked incredulously at his superior. 'Sir! With respect, you can't! The man I sent earlier was killed – the very second he broke cover. Then Cpl. Leighton volunteered to go, but that was it; we can only assume the worst. Sir, you *must* see reason! It's death to try it!'

'It's surely no more dangerous than waiting here, and without ammunition.'

'Then send another man.'

'I'd rather not' Elstob said.' Besides – I'm luckier than they.'

He slid rather than climbed down through the mounds of quarry-waste, catching his wounded side against a jutting outcrop. The pain of it overwhelmed him and he clawed his fingers into the spoil until it eased sufficiently for him to go on. Even as he stirred a bullet split a rock not an inch away from his head, and whined away. It was well directed, but not well enough. *Missed* Elstob thought; *I am lucky.*

Though his every movement was limited by his wounds he evaded the sniper by shifting from boulder to boulder until he reached the munitions store. Rummaging frantically about amongst the boxes and crates he retrieved three canvas sacks which he filled with small arms ammunition and bombs. Hurriedly lashing these together with rope he draped them around his shoulders, wincing as they chafed his neck; then, staggering under the burden, he made his way back to the quarry slope. Amidst the many bodies littering the quarry floor he saw that of the brave Leighton, still clutching the bag for which he'd died. In an instant Elstob resolved that his death would not be totally in vain; and prising the dead fingers away he added the bag to his load. Even as he stooped over the soldier's body the German sniper readjusted his sights, and fired. This time his aim was better, and the bullet would have struck Elstob fully in the chest had it not been deflected by one of the many Mills bombs he carried. Despite being a heavy man the impact flung him backwards onto the quarry slope and winded him, yet miraculously the grenade itself did not explode. *Lucky again* he thought wryly.

It took him almost a half hour to travel the hundred yards to the summit, where Sharples still kept up a fierce defence with his dwindling band of survivors.

It now became clear that the Germans had taken advantage of the brief lull after their last assault by hauling up their field-guns to within sixty yards of the 16th.with the intention of inflicting the final *coup;* and at a predetermined signal the encircling batteries now opened fire with one voice. As the bombardment grew in its intensity, acrid cordite fumes caused even breathing to become a life – struggle for the Manchesters. Common sense said that no living thing could withstand such an onslaught; but in defiance of all the odds the last remnants of the heroic 16th still fought on, still clung to the last shreds of their battered trenches.

Elstob stumbled into the crater which was now for all purposes Battalion Headquarters. Exhausted equally by the immense weight he'd carried and by loss of blood he sank down. Opposite him sat Sharples, wincing as a soldier bound a piece of rag around a splinter wound in his forearm. He looked at the hefty sacks which his Commanding Officer had brought. 'I never imagined you'd get back to us, sir' he said 'and certainly not with that lot.'

'You underestimate my powers of avoiding Bosche bullets, Norman.!'

And Elstob actually smiled.

All those who shared that desolate hole in the side of a French quarry saw him smile.

And all those who still defended it – still fought for it despite the certainty that they were done for – took heart from that smile and from the reassurance that here was one whom nothing could kill, nothing could overcome.

Elstob now beckoned to Sharples to follow him; and slithering over the broken earth the two made their way into the trench beyond. The scene which confronted them was terrible indeed. Bodies littered the floor and sides, crumpled in every attitude of death imaginable and unimaginable. The severely wounded squatted or kneeled or lay, holding limbs which bled through fingers; others gazed empty-eyed, remote,lost.

The firestep itself had largely collapsed, and those still able to had cut themselves makeshift firing positions out of the dilapidated walls. Now fully encircled, their riflefire had to be directed both forward and back.

A young officer wielding a pistol turned to them. From his pink young face he might have seemed barely out of his teens except for the feral eyes which glared at them. He saluted his seniors mechanically.

Elstob cupped his hand to his mouth 'How goes it, Jack?'he shouted

Second Lieutenant John Birchenough looked at him, and for reply shook his head. That and the expression in Birchenough's eyes said much.

'They've driven us back to the inner line, sir. All outer defences have been overrun. We're pinned down here, and barely half the trench beyond, – and I think they've taken the Forward Obs Post. They're within twenty yards of us now, on every side – within lobbing distance and – *Christ, here comes another one'* As if to bear out what he'd said a heavy iron object with a handle fell into the trench. They dropped as one, instinctively seeking whatever meagre protection there was; but in that second a soldier pounced on the grenade and was in the act of throwing it back when it detonated. His body was hurled back towards them, whirling through the air in some ghastly pirouette.

'*Enough! That's quite enough!'* The others turned in alarm at Elstob's outburst. He had seized a rifle and was checking the magazine. 'Give me a bag of bombs. *Bombs, and quickly!'*

Elstob was already out of the trench when he realised that others were with him. Four men – Frost, Edwards, Masters, and Southworth had risen without a word and followed.

'*Get back!'* Elstob was almost savage '*Get back, I say!'*

They hesitated, at first.

'You can't do it alone, sir' Frost said simply 'An' we wouldn't want you to try. You'll need help, sir.'

Elstob considered their loyal, brave faces from which hope had all but fled. For a moment he could not speak.

'Take us along, sir.'

'Good lads!' he said, in the tones of the school teacher he had once been. '*My good lads!'*

So armed only with rifles and grenades the five of them rose as one to assault the overrun Observation Post,driving out an enemy twenty times their number in a vain bid to protect the remnants of the 16th. from further bomb attack. Of the five, only Frost and Elstob returned.

The respite gained was at best temporary, as the latter saw only too well. And still the iron stranglehold of the siege continued to tighten about them. As the hands of his wristwatch counted away the final minutes of his command Elstob rose from his trench one more, and for the last time; and alone went in search of a sniper who had killed two of his men. But the sniper was cunning, and not easily taken; even as Elstob approached his lair he had the British officer in his sights.

It only took a single round.

On seeing the commander fall Norman Sharples climbed from the trench and despite his many wounds ran to where he had seen Elstob shot, in a hopeless attempt to save his life.

And again the German sniper did not miss.

With Sharples' death, and with no other officer left to take over the Battalion the last defenders of Manchester Hill finally laid down their arms.An unearthly silence fell as formations of grey figures swept over the ridge of the Brown Quarry and began the descent down the blasted and cratered slopes; the enemy's bombardment faltered, then abruptly ceased.

The Germans spoke in hushed tones as they made their slow way down past the corpses which littered the banking; and their British counterparts who sat amidst the carnage below said nothing at all as they awaited the arrival of their captors. Moans or cries rose up from time to time from the many wounded who lay about singly or in groups, and some looked wildly about them, expecting the worst as the end finally came.

But of these things Oliver Rusholme knew nothing at all. His head and arm swathed in some of the very bandages he had brought so far, he now lay motionless on a stretcher which one of his own wounded had given up for him. After the shell blast they had scraped him up somehow, and lifted his body gently from where it had been tossed. Captain Walker had crawled to him, but had shaken his head when he had seen Oliver's wounds.

'Poor chap' he muttered.'Poor young chap.'

Barely two hundred yards distant a German officer standing in the Havre Trench looked across to Manchester Hill from which the smoke of battle now slowly cleared, and as the final minutes of its hopeless defence were played out, turned away bitterly from the sight.

Roll call on the morning of 30th. March was a tragic affair.The extent of the 16th.'s losses had been inconceivable until the handful of battle weary and shellshocked survivors paraded for inspection. Until that moment a faint glimmer of hope had remained alive in many a heart that the initial reports percolating back had been alarmist, had grossly exaggerated what had admittedly been a tight situation. Division's natural reluctance to face up to the appalling facts had persuaded most that things could not possibly have turned out quite so badly for the 16th. They'd been knocked about, certainly; but this was something very different.

The Staff officers present exchanged uneasy looks between them.

'Is this *it*?'

'Sixteenth Battalion; present and correct, sir.'

'Good God!'

Of the twenty three officers and seven hundred and seventeen men who had marched behind the band to defend Manchester Hill, no less than twenty two officers and six hundred and one other ranks had been killed, wounded or were missing in action.

The 16th. Battalion The Manchester Regiment – that cohesive brotherhood of 'Pals' from warehouse, office and grammar school – had for all practical purposes ceased to exist. Its destruction had been complete and total. And of all the men of the 16th. who gave their lives on Manchester Hill only seven would ever have a known resting place.

Despite the efforts of those who after the Armistice returned repeatedly to the infamous Hill to seek his body, Lieutenant-Colonel Wilfrith Elstob *V. C.* would not be among them.

Chapter Ten

THE WEATHER had cleared sufficiently for Clarence Rusholme to be wheeled out into the upper garden at Millwain Place.He sat with a plaid rug wrapped tightly around his legs; for though the sun shone brightly there was sufficient of a bite in the Easterly breeze for Ida to have insisted that he wrap up warmly. She sat fairly close to him, dressed in a long black skirt and black woollen jacket. She habitually wore black, now. No other shade seemed to suit her, she would say to friends, though the colour accentuated the whiteness of her hair and skin.

Clarence peered into the bowl of soup which rested on a tray on his knees. He stirred it round absently with the spoon but did not seem any more inclined to eat it.

'You ought to try a little, you know' Ida said, patiently closing the book she was reading. 'The Doctor said very firmly that you need building up after your illness.'

'Leave me to decide what I need ' Clarence replied pettishly.' I don't like chicken at the best of times.You all know that, but you still... ' he paused, as if hunting for the right word, 'you still... persist, yes *persist*, on feeding me this sort of thing.'He placed particular emphasis upon the word, and seemed smugly satisfied with it, as if saying it had been an achievement in itself.

'Then what sort of things *would* you like to eat, dear?' she asked disarmingly.

'I don't know... I *really* don't. Get them to take it away, would you.'

He let the spoon fall noisily from his shaking hand. His wife reached for a little brass bell and rang it.

'Too loud!' Clarence snapped 'Too loud! Do you want to deafen me?'

'No, dear.'

Duly summoned Phoebe tripped down the steps from the kitchen and deftly cleared the things. She looked at the untouched soup but showed no surprise. Eaten meals were apparently the exception in the household, now.

Clarence began fishing uncertainly in the pockets of his trousers and jacket. As he searched his hands trembled more violently with his growing agitation.

'It's in your inner pocket, Clarence' Ida said gently 'The inner pocket of your jacket. I saw you put it there, only half an hour since.'

'Is it? What is? Ah, here!' And he drew out the case which contained Godfrey's Military Cross, as he had done a thousand times before. The leather cover was much polished from its constant handling and Clarence's fingers shook as he attempted to open the hasp. Ida did not offer to help him; she knew from bitter experience how her husband would react, how any such intervention nomatter how minor or well meant would be perceived by Clarence as an intrusion between him and the memory of his dead son. Since his partial recovery from the stroke his behaviour had become increasingly more petulant and self indulgent and now virtually excluded all others from consideration; and he did not or could not see that there should be any place for his equally bereft wife in this ritual. Whether she would have wanted to participate in her husband's daily acts of remembrance was not at issue, for her opinion on the subject was never sought; it was implicit in his general demeanour towards others that the grief he felt was an emotion unique to him; and at no time since the news about Godfrey had he offered the slightest emotional support to Ida.

His gaze lingered once more on the medal then he closed the case with a snap.

'When is Helene coming?' he demanded 'She said she would.'

'I don't think she did, dear' Ida said. 'You remember how busy she is at the hospital just now. She and Dulcie have a great deal to do, with the wounded soldiers. On her last visit she said how little spare time they get. But I don't think she minds too much.'

'Of course. I recall. Where's Oliver these days? He doesn't come, either.'

A shadow passed over Ida's face as if Clarence's reference to her son had caused her physical pain. Though Oliver was never far from her thoughts – she feared for him constantly- each recollection seemed like a stab nonetheless.

'You know Oliver cannot come, Clarence. He's at the Front' she said rather coldly. Though Ida made every allowance for what she liked to think were the changes in her husband's character – changes which the specialists insisted had been the consequences of the stroke – there were times when she suspected that he exploited his disability, using the impediment as a shield from behind which he could wound her. Clarence had never evinced much interest in Oliver prior to his joining up and had never missed an opportunity to disparage him – so why should he be so concerned about the boy now? Yes, Oliver *was* his son, and was no doubt facing some danger at the Front despite all his attempts to reassure them that the opposite was true; but whilst her more sanguine side felt grateful that at last her husband's paternal instincts were showing themselves her cynical other self whispered that Clarence had ulterior motives for mentioning him. He knew she doted on Oliver. Was her husband jealous in some way of this particular affection of hers for their youngest boy? Such thoughts had begun to recur more frequently, of late. In the past she had turned a deaf ear to them as a matter of course, but more recently she had begun to listen.

'Oliver cannot come. He is in France' she said again.

Yet despite it all, Helene and Dulcie did visit Desbury for a few days. It was noticeable to all that the two young women were not as they had been; Dulcie was more reserved than Ida remembered her, and though she still smiled her smiles were not as broad or as ready as they once were; her light heartedness now seemed less spontaneous and a little more forced, and Alice commented drily 'that young lady's lost a lot of her spark.' As for Helene, she had recovered to a degree from the initial shock of Gerald Warrington's death, but only to a degree. The unremitting harshness of her duties as a VAD nurse had provided her with a distraction for her thoughts, and had supplied a palliative for her wretchedness. But though she had assumed an outwardly more cheerful disposition it was largely a veneer.

'You have to put on a smile for the poor lads in the hospital.' she said to Alice ' the last thing they want around them is a misery-guts.' But she never ceased to pine for Warrington.She still mourned him, and on the evening of their arrival she wept again for him on Alice's comforting shoulder.

Though Helene was broken-hearted at the death of her lover, the scale of the suffering she and Dulcie now hourly witnessed and the seemingly endless stream of casualties they strove to help produced a reaction which differed from that of grief. It was a reaction not unlike that which had been experienced by Oliver two years earlier; but while in him it had brought about a reaffirmation of his commitment to medicine – insofar as any reaffirmation was necessary – in the two friends it had prompted a suspension of their emotions out of a determination simply to survive. Such had been the advice given them by the nursing authorities, and they did their best to follow it.

Compassion for the Tommies they had in plenty; but they had now to redefine the extent to which that compassion was allowed to invade and even compromise their own emotions. Too often it was easier in principle than in practice, when you were holding the hand of someone as he died. Nothing in their pre-war lives of sheltered affluence could have equipped them for the terrible realities which confronted them hourly in the hospital wards, and which had displaced the soiree and the studio as the hub of their social orbit. What they had witnessed and continued to witness was costing them the vital essence of their youth, and it could hardly have been otherwise; for circumstances had caused them to set aside the levity of young womanhood – perhaps to be retrieved again when the war was finally over, or perhaps not. Many thousands of their generation would never recover what they had lost, and in later years would find that the subconscious deep-freezing of their emotions had become irreversible.

The newspapers had been full of the unremitting build-up of German forces on the Western Front, and speculation was rife as to the implications. The United States' entry into the War had led to a misguided complacency amongst some armchair tacticians who rather smugly gave it out that it could only now be a matter of time- that this was the last throw of the dice by a defeated people and that victory was only weeks or a month or two away at most – while others took the less sanguine view that the very opposite was indeed the case, and that the concentration of enemy troops and munitions suggested his intention to prolong the conflict and if anything to seize the initiative and drive the Allies back to the sea. Too frequently speculation and in some cases wild guesswork had been permitted to substitute where there had been a dearth of hard fact. But the unleashing of the March Offensive was undeniable, and brutal, and again threw the position of the beleaguered Manchesters into stark perspective.

Oliver's letters from the Front had in preceding weeks been penned with that anodyne cheerfulness which too often hinted at the exact opposite. Though his letters to Dolly were filled with his love for her his efforts to reassure her as to his safety were too frequent and too fulsome; her late father had said similar things when, as she now knew only too well, he was engaged in a constant struggle with death.

She read Oliver's letters with a misgiving which deepened with each one she received. On her return from Millwain Place she would hurry into the kitchen where, if the postman had been, the envelope marked 'Field Post Office' would await, propped up on the mantle-shelf. And her mother would smile sadly and knowingly as she said 'he's written, love.' Tearing it open Dolly would stand in the privacy of the little parlour and drink in the affection couched in every line. Only later when she lay in bed would she re-read it by the light of a candle, and only then could she tease out the implications. Sometimes she would compare it with an earlier letter from the bundle she kept tied together with a piece of ribbon; and then she would try to rest, though sleep would always come slowly and fitfully, and be plagued with anxieties.

Sometimes Ida would call her from her work and invite her to the study for a few minutes where the girl would read out short passages more likely to be of interest to his mother – for Oliver's letters to Dolly were always appreciably longer than those to his parents or friends.

Ida had been troubled by the thought that when her daughter ultimately learned of the relationship between Oliver and Dolly she might well refuse to accept it, or them; she believed she understood Helene well enough to know what her likely reaction might be. Ida had in consequence dropped oblique hints about the 'understanding' to Helene in their correspondence in an attempt to smooth the way a little and deflect the potential for resentment. Ida's worries were to prove groundless, however. What only four years' previously would have been regarded by Helene as unthinkable was now received by her with equanimity, and with only mild surprise in contrast to the explosion of indignation that her mother had expected. If it had accomplished nothing else the passage of the war years had taught Helene to value people rather more for what they were than what they stood for. Social ranking and status held neither the attraction nor the kudos for her which they once had; though the barriers were still in place she saw through them now, through their shallowness and lack of substance, as if for the first time; and in her eyes this blurring of the distinctions had been further aided by the redeeming factor of Albert Chadderton.

Dolly fought stoically to master her fears for Oliver in her determination to maintain as normal and optimistic an appearance as possible; and in spite of the incessant anxiety which seemed to dog her every step she succeeded in carrying out her run of household tasks cheerfully and diligently.. Partly as a consequence of her promise to Oliver – but more because of her growing respect and fondness for the girl – Ida had been as good as her word towards Dolly and had done all in her power to make her welcome at Millwain Place – even ill-advisedly offering to relieve her of her domestic duties and have her with her in the role of companion, as more befitting the status of her son's future wife. Dolly's polite but firm refusal took her aback, and it was only when the girl explained that she welcomed her duties as a means of diverting her thoughts with trivial things rather than dwelling too much on her worries that she saw the practical common sense in it. In truth Ida's existence at Millwain Place had become increasingly solitary; their friends seemed to call less frequently, or gave up calling entirely, and sometimes her loneliness seemed to close in upon her. At such times and out of a genuine need for companionship she would look for Dolly and invite her to have tea with her. Whilst finding it at first something of an ordeal – for the formal stuffiness of middle-class tea was certainly daunting – with Ida's encouragement Dolly proved to be a less reticent guest, and showed signs of developing into an articulate and ready conversationalist.

To her credit Helene had made every effort to befriend Dolly on her infrequent visits.In his letters Oliver had written to his elder sister of the depth of feeling he had for the girl and had asked Helene to receive her with kindness. Whilst she thought it singularly unconventional Helene surprised herself by admitting freely that she was neither affronted nor disappointed by the news, and she was touched by the sincerity of her brother's words. She needed no reminders of her own tragic yet enduring affection for one now dead.

What if their relationship is at odds with convention? she asked herself. Life was and would continue to be a short affair for many of Europe's youth; why shouldn't they live it to the full in what time was left to them? She did not begrudge a single second which she had spent with Gerald Warrington; she recalled Weymouth with a beating heart – the closeness of their lovemaking, and the measuring of each minute; and she only wished she had given herself to him sooner so that her Gerald would have lived a little more in his brief life and there would have been more of him to remember as she confronted the future alone. She smiled through her tears as she reflected that she sounded like an old woman, though she was barely twenty eight. She could not turn her face against Oliver's plea for her acceptance of his and Dolly Chadderton's love.

She was even pleased about it, and she wrote as much to him. So whilst Dolly was still very much in awe of one whom she instinctively felt she ought to regard as her mistress still, there was undoubtedly a growing warmth between them. Helene strove to narrow the distance of their social divide, on the one hand consciously keeping in check any hint of superiority in herself while countering Dolly's misplaced sense of inferiority on the other.

It was the evening prior to Helene's return to the hospital. She had been engaged in packing her few things into her case ready for the trap and the early morning train when her attention was drawn to a faint knocking at her door.

'Come in.'

The handle turned softly and Dolly Chadderton entered.

'I'm sorry to intrude, Miss Helene. I just heard from Mrs. Rusholme that you were intending to leave early tomorrow morning.'

'I'm afraid we have to, Dolly. Miss Grady – Dulcie – and I were pretty fortunate to have got Matron round to allowing us the four days; some of the girls got far less, and some no leave at all. But one thing- please- just call me Helene.'

'I wanted to tell you' Dolly said, her face flushed 'I'm glad you came.'

'So am I, Dolly. I'm really glad… that we've had a chance to meet, on our new footing.'

'You've all been so kind to me, and made me so welcome,' Dolly said earnestly. 'Especially you... *Helene*. I know what a shock it must have been when Oliver told you, an' how disappointed it must have made you all when he said who he'd chosen.'

Helene sprung to her feet and took the other girl's hand firmly. 'Don't *ever* disparage yourself in that way, Dolly! You mustn't. If you can make my brother happy – and I see it in every atom of your being that you can and will – that is the most wonderful gift anyone can bring to their relationship. Without that gift there is nothing. All else is secondary to it. The world is changing, Dolly; and it is changing us, too; I'd like to think for the better, but I fear in many cases it is for the worse. So many people have sacrificed everything – *everything*- because of it, and have been scarred permanently as a result. I found out in the harshest way that we must never run from the chance of being happy, or of giving happiness to another And when this terrible war is finally over and done with… when the..the men c-come home… ' Biting her lip she turned her tear-filled eyes on Dolly. 'When we first agreed to be friends,' she continued, 'I did not know just *how* close you were to Oliver, and he to you.'

'I'm sorry I didn't tell you; you must have thought I was very deceitful, not to have mentioned it then.'

'Of course I didn't,' Helene said, 'and I don't think so now. It must have been very hard to speak of it to anybody'

'I think about Oliver all the time. I can't stop worrying about him, Helene. He says he's not in any danger but I know different. *I just don't know what I'd do if he didn't come back.*' She spoke so simply and so much from the heart that Helene put her arm about her shoulder and hugged her.

'Then he *must* come back, Dolly! We must *will* him to!'

Even as the two young women sat together arm in arm, the typesetters of New Cross were already busily at work on the newspaper headlines for the following day – headlines destined to burst on a Manchester public who would at first receive the news from the Western Front with incredulity; and then, when the appalling truth had been established beyond doubt, would attempt to reconcile themselves to the impossible – that the City's two most cherished battalions of 'Pals' had been virtually annihilated, and all in the space of two days. Once more the people of Manchester had to steel themselves to the loss of yet another thousand of their young men, and a cry of distress mingled with pride rose from the City with a common voice as details of the epic tragedy of Manchester Hill finally became known.

Chapter Eleven

THOUGH LESS than an hour from the City by train, Desbury might have been a hundred miles away, it was so remote from current affairs. There was no local telegraph office, and the population was even then so sparse and scattered that a news agency in the village was out of the question. Papers came by post – which meant that the news was often a day or two old, at least, and rather stale – or were brought back by visitors to Manchester or Stockport. And there was simply nobody who could telephone to inform the family of the disaster which had overwhelmed the 16th. Battalion, and Oliver; nobody to tell them of the upsurge of grief which had taken possession of the City, and of the mood of incalculable loss which pervaded every square and street. A small figure in a dark blue uniform dismounted from the bicycle which he had ridden all the way from Chorlton. Though the weather was overcast and cold he was hot from the exertion of pedalling along the unmetalled Desbury lanes. The boy pushed his pill-box hat to the back of his head and wiped his brow with a grubby handkerchief.

He looked about him,to the left and right, along the unfamiliar tree-lined road and toward the large houses which stood distant and half-obscured along winding driveways. The boy looked with misgiving at the wide expanse of gravel which trailed off and away between dark rhododendrons. It made him feel very insignificant, and very small.

'I wish these toffs'd put the name on proper' he muttered to himself 'how'm I supposed to know what the number is?' He stuffed his handkerchief back into the pocket of his jacket and fishing in the leather pouch which hung from his belt pulled out a number of papers. He read the address on each as he thumbed through them and finding the one he wanted looked again about him for some evidence of the house-name. This time he was more successful, for on the left gatepost he saw that a mat of ivy had overgrown a sandstone tablet let into the brickwork. 'Oh, this is it' he said as he read the name. 'This is the one, all right. *Millwain Place*.'

The doorbell rang just as Dolly Chadderton was coming downstairs with a book Ida had asked her to bring from her bedside table. Dolly had been told not to answer the door, leaving callers for Phoebe to attend to; but that morning Dolly knew that the maid was in the kitchen, and besides she didn't mind. Still clutching the book she approached the door and through the distorted glass could just make out the small dark shape which stood beyond. As the door swung open the boy mechanically thrust out the piece of paper with one hand while extending his receipt-book with the other.

'Telegram for Mr. and Mrs. Rusholme' he said mechanically. 'Will you sign for it, Miss?'

Dolly recoiled from the boy's outstretched hand, and instinctively placed her own behind her. She looked at the sealed paper for a moment, considering it with dread whilst it still lay beyond arms' reach. To take it would probably signal the end of all that mattered to her – would at the moment of its opening bring about the collapse of every real hope she'd ever had. She couldn't face what that piece of paper contained

It was not the first Official Telegram that the boy had delivered and he was no stranger to the reaction. 'I'm *very* sorry, Miss,' he said as he read the distress in her face and saw her reluctance 'but *someone's* got to take it.'

She stepped forward like an automaton and took the telegram from the boy. Her hand signed the receipt, though she was hardly aware of its motion. Then almost forgetting herself she gave the boy sixpence.

He took it and thanked her, but did not value the money much, for the young lady had been so pretty, and he wished he could undo the sadness he'd caused.

Ida Rusholme turned to Dolly as the girl entered the sitting room. She looked first to the book in Dolly's left hand, and smiled her gratitude.

'It was good of you to get it for me, dear. So it *was* where I thought I'd... 'The sentence remained unfinished as her eyes wandered to Dolly's face, and she took in the pallor of cheeks from which the blood had all but drained. Ida started to her feet, and the embroidery on which she had been working fell to the floor.

'Oh, *no*... ' she began in choking tones. She looked with staring eyes to the girl's other hand and saw what it contained, then shrank back wincing as though she had been physically struck.

'Oh no... please God... .not Oliver too? Not *Oliver*... .' Ida Rusholme covered her eyes with a trembling hand as Dolly – though stricken herself – stepped towards her.

'Open it... .open it, please. I cannot.'

Dolly hesitated as she looked again at the anonymous scrap of paper which at that moment seemed to be the determining factor on which the fate of her lover and herself entirely depended.

'Open it, Dolly. *Please'* She tore open the seal and unfolding the paper scanned the official print.

'It's Oliver' she said.

She heard her own voice repeat the words *Oliver... it's Oliver...* It seemed no more than a meaningless sound when you said it like that.

It's Oliver. Was that how you said it, when the news you'd dreaded every waking minute came through at last? She closed her eyes and tried to recall his face but the image appeared hazy and indistinct. *Oliver.*

She turned to the telegram once more.

> *Infantry Records Office*
> *Ardwick Station*
> *27th.March 1918*
> *Sir/Madam,*
> *It is my painful duty to inform you that a report has this day been received from the War Office notifying that* Oliver Rusholme Second Lieutenant 16th Battalion The Manchester Regiment *has been posted as Missing in Action...*

There followed some details about further news, personal effects and authority to dispose of them and to whom to apply, etc.

Dolly handed the paper to Ida who took it listlessly from her.

'Oh, God.' She spoke so inaudibly it was more like a sigh. 'Oh God.'

'He isn't *dead*, Mrs. Rusholme. It doesn't *say* so. He's *missing*.' Had Dolly been alone she would have collapsed; almost the worst blow of all had fallen; now she spoke with as much conviction as she could to reassure herself as much as Ida. Her heart and her head were equally in turmoil, but of one thing she was certain; she would not permit herself to think him dead, whilst there was the faintest hope. And she would not mourn; and she would not despair.

'No. It doesn't say so.' Ida repeated her words in a dull monotone from which conviction was utterly absent

'He might not be, Mrs. Rusholme.' Dolly persisted. 'Soldiers have turned up weeks or months later, in a hospital somewhere, or as a prisoner of the Germans. I've heard it can happen that way, sometimes.'

Ida returned her look with empty eyes. 'I'm sorry, Dolly; I'm sorry for you, more than anyone.'

'Don't be, *please*! I can't take it, Mrs Rusholme. Not yet, I can't. I *won't* hear that he's dead until I *know*. If you pity me like that, it seems that you've given up hoping, and that I couldn't bear.'

She moved towards Ida and gently took her hand. ' Please don't leave me alone to hope 'she said, as tears started in her eyes 'It's all we've got left, after all.'

Ida said nothing as she took the telegram from Dolly. She looked at the icy print once more, then turned and made her way out of the room. The door opened and clicked to behind her. She did not look back.

Dolly buried her face in her hands and wept.

She vowed that was the last time she would allow herself to cry.

To her, tears seemed a milestone on a bitter road to defeat, an indulgence which signified her capitulation to the pessimistic forces which beseiged her. She pushed the bleak realities aside, and hoped on regardless. She swore she would never accept Oliver's death until she was told the unequivocal truth by one who had *seen* him die, or who knew him to be dead. Until that point she would believe him alive, even yet; and as she lay alone in her bed in the dark she would repeat the words Helene had spoken to her, and managed to draw a little comfort from them. *Then he must come back... we must will him to.*

She kept herself fiercely busy at Millwain Place. It was all she could do, clinging as she did to the last vestiges of normality; and once more the welter of duties in which she engaged enabled her to occupy each day with trivial things and problems, and deferred the thought and the prospect of a lonely journey home. It was then than the demons of recollection rose to scourge her; for there was no alternative but to return by the path which she and Oliver had walked so many times. She knew the patination on the bark of each tree, every turn and undulation in the ground, every place where they had halted, and loved each other. At first she would turn her sight from them as she passed; but latterly she began to anticipate the bittersweetness of the memories which seemed to cling to them with their own distinctive fragrance.

In the sepulchral silence which now pervaded the house she was the only soul still awake to the possibility that Oliver was not dead; Ida had accepted the news about her youngest son with a disturbing resignation, for her spirit and indeed her will to go on seemed entirely broken by grief at this latest – and greatest – loss. The catastrophe which she had feared had in her mind finally come to pass; to her, *Missing* or *Killed in Action* was only a matter of degree – a matter of military tautology which said much the same. Ida Rusholme had finally given up the fight.

At first she had decided to tell Clarence of the telegram, her feeling of loss somehow coalescing into a desire for revenge against her husband – revenge for his lack of concern for her since they had lost Godfrey; and for his lack of concern for Oliver, which had been always. The telegram would have proved the ultimate weapon borne of a complex of grievances which she had no other opportunity to vent upon him. But compassion prevailed even as she grasped the handle of his sickroom, and she withdrew once more. In his feeble mental state she recognised that there was nothing to be gained from such an act; the motives were cruel, just as he had been cruel. and so she never told him. And why seek to breed misery?

In her spare time Dolly wrote letters, asking if the recipients knew anything of Oliver's whereabouts, or had heard any news of him. She wrote to Oliver's commanding officer and to several other officers from the 16th. 'Pals' – but she did not know they were dead, until the letters were returned with that ghastly endorsement which nearly broke her resolve, and her heart. She wrote to colleagues known in training and whom he had mentioned once or twice; they replied, occasionally. Their letters offered sympathy, but no help. Daily and with each disappointment she felt that she was groping in an ever more impenetrable darkness, a darkness which shrouded all of Oliver's doings in the days before his disappearance and on which no light could be shed. He seemed to have disappeared from the face of the earth.

It would have been a tedious journey to Ardwick from Desbury, but Dolly's steps were again buoyed with irrepressible hope, and she regarded her visit with a mixture of apprehension and anticipation. She had walked to the station to take the train, and from Manchester Oxford Road had caught the tram to the Green, where she got off.

A passer-by politely directed her towards the Barracks, and a few minutes walking brought her before its forbidding castellated façade. Several doors gave onto the cobbled square in front and she paused, wondering which one might be the best to try. She was hesitantly approaching the one to the left when it opened and a burly sergeant stepped out, turned and presented his broad back to her as he noisily locked up. He rattled the handle to make doubly sure and was on the point of leaving when he caught sight of Dolly standing there. He doffed his cap to her and walked a few paces then turned and looked back. 'Can I help you at all, Miss?' The kindness in his voice seemed at odds with his rather daunting appearance, and Dolly was encouraged. 'I hope you can, sir.' She briefly told him of Oliver, and of her search for him, and how she could find nothing out. Her earnestness touched the sergeant, and he felt he would like to help her, if he could.

'Well, Miss, the Adjutant's the man you'll need to see' He nodded toward the door on the right 'though I'm not so certain as he'll be about. We've been rather busy of late as I'm sure you'll appreciate.'

But the Adjutant happened to be in his office, and Dolly was informed by the sergeant that he would be free to speak to her in a few minutes, if she wouldn't mind waiting? She said she wouldn't, but as no seat was offered her inside she took up station hard by the door to his office.

It seemed to take an age, standing there, silently fingering the ruby engagement ring which Oliver had given her. A few soldiers sauntered past and eyed her up and down, and one winked at her. She looked away, and reddened indignantly. She peered up at the clock set high in the stone frontage. It couldn't have been only twenty minutes, surely? She thought it had been at least an hour. Then mens'voices could be heard from within as they prepared to leave, and at last she was ushered in. A fug of tobacco smoke cloaked everything in a bluish mist, and it was a moment before Dolly could make out exactly where the Adjutant was sitting.

'Take a seat.' The voice was clipped and to the point, though not sufficiently to render it exactly brusque. Rather the speaker sounded testy, and tired. He waved her to a chair.

'Yes? How can we help you?'

Once more Dolly explained, though in greater detail. She had brought along the last of the envelopes with Field Post Office frankings in the faint hope that they might give an indication of Oliver's whereabouts. The Adjutant took them from her and scanned them cursorily. He penned down a few details, though it was obviously only for form's sake.

'No.I'm sorry.There's little or nothing we might find out from these' he said, passing them back across the desk 'their very purpose is to give nothing away,y'see? I regret I can't help you. '

'There's nothing you can do, sir?'

'Nothing, I'm afraid. Everything over there is in a state of confusion, with the Enemy mounting his offensive and all.We hardly know where the Regiment *is* from one day to the next.There are no enquiries that I could make which could serve any useful purpose, other than to raise false hopes. You see our position.'

'Yes, sir.I see.'

As Dolly silently rose to leave the Adjutant had a change of heart.

'One moment, miss ' he called after her. 'Look' he said rather apologetically ' What I tell you is unverified, and essentially *off the record*. But whilst our casualties *have* been very heavy, we've got reason to think that perhaps the Germans managed to capture more of our men than we'd originally thought. Observers reported seeing large columns moving away from the battlefield, which suggests prisoners rather than formations of the enemy. But you mustn't hold out any hope on that score.'

'No, sir. I won't'.But she did, nevertheless.

'Damn' shame' said the Adjutant. 'What is, sir?' enquired the sergeant who was tidying a heap of files. The officer nodded towards the window and the lonely figure of Dolly as she made her way across the yard. The sergeant stooped and followed his gaze.'Oh, aye, sir. A pretty lass like that, an'all.'

'How many is that?'

'Must be thirty this week alone, sir.'

Chapter Twelve

THE SHOCK waves from those disastrous March days continued to reverberate until even the furthest corners of the country felt the tremors. The extent of the British losses – published at a time when so many believed the war to be all but won – cast a black cloud of apprehension over many a remote hamlet; and the incidental cost of the news would prove to be a heavy one indeed.

The appalling truth gradually became known; that the Germans had recovered *all* the territory lost by them during the Somme Offensive. The Battles of Arras, Passchendaele and Ypres might never have been fought – might count for nothing at all – for despite the incalculable bloodshed and misery, not a yard of ground had been gained.

Almost a month to the day after the publication of the casualties of Manchester Hill a letter arrived at Millwain Place. It was a bulky item and evidently contained a substantial document. The aspect which made it exceptional was not however its weight but the fact that it was addressed to Dr. Oliver Rusholme. Phoebe brought it to Ida who placed it by her on the occasional table. She was deeply puzzled by it. It did not seem to relate to his profession – Oliver had long since ceased using his former home as an address for medical correspondence – yet there was no doubt in her mind that it originated from a professional source. That the stamps on it had been franked with a Welsh postmark only deepened the mystery.

Long years wedded to a solicitor had sharpened her instinct for such things, and she felt that the packet ought to be opened, though she hesitated to open it. Dolly's opinion was not asked for – not as an intended snub but rather because Ida still regarded her missing son as part of *her* household.

For some days it lay there, sealed. Then on an impulse she took it up and tore the paper. It contained a number of large documents and what appeared to be a copy of a Will. The enclosed letter was from a firm of solicitors in Flint, North Wales. Mr Jones of that company was pleased to advise Dr Rusholme that he was the sole beneficiary in the estate of the late Captain Edward George Bonnard; that the Will of the deceased gentleman was at that moment in the process of Probate, and on receipt of sufficient proof of his identity the proceeds of the estate and the Deeds to the deceased's property in Ridland would be transferred to him.

It transpired that the lifeless body of the old man had been discovered on the rutted banks of the Clwyr, where he had apparently fallen. Setting out as usual from the cottage to buy a few necessaries from the store at Ridland, he had visited the post office to collect his mail and his daily paper.. He had said good day to the postmaster Owens who stated that he had seemed in reasonable spirits. When on the following two days he did not call Mr Owens became concerned and notified the local constable. It was the latter who on his way to the cottage on that overcast and bitter March day found the Captain's body lying beside the path. Though his groceries lay scattered about him in the mud, he still held tightly onto the newspaper which it appeared he had been reading at the moment of his death. It was clear, they all said, that he had tripped while his attention was diverted, and had died from the consequent fall. An inquest was deemed unnecessary as he had been a man of advanced years, and there was no evidence of foul play. The few locals that he was on nodding acquaintance with were sorry about it; but only the vicar, the constable and Mr Owens attended his funeral. As no-one had troubled to examine what he had been reading, none would ever know that they had been the lists of those missing in action on Manchester Hill.

Dolly Chadderton now spent more time at Millwain Place than she did at her own home in Desbury; in both houses she felt equally apart from the others, for in both she encountered the same dearth of hope. Though she could have had the sympathy of both her mother and Ida – sympathy from which she recoiled – neither had been able to vouchsafe one word of encouragement; they simply could not bring themselves to utter cruel falsehoods which they believed would prove ultimately to be no more than delusive; and each wished that the girl could reconcile herself to her loss, and brace herself for what would inevitably come. Nobody – not even the sorrowing Alice- believed that Oliver was still alive. So Dolly was acutely alone, and she felt that loneliness bitterly. Yet Millwain Place granted her a nearness to the missing Oliver – a communing with his past, and a proximity of spirit which she could not have gained elsewhere. For her the house was redolent with him; it echoed to his footsteps and to his voice, and she would pause by the door of his boyhood room and think of him as she fought back the tears which she had sworn never to shed.

Another month had almost past, and not a trace had been found nor a word received. It had been a month which had witnessed the Requiem for the 16th. and 17th. Battalions, held in the sombre nave of Manchester

Cathedral. It had promised to be a dignified and contemplative affair until the Bishop intervened, seizing on it as an opportunity to mount a vitriolic attack against the whole *degenerate German race*.

Ida had attended,clad in mourning black, and had invited Dolly to accompany her, but she had declined.It was too final for Dolly, and a Requiem was for the Dead.

The weather had closed in and Millwain Place was being battered by gales and squally rain. Dolly had finished every little chore to perfection, and the house shone. She bid goodnight to Ida who pressed her to stay over in one of the spare rooms, but Dolly thought of her mother's anxiety and decided to go home in spite of the weather. The walk down through the trees was alarming as branches heaved and groaned above her, and there were unseen movements in the night as cloud scudded across the moon and darkened her path. Finally and with a sense of relief she reached her own front door which now glistened with runnels of water. Removing her dripping coat in the twilight of the little lobby she made her way to the kitchen, guided by the thin light flowing from the crack beneath the door.

She entered slowly; nobody was there, though the coals in the grate had been freshly banked up and burned with a cheerful confidence. She sat herself close to the iron range, for the cold had penetrated her clothes and her thin body. Feeling more weary than she could ever remember she stretched herself back, then yawned and nodded, and let sleep take her.

She did not know how long she had lain there, but she was roused by someone gently shaking her shoulder.

'Dolly! *Dolly, love*! *Wake up*.' She rubbed her eyes blearily with the back of her hand.

'You must be right tired, Love. But *you need to wake up*.' She looked about her, still half asleep.Her mother was there, and beside her stood her Uncle Edwin. And her cousin Wilfred. And at this late hour...

She was fully awake in a moment. 'What is it? *Oh, Ma, what is it*? *Tell me!* I must know! Is it Oliver?'

Her voice was unnaturally high, for the exhaustion and the months of constant fear had taken a heavy toll of her strength. 'Oh, God! Please, no... ' Her mother looked anxiously across toward Uncle Edwin, and back to the blanched face of her daughter.

'It might well be, lass. This has come, in this mornin's post.' She held out a letter. 'It's very odd, Love. It's travelled all the way from Switzerland.' Dolly took it almost reluctantly, and turned it carefully as if doubting even its existence.

The envelope had foreign words impressed on the top in place of a stamp- words which she thought might be German – and beside them the symbol of a Red Cross.

Dolly looked imploringly to her mother and her uncle as if they had the power to intercede between her and it. Then with a trembling hand she began to open the letter.

A few sheets of wispy paper was all it contained – paper so translucent that the ink had penetrated through to the reverse, and made reading difficult. But not so difficult that Dolly could not read there what she had longed for.

Months of sustaining hope against the odds, and of fighting a rearguard action against despair, months of suspending misery and holding it at bay. Had she known it, Dolly Chadderton had reached the very last of her inner reserves. The constraints which she had through pure willpower imposed upon her emotions now snapped like cotton, and she was overwhelmed and swept away in the deluge.

The tears which she had sworn never to shed now fell in abundance, for the prop provided by her inner strength was now no longer needed. Her legs gave beneath her and she buckled physically under the sudden shock of release. Uncle Edwin rushed forward to catch her before she struck the stone floor, and helped her into an armchair.

There she covered her face with her hands and sobbed uncontrollably.

Her mother looked aghast. 'Oh, God, poor lad! An' our poor lass! Edwin ! Run to the *Sceptre* an' fetch a glass o' brandy, quick. She'll pass out, else.'

'N..no Mam ! Don't !' Dolly broke in, laughing amidst her sobs

'Oh, Mam! *Mam!* You've got it all wrong ! You don't *know*! You don't ! Oh, Mam! *He's alive! Oliver's alive!*'

Offizierenlager Vll
4116 Freistad
Hamburg
Germany

My Dearest Love

When I first picked up my pen to write this letter I knew exactly where and how I would begin; but now I'm not so sure. The last weeks have been pretty grim ones for me, but how much grimmer and more desperate have they been for you, my darling, as you waited for news which did not come at all; and if it had, could only have been awful. You, and the worry you must have suffered hourly, have been constantly on my mind. My enduring love for you and the thought that one day we will be reunited has kept me going throughout all these trials as has my determination to survive this war as I promised you I would, come what may.

You will see from the address I am now a Prisoner of War – a rather dismal term for one cooped up in a rather dismal and remote part of Germany. During a very terrible battle in which the 16th. were engaged, and about which you might have heard – I received a hefty bump on the head together with one or two other scrapes – as a result of which I appear to have been unconscious for a fair time.

It seems that the some of the survivors decided that I shouldn't be left behind when our position finally fell to the Germans, and so the silly beggars resolved to carry me insensible 'from the field' as it were.

I say 'silly beggars' but in truth I probably owe them my life, for one of the sergeants told me that between them they carried me over thirty miles on a stretcher,although there was not a man amongst them who was unwounded; and on that long hike they saw to my every need, 'out for the count' though I was.

I still find it impossible to put into words what I feel towards those men.

I was admitted to a German hospital on the outskirts of Hamburg; it's a place with a pretty good reputation for sorting out head wounds – and for fixing head-cases like me! When I finally came to I had the devil of a headache, and the staff were very surprised to find that Gefangene2308 (Prisoner 2308) was in fact a medical doctor. They were all very polite – deferential, even – and treated me after a fashion and as well as they could. The privations everyone is going through here – as a result of the Royal Navy's blockade, I suppose – mean that basic medicines and equipment are either entirely exhausted or worn out. So I'm lucky to have recovered to the degree I have. Many haven't, both our chaps and theirs.

I was transferred here from the hospital only a few days ago, and so this is the first opportunity I have had to write to you, though I have been desperate to do so, knowing too well what you must have been thinking, my poor Sweetheart.

I share a billet here with nineteen other officers, most of whom have been through far more than I, and whose only hope is to see an end to all of this, and get home in one piece.

The Kommandant and the camp guards are actually quite a reasonable bunch; there was a bit of officious pushing and shoving, at first – just to show who was 'boss' – but that has quite fallen off, and they seem to be a pretty decent lot on the whole who are suffering much the same privations as we, and are as keen as we are to 'call it a day.'

I hate to beg, my darling, but if you could find your way to make up a parcel – a little one will do splendidly – I would be immensely grateful. We are short of everything without exception so whatever you put in will be more than welcome. Don't be too imaginative or extravagant; basic stolid stuff will do just fine! You must mark all parcels and letters to be sent via Switzerland and their Red Cross. It's a wonderful system, isn't it? and all the chaps appreciate it immensely.

My prisoner number has been altered to OG 7358, for some reason. Don't forget to write it clearly on whatever you send.

I must close now, my Dearest Love, as Pte. Hartner, our hut guard (whom we've nicknamed 'Our Franz') has told us in no uncertain terms 'lights out'.

Goodbye my darling. Set aside all worries now, for we are 'on the homeward stretch'.

I count off every minute to the time when I hold you in my arms again, and we kiss as we once did.

Loving you always

Oliver.

P.S I shall write a letter separately to my parents, to tell them I am still 'alive and kicking' and likely to plague them for a while yet!

Dolly had recovered herself within a few minutes, and pulling herself upright with diminutive dignity had decided that she could not and would not contain the wonderful news. Though every fibre of her being rejoiced, her thoughts had turned almost immediately to the wretchedness of others and what that news would do for them. The Rusholmes should not suffer a minute longer. She washed her face under the scullery pump, and prepared to go out bearing the letter.

It was a motley group which arrived unannounced at the doors of Millwain Place that night, with Dolly leading. Uncle Edwin had insisted on accompanying his niece on the journey in the dark, as had Wilfred even though he hadn't been asked. Mrs. Chadderton had also come along, in part because she was concerned about her daughter in the mood which possessed her, but mainly because the euphoria was infectious *'and such grand news isn't received* every *day'*.

These, together with 'Perce' Bredbury the local trap-proprietor who had been persuaded to harness-up for an extra two shillings- now crowded beneath the white expanse of the house porch. Dolly applied herself both to the electric bell button and the older bellpull, not trusting to either. For once both rang simultaneously and Wilfred rattled the doorknocker as an accompaniment. At first the was no movement; but then a lamp was lit in the upper part of the house where Phoebe slept, and its glow cast distorted shadows as the maid descended to the landing and turned on the electric light. Other lights now went on in different parts of the house – at the front, where Mrs. Rusholme had her rooms, and at the side where Alice's firstfloor bedroom was. Now the hall lights flared on, and Phoebe could be seen through the glass panel, fumbling with the bolts. The door swung open.

''Ello' Phoebe said sourly 'What's the to-do?'

Shading her eyes from the sudden brilliance Dolly looked past her to where Ida was standing, white-haired and statuesque in her dressing-gown. Ida returned her gaze, and for the first time in years was able to read unbridled joy in the face of another. She involuntarily put her hand to her mouth. 'It's Oliver*! Isn't it*! Oh, Dolly, *tell me*! Isn't it?' Dolly nodded, her eyes lustrous.

Formality was cast aside in a moment, and the two women were in each others' arms hugging and crying and laughing at once.

It proved to be the oddest of impromptu parties, but it was the most memorable ever to be held in that house.. Old Alice was helped downstairs huffing and puffing but without complaint, and they gathered together in the drawing-room where the letter was read out again and again by Dolly, who blushingly omitted the more personal and tender lines. Phoebe had recovered from her ill-temper and now smiled and laughed with the rest, and was sent down to the cellars to fetch bottles of the finest Lafite. They'd no ice, but who cared? The corks were drawn and glasses raised to Oliver's speedy return. Outside the night wind howled and rattled wisteria stems against the windows, but those within paid it no heed. Heady with the wine and the news that only one there had hoped for they passed two unimaginable hours, until the grandfather clock signalled in the morning. The chimes reminded Perce Bredbury of something, and he started to his feet 'Damn' if I hadn't forgotten that I've left Snowball harnessed in the trap!' he said unsteadily. 'I wonder if she'll be alright?' He disappeared in the direction of the unfortunate horse while his passengers prepared for the homeward trip. Perce reappeared red – faced and blowing a few minutes later 'Damn' it, if the ole girl hadn't taken herself off down the lane a little way, an' was waitin' for me there! She looks at me is if to say *where've you been all this while?* An' no doubt my missus'll say t' same!'

As they left Ida drew Dolly tenderly aside. ' Thank you, my dear' she said softly ' For all you have done. You cannot imagine how much I – we all – owe to you.'

' Mrs. Rusholme, please! I did no more than… .well.'

'Dolly, you kept faith when all of us were doubting. You kept hope alive, though we had none. '

'Faith's not so difficult if you love someone' Dolly said simply.

'I'm proud that my – *our* – Oliver chose you.'

And Ida kissed her.

Chapter Thirteen

WITH THE tightening of the stranglehold imposed by the Royal Navy the balance of the Great War tipped ever more in favour of the Allies. Shortages which in Germany had been at first an inconvenience grew insidiously to become want, and want in its turn became full-blown starvation. The food parcels which Dolly and Ida together spent hours packing for Oliver now assumed a far greater significance; while intially their contents had been anticipated as something of a luxury they now increasingly became the lynchpin of survival.

Parcels arrived infrequently enough as it was, with the imposition of strict limits on the numbers which could be sent; but in spite of their value the contents were always shared amongst fellow-prisoners and even amongst their guards who looked on enviously as tins of sardines or sausages were opened and the rare smell of decent food filled the hut. For that one day the cabbage or potato soup which had been the staple for both prisoner and gaoler alike became secondary, relegated to a mere *hors d'oeuvre*; and the coarse grey bread ration served to mop up the very last traces of gravy, and wipe the tins clean.

While the warm summer weather held they could hold out, too; but with the damper chills of autumn the prisoners in their half-starved state began to weaken. Then with the onset of winter influenza arrived, and men began to die. With the adverse weather the tone of Oliver's letters descended by degrees from buoyant optimism and relief to a growing pessimism, and from that pessimism to a dark introversion fuelled by the spectre of suffering which he could do little to alleviate, and deaths which he felt acutely he was powerless to prevent. Such fragile mortality amongst men who had been through so much angered and embittered him and made him examine with a jaundiced eye the fundamentals of that society in which he had been raised, and which had nurtured him. He began to persuade himself that this was indeed war without end – all-consuming, all-destructive – and he wondered frequently if he should ever live to see its conclusion. He believed increasingly that the world he knew could not survive, when confronted by such realities, if it had not already passed away.

Had the resources been available for him to serve properly as the doctor he was and desperately wished to be, perhaps the interminable days and nights of incarceration in the camp would have been less of a burden; but Oliver Rusholme now began to ask himself whether it was the predestined lot of his generation to suffer, and perish before their time. Self-doubt, and doubt about so much in which he had hitherto believed, began to gnaw insidiously at him

Dolly sensed the change in his letters. They did not express his thoughts overtly, and were still full of his love for her; but she noticed the intrusion of a depressive element which seemed like a shadow behind everything he now wrote, and she suspected what its underlying cause might be. So she strove to keep her letters as light and as matter-of-fact as possible, using that inner strength which had served her so long and so well to communicate her affections and warm him with the glow of her enduring optimism.

October passed into November, and rumours began to spread in the camps – rumours originating from the guards in conversation with their charges – that peace overtures had been made to the Allies by certain senior German figures, and that the Kaiser was done for.

For a few days nothing more was heard, but the talk of peace continued undiminished; then on the afternoon of the 12th. November the surviving inmates of *Offizierenlager VII* were asked to assemble in the main concourse before the Kommandant's hut. In almost embarrassed tones he informed them that an Armistice had been signed at 11 o'clock on the previous day, and that the War between his country and Britain was finally at an end. He had already ordered the gates to be unlocked and any who wished to were free to leave immediately – but perhaps some might want to stay on a little longer to prepare themselves for the long journey home? He was sorry that no transport would be available, despite his efforts to secure some trucks. There was a railhead at Munster, though he could not vouch for there being any trains.

He concluded by wishing them all good luck.

Most reacted with an almost frenetic joy, cheering and hugging each other and jumping about like children freed from school; while some received the news with a strange reluctance, as if mistrusting what they had heard, and without celebrating sauntered over to the gates to check for themselves that the Kommandant's words had been genuine. A few felt simply too dulled and indifferent to absorb the full impact of what they had been told. The barbed wire still surrounded them, the huts were the same, and the mud still as cold. It was hard to grasp that it was all finished, that they were free to go, for home seemed so unattainable, and so infinitely far away. But for Oliver Rusholme it was not simply geographical separation but more the perception that he was confronting his earlier self from the opposite side of a temporal gulf. He felt immeasurably distant from the figure whom he saw only as a tiny dot on the far rim– a being whose features he could only discern in fragments, like the image reflected in a broken mirror – a being who seemed to belong elsewhere.and to an earlier epoch when his own ignorance seemed his greatest attribute.

His pre-war self seemed to him alien – a presence with whom he could not communicate nor identify, and the country of his birth both incomprehensible and foreign. He did not know the way back nor what he should do when he got there, for he was uncertain even as to who he was.

He returned slowly to his hut, exchanging congratulations with fellow officers with an outward show of warmth. He let himself back in through the flimsy wooden door, and closing it quietly behind him walked across to the window hard by his bunk. His breath formed a small fog as he drew close to it and looked through at the antics of some of the younger detainees. A thin layer of ice was already beginning to form on the surface making it increasingly difficult to see out. He wiped the glass with the cuff of his ragged coat, but it caused the ice to smear and refreeze the quicker. The marionette shapes of men still danced beyond, but obscurely now. He gave a heavy sigh and lay down on his bunk; and pulling the collar of his greatcoat over his head, fell immediately into a leaden sleep.

Chapter Fourteen

ALICE SHIFTED herself in her armchair and leaned forward to poke a little life back into the embers of the fire. Her rheumatism had begun to play up again with the winter closing in rapidly, and despite the tablets and the new hot waterbottle which Miss Helene had kindly sent her, her joints ached with a vengeance. Still, there were far worse places to be than in that warm firelit kitchen, with just the cat for company.

A whistle shrilled in the far distance, signalling that the last train of the evening was departing from Desbury station. The engine's metallic voice traversed leafless trees and coverts white with frost, reverberating from the ice-bound banks of the Mersey until it floated away on chill airs.

The old woman turned her head and listened – for no other reason than the sound was one rarely heard in the house. She envisaged the train's slow departure as it rattled away into the dark, reminded of days when the railway was still her artery to the outer world.

'Ah, well' she said with feeling, expressing a hundred different thoughts in the simple words, and shook her head sadly.

She retrieved her glasses from a worktable and picked up the book she had been reading. It was a romance – a genre of which she was particularly fond – and she became so engrossed in the story that she did not notice the passage of another hour until the clock struck ten.

The sound of the chimes had barely died away when the cat suddenly pricked up its ears as though its attention had been drawn to a movement outside. 'What is it, Puss?' asked the old lady as the animal slipped noiselessly from her lap, 'I should think you'll need to go out before I lock up; it's gettin' late for us both.' Alice heaved herself upright and stood a moment getting her breath and trying her legs. She decided to have a hot cup of tea before retiring to bed, and drew some water from the boiler by the fire.

She hobbled to a door leading to the adjoining pantry where the milk-jugs were kept. The outer wall was in turn pierced by another door which gave onto a flight of steps leading down to the laundry and garden. As she opened the door she was met by a blast of cold air. The cat which had accompanied her thus far, retreated briskly to the fireside.

'Well!' she exclaimed to the cat, 'An' would you believe it? That silly girl Phoebe's left the door off the latch again.'

Returning to the kitchen to fetch an oil-lamp she made her way back into the pantry. Her attention was on the unlocked door as she shuffled towards it. At that moment she sensed a movement in the shadows on her left. Alarm caused her to spin round.

'Who… who is it? Come on out at once, or I'll call the policeman!'

'Please don't, Alice' said a hoarse voice. 'I'd rather you didn't.'

'Who is it? ' she demanded furiously as her courage reasserted itself. 'Who *are* you? Show yourself this minute!'

A shape detached itself from the darker shadow behind and stepped unsteadily towards the lamp she held aloft. Its light fell on the thin figure of a man whose gaunt features were accentuated by a few days' growth of beard. He was clad in a tattered military coat which seemed several sizes too big, and which drooped heavily from him. He halted with shoulders bowed, and glittering eyes. He made another movement towards her and raised his hand lamely

'Don't you recognise me, Alice?' he said hoarsely ' Don't you *know* me?'

Alice took an involuntary step forward as if doubting her own eyes and ears.

'Oh, Lord! Lord! Oh, my darlin' lad!' she said at last. 'Oh, you're safe, an' you're home! God forgive me for not knowin' you.' She held out her fat arms to him. 'Give your old Alice a big hug' she choked, using words of endearment recalled from Oliver's childhood days.

'I… I don't know that you'd want me to, Alice,' said Oliver faintly, 'you see, I'm not very clean and… '

'Do you think I mind a bit o'dirt' she cried ' when my favourite lad's come home from the wars?'

Oliver succumbed and she enfolded him in her arms and clasped him to her; and he hung as limp as a rag doll in her embrace.

He slept for two days solidly and without waking, though his sleep was feverish and troubled with dark dreams; and when he finally roused himself he felt as leaden as the overcast morning which trickled greyly through chinks in the curtains. He heard the muffled sound of voices below in the unfamiliar surroundings of a house which had long before ceased to be his home. He wondered who they might be, though he guessed that Dolly might be among them. And so she was, sitting with Ida and Helene and laughing more lightheartedly than she had done in many months. Yet ever and anon her eyes would stray upwards in the direction where she imagined Oliver to be lying, and as her gaze lingered there she wondered if he was awake at last, and when he would finally come down to her. She longed for him with a overbrimming heart; and now he was so close. She rehearsed what she would say to him when they met again, and thrilled at what she imagined he would say to her.

Oliver thought of her no less constantly than he had during all the days of his imprisonment; but now his mind was turned not to the prospect of their reunion and the fulfilment of something for which he had yearned, but dwelt instead upon the invasive and cankering doubts which had increasingly plagued him in the weeks before his liberation; doubt as to his own worthiness as a doctor and as a man, and growing doubt as to the depth of his love for Dolly.

His brain ordered a limb to move, and it still moved; his jaws chewed the food he had of necessity to place between them, and his tongue articulated his simpler sentiments. But he had returned mentally drained and emotionally scarred; and he drifted through the motions of living and paid only lip-service to them, harbouring reservations as to whether he were even truly alive; for there was so much that he seemed dead to. The man who had loved Dolly Chadderton and been loved by her seemed a universe away. She did not suspect what he had become, for he did not know himself. And he did not know how he would cope with the outrush of affection from those who loved him and who thought that they had got him back whole, when he had scourged and lacerated himself with constant recrimination. He was uncertain as to how much of that self remained and whether any of the substance which he believed lost could ever be salvaged from the ruins. But he saw that he would have to go through with it, for others and for the sake of Dolly in particular.

As for the future,he could not see how any society calling itself remotely civilised could be expected to rise from the charnel-house which from his perspective Europe had become. On Manchester Hill and afterwards his innate resilence had risen like a sea wall to get him through, though it had been tried to the utmost; but now the defences were down and the tides of despair poured in and overwhelmed him. He had witnessed too much and in too short a time; first hand he had seen the predisposition of European society for genocide, and its ready capacity for visiting mass destruction as much upon itself as upon its enemies. He could hardly bear to think of what the consequences could be, and what sort of new world might be destined to emerge in the post-armageddon years.

Frowning into the mirror at his own attenuated reflection he shaved off his beard and put on an old outdoor-suit which he had worn when he had last gone rambling with Godfrey. He had no difficulty in fitting into it, for the privations of the camp had left him painfully thin.

As he made his way down by the rear stairs he recalled how he and Godfrey had done much the same almost three years before. He wondered if his brother's feelings then had been similar to his own. Only now could he begin to understand Godfrey fully.

Oliver Rusholme gripped the handle of the door with all his strength and swung it open onto peacetime, and all that it entailed for him. He stood framed in the doorway, uncertainly blinking in the brighter light of the room. Faces were uplifted to him, faces which radiated the joy which his survival and return had brought them.

His mother was there, and Helene, and sitting between them was Dolly. All three rose with their eyes fixed upon him, smiling away their initial shock at his appearance. But the eyes which glowed most brilliantly, which drank in his presence, were Dolly Chadderton's.

She looked on him with adoration; he looked on her with something else. What she saw was her Oliver – haggard, thin, maybe – but despite it all, it was still him. What he saw was an extraordinarily beautiful woman, but one who might have been a mannequin in a St Ann's Square window, for all he was able to feel. He looked at the immaculately coiffeured hair- the fruits of Helene's labour – and considered the slim figure and the full breasts set to perfection by the dress she had made in readiness for his homecoming; yet his admiration of her beauty was oddly dispassionate and objective. He found he felt no stirring of desire for her.

Sensing something in his demeanour she approached him slowly and with a measure of apprehension.

'Hello, Oliver' she said, her voice low and resonant with love for him.

He smiled, but not broadly.

'How are you, Dolly?'

'Well. And you, Oliver?'

'Well enough.'

She glanced over her shoulder at her companions as though seeking their approval of her conduct while at the same time entreating them to depart.

Helene took Ida's arm. 'Shall we go, Ma? Into the study?'

Ida accompanied her with evident reluctance; there was enough of the nineteenth century left in her to make her uneasy at the lack of a chaperone. As they passed him they kissed him tenderly and caressed his hands with theirs. He returned their smiles but with eyes which shifted uneasily as they left.

His mother and sister assumed that his diffidence came from a natural desire to be alone with Dolly. In her heart Dolly hoped it was so, too, but there was something that persuaded her otherwise. Perhaps it was that his gaze did not linger on her as it should, and as she had a right to expect it would. Though certainly no slave to vanity, Dolly knew that she looked nice; Helene had made her stand in front of a wardrobe mirror just to prove the point. So what was wrong?

Why was he so changed, and how profoundly? A difficult silence fell between them as Oliver shifted uneasily where he stood. His eyes flitted from her to the wall, then down to the carpet and back to her again.

She gazed back steadily and unflinchingly into his face, and though she dearly wanted him to hold her, knew that there was a reason why an embrace would be inappropriate. Instead she took his hands in hers. They felt skeletal, and icy cold.

'Oh, Oliver! Sweetheart... ' she breathed, and drew closer to him. 'I can't say how much I've missed you, every day since you went... there are words for it, I'm sure. We never did give up hope.'

'Well, I'm alive as you can see, so your hopes were well founded.' Oliver intended it to be light-hearted, but failed utterly; too matter-of-fact, too flippant, even, the effect was only partially disarmed by her faith in him, and her growing conviction that he was still suffering. He laughed hollowly and with such insincerity that she wished he hadn't, and she could hardly disguise the perplexity which registered in her face.

'I... I'm so sorry, Dolly' he said, with sudden feeling 'I didn't mean it to come out like that. I'm very weary. Not had much sleep, you know! and I need a rest. I'm truly sorry if I'm not as sparkling as I might be.'

'Don't say that! I'm just happy to have you home in one piece... ' she squeezed his hands firmly and fixed her eyes on him. '*One piece*, Oliver' she repeated emphatically. 'No-one could expect any more from you, after all you've been through and how far you've had to come.'

How far you've had to come. That was certainly true, and he inwardly winced at the innocent significance of her words. He reflected uneasily that he had still a way to go, though how far he could not say; he had been to the brink of the abyss; had approached it and gazed down into its unfathomable depths with horror yet had been drawn inexorably further until he had toppled.

He was still falling, spun off in some vortex which drew him downward and away from the light; he had struggled desperately against it at first; but every effort to resist had proved futile; you could not swim against such a tide. Though intangible and without form it had overwhelmed him and he felt he was drowning beneath it as his efforts weakened and failed him.

She rose on tiptoe and kissed him on the lips and he responded mechanically.

'What's wrong, Oliver? Won't you tell me?'she asked.

He could not reply, but turned away from her.

He kept to the house, though he hated it; hated it partly because of the uncomprehending normality which prevailed there, partly because it was a place of recollections which pained him, and partly because he had nowhere else to go. He had given up his rooms on joining up for the army and now his few cases of clothes and books were delivered to Millwain Place from the storage warehouse where they had been kept. With their arrival by the carriers it seemed to Oliver that his life had described a full circle; he felt he had progressed nowhere, and had fulfilled nothing. Though still technically a member of His Majesty's Armed Forces he had received no indication that they had any further interest in him now that hostilities had ceased; and besides, he lacked the desire and the energy to return to his pre-war duties at the hospital. Finding himself in a twilight world of irresolution and doubt, he simply drifted.

As far as Clarence was concerned, Oliver visited him less and less frequently. The old man had descended further into senility and though Oliver pitied him, he found he lacked the patience to withstand his father's unending monologues about his own sufferings – monologues to which every visitor was subjected – and the increasingly exaggerated eulogies about Godfrey. Though Ida had prompted him often enough, Clarence made few references to Oliver's own war; and those he did make were fleeting, and entirely devoid of paternal feeling.

The news about Captain Bonnard was wisely withheld by Ida until Oliver asked one day whether the family had heard from his friend the former schoolmaster. Then she told him, and handed him the papers which she had kept by her. Silently Oliver took them; and reading them through discovered how that kind old man, who had loved Oliver like his own lost son and had adopted him in all but name, had left him all he possessed.

Oliver spent the rest of that day alone, pacing the gardens from which he could gain a sight of the country lying to the west, as he had once done as a boy. When he returned, he was changed.

Dolly Chadderton's position became an increasingly difficult one now that Oliver had come back. Part-employee, part-companion, and on the verge of being part – related by marriage – should that marriage ever take place – she became more certain that her presence was a growing source of agitation for Oliver – as indeed it was, for he was visibly uneasy whilst she was there. And so with a sorrowing heart she reluctantly gave in her notice – suggesting as a replacement a pleasant and well-favoured girl from the village who would do as well as she. Ida tried desperately to prevail upon her to stay, but she held firmly to her decision. When Dolly told him she was going he felt a surge of regret that almost amounted to physical nausea, yet he let her go nonetheless, without uttering a word to dissuade her; then he went to his room and cried like a child.

The aftershocks of the Hill and the prison-camp still resonated in his mind like a distant barrage, and the bad dreams continued unabated and without mercy. As a doctor he had depended upon his professional detachment to shield him – or so he had told himself over and over again; but the images of hospital wards, of the stretcher-cases, of the mutilations and the expressions in the eyes of the dying had discovered the chinks in his armour; and having invaded the soft inner man, had set about lacerating his mind. And there was nobody in whom he could confide his misery, for he feared what would happen to his own sanity if he were to speak of such things. So he buried them deep in his soul, in the belief that the wounds would cure themselves.

Dolly hoped that by being a little more distant and by seeing less of each other it might somehow reignite his love; she of course could not see enough of him; but she freely acknowledged that that was *her* way; and wisely saw that if nothing else, Oliver needed both time and space if he was to get better. They maintained the outward appearance of lovers by meeting openly most evenings in the village and walking together arm in arm through Desbury. But for one of them it was done for form's sake only, and to avoid the deeper hurt which his total rejection of her would have caused.

A people in denial of bitter truths are easy prey to myth – particularly when that myth has its origins in fact, and particularly when popular attention needs to be diverted from asking uncomfortable questions.

The City had an aching need to justify the massacre of Manchester Hill in terms of the undoubted and genuine heroism of its defenders; but to give the abstract concept of heroism a more tangible focus it had to be given a face and a name, and point to a particular act.

The dead Wilfrith Elstob was rightly destined to receive the ultimate honour for his gallantry and fearless leadership; but there were whisperings from those who had survived capture and the camps that there was another deserving of recognition for his exemplary bravery, and his sacrifice for the beleaguered 16th. Enquiries were made, a name obtained; and the Press seized upon the opportunity to create a second hero of Manchester Hill.

Chapter Fifteen

OLIVER HAD taken a solitary walk along the iron-hard banks of the Mersey. All his walks were solitary now. Indifferent to the biting cold he sat for an hour on the same old stump of willow near where the river cut deep into the sandstone cliff. It was a familiar spot, one which had not changed and one which had always held an attraction for him, for some reason. Perhaps, he thought, perhaps it would be an ideal place to fish, if the river had not long ago been poisoned.

The banks were narrow, channelling the black waters which ran particularly deep and treacherous here beneath the undercut banking; and he watched as they sucked and eddied, visualizing where he would cast a fly, and how the imaginary quarry might react.

It occurred to him suddenly that he could not recall when he had last been fishing. He was saddened by the thought that it would have been with the Captain, and was ashamed that he could not remember anything of it. He suddenly tired of the river, and standing stiffly, turned to make his way back to Desbury.

He emerged from an obscure field-path onto the lane just below Millwain Place. At first he did not notice the two cars parked by the gates; and when he did, dismissed them as having nothing to do with him. He walked up the driveway and round to the rear of the house, where he deposited his old boots in the boiler-room, placing them reverently side by side with Godfrey's. It always hurt to do this, but he did it nonetheless; for Oliver it was another private act of remembrance.

He ascended the laundry-steps and was on the point of going up to his room when the lounge door opened suddenly.

'Is that you, Oliver?' It was his mother's voice, certainly; but it had a most peculiar quality about it- animated, bright, even excited.

'Yes, Ma. It's me.' He turned and saw his mother looking up at him. Her eyes were shining.

'Will you come down for a moment, Oliver darling? There are some gentlemen here who wish to speak to you.'

'Me?'

'Yes, if you'd spare them a minute.'

Oliver entered the lounge. It was blue with cigarette smoke.He scanned the faces which turned as one to him. He took out one of his own cigarettes and lit it nervously.

'How can I help you?'

A corpulent man with a bald head stood up, as if he had been delegated as spokesman.

'You *are* Second Lieutenant Oliver Rusholme, of the 16th. Battalion The Manchester Regiment?'

'Yes.'

'We have the very man!' exclaimed the other. 'The very man!' He strode forward officiously and shook Oliver's hand.

'These gentlemen are from the Press, Oliver.' Ida explained. ' They have told me a story of astonishing bravery… of what you did for the trapped soldiers, on that terrible hill in France. I'm so very, very proud of you, my darling.' Her eyes shone with pride. It troubled Oliver that his mother of all people should have succumbed to this stuff – she who had particular grounds to feel bitter against the whole business of war

'What do they say I did?' he said guardedly.

'You broke through the Jerry lines single-handedly, dragging a box of vital medical supplies to the defenders' one of the others interrupted.

'The supplies *were* vital, otherwise I wouldn't have taken them' Oliver said blankly.

'*There* you are!'

'But as to breaking through, I didn't. A German officer helped me, and gave me safe conduct onto the Hill.'

The men exchanged looks.

'Genuine heroism always denies itself' said one. 'We wouldn't have expected anything less.'

'We don't want – or need -a Bosche perspective' said the fat man.

'But you want the truth of it, surely?' asked Oliver.

'We already have it.'

'Then why do you need to speak to me? Look. I'm no hero' said Oliver desperately 'You've got it wrong. Terribly wrong! And I didn't do it single-handedly, as you choose to put it. There was another, braver man than me. He was an orderly, called Burton, if you want to know. I never had time to find out his first name. He was *killed* carrying that box. Without him I should have got nowhere. He gave his life to get it that far. *Do you hear me? He died for it!'*

Oliver took out his handkerchief and wiped sweat from his forehead with a trembling hand.

'We hear you, Lieutenant' said the first man placatingly 'and we respect you even more for the way you generously give credit to others for what happened. It *was* you who carried the box, wasn't it. And it was you who broke through to Manchester Hill. '

Oliver sensed that these were no longer questions but statements which he was being required to corroborate or deny. If he adopted the former course they would believe him; if the latter, they would simply ignore what didn't fit their version of events.

'I can't... can't tell you more... there's nothing more to tell.'

'We know enough to complete the story, as it is.'

'Complete *what* story? What story are you talking about? Just what are you proposing to write about me? I forbid it!'

'It's a little late for that, Lieutenant.'

The first man handed Oliver a copy of a newspaper. The front page proclaimed:

Manchester's Angel Of Mercy

Anonymous hero found at last

'It's outrageous!' he shouted as he read. 'How dare you take such liberties?'

'Oliver, please!' interceded his mother 'Please calm yourself! These gentlemen are only reporting what you did, and for others.'

'You didn't hear me, did you?' Oliver said, scanning their faces. 'None of you. And you don't hear me now – not at all.'

'Look at it this way' said the bald man. 'There are at least ten thousand bereaved families in the City alone. Probably more. Don't you think you owe it to them to let them think their husbands or sons died for something worthwhile? The *world* will regard what you did as magnificent, deny it as you might. And it's how the world perceives you which counts. When you chose to act in that way you became public property whether you wanted it or not. The public are entitled to know, and to feel good about something for once. You have no right to deny them that.'

'I never saw *anyone* who died for anything worthwhile.' Oliver retorted between clenched teeth ' All those I saw died for *nothing*. Put *that* in your bloody paper.'

The journalists ignored the comment.

'You attended Hugh William's, didn't you. Isn't their motto *Per Valore Venit Victoria?* (Actually, that bit's worth putting in.)'

The man jotted something down in a small notebook, and smiled fatuously 'Can we have some photographs, please, Lieutenant?'

A man produced a large camera.

'Standing with your mother would be nice.'

Oliver did not reply, but turning on his heel strode from the room.

He heard Ida's voice calling him back, but he ignored it. Slamming his bedroom door behind him he threw open the window, though the frost was settling on the laburnums in the garden below. He felt asphyxiated by his mother, those men,the house, and peacetime.

He tugged at his collar and in loosening it tore the button off his shirt. Regardless of the cold he inhaled deeply, with eyes tightly closed. He waited until he was sufficiently calm. Closing the window decisively he walked to his wardrobe, and pulled out a dog-eared old backpack. Rummaging through drawers he crammed some warm clothing and his washing-kit into it. Then he picked up some small photographs which he had carried with him in France. He looked at the picture of Godfrey, and carefully placed it in a side pocket. He turned to one of Dolly which she had sent him and which had been his most treasured possession while a prisoner. He placed it to one side, on his bedside table.He thought he would leave it behind.

Having pulled on an oiled canvas jacket and a knitted woollen hat he stepped toward the door and turned off the light. At that moment he had a change of heart and flicked the switch on again briefly. He went to his bed and retrieved the picture of Dolly, stuffing it into his breast pocket. Then once more he turned off the light and slipped away down the rear stairs.

Once out in the garden he skirted the shrubs on the left as he had done long ago when escaping into the night world. Descending to the stile he climbed over it and dropped onto the stubble of the field. Without hesitation he struck out diagonally across it and within a few minutes had attained the sunken trackway which lay beyond. He paused briefly to look back at the distant lights of the house. Then hitching up his pack, he was gone.

Oliver's disappearance excited considerable alarm in Millwain Place and the immediate vicinity of the village. Well aware of her son's fragile emotional state Ida was beside herself with worry, and wondered seriously if he had set out to harm himself. She pleaded with the local constable to organise a search of the country round about, but despite the considerable number of volunteers who turned up – for Oliver's reputation as the reluctant war hero had begun to spread already – not the slightest trace of his whereabouts could be discovered, even in the places where he most often walked. The Mersey's banks were scoured and every deep pool dragged; but nothing was found.

Even the offer of ten guineas' reward for information drew a complete blank, though there were more than a few whom the money tempted to take a few days off work. It was as though the earth had opened before Oliver Rusholme and swallowed him completely.

The long months which Oliver had passed at the Front and as a prisoner of war had told heavily upon Dolly's resources; but her unshakeable belief that he would ultimately return had helped her to withstand the strain. She had schooled herself to say that it would only be a matter of time, and that time would ultimately pass. She'd never had cause to doubt his love for her, and this had been an additional and constant comfort when coupled with knowledge of his whereabouts.

Now the situation was fundamentally different. Where hitherto she had never doubted, now she was beset by fears. His homecoming was a far cry from all she had hoped for; the man returned to her was a stranger compared to the lover she had known, and had all but rejected her in the few weeks he had been back. The tears which she had so steadfastly resisted now seemed to flow in profusion, and few nights passed without her turning a wet face into her pillow to stifle her sobs. After one such wretched and sleepless night she had considered the ruby engagement ring which Oliver had given her and which she had worn religiously; now with tears coursing down her cheeks she removed the ring and returned it to its little leather box.

She imagined that her mother could not hear, and that she had no inkling of what had passed between them. But Mrs.Chadderton was no fool, and was hardly deceived as she lay in her own room and listened with a heart aching for her daughter. But she said little, for Dolly seemed to have moved so far beyond her that she felt unable to offer any words in the way of comfort.

The weeks passed, and still not a word of Oliver's whereabouts reached Desbury. The story of his role at Manchester Hill was run by the Press, and he was hailed a hero; but the stories were in the main so sanitised and embroidered that the focus of all the attention would have had the greatest difficulty in recognising anything of himself in them.

Calls were made for Oliver to receive some form of tangible recognition; a medal was suggested, and a petition was circulated and passed to the appropriate Authorities. And there the petition languished. So Oliver Rusholme was at least spared the sense of guilt and remorse that the award of a decoration would have caused him – an award which he would have believed completely undeserved and which he would have rejected out of hand.

Dolly had meanwhile written to all the friends whom Oliver had mentioned to her, and whose addresses she was able to trace. None knew anything of his whereabouts. A few unhelpfully suggested that he might have left the country – for rumour had it that quite a few disillusioned or troubled ex-officers had abandoned Britain for the furthest corners of the planet – and this only added to her distress. Others suggested London as a possibility, but without giving any idea as to where. But it was her letter to Archie McLeish – who still worked at Levenham amidst his dwindling gas cases – which ultimately bore fruit.

Oliver's old friend was shaken by the news, and viewed it very seriously indeed. He suggested that he might visit Desbury as soon as possible so that they could meet to discuss the possibilities as to where to continue the search; would next weekend suit? When Ida learned of this she immediately invited McLeish and Dolly to Millwain Place. He wrote back by return, accepting her offer gratefully.

His near-four years at Levenham had aged Archie McLeish considerably. He had always possessed a careworn look, accentuated by his stoop; but now the few hairs he had possessed had got fewer, and carried a hint of whiteness which gave him the air of a man long past his prime. He now sat facing Ida and Dolly in the lounge.

'It came as a shock, I have to confess' he said in his soft Edinburgh tones 'though when I read in the papers about what he was involved in and what he did – well, every man has to have his limits; I think he must have been well beyond his.' Immediately the tears filled Dolly's eyes, and he could have bitten his tongue for what he'd said. 'Och, I'm terribly sorry Miss Chadderton; I didn't mean to suggest anything *untoward* might have happened to him.' McLeish leaned forward to emphasise his point. 'I have to say that he impressed me as being more able to cope with the sorts of things which arise from time to time in our line of work, than most… Not from indifference, y'understand, but on the contrary,from strength of character.' Dolly smiled her thanks to him. 'Can I speak frankly, Madam?' he enquired, turning to Ida.

'Please do, Doctor McLeish. We all want answers, and I'll be deeply grateful for any light you can shed.'

McLeish nodded his acknowledgement. 'My feeling is, that he's had a dreadful time – particularly so, in view of what we know now. We can only speculate as to how he conducted himself in the prison-camp, but we can have a pretty shrewd idea nevertheless. Forgive me for saying it, but I know him better professionally than either of you ladies.'

'I'm sure you do, Doctor.'

'I *know* that he would have worked himself to a standstill, and without resources too. I believe that on his return a safety-valve blew in him as the pressure built up... Y'say he was very distant... very strange, Miss Chadderton?'

'I hardly recognised him, Dr McLeish.'

'I'm more convinced than ever that he left to be by himself – to seek solitude in which he could get well again, and become himself once more. It's no reflection of his feelings for you, Miss Chadderton, nor you Madam.'

'You think not?'

'I doubt very much if he truly knows what his feelings are, at this moment. I have every confidence that he will not harm himself – that certainly would not be his way- but that is not to say I believe we should abandon the search for him. He still *has* to be found.'

They fell into a silence punctuated only by the ticking of a black slate mantel-clock. McLeish's eyes settled idly upon it. It was fashioned in the French style, with gilded feet on swept-back wings. It whirred, and chimed four. He looked at the numerals, and saw how they stood out golden against the black face. There *had* to be some clue to his whereabouts as prominent as those numbers, if he could only see it...

'I'm sorry ladies' he said, rising reluctantly. 'I have to take my leave, though I regret we haven't made any particular progress. But I'm sure it'll come, sooner rather than later.'

Ida thanked him, and Dolly shook his hand. He smiled gently at her as he shuffled into his heavy driving-coat. 'I know it's easy for me to say, but don't fret yourself, lassie' he whispered. She smiled back wanly as he made his way down the steps. He stopped at the bottom of the flight, and turned to them once more. 'There was nothing else that you've omitted to mention?' he asked as an afterthought 'nothing out of the ordinary that might have occurred which could give us the slightest inkling?'

Ida shook her head. 'Nothing that I recall, Doctor. Only... .'

'Yes, Madam? Only what? *Was* there something else?'

'Well, Oliver was very upset when I told him that a dear friend had passed away. But he chose not to discuss it at all. Did he speak to you of it, Dolly?'

The girl shook her head. 'He said nothing about it to me. Who was it?'

'It was Captain Bonnard.'

'Captain Bonnard! Oh, poor Oliver! I never knew' said Dolly. 'He had a great affection for the old gentleman.'

'No more than the Captain had for him' said Ida; 'he left his whole estate to Oliver in his will.'

McLeish halted with a pensive look as a faint possibility occurred to him. He turned once more and briskly ascended the steps with a curious light kindling in his eyes.

'Captain Bonnard… the person who taught Oliver to fish?'

He fired the question at them even before he had reached the top.

'Yes.'

'On the Clwyr, in North Wales? *Rusholme often used to tell me about it…* ' McLeish was becoming increasingly animated. 'There was a cottage, wasn't there?'

McLeish did not wait for a reply, but continued speaking as though to himself 'A *remote* cottage, he said it was… .which belonged to the old gentleman?'

Ida and Dolly simultaneously perceived his drift.

'*And who owns that selfsame cottage now?*'

The engine of Archie McLeish's motor car sputtered and fell silent. It freewheeled onto the grass verge, bumping over loose pieces of limestone which had fallen from walls bordering the road. McLeish climbed from the driver's seat with a resigned air; and delving into the pocket of his travelling-coat produced a box-spanner and a wrench. Wielding the tools he disappeared under the hood. A few minutes later he emerged from the engine compartment and issued some instructions to his travelling companion.

A bundle of rugs parted and Dolly Chadderton's arm appeared.

'Advance it a little, as I turn the starting-handle.' McLeish shouted. Dolly did as she was told.

He cranked the handle, but nothing happened. 'Now a little more… ' Still nothing.

'And a little more… ' Suddenly there was a loud backfire which shook the whole vehicle's superstructure and the tiny engine once more rattled into life.

'Now… how far is it to Ridland?' McLeish said as he climbed back into his seat.

Chapter Sixteen

DWARFED BY one of the castle's huge bastions which loomed above it was a general stores. It was an Aladdin's cave of candles, food, paraffin, tinned goods, brooms and a thousand other items piled almost to the top of its mullioned windows, with only a thin band of uncluttered glass left to let in the daylight.

'If anything's been heard of him in Ridland, I'll bet they'll know it in here' Archie McLeish said encouragingly. They entered the shop, and rang the little brass bell on the counter.

They were not disappointed. The bustling round ball that was Mrs. Megan Jones made it her business to know everything that went on in those parts; and in reponse to the polite enquiry of the Scottish couple whom she could tell at once were honeymooners about the remote cottage down by the river she was able to inform them in detail about the unfortunate death of the English gentleman who had retired there. Oh yes… there *was* another man there now, she'd heard, but he was something of a hermit, keeping himself to himself, and he hadn't told anyone his name, though he came to buy things in the shop from time to time- basic things mainly like soap and powdered milk and he bought a towel when he first appeared – very good quality too- though he hadn't bought one since, well at least not from her he hadn't. And there were those round about who thought him a bit odd, not that she held an opinion one way or the other, you understand. McLeish managed at last to stem the flow, and ask her how they might find their way to the cottage in question. She provided them with directions but suggested that if they could wait a few minutes her son who was out on a delivery would soon be back, and he'd be happy to show them the way. This seemed a more sensible suggestion, and there could be no question that the stocky red-haired lad who moments later entered the shop in a rush was their intended guide.

'Are you related to him then?' asked the proprietress, raising a quizzical eyebrow as they left.

'Oh, no. Just friends o' his' replied McLeish.

'Oh, just friends, is it?' said the lady to herself as the shop door closed on them; and she nodded knowingly. 'What's the world coming to?'

It was obvious that Dolly was ill-equipped to walk the path along the river bank to the cottage. The lad Dewi looked contemptuously at the neat little court shoes on the young lady's feet.

'You're not expectin' to go anywhere in *those,* Miss, I hope' he said, pointing at them. 'You'll not get ten yards wearin' totty little shoes like that.'

'Why won't I?' she demanded defiantly. 'What's wrong with the path? I've walked before.'

'Not 'ere you 'avent!' Dewi declared. He seemed to be enjoying himself. 'Take a look!'

Waving his arms he beckoned them across the road to the parapet of the old bridge and they peered over, unwittingly gazing on the same path which Oliver had so frequently trodden in his boyhood.

'See!' Dewi declared triumphantly. 'It's been high tides for a week now. The river's been right over the sheep-paths, an' even into Mr. Parry's meadows. It's down now, but there's the mud!'

They had to admit he was right. It was impassable to all but those clad in knee-height gum-boots – a pair of which McLeish had had the presence of mind to bring along. Such a thing had never occurred to Dolly, at the early hour which McLeish had collected her from Desbury. Her disappointment was great, yet it was tempered by a curious sense of relief that McLeish and not she would be the first to encounter Oliver. She instinctively felt that this young Scot whose friendship had proved so steadfast might feel the need to speak in a manner which her presence there might compromise. No, she did not regret having to stay behind, and though she yearned to see Oliver again was almost grateful of the opportunity to do so.

'I'll stay in your motor-car, if you don't mind, Doctor McLeish.'

'Do ye not want to come, Miss Chadderton? After all it's been a long time and a long way, for you particularly.' He looked into her eyes and read the reluctance in them. 'Aye, well, perhaps not straightaway. Maybe you're right' he said ' But you're not sitting in my draughty car!'

He led her back to the main road and into a low and comfortable inn nestled back from the pavement. Yes, the landlord would be happy to accommodate the young lady for a few hours, and if she didn't object there was a fire just banked up in the Snug. She could sit there and read the paper – it had just this minute come from the post office – and he would call his daughter down to serve her with tea. McLeish looked across to Dolly and she smiled her agreement to him..

If only I could meet a girl half as good he thought as he and his guide slithered their way along the riverbank. For the first time McLeish realised how beautiful Dolly Chadderton truly was, and he envied his friend for the uncompromising devotion and love she bore him.

'Over there, it is. You see it?' Dewi pointed out the little white cottage lying by the river. He was about to continue walking when McLeish signalled him to stop.

'This'll do just fine, thank you' he said, and fished out a shilling which he gave to the boy.

For the first time Dewi smiled. 'I'll guide you to the door, if you like' he said.

'No..no thanks. I can easily find my way from here.' McLeish said with affected brightness 'I think I'll give my friend a surprise.'

'Well, that's all right then, isn't it? And thank you again for the shillin' sir.'

Now that he was actually there he was unsure as to what to do next. A vague plan of action had occurred to him while driving; but it *had* been vague.

And now he was confronted by the immininent need to do something it seemed insubstantial and very thin indeed. He had thought he would saunter up and present himself as if he had been casually rambling in the vicinity; but the patent absurdity of this struck him immediately. Suspecting how fragile Oliver might be, he had to take particular pains to avoid his appearance causing a shock or precipitating a crisis. But by the same token McLeish's point of view had shifted imperceptibly, away from an unquestioning sympathy to sympathy with reservations. He had met Dolly for the first time only the week before, but had got to know her quite well on their long and gruelling trip together from Desbury. He had begun not only to admire her for her looks, but for her resilient and loving nature. He thoroughly liked the girl, and had begun to feel that perhaps she had received less than her due.

He stood indecisively in the mud. It was particularly glutinous in the vicinity, and in order to move in any direction at all he had to twist his feet sideways to break the clinging viscosity of the stuff. He clambered away from the river and further up the high banking, from where he was able to gain a clearer view of the cottage. A thin wisp of woodsmoke curled from the stubby little chimney, and that small domestic detail and the homeliness it implied, heartened him. There was no sign of the occupant, however. He resolved to wait on events, and made his way to the field–stile at the end of the nearby meadow, where he sat down on the stone wall.

After an inert half- hour McLeish decided to seize the initiative and approach the cottage. He had slipped down from his perch and was brushing down his clothing when he heard the distinctive *chop-crack* of logs being split. Someone was outside, and cutting wood.

Bracing himself McLeish walked as casually as he could across the meadow and round the back of the small garden-cum-lumberyard to where the sounds originated. The property was bordered by a low and scrubby thorn-hedge, and McLeish halted some few yards away from it. Peering over he judged the occupant to be a youngish man though it was difficult to tell. As each log was placed on the block the axe was raised and brought down with considerable skill and force; the man rarely needed to strike twice.

He worked mechanically as he lifted and chopped and stacked, but in observing him labour McLeish guessed from the man's physical attitude that he gained considerable satisfaction from it – from a simple manual job which he knew he did well. There was a distinct sense of achievement communicated by the way he aimed and struck, and McLeish almost wished he might give it a try himself.

The man paused for a moment to rest; and throwing down the axe half-turned, revealing his face in profile. Whether it was Oliver was impossible to say, for the old walking-cap he wore made his brow and his eyes invisible, while the lower portion was obscured by a dark and untidy beard. This and the unkempt clothes suggested a character utterly indifferent to his appearance and one who paid little heed to the opinion of others. He hitched up the braces of his trousers and having retrieved the axe was about to begin his work once more when he caught sight of Archie McLeish on the other side of the hedge. The man started, evidently taken aback by the unexpected appearance of anyone in such a remote spot.

'Good afternoon ' said McLeish, doffing his hat.. 'I'm sorry to intrude. I'm trying to trace the whereabouts of a friend of mine. I wondered if you might be able to help… '

The figure's arms slowly dropped to his sides, and the axe slid from his grasp. He took one or two faltering steps towards the hedge and McLeish, then stopped. His left hand rose uncertainly to his head, and pulled off his cap.

The eyes that returned Archie McLeish's gaze were indeed those of Oliver Rusholme.

They sat facing each other from opposite ends of the table. In the green semi-darkness of the kitchen it was difficult for one man to read the facial expressions of the other – a handicap in other circumstances, maybe, but not now; for now the focus was on what must be said, and glow of the wood fire in the hearth invested that one room with an intimacy which fostered openness.There was a tacit agreement to dispense with superficial chat; it would have been difficult at best.

'I think I owe you some sort of explanation.' Oliver said.

'You owe me nothing, old chap; explanations may well be due, but there are those who deserve them far more than I. I'm only a newcomer to the situation.'

'Yes… you're right, of course. You mean Dolly, and my mother.'

'To them, certainly.'

'I came here… well, almost directly after I left the house.' Oliver said quietly. 'I walked all night, and the next day too. I just kept walking until I got here.'

'My god, Rusholme! that's over seventy miles.'

'Is it? I suppose it is. I wasn't particularly conscious of the distance. I just felt the need to walk'

'Where did you sleep?'

'Wherever I could find somewhere. It wasn't too bad, out in the open air like that. I didn't particularly want to be with people. Even now I can't fully explain why.'

'You slept rough?'

'If you choose to put it like that. It was no inconvenience.'

'Then you arrived at the cottage?'

'Yes – after a few days. I wandered about a bit before finally landing here. At first, I wasn't sure that I ought to come. Or that I had any right to.'

'Why did you think that?'

'Because I felt a coward. Once I entered this cottage I capitulated to my own failings. It's the ultimate funk-hole, isn't it? But I wound up here anyway. A yellow streak a foot wide runs down my spine.' He shot a glance at his friend, and smiled bitterly 'Nowhere else to go, you see.'

'I think I do. How have you kept yourself occupied here, since you came??'

'Avoiding people mainly, and trying most of all to avoid myself.'

'That was not my meaning.'

' I'm sorry for being deliberately obtuse. Well, if you must know, I've walked the river and fished, and watched the birds on the estuary, and thought a lot, about a lot of things.'

'Has it helped, at all?'

'Helped? Well yes, I suppose it has – to a degree. My mind has been in an awful tangle, and the threads of my thoughts seemed so horribly knotted up together, that I doubted I'd ever sort anything out.'

'And have you?'

'I've managed to sit and think; being close to the river seemed to help me unravel a few ends, and salvage something from them. '

'I'm not sure I understand you, Rusholme'.

Oliver paused and inspected the grain of the old oak table.

'I'm not sure I understand myself. In the days before… there were so many things we felt confident in – things we remained faithful to as long as we could until they were shown up for what they really were.'

He raised his eyes from the table and looked directly at McLeish. 'They were false, you see, and when exposed in the cold light of the War they were unable to survive.'

'What things, precisely?'

'Oh, ideas – like loyalty, and duty- one's professional duty, I mean. Anyone who believes he can hide his vulnerable inner self behind that is a fool, or heartless, or both; and if either case applies to him he's unfit to be a doctor anyway. All we can do is delay the inevitable erosion of our wits by affecting medical objectivity. But it's all self-deception; your nerves and your mind and your conscience get you in the end.'

'Do you feel that about yourself? Do you feel you have to blame yourself?' It occurred to McLeish that he was speaking to Oliver in a manner similar to that which he adopted with the neurasthenia cases at Levenham.

'Of course I do. I ended up a bloody sham. I did *nothing* for those poor buggers out there. I think they would have died the same whether I had been there or not.'

'That's certainly not what I heard, Rusholme. On the contrary… '

Oliver rounded on McLeish 'What can you *possibly* know about it? What would you *know?'* he flared. McLeish kept outwardly calm.

'Nothing, old chap' he said evenly ' except what three long years at Levenham taught me.'

Oliver looked at his friend; then slowly he reached out his hand to him across the table.

McLeish took it and held it firmly.

Tears started in Oliver's eyes, then coursed downwards as his whole frame was wracked with sobs. They just sat there as Oliver let his wretchedness pour out, and his friend held his hand.

'Archie, forgive me! I don't know what I'm saying. I still have bad nights – often – when I can see nothing but *them*… I can hear their voices,and the reek of it is as real to me as if I was back there.

I walk the river, at such times; but in the dark the banks remind me of the trenches near St Quentin… near where it all happened. I can't exorcise the demons, Archie. I'm cursed with them, and they hover round my head like flies. '

'I think a part of you is utterly worn out. You've seen and experienced too much misery, my dear friend. I think you are right in one particular – that any conscientious doctor *will* be moved ultimately by what he sees, and begin to indict himself for real or imaginary failures. If he's any good as a man, what he bears witness to is bound to affect him profoundly, as it has you. It oughtn't to be otherwise.'

'Do you think so?'

'I most certainly do; we are only human, when all's said and done.'

'But what use is a doctor who has lost all faith in himself? I'm still no good. I don't see how I can continue to practise as a fraud and a failure.'

'Those whose lives you saved will never regard you in that light.'

Oliver drew out a handkerchief and wiped his eyes.

'They were too few.'

'Of course they were too few! If we were magicians we'd wave magic wands! But we're in the real world, a wicked and a harsh world, where such things exist in fantasy only. We're simple men, and we've done our best, and continue to do it, despite our failings and our weaknesses. Do you think I don't still ache for bairns like Billy Holcroft? I confine his suffering to the darkest recesses of my memory, but he's still there and always will be – one of *my* many failures.'

'You didn't fail him, Archie.'

'It was hardly success. But the point is, I *live* with it. And so, my dear friend, must you. I think, Oliver, that you need to return. You have to. There is no option, for someone of your talents. Your devotion and your gifts as a doctor are needed more desperately now than you could imagine. Will you come back with me and let me show you?'

'I can't. You've no idea how debased my skills have become.'

'Then do something about it, man! Relearn them ! Retrain, if you have to, though I cannot conceive it'll be remotely necessary. You have to rebuild your faith in yourself – and might I say, learn to recognise the faith that others have in you still.'

'I think it's misplaced.'

'We've known each other a long time. Rusholme; and that's the very first time I've heard you become self-indulgent. It ill becomes you.'

Oliver made no reply.

'Do you naively imagine that the suffering has ended with the War?' McLeish continued 'Is *that* it? That with the Armistice everything's been neatly wrapped up? I assure you that it hasn't been. We've only just begun to pick up the pieces, at Levenham and a hundred other such places. The challenge is immense'

'I said I cannot come back.' But McLeish was in no mood to listen to prevarication.

'I won't hear such nonsense! When you first came to see me at Levenham I was impressed by the passionate way you spoke about medicine and your ambition to become a doctor. Bill Aplin spotted you early – did you know that? – and here's something you *don't* know; he said you were perhaps the most promising student he'd ever taught. He was *fiercely* proud of you! And now because you've been 'through the mill' you're prepared to consign it all to the dustbin.'

McLeish stood up suddenly 'You have no right to deny what you have. It's a rare gift, and to refuse to practise it is mean-minded, or worse. You disappoint me, Oliver. I thought you were made of better stuff.'

'Then you were wrong.'

'Don't tell me what's right or wrong, laddie! I'm standing on the outside looking in on all this, and I can see clearly enough. I see someone whom I liked and respected as a fine doctor now hell-bent on self immolation. It's wilful of you, Rusholme!'

McLeish animatedly paced back and forth as if debating a difficult point 'You suffered, I know that,' he said, 'but so have countless others, and in ways we can't begin to imagine. The difference between you and them is that you have it in your power to do something both for yourself *and* for them – *if* you have the backbone for it, which I'm beginning seriously to doubt. Shake yourself out of this lethargy, Rusholme! If you persist in wallowing in this destructive self-pity I'm afraid I'll have no option but to consider our friendship at an end.'

Oliver shook as if he had received a physical blow. He raised his eyes from the table and returned McLeish's angry gaze. For a moment there was an opposing polarity between them, a force of electric intensity running from one to the other.

'That was below the belt, McLeish. You know the regard in which I hold you, and the value I set on you as a friend.' The turning point had come, and his resolve wavered fatally. He rose from the chair and pushed it away from him.' I might still have returned, though I can't see what use I will ever be again… but there is one insurmountable obstacle which prevents it; that tissue of warped truths about St. Quentin; I don't know how I could confront it all a second time.'

'Insurmountable? Don't flatter yourself in that regard !'McLeish goaded. ' You're not as important as you think !You're already ancient history. The newspapers have moved on to other more fertile territory since your disappearance.Bear in mind that the public's fickle! They rapidly tire of something unless it's constantly revived. Nomatter what you did... or *didn't* do' he added politically, seeing Oliver's hackles begin to rise, ' you were a Seven-Day Wonder to them; they milked the story for what it was worth, then shifted to something new which had greater potential for running a little longer.'

Oliver looked visibly relieved; McLeish's strategy had begun at last to work Then his face clouded once more.

'But there is Dolly. I've wronged her terribly and I've treated her with complete indifference. It was shameful and very cruel of me to behave in that way towards anybody, let alone one who loved me.'

'Do you still feel for her in the same way?' McLeish asked.

Oliver was slow to reply. ' Yes, I *think* I do' he said, unaware of the emotional upheaval his words caused in his friend. McLeish was at once gladdened that Oliver was returning from that grey limbo which continued to blight the lives of so many, and had begun the long process of finding himself again, yet nevertheless he felt a sinking in his heart, the origins of which he would be forced to deny for the rest his life.

'I do now' Oliver continued ' but when I got back I felt nothing; just numbness. I saw her, but did not recognise her. She was like just another face in a crowd. Worst of all, I didn't want her – not in the way one *should* want a woman. I'd dreamed of her constantly, when I was in the camp; she was hardly ever out of my thoughts. But when I returned I seemed to have been emasculated.' He sighed deeply. 'Nothing can be the same as it was' he continued. ' Things have been irretrievably altered, and in most cases for the worse. Though my sight is less clouded than it was – due to just being here, I think – I still can't banish the War; everything seems to be tainted by it. Archie,it's like looking at a picture through a different lens. What I thought I had seems all distorted, somehow – like a caricature of what it used to be. And now I' m at a complete loss as to how to make it right, or whether it's even possible. I wouldn't blame her if she told me it was all over, though I know now I still love her.'

'Then you need to speak with her.'

'How can I? I can't simply return to Desbury and present myself on her doorstep, as if nothing had happened.'

'I don't think distance will be a problem. You won't have to go nearly as far as Desbury if your mind is made up to see her.'

'I've missed her terribly, McLeish. Every day that passes here I realise just how much, and what a heartless fool I've been.'

'You're neither heartless, nor a fool. It's probably the very absence of those traits which has ironically brought you to this. And as for the feeling of impotence, my opinion on that subject both as a colleague and as a friend… yes, *friend,* Rusholme' he said, catching Oliver's searching look ' is that it is a temporary phase originating from a combination of protracted shock and exhaustion- one which will almost certainly pass.'

Oliver looked thoughtful. 'You said I wouldn't have to go to Desbury… I'm not sure what you mean.'

'How do you think I found you here? Guesswork's one thing, but coming here certainly wasn't my idea. If you wish to see Miss Chadderton, she's waiting for you at Ridland.'

Oliver's head spun, as he was struck by a welter of possibilities tempered by his usual reservations. *Ridland!* So close! 'Does she want to see me? *Truly?*'

'Do you imagine that she'd have risked a long voyage in my motor-car if she hadn't? Will you let me take you to her?'

'Yes; I will.'

'Then you had better do something about your appearance; you look absolutely awful. For a start you're in desperate need of a shave; you'd frighten the poor young lady to death if you appeared with *that* growth around your chops. A haircut will have to wait, for now. ' Oliver peered into the little shaving-mirror which hung from the kitchen door. It was the first time in many months that he'd considered what he looked like, and he was shocked by the bedraggled and bearded image which confronted him.

He looked from side to side, trying to recall where he'd last placed his razor and brush. Some opening and slamming of cupboard-doors later the articles finally came to light, and whilst McLeish drew buckets of hot water from the boiler he set about shearing away at the outward signs of his breakdown. Then, clean-shaven at last and stripped to his underpants he soused himself down in the little yard, scrubbing himself mercilessly with a hard block of carbolic soap and a brush, as though he were determined to erase the stains of the past entirely from his body. Sitting nearby McLeish noticed a livid scar running across the back of his friend's head – the wound received even as he attended to casualties in the last tragic minutes of Manchester Hill. McLeish guessed its origin immediately for he had read about it all in the papers. He had admired his friend's selfless bravery though it had not surprised him; from what he knew of Oliver's qualities he judged he would have done no less, nor any differently. A lump rose inadvertently in his throat and he looked away and said nothing, but thought much.

Oliver stood before the panelled oak door of the 'snug'. After delivering his friend, McLeish had slipped away into the public bar leaving Oliver standing alone in the flagstoned corridor. Despite the warmth generated by several coal-fires Oliver broke into a sudden chill sweat. He raised his hand uncertainly to knock on the door then let it fall back limply to his side once more. It seemed absurd to be knocking like this, as if he were visiting someone's house.

'Dolly?' he said huskily to the closed door. 'Could I speak to you, please?'

There was no reply from within. He cleared his throat and began again. ' Dolly, could I speak to you?'

Someone moved to the door and opened it slowly. Dolly Chadderton looked steadily up at him. There was no smile of greeting – neither on her lips nor in her eyes; and the reserve with which he was received was as unexpected as it was unwelcome. She stepped back a few paces into the little room.

'Shall I come in? ' he asked almost inaudibly. She looked elsewhere to avoid his gaze and nodded. 'If that's what you want.'

'I do.' He reached out his hand tentatively toward hers. She placed her own firmly behind her and drew away from him.

They stood thus for a moment without speaking, both equally ill at ease. Then Oliver entered the room and stood with his back against the wainscotting. Dolly turned and looked towards the window sunk in the wall.

'*Why* didn't you at least say goodbye?' she began ' and why didn't you write, if only to tell me where you were? Didn't I deserve it? Didn't I matter even *that* much to you? '

'I have no excuses, Dolly.'

She looked levelly at him. 'No, you haven't Oliver. You knew very well how much I loved you; everyone knew. Only you seem to have chosen to forget it – and how much I'd worry about you if you were ever to do such a cruel thing, but you went ahead and did it anyway. You didn't care anything for my feelings... not in the slightest, you didn't.' As the tears pricked her eyes, her voice became ever more charged with emotion.

'I know it sounds pathetic, Dolly; but at the time it seemed that I didn't have any feelings left worth the name. I searched my heart desperately but found nothing there which was worthy of you.'

'I don't believe you were thinking of me at all.'

'No, in a way I wasn't Dolly. I thought of you, but without any stirrings of my old love.'

She recoiled involuntarily, and alarmed by his own stark admission he took a step forward.

'Please just keep back from me, Oliver' she choked.

'Dolly! Just hear me out, and then I'll go, and if you wish it I'll never trouble you again. I still don't know what came over me; it just overwhelmed me completely. There was a constant ache deep inside me. It was all grey, Dolly, and at times I could feel nothing beyond the pain in my mind. I couldn't make out any brightness or hope, and everything appeared shapeless and indistinct except for the things I remembered about France, and the camp. They stood out too prominently. They dwarfed everything else and shrouded everybody who mattered to me in darkness.. But it was never your doing, my darling; never your doing. It was when the light which you shone on me finally started to go out that I realised I was pretty well washed up, and I desperately felt the need of some time alone. I had to come to terms with myself and my having let everyone down. And now I see that I let you down all the more. McLeish's been kind, and told me it's not so. But Dolly, I know it to be different. My conduct till now has been indefensible. I realised then even as I realise now, that I should have written to you immediately to spare you the heartache – but my darling, believe me when I say I simply couldn't. To try to express it even indirectly caused me unspeakable anguish. I started letters – how many I don't know – but never got beyond the first few lines. I hope one day you might understand, and then perhaps you can find it in your heart to forgive me, a little.'

'I *could* forgive you, Oliver, if I knew beyond anything that you'd never treat me in such a way ever again.'

'I can only vow to you that I will not.'

A silence fell between them, as Dolly looked through the window onto the street beyond. She cast her eyes downwards and away from the commonplace scene, glancing at the hand where she had once worn the ruby he had given her. Oliver followed her gaze and as he divined her thoughts tears welled up involuntarily in his eyes. 'I don't blame you' he said indistinctly.'What were you to think?'

'I think, Oliver. that we both deserve a bit of happiness after all that's passed' she said.

Chapter Seventeen

OLIVER DID not go back to Desbury with them. Explaining that he had a number of things to attend to in shutting-up the cottage, he promised that he would return by the afternoon train on the following day. But the real truth lay more in a determination to re-emerge from his self-imposed banishment on his own initiative rather than suffer the stigma of being brought back by friends nomatter how good their intentions. He could not have faced being returned like some delinquent child, nor the long journey to Manchester sitting in the car with Dolly and McLeish.

At first his friend had pressed him to accompany them; but Dolly's silence had been sufficient to alert McLeish and he had quickly followed suit, hazarding a guess as to the underlying reason for Oliver's reluctance.

The rail journey was long and tedious, and as solitary as Oliver had contrived it to be, for he had taken the trouble to search out an unoccupied compartment. It wasn't difficult to do, for the train was more than half empty and the warmer weather and the holidays were still many months away. But as the familiar scenes passed him and as the momentum of his return seemed to gather pace the doubts once more began to assail him. Why was he returning, and what was he returning to? Panic suddenly seized him as his imagined shortcomings as a doctor rose once more to confront him, and as the train began to slow down on its approach to Chester he had all but made up his mind to get out.

The carriages squealed to a juddering halt and he had risen to grab his bags when the door was flung open. Like a schoolboy caught red-handed in some trifling offence he guiltily recoiled from the baggage-rack and sat down as if nothing had happened. A large woman clad in a VAD nurse's cloak came into the carriage backward, leading a soldier by both hands. Her face was obscured by virtue of her reverse manoeuvring, though the man could be seen plainly enough. He was clad in the blue jacket of an invalid, and the reason for his being led became immediately apparent as Oliver looked up at his face. There hadn't been much remaining after the shellblast, though by the look of it the surgeons had done what they could; and he was evidently blind.

The nurse spoke continuous words of encouragement and affection, and as he struggled forward the man laughed through his broken lips, feeling his way with his feet.

'Come *on,* Ernest!' said the nurse ' if you don't stir your stumps we'll end up leaving our cases behind !'

'Now, lass! Don't you hang on for me!' chuckled the soldier, turning his head in the direction of his nurse companion. Oliver started to his feet and shot down onto the platform where two welltravelled suitcases stood. He grabbed them, one in either hand, and swung himself back into the compartment.

'That's very kind of you, I'm sure!' said the nurse

'What is?' asked the blinded man.

'Not *you*,silly!' retorted his companion with mock severity 'a chap's just helped us with the cases. There's someone else in the compartment with us.'

'Is there? I'm forgetting my manners.' Ernest doffed his cap gracefully, and addressed himself to the empty seats in front of him. 'Good afternoon, sir, and thank you for helping.'

'Think nothing of it ' Oliver said as lightly as he could. He stacked the cases in the baggage rack and turned back to his seat. As he did so the nurse also turned. From the very outset something had struck him as vaguely familiar about her voice. Now as he caught sight of her face he was convinced that he knew her. She in her turn smiled her thanks to him and sat down beside her companion, linking her arm affectionately with his. He felt for her hand and patted it.

Again she looked across to Oliver who did his best to avoid her gaze

'Pardon me for asking, but don't I know you from somewhere? Mere, maybe? Or Chester General

'I'm afraid not' he said ' I've worked at neither.'

'Oh, well, perhaps I'm mistaken. We met a lot of chaps during the War; can't remember every face, can we?' She leant over and offered Oliver her hand. 'My name's Dulcie Grady' Oliver became visibly tenser as he returned the greeting

'How do you do?' he asked flatly.

'Well enough, thank you,' she replied, 'and this gentleman I'm with is my fiancé, Ernest; Ernest Woodleigh.' She saw from Oliver's expression that he recognised her, and her eyes narrowed; yet she remained at a loss to place this tanned, rather windswept looking person. Despite his weatherbeaten exterior she thought him refined, and she was held by eyes which seemed to her sensitive and profoundly sad. There was something particularly familiar about them, some factor which she knew but couldn't place.

'Pardon me for prying' she persisted ' but were you ever a soldier at... '

'No. I've never been a soldier,' he interrupted. She was still wide of the mark, but was getting nearer. Suddenly a look of recognition flashed across her round face.

‘I remember!’ she laughed ‘Aren’t you Helene’s brother… let me think… Oswald… no, not that… Oliver! That’s it! Aren’t you *Oliver Rusholme*?’

‘No. I’m afraid you’ve mistaken me for somebody else.’

Dulcie Grady looked nonplussed. ‘Well! I do beg your pardon! It’s been a very long time, though I rarely forget a face… but no matter! Do forgive me. I have this awful habit of running on, sometimes!’

‘Who did you think he was, Dulcie?’ asked Ernest.

‘You know Nurse Rusholme… at the hospital?’ she said, turning to him ‘Well, she and I have been the best of friends for years. Her brother is – or was – a doctor. A very fine doctor, so everyone says.’ Oliver cringed inwardly, but kept his silence. ‘He volunteered to help with the casualties at one of the Manchester hospitals even before he’d qualified.’ Dulcie continued ‘ and when he *had* – and he’d come out at the *very* top, mind – of all the places he chose to work in was a Poor Hospital in the north of the city! Apparently they all thought the world of him there, and when he went to join up they all missed him awfully. And then to cap it all he turned out a War hero… ’

Oliver had heard quite enough.

‘Tell me,’ he burst out, ‘are you on your way to visit friends,… or family… or for some other reason?’ The enquiry sounded rather lame and not a little rude, so he added ‘ I... I only ask because… I’m on my way to Manchester.’ Dulcie Grady gave him an odd look.

‘Well since you ask, we’re going to have Ernest’s eyes checked up at The Royal Eye Hospital. Mr. Milliner’s your specialist now, isn’t he Love?’

Ernest smiled. ‘He’s the best in the North’ he asserted with confidence ‘or so we’ve been told. And he *thinks*… well, you tell the rest, Dulcie.’

‘He thinks that with a few of the new type of operations they’re developing, Ernest might get a little of his sight back. Mr. Milliner’s a wonderful man,’ she concluded with feeling. ‘If only he can give us that… .’ She squeezed Ernest’s arm and turning to the battered mask of his face smiled wanly into the sightless eyes.

Oliver averted his gaze; and though he looked out at the Cheshire Plain as it passed he saw nothing of it, blinded as he was by remorse and a growing conflict of heart and mind.

On their arrival in Manchester Oliver, having shouldered his own bags, gave a hand with the couple’s cases. By the time the trio had shuffled to the platform gate the ruck of passengers had long dispersed, and they were through very quickly. Oliver insisted on calling a taxi for them, though they said that a bus would do. As they were helped in by the cabbie Dulcie turned to Oliver

'Thank you, Mr…' she said warmly, 'I'm sorry, I don't think you mentioned your name.'

Oliver was momentarily lost. 'Didn't I?' he fumbled for a second or two, then lit upon a name which seemed appropriate, 'It's Bonnard, actually.'

Some months previously Archie McLeish had transferred from Levenham to one of the non-military hospitals in North Manchester. Many of the wounded and gas-cases who had passed officially through their period of convalescence were returned shellshocked and ill to their families to scrape a living as best they could; and for thousands it was subsistence, and no more. McLeish and many like him recognised that their task was far from done. A visitor to any poor residential quarter in any British town or city could see the bitter truth of that.

So it was that McLeish had invited Oliver to join him at the free Outpatients Clinic which was held every morning at the North Manchester hospital where he now practised. Oliver rose before dawn at the small hotel where he had spent the night and retrieved one of his freshly-pressed suits recently collected from storage.

By seven, shaved and breakfasted, he presented himself at the clinic. He knocked as he had done years before and the door was opened to him. McLeish ushered him in and offered him a seat.

'Well, Rusholme; its good to see you, my friend.' He shook Oliver's hand and patted him reassuringly on the shoulder 'Very good indeed! I knew you'd make it back.' He turned to a side table on which medical records were stacked. 'These are this morning's cases, though no doubt there'll be more yet.' McLeish looked quizzically across to Oliver, 'would ye like a quick glance?' he asked casually. And as he had done once before he pushed one of the brown heaps towards his friend.

Oliver could not resist; he picked up the first of the files and began to read.

By nine it was clear that McLeish had woefully underestimated the number of that morning's patients. Almost as if in answer to a prayer the numbers in the waiting – room swelled steadily until there was barely space left to stand. Oliver sat at a corner of his friend's desk and observed the steady stream who were brought in and greeted with McLeish's habitual courtesy, sympathy and genuine concern for their condition – which as always he was fully acquainted with.

By nine-thirty the nurse in charge of registration put her head round the door whilst McLeish was in between patients. She appeared to be rather harassed

'Doctor, we're already exceeded this morning's fixed appointments. Shall I tell all those without one to go away?'

'How many are there?'

'Some thirty-odd, already.'

'How are Doctors Pearson and Klein situated?'

'Rather snowed under, but coping. Like yourself, Doctor, if you'll excuse me for saying so. I doubt you'll be finished by mid-afternoon, the way things are going.'

McLeish looked meaningfully across at Oliver. 'Well?'

'I… I'm not sure. I don't feel that… '

'Over there on the peg.' McLeish said shortly, ignoring Oliver's vacillation. He nodded to a fresh-laundered white coat hanging from the back of the door. 'Sister Williamson?' he asked in a matter-of-fact way 'is there a consulting-room available?'

'Room 6b is certainly free.'

'*Excellent*, Sister. Could I introduce you to a highly valued friend and colleague of mine, Dr. Rusholme?' Sister Williamson smiled. 'Good morning, doctor.' Oliver felt an apprehensive chill sweep through him as he returned her greeting.

'He'll be joining us for clinic this morning' continued McLeish. 'Take some of the pressure off us. Won't you, Dr. Rusholme?'

As Oliver looked across to his friend he was reminded of the exchange which took place between them at the cottage. He was fixed in the same firm stare. 'Won't you?' McLeish said again.

Oliver cleared his throat: 'Yes… well… I certainly hope so.'

'Could he start with these, if you'd be so kind?' McLeish pushed the familiar pile of records across to her.

'With pleasure, Doctor. I'll see that 6b is made ready at once.'

As the door closed behind her Oliver turned rapidly on McLeish.

'Look here !' His tone was more frantic than angry 'I'm not sure that I'm up to it. What if I get it wrong? What if...'

'It's now or never, Rusholme. I have sufficient faith and confidence to stand by you in any decision you may make. I couldn't entrust the wellbeing of those poor sods out there to anyone better.' McLeish's face cracked into a smile ' I know you better than you do yourself, my *dear* friend.'

Oliver walked slowly to the door as if making to leave the room. He grasped the handle, then paused. The coat hung there before him, and at that moment he recalled Dulcie and Ernest on the train from Chester, and the hope which Milliner had given them. He released his grip, and slowly he found himself lifting the garment down.

'Let me help you' McLeish crossed the room in a second.

Oliver adjusted the collar, and straightened his tie. 'Good man!' McLeish beamed as he opened the door. 'Now get back to where ye belong!'

Oliver stood alone in Room 6b. He breathed in the pervasive smell of medicines and disinfectant, and ran his hand over the surface of the desk. The notes lay neatly arranged on the left by his chair. There was a slight knocking at the door. 'Come in'

Sister Williamson entered: 'Are you ready for the first appointment, Doctor?'

Oliver took a deep breath. 'Yes, Sister. Yes I am. Send them in please.'

She turned and then said 'I hope it's not out of place to say it, but I hope you' ll like it here. Thank you so much for coming.'

A young mother and her little girl stood before Oliver's desk. As he rose he seemed to dwarf them as he offered a chair to the woman. She seemed unused to such civility and was at first unwilling to sit down, but his kindly manner prevailed over her reluctance and she covered her toothless mouth with her hand as she smiled. The girl had retreated behind her and her mother drew her out by a frail arm and placed her before Oliver. The child's thin face accentuated the round eyes which now stared fearfully up at him. Oliver had read the notes, and the signs.

The woman pulled off the child's coat to reveal a dress of bleached-out cotton which barely covered the emaciated little body beneath.

'Hello, Mary! ' said Oliver, gently taking the child's hand in his. 'My name's Dr. Rusholme. And let's see how *you've* been getting along, shall we… ?'

Chapter Eighteen

OLIVER SPENT a week at the hospital. On the afternoon of the first day he had penned an affectionate and apologetic letter to Dolly, telling her of his arrival in Manchester and of the work he had undertaken to do for Archie McLeish. The letter was filled with praise for his friend, and remorseful love for her.

She read it repeatedly – as she had once read his letters from the Front- and it seemed to her that the voice of the old Oliver sounded in it once again.He said he'd decided to continue at the hospital, for now; his decision to stay on there was not because of her, or because of his feelings for her; but he rather hoped she'd understand.

It was fortunate for him that Dolly Chadderton did; for she divined from what he'd said – or more particularly from what he hadn't had the courage to say – that it was a most significant step in his recuperation.

The three fifteen train wheezed its way into Desbury Station and shuddered to a halt. A few doors opened and a few passengers climbed out – a lady with a small boy dutifully carrying her parcels, an old man in plus fours with a bicycle, and a young man in his mid-twenties. He was smartly dressed in a tweed suit and trilby hat, and he carried with him a leather grip-bag which he set down on the platform as he searched for his ticket. As he did so he paused for a moment, recalling with a pang of sadness that he was re-enacting a scene which he had witnessed years before, and on that very spot. It seemed an age ago as he fondly remembered his reunion with a brother whom he'd found there.'Ah, Godfrey' he murmured to himself.

Picking up his bag he made his way past the grousing porter and on up the lane towards the centre of the village, out past *The Sceptre* and on towards *The Hen*. As he passed the familiar squat windows of the inn he felt a pang of nostalgia as he thought of his boyhood there – of going to see Albert with a message from Millwain Place, and of the little girl with the flaxen hair; and he remembered how he and Godfrey had swung along down through the fieldpaths and across the meadow carefree, and together; and their laughter seemed to echo down the years to him, and the words he had planned to say to Dolly Chadderton seemed to blur even as he considered them.

And now he stood before her door once again, that neatly painted, familiar door. His heart pounded in his ears, reverberating with each blow as he knocked.

'Oh… Doctor Rusholme. This *is* a surprise, sir.' Mrs Chadderton wiped her hands on the immaculate pinafore covering her black dress. 'Would you kindly step into the parlour? Dolly wasn't expecting you but I'll tell her you're here.'

Oliver waited impatiently in the half-light, in an atmosphere charged equally with expectancy and apprehension. He heard remote voices from the adjoining kitchen – voices raised in an indistinct babble of excitement. The kitchen door opened, followed rapidly by the door of the parlour. He jumped to his feet as Dolly came in. He'd always thought her beautiful, but now her looks surpassed all recollections he'd had of her. Her hair shone like burnished gold from the brushing she'd given it, and her eyes…

'Hello, Oliver,' she said softly 'and how *are* you?'

'Better, Dolly… so much better.'

'I got your note. Thank you for it.'

'I... I'm sorry I couldn't let you know I was coming. I didn't want to catch you unawares, or anything like that… in fact, I didn't even know I was coming to Desbury at all… to see you… until barely two hours ago.'

'I'm glad you've come.'

Oliver took a step towards her. This time she did not draw away, and when he took her hand she did not snatch it back.

He looked steadily into her face. 'Dolly,' he said simply, 'I've come back. I've been far away for a very long time. I lost myself, Dolly. But I know that I've found my way back, for always.'

She drew closer to him and looked up into his face.

'Will you let me come back, Sweetheart?' he asked huskily. 'Will you let me finally come back?'

On a day which dawned brilliantly in a cloudless June sky, a day when the aspen-leaves in the neighbouring wood fluttered silver as though applauding, Miss Dorothy Victoria Chadderton was married to Doctor Oliver Rusholme at the ancient red stone church of St. James, in Desbury. It was a day which seemed to proclaim that the longed-for peace had indeed come at last, with the uniting of two young people who deserved so much from life. And as the couple ran the gauntlet of medical friends and colleagues lining the path to McLeish's diminutive motor car, Oliver slipped his arm round his new wife's slender waist.

She turned to him and breathed the words, '*I love you.*'

The car's proud owner had agreed to officiate both as Best Man and sole Chauffeur, while Drs.Wilfred Hallett and David Pottinger's shortcomings as Ushers were compensated for by their loudness.

As the bride and groom were stowed behind the driver's seat McLeish – red-faced and blowing – went through the ritual cranking of the engine, accompanied by a chorus of well-intentioned medical advice as to which chest specialist he ought to see.

Ida Rusholme was there, though Clarence was too ill to attend.

When her son had come to her she embraced him silently and kissed him tenderly on the cheek. Helene had approached them, smiling as much as she could, and genuinely wished them all the happiness in the world. Dolly caressed the other's hand in a brief gesture which said much. And the widowed Mrs. Chadderton, who had bought a lighter hat to mark the occasion of her daughter's wedding though the rest of her outfit was black, even yet.

And then there was Mr.and Mrs.Ernest Woodleigh. As Oliver passed them Dulcie grinned, wagged a fat finger at him and giggled, 'you *naughty* boy! Bonnard indeed!' And the pair roared with laughter.

They slipped off from the reception which was being held at the *Sceptre*, and were spirited away by Archie McLeish to Altrincham. There they piled into a First Class compartment of the evening train to Llandudno, where the bridal suite of The Royal Hotel, booked secretly by Oliver some weeks earlier, awaited them.

Whistles shrilled and McLeish waved farewell to them; and as the carriages jolted into motion he watched them away into the gathering dusk, then he turned and walked back to his car alone. His habitual stoop seemed more than usually pronounced.

They had the compartment to themselves, at least until Chester. Dolly looked across at her new husband who stood by the window watching the velvet night scud past. She rose from her seat and wrapping her arms around him inclined her head against his shoulder. He kissed her hair, then her cheek, then her lips. She snuggled into him and turning her head followed his gaze out into the dark. She considered the immeasurable heavens whose faint starlight created silhouettes of the darker trees as they passed.

'Do you think they see us as we see them?'she asked.

Oliver stirred as if woken from a dream. 'I very much doubt it ' he said smiling ' but I don't think I'll chance it anyhow ' and turning to face Dolly he drew down the blinds.

Chapter Nineteen

A LARGE car drew up at the crossing of Tannery and Canal Streets and the driver turned off the engine. The uniform greyness of the cobbles was complemented by the greyer sky which hung sullenly overhead,and grubby brick walls which formed a junction of uncompromising ugliness. It was difficult to believe that it had ever been other than it was.

The driver deftly skipped out and opened the car's rear door with a practised sweep of his hand. As he waited for his passenger to alight he looked about him from out of the corner of his eye. What he saw of the neighbourhood filled him with a distaste which he made no effort to conceal. A crowd of unkempt children, as anaemically colourless as the sooty street in which they stood, gathered open-mouthed around this coachpainted vision from a wealthier, alien world.

What the Hell's possessed the Guv'nor to visit this of all dumps the driver wondered *and can't he hurry up?*

A small curly-haired lad with bare feet detached himself from the ruck which now surrounded the car.

'Hey, mister? ' he said ' 'Ow fast does it go?'

'Is it a Rolls Royce?' asked another.

'I bet it is'

'An' look at its posh wheels. *An*' them winders.' Gasps of admiration rose from the crowd as the curly lad pointed out its qualities.

The chauffeur distained to reply;*'Gerroutofit!* he hissed through clenched teeth,*'Beat it, all of yer!'*

His passenger had by now climbed from the car. He was a tall man of imposing stature and was dressed expensively in a dark suit, overcoat and hat.His shoes sported white spats. He stood for a moment and surveyed the street with a disinterested air.

'Stay here would you, Glover? I'll walk the rest of the way; it's roundabout here, I think.' The man's accent was refined but certainly not British. He set off across the street with a knot of children at his heels – mainly little girls who, tired of gazing at the car, now wanted to find out where the visitor was heading. They did not have far to go.

Having crossed the road he looked about him uncertainly; then he spotted the place he was searching for. Striding up to the entrance of a double-fronted house he scanned two brass plaques screwed to the wall.

Archibald McLeish, M.D.(Edin)

said one. And the other

Oliver Rusholme, M.D. Vict. Univ. Manch. {Hons}.

The stranger humphed and taking off his hat, gripped the door handle and entered.

The small hallway within opened onto a waiting room on the left, while further down to the right were two cream-painted doors which he judged to be the doctors' consulting-rooms. Having appraised his surroundings with a critical eye he walked purposefully into the waiting room. It was brightly lit and warm, with a gas fire burning away in the hearth; but as the visitor looked around him he saw at once how sparsely furnished it was. Cheap bentwood chairs lined the walls on three sides. On these sat a complete cross section of the district's population – from a sickly infant with its hollow – cheeked mother to the aged ex mill-hand, snowy haired and bowed by a lifetime of work. And poverty – of the sort that could be smelled as well as seen- was evidently the common denominator between them. All eyes followed him in amazement as he approached the frosted glass window let centrally into the further wall, and rang the bell.

The window slid back to reveal a remarkably pretty young woman who smiled pleasantly and took his visiting-card.

'Would you take a seat?' she said;'Doctor Rusholme will be available to see you shortly.' The visitor sat down where she had indicated, between a thin-faced man whose missing leg and threadbare smartness suggested a former soldier, and an old woman racked by a ghastly cough. The others watched intently, expecting the well-heeled gentleman to recoil from his neighbours; but to their surprise he did not, and as he seated himself he nodded affably to those nearest to him.

Oliver's previous patient had just departed when Dolly slipped into the surgery. As she came behind the desk he put his arm round her waist, then let his hand drop a little lower.

'Oliver, don't!' she said demurely, 'at least,not here! What would the patients think if they could see?'

He released her reluctantly.'How's Jamie getting along?'

She glowed with motherly pride ' He *loves* those bricks which Helene bought for him. He made a little house, with a roof. Well..until it collapsed. Oh, a gentleman's asked me to give you his card. He looks very important.

He's in the waiting-room.'

Oliver took it from her curiously, but paled as he read it. '*Good God*! Today of all days, *and in the waiting room too*!' He sprang to his feet and made for the door, 'Dolly! he gasped, turning 'd'you know who it is?' She was about to reply, but he forestalled her. 'It's only Bill Aplin – *Sir William Aplin* – in person, that's who. Oh, God. What can he possibly want here?'

'Bill' Aplin sat in the only comfortable chair that the practice possessed. He carefully placed his cup and saucer down on Oliver's elderly desk.

'Well, Rusholme,' he said, 'and how are you finding things here? Hard, eh? Thought they might be, when I was told what you'd proposed.'

'It's hard enough, sir,' Oliver conceded, 'and it may sound odd, but McLeish – my colleague in the practice – and I are kept so busy that we neither of us have time really to consider it. There's such a need, you see. Sometimes, I feel we're barely scratching the surface.'

Aplin pursed his lips.'From what I hear you're doing more than that. But the thing is, do you think you'll stick it out?'

'I believe we have to, sir. I don't think we could quit now even if we wished to. The local people have invested a lot in us… .. just as we've invested in them, I suppose. We couldn't let them down. Setting up here was not a decision which we took lightly. McLeish and my wife and I had to think hard and long before committing ourselves.'

'Are you *happy* with it, Rusholme?'

Oliver considered a moment.' I wouldn't say *happy*, exactly. It's not the right word. I'm certainly *content* with what I have and what I am. And I find what I do here fulfilling.'

'I'm truly glad to hear it. Truly glad.' Aplin picked up his gloves and hat, and rose to leave.

Oliver showed him to the door and the older man surveyed the dingy street as he stood on the pavement once again. 'You know, I'd always believed that you'd go a long way in the profession, Rusholme.'

Is he saying he's disappointed in me? Oliver thought with a sudden pang of shame. But Aplin smiled broadly as he turned once more and offered Oliver his hand. 'I'm proud to say that I was right.'

Some days later Dolly opened an envelope which had been pushed through the letterbox. Within she found a cheque for two hundred pounds, signed by W. Aplin. There was no covering note with it, but the back was endorsed *to be spent on necessities.*

Time seemed to slip away at an ever increasing pace. Six full years had elapsed since the Armistice, yet to Oliver and to many others of his generation the events were as immediate as if they had occurred only yesterday. Each man had his own way of dealing with them, and each experienced a varying degree of success. Oliver immersed himself in his growing family, his wife and his work. These things did not make him forget, but enabled him to regain his sense of proportion – to readjust it to the present, and dwell neither too heavily nor to long on the past; and like the storm-filled Clwyr of his pre-war years – now so remote that they seemed a different epoch – he too had reshaped his own course, and adapted to it as well as circumstance allowed.

Then came November 11th. 1924 and the announcement in the *Evening News* that the long awaited memorial to the Manchester Pals would be unveiled on the following Remembrance Sunday. Dolly walked into the lounge where Oliver sat with Jamie on his knee. She leant over them, and tenderly caressed Oliver's hair as she placed the article before him.

'Read this, love. Do you want to go? I'd understand if you didn't... ' He quickly scanned it. Jamie, puzzled by his mother's tone, stopped playing with his father's tie. Reaching up Oliver took her hand.

'It's been rather on my mind, of late. I think I ought to,' he said simply, looking into her face.

'Alright, love; then we'll go.

It was a bitter day. From first light a patchy drizzle had conspired with a troublesome wind to soak everything; and though a canopy had been erected for just this eventuality the damp had managed to find its way beneath it; rows of Union Jacks suspended from the podium now hung limply and lifelessly while a pool of water collected around the feet of the great and good of the city.They shuffled uncomfortably on their chairs and cast the occasional wistful glance up to the town hall clock. Behind them stood the newly erected memorial, a large semi-circle of masonry draped similarly in Union flags. Before it a sea of black umbrellas eddied and shifted with the movement of the crowd and the stiffening wind. The thousands assembled there stood in silence.What little conversation there was, was muted; and without gaiety; coughs could be heard, but few words were spoken.

As the rain steadily fell Oliver took in those nearest to Dolly and himself. On their left stood an elderly couple, a man and a woman. The old man's toothless mouth worked constantly as he gazed before him, while his wife cupped her ear in case the speeches had already begun. To their right was a youngish man who somehow stood apart despite the crush hemming them in; impeccable in pressed suit and polished boots he stood rigidly upright as if to attention, without motion other than the twitching of a muscle in his cheek. Beyond him was a woman of uncertain age. Her shabby black bonnet was tied tightly down against the weather and as she waited she busied herself with cleaning the face of a small resentful boy.

As he considered them Oliver wondered what diverse and secret purposes had caused them to be there. Of course it was remembrance; but the phrase rolled off the tongue too glibly. Was it to bear witness to the immortalising of a loved one's name in bronze? Or to recall the comradeship of the Western Front and by doing so regain something of the spirit which had infused the Pals? Or were they there in the faint hope of hearing new words of comfort which might succeed where all the old ones had failed?

Whatever their other reasons might be, he felt certain that the common bond which united them was a sense of irredemable loss.

The usual stuff was declaimed by the usual civic dignitaries. Oliver paid them little heed as he stood silently lost in his own thoughts. Dolly saw the remoteness in his face and squeezed his hand reassuringly. With the final speaker's closing words the Union flags slowly fell away, to solemn music from the Manchester Regiment band.

Even as the great work of bronze was revealed a whisper like the exhalation of breath rose from the onlookers gathered nearest to it. Many uncovered their heads instinctively, as though the Square had been transformed into hallowed ground by the very presence of the memorial. Even now the magnitude of the City's losses came as a redoubled shock for some; for few could have visualised just how many young Manchester men had died. Now the appalling reality confronted them at last – in the form of plaque after plaque bearing thousands of little bronze names, ranged precisely and alphabetically in rows.

Still others were affected by the monument itself – for it was a concept of melancholy beauty realised by a sculptor of rare gifts. Life-sized figures cast in relief progressed from left to right across the curving stonework; figures in the everyday clothes of millgirl, engineer and mason bent to their peacetime tasks while others stood and gazed unflinchingly towards the 1914 horizon, and war.

Then began the gradual metamorphosis from labourer into soldier or nurse as some donned jacket and helmet, some bound up leggings and still others took up rifles. Every figure epitomised movement – sinuous liquid movement which the artist had encapsulated in bronze and stone.

And then there was battle. As Oliver's eyes followed them, the figures could be seen in the zero-hour crisis of an attack as they ascended trench-ladders; and led by their officer, went 'over the top'; and as Oliver looked to the horizon the same figures, though diminished now and indistinct, could be seen to fall. And in the last panel a nurse tended a dying comrade as a Tommy, helmeted and backpacked, leaned on his rifle and looked sadly down upon them both.

Oliver saw that in its progression the sculptor had intended to depict a tragic Rite of Passage, a profound and intensely moving vision realised in art which while it did not indict, neither excused nor ratified. It commemorated the Fallen with simple dignity,celebrating in its bronzes a people's stoicism and generosity of spirit, but not their deaths.

As his gaze rested upon the memorial Oliver felt the pain return to him, like the reopening of an old wound. Dolly looked up at him anxiously, and saw that tears were silently coursing down his cheeks.

'We can't go on with this' she said emphatically. 'Oliver, we *can't*. Shall we go home, love?'

Without a word Oliver Rusholme turned; and slowly he and Dolly made their way through the crowd, many of whom were affected even as they themselves were. Holding on tightly to each other they passed along the glittering rainwashed streets of Manchester until the lights of the surgery, their home, shone out like a beacon before them.

They left the seeking-out of names for another time; names of the Pals whose comradeship was enshrined for an eternity in bronze – and who would await them there, until they were ready at last;

Percy Crossley, George Gilbank, Gerald Warrington, Tom Burton, Albert Chadderton, Godfrey Rusholme and Wilfrith Elstob.

THE END